THE DESCENT
OF
MANUSCRIPTS

THE DESCENT OF MANUSCRIPTS

BY

A. C. CLARK

CORPUS PROFESSOR OF LATIN IN THE UNIVERSITY OF OXFORD

Wipf and Stock Publishers
199 W 8th Ave, Suite 3
Eugene, OR 97401

The Descent of Manuscripts
By Clark, A. C.
ISBN: 1-59752-576-6
Publication date 6/14/2005
Previously published by Oxford, UK, 1918

PREFACE

THIS work has been in type for some time, but its appearance has been delayed by the great European war, which has disorganized industry and extinguished interest in philological studies. It seems hopeless to wait for more favourable times, so it is now published under very unpropitious circumstances.

The book was not constructed according to a definite plan, but took shape gradually in the course of a protracted inquiry. It may, therefore, be well to indicate the order in which it was composed. The method which I have employed was based upon a study of Cicero's *Philippics*, and the chapter in which I treat them was more or less completed before I proceeded to other writings. I went on to other speeches of Cicero, chiefly the *Verrines* and the collection of orations *post reditum*, &c., found in Paris. 7794, also to the *corpus* of philosophical works (*Nat. D.*, &c.) discussed in Chapter X, and Asconius, together with the pseudo-Asconius. While my work upon these was in an inchoate condition, it was broken off (in 1913) by an incursion into a different field.[1] On my return to my former studies, I completed the chapters which I had begun, and extended my inquiries to the Ciceronian palimpsests. At this period I became interested in omission marks, and found a rich store of material in old Latin MSS., chiefly patristic, in which passages added by the corrector are accompanied by symbols denoting previous omission. I have dealt with a selection of these in Chapter III. The chapters upon the MSS. of Plato and the Paris MS. of Demosthenes were added after the rest of the work had been for some time in print, since it seemed well to exemplify the application of the method to Greek authors.

[1] *The Primitive Text of the Gospels and Acts*, Oxford, 1914. Cf. *Journal of Theological Studies*, *Jan.* 1915, pp. 225–40 (an answer to objections).

The inquiry has developed as I went on, and fresh material has continually accumulated. Since I wished to keep this volume within bounds, I have not included in it references to other MSS., some of which are very instructive, which I have used since Chapter III was written, or certain studies which I have sketched in the case of other classical authors. The method is equally applicable to all ancient prose-texts for which we have good MSS., and the material is therefore inexhaustible.

The general object of this book is to show how internal evidence furnished by MSS. can be utilized to cast light upon the filiation of *codices*, and in some cases upon the archetype from which they are derived; also to apply such knowledge to the criticism and emendation of the text.

The argument rests mainly upon two principles, viz.:

(1) the regularity of writing in ancient MSS., which, as a rule, contain a similar, or even the same, number of letters to a line.

For proof of this I refer to pp. 9–18.

(2) the frequency of line-omissions in MSS.

It is always easy to omit, when one is making a copy. Sometimes there is no reason at all for the omission beyond human frailty. Most frequently there is a contributory cause, viz. ὁμοιότης (p. 1). This is often assisted by line division. Sometimes lines are omitted without any other cause than line division. The most instructive cases are where the sense is destroyed by the omission, or where a word is actually bisected (pp. 3–4).

I have illustrated this process (pp. 18–24) from *W*, a fifteenth century MS. of Cicero's speeches, which is derived, probably through an intermediate copy, from Σ, a MS. written in the same century. I have noticed 10 cases, where *W* omits complete lines of Σ, in three of which a word has been bisected; and 33 cases, where the scribe has passed from a certain point in one line to the same, or nearly the same, point in a line below. It would appear that the second process is the easier of the two, and it is probable that most omissions took place in this way.[1]

Σ is written in irregular script, with a quantity of abbreviations.

[1] In the course of this work, when I attempt to rearrange the model, I place the omitted passages in complete lines. This is merely for purposes of convenience.

The number of letters, however, contained by the omitted lines, shows a well-marked average. Thus, there are 15 examples of 47–9 letters. In an ancient MS. the uniformity would have been much greater.

In default of the model from which the copy is taken valuable evidence is sometimes supplied by MSS. which possess marginal supplements ticketed with omission labels. Here a numeration of the letters in the supplements gives unequivocal evidence of line-omission. Some simple examples where very few figures are involved will be found collected on pp. 37–8. Thus, Harl. 3063 has only two such additions, one of which contains 66 and the other 132 letters. As a rule, we find more than one unit, testifying to the presence of more than one ancestor, with corresponding bulges in the curve of omissions.

We have now a method which can be used where we possess MSS. belonging to different families. One of the chief problems in textual criticism is caused by the presence in some MSS. of passages not found in others which possess a better reputation. The general tendency of editors has been to throw in their lot with what they term 'the best MS.', and to regard with great suspicion all passages not found in it. Some go so far as to tar with the same brush passages omitted by the first hand in the 'best' MS., or the only MS. Thus Halm regarded as interpolations the additions of the second hand in the palimpsest of Cicero's *de Re Publica*. Some editors occasionally admit passages necessary to the sense, especially if their omission can be defended by ὁμοιότης, but reject others which are not absolutely necessary, though the omission can be explained in the same way. It is, I think, unlikely that an interpolator would have been so cunning as to conceal his inventions by a device intended to show that their omission was palaeographically possible. Other passages not defended by ὁμοιότης met with a short shrift. The first duty of the critic was to prune the text, and the fatal maxim *brevior lectio potior* still holds sway.

In these cases of doubt an arithmetical test is of great value. If the suspected passages are due to interpolation, then we should expect them to be of unequal length, and to show no relation to each other. If, however, we find a well-marked unit, or units, rising by multiples at regular intervals, there must be a cause, and the obvious cause is to be found in line-omission. To any one who fights against arithmetic I can only say σκληρόν σοι πρὸς κέντρα λακτίζειν.

The method which I have followed is to tabulate the omissions of a particular MS., to arrange them in order of magnitude and to let them tell their own story. There is a constant feature in all such tabulations which I have conducted, viz. that the figures become more and more striking as they increase in size. It is common to find that the largest figures form a series of multiples, closely correlated with each other. The reason is that single lines differ in length, some being abnormally long or short. If, however, we take a sufficient number the average appears and becomes more and more constant.

The large numbers are of special importance, where the unit is small, as in the case of MSS. written in narrow columns. Here we may detect a unit or even a multiple of a unit, but as the numbers rise they may be explained as multiples of any unit. If, however, the largest numbers are exact, or almost exact multiples of each other, and looking backwards we find a series of correlated numbers which support each other and form part of a scheme, we can work back from the larger multiples to the smaller and from them to the unit (p. 40).

In order to guard against a misconception which I find it hard to remove, I must point out with some emphasis that this method does not attempt to explain all omissions, but only those which are due to the lineation of an ancestor. There must always be omissions due to chance, especially if ὁμοιότης is present. These it is impossible to control, and they do not affect the argument. We can only tell from the figures where a line has been skipped.

There are also other sources of evidence, e.g. the dittography (p. 6). Here also the tendency is for the scribe to write twice a line or more. Thus, in Burn. 340 out of nine omissions seven contain 27–9 letters: there is also one dittography which consists of 56 letters (p. 55). Dittographies must therefore be tabulated together with omissions. Frequently we find contiguous omissions, or an omission followed shortly afterwards by a dittography of similar length. In such cases it is easy to write out the whole passage as it appeared in the model (p. 37, &c.).

Much convincing evidence is given by transpositions. When we compare the length of the passages which have changed places, it is a common experience to find that one is a multiple of the other, or that both are multiples of a unit for which there is other evidence. The reason for the inversion is therefore obvious. For a large succession of transpositions I would refer to the chapter on the Pseudo-Asconius.

The most interesting evidence is given by variants, frequently corruptions, which have got into the text (p. 49). These have a tendency to invade the text at regular intervals, i.e. at a distance of a line or several lines from the passage to which they refer. The testimony of papyri and palimpsests shows that *duplices lectiones*, or doublets, go back to a very ancient date. Sometimes they are corruptions or *voces nihili*, which were recorded in the margin. In some cases we find a doublet embedded in the text at a considerable distance from the variant for which it is an alternative. Here it is probable that it has been entered in the wrong column, or on the wrong page or folio of an ancestor. It is therefore important to tabulate and compare the distances between the two passages. The results are sometimes very surprising. Thus in *Phil.* xiv. 13, where a variant has found its way into the text from § 15, the intermediate space consists of 951 letters: in *Phil.* ii. 106, where the MSS. have a *vox nihili* (variously corrupted) which I take to be a doublet for a word in § 104, the intermediate space consists of 953 letters (pp. 199–201).

I desire to call particular attention to some singular evidence which throws light upon the formation of 'shorter' texts. I refer first to the abridgements which I have pointed out in the Berne Horace, and particularly to the version which it gives of *Sat.* i. 3. 75–125 (pp. 30–1). Here the abbreviator has reduced 51 lines to 23 by the simple expedient of striking out lines regardless of the sense, on one occasion 14 consecutive lines. His method is like that of a modern schoolboy who tries to cheat when he has been set to copy out a long imposition. He does not, however, endeavour to 'botch' the sense by consequential alterations, such as are often found (p. 123) where a passage has been doctored after an omission.[1]

I come next to a singular series of omissions found in an abridged text of Cic. *Fam.* vi. 9 § 1–10 § 6, which is given by a palimpsest leaf (pp. 147–53). Here there is a striking numerical relation between the portions excised by the abbreviator and those which he retained. The first passages which I examined yield the following figures: 94, 187, 284 (94 × 3 = 282), and similar relations exist throughout. I see no explanation except that the abbreviator struck out lines of his copy. Some of the excisions are self-contained. In others the sense is vitally affected by the omission, but the passage can be construed without any doctoring. Thus in 10. 1 he retains *itaque*, the first word in a sentence, leaves out the rest of the sentence, which contains names and details, and goes on with the next. The most interesting case is in § 2 of the same letter, where after a long cut, which appears to represent a passage of 22 lines in his model, he disguises his handiwork by inserting *nihil erit saltem.*

A minor example is to be found in the pseudo-Platonic Ὅροι as given by Par. 1807 (*A*). Here we have a series of excisions which exhibit numerical relations with the passages retained. Thus, one of the excisions which consists of 57 letters is preceded by a retained passage of 111 letters, and followed by one of 578 (p. 395).

More curious evidence is furnished by a remarkable series of obelizations in Demosthenes, *Midias*, found in three MSS. The

[1] A good example is to be found in the MSS. of Juvenal vi. 346–8. I quote Professor Housman, p. xxix:

'We now know that at some remote epoch twenty-nine verses were omitted after vi. 365, and left this headless sequel,

consilia et veteres quaecumque monetis amici,
"pone seram, cohibe." sed quis custodiet ipsos
custodes, qui nunc lascivae furta puellae
hac mercede silent? crimen commune tacetur.
prospicit hoc prudens, et ab illis incipit uxor.

In our MSS. these lines have been battered into the following shape:

audio quid veteres olim moneatis amici,
"pone seram, cohibe." sed quis custodiet ipsos
custodes? cauta est et ab illis incipit uxor

and have been transported to a new station between 345 and 349 in the vain hope of providing them with an appropriate context.'

first obelized passage consists of 54 letters, and the next of 107. Shortly afterwards two obelized passages both contain 110 letters (pp. 441–2). There is a constant relation between the excisions and the portions retained. Thus one obelized passage (§§ 217–18) and one intermediate block (§§ 98–9) both consist of 507 letters. These figures seem to shew that the author of the obelizations, who, as W. Christ says, 'was no Aristarchus', pursued the easy method of striking out lines in his copy.

This reference to Aristarchus induces me to mention a curious passage in Homer, *Il.* xviii. 603–6:

πολλὸς δ' ἱμερόεντα χορὸν περιίσταθ' ὅμιλος
τερπόμενοι· μετὰ δέ σφιν ἐμέλπετο θεῖος ἀοιδὸς
φορμίζων· δοιὼ δὲ κυβιστητῆρε κατ' αὐτοὺς
μολπῆς ἐξάρχοντος ἐδίνευον κατὰ μέσσους

The words μετὰ δέ . . . φορμίζων are not found in any MSS. or scholia. They are also absent from the Harris papyrus and B. M. 127. They are read by editors since Wolf, on the authority of Athen. 181 b–d, who ascribes the shorter version to Aristarchus, and accuses him of cutting down the text (ἐπιτεμὼν τὰ ποιήματα τὸν τρόπον τοῦτον). It is to be noticed that without the missing words ἐξάρχοντος[1] (i.e. ἀοιδοῦ) is very awkward.

The facts to which I have drawn notice are of importance in connexion with the shorter text of the Acts and the longer version, for which our chief authority is the codex Bezae. My excuse for mentioning this subject here is that it happens to be the part of my previous work to which I attach most importance, and that it has been passed over by my critics in significant silence. I therefore draw attention to it in the hope of eliciting an answer. My contention is that the oldest Greek MSS. *B* and ℵ—together with those of later date, apart from some insignificant exceptions—are derived from a MS. arranged in cola and commata resembling those found in the codex Bezae (*D*).

My argument is founded in the first place upon omissions. I have put together 41 cases where *B*ℵ &c. omit passages which occupy lines in *D*. To illustrate the character of these omissions I take Acts i. 5. Here *D* gives, with support from the versions:

υμεις δε εν πν̅ι̅ αγιω βαπτισθησεσθαι
και ο μελλεται λαμβανειν

[1] So Athenaeus; our MSS. have ἐξάρχοντες, so *Od.* iv. 17–8.

ου μετα πολλας ταυτας ημερας
εως της πεντηκοστης

*B*א &c. omit lines 2 and 4.

In another block of 20 cases the construction in *B*א &c. seems to have been botched after an omission. I instance as an example, ii. 37. *D* gives, with the Syriac (Harkl. *mg.*):

τοτε παντες οι συνελθοντες
και ακουσαντες κατενυγησαν τη καρδια

*B*א &c. give:

ἀκούσαντες δὲ κατενύγησαν τὴν καρδίαν

In other cases, no explanation is possible except that of bold abridgement, apart from line-omission.

Formerly I spoke of abridgement with caution, and only in connexion with the longer cuts, since it did not occur to me that an abbreviator would deliberately reduce his text by the excision of lines. I therefore treated all the omissions of *B*א &c. as due to accident. In view of the new evidence as to the methods of abbreviators, I now think that many of them may have been deliberate. This removes certain difficulties, since it seemed strange that a copyist should be so careless.

The instances which I gave were collected from the notes in Souter's edition. Since then I have noticed 14 other cases, not mentioned in his notes, in which passages omitted by *B*א &c. form lines in *D*. I mention the following as specimens:[1]

ii. 37: τι ουν ποιησομεν ανδρες αδελφοι
υποδειξατε ημειν *D*

*B*א &c. omit the second line.

xv. 23: γραψαντες επιστολην δια χειρος αυτων
περιεχουσανταδε *D*

*B*א &c. omit the second line.

[1] The other cases are v. 21 ἐγερθέντες τὸ πρωΐ, vi. 1 ἐν τῇ διακονίᾳ τῶν Ἑβραίων, vii. 24 καὶ ἔκρυψεν αὐτὸν ἐν τῇ ἄμμῳ, 26 καὶ εἶδεν αὐτοὺς ἀδικοῦντας, 37 αὐτοῦ ἀκούσεσθε, x. 33 παρακαλῶν ἐλθεῖν πρὸς ἡμᾶς, xii. 21 καταλλαγέντος δὲ αὐτοῦ τοῖς Τυρίοις, xiii. 41 καὶ ἐσίγησαν, xvi. 19 ἧς εἶχον δι' αὐτῆς, 38 τὰ ῥηθέντα πρὸς τοὺς στρατηγούς. All these occupy single lines in *D*, of very various length. Also, in xiii. 33 *D* has a passage of five lines, αἴτησαι παρ' ἐμοῦ . . . τῆς γῆς, not found in *B*א &c.

38 : τον αποστησαντα απ αυτων απο παμφυλιας
και μη συνελθοντα εις το εργον
εις ο επεμφθησαν *D*

*B*א &c. omit the third line.

I have also observed two more cases in which the text as found in *B*א seems to have been mended after an omission, viz.:

ii. 1 : και εγενετο εν ταις ημεραις εκειναις
του συμπληρουσθαι την ημεραν
της πεντηκοστης *D*

*B*א &c. give :

καὶ ἐν τῷ συμπληροῦσθαι τὴν ἡμέραν τῆς Πεντηκοστῆς

xii. 23 : και καταβας απο του βηματος
γενομενος σκωληκοβρωτος *D*

*B*א &c. give :

καὶ γενόμενος σκωληκόβρωτος

If this new evidence is taken into account, we have 55 cases where lines of *D* appear to have been omitted by *B*א &c., and 22 where, after an omission, the text has been slightly doctored. It will be seen therefore that my case is even stronger than I had supposed.

I now address a few words to those who may care to make trial of the method which I have employed. I venture to suggest that the student before trying his hand upon an author should select a MS. possessing a number of marginal additions prefaced by omission marks, and treat it in the manner set forth in Chapter III. It is best to choose a patristic MS. since, so far as my experience goes, these are richest in such marginalia. It is highly probable that in the great libraries of Europe there are many MSS. more suitable for this purpose than any of those which I have employed. The task is an easy one, since the additions and alterations of the corrector are obvious. The student will have some exciting moments. It is quite likely that the two first additions which he notes will prove to be of the same length, or that one will be twice the length of the other. As a rule he will get upon the track in the course of ten minutes. If he finds a 'telescoped' passage (p. 3), he has a sure clue. When the tabulation is complete, the large figures are likely to be of great interest.

After this preparation the method may be applied to a classical author. It will be well to select one for whom we have MSS. belonging to more than one family and of considerable antiquity. The inquiry is more difficult if the MSS. belong to a single family, or if there is only one MS., especially if this MS. is late. It is possible to elicit much information from corruptions of various kinds, particularly from dittographies (p. 159), but we are without the more cogent evidence furnished by the omissions of the various families.

It is best to analyse the MSS. singly, beginning with the one to which special importance is attached by critics. The student should abstain from guesses about the archetype until he has put together his results in the case of the various MSS. and the groups and families into which they fall. It is probable that several intermediate MSS. intervene between any particular MS. and the archetype. The possibility that a MS. is derived from a model very like itself must always be borne in mind.

It is necessary to be cautious and to avoid hasty conclusions. Figures are curious things and the limits of coincidence are large. It is only when we have a large number of facts all tending in the same direction that chance becomes unlikely or impossible.

I have to thank various friends for generous help which I have received from them. Dr. S. G. de Vries, whose kindness I have had to acknowledge on various occasions, lent to the Bodleian Library for my use the two chief MSS. for the philosophical *corpus* (*Nat. D.*, &c.), both of which belong to Leiden. Monsieur L. Dorez, of the Bibliothèque Nationale, verified for me a large number of passages in Paris. 14749, where I suspected that lines had been omitted by *W*, supplying me with the abbreviations used. Professor U. von Wilamowitz-Moellendorff obtained for me (in 1913) photographs of the Berlin leaves containing portions of Cicero, *pro Plancio*. Mr. Percy Simpson furnished me with a number of parallels in English literature for omissions similar to those which occur in classical texts. The Rev. H. M. Bannister verified for me various passages in Vatican MSS., and when in Oxford frequently advised me upon points of palaeography.

CONTENTS

INDEXES

CHAPTER I

OMISSIONS IN MANUSCRIPTS

THERE are certain forms of error to which all copyists are liable. The most fertile and insidious of these is generally known as *omissio ex homoeoteleuto.* The eye of the writer wanders from a particular word, or portion of a word, to a similar word, or portion of a word, elsewhere in the context, with the result that the intervening words are omitted. I take as an example

Thuc. iv. 39 ἐν τῇ νήσῳ ἐπολιορκήθησαν ἀπὸ τῆς ναυμαχίας μέχρι τῆς ἐν τῇ νήσῳ.

In an Oxyrhynchus papyrus (no. 16), written in the first century A.D., the words ἐπολιορκήθησαν . . . ἐν τῇ νήσῳ were omitted by the writer. They are added at the top of the page with reference marks, viz. κάτω at the top of the page and ἄνω above the place in the text where the insertion is to be made.

Frequently the similarity comes at the beginning, not at the end, e.g. Cicero, *pro Caelio*, § 27:

qui in hortis fuerit, qui unguenta sumpserit, qui Baias viderit.

The first clause, *qui in hortis fuerit*, which has been preserved by Donatus, is omitted by our MSS.

In such cases *homoeoteleuton* is a misnomer, and some critics use the term *homoeoarcton*. I prefer to use the single word ὁμοιότης for all such cases of 'skipping', and denote this by the symbol ὁμ. A French phrase is *saut du même au même*.[1]

The ravages of ὁμ. are widespread and in some cases difficult to control. Frequently, however, there is a contributory cause, viz. the coincidence of ὁμ. with line division. I illustrate by an example furnished to me by Dr. Wickham Legg. Recently he had occasion to quote in a work of his own a passage from R. C. Trench's *Sacred Latin Poetry*, which is printed thus:

The book, which is rather
scarce, was till very lately of absolute necessity for the
student of the Christian hymnology, above all for the
student of Adam of S[t] Victor's hymns.

[1] L. Havet, *Manuel de critique verbale*, p. 130.

When revising his proofs, he found that he had omitted l. 3, *student of the . . . for the.* The error was due to *homoeoarcton* as well as *homoeoteleuton.*

I have myself not infrequently fallen into the same trap. On one occasion I was engaged in copying out a long passage, previously unpublished, in Acardus (Achard d'Arrouaise) *de Templo Salamonis*[1] from an Oxford MS. (Bodl. 603), in which the following lines occur:

> labiumque singulorum ut repandi lilii
> mare quoque fecit unum cuius luter fusilis
> erat et in altum denis tendebatur cubitis
> trium unciarum erat grossitudo labii
> labiumque eius quasi calicis uel lilii

On comparing my proofs with the MS., I found that I had omitted ll. 2–5, having passed from *labiumque . . . lilii* in l. 1 to the same words in l. 5.

So also, when copying out for this work a passage of Primasius, which in Douce 140, cent. vii/viii, is written thus:

> sicut mosi di
> cit ego sum qui sum sic dicis filiis israhel qui est misit
> me ad uos et tu uero idem ipse es et per malachiam
> ego sum dn̄s deus

I found that I had written:

> sicut mosi dicit ego sum dn̄s deus (*om. med.*)

Here the *saut du même au même*, viz. from *ego sum* to *ego sum*, does not exactly correspond to the line division, but very nearly so. This is a very instructive error.

I owe to the kindness of Mr. Percy Simpson the following examples from English literature.

Chaucer, *Shipman's Tale* (*Canterbury Tales*, B. 1374–80):

> And if myn housbonde eek it myghte espye
> I were but lost and therfore I you preye
> [Lene me this somme, or ellis moot I deye.
> Daun John, I seye, lene me thise hundred frankes:
> Pardee, I wol nat faille you my thankes,
> If that you list to doon that I you praye.]
> For at a certeyn day I wol you paye

Harl. 7334 omits the bracketed lines (ὁμ.).

[1] *Revue de l'Orient latin*, xii, pp. 263–74.

Shakespeare, *Troilus and Cressida*, II. iii. The First Folio has:

Ther. Ile declin the whole question: Agamemnon commands Achilles, Achilles is my Lord, I am Patroclus Knower, and Patroclus is a foole.

[*Patro.* You rascall.

Ther. Peace, foole, I have not done.

Achil. He is a priuiledg'd man, proceede, Thersites.

Ther. Agamemnon is a foole, Achilles is a foole, Thersites is a foole and as aforesaid, Patroclus is a foole.]

The 1609 Quarto omits the bracketed lines (ὁμ.).

Hamlet, V. i. The First Folio has:

Clo. He was the first that ever bore Armes.

Other. [Why he had none.

Clo. What, ar't a Heathen? how dost thou understand the Scripture? the Scripture sayes, Adam dig'd; could hee digge without Armes?] Ile put another question to thee.

The 1604 Quarto omits the bracketed passage (ὁμ.).

Hamlet, V. i. The First Folio has:

This fellow might be in's time a great buyer of Land, with his Statutes, his Recognizances, his Fines, his double Vouchers, his Recoueries: [Is this the fine of his Fines, and the recouery of his Recoueries,] to haue his fine Pate full of fine Dirt?

The 1604 Quarto omits the bracketed passage (ὁμ.).

These instances will suffice to show the danger of omission due to ὁμ. which threatens every copyist, even if he is writing what he understands. It must be remembered that many of the scribes by whom Latin texts have been transmitted were very ignorant, and unable to grasp the sense of what they were writing. It is, therefore, not to be wondered at if they were often helpless victims to ὁμ.

I now proceed to consider further the phenomena of line omission. In some cases there is an obvious rent in the text. This is most noticeable when a word has been cut in two in consequence of an omission. I use the term 'telescoped' of such passages, e.g.:

Harl. 2686, f. 55r. Here the first hand gives:

inuicẽ se humogore temperat

A second hand adds, after *humo*:

-re siccitate calore et fri-

A previous MS. appears to have had:

humo
re siccitate calore et fri
gore

The scribe omitted a line. Here there is no ὁμ.

Laud. Misc. 134, f. 80^{v}. The first hand gives:

consuetu omnes

A second hand adds after *consuetu*:

dine uetus testamentum et lex ꝓphetae

The model must have had:

consuetu
dine uetus testamentum lex et ꝓphetae
omnes

Harl. 3012, f. 44. The first hand gives:

ecce aperti sunt caeli et uidit spm̄ dī descendentem sicut colummeus dilectus in quo mihi complacui.

A second hand adds, with reference mark for insertion after *colum-*:

bã uenientẽ sup̧ se et ecce uox de caelis dicens hic ẽ filius

The model must have had:

ecce aperti sunt caeli et uidit spm̄ dī descendentem sicut colum
bã uenientẽ sup̧ se et ecce uox de caelis dicens hic ẽ filius
meus dilectus in quo mihi complacui.

I mention as an illustration of these telescoped lines a paragraph which appeared in the *Globe* of May 1, 1914, viz.:

That speculators who dabble in oil shares, and
particularly in those of companies possessing
individual propositions as distinct from the
shares of trust companies, undertake consider-
had further advanced to ·970. The directors ex-
of this has just been provided by the Egyptian
group.

Shortly afterwards we read:

telegram received from Gemsah stated that the
specific gravity of the oil yielded by Well 13
had further advanced to 970. The directors ex-
plained.

Here it is obvious that a line has dropped out after *consider-*. The loss was repaired in a later edition, in which ll. 4–7 appeared correctly, viz.:

shares of trust companies undertake consider-
able risks is well known. A striking example
of this has just been provided by the Egyptian
group.

The missing line was expelled by a corrected version (·970 for 970) of a line which occurs later on *loco suo*. The confusion was due to ὁμ. (viz. *example* and *explained*).

In other cases the sense is mangled, although the words are intact. Thus, the *Globe* of August 3, 1915, gave the following:

> The Press Bureau announces:—
> General Sir Ian Hamilton reports on
> August 2 that on the right of the
> position held by the Australian and the
> was carried out against a network of
> Turkish trenches, which were about
> to threaten the safety of an advanced
> post called 'Tasmania Post'.

Here there is a lacuna at the end of l. 4. The report, as given in other journals, after *and the* adds, *New Zealand Corps a successful attack*. Here a complete line has fallen out.

I would here quote M. Havet, who says:

'Quand un MS. omet de suite plusieurs mots sans qu'ils forment ensemble une unité de sens et sans qu'il y ait saut du même au même, il est à présumer que la suite de mots en question formait une ligne du modèle.'[1]

In the following examples, I arrange, for the sake of brevity, the passage as I conceive it to have stood in the model, enclosing in brackets the line omitted by m. 1.

Harl. 3034, f. 80ʳ:

> non enim inquit est tibi pars neque
> [sors in sermone hoc separans eum]
> ab eis

Brit. Mus. 21215, f. 20ʳ:

> per hoc xp̃s ẽ
> [d̃s anima rationalis et caro qua veritate]
> recognita

Laud. Misc. 92, f. 129ᵛ:

> si per se ipsum quasi fidelium
> [coniugum commixtione ducẽ rationẽ consideret et culpabilis usus]
> non in coniugali c̄cubitu

[1] *Manuel*, p. 200.

Laud. Misc. 139, f. 11^{v}:

de hac aqua uiua dare mihi non potes
[quoniam hauritorium non habes, forte alium]
fontem promittis

Laud. Misc. 256, f. 81^{v}:

ꝑ speluncis
[et lenis nidos et catulos LXX transtulerunt]
in ceteris idẽ sensus est

Laud. Misc. 275, f. 12^{r}:

in
[cottidiana urbis sollempnitate]
laborantibus pauca loquenda sunt

Laud. Misc. 452, f. 166^{r}:

et eum qui orbem terrae
[extenta manu quatiebat nunc lepusculi alicuius]
aut ranae timiditatem adtractum latitare

In order to avoid misunderstanding, I would here state that the length of line, which I ascribe to the model in these examples, is inferred from a number of similar omissions in the same MS.

I now proceed to consider the opposite phenomenon to omission, viz. repetition, or dittography. A dittography, like an omission, may be due purely to chance, especially when one word or two or three only are repeated. Longer dittographies are generally due to line division, frequently aided by ὁμ. Repetitions of a line are not uncommon in newspapers. Thus, in the *Globe* of July 9, 1915, I noticed among the Stop Press Telegrams:

The "Echo de Paris" publishes a
message from Cettinje announcing the
message from Cettinje announcing the
appointment as Governor of Scutari of
Bojo Petrovitch.

The same journal contained a more complicated error in its issue of April 20, 1914, viz.:

Plans are reported to be quite ready for a
seizure of strategic points and a complete
blockade of the two coasts. A very powerful
forces, and a direct appeal from Huerta to
within thirty or so hours.

> Federal hopes seem to be that the intervention will be followed by a fusion of Mexican forces, and a direct appeal from Huerta to Carranza is reported.

Here l. 4 is a dittography of l. 8, which has taken the place of a missing line. A later edition contained the correct version, viz.:

> A very powerful force will be concentrated on the scene within thirty or so hours.

The corruption in l. 4 is due to ὁμ. (*force* and *forces*).

Prof. Skeat has pointed out an interesting dittography in Thomas Usk's *Testament of Love*, iii. 4:

But thilke to wilne nedeful is, for impossible to him it is oon thing and the same to wilne and not to wilne (SKEAT).

The first edition (Thynne's) has:

> but thilke to wylne nedeful is for impossyble
> to him it is one thing and the same to wylne
> he may not wylne [but thilk to wylne nedeful
> is for impossyble to him it is one thyng and
> the same to wylne and not to wylne]

I have enclosed in brackets the repeated words.

Dittographies are especially frequent in MSS. written in very narrow columns. I would refer to my analysis of the palimpsest containing Cicero, *de Re Publica*, and to that of the Scholiasta Bobiensis. Copyists seem to have found these short lines very confusing. As a typical example of dittography, due partly to line division and partly to ὁμ., I would quote an instance from Burn. 340 (Brit. Mus.), f. 27v.

The model, as is shown by other evidence, had

> considerantes
> quae per spm̃ scripta sunt et spiri
> talibus spiritalia comparantes

The first hand in Burn. 340 wrote twice the words *quae per* . . . *comparantes*. The scribe looked back from *comparantes* to *considerantes* and he repeated the intervening passage.

Before I go further, I would point out the great importance of line omission as a clue to parentage. When we are dealing with two allied MSS. we may often suspect that one is derived from the other, but it is difficult to prove the point, unless we find that a passage omitted by one MS. occupies a complete line in the other. If the line is very short, the occurrence may be due to accident. If, however, the line is fairly long, the hypothesis of accident becomes unlikely. If the same phenomenon occurs more than once, the proof is complete. This test is of special value when both MSS. appear to be of the same age. I take as an example two tenth-century MSS., which contain Cicero's *de Natura Deorum*, viz. Leid. Voss., Fol. 86 (*B*), and Flor. Marc. 257 (*F*). Schwenke has shown that *F* is derived from *B*. The proof is furnished by the fact that on two occasions *F* omits lines of *B*: viz.

N.D. i. 12. *B* has:

qui hac ratione
philosophentur ii nihil habeant quod sequantur. Dictum est omnino
de hac re alio loco

F omits *philosophentur . . . omnino.* Here there is no ὁμ. to assist the omission.

N.D. ii. 81. *B* has:

pos-
sent et ex sese similia sui gignere. Sunt autem qui omnia naturae nomine appel-
lent ut Epicurus

F has possent ut Epicurus *om. med.* Here the writer passed from one line to the text, the mistake being due to ὁμ. *F*, therefore, is no longer quoted as an authority, but is merged in *B*.

When we are dealing with fifteenth-century MSS., where the pedigree is often mixed, this test is of special value. Thus a British Museum MS. of the *Verrines*, Harl. 2687, appears to be derived from a Florentine MS., Laur. XLVIII. 29, known as Lag. 29, since in *Verr.* v. 168 it omits the words

crucem tollerentur. Sed quid ego de Gauio? quasi tu Gauio tum fueris

which form a complete line in Lag. 29.

The same test shows that another Florentine MS., Laur. XLVIII. 24 (Lag. 24), is descended from different ancestors in the speeches *in Rullum* and *in Pisonem.* The decisive passages are *Rull.* ii. 86:

altera Roma quaeretur. In id oppidum homines nefarii rem publicam uestram

This passage, which is omitted by Lag. 24, forms a complete line in another Florentine MS., Conv. Soppr. 13 (Lag. 39).

Pis. 1:

mentis est hic in fraudem homines impulit hic eos quibus est ignotus

This passage, which is omitted by the first hand in Lag. 24, forms a complete line in Laur. XLVIII. 13 (Lag. 13).

I would draw particular attention to certain excerpts from the *Verrines* which are found in a British Mus. MS., Harl. 2682, cent. xi (*H*), formerly belonging to Cologne Cathedral, and a MS. from Erfurt, cent. xii/xiii (*E*), now at Berlin. On two occasions *E* omits lines of *H*.

The first case occurs on f. 162ʳ of *H* (*Verr.* iv. 63). Here *H* has

libentissime dedit. Mittit etiam trullam gemmeã rogatum uelle se eam diligentius considerare,
ea quoq' ei mittitur. Nunc reliquũ iud' adtendite.

E omits *mittit . . . mittitur*. The copyist looked forward from *dedit* to *nunc* in the following line.

The other case occurs on f. 164ʳ of *H* (*Verr.* iv. 110). I here write out three lines as given in the MS., numbering the letters.

corpore ꝑhorrescam. Venit enim mihi fani loci religionis illius in mentẽ uersañt ante oculos omnia
dies ille cum ego hennã uenissem presto mihi sacerdotes cereris cum infuli[s] ac ũbenis fuer̃t contio
conuentusq; ciuiũ in quo ego cum loquerer tanti gemitus fletusq' fiebant ut acerbissimus tota urbe

E omits *dies . . . contio* (82). The previous passage, *mittit . . . mittitur*, contains 79 letters. The passages, therefore, are almost equal in length.

A page of *H* (f. 150ᵛ) will be found in facsimile in my collations from this MS.[1] It is written in a fairly regular hand with a number of abbreviations.

The contents of the page (36 lines) are as follows: 86, 81, 85, 83, 80, 86, 85, 83, 77, 79, 78, 81, 84, 85, 86, 85, 83, 86, 83, 85, 82, 85, 79, 80, 81, 76, 79, 82, 75, 83, 78, 80, 73, 75, 75, 76 = 2920.

The average here for a line is 81 ($81 \times 36 = 2916$).

Since I made this calculation, I have noticed that Dr. Purser, who collated *H* for the Letters *ad Familiares*, says of them that they are written in lines which contain about 82 letters.[2] The agreement between his calculation and mine is somewhat striking.

We now have an arithmetical equivalent for a line of *H*, viz. about 81 letters. It follows that in a MS. copied from *H*, if the scribe omitted two lines, the passage would be likely to consist of about

[1] *Anecdot. Oxon.* Part VII (1892). [2] *R. Irish Acad.*, 1885, p. 366.

162 letters, and that if he omitted three lines the passage would probably contain about 243 letters, and so on. Unfortunately *H* is ἄπαις, except in the excerpts from the *Verrines*, so these figures cannot actually be produced.

Let us now invert this process and suppose that we are dealing with three passages omitted by an important MS., or by the first hand in an important MS., the genuineness of which has been suspected. If, on counting the letters, we found that they consisted of 81, 162, 243 letters, or of numbers closely resembling these, we should be justified in concluding that they represented lines of a previous MS.

I have selected a MS. written in long lines for this preliminary demonstration of the method which I have followed in these pages, since, where the unit is so large, the argument may be stated simply. The theory, however, is the same, whatever the unit may be.

I would now point out that single lines in *H* vary a good deal in content, viz. from 73 (one example) to 86 (four examples). The average 81 emerges when we take 36 lines, some of which are exceptionally large, while others are exceptionally short. It follows that if a MS. copied from *H* omitted e.g. 10 lines, the contents of those 10 lines would be likely to exhibit a multiple of 81, rather than of the exceptional numbers. If the passage omitted were e.g. 20 lines, the average would appear still more unmistakably. This fact accounts for the importance of the large numbers to which attention will be called in the course of this discussion.

I now pass to more ancient documents. Before minuscule came into use, i.e. roughly speaking before the eighth century A.D., MSS. were written in capitals or uncials, without any division between the words. It is, therefore, likely that the content of lines would be more stable than in a minuscule MS., where the words are separated. Also, the lines were generally very much shorter in length and very narrow columns were often employed. There is, therefore, less scope for accident than in long lines of e.g. 80 letters. Further, whereas in *H* there are a number of contractions, which introduce an element of complication, in very ancient MSS. there were hardly any contractions, apart from certain recognized abbreviations, in Greek theological texts for *nomina sacra*, and in Latin MSS. for official titles. We can, therefore, take an ordinary printed text and arrange it with some certainty as it would be written in the second or third century A.D.

Since this principle that the contents of lines in ancient MSS., apart from certain disturbing causes, which will be dealt with later on, were very uniform, is the foundation of much of the reasoning to be found in this work, I propose to illustrate it by a number of examples. My excuse for so doing must be that there is not in existence, so far as I know, any similar collection of evidence. In several cases I give statistics concerning the number of letters in columns, pages, and folios of MSS. It was the rule[1] in ancient MSS. for every page to contain the same number of lines. It follows, therefore, that the contents of columns, pages, and folios constantly agree, like the smaller units of which they are composed.

Since we have no Latin documents which approach in antiquity some of the Greek papyri, I select as my first example a Greek papyrus written in the third century B.C.

Hibeh 26, Ῥητορικὴ πρὸς Ἀλέξανδρον. I take 20 lines from col. x. Here and elsewhere I use, for the sake of convenience, minuscules instead of capitals, and separate the words. I retain orthographical peculiarities.

επικεισθαι τιμωριας τοις παρα	(26)
βαινουσιν ταυτα χρη και τοις εν	(26)
τωι πολεμωι τελευτησασι ταφην	(26)
δημοσιον χωριον εγ καλωι προ της	(27)
πολεως αφωρισθαι καιτοι πασιν αν	(28)
των εως ηβησωσι εις τροφην διδοναι	(29)
τωμ μεν ουν εν ταις δημοκρατιαις	(27)
νομων τοιαυτην δει την θεσιν	(24)
ποιεισθαι· περι δε τας ολιγαρχιας	(28)
τας μεν αρχας δει τους νομους	(24)
κατανεμειν εξ ισου πασι τοις της	(27)
πολιτειας μετεχουσιν τουτων	(25)
δ ειναι τας πλειστας κληρωτας	(25)
τας δε μεγιστας κρυφαιαι ψηφωι	(26)
μεθ ορκων και πλειστης ακριβει	(26)
ας διαψηφιστας δει δε και τας ζη	(26)
μιας εν ταις ολιγαρχιαις μεγι	(25)
στας επικεισθαι τοις υβριζουσιν	(28)
τινας των πολιτων επιχειρουσιν	(27)
το γαρ πληθος ουχ ουτω των αρ	(23)
	523

[1] For exceptions see p. 46.

The figures are thus distributed:

(23) 1	(26) 6	(28) 3
(24) 2	(27) 4	(29) 1
(25) 3		

The curve bulges at 26, and this is the average for the 20 lines ($26 \times 20 = 520$).

The oldest documents which we have in Latin are palimpsests of the fourth and fifth centuries A. D. The examples which I take are from Ciceronian palimpsests.

Cicero, *de Re Publica*, cent. iv, Vat. 5751 (*C*).

A transcript of this important palimpsest has been published by Van Buren, from which I quote. It is written in two columns, with 15 lines to the page. I take as a specimen p. 24 (*Rep.* iii. 7):

col. 1		col. 2	
niam id est ĩ	(10)	si aut italiae	(12)
rerum natu	(9)	latium aut eius	(13)
ra longe ma	(9)	dem sabinā	(9)
ximi consili	(11)	aut bolscā	(9)
constituere	(11)	gentem si sā	(10)
eam remp. quae	(11)	nium si etru	(10)
possit esse diu	(13)	riam si mag	(9)
turna si sin	(10)	nam illam	(8)
gulos nume	(9)	graeciam cō	(10)
remus in sĩ	(9)	lustriare ani	(12)
gulas quanta	(11)	moue tueri	(9)
iam reperia	(10)	mus si deinde	(11)
tur uirorū	(9)	assurios si	(10)
excellentiū	(11)	persas si poe	(11)
multitudo	(9)	nos si haec	(9)
	152		152

Here the lines vary in content from 8–13, but the total is the same in both columns.

The columns vary slightly in breadth, but similar agreements between the contents of two columns in the same page are frequent, e.g.:

	col. 1	col. 2
p. 36	143	146
51	167	169
80	152	151
92	164	163
129	146	144
205	157	154

I tabulated the contents of 20 pages in this MS., which I chose as examples of different formation. Single columns vary from 135 to 174 letters. The total number of letters in 20 pages is 6112, divided between the two columns, thus:

Col. 1 = 3057.
Col. 2 = 3055.

This is an interesting example of the way in which the average asserts itself. I may add that it is not usual for two (or three) columns to be so similar. As a rule one column tends to 'squeeze' a second column, and when three columns are employed one of them generally suffers.

The total 6112 = 20 pages of two columns, i.e. 40 columns. If we divide 6112 by 40, we obtain as average 153 nearly (153 × 40 = 6120). The average number of letters to a line over 20 pages is 10·2.

I next take a palimpsest, also written in very narrow columns, but with three columns to the page (24 lines to the page), viz.:

Ambros. R. 57 sup., cent. v (*A*).

This MS. contains Cicero, *pro Scauro*, *pro Tullio*. A facsimile has been published by Peyron. I have counted the letters in 10 pages, choosing those in which the text was perfect, or nearly so, and found the totals to be as follows:

p. 15	= 836
16	= 833
17	= 843
21	= 843
22	= 828
25	= 840
26	= 834
31	= 833
32	= 894
39	= 852
	8436

The average for a page is 843. It is to be noticed that the figure 843 occurs twice. There are also two examples of 833, reinforced by one of 834. The contents of p. 32 are exceptionally large.

I add the contents of the columns in the two cases of 833 and 843 letters:

	col. 1	col. 2	col. 3		
p. 16	292	270	271	=	833
31	273	285	275	=	833
17	286	281	276	=	843
21	284	277	282	=	843

Here again considerable variety appears in the unit, but the totals coincide.

The totals for the 10 pages are:

col. 1 = 2835, avg. 283
2 = 2773, avg. 277
3 = 2828, avg. 282.

The general average for a line is nearly 12 letters (12 × 24 = 288).

I now take a palimpsest written in two columns, but with rather longer lines, viz.:

Taur. A. ii. 2*, cent. iv (*T*).

This is not now extant, having been burnt in the fire at the Turin Library. It also contained Cic. *pro Scauro*, *pro Tullio*, together with other fragments. Peyron has published a facsimile of *T* for the *pro Scauro* and *pro Tullio*, together with *A*. It had 21 lines to the page.

The contents of 10 pages in Peyron's transcript are as follows:

	col. 1	col. 2		
p. 13	379	404	=	783
14	368	377	=	745
19	361	370	=	731
20	377	393	=	770
23	397	390	=	787
24	358	388	=	746
27	374	380	=	754
28	371	384	=	755
41	374	388	=	762
42	357	367	=	724
	3716	3841	=	7557

Here the averages are: col. 1 = 371, col. 2 = 384. It is to be noticed that 371 occurs once in col. 1, and that there are two examples of 374. Also, that in col. 2 there is one case of 384, and two of 388.

The average number of letters to the line is a little over 18 for col. 2, and a little less than 18 for col. 1 (18 × 21 = 378).

The largest Ciceronian palimpsest is Vat. Reg. 2077 (*V*), containing portions of the *Verrines*, cent. iv. Of this we have 101 folios written in two columns, with 20 lines to the page and 18–19 letters to the line. I postpone discussion of *V* at this moment, since I describe it fully elsewhere.[1] I merely remark that throughout the *Verrines* the average contents of a page in *V* correspond with great regularity to 35 lines of Teubner text.

[1] pp. 212–26.

The examples which I have hitherto given from Latin MSS. are written in columns. This, however, was not the only method of writing. We also find MSS. at the same date written in long lines, i. e. across the page. Thus *T*, in addition to the fragments written in columns (*Scaur.*, *Tull.*, &c.), also contains two leaves obtained by Peyron from other sources. One of these contains a fragment of the *Verrines* written across the page with an average of 20 letters to the line. The other contains a fragment of Cicero's Letters *ad Familiares*, written in long lines with an average of 37 letters to the line.

As a specimen of writing in this formation, I will take:

Berol. Pap. 13229, cent. v.

This consists of two parchment leaves, containing Cicero, *pro Plancio*, §§ 27–8, 46–7. There are 17 lines to the page. The first leaf is perfect, except for some lacunae, the other is mutilated; but its contents can be inferred. The leaves were noticed by M. Seymour de Ricci in the Berlin Library; and I quote from his transcript.[1] I have not thought it necessary to mark the few lacunae. The verso of f. 1 contains §§ 27–8.

primum macedonia sic diligit hunc (29)
ut indicant hi qui principes ciuitatũ (32)
suarum cum missi sint in aliam (25)
causam tamen huius repentino (25)
periculo commoti huic adsident pro (30)
hoc laborant huic si praesto fue (27)
rint gratius se ciuitatibus suis fa (30)
cturos putant quam si legationem (28)
suam et mandata confecerint. (24)
L. uero apuleius tanti facit ut mo (27)
rem illum maiorum praescribit (26)
in parentum loco quaestorib. suis (28)
praetores esse oportere officiis (29)
benebolentiaq. superarit. (22)
Tr. pl. fuit non fortasse tam uehemens (30)
quam isti quos tu iure laudas set (27)
certe taliis quales si omnes semper (30)

469

[1] *Mélanges Chatelain*, pp. 442–7.

The average number of letters to the line is nearly 28 (28 × 17 = 476). It is to be noticed that ll. 9 and 14, which come at the end of paragraphs, are exceptionally short.

I now take two very important MSS. of Livy, viz. Vindobon. 15, cent. v, and Paris 5730, *cod. Puteani*, cent. v/vi. The Vienna MS. has been reproduced in facsimile by Messrs. Sijthoff (Leiden), and the Paris MS. (reduced) by the authorities of the Bibliothèque Nationale.

The Vindobonensis (*V*) contains Livy xli–xlv. It is written in long lines, with 29 lines to the page. I took at haphazard ff. 127^v^ and 128^r^ for examination.

As it would occupy much space to copy out the contents, I give the figures for the two pages.

f. 127^v^ = 27, 28, 27, 28, 27, 30, 30, 28, 27, 29, 27, 29, 28, 30, 31, 26, 30, 27, 27, 28, 28, 26, 27, 26, 23, 28, 25, 25, 28
= 800

f. 128^r^ = 29, 25, 27, 31, 28, 26, 30, 30, 26, 27, 28, 28, 28, 27, 27, 28, 31, 29, 28, 29, 28, 27, 29, 27, 28, 26, 29, 24, 29
= 809

The average content of a line is nearly 28 (28 × 29 = 812).

The 58 lines are thus distributed:

23	1 ex.	28	16 exx.
24	1 ex.	29	8 exx.
25	3 exx.	30	6 exx.
26	6 exx.	31	3 exx.
27	14 exx.		

It will be seen that out of 58 lines 30 consist of 27–8 letters.

The *Puteaneus* is written in two columns, with 26 lines to the page. I selected f. 13 for examination. The contents are as follows:

recto. col. 1 = 17, 18, 16, 16, 16, 19, 16, 18, 18, 16, 16, 17, 16, 16, 14, 17, 17, 15, 16, 13, 18, 17, 18, 17, 19, 18
= 434

col. 2 = 18, 18, 16, 17, 16, 20, 16, 17, 16, 19, 17, 18, 15, 17, 17, 17, 16, 16, 18, 15, 17, 16, 17, 16, 16, 15
= 436

verso. col. 1 = 16, 18, 14, 18, 16, 17, 14, 15, 19, 15, 15, 19, 14, 17, 15, 20, 16, 18, 16, 16, 16, 16, 18, 17, 17, 16
= 428

col. 2 = 18, 16, 17, 15, 16, 16, 16, 16, 15, 18, 16, 16, 14, 13, 16, 17, 16, 14, 17, 18, 16, 18, 17, 18, 15, 19
= 423

The average content of a column for this folio is 430, and the average content of a line is 16½ letters (16½ × 26 = 429).

The 104 lines are thus distributed:

13	2 exx.	17	22 exx.
14	6 exx.	18	19 exx.
15	11 exx.	19	6 exx.
16	36 exx.	20	2 exx.

Out of 104 lines, 53 consist of 16–17 letters.

I now pass to the end of the eighth century and take the first quaternion of

Basil. S. Petri H. 25 (*V*).

The MS. is written throughout in three columns, with 30 lines to the page. In the first quaternion, which contains part of Cic. *in Pisonem*, the script is semi-uncial. The rest of the MS., which contains the speeches *pro Flacco*, *pro Fonteio* (both fragmentary), and *Philippics*, is written in ninth-century minuscule.

Chatelain (Pl. xxvi) has a facsimile of f. 3r, and I possess a photograph of 4r. The contents of these pages as written are:

		col. 1	col. 2	col. 3		
f. 3r	=	509	498	471	=	1478
f. 4r	=	534	468	436	=	1438

If we take the whole quaternion, allowing the usual official abbreviations, the totals for the three columns are:

col. 1 = 8642
col. 2 = 8321
col. 3 = 8184

The average contents of a line are, in col. 1, 18; in col. 2 a little over 17; and in col. 3, 17. The tendency of col. 1 to 'squeeze' the others is to be noticed.

There are some interesting coincidences in the first quaternion, e.g.:

		col. 1	col. 2	col. 3		
1r	=	546	481	511	=	1538
2r	=	529	495	514	=	1538
2v	=	531	515	488	=	1534

In the later *Philippics* two passages (xii. 12–23, xiii. 1–10) have changed places owing to the dislocation of folios in an ancestor. The contents of the two blocks, if we allow the ordinary official abbreviations, are:

xii. 12–23 = 5828 letters
xiii. 1–10 = 5826 letters

I now pass on to the fifteenth century and select a MS. written in France, probably about 1400 A.D., viz.:

Paris. 14749, *olim S. Victoris* (Σ).

This is written in more than one hand. The earliest part of the MS. is written in a large, clumsy hand: the later part in smaller and more cursive characters. Neither hand has any pretence to neatness or uniformity. The interest of the MS. lies in the fact that part of it is derived from a very ancient MS. belonging to the Abbey of Cluni, no. 496 in the twelfth-century catalogue,[1] which contained Cicero *pro Milone*, *pro Sex. Roscio*, *pro Murena*, *pro Cluentio*, *pro Caelio*. The extant MSS. of the *pro Sex. Roscio* and *pro Murena* are all derived from Clun. 496, which came into the hands of Poggio in 1414 and was by him sent to Italy, where it subsequently disappeared. The writer of Σ copied from it the speeches *pro Sex. Roscio* and *pro Murena*, while in the other speeches which it contained he extracted from it marginalia and supplements, taking his text from a more legible MS.

In a work which I have published upon this MS.[2] I have given a reproduction of a page which contains Cic. *pro Caelio*, §§ 43–7. The contents of this, as written, are: 50, 51, 49, 54, 52, 51, 56, 49, 51, 52, 53, 47, 49, 50, 51, 51, 52, 52, 52, 54, 58, 55, 51, 52, 49, 52, 54, 52, 52, 54, 49, 52, 54, 52, 54, 55, 52 = 1923.

Σ contains 37 lines to the page. The average number of letters to the line, therefore, is, in this page, 52 ($37 \times 52 = 1924$). The script turns out to be more regular than might have been supposed.

The interest of Σ for the purposes of this discussion lies in the fact that it is a parent. Its offspring is a Wolfenbüttel MS. 205 (*W*), the readings of which have been published by Wrampelmeyer. We can therefore learn from Σ and *W* what actually happened when a copy of Σ was made.

Here, and elsewhere, I mark with an asterisk omissions not helped by ὁμ. and with double asterisks telescoped passages.

W omits the following complete lines of Σ. I add the number of letters.

[1] Manitius, *Philologisches aus alten Bibliothekskatalogen*, p. 15.

[2] *The Vetus Cluniacensis of Poggio*, Oxford, 1905.

(45) *Dom.* 116:
homo religiosus cum edis meas idem emeret et uenderet

(47) *Sest.* 27:
* cũ hoc satis ẽet signi ẽe impbũ qui mutata ueste nõ eẽt hac

(48) *Mur.* 6:
* dignitas in sũmo piculo ciuium postulabat. Quod si tum cum

(48) *Mur.* 79:
** magni interest iud. id qd ego multis repugnantibus aegi at-

(48) *Dom.* 72:
* poena dãpnati. Vtrũ igit' pcco meo nomẽ subeo an re iudicata

(49) *Vat.* 19:
** -nique cogitaris. Est enim res ei'modi ut si tibi modo in mentẽ

(50) *Mur.* 30:
* bon9 horridus miles amatur uestrũ uero studium totum iacet

(51) *Balb.* 29:
coniũcta ita m maxime cõmunionẽ beneficiou pmiou ciuitatis

(52) *Mur.* 5:
* michimet ipĩ iã pridẽ tulerĩ de ciuium piculis defendendis nõ

(52) *Balb.* 53:
** -ma uirtute et dignitate nepotes T. et C. coponios nostis damnato

It is to be noticed that there are three examples of 48, also two of 52, the number which came out as the average for *Cael.* 43–7.

In the following cases *W* passes from one line of Σ to another:

(41) *Dom.* 120:
et [TR. PL. idem ẽẽ potest. M. drusus ille clarissimus
uir] TR. PL. pontifex fuit

(42) *Sest.* 144:
tum ei' filium oculis lacrimãtibus [me intuentẽ uideo
milonẽ uindicem ũre libertatis] custodẽ salutis mee subsidiũ

(43) *Mur.* 60:
asperior et durior quã aut ueritas aut natura [patitur. Et quo
niam non est nobis hec oracio habenda] aut in ĩperita multitudine

(43) *Sest.* 46:
suspicione piculi sui nõ defenderẽt. [Alii uet'e odio bonorũ
incitarentur, alii inuiderẽt,] alii obtestare sibi me arbitrẽt'

(44) *Sest.* 95:
* etiam diem [dixit et accusauit de ui milonẽ. Neque hic tamen
nulla] umquam iniuria adduc'et˜ ut eũ tali uirtute tantaque firmi
tate

(44) *Sest.* 141:
** exemplis iracundiae leui[tatisq3 popularis tamẽ suã R.
P. illam defenderũt quid] nos tandem facere debemus, primum

This is a very remarkable case:

(45) *Rosc. Am.* 101:
uideremus nisi ipsos caecos redderet cupiditas et auaritia [et
audacia. Alter ex ipã caede uolucrem nuncium ameriã] ad socium

(45) *Vat.* 41:
eo quẽ [tu unũ improbiorẽ ẽẽ quã te numquã soles con
fiteri alt'] tuis consiliis illo tamẽ adiuuante q̃ro q[i] possis

(46) *Rosc. Am.* 120:
defectus iniquom est at ne quaeritur. [Sex. enim roscius reus
est neq; enim cum de hoc quaeritur] uos enim dominos esse

(46) *Sull.* 82: *loqui
tur neq; [cui'qã ornãenta oratiõis desiderat potest quisqã
dice'] umquam meliores

(47) *Quir.* 23: pecu
nia debita ꝓpt'ea qđ pecuniã qui retinet nõ dissoluit [q[i] reddidit nõ hẽt
grãm et qui retulit hẽt et q[i] hẽt desoluit] quaꝓpt' memoriã ũri

(47) *Dom.* 90:
*facinorosis ex egentib' congregatã. Illa [fuit pulcritudo populi
R. illa forma quã in campo uidisti] tũ cũ etiã tibi cont˜ senat' tocius

(47) *Har. Resp.* 43:
*foedere imꝓbando senat' seueritas dolori et timori [fuit.
Itaq; res illũ fortẽ et clarũ uirũ a grauitate patrũ] desiste
re coegit

(48) *Rosc. Am.* 147:
*possis nisi hoc [indignũ putas quod uestitum sedere in iudi
cio uides quem] tu e patrimonio tamq̃m a naufragio nu
dum

(48) *Mur.* 29: non po
tuerint. [Sic nonnullos uidem9 qui oratores euadere non potue
rint] ad iuris studiũ deuenire

(49) *Rosc. Am.* 56:
accusatores multos esse in ciuitate utile est [ut me
tu contineatur audacia. Verum tamẽ hoc ita est utile ut] ne plane il
ludamur

(49) *Quir.* 8:
pulcro quidẽ se a me ẽẽ seiunctũ [ꝑ me p̃sente senatus hominũq;
p̃terea XX mil. uestẽ mutauerũt] ꝑ eo absente unius squalorẽ sor
desque uidistis

(49) *Sull.* 48:
uelis ac defendere quẽ uelis [Imo seruit' est non dic'e in quem
uelis et defendere quẽ uelis] At si considerare cepis utrũ

(50) *Pomp.* 62:
priuatũ pro consule. [L. philippus dixisse dicit˜ nõ se illũ sua sententia ꝑ consule] sꝫ pro consulib' mittere

(50) *Vat.* 37:
sit amẽcia ut in ipã petitione gladiatores [audeas dare nunc quẽ putes illi' tui certissimi gladiatoris] similem

(51) *Quir.* 8:
desi
* derium mei [lacmeqꝫ pueriles. Aut itineribꝫ necessariis aut magna parte] lectis ac tenebris

(51) *Dom.* 95:
* fugisse. ad id qđ in crimine dabat˜. Non mo [pc̃cm nõ erat sꝫ erat res post natos hõies pulcherrima iudiciũ] populi ꝑtimuis se

(52) *Rosc. Am.* 39: inter
fuisse [nihil autem umquam debuit cupiditates porro quae possũt esse] in eo

(52) *Cael.* 63:
* impetrauisset. Sꝫ quid ego de dignitate istoꝝ testiũ loquor [uirtu tem eoꝝ diligentiãqꝫ cognoscite. In balneis delituerũt] testes egre gios

(53) *Rosc. Am.* 92: multi
titudine occiderit. Ac non hoc quaeratur eum qui [romae sit occi sus. Vtrum ueri similius sit ab eo esse occisum qui] assiduus eo tem pore

(53) *Rosc. Am.* 100:
* multas esse infamius [palmas, hanc primam esse tamẽ lemniscatam quae romae deferatur]. Nullum modum esse hominis occidendi

(54) *Pomp.* 7:
et ita regnat ut se nõ põto [neque capadocie latebris occultare uelit sed em̃g̃e patrio regno] atqꝫ in ũris uectigalib' hoc est in asie luce uer sari

(55) *Sest.* 135:
nõ tam admiror qđ meã legẽ [contẽpnet hominis inimici quã qđ se statuit om̃no consularẽ legẽ] nullam putare an

(56) *Cael.* 56:
herenniũ dicere [audistis uerbo se molestũ nõ futurũ fuisse caelio in iterũ eadẽ de re] suo familiari absoluto nom̃ hic detu lisset

(94) *Sest.* 109:
illa ruina rei p. dicet se legẽ tulisse [Quis est qi secũ cont˜ me ferebat˜ inisse suffragiũ confiteat˜. Cũ aũt de me eodẽ ex S. C. comiciis centuriatis ferebatur] Quis est qui non ꝑfiteat˜ se adfu isse

To these is to be added a case of dittography:

(49) Mur. 86: Quae cum ita sint iud.
primum rei p. cum qua nulla [res cuiqm̃ pocior debet esse uos ꝑ
mea summa et uobis cognita] in re p. diligentia

The words *res . . . cognita* are written twice in *W*. The scribe looked back from *cognita* to *nulla* (ὁμ.).

I would also illustrate a frequent cause of corruption from *Rosc. Am.* 45. Here Σ has:

haec tu non intelligis sed usq; eo quid arguas non habes ut non
modo tibi contra nos dicendum putes uerũ etiam contra rerum

W after *eo* has *quid putes arguas*. The writer dropped a line and then discovered his error.

If we put these figures together, their distribution is as follows:

(41) 1 ex. (*Dom.* 120)
(42) 1 ex. (*Sest.* 144)
(43) 2 exx. (*Mur.* 60, *Sest.* 46)
(44) 2 exx. (*Sest.* 95, 141)
(45) 3 exx. (*Rosc. Am.* 101, *Dom.* 116, *Vat.* 41)
(46) 2 exx. (*Rosc. Am.* 120, *Sull.* 82)
(47) 4 exx. (*Quir.* 23, *Dom.* 90, *Har. Resp.* 43, *Sest.* 27)
(48) 5 exx. (*Rosc. Am.* 147, *Mur.* 6, 29, 79, *Dom.* 72)
(49) 5 exx. (*Rosc. Am.* 56, *Mur.* 86, *Quir.* 8, *Sull.* 48, *Vat.* 19)
(50) 3 exx. (*Pomp.* 62, *Mur.* 30, *Vat.* 37)
(51) 3 exx. (*Quir.* 8, *Balb.* 29, *Dom.* 95)
(52) 4 exx. (*Rosc. Am.* 39, *Mur.* 5, *Cael.* 63, *Balb.* 53)
(53) 2 exx. (*Rosc. Am.* 92, 100)
(54) 1 ex. (*Pomp.* 7)
(55) 1 ex. (*Sest.* 135)
(56) 1 ex. (*Cael.* 56)
(94) 1 ex. (*Sest.* 109)

Here we have to notice the pronounced bulge in the curve at 47–9 (14 exx.), together with the largest number, 94. There is also a minor bulge at 52 (4 exx.). It is interesting to observe that the average for a line of Σ in *Cael.* 43–7 (cf. p. 18) is 52. I would also remark that out of 40 cases where a single line has been omitted, 33 range from 44–53. If we consider the irregularity of the script in Σ, this is a striking result. It cannot be doubted that if the model of *W* had been an ancient MS. written in capitals, the similarity between its omissions would have been even greater.

These examples are taken from ff. 1–168. After this point the hand changes and becomes more cursive. I have noticed the following cases of omission in *W*, due to the fact that the copyist passed from one line of Σ to another:

(58) *Quinct.* 78:

etẽm cũ artifex eiusmodi sit ut solus [dignus uideatur ẽẽ qui in scena spec
tetur tñ uir eiusmodi est ut solus] dignus uideat˜. qui eo non accedat

(123) *Clu.* 63:

exitus illi' iudicii futur' esset, uerisimili' tñ ẽẽt eũ [poti' corrupisse qui me
tuisset ne ip̃e condempnaret˜ ꝗ ille qui uerit' ẽẽt ne alt' absolũẽtur. Deinde
cũ ẽẽt nemini dubiũ ꝗ iudicãĩ necesse esset eũ certe] poti' qui sibi aliqua

(132) *Clu.* 88:

tra inuidiam his iudicibus freta miserit. Verũtñ multa ista iudicia [que sunt ego
enĩ me ad om̃ia confirmaui et sic paraui ut docerem que fc̃a postea iudicia de illo
iudicio dicerentur ꝑtim ruine similiora aut tempestati q̃ iudicio] et disceptatõni

There is a noticeable difference between this list and the first, in which omissions of whole lines were given. In the first list only two cases out of ten were due to ὁμ. In the second ὁμ. is present in 24 cases out of 33. It appears to follow that where ὁμ. is present, it is more likely than not that a writer has passed from one line to another, and that where it is absent, or where the passage is telescoped, it is probable that the writer has skipped complete lines. On the other hand, the telescoped passage, *Sest.* 141 (44), shows that it was possible for a scribe to jump from one line to another in a very unaccountable way.

We have seen that *W* omits a line, or lines, of Σ on 43 occasions in all. I may add that *W* has a large number of further omissions, which I have not attempted to deal with, since they find no explanation in Σ. Many of them are short passages, and the loss is without doubt frequently due to chance or the carelessness of the transcriber, assisted by ὁμ. Also, there is reason to believe that an intermediate MS. intervened between Σ and *W*. If so, it is likely that many of the unexplained omissions represent lines of this intervening ancestor.

I have said elsewhere,[1] 'A text is like a traveller who goes from one inn to another, losing an article of luggage at each halt.' In the case of certain speeches contained by Σ, it would be possible to extend the inquiry further than I have done. I refer to the sylloge contained in Paris. 7794 (*P*), cent. iv, viz. *post reditum*, *Sest.*, *Vat.*, *Cael.*, *Prov. Cons.*, *Balb.* I had previously remarked that in these

[1] *Journal of Theological Studies*, xvi (1915), p. 233.

speeches Σ is derived from *P*. Peterson has shown that Σ is not a direct copy, but that it has been taken from Bern. 136 (*B*), cent. xii, which is itself copied from *P*.[1] It would be interesting to trace the transmission of the text from *P* to *W*, through *B* and Σ. It has not, however, been possible for me to do this at the present time.

The only other case in which I have myself collated two MSS., one of which is certainly derived from the other, concerns Asconius and the pseudo-Asconius. The MSS. in question are

Pistoriensis, Forteguerri 37 (*S*)
Paris. 7833 (*σ*).

The first of these is the most authoritative MS. of Asconius. It is a copy made by Sozomenus, a friend of Poggio, at Constance in 1417. The second is derived from it, but is not a direct copy, being drawn from an intermediate MS., which had received a number of corrections taken from the Poggian family.

At first sight *S* would seem a most unpromising MS. for the purposes of this inquiry, since it is written in a semi-cursive hand with no pretence to regularity. The results, however, are more satisfactory than could have been expected.

The references which I give are to Stangl's *Ciceronis Orationum Scholiastae* (1912).

There are three occasions on which *σ* omits complete lines of *S*. The first does not concern us here, since it is not a line of the text, but a title, written in capitals, viz.:

24. 1-2. ENARRATIO CIRCA VER. PRIM. XXXX

The other two are:

(40) 65. 12: cum peregrino negauit se iudicio aequo certare
(77) 203. 16: sunt accusare atque ille GN. pompeius propiora
exempla et magis similia posteriora ponenda

There are nine cases in which the writer has passed from one line of *S* to the next, viz.:

(33) 212. 2: nonis Augustis [et comitia
consularia fuerũt VI k̄l. Augu.] nec multo post
(35) 247. 8: conficeret [quo modo ergo
dicit uerrem tabulas non hr̃e] sed aliquo

[1] *Class. Quarterly*, iv (1910), p. 168.

38) 187. 18-20: de
fensioẽȝ [et inire defensiõem uult esse nõ accu
satioẽȝ] saepe

200. 23-4: uel gestum [quartum
quem sit habiturus duos dixit quõ quõ] quartum

232. 29-30: * si quam diem [illi ĩ ꝓmittendo elegerãt ego ĩ
accusando non] effugissem

240. 19-20: postea ꝓcreare [uideant si in promptu ẽ res
inuestigent qua nõ] uideant

(39) 221. 9-10: patrocinium [meruerit aut assentatione aliqua
defendendi] meruerit

(42) 255. 22-3: accusatus est [a cluentio reiectiõe utrimqȝ
fc̃a subsortitus est] in eorum

(43) 225. 25-6: intelligi conuenit [ibi enim reie
ctio iudicum ubi et retentio continet˜] in reiectiõe

There are also two dittographies, viz.:

(36) 213. 10-11: nomẽ est propriuȝ romula
[nomẽ tribus ablatiui casus ut sit ex romula] tb' (with "i" written above)

The words *nomẽ . . . ex romula* are written twice. The writer looked back to *romula* in l. 1 and repeated the intervening passage.

(71) 231. 12-14: dabãt quod significabat [nõ liquere unde
ampliatio nascebat˜ iudicari dici sñia absolu
tionis hoc significat] id quod sequitur.

The writer looked back from *significat* to *significabat* and repeated the passage.

If we put together these figures we have:

(33)	1 ex.	(40)	1 ex.
(35)	1 ex.	(42)	1 ex.
(36)	1 ex.	(43)	1 ex.
(38)	4 exx.	(71)	1 ex.
(39)	1 ex.	(77)	1 ex.

The bulge in the curve at 38 is noticeable, also the relation of 77, the largest number, to 38. There is also a relation between 71, the next largest number, and 36.

The results in the case of *S* and σ are very similar to those observed in that of Σ and *W*. They are striking, because in both cases the parent MS. is written in an irregular minuscule.

So far I have dealt with the relation of two existing MSS., both written in the fifteenth century, to their existing ancestors, also written in the same century. It is obvious that several ancestors must have intervened between a MS. of this period and the distant archetype. It is to be remembered that a text ran the same risks on each occasion when it was transcribed, since all copyists were subject to the same infirmities. Let us suppose an archetype written in about 28 letters to the line, succeeded by a MS. with about 35 letters to the line, and again by one with about 45. It seems probable that on each occasion a certain percentage of the omissions would show the units 28, 35, 45, or multiples of these units.

It is manifest that in course of time the losses thus sustained would become considerable. There was, however, a restraining influence, that of the corrector, who took the place of the modern proof reader. When a MS. was written, it was generally, though by no means always, read by a corrector, who compared it with the model, or possibly with other MSS. One of his chief duties was to repair omissions, and this we find him doing in papyri, palimpsests, and MSS. of all periods. The additions which he makes are frequently accompanied by omission-marks, which show that the passages had been left out by the first hand. In several MSS. there are references to other MSS. from which losses have been repaired. In this way the marginalia may take us back to a previous stage in the transmission of the text. We should, therefore, expect to find in them the operation of more than one unit.

In this connexion it is to be noticed that it is frequent to find the same additions in the margin of various MSS. belonging to the same family. In this case they are traditional variants taken from another family. This is notably the case with four tenth-century MSS. of Cicero, *de Senectute* (*ALPV*). A scribe sometimes incorporated a supplement and sometimes reproduced it in the margin, without any apparent reason. Sometimes we find an entire collection of marginalia, including notes of all kinds, in two or more MSS. I would give as an example Paris. 14749 (Σ) and Vat. Palat. 1820 (*p*) in the *Planciana* and other speeches.

So far I have considered omissions due to accident. I now come to another cause, viz. deliberate abridgement. In order to illustrate this, I will turn to an author whose text is well attested, viz. Horace. The particular MS. is:

Bern. 363, cent. ix (*B*).

B was written by an Irish scribe, apparently in the North of Italy.[1] It has been reproduced in the Leiden series of facsimiles with a very valuable preface by H. Hagen, who describes it as '*omnium quotquot exstant Horatii librorum fere vetustissimus*'. It is the only ninth-century MS. in Vollmer's class i, though there are three ninth-century MSS. in his class ii. It will be seen, therefore, that it has great claims to respect.

B has a number of omissions which appear to be involuntary. I mention these first. Some are due to ὁμ., viz.:

Carm. iv. 2. 32–3: carmina fingo
[concines maiore poeta plectro]

Carm. iv. 13. 1–2: audivere, Lyce, [di mea vota, di
audivere Lyce] fis anus et tamen

Epod. xvi. 51–2: nec vespertinus circumgemit ursus ovile
[nec intumescit alta viperis humus]

Sat. i. 1. 78–9: [ne te compilent fugientes, hoc iuvat horum]
semper ego optarim pauperrimus esse bonorum

Sat. i. 3. 9–10: nil aequale homini fuit illi: saepe velut qui
[currebat fugiens hostem. persaepe velut qui]

Sat. i. 3. 51–5: postulat ut videatur: at est truculentior atque
[plus aequo liber: simplex fortisque habeatur
caldior est: acris inter numeretur: opinor,
haec res et iungit, iunctos et servat amicos.
at nos virtutes ipsas invertimus atque]

Sat. i. 3. 75–80: peccatis veniam poscentem reddere rursus.
[denique, quatenus excidi penitus vitium irae,
cetera item nequeunt stultis haerentia, cur non
ponderibus modulisque suis ratio utitur ac res
ut quaeque est, ita suppliciis delicta coercet?
si quis eum servum, patinam qui tollere iussus]

To these should probably be added

Carm. iii. 4. 17–20: ut tuto ab atris corpore viperis
dormirem et ursis, ut premerer sacra
lauroque conlataque myrto
non sine dis animosus infans

The next stanza begins with *vester*, which in *B* is written *ũr*. Probably the writer passed from *ut* to *ũr*.

In other cases there is no ὁμ., but the scribe appears to have omitted lines by accident, viz.:

[1] Cf. Lindsay, *Notae Latinae*, p. 448. The MS. is connected with the circle of Sedulius.

Carm. i. 10. 14: Ilio dives Priamus relicto
Carm. i. 17. 15–16: manabit ad plenum benigno
ruris honorum opulenta cornu
Carm. i. 19. 11–13: aut versis animosum equis
Parthum dicere nec quae nihil attinent
hic vivum mihi caespitem, hic
Carm. i. 19. 15: bimi cum patera meri
Carm. i. 26. 7–8: gaudes apricos necte flores
necte meo Lamiae coronam
Carm. ii. 17. 6–9: maturior vis, quid moror altera
nec carus aeque nec superstes
integer? ille dies utramque
ducet ruinam. non ego perfidum
Carm. iii. 4. 29: ut cumque mecum vos eritis, libens
Carm. iii. 4. 66–8: vim temperatam di quoque provehunt
in maius, idem odere vires
omne nefas animo moventes
Carm. iii. 5. 31–4: si pugnat extricata densis
cerva plagis, erit ille fortis
qui perfidis se credidit hostibus
et Marte Poenos proteret altero
Epod. viii. 18: minusve languet fascinum
Epod. xvi. 23–6: sic placet? an melius quis habet suadere? secunda
ratem occupare quid moramur alite?
sed iuremus in haec: simul imis saxa renarint
vadis levata, ne redire sit nefas
Sat. i. 3. 84–5: maius peccatum est: paulum deliquit amicus
quod nisi concedas, habeare insuavis, acerbus
Sat. i. 3. 92: aut positum ante mea quia pullum in parte catini
Ars Poet. 2: iungere si velit et varias inducere plumas
Ars Poet. 283: dignam lege regi: lex est accepta, chorusque

B contains various transpositions, viz.:
Carm. iii. 15. 15–16 are given thus:

(16) nec poti vetulam faece tenus cadi
(15) nec flos purpureus rosae

Ars Poet. 424–5. The order in *B* is:

(425) noscere mendacem verumque beatus amicum
(424) litibus implicitum mirabor si sciet inter

In *Epod.* xvi, line 32 is placed after 39. The order, therefore, is:

(39) vos quibus est virtus, muliebrem tollite luctum
(32) adulteretur et columba miluo
(40) Etrusca praeter et volate litora

The effect is somewhat curious, since nonsense is produced.

I have noticed an occasion where *B* corrects a mistake in the making, viz.:

Carm. Saec. 55: iam Scythae responsa petunt superbi

The writer originally went on to l. 57 (ὁμ.):

iam Fides et Pax et Honor Pudorque

omitting ll. 55–6. He then struck out the line, and went on correctly with l. 55. The correction shows that some at least of the writer's omissions were involuntary.

I now come to the evidence for design, as apart from accident. The order in *B* is curious. First comes a short selection from the *Odes* and *Epodes*, also the *Carmen Saeculare*, then the writer goes back to the poems previously omitted. Thus he had previously given *Epod.* xvii. 53–81 (p. 345 of the facsimile), and afterwards (p. 364) has 1–80. On p. 345 *Epod.* xii ceases at l. 6, and on p. 363 it is given in full.

In a large number of cases the writer omits the end of the poem, in some cases the greater part of the poem, entering in the marg. *rt* (= *reliqua*), or *et rt*. This happens on the following occasions:

Carm. i. 16. 15–28; 29. 7–16.
ii. 7. 19–28; 15. 12–20.
iii. 2. 17–32; 6. 15–48; 16. 29–44; 22. 5–8; 23. 12–20; 24. 30–64.
iv. 2. 41–60 (*rt* is here omitted); 14. 5–52.
Epod. i. 1. 9–34; 3. 9–22; 9. 13–38; 11. 13–28.
Sat. i. 3. 135–42.
Ars Poet. 441–76 (*rt* omitted).

On several occasions there are minor cuts, just before the writer breaks off and adds *rt*. It is probable that these also are intentional.

Carm. ii. 15. 8–11 are given thus:

fertilibus domino priori
non ita romuli praescriptum et intonsi catonis *rt*

Here ll. 9–10:

tum spissa ramis laurea fervidos
excludet ictus

have disappeared before *non ita Romuli*.

iii. 2. 5–12. *vitamque* . . . *caedes.* These two stanzas are omitted, the next stanza is spared, then comes *rt.*

iii. 6. 11–13. *nostros.* . . . *seditionibus.* These lines are omitted just before the final cut. The poem ends in the following manner:

10 inauspicatos contudit impetus
14 delevit urbem Dacus et Aethiops *rt*

iii. 16. 6–44. *B* has:

6 custodem pavidum Iuppiter et Venus
28 magnas inter opes inops *rt*

This is a very singular case.

iv. 9. 37–46. *B* has:

37 vindex avarae fraudis
41 iudex honestum praetulit utili
46 recte beatum rectius occupat

The rest of the poem is not omitted.

There is a remarkable series of omissions in *Sat.* i. 3, viz. 76–80, 84–5, 92, 95–100, 111–24. I have already mentioned δμ. as a cause for the omission of 76–80, and suggested that the omissions of 84–5 and 92 may be due to accident. No such explanation can be given for the long cuts 95–100 and 111–24. As *B* breaks off with *rt* after 134, it would seem that the writer was getting impatient.

I add the passage as given by *B*:

75 peccatis veniam poscentem reddere rursus
81 semesos pisces tepidumque ligurrierit ius
in cruce suffigat, Labeone insanior inter
83 sanos dicatur, quanto hoc furiosius atque
86 odisti et fugis ut Rusonem debitor aeris
qui nisi cum tristes misero venere kalendae
mercedem aut nummos unde unde extricat amaras
porrecto iugulo historias captivus ut audit
comminxit lectum potus mensave catillum
91 Evandri manibus tritum deiecit ob hanc rem
93 sustulit esuriens minus hoc iucundus amicus
94 sit mihi? quid faciam si furtum fecerit aut si
101 unguibus et pugnis dein fustibus atque ita porro
pugnabant armis quae post fabricaverat usus,
donec verba quibus voces sensusque notarent
nominaque invenere: dehinc absistere bello,
oppida coeperunt munire et ponere leges
ne quis fur esset neu latro neu quis adulter

nam fuit ante Helenam cunnus taeterrima belli
causa sed ignotis perierunt mortibus illi
quos venerem incertam rapientes more ferarum
viribus editior caedebat ut in grege taurus
et sutor bonus et solus formosus et est rex

It will be seen that the sense is wholly destroyed by the omissions.

It is difficult to discover any principles upon which the writer of *B* acted in his abridgements. That he was not influenced by delicacy will be seen from the passages retained in *Sat.* i. 3. 75–125. Also, it is noticeable that while on p. 345 *Epod.* xii ends at l. 6 (*rt*), on p. 363 it is given in full, this being the only case except *Epod.* xvii. 1–80, where such an omission is repaired.

He cannot have been influenced by religious considerations, since he leaves out, e.g., the magnificent passage upon *virtus* in iii. 2. 17–32. His excisions show a total want of taste, since he mutilates some of the finest poems, e.g. iv. 14, in which he leaves out 5–52, an unusually large cut. The hypothesis of dishonesty would explain some of the long cuts in the middle of a poem, but the question arises, why did he indicate his omissions at the ends of poems by *rt*? In any case *B* is very interesting as a clear example of deliberate abridgement, and it throws much light upon some similar cases which will be pointed out in the course of this work.

CHAPTER II

OMISSION MARKS, ETC.

In the previous chapter I have given examples of line omission in the case of two MSS. (*W* and σ), derived from two other MSS. (Σ and *S*) now extant. I now turn to another source from which valuable information can be gained.

Most MSS. contain much evidence concerning their ancestry which can be collected by any one who will take the trouble to turn over their pages. I refer in the first place to erasures where the writer has corrected some error due to mechanical causes, and to dittographies which have been struck out. Also, in many MSS. there are a number of additions made by a second hand, generally introduced by omission marks.

It occurred to me that it might be worth while to make a systematic examination of such additions in a few ancient MSS., in order to see if they showed the operation of a unit, or more than one unit. If so, the conclusion would seem to follow that the unit or units represent lines of one or more ancestors. I soon found that the inquiry was fruitful, and I was encouraged to conduct it on a large scale. I therefore looked through all the Latin MSS. (over 100 in number) prior to the tenth century which I could find in the Bodleian Library and in the British Museum; also a few of later date. I am aware that better and more interesting examples than many of the MSS. which I have used might be furnished by the great continental libraries, but the times at which I write are not favourable to travel, and I wished to get this work off my hands as soon as possible. I have, therefore, contented myself with the evidence furnished by two English libraries. I venture to think that the phenomena which I have observed in the MSS. which I have used will be found to be normal in MSS. generally.

The MSS. which I have examined differ greatly in regard to marginalia. Some possess few or none. Thus I found none in

Harl. 2664, cent. x/xi (Quintilian), or in Harl. 2767, cent. ix/x (Vitruvius), and only three in Harl. 2672,[1] cent. x (Livy). Speaking generally, I should say that classical MSS. of the Caroline and post-Caroline period are not a good hunting-ground for such evidence. On the other hand theological MSS. at all periods are much more instructive, and sometimes present a veritable *embarras de richesses*. One particular collection I found to be of extraordinary interest. This consists of MSS. from the Irish foundation of St. Kilian at Würzburg, given to the University of Oxford by Archbishop Laud. Most of these now form part of Laud Misc., in the Bodleian Library.

The method which I have followed is to copy out all the additions made, either by the scribe himself, or by a second hand, to register dittographies in the same way, to collect any other evidence in the shape of corruptions which seemed due to the lineation of the model, or of previous ancestors, and to tabulate the figures in order of magnitude. The figures then tell their own story. It would be possible for me to put the results in a more striking way, if I were to ignore those omissions which are due to mere chance and only confuse the issue. I think it best, however, to present the reader with all the evidence, and therefore include much superfluous matter.

The theory is that a certain percentage, in some cases a very large percentage, of omissions is due to the lineation of the model, or of a previous MS. What this percentage is can only be determined by the figures. I have said elsewhere:[2]

'My contention is not that all omissions are to be explained in the same way. Chance is always an important factor, and any omission of any length may be due to ὁμοιότης' (i.e. without line division). 'What I maintain is that a certain proportion of omissions is due to a definite cause, viz. the loss of lines in a previous MS., and that where the curve of variations shows recurring bulges, as we rise from multiple to multiple of the unit, while the larger numbers are correlated and support each other, we are justified in considering that something more than blind chance is at work.'

Before I go further, I will say a few words about omission marks.

[1] According to Conway and Walters, Harl. 2672 omits freely, generally on account of ὁμ. (Praef. p. xxv.) These omissions were not repaired by a corrector.

[2] *Journal of Theological Studies*, xvi (1915), p. 235.

The best discussion of these is to be found in a paper recently published by Prof. Lindsay.[1]

Sometimes a mere *signe de renvoi*, e. g. ;, ⋇, ∸, is used. As a rule, however, the letter *h* (= *hic*) is employed, either by itself or in combination with another letter, in order to arrest the attention of the reader. Lindsay observes that *hic*, in full, occurs in this sense in Paris. 8084, Prudentius, cent. vi. I have noticed in a dictionary of Tironian notes, Brit. Mus. 21164, cent. x, f. 11^{v}, that *h* is given as the sign for *hic*.

The letter generally combined with *h* is *d* (= *deest*). Other combinations are h̄s (± *hic supple*), h̄p (= *hic pone*), h̄l (= *hic lege*). We also find h̄h, where the *h* appears to be doubled for the sake of emphasis.

A rarer sign is *h. m.*, which apparently = *hic minus*. Other signs are s̄r̄ (= *super*), or $\bar{d}^{m}$ (= *dimissum*). In Harl. 5792, cent. vii, I have noticed *deletum* where lacunae occur.

The usual method is to employ a pair of signs, e.g. h̄d in the text and d̄h in the margin (or elsewhere) before the addition. Lindsay points out that some of these signs are peculiar to certain *scriptoria*. Thus h̄l is specially characteristic of Lorsch.

These symbols are frequently received into the text of MSS.[2] In this case they bear witness to a previous stage, when an omitted passage was placed in the margin with a label attached to show its status. When it was taken back into the text the ticket was not removed. Thus I have noticed in Douce 140, cent. vii/viii, three passages in the text (one of them *loco alieno*), which are preceded and followed by omission marks (cf. p. 108). In the *Philippics V* has received *hs* into the text in i. 11, and *h. m.* in v. 4. On both occasions the insertion has been made in the wrong place. One of the most curious of such insertions is:

Lucr. iii. 4: ficta pedum pono pressis vestigia signis

The Vienna fragment, cent. ix (Chatelain, Pl. lx), has:

ficta pedum pono presis uestigia signi hd̄s

Chatelain thinks that *s* was originally omitted. It seems more

[1] *Revue des Bibliothèques*, 1914.

[2] For corruptions due to such insertions cf. W. C. F. Walters in *Class. Rev.* xvii (1903), p. 162, on 'Some symbols of omissions in Livian MSS.'

probable that the whole line was omitted, and that *hđ* was introduced before *-s*.

I will here mention another critical sign which is very common in MSS., viz. *R̸* (= *require*). This occurs in a seventh century MS. of Orosius (Steffens, Pl. 26). In Laud. Misc. 120, cent. ix, I have noticed it nine times on one page. Its meaning is explained by Ekkehart, who wrote in the eleventh century:

ego quidem corrigere per me, exemplar aliud non habens, si poteram, temptavi. Ergo, ubi minus potui, ℞ litteram apposui.[1]

It is also found in the forms *Req̃* (Laud. Lat. 117) and *Rq̃* (Brit. Mus. 21215). In Cic. *pro Milone*, where Harl. 2682 omits §§ 18–37, it has received into the text the critical mark *RQ̃*. So in Cic. *Phil.* vii. 11, where *V* has a curious dislocation, there is a mysterious *R* in the text, which I take for this symbol.

Sometimes *R̸* is combined with other critical signs, e.g. *t* (=*uel*) or *Z* (= ζήτει), a sign used to show the existence of some difficulty. Thus Laud. Misc. 126, cent. viii, a MS. in which *Z* is frequently used, has *ZR̸* (f. 79r) and *R̸tZ* (f. 77v). Another sign used like *R̸* is *Q̃* (= *quaere*). This occurs in Bern. 366, Valerius Maximus, cent. ix (Steffens, Pl. 60). In a Milan MS., Ambros. C. 29 *infr.*, cent. x (Cic. *in Catil.* etc.), I have noticed it used as frequently as seven times on a page. In Harl. 2736, cent. x (Cic. in *Catil.*, etc.), it is often combined with *t*. Onions has remarked that in Harl. 2719, cent. ix/x, Nonius, which is derived from a Florentine MS. (Laur. xlviii. 1), cent. ix, the adscript *q̃* found in the margin of Laur. xlviii. 1 is on two occasions received into the text (corrupted to *quae*).

I have selected for publication the results at which I arrived in the case of certain MSS. I fear that I may be criticized for including so many, but my difficulty has been to exclude many more which possess great interest. However, as I do not wish to weary the reader, I have had to steel my heart.

The following instances, taken from two MSS. which I have not included, are interesting as illustrating mechanical error:

[1] E. Dümmler, *Ekkehart IV. von St. Gallen*, in *Zeitschrift für deutsches Altertum*, *neue Folge*, ii (1869), p. 21.

Laud. Misc. 271, cent. ix, Gregory on St. Luke.

On f. 47^v the first two lines are:

> pedes eius et unguento unguebat, uidens autem pharisaeus qui
> uocauerat eum ait intra se dicens.

It is frequent to find in MSS. that an illiterate scribbler copies the first line at the top of the page or the last line at the bottom. Here there is at the top of the page a rough scrawl.

> pedes eius et unguento unguebat, uidens autem phariseus qui pedes
> et unguento unguebat uocauerat eum ait intra se dicens.

Here we see a blunder in the making. The writer, after copying l. 1, *pedes eius . . . pharisaeus qui*, instead of going on to *uocauerat eum*, looked back to l. 1 and repeated *pedes . . . unguebat*, omitting *eius*. He then detected his error and went on with l. 2.

Laud. Misc. 139, cent. ix, St. Augustine on St. John.

The model from which this was copied did not contain Sermons xvii, xviii. Consequently the scribe, after finishing Sermon xvi, went on with Sermon xix on the same page. Subsequently the missing Sermons xvii, xviii were inserted. They are written in a different hand and form two quaternions. The result of this insertion was to separate the end of Sermon xvi by two quaternions from the rest of the Sermon. To remedy this a fly-leaf was inserted before the two quaternions, containing the end of Sermon xvi, to come immediately after the previous part.

The fly-leaf was copied from the leaf (f. 39^r) on which the end of Sermon xvi is given, and followed by Sermon xix. On f. 39^r we find the following passage:

> iste qui dicit mater sion factus est in ea homo fac
> tus est in ea, nam ds̄ erat antea et homo factus est
> in eam. Qui homo factus est in ea, ipse fundavit

On the fly-sheet (f. 22) we find:

> iste qui dicit mater sion factus est in ea. Homo factus est in ea
> Qui homo factus est in ea, ipse fundavit *om. med.*

Here the writer has passed from *in ea* in l. 2 to *in ea* in l. 3.

It happens not infrequently that omissions of equal length occur in close proximity to each other. Thus Laud. Misc. 139, f. 145^v, has at the top of the page:

> .ᵭ. In errore arrianorum alius quidem pater est alius filius (48)

There is a corresponding *.đ.* over the place where the insertion is to be made.

At the foot of the page we have:

> *ħ.* sabellianus, cũ au͞t audit unũ, abscedat arrianus confusus (48)

There is a corresponding *ħ.* over the place where the insertion is to be made.

The intervening passage as written in Laud. Misc. 139 consists of 238 letters (48 × 5 = 240).

We can now with certainty arrange the text as it stood in the model,[1] viz.:

ipse est pa͞t qui filius
in errore arrianorum alius quidem pater est alius filius (48)
sed apud arrianos ipse filius ñ solum alius sed etiam ali (47)
ud. Tu in medium quid, exclusisti sabellianum, exclude et ar (48)
rianum. Pa͞t pater est filius filius est, alius non aliud quia (49)
ego et pa͞t inquit unũ sumus. Sicut etiam hesterno die quan (47)
tum potui commendaui. Cum audit sumus abscedat confusus (47)
sabellianus cũ au͞t audit unũ abscedat arrianus confusus (48)

The omissions of ll. 2 and 8 are both due to ὁμ.

Similar information is yielded by the combination of dittographies with omissions. I take as an example:

Laud. Misc. 252 (Jerome's Letters), cent. ix/x.

In this MS. there are no less than eight omissions of 45 letters, besides a number of very similar length. On p. 218 we find an omission of 45 letters, also a dittography of 90 letters. The intervening passage, as written in the MS., consists of 1175 letters. Here 45 × 26 = 1170. We may, therefore, conclude that it occupied 26 lines in the model.

Sometimes the additions of the second hand show traces of one unit only. In this case we are without doubt concerned with lines of the model.

Thus in Harl. 3063, a MS. containing 192 folios, there are two additions, and two only. As written in the MS. one consists of 66 letters and the other of 132 (66 × 2 = 132).

In Brit. Mus. 11878 there are only three additions, the figures for which are 41, 45, 176 (44 × 4 = 176).

[1] I ascribe to the model the abbreviations which occur in Laud. Misc. 139.

Burn. 340, a seventh century MS., furnishes us with ten figures. Seven of these contain 27–9 letters, while four out of the seven contain the same number, 29. The largest number furnished by a dittography is 56 ($28 \times 2 = 56$). There remain two numbers, viz. 25 and 41. The first of these probably represents a short line, while 41 has nothing to do with the lineation, but it is due to accident assisted by ὁμ.

These simple cases are not common. As a rule we find more than one unit. I take as an example:

Laud. Misc. 148, cent. ix, Jerome, on Prophets.

Here, after a few short omissions, due to accident, we have the following series, without any intermediate figures:

36, 41, 48, 72 *bis*, 81, 82, 97.

Here $36 \times 2 = 72$, $41 \times 2 = 82$, $48 \times 2 = 96$.

The natural explanation here is that 48 and 97 represent lines of the model, while 41 and 81–2, 36 and 72 represent lost lines of previous ancestors, which have been recovered by collation with another MS.

To illustrate this remark I would call attention to:

Laud. Misc. 134, cent. ix, Augustine, *de Spiritu*.

In the marginalia there is a notable bulge at 27–31 (16 examples). This appears to be the predominant unit, which represents a line of the model. There are also 10 omissions of 21–5 letters, together with one dittography of 21 letters and another of 24.

On f. 92ᵛ we find in the text:

non crimen primi hominis transisse in genus humanum ħ dicunt

In the margin is placed ℞, to mark the corruption. A second hand adds for insertion after *humanum*

neq. ꝑ carnẽ quã nũquã fuisse (23)

Here the model of Laud. Misc. 134 appears to have had *ħ* above the line, to mark an omission already made. The omission, therefore, goes back to a previous stage.

I would call attention to the difference in the phenomena when two MSS. have been bound up together in one volume. Thus Laud. Misc. 134, the MS. which I have just mentioned, consists of two parts. I have already shown that in Part II, Augustine *de Spiritu*, the model seems to have had 27–31 letters to the line. Part I, Augustine *in Rom.*, consists of 14 folios only. There are here seven additions made by the second hand. Three out of these contain the same number of letters, viz. 72, while three others contain 76–8. We, therefore, find ourselves in a new world.

There are two features which are prominent in these lists and in all similar investigations which I have made, viz.:

(1) There is considerable variety in the smaller numbers, and, if we were wholly dependent upon them, it would in many cases be difficult to draw conclusions with any certainty.

(2) The larger numbers are usually decisive. They rise gradually from multiple to multiple of a particular figure and thus reveal the unit. They exhibit numerical relations to each other and show the operation of a common cause.

I take as an example:

Laud. Misc. 121, cent. ix, St. Augustine, *de doctrina Christiana.*

Here I have noted 51 additions of the second hand with omission marks, also two dittographies, ranging from 14 to 85 letters. The five largest omissions exhibit the following figures:

101, 102, 224, 399, 425.

Here $25 \times 4 = 100$, $25 \times 9 = 225$, $25 \times 16 = 400$, $25 \times 17 = 425$.

In one passage, f. 50[r], the MS. has a senseless repetition or anticipation of a passage which occurs shortly afterwards. The writer appears to have looked forward. The intermediate words, as written in the MS., consist of 653 letters. Here $25 \times 26 = 650$.

If now we look at the smaller figures, we find:

21–9, 17 examples (including two dittographies); also, two corruptions which point to a line of 26 letters.

50–2, two examples.

75, one example.

We now have the series: 21–9, 50–2, 75, 101–2, 224, 399, 425, 653.

The superior regularity of the large figures is due to the fact that the average asserts itself and becomes dominant.

This is a typical case, for which a very large number of parallels will be found, both in the analysis of these marginalia and scattered throughout this volume.

The large figures are of special importance where we are dealing with a very small unit, e.g. 10–11, especially when there is considerable variety in the unit. I can give no better example than the MS. of the Gospels known as Syr.sin. This is a Syriac translation, in which the Greek text is rendered very literally. When Syr.sin. omits, which it does with the utmost freedom, we can infer what the Greek words which were omitted were. The smaller omissions present what I call[1] a 'welter of confusion', the only point which is clear being that the predominant unit is 10–11. As the figures become larger they begin to group themselves. The five largest are 83, 128, 132, 167, 262.

Here 83 × 2 = 166, 132 × 2 = 264. Also, 128 is very near to 132.

If we look back, we find three omissions of 41 letters, one of them a 'telescoped' passage, which are in relation to 83; also one of 65, which is in relation to 128–32.

Thus, while Chaos seems to reign in the smaller figures, this is replaced by Cosmos in the larger. As the figures increase, the burden of proof passes away from the small unit and resides in the correlation of the large numbers, not on the fact that they may be explained as multiples of the small unit.

I have made a somewhat elaborate study of one MS., viz. Douce 140, Primasius, cent. vii/viii. I was led to do this by the fact that this MS. contains a good deal of material hitherto unpublished. Migne's text is extensively mutilated, and the Bâle text, which is much more complete, also omits a number of passages found in this MS. (*D*). Thus Migne gives a short text, the Bâle edition a longer text, and *D* one that is longer still. It cannot be doubted that *D* is the most faithful witness. If so, its evidence throws much light upon the development of abbreviated texts. The portions of text omitted by Migne, or by the Bâle edition, or by both, show some singular numerical relations which point to the omission of lines and folios in an archetype. Also, there are places where some doctoring seems to have taken place after omission.

I have included in my list one MS., of which my knowledge is gained from a transcript, not from personal collation, viz. the *codex Rehdigeranus*, containing the Old Latin Gospels. This MS. is of

[1] *Primitive Text of the Gospels and Acts*, p. 38.

special interest, since, as is shown by the editor, H. J. Vogels, it was copied from its model line by line and page by page. Such a method was admirably suited to prevent omissions. In spite, however, of all precautions, the writer could not escape from human infirmities. From time to time he left something out, and rather than add anything in the margin, he erased six or seven lines of text and rewrote the passage. On one occasion he repeated an entire page. He then rubbed this out and wrote the correct passage on the palimpsest. The MS., however, has a number of additions made by a second hand, which appear to represent omissions made by an ancestor of similar formation. On one occasion (f. 252), two columns of 20 lines, the same number as those found in the *Rehdigeranus* itself, are added in the margin with omission marks.

The possibility that a MS. is a reproduction, more or less exact, of its model must always be borne in mind. M. Havet says:[1]—'Parfois deux copies d'un même modèle ont des pages qui coïncident exactement.' He refers to two MSS. of Plautus, Palat. (Heidelberg.) 1613 and Vat. 3870, both belonging to the eleventh century, in which *Merc.* 1–43 occupies exactly one page (Chatelain, Pl. iv, 1 and 2); also to two MSS. of Horace, Harl. 2688 and 2725, both belonging to the tenth century, in which *Epod.* xvii. 74 . . . *Carm. Saec.* 1–17 occupy a page (Chatelain, lxxxiii, lxxxviii). As I have myself examined the two MSS. of Horace, I must remark that this is the only such coincidence. Harl. 2688 (*d*) generally has 28 lines to a page, while Harl. 2725 (δ) generally has 27. The coincidence is made possible by the fact that *d* here has three lines for the title to the *Carmen*, while δ has two. Also δ is the parent of *d*, a fact which has escaped collators, not a *gemellus*. This is proved by an omission of *d* in f. 32^r, l. 22. Here after *Epp.* i. 1. 102 (*nec medici credis nec curatoris egere*) *d* goes on with i. 18. 47, omitting 860 lines. The lacuna is noted by a later hand. In δ i. 1. 102 comes at the end of a gathering (f. 83^v). The reason for the omission in *d* is therefore obvious. The parent MS. has 54 lines to a folio. It appears, therefore, that *d* has omitted two quaternions of δ ($54 \times 16 = 864$).

In various MSS. which I have used I have noticed indications

[1] *Manuel*, p. 192.

that the writer was trying to reproduce the formation of his model. The symptoms to which I refer are :

(1) Words or portions of words are added at the foot of the page immediately after the last line, or, conversely, part of the last line is left blank. Both phenomena are common in Douce 140 (Primasius).

(2) The writer spaces out his words, so as to fill more room than they would naturally do. This practice is frequent in MSS. at the end of a quaternion, where the scribe wished to fill up the space allotted to him, e.g. in Laud. Misc. 120, 451 ; Brit. Mus. Arundel 129 : so also we find blank spaces at the end of several quaternions, e.g. in Laud. Misc. 135. Sometimes, however, spacing out is to be observed within the quaternion where there is no explanation except that the writer was trying to preserve the pagination of his model. In Brit. Mus., Cotton, Vesp. B. vi, I have noticed spacing in close proximity to omissions (e.g. ff. 44r, 58r, 60r).

(3) The most significant evidence is given by passages marked for insertion at the end of a line, or the end of a page. Thus Laud. Misc. 452 on two occasions has added by a second hand at the foot of a page a complete line of similar length, one of them being a telescoped passage, viz. :

ff. 233v, 234r :

lepus quõ reducit rumigationẽ et ungulam non diuidit inmundũ hoc uo (57)
[bis et erinacius quia reducit rumigationem et ungulã et inmundũ hoc uo] (59)
bis et sues et cetera.

Here l. 2 is written at the foot of f. 223v underneath l. 1, which is the last on the page. The conclusion seems to be that the scribe was reproducing the lineation, but not the pagination of his model.

In the same MS. (f. 255v) a marginal addition in the middle of the page is marked for insertion at the end of a line.

Similar phenomena are to be observed in Cotton, Vesp. B. vi (ff. 38v, 58r).

Sometimes we find a complete line written twice by the first hand, e.g. in Laud. Misc. 139 (f. 111r), the first hand wrote :—

creden
do amare, credendo diligere, credendo in eum ire
do amare, credendo diligere, credendo in eum ire

The inference appears to be that the words formed a line in the model.

In Douce 140 (f. 23[r]) the last two lines of the page were written thus by the first hand:

optionem dicimus et nomen ciuitatis dĩ mei
tionem dicimus et nomen ciuitatis dĩ mei

Probably here the dittography already existed in the model, this being copied from a MS. which had:

op
tionem dicimus et nomen ciuitatis dĩ mei

Even when there is no attempt to reproduce the lineation or the pagination of the model, it is frequently clear that the formation of the model was very similar to that of the copy. I would invite attention to my analysis of the corruptions in the palimpsest of Cicero, *de Re Publica.*

We must not suppose that violent changes in formation took place on every occasion when a text was transcribed. It was far easier for a copyist to reproduce the method of writing, whether in columns or in long lines, which he found in his model, and it is probable that in many cases there were several intervening copies which did not greatly differ from each other.

I now venture to say a few words about the length of lines in different MSS. It is not long ago since Birt, following up the stichometrical speculations of Graux, spoke of a 'normal line' in papyri, consisting of 35–7 letters. I do not propose to discuss on this occasion the views of Graux and others, which I mention with respect. I am, however, concerned with facts, not with theories, and I can only say that subsequent discovery does not support the doctrine of a normal line.

I have made some examination of the classical and theological fragments published by Messrs. Grenfell and Hunt, whether from papyrus rolls or books written on papyrus or vellum. These are of all sorts and sizes, and the only conclusion one can draw is that any shape is permissible.

The supposed 'normal line' is found, but cannot be called common. I have noticed as specimens:

Ox. 418. Scholia on *Iliad* i, cent. i/ii.
880. Thucydides v, cent. ii.

Also, two Latin texts, viz.:

Ox. 668. Epitome of Livy, cent. iii/iv.

884. Sallust, *Catiline*, cent. v (papyrus book).

The most frequent sizes appeared to me to be 16–19, 24–5, 27–9 letters. I mention a few well-known papyri as specimens of these favourite formations.

(1) 16–19:

Ox. 1. Sayings of Jesus, cent. ii/iii (papyrus book).

225. Thucydides ii, cent. i.

228. Plato, *Laches*, cent. ii.

844. Isocrates, *Panegyric*, cent. ii.

(2) 24–5:

Grk. Pap. ii. 9. Demosthenes, *Fals. Leg.*, cent. i/ii.

Ox. 19. Herodotus, cent. ii/iii.

208. St. John's Gospel, cent. iii (papyrus book).

231. Demosthenes, *de Corona*, cent. i/ii.

(3) 27–9:

Ox. 2. St. Matthew, cent. iii (papyrus book).

221. Scholia on *Iliad* i, cent. ii.

843. Plato, *Symposium*, cent. iii.

1087. Scholia on *Iliad*, cent. i B.C.

As specimens of intermediate sizes I may cite:

(21) Ox. 16 and 696. Thucydides iv, cent. i.

(26) Hibeh 26. Ῥητορικὴ πρὸς Ἀλέξανδρον, cent. iii B.C.

Some of these documents are written in very narrow columns (9–12 letters), e.g.:

Ox. 883. Demosthenes, *in Aristocratem*, cent. iii.

1084. Hellanicus, cent. ii.

1093. Demosthenes, *in Boeotum*, cent. ii.

1176. Satyrus, *Life of Euripides*, cent. ii.

1182. Demosthenes, *de Falsa Leg.*, cent. ii.

1364. Antipho, cent. iii.

1375. Herodotus vii, cent. ii.

Among larger sizes than those previously mentioned are:

(38–40) Ox. 842. *Hellenica*, cent. ii.

(41–3) Ox. 459. Demosthenes, *in Aristocratem*, cent. iii (papyrus book).

697. Xenophon, *Cyropaedia*, cent. iii (papyrus book).

Sometimes exceptionally long lines are used, e.g.:

(60–70) Ox. 1086. Scholia on *Iliad* ii, cent. i B.C.

(70–80) Ox. 1097 and 1251. Cicero, *pro Lege Manilia, in Verrem, pro Caelio*, cent. v.

In Latin both systems of writing, viz. in columns or in long lines, were used, apparently at the same date. The arrangement by columns seems to have been preferred, if we may judge from the specimens which have come down to us.

Latin scribes appear to have had a liking for very narrow columns (10–11 letters), such as are used in the palimpsest of the *de Re Publica* and the Ambrosian palimpsest of Cicero, *pro Scauro*, etc. These narrow columns are especially frequent in MSS. of the Old Latin Gospels, e.g. the *Vercellensis*, cent. iv; *Palatinus*, cent. v; *Veronensis*, cent. v/vii. They are also employed in the oldest MS. of the Latin Pentateuch, Lugd. 54, cent. vi.

As specimens of larger columns we may take the Turin palimpsest of Cicero, *pro Scauro*, &c. (avg. 18 letters), the Vatican palimpsest of the *Verrines* (avg. 18–19), and the palimpsest of the *Scholiasta Bobiensis* (avg. 16).

For the use of long lines at the same period we may notice the leaf from the *Verrines* which Peyron has bound up in Taur. A. ii. 2* with the fragments of Cicero, *pro Scauro*, etc. This is generally ascribed to the fourth century, but Chatelain thinks that it may belong to the third century. The same volume contains a leaf taken from a MS. of Cicero's Letters *ad Familiares*, which has an average of 37 letters to the line, but the date of this seems doubtful. I have already mentioned the vellum leaf discovered by De Ricci (Cic. *pro Plancio*), cent. v, which contains an average of 28 letters to the line; also the Oxyrhynchus fragments of Cicero (*Verr.*, *pro Lege Manilia*, *Cael.*), in which the lines are abnormally long. As an example of a complete MS. written in long lines in the fourth century, we may take the Vienna Livy (avg. 27 letters to a line).

MSS. also vary greatly with regard to the number of lines to a page. The most common numbers are 25–30, but we find all sorts of variation. As examples of short pages I quote:

Harl. 5041 (Theological Tracts), cent. vii, 14 lines.

Laud. Lat. 22 (Maccabees), cent. viii/ix, 16 lines.

Voss. O. 79 (Cic. *de Sen.*), cent. ix, 18 lines.

It will be remembered that the palimpsest of the *de Re Publica* contains 15 lines to the page, and Ricci's fragment of the *pro Plancio* has 17.

As examples of long pages we may take:

Laud Misc. 464 (Authpertus), cent. ix, 36 lines (two cols.)

Paris. 7794 (Cic. *post reditum*, etc.), cent. ix, 36–43 lines (two cols.).

Laud. Misc. 132 (St. Augustine), cent. ix/x, 39 lines (two cols.).

Bodl. 218 (Bede), cent. ix, 40 lines.

Brit. Mus. Add. 11875 (St. Augustine), cent. ix/x, 43 lines (two cols.).

Toletanus 15.8 (Isidorus), cent. viii/ix, 47–60 lines (two cols.).

It is to be noted that some very early MSS. were extremely bulky. Thus the *Puteaneus* of Livy (Par. 5730), cent. vi, which is now incomplete, contains nearly 55 quaternions. So Harl. 1775 (Gospels), cent. vii, contains 57 quaternions. Some interesting evidence is given by the signatures in various palimpsests. Thus the palimpsest of the *Verrines* (V) has at v. 120 the signature Q. XXXXII. When complete it must have consisted of about 45 quaternions. The palimpsest of Fronto, according to Niebuhr, contained over 42 quaternions, while that of the *Scholiasta Bobiensis*, which on p. 189 in Ambros. E. 147 *sup.* has the signature Q. LXX, is said by Hildebrand to have contained, when perfect, 73 quaternions. The palimpsest of the *de Re Publica* has at iii. 48 the signature Q. XLI. If it contained all six books of the treatise, it must have rivalled, or surpassed, the *Scholiasta Bobiensis* in size.

In the preceding pages I have shown that it is possible to base arguments upon the general uniformity which is to be observed in the content of lines, pages, folios, and quaternions. I now point out some circumstances which may disturb such calculations.

Some MSS. are not written in lines of the same length, but in *commata* or *cola*, i.e. sense-lines of various length. This is the method employed in the *codex Bezae* of the Gospels and Acts. Here we get such στίχοι as (Acts ii. 21)

και εσται πας ος αν επικαλεσηται το ονομα του κ̅υ̅
σωθησεται

In the case of a MS. copied from a model in this formation we cannot expect to find any numerical relation in the omissions. Sometimes, however, we find among the marginalia additions in which the στίχοι are reproduced as written in the model. I take as an example Harl. 1775 (Gospels), cent. vii. This on f. 399r has:

non moses dedit uobis
panem de caelo *hs*

At the top of the page is:

sed pater meus dat uobis panem
panem de caelo *hd*

The model must have had:

non moses dedit uobis
panem de caelo
sed pater meus dat uobis
panem de caelo

The scribe originally made a slip and then corrected himself, so as to retain the arrangement which he found in his model.

In classical MSS. we sometimes find an arrangement by paragraphs. I have already referred to occasional short lines in various palimpsests and early MSS. due to this cause. In *V* (Cic. *Philippics*, etc.) we find occasional paragraphs, especially in *Phil.* ii. While an arrangement by paragraphs simplifies omission, the occasional short lines disturb, though often very slightly, the minute correspondence which would otherwise exist.

Various small accidents may occur. Thus omissions, dittographies, supralineal insertions are sufficient to prevent exact correspondence in content. Sometimes we find a flaw in the parchment, with the result that a piece is cut out or left unused. For the same reason pages or folios are left blank. I have noticed examples of this in Harl. 1775, 2736, Brit. Mus. 11878, Cotton Vesp. A. 1, Laud Misc. 139, 148. According to Mai, there are a number of blank pages in the palimpsest of the *Verrines*. If his statement is correct, these pages generally form the verso of the last folio in a quarternion, or the recto of the first page in a new gathering. In this case no defect in the parchment is to be observed.

A writer sometimes expands or contracts his hand. Thus in Laud. Misc. 252 I have observed six omissions of 45 letters in 33 pages, while the number 45 does not occur among the omissions in the next 105 pages. The obvious explanation is that the writing in the model was less regular after this point. The tendency is for the scribe to compress his script towards the end of his work. A striking example is to be found in *V* (*Philippics*, etc.). In the later *Philippics* the average number of letters to the line in this MS. rises from 17–18 to 24–5. In the Holkham MS. of the *Verrines* (*C*) the script contracts slightly after f. 34, and there is an extra line to the page. I would call attention to some suggestions which I have made concerning the archetype of Cicero, *de Natura Deorum*, etc. (p. 337). The evidence here seems to show that the scribe contracted his script considerably at the end of the MS. when he was writing the *de Legibus*.

Many MSS. were the work of several scribes.[1] In such cases the length of a line varies somewhat in different quaternions. Sometimes a new writer introduces variety not only in the character of the hand, but also in the number of lines to a page, e.g. in Douce 140 (Primasius).

A further point relates to the gatherings. The arrangement by quaternions is normal, but other gatherings are also employed. Thus in Harl. 3024 I have noticed the following consecutive gatherings: 8 ff., 4 ff., 8 ff., 6 ff., 8 ff., 8 ff., 5 ff., 9 ff., 9 ff.

If Mai's account is to be trusted, the palimpsest of the *Verrines* appears to have had a number of gatherings which consisted of ten folios, with a blank page at the beginning and end.

There is also a disturbing influence to which I refer frequently throughout this work, viz. that in MSS. written in columns it is normal for one column to be slightly 'squeezed' by the other (or others, if three columns are used). As a rule it is the left-hand column which is a little broader than the right, but to this there are exceptions.

It will be seen that there are various circumstances which may interfere with the general uniformity which I have pointed out, and derange calculations based upon this principle. The possibility,

[1] In Vat. Reg. 762 (Livy) seven scribes, all monks of St. Martin at Tours, have signed the portions of the MS. for which they were responsible. Cf. Shipley's paper, *Class. Quart.* iv (1910), pp. 277–81. In Brit. Mus. Arundel 129 (Isidorus) I have noticed the signatures *Ebo*, *Sigebolt*, *Heicil*, and in Harl. 5642 (Glossary) *Ripoinus*, *Odnand*, *Vuiniger*. Cf. Steffens, Pl. 50.

however, of such accidents in no way affects the validity of the evidence given by minute numerical agreements unaffected by such accidents.

I conclude this chapter with a few remarks upon a subject to which I frequently refer, viz. the phenomena of insertion *alieno loco*.

When a passage has once been omitted, there is always a danger that it may be inserted into the text elsewhere.[1] I take an example from a papyrus, Ox. 223, cent. iii (*Iliad* v). The first hand omitted l. 75:

ἤριπε δ' ἐν κονίῃς ψυχρὸν δ' ἕλε χαλκὸν ὀδοῦσι.

The corrector inserted it after l. 83, in a similar context.

Sometimes it is not easy to distinguish a correction from the text. Thus, in the *cod. Bobiensis* (*k*) of the old Latin Gospels, cent. v, some passages which had been omitted by the scribe are added at the foot of the page after the last line in a similar script, and are only to be distinguished from the text by the omission symbol (*hs*) which follows them. Sometimes the reference marks over the text, where the insertion is to be made, are hard to find. Thus in Laud. Misc. 464 (Authpertus) the only reference mark is ·//., and in Harl. 208 (Alcuin) the only symbols are ┌ or ᴜ. These are much less easy to follow than *ħ*, *hđ*, ⁜ &c.

For a simple case of insertion in the wrong place I take an example from Cic. *de Sen.* 60. Here Simbeck says:

'*voluerunt* om. *P'*, add. m. 1 una linea infra.'

I have noticed in Laud. Misc. 256 (Jerome) three passages where a subsequent writer might be misled:

f. 12v: siro quo LXX transtulerunt in ęclesia dn̄ī

These words are added by the corrector at the top of the page with an omission mark. Their proper place is in l. 20, after *in coetu domini*. There is, however, no reference mark here.

f. 24r: ibi non erit et ubi iactatis uaticinium ꝑphetale

These words are added in the margin, two lines below the reference mark *ħ* (over the text).

[1] Cf. Havet, *Manuel*, pp. 367–74. Conway and Walters (*Class. Quart.* 1911, p. 9) remark, 'When these words once got into the margin, heaven help them.'

f. 59^{v}. In the margin an omission mark is entered, but there is no insertion.

For frequent insertions in the wrong place I would mention Laud. Misc. 456 (excerpts from Gregory on Job), cent. ix/x. In this MS. a second hand makes a number of additions to the excerpts, prefaced by *M* (sometimes combined with *h*). These additions are often entered for insertion in the wrong place. I take as an example:

f. 94^{v}: minime sperat. Seqr̃. Numquid clamorẽ ei' audiet d̃s quũ uenerit sup̱ eũ angustia? Clamorem ei' angustiae tempr̃ dn̄s non audiet

The second hand adds, with a reference mark after *angustia* in l. 2:

scriptũ nãq̧ est qđ enĩ uidet quis quid sperat. Idcirco
ergo ypocrita̧ ad ẽtna p̃mia ꝑ spẽ minime tendit'
qꝫ qđ alio quȩrendũ fuerat hic se tenere
gloriatur.

The passage should come after *sperat* in l. 1.

A more striking example is to be found in Laud. Lat. 117 (Servius), cent. x/xi. The first hand omits, with four of Thilo's MSS. (*ARSH*), in the note of Servius on *Aen.* vi. 72, the passage:

reversa est et tantumdem poposcit, item tertio aliis tribus incensis (ὁμ.)

There is a reference mark (đ) in the margin between two lines of the note on l. 64. The missing passage is added in the margin of the note on l. 66. The note on l. 72, to which it really belongs, comes 18 lines further on in the text.

In MSS. written in columns there were great possibilities of confusion, since notes and various readings were frequently written between the columns. Thus in Brit. Mus. 11875 (St. Augustine), cent. ix/x, various readings are sometimes placed in their proper margin and sometimes between the two columns. Professor Lindsay has drawn my attention to a Bodleian MS. (Ambrose), no. 206, cent. xii, written in two columns. In this, as a rule, the marginalia on the recto are on the right margin, while those on the verso are on the left margin, to whichever column they belong. There are, however, exceptions, e.g. on f. 56^{v} there are two variants on the right margin also. I quote a few examples of these marginalia, giving the parallel lines in the two columns:

f. 27^r:

<table>
<tr><td>cinctos cet'asq: gemmas fulgere

existimas choruscare indicos al
barum emicare grãm</td><td>et procera sit spaciis nec onerosą
o
parietib: Lacunarib: qq: com
mendandis</td></tr>
</table>

In the right margin, adjacent to col. 2, is the note:

indicos uocat quosdam lapides qui de india feruntur

It really belongs to col. 1.

f. 49^v:

<table>
<tr><td>
utrum consulti' euolassẽ an uti
liber ũra in retia sim relapsus
nec uereor ne fastidium nobis</td><td>i
alti' g et inusitati' in tali genere
scriptionis. sermo nr̃ canorus
resonet ac resultet</td></tr>
</table>

In the left margin, adjacent to col. 1, is the variant:

Aliter Aui' et inusitat'
itali gñis auib: sermo
resonet ac resultet.

It really belongs to col. 2.

f. 52^v:

<table>
<tr><td>
al. politia</td><td>e
in illis enim deuotio qdam et
militia naturalis in nob̄ coacta
atq: seruilis quã uiro ꝑprio et

uoluntario usu. Grues in nocte
sollicitã exercent custodiã. Dis
positos</td><td>
om̄s uoluntaria sorte transcribi
antiqua hoc rei publicę munus
et instar liberę ciuitatis est. Sic
i
a pncipio acceptã a natura ex
emplo auium policiã homines
exercere</td></tr>
</table>

Here *politia* in the margin of l. 1, col. i, is a variant for *policiã* in l. 5 of col. 2.

Sometimes a variant is embedded in the text at a considerable distance from its doublet. I take as an example:

Laud. Misc. 252, pp. 26–7.

On p. 27, ll. 4–6, we have:

quã ob rem
obtestor beatitudinẽ tuam ꝑ cruci fixum mundi salutem ꝑ homo usiã
trinitatem

Here *homo usiã* = *homousiam* (ὁμοούσιον).

On p. 26, l. 6, we find:

quid ue
neni in sillabis homousion trinitatem latet clamamus si quis tres

Here *homousion trinitatem* is a variant for *homo usiã* on p. 27. In the case of such roving variants there are two possible explanations, viz. (1) that a variant was entered at the top or the foot of the page and incorporated in the text at that point, or (2) that it was entered by error on the wrong page or folio. M. Havet remarks:[1] 'Un correcteur, se trompant de page, exécute sur telle page, au bout d'une ligne, ce qu'il doit exécuter à la même place, également en bout de ligne, sur la page voisine.'

Such variants may therefore throw light upon the pagination of a previous MS. It is dangerous to draw an inference from an isolated case, but, if two occur, each at the same distance from the doublet, we may conclude with certainty in favour of the second explanation. I would call attention in particular to *Phil.* ii. 106, xiv. 13 (pp. 200–1). In the first place, a variant for *vicinus* in § 104, and in the second a variant for *impetus* in § 15, has found its way into the text. The intervening words consist in *Phil.* ii. 104–6 of 953 letters and in xiv. 13–15 of 951. This minute agreement cannot be due to chance. We may therefore conclude that in both cases a variant was entered on the wrong folio of the archetype.

[1] *Manuel*, p. 375.

CHAPTER III

THE EVIDENCE OF MARGINALIA

Harl. 3063. cent. ix

Theodorus of Mopsyestia on the Epistles to the Galatians and Philemon.

In this MS. there are only two occasions where omissions of the first scribe have been supplied by the corrector, with omission marks (*ħ*), viz.:

(66) 56r : eo qđ necdũ reb: ipsis in illis sumus sed interĩ credim: de illis pro- missionẽ ũō

(132) 78v : quale ē illud qđ dix̃ p̃elegit nos adhuc etiã et affectũ de reb: hui' modi implens ostendit. Nã qđ dix̃ in caritate 7 secundũ bonũ placitũ uoluntatis sue hęc ostendit.

Here 66 × 2 = 132.

Both omissions are due to ὁμ. It is noticeable that both supplements contain many abbreviations, so the exact correspondence is very remarkable.

Brit. Mus. Add. 11878, cent. vii (Merovingian script).

Gregory on Job (Migne, vol. 76).

The omission symbols are *hđ* over the text and *ħs* at the foot of the page. Three passages have been added by the corrector, viz.:

(41) 68v (Migne, 297 A):
uirtute accenditur nec tamen in summa scientiae

(45) 58v (Migne, 287 C):
ab homine non poterat d͠s ergo homo factus est ut uideri

(176) 67v (Migne, 295 B–C):
et iudicati sunt mortui ex his quae scripta erant in libris quia in ostensa uita iustorum quasi in expansione librorum legunt bonum quod agere ipsi noluerunt atque ex eorum qui fecerunt comparatione damnantur.

Here 176 = 44 × 4.

All three omissions are due to ὁμ.

Brit. Mus., Burney 340, cent. vii (Corbie).

This MS., written in uncials (ff. 1–60), contains Origen's *Homilies on Numbers*, xv–xix (about Balaam), Migne, xii, pp. 683 C–726 A.

I would recommend this MS. to any one who wishes to test the method which I have employed. Ff. 1–27 contain some additions and corrections which I will take in the order in which they come, giving references to Migne's text. I call the MS. *B*.

5ʳ: potest ergo dici veni maledic mihi Iacob et veni supermaledic mihi Israel (Migne, 686 A).

B^1 wrote: *potest ergo dici ueni maledic mihi Israel*, omitting *Jacob et ueni supermaledic mihi* (27). B^2 adds the omitted words partly above the lines and partly *in ras.*

ib.: tunc non solum maledictis ab inimico sed et supermaledictis.

B^1 omitted *ab inimico sed et supermaledictis* (29). The words are added at the foot of the page. The omission symbol *d̄r* (*desuper*) is placed over the text, and at the foot of the page is *dh̄* before the addition and *sūr* (i.e. *super*) after it.[1]

6ʳ: Graeci sermonis rationem, vim verbi ostendere ex praepositionis (pronominis *B*) augmento cupientes (Migne, 686 C).

B^1 omitted *vim verbi ostendere ex pronominis* (29). B^2 rewrote the passage (*in ras.* and above the line).

9ʳ: et credidit Abraham deo et reputatum est illi ad iustitiam (Migne, 688 C).

B^1 omitted *et reputatum est illi ad iustitiam* (29). B^2 adds the words in an extra line (above the text).

11ʳ: igitur Balach rex veluti attonitus et percussus ex iis quae contra spem dici videbat a Balaam (Migne, 690 B).

B^1 omitted *rex veluti attonitus et percussus* (29), having passed from *rex* to *ex*. B^2 adds *rex* at the end of the line, and inserts an extra line containing *veluti . . . percussus*.

19ᵛ: quia neque proprie bonum dici potest quod aliquando a malo venit neque proprie malum quod aliquando a Deo descendit (Migne, 696 B).

[1] The use of this sign is said by Lindsay to be Spanish. It is employed regularly in the Toledo MS. of Isidorus. Cf. Beer's preface to the facsimile (p. xxi).

B^1 omitted *a malo venit neque propriae* (*sic*) *malum quod aliquando* (41). B^2 inserts an extra line.

21ᵛ: vel pecudum vel fibrarum motus aut sortium secundum ea signa quae docuerunt iidem daemones (Migne, 698 A).

B^1 omitted *motus aut sortium secundum ea* (25). B^2 adds the words at the foot of the page with omission marks, viz. *d̄r* above the text and *s̄'* (= *super*) at the foot.

27ᵛ: in Spiritu Sancto considerantes quae per Spiritum scripta sunt et spiritalibus spiritalia comparantes (Migne, 702 B).

The words *quae per spm̄ scripta sunt . . . comparantes* (56) were written twice by B^1 (corr. B^2). The dittography is due to ὁμ.

The corrections cease after f. 27. I made a hasty collation of the remaining folios with Migne's text and found that *B* has omitted two passages, viz.:

34ʳ (Migne, 712 A):

caveamus ne propter (per opera et *B*) actus nostros Christi nomen blasphemetur sed magis id agamus ut . . . mereamur.

B omits *xp̄i nomen blasphemetur sed magis* (28). Here there is no ὁμ.

39ʳ (Migne, 705 D):

ut evidentius elucesceret qui sunt oculi qui claudantur et qui sunt oculi qui revelentur.

B omits *qui claudantur et qui sunt oculi* (27).

I now put together the figures in order of magnitude and leave them to tell their story.

(25)	21ᵛ:	* motus aut sortium secundum ea
(27)	5ʳ:	Iacob et ueni supermaledic mihi
	39ʳ:	qui claudantur et qui sunt oculi
(28)	34ʳ:	* xp̄i nomen blasphemetur sed magis
(29)	5ʳ:	ab inimico sed et supermaledictis
	6ʳ:	* uim uerbi ostendere ex pronominis
	9ʳ:	* et reputatum est illi ad iustitiam
	11ʳ:	rex ueluti attonitus et percussus
(41)	19ᵛ:	a malo . . . aliquando
(56)	27ᵛ:	quae per spm̄ . . . comparantes

Here, out of 10 cases, four contain the same number of letters (29), while seven contain 27–9. The dittography of $56 = 28 \times 2$. The omission of 25 letters may represent a short line. Only one case remains recalcitrant (41), and here ὁμ. is present.

This is a very remarkable result.

Two of the omissions, viz.:

Iacob et ueni supermaledic mihi (27)
ab inimico sed et supermaledictis (29)

occur on the same page (5^{r}), in immediate proximity to each other. The intervening passage *Israel . . . maledictis* is written thus in *B*:

israhel per quod (14)
ostenditur idcirco sermo repetitus (31)
ut ampliore ui et maiore intentione (30)
maledictionem in israhel quam in iacob (33)
balaac uideatur exposcere donec (28)
enim quis tantum iacob est hoc est (28)
in actibus solum et operibus positus (31)
inferioribus maledictionibus (27)
inpugnatur ubi autem profecerit (28)
et interiorem hominem ad uidendum (29)
dm̃ reuelato mentis oculo exacuere (29)
et prouocare iam coeperit tunc non (29)
solum maledictis (15)

This gives a total of 352 letters, i.e. 12 lines in the model (29 × 12 = 348). We can now reconstitute the whole passage as it stood in the model:

potest ergo dici ueni maledic mihi (29)
iacob et ueni supermaledic mihi (27)
israhel per quod ostenditur idcirco (31)
sermo repetitus ut ampliore ui et ma (30)
iore intentione maledictionem in (29)
israhel quam in iacob balaac uidea (29)
tur exposcere donec enim quis tantum (31)
iacob est hoc est in actibus solum et (30)
operibus positus inferioribus ma (29)
ledictionibus impugnatur ubi au (28)
tem profecerit et interiorem homi (29)
nem ad uidendum dm̃ reuelato mentis (29)
oculo exacuere et prouocare iam (27)
coeperit tunc non solum maledictis (30)
ab inimico sed et supermaledictis (29)

B omits l. 2 and l. 15, the omission in each case being assisted by ὁμ.

It is to be noticed that the formation of *B* itself is almost precisely the same as that of the model. Thus, if we take the eleven complete lines (2–12) as written in *B*, the total is 323 ($29 \times 11 = 319$).

Laud. Misc. 148, cent. ix.

Jerome on Minor Prophets.

(9) 133^{v}: pericuľis
(16) 31^{r}: diabolū ēē ł demonē
132^{r}: * certū quid nouimus
170^{v}: ancille ūō niniuen
(22) 104^{r}: in ebreo ꝑ hereditate gath
203^{v}: dicͦ dn̄s exercituū et ꝑ leui
(24) 15^{r}: uincula corpore non uruntur
(25) 124^{r}: et bruto et cassio aug’to eodem
(28) 118^{r}: erit diuisione et tenebrae eř uoƀ.
(36) 3^{r}: * et tradidit dn̄s in manū ei’ ioachim regē iuda
e o o
(41) 5^{r}: dicem’ in ɔseqntib’ qm qui usq: ad ānū ꝓmū cyri regis
(48) 2^{r}: * p̄notauimus significantes ea^{s} ĭ hebraico n̄ haberi et miror
(72) 45^{v}: * claudius annis XIII mensibus VIII nero annis XIII principatum romani apicis obsedit
161^{v}: * nec erit ulla anima quę n̄ paueat ad iudiciū dĭ cū astra quoq; n̄ munda s̄t in conspectu eius
o
(81) 126^{r}: * $iudicab^{t}$ illos u ut ĭpios et negatores n̄ iudicabit s; arguet ɔdempnatos. Semꝑ inuidis respondemus.
162^{v}: LXX. et in diluuio transeunte consummationē faciet consurgentes et inimicos ei’ ꝓsequenť tenebrę
(97) 127^{v}: ad quam uenturus est inquid dn̄s et potestas prima et regnum quare nunc merore contraheris aut quare cognouisti mala *bis scr.*
(875) 182^{v}: * colligentiū sed statim in os deuorantis cadent. Hęc dicta sint παρηφραστικος iuxta LXX inťp̄tes semel enĭ propositū in nobis ē et uulgatā editionē sequi ne aliquā sardanapallo rep̄hendi occasionē p̄buisse uideamur ceterū n̄ satis mihi uidetur congruere exemplū euersionis nineue cum filiis lot qui uocantur ammon. primū enĭ ammon dr̄ sed n̄ ammon deinde amman quę nunc uocatur filadelfia n̄ est sita suꝑ flumina nec opes illius de mari congregantur quippe quę mediterranea sit nec aquę sunt muri eius nec habet aethiopiā et ęgiptū et africā et libes federatos cum haec omnia et iuxta potentiam et iuxta exemplum et iuxta scriptionē loci et regionis et amicarū gentiū magis alexandrię coaptanda sint et numquā potentissima $ciuita^{s}$ niniue minori filadelfię comparata audiret ait ꝓpheta numquid melior ē. Cui autē dr̄ numquid melior es ostenditur minor ēē ea cui comparatur et n̄ debere eā indigne facere si apta sit cū maior et firmior et potentior tam natura loci quā

uiris fortib: ab eodē sit hoste superata quia uero niniuen et mundũ istum interp̃tati sumus

I would also draw attention to the following corruption (f. 82^{v}):

et quia consuetudinis est
ere uestimenta
ut in tristibus atq: aduersis scindatis uestibus qđ et pontifex
ad dñi saluatoris crimen augendum in euangelio fecisse
memoratur et paulum et barnaban audientes uerba blasphe
mię legim' perpetrasse. Idcirco ego p̃cipio uobis ut nequaquã
scindatis uestimenta

Here the eye of the scribe appears to have been caught by *scindatis* further on. The passage *scindere vestimenta . . . nequaquã* consists of 175 letters.

The striking point in these figures is that there are two examples of 72 and two of 81–2. This is extremely significant. Also, we have one example of 36 and one of 41. Further it will be noticed that $48 \times 2 = 96$, cf. 97.

The two largest figures are exact multiples of 35 ($35 \times 5 = 175$, $35 \times 25 = 875$). They appear to be in relation to 36 and the two examples of 72.

The conclusion is that three units are to be observed here, viz. 36, 41, 48. I abstain from drawing any further conclusion as to whether they represent successive ancestors. The difference between 36 and 41 is not great.

Laud. Misc. 121, cent. ix (Würzburg).

St. Augustine, de doctrina Christiana.

The MS. (*L*) contains references to MSS. with which it was collated, e.g. f. 9^{v} *alius sic, alius sic ƚ*, 13^{r} *aliter*.

The usual omission mark is *ħ*, but others are frequent, e.g. ⋇, ;, ÷. Many additions are entered over the line without any sign. The longest passage (425) is added on a fly-leaf.

The following is a complete list of omissions and dittographies:

(14) 5^{r}: si tamen et causa
(15) 52^{r}: cor quippe carneũ
(16) 6^{v}: et q̃si nauigationẽ
11^{r}: ut ex tota mente tua
11^{v}: in quantum peccator
18^{r}: et ambiguitatibus
(17) 3^{v}: * magnũ honus et arduũ
50^{r}: et semitas quas ñ nor̃

(19) 15^{v}: ꝑpt̃ illud id qd̃ ferimur
40^{v}: qui enĩ sequit' litterã
61^{v}: in bonis quae rependit
(20) 7^{r}: * qua se insinuet auribus
(21) 19^{r}: * quo cogitat de iudicio dĩ
49^{v}: * in scripturis canonicis
51^{v}: et mandabo uos ex omnibus
(22) 5^{r}: quo modo autẽ a me dictũ est
77^{r}: non contemptibilĩ uiuit
77^{v}: potius quã dicat eloquent̃
(23) 57^{r}: multitudo eloquentium sed

Cf. 58^{v}, where 23 letters have been erased.

(24) 15^{v}: * sed tamen ut dicere coeperam
65^{r}: fecit ꝑ hunc ipsum prophetam
(27) 13^{v}: nob̃ sed utitur nã si neq; fruitur
77^{v}: et rursus alio modo ipsi ñ dicunt
(28) 50^{r}: * debuit appellare non enim reuera
72^{v}: portat integritas s̄c̄ītas portat
(29) 5^{v}: partim eis quae ad corporis sensum
63^{v}: ubi non ipse sed motus quod dicuntur *bis scr.*
64^{r}: sit ut sciant sed ut agant qd̃ agendũ
(31) 50^{r}: * sicut sponso imposuit mihi mitram et
(32) 39^{r}: et x̄p̄m non condemnaturum electos suos
77^{v}: aufer̃ uerbũ autem d̄ī ñ est ab eis alienũ
(33) 22^{r}: alius aũt ait et carnẽ tuã ne despexeris
55^{r}: et modus ꝓferendo quae intellecta sunt
(36) 29^{v}: et quia diuersa consensio ẽ diuersa mouent
(38) 41^{v}: ꝓ ipsa re sequi cui significandae institutum
(39) 13^{v}: nos uero inuicẽ nr̃i miseremur ut illo ꝑfruamur
(41) 6^{r}: at uero ipsa sapientia nec fuit umquam insipiens
8^{r}: et quae ligaret in terra ligata essent et in caelo
(42) 55^{r}: de ꝓferendo pauca dicemus ut si fieri potuerit uno
(44) 30^{r}: quorum partim suꝑflua luxuriosaque instituta sunt
(45) 48^{r}: ꝓuidit, nã quid in diuinis eloquiis largius et uberius
68^{r}: * facta est lex non infirmata ad euacuandas ꝓmissiones
(49) 67^{r}: neque enĩ parua est iustitia quã ꝑfecto et in parua pecunia
(50) 24^{r}: inspecta atq: discussa tantum absit falsitas nã codicibus
(52) 6^{r}: quantalibet luce p̃fulgeat quantalibet magnitudine p̃mineat
30^{r}: s; aut transacta tẽporib' aut diuinit' instituta inuestigando
(57) 46^{r}: * et quia non potuit non orbitatem doluit in eius interitu sed nouerat
(58) 16^{r}: et si sperando diligimus quo ñdũ ꝑuenimus quanto magis cũ ꝑuenerimus
37^{v}: et laetitiam deinde consequenter adnectit ut ostendat purgationem
(69) 13^{r}: sed nescio quomodo etiam nostra fit consequens cũ eam misericordiam quam facimus

(75) 52v: adiuncta etiã p̃terita et nox in cuius parte ultima resurrexit nisi totus dies accipiatur

(85) 75v: in quocumque istorum trium genere dicere ad persuasionem finis aũ id qđ intenderis ꝓsuadere dicendo

(101) 3r: cur ipse alius affectat exponere ac non potius eos remittit dõ ut ipsi quoq: ñ ꝑ hominẽ sed illo intus docente intellegant

(102) 33r: errorẽ illius cũ quo agit quae tamen ad hoc inferunt˜ a bono et docto homine ut in his erubescens ille cuius errorẽ consecunt˜

(225) 2v: legens non intellegebat ad quem apostolũ ñ angelũ misit instruendũ nec ei ꝑ angelũ id qđ ñ intellegebat et positũ aut diuinitus in mente sine hominis ministerio reuelatũ est sed potius suggestione diuina missus est ad eũ seditq: cũ eo Philippus qui nouerat Esaiã ꝓphetã

(399) 67r: * et fraudatis et hoc aput fratres. an nescitis quia in lustris regnũ dĩ ñ haereditabunt. quid est qđ sic indignatur apostolus sic corripit sic exꝓbrat sic increpat sic minatur. quid est qđ sui animi affectũ tam crebra et aspera uocis mutatione testat˜. quid est postremo qđ de rebus minimis tam grandĩt dicit'. tantum ne de illo negotia saecularia meruerunt, absit sed hoc fecit ꝓpt̃ iustitiã caritatẽ pietatẽ quae nulla sobria mente dubitante etiã in rebus quamlibet paruulis magna sunt.

(425) 38r: discutienda atque soluenda ut autẽ signis ambiguis non decipiatur quantum ꝑ nos instrui potest. fieri h' potest ut istas uias quas ostendere uolum' tãquã pueriles ł magnitudine ingenii ł maioris inluminationis claritate derideat, sed tamen ut coeperam dicere quantũ ꝑ nos instrui ualet qui eo loco animi est ut per nos instrui ualeat. sciat ambiguitatem scripturae aut in uerbis propriis ẽẽ aut in translatis quae genera in secundo libro demonstrauimus sed cum uerba propria faciunt ambiguitatẽ scripturarum.

To these omissions may be added some significant corruptions, viz.:

(26) 67v: docetur temperate cum aliquid docetur (with "uituperatur" written above the dotted "docetur")

This indicates in the model:

docetur temperate cum aliquid (26)
uituperatur

68r: repromissione abrahae autem per repromissionem donauit d̃s

This indicates:

promissione abrahae autem per (26)
repromissionem donauit d̃s

(56) 64v: eloquium (o written above) agitur neque hoc attenditur ut uel ipsa uel ipsum delectet eloquium

This indicates:

eloquio agitur neque hoc attendi (28)
tur ut uel ipsa uel ipsum delectet (28)
eloquium

The eye of the writer was caught by *eloquium* further on.

(125) 41[r]: quia ꝓximi sp̃italibus fuerunt ipsi enim temporalibus et carnalibus notis atque signis quamuis quomodo sp̃italiter essent intellegenda nescirent q̣ụịạ

Here *quia* has been repeated from five lines above ($5 \times 25 = 125$). I reserve for the moment a more complicated case.

Here, as usual, the shorter omissions are very indecisive. For light we must turn to the longest, viz.: 101, 102, 225, 399, 425.

The first two, 101 and 102, are practically identical, while 399 is at most 100×4. If we subtract 399 from 425, the result is 26. I now draw attention to the following multiples:

$$25 \times 4 = 100,\ 25 \times 9 = 225,\ 25 \times 16 = 400,\ 25 \times 17 = 425.$$

The same unit appears in other omissions, viz. $25 \times 5 = 125$ (41[r]), $25 \times 3 = 75$ (52[v]), $25 \times 2 = 50$ (24[r]), cf. 52 (6[r], 30[r]).

It will be seen that there are 15 omissions of 21–9 letters, also a dittography of 29 letters. Also, there are two corruptions (67[v], 68[r]) which point to a line of 26. The conclusion is that single lines differed a good deal in length. The average asserts itself in the longer passages.

It is probable that more than one ancestor is responsible for omissions. Thus the only one of the longer omissions not accounted for is 85 (75[v]). There is a relation between 85 and 41–5 (six cases), and again between 41–5 and 20–2 (seven cases). The probability, therefore, is that there is in the background an ancestor with shorter lines, i.e. with an average of 20–2 letters.

I now proceed to mention the more complicated case of corruption to which I referred previously.

50[r]. Here *L* has:

sed dicendũ
fuit de dñi corpore uero atque ꝑmixto [bonorum et malorum] aut
quic
uero atque simulato. ł quod aliud quia non solum in aeternũ uerũ etiã
nunc hypocriptę non cum illo ēē dicendi sunt. quamuis in eius esse
n
uideatur eccła unde poterit ista regula et sic apellari ut diceretur
de ꝑmixta aecclesia quae regula intellectorem uigilantem requi
rit quando scriptura cum ad alios iam loquatur tamquam ad eos
ipsos ad quos loquebatur uidetur loqui uel de ipsis cum de aliis iam
loquatur tamquam unum sit utrorumque corpus ꝓpter tempo
ralium commixtionem et communionem sacramentorũ ad hoc per
tinet in cantico canticorum fusca sum et speciosa ut tabernacula cae

> i
> dar speciosa sum ut pellas salamonis. non enim ait fusca fui ut
> i
> tabernacula caedar et speciosa sum ut pellạs salamonis sed utrũ
> que esse se dixit ꝓpter temporalem unitatem. Intra unum rete
> piscium bonorum et malorum

Here the words *bonorum et malorum* in l. 1, which I have enclosed in brackets, are an insertion from l. 15, where they occur in their proper place. This is the sort of mistake which appears to throw light upon the pagination of an ancestor. The natural explanation is that the scribe 'looked forward' and inserted something which caught his eye on the next page at the same place.

The intermediate passage *aut vero . . . rete piscium*, as written in *L*, contains 653 letters. This appears to represent 26 lines of the model (26 x 25 = 650).

We are now in a position to arrange a page of the model, viz.:

aut uero atque simulato ł quia	(25)
aliud quia non solum in aeternũ	(26)
uerũ etiã nunc hypocriptę non	(25)
cum illo ēē dicendi sunt quam	(24)
uis in eius esse uideantur ec-	(24)
cl͞a unde poterit ista regula et	(26)
sic apellari ut diceretur de	(24)
ꝑmixta aecclesia quae regula	(25)
intellectorem uigilantem re	(25)
quirit quando scriptura cum ad	(26)
alios iam loquatur tamquam ad	(25)
eos ipsos ad quos loquebatur ui	(26)
detur loqui uel de ipsis cum de	(25)
aliis iam loquatur tamquam unum	(27)
sit utrorumque corpus ꝓpter	(24)
temporalium commixtionem et	(25)
communionem sacramentorũ ad	(25)
hoc pertinet in cantico canti	(25)
corum fusca sum et speciosa ut	(25)
tabernacula caedar speciosa	(25)
sum ut pellas salamonis non enim	(27)
ait fusca fui ut tabernacula	(24)
caedar et speciosa sum ut pel	(24)
las salamonis sed utrũque esse	(26)
se dixit ꝓpter temporalem uni	(25)
tatem intra unum rete piscium	(25)
	653

Laud. Misc. 134, cent. ix (Würzburg).

Augustine, Ep. ad Rom., de spiritu et littera.

This MS. consists of two parts, the first of which, ff. 1–14, contains *Ep. ad Rom.*, and the second (ff. 15–110) the treatise *De spiritu et littera ad Marcellinum.*

Its interest resides in the fact that the passages omitted by the first hand are wholly different in the two parts. Part I is derived from a MS. written in long lines, and Part II from one written in short lines. The usual omission sign in both parts is *ħ*: in Part II ⋇ and ; are also frequent.

(A) Part I.

(72) 2^r: * non eas quę populo hębreorum s̄ diuinitus creditę, satis oportune mihi uidet' adiungere

3^r: * dĩ in uirtute secund̃ spm̃ sc̄ificationis factus est ergo ex semine dauid, id est filius d̄d̄

10^r: quia non ignorantiae tempore peccatum est et aliam causam ēē cũ d̄r ꝑpterea non ignosci

(76) 14^v: non potest recte intellegi nisi ut factis dicere intellegatur, non enĩ hoc in spũ sc̄o dicere

(77) 1^r: * iustificati deinceps iuste uiuere inciperent, hoc ergo docere intendit ap̄s omnib; uenisse

(78) 11^r: tamquam si diceret leuiter emendatus ad ueniam ꝑtinebit in eo enim quod dictum est uapulabit.

(257) 4^r: ex resurrectione enĩ ceterorũ mortuorũ ñ est p̃distinatus quos non ꝑcessit ad gloriã uitae aeternae ñ utiq: secuturos quõ ad penas suas impii resurrecturi sunt. ergo ille tamquã filius dĩ unigenitus etiã primogenitus ex mortuis p̃distinatus est ex resurrectione mortuorũ. quorũ mortuorũ. nisi ĩhu xp̄i dñi nr̄i

(399) 12^v: acceperit ꝑpter quorundã posteriorem ꝑuectum ł miserabilẽ neglegentiã et tamen illud sacrificium de quo loquebatur id est holocaustum dñi quod tunc ꝓ uno quoque offertur quodam modo cum eius nomine in babtizando signatur iterũ si peccauerit offerri non potest. Non enim possunt denuo babtizari qui semel babtizati sunt quamuis etiam post babtismum per ignorantiam ueritatis peccauerint ita fit ut quoniam sine babtismo nemo recte dicitur accepisse scientiam ueritatis *bis scr.*

Here, out of eight omissions, six consist of 72–8 letters, and no less than three exhibit the same figure, 72. The dittography of 399 letters seems to represent five lines of the model ($78 \times 5 = 390$).

There are fewer abbreviations used in the text than in the supplements, hence the unit (78) is a little higher than the average.

The remaining omission of 257 letters seems due to accident (ὁμ.).

Part II.

De spiritu et littera ad Marcellinum (*Letters*).

(13) 90v: iam ñ sit gratia
(14) 104v: nisi quia lucrum
(16) 35v: legis sed factores
69v: sed ei cui redditur
105v: ꝑ liberũ arbitrium
(17) 22r: ꝑ legẽ ñ iustificati
23v: aut gratias egerunt
(18) 30r: ñ secundũ testamentũ
(20) 38r: apparuit ł ut audiretur
74r: dš dat ut ꝑ se ipso habeat
(21) 18r: uocauit ut iustificaret
19r: ubi aũ abundauit delictũ
34v: dš sit ipse quem diligunt
47r: uel in ipso corde aliquid *bis scr.*
(23) 72v: nec tamen cupimus omne quod
92v: * neq. ꝑ carnẽ quã nũquã fuisse
(24) 75v: quis aũt ambulat secundũ spm̃
ib.: non sunt itaq: filii liberae
78r: uult potius ad nos pertinere *bis scr.*
(25) 38r: porro aũt si ñ gratis mortuus ẽ
68v: * non solũ actus et euenta uerum
78r: Abrahae aũt per promissionem
(27) 80v: * eadem gratia ꝑ spm̃ scm̃ unde dicit
81v: ueterẽ a quo necesse est hominem
88r: * diaboli p̃cipites ire ꝑsuadeant
89r: tribuunt cũ sit nostrae naturae
98r: ꝑ quẽ sunt omnia in quo sunt omnia
101v: uoluntas dĩ quae ut fiat in nobis
(28) 85v: legis ñ impleri secundũ iustitiã
93v: * et hoc quid est nisi peccatum, unde
(29) 91v: et pelaiani laudando se occultant
95r: liberum arbitrium, sic enim uolunt
(30) 75r: non litigant ut nũquam intellegant
80v: Abrahę dictę sunt ꝑmissiones de quo
Cf. 33r: non enim ipse ꝑmittit et alius fecit. After this the first hand adds *non enim ipse promittit*
(31) 39r: sibi congrua hoc ẽ in iustificatione

104v: * hic uobis p̃cipit' iustitia cũ dicitur
(32) 47r: uel linguam alicui quae dicenda ñ e̅e̅nt
80v: * * -dine uetus testamentum lex et ꝓphetae
82r: * si non in dm̃ fidem rectam et catholicam
84v: necessaria medicina et hoc factum est
101v: orationibus nr̃is sed qđ petamus a dõ ut
(33) 18v: intrasse in genus humanũ et ꝑ unũ hominẽ
88r: * ne gratiam dĩ qua iustificamur ñ gratis
(35) 104v: * eorũ hic in p̃cepto curanda est actio illic
(39) 30r: in facie xp̃i ih̃u haec est scientia gloriae eius
73r: et a dñõ responsio linguae quia homo p̃parat cor
(48) 98v: quapropter et in babtismate dimittuntur cuncta peccata.
(54) 76r: quale peccatum sit sicut apostolus cũ dicitur si non exprimatur
(57) 92r: et dm̃ creatorem credite et corporum quia non potest e̅e̅ templũ sp̃s sc̃i
(58) 25r: quamuis utriq: horũ preferendus sit qui et habet et nouit a quo habeat
(61) 36r: alit̃ aũt s̃cificetur nomen tuũ, nam illud ideo quia ipse illos fecit e̅e̅ sc̃os
(64) 31v: * congruebant talia contineat p̃cepta iustitiae qualia nunc quoq: obseruare
(88) 92r: aduersus eos isti non solum ueram sed et ipsam et animam nulla peccati macula respersam fuisse defendunt
(100) 89r: quod uero et ipsis quamuis iustis et dõ placentibus ꝓpitiationẽ dñi fuisse dicimus necessariam aduersũ est pelaianis
(156) 31v: * scriptae in cordibus nisi praesentia sp̃s sc̃i qui est digitus dĩ quo presente difunditur caritas in cordibus nr̃is quae plenitudo est legis et finis praecepti. nam quia ueteris testamenti

These words are added by m. 2 *in lac.* In the margin is written *Quere in aliis codicib;*

(235) 55r: sed habitet in me peccatum id repetiuit inculcans tamquam tardissimos de somno excitans. inuenio ergo inquid mihi uolenti facere bonum quõ mihi malum adiacet. illa ergo bonum uolenti facere adiacet autem malum ex concupiscentia cui non consentit qui dicit iam non ego operor illud *bis scr.*

Here the most noticeable point is the bulge in the curve of omissions at 27 and again at 32. It is to be observed that one omission of 32 is a 'telescoped' passage. The dittographies of 21 and 24 should also be noticed.

The omission on 92v (23) requires especial attention. The passage as printed by Migne is:

non crimen primi hominis transisse in genus humanum neque per carnem quam numquam fuisse dicunt

For this the MS. (L) gives:

non crimen primi hominis transisse in genus humanum ħ dicunt.

In the margin is ℞ (=*require*). A second hand supplies the omission (23) in the margin.

Here *ħ*, the sign of omission, has been received into the text. This postulates a previous stage, when *ħ* was written above the line to signify that something was lost. The original loss, therefore, goes back beyond the model. We may, therefore, recognize in 21–4 traces of a previous ancestor.

The telescoped passage 80ᵛ indicates in a previous MS.:

legendi consuetu
dine uetus testamentum lex et ꝑphetae (32)
omnes qui usque ad iohannem prophetã

L^1 gives *legendi consuetu omnes*, etc., *med. om.*

It must remain doubtful whether the six omissions of 27 letters point to another intermediary MS., or, as I think more likely, one column in the model was slightly 'squeezed' by the other.

With regard to the larger numbers we may notice the relation of 235 to 58 ($58 \times 4 = 232$), while $100 + 56$ (cf. 92ʳ) $= 156$. The unit here seems to be 28–9.

Laud. Misc. 252.

Jerome, Letters, cent. ix/x.

In this MS. the numeration is given by pages, except in a few cases where the marking is by folios.

(17) p. 231: alium fuisse mundum
(18) p. 194: et flos de radice eius
(20) p. 95: * animaduerte quid dicat
p. 190: * negotii cardo uersatur
(21) p. 137: * referant egressus est aũ
(22) p. 52: * compellit me tua dilectio
(23) p. 60: * ꝑ quib:libet tribulantib:
p. 86: inanis est praedicatio nr̃a
p. 235: pater quo modo cognoscitur
(27) p. 100: sed gaudeas quod talem habueris
p. 161: primum spiro solus nr̃a obmutuit
(29) p. 222: nisi sexus meus et hoc nũquã obicit˜
ib.: aut ñ fictũ ut fingatur impellitur
(31) p. 72: qui simul mecũ dulces capiebas cibos

(32) p. 62: dispensatores domorū alienarū atque
p. 136: spoliorū et habrahae dederit decimas
p. 221: dicatur qđ minime luceat et parce ab eo
(36) p. 163: sed iustificati estis sed sc̄ificati estis
p. 213: flores et gemmas artificis manu non textas
p. 229: mundos ēē contendunt et iterū triplex ergo
(37) p. 202: * fugerat quondam et ionas animosus propheta
(38) p. 23: ita intep̄tatus ē obsecro dn̄e libera animā meā
p. 67: mansionū mysteria continent deuteronomium
p. 102: uigilans in p̄cando lacrimas dō non hominibus
p. 128: qui temporum scripsit historiam et theodori
p. 146: quantum acciperis uestiaris quod acciperis
(39) p. 75: * laudant hoc philosophi et caelum usque ferunt
p. 220: * aut corrigendum putauerint aut non diuinitus
(40) p. 172: ad altare aut ira ꝑmanente sine causa optulimus
p. 224: aput triueris manu mea ipse descripserā aequae
(41) p. 189: * interrogare eos qui malitiam prudentiam uocant
f. 196v: filio saar nec sepultus est in sychem sed in ebron (ch above ebron)
(42) p. 23: quod nos corrupte ꝓpter ignorantiam dicim' osanna
p. 128: et eustachii antioceni et athanasii alexandrini
p. 192: * tu q:re sententias dies me deficiet si omniū qui ad
(44) p. 196: * quando necesse habuit et esuriuit ipse et socii eius
(45) p. 47: * quo hierusalem cęlestē uir fortis coronatus incedes
p. 57: * qui te in omnibus quae sc̄ā sunt docuit. Illud etiam dico
p. 59: atq: diuitiis simplex nos delectat historia cum auro
p. 61: * et dum delicias sectamur a regno caelorum retrahimur
p. 77: torqueri alios necari alios absorbi fluctibus alios
p. 80: potest enim fieri ut tibi uideatur aliud quam ueritas
p. 218: * ne doctrinae auctoritas cassis operibus destruatur
p. 235: contendet ut dicat et in cognitione filii patrem esse
(46) p. 185: ** quę fuit unius uiri uxor in bonis operibus habens testi-
(47) p. 111: ecclesias frequentius ceperit lectitari quod a grecis (o above ceperit)
(51) f. 167r: ab omnibus inmunditiis ūr̄is. Dabo uobis cor nouum et sp̄m nouum
(55) f. 196v: sepelieruntq: in ea sarram uxorem suam atq: in eodem libro postea
p. 224: satis habeo si splendorē morū eius et inbecillitas oculorū meorū
(58) p. 179: conpellaris simulabitur mariti infirmitas et qđ te moritura facere
(67) p. 189: * qua cuncta loquitur et impunitate qua sibi licere omnia putat. Me quoque apud uos
(76) p. 194: ꝓ quo in eodē loco LXX transtulerunt quia paruulus ē israhel et dilexi eū et ex egipto uocaui
(78) p. 114: legi esse subiectos ut ꝓ utrarumque ꝑsona et paulus recte rep̄henderet eos qui egē seruarent

(90) p. 218: significant et eclesiã XII apostolorũ qui ad prȩdicationẽ missi sunt nomina continentes uel literã et sp̃m *bis scr.*

The striking feature here is the bulge in the curve at 45 (eight examples).

The example of 46 is interesting. Here an ancestor appears to have had:

non minus annorum lx
quȩ fuit unius uiri uxor in bonis operibus habens testi (46)
monium

The writer of the present MS. (*L*) wrote *non minus annorum lx monium*: then he deleted *monium* and added the passage at the top of the page.

The example of 42 (p. 192) is also interesting. Here an ancestor seems to have had:

alii sillibas aucupentur, alii litteras
tu q:re sententias dies me deficiet si omniũ qui ad (42)
sensum interp̃tati sunt testimonia replicavero

L^1 omits line 2, destroying the sense.

The largest number, 90, is exactly 45 × 2. Here we have a dittography of two lines in the model. This occurs on the same page (p. 218) as an omission of 45 letters. The intervening passage between the dittography and the omission, as written in *L*, contains 1,174 letters. Here 45 × 26 = 1,170. It appears that the intermediate words occupied 26 lines in the model. I therefore reconstitute it thus:

significant et eclesiã XII apostolorũ qui ad prȩdica (45)
tionẽ missi sunt nomina continentes uel literã et sp̃m (45)
in quibus tenentur legis uniuersa mysteria. In dextra (45)
sp̃s in leua littera ẽ p̧ litteras ad uerba descendimus p̧ (45)
uerbum uenimus ad sensum quã pulcher ordo et ex ipso ha (45)
bitu sacramenta demonstrans in humeris opera sunt in (45)
pectore ratio unde et pectusculum condunt sacerdotes (46)
hoc aũ rationale duplex ẽ aptũ et absconditũ simplex (44)
et mistycũ XII in se lapides habens et IIII ordines quos (46)
IIIIor[1] puto ẽẽ uirtutes prudentiã fortitudinẽ iusti (45)
tiã temperantiã quae sibi haerent inuicem et dum mutuo (46)
miscentur duodenariũ numerũ efficiunt uel quattuor e (46)
uangelia quae in apocalipsi discribuntur plena oculis (47)

[1] Probably the model had IIII with "or" written above. Cf. l. 14.

et dn̄ī luce radiantia mundum inluminant in uno IIIIor (45)
et in quattuor singula unde et aeaωcιє et aacia[1] idē doc (45)
trina et ueritas in pectore sacerdotis ē cum enī indu (44)
tus quis fuerit ueste multiplici consequens ē ueritatē (47)
quā corde retinet sermone proferre et ob id in rationa (45)
li ueritas est idē scientia ut nouerit quae docenda (43)
sint et manifestatio atque doctrina ut possit instru (45)
ere alios quod mente concepit ubi sunt qui innocentiā (45)
sacerdotis dicunt posse sufficere uetus lex nouę con (45)
gruit id ipsum moyses quod apostolus ille sacerdotis (45)
scientiā ornat in uestibus iste timotheū et titū instru (47)
it disciplinis sed et ipse uestimentorū ordo p̃cipuus. (45)
legamus leuiticū non prius rationale et sic suꝑ hume (44)
rale sed ante suꝑ humerale et deinceps rationale. A man (45)
datis tuis intellexi prius faciamus et sic doceamus (44)
ne doctrinae auctoritas cassis operibus destruatur (45)

ll. 1–2 *bis scr.* L^1 : l. 29 *om.* L^1.

It is to be noticed that six out of the eight omissions of 45 letters occur on pp. 47–80. After this point 45 does not occur until p. 218, though we have a telescoped passage of 46 on p. 185. The conclusion appears to be that after the fifth quaternion (p. 80) the hand changed. As there is only one omission of 47 letters, while there are fifteen of 38–44 letters (eleven after p. 80), it is probable that the script became larger. There is an instructive case on p. 128, where an omission of 38 letters is followed by one of 42. The intervening passage, as written in *L*, contains 201 letters (40 × 5 = 200). This suggests the following distribution:

exstant et iulii africani libri
qui temporum scripsit historiam et theodori (38)
qui postea gregorius appellatus ē uiri apostoli (41)
corum signorum atque uirtutum et dionisii ale (39)
xandrini ep̄ī anatolii quoque laudicenę ecclesi (41)
ae sacerdotis nec non presbiterorum panfili py (40)
eri luciani malcyonis eusebii cesariensis ep̄ī (40)
et eustachii antioceni et athanasii alexandrini (42)

L^1 omits ll. 2 and 8.

If this suspicion is correct, the two largest omissions, 76–8 letters, may each represent two lines written in a larger hand. It is to be noticed that there are seven examples of 38–9 (four after p. 80).

1 = δήλωσις et ἀλήθεια (Migne, 22, § 370).

The question may now be asked whether these figures (38–45) represent a unit or multiples of a unit. There is something to be said in favour of the second explanation. It is to be noticed that several omissions of 20–3 letters are not due to ὁμ., also that 45 + 21 = 66 (cf. 67, p. 189). It is tempting to arrange the figures thus: 20–3, 40–6, 67, 90.

On the other hand, I am struck by the great number of omissions of 40–5 letters (16 cases). Generally, the unit is predominant and multiples are less frequent. I, therefore, incline to consider that we are dealing with the unit and to look on the omission of 67 letters as due to chance, or to some other ancestor.

There is an important passage which shows the existence of a smaller unit, probably representing a line in a previous MS. I refer to p. 222, where an omission of 29 letters is shortly afterwards followed by another of the same number. The intervening passage, as written in *L*, contains 235 letters. Here $29 \times 8 = 232$. This suggests the following distribution in a previous ancestor:

nisi sexus meus et hoc nũquã obicit˜ (29)
nisi cum hierosolimã paula profici (30)
scitur. esto crediderunt mentienti (30)
cur non credunt neganti idem ẽ homo (29)
ipse qui fuerit fatetur insontẽ qui (30)
dudũ noxiũ loquebatur et certe ueri (30)
tatẽ magis exprimunt tormenta quã (29)
risus nisi quod facilius creditur (29)
quod aut fictum libenter auditur (28)
aut ñ fictũ ut fingatur impellitur (29)

L^1 omits ll. 1 and 10 (ὁμ.).

It is to be noticed that there are four examples of 31–2 letters. It is possible that 67 is to be taken in connexion with a unit of 29–32 in a previous MS.

Laud. Misc. 92, cent. viii/ix (Würzburg).

Fulgentius.

Omissions are often introduced by *hp*, also by *hd* and *h*.

There is an interesting note on 47^v, where various heretical objections are stated without an answer, viz.:

℞. Hic requirat lector ℞ diligenter. aut rectũ ñ est aut intellegi ñ potest

Shortly afterwards the whole passage is written out correctly with the answers, as in Migne, lxv, p. 206.

Omissions.

(37) 160^{r}: nunc autem necdum uidemus omnia subiecta ei

(38) 59^{r}: quae dš non sit aut alterã lucem p̃t. sapientiam

(39) 22^{v}: sed qui seminat in spm̃ et de spũ metat uitã aet'nã

39^{v}: non tamen in illo ẽẽt extra illũ ñ intra illũ ẽẽt

(41) 41^{r}: exterius est. quo arrianos uerbum quod apud dm̃ est.

116^{r}: cũ ergo non dixerit xp̃s tristis sum usq: ad mortem

141^{v}: et ieiunabat uidit omnibus dieb: uiduitatis suę

(43) 76^{v}: humanum assignant et animam denegant in sola carne

(45) 8^{r}: sicut iohannes ꝑ opere iustitiae iustitiã autẽ dixit

(46) 125^{v}: occidi ꝑmisit, ipse dignatus est mori. sic in eo quod in eo

(49) 60^{v}: ex hoc iam filius subiciat ambob: et saltim sic paraclytus

68^{v}: quia reuera si localis non inmensus, si mutabilis non est dš

133^{v}: debita sic infirmitatem carnis usus excipiat coniugalis

(50) 113^{r}: erit excepta diuinitus quę particeps passionum generibus

127^{v}: et alio loco scire etiã supeminentẽ scientię caritatem xp̃i

(51) 76^{r}: * sic et xp̃s non semet ipsũ clarificauit ut pontifex fieret sed

(52) 13^{v}: sic nemo potest habere ueram gloriã nisi fuerit glorificatus

19^{v}: qui seruiunt mihi exultabunt in laetitia, uos autẽ clamabitis

98^{r}: * et filiũ demonstrauit ubi se ad ĩmana et iam in nouissimo maris

(54) 34^{r}: hoc itaq: spiritalis ędificatio corporis xp̃i q̃: fit in caritate

144^{v}: * nec deputes posse deficere si te ille dignatus fuerit custodire

(56) 129^{v}: * coniugum commixtione ducẽ rationẽ consideret et culpabilis usus

(57) 149^{v}: ad spiritalia recurrere et s̃carũ coniugatarum cogitationem magis

(58) 167^{r}: uelle nullatenus poterit propt̃ quod beatus apo̅l̅s non solũ bona opera

(67) 12^{r}: opera bona ꝑ quib: glorificabunt' iusti sic credenda sint p̃distinata diuinitus

(80) 101^{r}: ac ne quis eoꝝ qui spm̃ scm̃ in morẽ patre filioq: constituunt hic ubi dictũ ẽ sp̃s dĩ habitat in uobis

(86) 144^{v}: tesaurizate aũ uobis in cęlo ubi neq: erugo neq; tinea exterminat et ubi fures ñ effodiunt nec furantur

(90) 5^{r}: malo p̃distinationem ter elegisse diceres, ipse edocens aiebã. ad poenam debitam. non ad malum faciendũ posse (*m.* 2 *in lac.*)

(96) 143^{r}: teneas in corde diuitias. non enĩ illi soli peccant qui pro diuitiis quas habent aliquas gestam in corde iactantiam

To these may be added the following corruption:

(51) 61^{r}: sumus [unum written above] agnoscatur non aliud ẽẽ quam pater est et in eo quod dixit sumus agnoscatur.

This points to the following arrangement in the model:

unum agnoscatur non aliud ẽẽ quam pater est et in eo quod dixit
sumus agnoscatur

The striking points here are the bulges in the curve at 41, 49, 52. It will be noticed that there are nine examples of 49–52, reinforced by the corruption on 61^{r}. These appear to represent a line of the model.

On the other hand the larger numbers 80, 86, 90 seem to be in relation to 41–5 (five cases). These probably represent lines of a previous ancestor.

The largest omission, 96, seems connected with the three cases of 49, i. e. with the model.

It is to be noticed that all the omissions of this MS. are due to ὁμ. except 76^{r} (51), 98^{r} (52), 144^{v} (54), 129^{v} (56). In 129^{v} the model seems to have had:

igitur si per se ipsam quasi fidelium
coniugum commixtione ducẽ rationẽ consideret et culpabilis usus (56)
non in coniugali ɔ̃cubitu sed in concũbentiũ repperiebatur excessu

L^1 omits l. 2, destroying the sense.

Laud. Misc. 120,[1] cent. ix (Würzburg).

Augustine, de Civitate Dei.

This MS. (L) has received much attention in the way of critical notes. The symbol ℞ (= *require*) is very frequent. Thus it occurs nine times on f. 155^{v} and eight times on f. 156^{v}. It contains references to other MSS., viz. 13^{v} *sicut in alio codice*, 16^{v} *alter codex aliter habet*. The usual omission mark is ħ, but đ and ħħ are also used.

Omissions.

(16) 31^{r}: insani secarentur
(17) 100^{v}: alteri non obueniat
102^{v}: *temporib: diuersis
158^{r}: magnã qđ cibũ pariat
(19) 52^{r}: troiana amasse romana
(20) 59^{r}: asscanii posteris nisi

[1] Cf. *Pal. Soc.*, ser. ii, plates 67, 68.

128v: quando agant quid agant
149v: statuendi stabiliendi
158r: *quod se apud deã iactare
(21) 22r: cur nõ tunc potissimũ fit
48v: laudandis decus latet et
118r: *uolens bonus uideri qđ ñ ē
(22) 135r: non tamen om̃s natura ds̃ est
135v: inꝓbare hanc non audebant
143r: et sentimus sensificator
153v: *pater ēēt et ioui regnanti
158r: non tã deę multę quã nomina
159r: **mulierumq· uerecundiã con-
(23) 6r: ille mirabilit̃ temperauit
88r: *non enim malignis demonib;
127r: *contra quos iam quinque prę (*m. 2 in lac.*)
144v: dea minerua et oscurata est
(24) 86r: cũ a suis partib: non colatur
87v: et suis contemtorib: aereat (h)
143r: sicut enĩ quę ratiocinantur
(25) 23r: istarũ occursũ est imminenti
161v: *rationẽ illã orium deorũ quib;
(26) 133v: ut non sint statuae delubrorum
(27) 17v: *extendere ut ex hoc nullum etiam
26r: luxuria flueretis nec contriti
80r: suoꝝ sic incipit principio rerũ
120r: in quib: sibi displicet quã in ea
131v: *ubi est nisi in urbe, qui (s) theatrum
161v: *mortuos et ad daemones pessimos
(29) 57r: siue quandoq: alba euersa fuerant
78v: *sibi sufficientem carissimũ suis
(33) 37v: hoc sane utilius feliciusq: successit
(39) 21r: inrapturũ atq: necaturum se fluuiũ ꝓiecerunt
(40) 101v: uaniloquia conuincantur, quid idem ipsi quorum
(44) 15v: perdita quocirca proposito animi ꝑmanente ꝑ qđ etiã
(45) 143r: ianus aditum et quasi ianuam semini confert selectus
(46) 15r: *atq: in se ꝑpetret peccatum proprium ne in eo ꝑpetretur
(48) 43r: sentirentur atque dicerentur quis non istorũ ea x̃pianis
(49) 5r: *ferire uel captiuare non ausi sunt sed uergilius poetarum
6r: unde captiuandi ulli nec a crudelib: hostibus abducerent̃.
(54) 97r: *contra uetustatem tanti possit erroris. profecto et unum dm̃ a quo
(61) 17v: a semet ipso dilector accepit quando quidem scriptũ est diliges proximũ
(79) 17v: sicut falsum testimoniũ cũ uetaret, falsum inquit testimoniũ non dices aduersus proximũ tuum

(108) 72^{v}: *postea cinna cũ mario tũ uero clarissimis uiris interfectis lumina ciuitatis extincta sunt. ultus ẽ eius uictorię crudelitatem

(110) 63^{r}: nam et idem brutus consangineus tarquinii fuisse ꝑibetur sed con-
do
latinũ uidelicet similitu nominis pressit qui etiam tarquinius

(271) 96^{r}: ut sibi sui liberi suꝑstites ẽẽnt, suꝑstitiosi sint appellati. quis non intellegat eũ conari dum consuetudinem ciuitatis timet. religionem laudare maiorum eãque a superstitione uelle seiungere, sed quomodo id possit non inuenire. si enĩ a maioribus illi sunt appellati suꝑstitiosi qui totos dies precabantur et immolabant.

(406) 8^{v}: *ad quam consequendam si nollent ẽẽ socii ferrentur et diligerentur inimici, quia donec uiuunt semꝑ incertum est utrum uoluntatem sint in melius mutaturi. qua in re non utiq: parem sed longe grauiorem habent causã quibus ꝑ prophetã dicit˜, ille quidẽ in suo peccato morietur, sanguinẽ aũt ẽĩ de manu speculatoris requirã. ad hoc enim speculatores, hoc ẽ populoꝝ p̃positi constituti sunt in aeclesiis ut ñ parcant obiurgando peccata. nec ideo tam̃ ab huius modĩ culpa penitus alienus est qui licet (*m.* 2 *in lac.*).

To these I would add the following corruption.

(138) 148^{v}. Here *L* gives:

> a
> quam ille q: fit quaꝑpter si ad ianum ꝑtinent initia
> e
> factoꝝ non ido priora sunt efficientib: causis quas io
> ui tribuunt. sicut enim nihil fit ita nihil inco
> atur ut fiat quam illa q: fecit.

Here *quam illa q: fecit* is a v. l. for *quam ille q: fit*, which has found its way into the text later on (*quam ille q: fit . . . ut fiat* = 138).

In this MS. the bulges in the curve come at 22–3 (10 examples), and at 27 (six examples).

The telescoped passage 159^{r} (22) is interesting: the model seems to have had:

> item
> que de mollibus eidem matri
> magnę contra omnem uirorum
> mulierumq· uerecundiã con
> secratis

L^1 omits l. 4, thereby producing nonsense.

It will be noticed that there are seven examples of 40–9, corresponding to this unit.

On the other hand the larger figures show that the other unit, 27, plays the predominant part. I give the following multiples, with references to the actual figures in the tabulation.

$27 \times 2 = 54$ (97^r).
$27 \times 3 = 81$. Cf. 79 (17^v).
$27 \times 4 = 108$ (72^v). Cf. 110 (63^r).
$27 \times 5 = 135$. Cf. 138 (148^v).
$27 \times 10 = 270$. Cf. 271 (96^r).
$27 \times 15 = 405$. Cf. 406 (8^v).

The conclusion, therefore, is that 27 represents the average length of line in the model and 22–3 that in a previous ancestor.

Laud. Misc. 452, cent. ix/x (Lorsch).

This volume contains two MSS. bound up together. Both of them have the library mark of Lorsch (*codex de monasterio Scĩ Nazarii*). The first MS., ff. 1–191, contains works of Chrysostom, the second, ff. 192–277, has Origen on Leviticus.

The evidence furnished by omissions, &c., differs in the case of the two parts, as in Laud. Misc. 134. The second part is the more interesting, but I add omissions of the first MS. for the sake of completeness.

Part I. Chrysostom.

(16) 151^v: diuites epulantes
(18) 145^r: et iniuriã patiuntur
172^v: neq: amicus neq: fraĩ
(22) 51^r: sedes iudicantes duodecĩ
161^v: sed et mortis tollerantiã
(24) 173^r: quã uulnerib: sanitas animę
184^v: animã aũt ñ possunt occidere
(25) 75^v: quare iudaei pacem non habent
175^v: et exacerbauerat qui fecit eũ
(26) 39^v: si enim hoc fecero mors mihi est *bis scr.*
57^r: non sub tali condicione posito
111^r: claustra nobis ualida quamvis
(30) 81^r: et gaudiũ quod quidem maximũ lucrum
163^v: si ait ex fructib' eoꝝ agnoscetis eos
183^v: *in corporib: tanta est differentia
(32) 68^v: in nube leui et quia pater sed et in urbe
(33) 179^v: corpora patietur sed incorruptibilia
182^r: arbitrio sollicitudo nobis immineret

(35) 103^{v}: et habitauit in nobis uerbũ caro factũ est
(40) 61^{v}: crux scutũ ꝑpetuũ crux insensatorum sapientia
79^{r}: tribuit enim ds̃ petentib: se quo quis desiderat
85^{v}: de terra carnem fecerit quo modo neruos quo modo
168^{v}: neq: in furore quod est absq: uenia corripiatur
(41) 116^{r}: *extenta manu quatiebat nunc lepusculi alicuius
(42) 163^{v}: sed in hoc gaudete quia nomina uestra scripta sunt
(44) 129^{r}: terrarum morib: de quib: dicit ds̃ quia in saturitate
(45) 190^{r}: ista pellatur quia illa bona quae egimus et emendatio
(51) 104^{v}: ñ mireris me tangere quem in sepulchro queris noli me tangere
(55) 190^{v}: immo uero etiam illud addo quia si quis parua ñ contemnat et minima
(58) 188^{r}: *apparente sibi eadem monetur, tunc uero instantius perunguentes eum
(64) 93^{v}: capituli in alio propheta melius dicitur et ipse dicit euangelista iste est
(79) 121^{v}: et discite a me quia mitis sum et humilis corde et inuenietis requiem animabus ũis iugũ enĩ meum
(108) 166^{r}: et iam si trahat aliquis corpus etiam si propellat' talis erit beatus paulus qui in tantum absens erat ab his inter quos conseruari

Here we have to note the relation of 108 to 55, also of 79 to 40 (four examples), and of 64 to 32. It is probable that more than one unit is present in these figures.

The most striking bulge is at 40, while there are eight examples of 40–5. I have also noticed the following corruption:

mutatur
f. 56^{r}: nox sicut dies inluminabitur, infidelibus autem et dies nocte inluminabitur.

This suggests in the model:

nox sicut dies
inluminabitur infidelibus autem et dies nocte (40)
mutatur

The most interesting omission is that of 41 letters on f. 116^{r}, since it destroys the sense. The model seems to have had:

et eum qui orbem terrae
extenta manu quatiebat nunc lepusculi alicuius (41)
aut ranae timiditatem adtractum latitare

I have treated 40–5 as a unit, since these numbers occur so frequently, while short omissions are rare. I have done so with some hesitation on account of two corruptions, which may possess significance, viz.:

ex uirtutibus suis
f. 183^{v}: ex uirtutibus suis tamen alias tibi decus eius conabor

This suggests in a previous MS.:

tamen alias tibi decus eius	(23)
ex uirtutibus suis	

f. 85ᵛ: neminem debere desperare salutem quia naturalis malignitas non est liberi quippe nos arbitri creauit d̃s ut uoluntate nostra cum adiutorio dĩ quod uolumus faciamus. Si publicanus es, potes fieri euangelista. Si blasphemus es, potes fieri a nemine disperare debere apostolus

Here the words *neminem debere desperare* = 22 letters, while the whole passage *neminem . . . fieri* = 198 ($22 \times 9 = 198$). This suggests:

neminem debere desperare	(22)
salutem quia naturalis ma	(22)
lignitas non est liberi quip	(24)
pe nos arbitri creauit d̃s	(21)
ut uoluntate nostra cum	(20)
adiutorio dĩ quod uolumus	(22)
faciamus si publicanus es	(22)
potes fieri euangelista si	(23)
blasphemus es potes fieri	(22)
apostolus.	

The words *a nemine disperare debere* look like a variant for l. 1, which has got into the text after l. 9.

Part II. Origen on Leviticus.

(18) 205ᵛ: siclo aut qualicumq:
(24) 255ᵛ: separate a terrenis actibus *bis scr.*
(45) 242ʳ: nunc pili nominantur iubeatur abicere peccator enim
(52) 217ʳ: aegyptius enim tertia generatione intrabit in ecclesiam dñĩ
(54) 276ʳ: *et nati aspidum uolantium qui portabant super asinos et camelos
(56) 273ʳ: **numquid hec apostolus de terra hac dixit, sed nec accepit terra bene-
(58) 245ʳ: a populo uero munera iubentur offerri aries a principib: et hirci duo
(59) 233ᵛ: **-bis et erinacius quia reducit rumigationem et ungulã et inmundũ hoc uo-
(60) 255ᵛ: *tu ergo qui hec audis, cui lex diuina recitatur, quem ipsius etiam dĩ sermo
(62) 249ʳ: achab illum impiissimũ de quo dicit dñs uidisti quo modo conpunctũ est cor
(64) 201ᵛ: *et consumat te et quinquaginta tuos, uis autem audire de ouibus dĩ dicitur per
(68) 221ʳ: contingantur aliam in eis qui edit carnes sacrificii inmundus sit et inmunditia

(75) 216^{r}: difficile esse ad intellectum illud enim quod edendum dicit ad peccatum referri uidetur

(80) 206^{r}: si ergo ipsius saluatoris uoce didicimus quia uerba quae loquutus est apostolis sp̃s et uite est.

Here there are two telescoped passages, viz. 56 and 59. The first is not striking, since *benedictiones* might be taken as two words. The second, however, in which *vobis* is divided at the beginning and end of the line, is very remarkable. Also, the omitted passage comes after the last line of the page. The same phenomenon is to be observed on f. 201^{r}, where 64 letters are added: while on f. 255^{v} a passage of 60 letters is marked for insertion at the end of a line. The explanation appears to be that the scribe copied his model line by line, but that the number of lines in a page was not the same. In order to make the point clear, I write out the passages as they are given in the MS. (*L*), merely inserting the line which has been added by the second hand.

233^{v}, 234^{r}:

lepus quõ reducit rumigationẽ et ungulam non diuidit inmundũ hoc uo (57)
[bis et erinacius quia reducit rumigationem et ungulã et inmundũ hoc uo] (59)
bis et sues ẽt cetera

201^{v}, 202^{r}:

[et consumat te et quinquaginta tuos uis autem audire de ouibus dĩ dicitur per] (64)
prophetam

In both cases the omitted passage is entered as an extra line after the last line (l. 30) of the page. It is to be noticed that the first lines of 202^{r} are written over an erasure.

255^{v}. If we add the line inserted by the second hand, the passage runs as follows:

de talibus ipsi enim sentire et uidere possunt quam sibi elegerint partem (62)
[tu ergo qui hec audis cui lex diuina recitatur quem ipsius etiam dĩ sermo] (60)
conuenit dicens sc̃i stote quia ego sc̃s sũ dñs d̃s uester. Sapienter intellege (63)

The same explanation appears to apply to some other passages, viz.: f. 221^{r}:

causas hic legislator exposuit unam ne carnes sacrificiorum aliqua inmun (63)
dicia eius in ipso sit tertiam quod et si carnes mundę sint et ipse qui edit mun (64)
dus sit

The corrector adds *contingantur . . . et inmundicia* before *eius*. This implies in the model:

causas hic legislator exposuit unam ne carnes sacrificiorum aliqua inmun (63)
dicia [contingantur, aliam in eis qui edit carnes sacrificii inmundus sit et inmun (68)

dicia] eius in ipso sit, tertiam quod et si carnes mundę sint et ipse qui edit mun (64)
dus sit

f. 249^{r}:

corri
gere uias suas cógitet et obliuisci praeterita et praeparare se ad futura saltim secun (73)
dum achab sed in his omnib: quid de illis dicam qui nec audiunt auribus haec nec (65)

The first line here is exceptionally long. The second hand adds *achab . . . cor*. This seems to imply:

gere uias suas cogitet et obliuisci praeterita et praeparare se ad futura saltim secun (73)
dum [achab illum impiissimū de quo dicit dñs uidisti quomodo compunctū est (62)
cor] achab sed in his omnib: quid de illis dicam qui nec audiunt auribus haec nec (65)

It appears, therefore, that all the omissions between 59 and 68 are to be explained in this way.

Those of 75 and 80 do not admit of such an explanation, since they are preceded by lines of 62 and 65 letters respectively. They are, therefore, due to chance assisted by ὁμ.

For the sake of completeness I now take the cases of 52–8 letters.

(52) 217^{r}. The line before this contains 70 letters and the next contains 64. It is highly improbable that one of 52 would come between these.

(54) 276^{r}. Here *L* gives (*sine sensu*):

prophetico spū de bestiis loquitur. in tribulatione quidem et angustia. leo (63)
et catulus leonis inde diuitias suas ad gentem que non proderit eis (56)

L^2 adds after *inde* the omitted passage:

et nati aspidum uolantium qui portabant super asinos et camelos. (54)

Here the words *et catulus . . . eis* form the last line of the page. This line is obviously rather short. I should hesitate to ascribe to the model another short line before it.

(56) 273^{v}. *L* has:

benedictiones a dō. Quę autem protulerit spinas et tribulos reproba est et male (66)
dicto proxima cuius finis ad exustionem. Dictiones a dō cum imbres biberit et (64)
fructū produxerit sed neq: si spinas ac tribulos post pluuiam protulerit conse (67)
quitur

L^2 adds after *exustionem* the missing passage:

numquid hec apostolus de terra hac dixit sed nec accepit terra bene- (56)

Here there are various points to notice, viz.:

(1) The passage is telescoped;

(2) It is not likely that a line of 56 letters came among lines of 66, 64, 67;

(3) The capital letter in *Dictiones* is a further corruption after the omission of *bene*.

The conclusion appears to be that we have now got back to a previous MS., in which the words were arranged thus:

benedictiones a dõ quae autem protulerit spinas et tri
bulos reproba est et maledicto proxima cuius finis ad exustionem (55)
numquid hec apostolus de terra hac dixit sed nec accepit terra bene (56)
dictiones a dõ cum imbres biberit et fructũ produxerit

(58) 245^{r}. *L* has:

animal aries est quod in ouibus sine dubio praetiosus est a populo unus qui demit (67)
titur in heremum qui et pompeius nominatur et unus qu^{i}aȩ dñõ offertur. Si esset (64)

The omitted passage, which is added by L^2 before *a populo*, is not likely to have formed a line in the model between lines of 67 and 64. It may, however, have formed a line in the previous MS.

L therefore seems to have been copied line for line from a model with 60–70 letters to the line. Behind the model there is a previous MS. with 50–60 letters to the line. The interesting point is that the formation of *L* itself enables us to distinguish omissions made by *L* from those previously made by the model.

Laud. Misc. 464, cent. ix (St. Denis).

Authpertus on the Apocalypse.

The writer Ambrosius Authpertus (or Authbertus) is said to have died in A.D. 778. If so, the MS. appears to have been written within a hundred years after the work was composed. It is written in an Irish hand and once belonged to St. Denis. The only sign used to mark omissions is ·//.. There are two columns to the page.

Omissions.

(16) 71^{v}: uigore capitis sui
186^{r}: qđ x̃ps ñ resurrexit
(18) 199^{v}: tolle regnum peccato
(21) 61^{r}: carnis neq: et uoluntate
(24) 63^{r}: et patientiã tuã ministeriũ
(26) 13^{r}: oculis uero carnis humanitatẽ
75^{v}: *quid autẽ ꝑ hoc dictũ insinuare
(28) 7^{r}: *aliud significet quã qđ enarrare
(30) 180^{r}: *etiã quando patiendi tempus minime

(31) 164r: *in hac uita mortali uisibilis ꝑ carnẽ
(32) 81r: *sed occisione illius uituli saginati
105v: indicia legentib: dare ut intra ipsos
122r: intellegitur aut ubi filius et sp̃s. sc̃s
(33) 15v: quod si amplexus destitutae ñ abnueris
(34) 88v: qui nisi desuꝑ acceperit ñ habet quod det
(35) 5r: **-dẽ ꝑsonas plerũq: non ad se sed sibi inuicẽ
71v: nolite condemnare et non condemnabimini
(42) 18r: grando et carbones ignis p̃ fulgore nubis transier'
(43) 55r: ipse enĩ dixit omnes qui pie uolunt uiuere in xp̃o ih̃u
(44) 1r: cum in hac sententia audiat non ẽẽ a clamore cessandũ
(47) 70r: alia uero uitę ꝑagendę et quidẽ prę̨cepta uitę figurande
(49) 32r: eadẽ designatur ecclesia et sicut in simili filio hominis
(57) 62v: candido annon ipsũ caritatis uestimenti qđ constat ex lapide mundo
(66) 78v: et corã angelis ei' et qui me negauerit corã hominib; negabo et ego corã patre meo
(69) 93v: in uera carne ueraciter ꝓ nob̃ mortuum in uera carne ueraciter a mortuis suscitatum
101v: alas de se reddunt tamquã scilicet duodecim pinnata animalia in uiginti quattuor
(71) 115v: sic eiusdẽ operationis sũma in istis septẽ excellentissimis munerib; p̃signabatur
(84) 190r: in fortitudinẽ diuine uirtutis excreuit paulo attestante qui ait et s crucifixus ẽ ex infirmitate
(97) 32r: ipsa inueniuntur candelabra. una itaq: ẽ xp̃i ecclesięq: ꝑsona quę et in septẽ candelabris et in simili filio hominis
(124) 46v: regulã tenere profitentur quanti pseudoapostoli inuenirentur, tentarentur dico, de ea fide interrogarentur, occultus si quidem intra sinum fidei
(168) 122r: quem dicunt homines esse filiũ hominis et illi responderunt alii iohannẽ baptistã, alii autem heliã, alii uero hieroniam aut unũ ex prophetis, quinam illi essent quos talia interrogaret aperuit dicens.

Here the most striking case is the telescoped passage, 5r. The model seems to have had:

idem iohannes eas
dẽ ꝑsonas plerũq: non ad se sed sibi inuicẽ (35)
colloquentes introducat

The scribe omitted l. 2.

Next in significance to this are those passages where there is no ὁμοιότης. It is to be noticed that there are only five of these, and that all of them are omissions of 26–32 letters.

The three omissions of 66–9 letters (two examples of 69) correspond to the omissions of 32–4 letters. The same unit appears in 97 and 124.

On the other hand 168 is in manifest relation to 84, corresponding to which we have three examples of 42–4 and two examples of 20–4. As usual, there is variety in the short passages, and it is impossible to say whether such numbers as 26–8 represent short lines of the model or long lines of a previous ancestor.

Laud. Misc. 132 (Eberbach).

St. Augustine, Psalms, cent. ix/x.

This MS. (*L*) is written in two columns with 39 lines to the page and an average of about 32 letters to the line. The usual signs for omissions are *h̶* and *h̶d̶*.

Omissions and Dittographies.

(20) 49ᵛ: quantum sibi iunguntur
63ʳ: ñ autẽ sit ipso locus dño
(21) 73ʳ: *ad barbam qui pertineant
(23) 5ᵛ: si sẽp flebunt ualde miseri
11ᵛ: sed monemus ne mundũ ametis
(27) 71ᵛ: nã et in turba est unus sed una cum *bis scr.*
(28) 2ᵛ: immo laudandi xp̃m a xp̃o prohibeas
(29) 57ʳ: uident et audiunt oculi et aures et
(30) 63ʳ: nisi enim in te non fiat quod quaeris
(31) 22ᵛ: tunc autem uidebimus facie ad faciem
(32) 4ᵛ: ascendit ascensiones inquit in corde *bis scr.*
(34) 6ʳ: auxiliũ enĩ ñrm a dño qⁱ fecit celũ et terrã
(41) 18ʳ: quis unus homo diffusus est usque ad fines terrae
22ʳ: unde abundant nam nisi abundarent supbi ñ essent
(42) 6ʳ: et moto pede cecidit et de angelo factus ẽ diabolus
44ʳ: sed nondũ ẽ ille castus pmanens in saeculũ saeculi
(43) 34ʳ: in os intrat aliquid quid uoluit dñs dicere non quod
(44) 56ʳ: numquid illi qui uoluerunt facere spelucã latronum
(49) 25ᵛ: de torrente inquit in uia bibit propterea exaltauit caput
(53) 64ᵛ: sicut dicit apostolus et pax xp̃i quae p̃cellit omnẽ intellectum
(66) 68ᵛ: ceciderunt illi de quib: p̃sũserunt et inuoluerunt eos qui de se praesumserunt
(78) 47ᵛ: quid est sup numerũ. non solũ illi qui crediderunt qui ptinent ad numerũ s̃corũ sed et sup numerũ
(104) 44ʳ: sed nondũ ẽ ille castus pmanens in saeculũ saeculi in quo ẽ castus. iã iterũ aliquid interrogo quod uosmet ipsos interrogetis (*m.* 2 *in ras.*)

The omission of 78 letters requires some comment. The first hand wrote:

> intrarunt multi iusti sed plures iniqui et ꝑtulerunt iustum quos quando in ecclesia. numquid

These words also contain 78 letters.

He then struck out what he had written and rewrote the whole passage (78 + 78 = 156).

The three largest numbers therefore are: 78, 104, 156.

Here 78 + 26 = 104 and 104 + 52 = 156. The same unit, 26, appears in all three cases. It is to be noticed that there is an omission of 53 letters, also three cases of 27–9. We have, therefore, the following sequence: 27–9, 53, 78, 104, 156.

There is also evidence for two other units, viz.:

(1) There is a notable bulge in the curve at 41–4 (six examples), with which we may connect 20–3 (five examples);

(2) The dittography of 32 letters on f. 4^{v} is very significant. It is not a case of simple repetition, but comes after the intervening words:

> si ergo ascendit in corde non ascendit (32)

This indicates in a previous MS.:

> ascendit ascensiones inquit in corde (32)
> si ergo ascendit in corde non ascendit (32)

The omission of 66 letters (68^{v}) may be explained as three lines of 22, or more probably two lines of 33.

There is, therefore, evidence for three units in the figures, viz. 20–3, 26, 32. It is to be observed that in *L* itself the average number of letters to a line is 32. We may, therefore, with confidence ascribe the unit 32 to the model.

Laud. Misc. 124, cent. ix (Würzburg).

Augustine on St. John.

Omissions.

(22) 6^{v}: nunc qđ sequitur uideamus
(25) 66^{r}: querentibus respondentibus
88^{v}: seruabat quos in nomine filii
99^{r}: quando palã fuerat locuturus
(26) 119^{v}: et eũ plus a quo minus diligitur

(27) 22r: abiit cũ ꝓfecto nos ipsos p̃paret
(29) 88v: intellegimus hominẽ in eo qđ rogat
(30) 6v: sed angeloꝝ et dñs non tantũ ipsorum
96v: notum faciam sine fine regnantibus
111r: qđ fuerat ablatus de monumento quam
(31) 5v: quid est ego dormio et cor meũ uigilat
(32) 48r: nondum in satietate et ipso desiderio
(33) 13v: quam mercedem significam redemptoris
61r: et tamquã ipsa sit iustitia ñ uidere xp̃m
(34) 20v: sed in domo patris mansiones multae sunt
43v: nemo autem potest desperare qui diligit
(35) 20r: sapientior alius alio iustior alius alio
(36) 17v: quia ex isto uetere induit nos hominẽ nouum
95v: qđ ibi iam esset de nobis autem uelle se dix̃t
117v: uel adquirendi cupiditate non oboediendi
(37) 91v: quia unius substantiae nos et ipsi non sumus
(40) 33v: exaudiuit de dilectione atque manifestatione
(45) 104r: id est ut iudicio ac potestate p̃sidis crucifigeretur
(66) 9r: qui accipit si quẽ misero accipit. tantũ et filius distat a patre, quãuis dixerit
(121) 106r: et tamen si uoluntates si insidias si operam si traditionẽ postremo si extorquentes clamores eorum cogitemus magis utiq: iudei crucifixer̃ ih̃m
(126) 103r: in mentem illi uenisse continuo consuetudinẽ iudeorũ quá solet eis dimitti unũ in pascha et ideo non expectauit ut responderet ei ih̃s quid est ueritas
(160) 72v: et sp̃s sc̃s de patre ꝓcedit, pater autem nec natus est de alio nec procedit nec ideo sane aliqua disparilitas in summa illa trinitate cogitationi occurrat humanae, nam et filius ei de quo natus est

The last case requires some explanation. The first hand (L^1) inserts the words out of place, viz. after *sine initio*, instead of before *et sp̃s sc̃s ei*. They must have been in the margin of the model, i.e. they were omitted by a previous MS. I write out the passage as given by L^1:

et sp̃s sc̃s ei de quo ꝓcedit aequalis est, quid autẽ illic intersit inter procedere et nasci, et longum est quaerendo disserere et temerariũ cũ disserueris definire quia hoc et mentis utcũq: comprehendere et si quid forte mens inde conprehenderit linguę difficillimũ est explicare, quantuslibet p̃sit doctor, quantũlibet adsit auditor. non ergo loquetur a semet ipso quia non est a semet ipso. sed quaecumque audiet loquetur ab illo audiet a quo ꝓcedit. audire illi scire est. scire uero esse, sicut superius disputatum est. quia ergo ñ est a semet ipso, sed ab illo a quo ꝓcedit. a quo illi est essentia, ab illo est scientia ab illo igitur audientia. quod nihil est aliud quã scientia, nec moueat quod uerbum futurum temporis positũ est. non enim dictũ est quaecũq: audiuit aut quaecũq: audit sed quęcũq: audiet et loquetur illa quippe audientia sempit'na est quia sempiterna scientia. in eo autẽ qđ sẽpiternũ est sine initio [et sp̃s sc̃s de patre ꝑcedit, pater autem nec natus est de alio nec ꝑcedit nec ideo sane aliqua disparilitas in summa illa trinitate cogitationi occurrat humanae nam et filius ei de quo natus est] et sine fine.

The intermediate passage *et sp̃s sc̃s ei . . . sine initio* should represent lines of the model. It consists of 751 letters.

The omissions of 66, 121, 126 furnish an obvious sequence. Also, there are nine cases of 30–34. Here, therefore, there is clearly a unit. As this is about the average length of a line in *L*, it appears that the model was very similar to *L*. It is interesting to observe the relation of 126 to 751 ($126 \times 6 = 756$). L^1 seems to have inserted the marginal supplement twenty-four lines further on, probably on the next page.

It is tempting to connect the omission of 160 letters by a previous MS. with those of 40 and 45, but the evidence is too slight to justify a conclusion.

Laud. Misc. 427, cent. ix (Lorsch).

Homilies (Pseudo-Bede).

The ordinary sign for omissions is *h̄*, not *h̄d*, the sign specially affected by Lorsch scribes.

Omissions.

(38) 4^r: *sed ꝑmanens aeterna ꝑuenire digni efficiamũ
(43) 7^r: *qua tamen iustitia dũ humanũ careret genus misit ds̃
8^v: et spiritui qui loquebat' in eo quia armis iustitiae
24^r: nouerimus nõ eos magnitudine uirtutis suae posset
25^v: *ecce nunc tẽpus acceptabilę, ecce nunc dies salutis
37^r: inter cetera hortatur dicens, sunt deniq: mulieres
(46) 44^v: dñõ dõ nr̃õ ih̃u xp̃õ et tales nos bonis operibus exibeamus
8^r: et diuinae cõsors factus naturę caue in ueterẽ malitiã
19^r: totum bonũ habet quia ds̃ ipse est caritas quem qui habet
(50) 36^v: *ne fiduciã habeamus et splendore terrestriũ aedificiorum
(51) 51^r: iustitiã in pectore renis et cordis inuocat dm̃ ut ipse reddat
(55) 132^r: sint diuersa passuri tormenta ita et iusti ꝑ qualitate meritorum
(66) 7^r: ꝑ baptismũ ergo peccata omnia dimittuntur et regni caelestis aditus aperitur
(68) 54^r: hodie crux fixa est et demones disꝑsi sunt, hodie crux fixa est et mors subuersa est

(78) 52^{r}: uerum corpus hominis et uerã demonstrat animã in ipso qui sciebat humanã ferre infirmitatem

(107) 38^{v}: et seruit cũ filiis suis siue in lege litterae siue etiam in carnali opera in ecclesia commorantes illa au͞t quae sursũ ẽ hierusalẽ

(117) 78^{r}: manifesta enim praedicatio est unius deitatis uniusque substantiae patris et filii et sp͞s sc͞i qui sua potestate dn͞s ds̃ singulis quibus quã *bis scr.*

(132) 2^{v}: xp͞s XII misit aplo͞s inter numerositatẽ omniũ gentiũ euangelizare regnũ dĩ ut de illis psalmista ait, in omni t'ra exiit sonus eorũ et in fines orb͞ te^{re} uerba eorum

The dittography of 117 letters does not take place immediately, but after an interval of 20 lines. It is due to ὁμ., viz. the recurrence of the words *operatur unus atq: idem sp͞s.*

I transcribe the passage as given in the MS. (*L*):

dicendo enim semp idem om
nia se dicere de sp͞u sc͞o declarat. haec autem omnia ope
ratur unus atq: idem sp͞s. manifesta enim praedicatio est
unius deitatis uniusque substantiae patris et filii et sp͞s sc͞i
qui sua potestate dn͞s ds̃ singulis quibus quã pro ut uult gra
tiarum dona largitur unicuique autem datur manifes
tatio sp͞s ad utilitatem, ut appareat illum sp͞m sc͞m ac
cepisse, ut increduli credant et credentes firmentur
alii autẽ datur ꝑ sp͞m, sermo sapientiae. sapientiae ser
mo est sapienter et aperte et rationabiliter loqui et pos
se disserere uel docere quę nouerit. sane qui ex dono
habet sapientiã sine suo conatu loquitur et labore et ne
mo illi potest resistere. sequitur. alii autem sermo sci
entiae, secundum eundem sp͞m, ut sciat legis mysteria
explanare et de praeteritis etiam futura cognoscere.
alteri fides, in eodem sp͞u, quia alii ueraciter atque
perspicatior intellectus datur ad fidem. alii gra
tia sanitatum in uno spũ, per ipsum datur sp͞m sc͞m
ut curare possit aegrotos, alii prophetatio, ut futura
praedicat, alii discretio spirituum, ut qualis quis sp͞u
ueniat uel loquatur intellegat, alii genera linguarum
ut multis ac diuersis linguis ualeat loqui, alii interpretatio
sermonum, ut quod alii diuersis locuuntur (*ex* loquuntur) linguis
is per donum sc͞i sp͞s poterit interpretari aliis ad notitiam
haec autem omnia operatur unus atque idem sp͞s. manifesta
enim praedicatio est unius deitatis uniusque substantiae patris
et filii et sp͞s sc͞i qui sua potestate dn͞s ds̃ singulis quibus quã

The block of text, ll. 3–25 *manifesta enim . . . unus atque idem sp͞s*, consists of 1,019 letters.

I have only noticed seventeen omissions in this MS. (*L*). Among these there are five cases of 43 and three of 46 letters. We have therefore eight cases of 43–6. This is an unusually high proportion, and this unit is beyond question. The average number of letters in a line of *L* is about 45. It appears, therefore, that it was preceded by a model very similar to itself.

The other omissions are also interesting. They exhibit two clearly-marked sequences, viz.:

50, 51, 55, 107
66, 68, 131.

The first of these shows a unit which differs but little from that previously observed, and probably means nothing except that the scribe contracted his hand, or was succeeded by a new writer. It is to be noticed that 1019, the block of text before the dittography *manifesta . . . quã*, seems to take its place in this series.

The second sequence cannot be explained in this way. As there is no evidence for a unit of 33–4, it is possible that the model was preceded by a MS. written in longer lines than itself.

Laud. Misc. 256, cent. ix (Würzburg).

Jerome on Minor Prophets.

This MS. is of considerable interest from a palaeographical point of view. The first part (ff. 1–54) is written by an Irish scribe, then comes a German hand, and after this ordinary Caroline script. Various arbitrary signs are used for omissions in addition to *ħ*. On f. 103^r^, where a long passage has been omitted, there is a note:

huc usq: errauit scriptor, dehuc sequitur expositio prophetalis ordinem suum.

Omissions.

(17) 46^v^: pro peccato animę mę
(18) 6^v^: et non solũ nascentur
(19) 113^v^: iudam conculcauerint
144^r^: omnis eius solemnitas
(20) 2^v^: ezechia in patris achaz
68^r^: ulciscens dn̄s cũ furore
(24) 72^v^: quinta a consurgentib: illi

133^v: regia et alter iesus de tribu
148^v: cũ mitteretis incipselen. XX
(33) 25^v: dĩ sed iudices et sacerdotes et ꝑphetas
(34) 25^v: *et cum dicatur ad sc̃os gratis accepistis
(35) 12^v: siro quo LXX transtulerunt in ęclesia dñĩ
(37) 18^v: corrupti estis ut sit ordo ꝑpter immundiciã
81^v: *et lenis nidos et catulos LXX transtulerunt
(40) 12^r: et de conditione humana posse accipi ut dĩ ad adã
(41) 24^r: ibi non erit et ubi iactatis uaticinium ꝑphetale
(42) 20^v: quam in ueteri testamento ubicunq: sine augmento
136^r: quõ paup ẽ et in ipso habet spẽ sed et hoc eis accidit
(43) 41^v: nemo potest resistere in iumentis et catulo leonis
143^r: scripturarũ de quibus dicitur eloquia dñĩ eloquia
(45) 5^r: et fundamenta eius reuelabo et omnia sculptilia eius
(48) 59^v: *in hominib: et de mari usq: ad mare et de monte usq: ad montẽ
(57) 45^v: et quanta uobis bona fecerim et meã in uos misericordiã cognoscetis
(63) 77^v: pater mundat ut fructũ magis adferat quod aũt in me manet et fructũ ñ adferat.
(64) 4^v: **-relinquat eos nã et de apĩis egrediebatur sermo dñĩ ad audientes et tamen non
(69) 11^v: iterum secũdũ litterã ut uel x trib. accipiamus in samaria uel in commune omnẽ isrl̃
116^r: si ergo hierusolima in qua crucifixus est uocatur spiritaliter sodoma et egyptus
(83) 32^v: *ita et discipulis suis donat ut ipsi quoque lumen uocentur mundi dicitque ad eos, uos estis lux mundi
(87) 109^r: facta est cum festinatione et non solum illius sed cunctis terrae iudae habitatoribus in consumatione
(332) 102^v: *et sensus et ipsam animã quae debet ẽẽ hospitiũ regis et iuxta superiorem expositionẽ indumenta quoq: aliena et omnia quae secuntur referamus ad unum quemque credentium, qui cum debuerant induti esse xp̃o et semp uersari intrinsecus uariis se peccatorum operuerunt uestimentis et egressi de ecclesia, id est congregatione sc̃oꝝ pro uirtutib: inpleuerunt templum corporis sui iniquitate et dolo

This long omission coincides with a change of hand at the end of a quaternion. The new writer seems to have begun at the wrong place. It is here that the marginal note quoted above occurs. The omission has been repaired by two supplements, viz. *et sensus . . . uariis se* (203) at the foot of 102^v, and *peccatorum . . . et dolo* (129) at the top of 103^r.

Here the first point which meets the eye is the manifest relation of the largest figures, 83, 87, 332 ($83 \times 4 = 332$). In the descending scale we have 63–9 four cases, including two of 69, and eight cases of 40–7. The omissions of 20–4 are only five in number, but it is noticeable that there are three cases of 24.

I must add that the examples of 63–9 admit of a rival explanation, viz. that they are multiples of another unit shown by the five omissions of 33–7.

I have marked 4ᵛ as a telescoped passage. If arranged in three lines it would run:

de	
relinquat eos nã et de ap̄tis	(23)
egrediebatur sermo d̄n̄i	(20)
ad audientes et tamen non	(21)
relinquebat eos	

The MS. has *derelinquebat eos* med. om.

Laud. Misc. 417 (Lorsch), cent. x.

Jerome on Jeremiah.

The usual sign for omissions in this MS., as in others connected with Lorsch, is *h̄l.*

Omissions and dittographies.

(24) 133ᵛ: et ipsius sed nec hoc habetur *bis scr.*
(28) 135ᵛ: hoc est nebeim, LXX pseudoṗphetas
(29) 5ʳ: pulchraeq: posuit consolata sunt
(34) 126ʳ: *dereliqui hereditatē meã, reliquit autē
(35) 125ʳ: siue tempestas egreditur a summitatibus
(36) 40ᵛ: *immolarent et omnis prauę superstitionis
52ʳ: ds̄ pater est, fecit autem in fortitudine sua
70ᵛ: non exaudiam preces eorum et si obtulerint
103ᵛ: et iterum haec dicit dn̄s sup domũ regis iuda
(37) 134ᵛ: et populo eius et uiuetis, quare moriemini, tu
136ᵛ: quod si dixisset, poterat et pseudopropheta
(40) 58ᵛ: in gladio filii eorum et filiae eorum morientur
(42) 46ʳ: siue docuerunt enim linguam suam loqui mendacium
(43) 9ᵛ: et deletę sunt qȝ non habent habitatorem dm̄ dicente
46ᵛ: siue quia faciam a facie malitiae filiae populi mei
(44) 144ᵛ: hoc dn̄s loquitur non propheta qđ uisitet sup semeiam
(48) 15ʳ: *et huc illucque circumspice et uide ubi non fornicatione
(53) 88ʳ: oblitus est mei, sequitur enim, quia oblitus est mei populus meus
144ʳ: *fuit qui ioas post interfectionem gotholiae imperiũ tradidit

(60) 136^{r}: babilonẽ, hic autẽ e contrario etiam ea quȩ translata fuerant referenda

(67) 64^{r}: et dicent ad te, numquid ignoramus quod omnis laguncula siue uter impleatur uino

(72) 54^{r}: referamus tempora quãdo tabernacula dñi subuertuntur et omnis habitatio ecclesiae

(90) 69^{r}: et onagri steterunt in rupibus, traxerunt uentum quasi dracones, defecerunt oculi eorum quia non erat herba *bis scr.*

(157) 32^{v}: pressius hoc legendum est iuxta hebraicum et cum inquit tanta fecerint, numquid confusi sunt? numquid erubuerunt in scelerib: suis, quin potius auxere contemptũ et erubescere nescierunt.

To these may be added the following corruptions:

22^{v}: in praesentemtiarum quid significet ignoro et aquila autem

This indicates:

in praesen
tiarum quid significet ignoro et aquila au (36)
tem

19^{r}: si abstuleris quando ergo offendicula tua a facie mea non commoueberis. quando ergo mouemur

This indicates:

si abstuleris
offendicula tua a facie mea non commoueberis (38)
quando ergo mouemur

140^{v}: promiserat sed hortatur eos ad preces ut quod promiserat [sum written above]

This indicates:

pro
miserat sed hortatur eos ad preces ut quod pro (38)
missum

140^{r}: in ezechiel ꝑpheta testatur scribens contra eos quib: hieremias quoq: prȩcepit non credendum necdũ autem eo tempore quo haec epistula dirigebatur hiezeciel propheta

Here the words *ꝑpheta testatur . . . hiezeciel* = 124 letters.

The most striking point in these figures is that 36 occurs four times. For 34–7 there are eight examples. We have also one of 72. Here clearly is one unit.

Also, there are six cases of 40–8, including two cases of 43. One case, 15^{r} (48), may be mentioned since there is no ὁμ. and the omission destroys the sense. A previous MS., probably the immediate ancestor, seems to have had:

leua oculos tuos o hierusalem
et huc illucque circumspice et uide ubi non fornicatione (48)
prostrata sis

Corresponding to 40–8, we have 90 (i.e. 45 × 2). The longest omission, 157, may be connected with the two omissions of 53 letters. It would seem likely that the lines of the model varied in length.

Laud. Misc. 433, cent. ix (Lorsch).

Taio's excerpts from Gregory.

This MS. is written in two columns. Omissions are sometimes rectified by the usual symbols, *hl*, *hd*, but some passages have been rewritten. It is clear that the model closely resembled it in formation. This is shown by various corruptions in the MS. (*L*), e. g.:

(20) 163r: stultam sapientiam deserant
em
et sapientiam dĩ stultitiam

This indicates in the model:

stultam sapien
tiam deserant et sapien (20)
tem dĩ stultitiam

(21) 64r: archano
est iudaico cordis infixus
iudaico
ex populo uel gentili

∴ archano est
cordis infixus ex populo (21)
iudaico uel gentili

(43) 28r: uocarentur
quia p uitae meritum ad caelestia
uerunt
propinquarentur

∴ uoca
rentur quia p uitae meri (20)
tum ad caelestia propinqua (23)
uerunt

The writer looked back to l. 2 (*-rentur*).

(71) 54r: eamque
fideliter inherendo circum (24)
dant. tot nunc quasi uestibus (24)
sc̃a aeclesia induitur. Quot (23)
v
fideliter

So *L*. The order in the model may have been the same.

(93) 71r: necesse est
igitur ut qui ad officium p̃
dicationis studio non recedunt
uectes esse
ad hoc namque necesse in circu
lis arcę semper iubentur

The second hand adds *ħt excubant a sacre lectionis*, to be inserted before *studio*.

∴ necesse est igitur ut qui ad (23)
officium p̃dicationis excu (23)
bant a sacre lectionis studio (25)
non recedant ad hoc namque (22)
uectes esse

The scribe responsible for most of *L* writes in a neat hand. After 153v his work is shared by a new writer, who uses a larger and more clumsy script. On two occasions the change of scribe led to the loss of a line, viz.:

f. 155 (Migne 76, § 123):

quia dum caro in delectatione rapitur etiam sua rectitudine spiritus infirmatus inclinatur. Requisitus Adam confiteri culpam noluit.

Here 155r, col. 2, ends with:

quia dũ caro in delectatione
rapitur etiã sua rectitudi

A new hand begins on the verso:

requisitus adam confiteri
culpam noluit.

Thus omitting a line:

-ne sp̃s infirmatus inclinatur (25)

This is added at the foot of 155r, but without *-ne.*

f. 159v. The clumsy writer ends in col. 1, l. 20, with:

pondus habent ad quod

The neater hand goes on with *pensant proximo ad dandum*, omitting an intermediate line *pensant sibi aliud ad quod*, which is added by a corrector. The model seems to have had:

pondus habent ad quod (18)
pensant sibi aliud ad quod (22)
pensant proximo ad dandum (22)

The appearance of the passages written in the rougher hand indicates that the writer was reproducing closely the formation of the model. Thus f. 154^{r}, col. 1, is spaced out in a curious manner, and on several occasions an extra half-line is added at the end of a page.

I now tabulate the omissions of *m.* 1.

(16) 25^{r}: id est transiturũ ẽ
(17) 71^{v}: *speciosum appareat
171^{r}: *si terrorẽ dĩ ad m̃tem
(18) 24^{r}: *dĩ et hominũ remoueri
72^{r}: namq: et hoc quaestio
75^{v}: officiunt quod aliis
132^{v}: simul et reuelatione
(19) 118^{r}: quatenus os discretum
121^{r}: quid per culpã fecimus
(20) 36^{v}: cernimus clausis nihil
48^{v}: dicitur quando amplius
56^{v}: scriptum ẽ qui producit
(21) 11^{r}: alteri fides in eodem spũ
74^{r}: amore se nesciunt libere
(22) 93^{v}: ex parte constructa sit et
95^{v}: pueritia ad adulescentiã
159^{v}: pensant sibi aliud ad quod
(23) 29^{r}: gignitur et ꝑ amorẽ proximi
71^{r}: excubant a sacre lectionis
71^{v}: omni poscenti uos rationem
163^{r}: *huius sc̄li quia multimodis
(24) 86^{v}: *nullius uos esse monstratis
(25) 42^{r}: uenit reus fraterno sanguine
155^{r}: **-ne sp̃s infirmatus inclinatur
(27) 119^{v}: conuertit sed adhuc se perfecte
(29) 49^{r}: loquuntur magnis ut tam̃ in quib;dã
(31) 54^{r}: dicitur sic indum̃tum sunt ecclesiae
(34) 44^{r}: iusti requiescerent et in inferioribus
134^{v}: iam se obtinuisse ꝗ concupierat exultat
158^{r}: iniquitas namq: in funiculis uanitatis
(39) 152^{v}: et quasi gubernator amisso claui in medio mari
(40) 84^{v}: *pietatis gratia benigni iustitiae seueritate
(61) 53^{r}: quod erat in maxillas populorũ canticum erit uobis frenũ quippe erroris
(94) 71^{v}: quorum uidelicet terror ac tremor quia esse suꝑ animalia terrae p̃cipitur profecto esse suꝑ homines prohibetur

With these omissions should be combined the corruptions before mentioned. The corruption on 71ʳ, after an interval of 93 letters, is interesting in connexion with the omission of 94, especially as it occurs on the same folio. Also on this folio (71ʳ) we have an omission of 23 letters. We are therefore entitled to explain 93–4 as 23×4 ($= 92$). The general phenomena here are such as we should expect when the columns in the model were of unequal length, as is also the case in *L*.

I now draw attention to a passage on 10ʳ:

> dš iacob. Unde paulus apostolus uolens
> nuncupatiuum dī nomen ab essentia
> li discernere ait quorum patres
> et ex quibus xp̄s secundum carnē
> qui est sup̧ omnia dš benedictus in se
> cula. Nuncupatiuus autem dš inter
> omnia, essentialis aū dš sup̧ omnia
> Paulus apostolus ut ostenderet xp̄m
> naturaliter dm̄ non hunc dm̄ tantū mo
> do sed dm̄ sup̧ omnia memorauit quia
> et iustus quilibet dš ē sed int̄ om̄ia quia nun
> cupatiue dš xp̄s autem dš est

All the passage after *dš iacob* is written in a contracted hand, and occupies 12 lines instead of nine. There is, however, no erasure, and the verso begins:

> super omnia quia naturaliter dš

The inference is that the exemplar had in the margin a passage previously omitted, and that the scribe wished to incorporate it, while beginning the verso with *super omnia.*

If so, the error must be due to the repetition of *super omnia.* Probably the model had in the margin:

> sup̧ omnia memorauit quia et iustus quilibet dš ē sed int̄ omīa quia nuncupative dš xp̄s autem dš est (80)

In another passage, f. 171ʳ, a passage of some length is written upon an erasure, and it overflows into five long lines at the foot of the page. There are three consecutive passages which begin with *Omnis hypocrita*, and the natural inference is that the scribe passed from one to another of them and then rewrote the whole. These passages are:

(161) omnis hypocrita cum' iniquus sit dici scs ab hominib; non ptimescit, etiam si iniquũ se tacita cogitatione rephendit. Tam dũ sepius scm audire se coeperit hoc qđ de se intrinsecus tenebat amittit

(185) omnis hypocrita dũ cor exterius fundit, quia libent foris falsum de se testimoniũ reddit, qualẽ se intus habeat non requirit, unde fit ut uacue laudis fomta etiam cum defuerint quaerat et oblitus qđ est appetit uideri qđ ñ est

(391) om hypocritae dũ iustos se ante humana iudicia simulant ad actiones sę laudib; dignas intuentiũ oculis ostendunt. occulta dĩ iustitia agitur ut quo nituntur foras alios fallere, eo de se intus etiam ipsi falluntur. quib: bene p pphetã dicitur, Redite puaricatores ad cor. si enim ad cor redirent, p exteriores attestationes se uerba ñ funderent. laus psentis scli iustos cruciat, simulatores exaltat, sed iustos dũ cruciat purgat, simulatores dũ laetificat repbos monstrat

These larger figures seem to reveal behind the model a previous MS. of similar formation. We have to notice the relation between 80, 161, 391 (80 × 5 = 400). Also, if we subtract 161 from 185, the result is 24.

Brit. Mus., Egerton 2831, cent. viii/ix (*Old French*).

Jerome on Isaiah.

The MS. is written in two columns, except in one quaternion (ff. 56–63), which is in long lines, though written by the same scribe.

Omissions.

(26) 50r: *q̄: de D experierat reperiuntur
(28) 93v: dni et quasi diadema regni in manu
(31) 43r: sabbatũ ne polluat illud custodiens
63r: tuine despicies domesticos seminis
101v: *per patriarchas moysen et pfetas sed
(36) 42v: cum uideretis ait signũ filii hominis quod
(37) 49r: *translationem ueteris instrumenti ɔcussâ
(38) 107v: *et uita est et scs precatur non ueniet mihi pes
(40) 32r: de quibus aedificat xps aeclesiam super terram
(51) 117v: ut aperiat intellegentiam illius, idcirco enim uallis achor
(52) 19v: *de qua et paulus apostolus loquebatur, induite uos armaturã dĩ
(59) 29r: et gloriam quam accipit is per cuius opera ds glorificatur in gentibus
(62) 60r: *comedunt et rursũ quare tacuistis impietatẽ et iniquitatis eius frumẽtũ
102v: id est gregis dni sm autem hic angelum debemus intellegere qui ductor fuit.

To these must be added the following dittography:

(159) 73v: propterea recessit iudiciũ ab eis et non adprehendit eos iustitia. Cum expectarent lucem factae sunt eis tenebrae praestulantes eam in tenebris ambulabunt, palpabunt quasi caeci parietem.

This passage, which occurs shortly before, is repeated before *propheta* in the sentence, *mirorque cur LXX quasi propheta.* The dittography is due to ὁμ. (*propterea* and *propheta*).

The striking feature in these figures is the relation of 31 (three cases) to 62 (two cases). It cannot be doubted that 31 represents a line in an ancestor.

The examples of 51 and 52 are also highly suggestive in view of those of 26 and 28.

Also the four cases of 36–9, two of which cannot be explained by ὁμ., are very significant. It is to be noticed that after 39 the next figure is 51.

The probability, therefore, is that here there are three units, representing lines in three previous MSS., viz. 26, 31, 36–9.

The dittography may be explained as $31 \times 5 = 155$, or $26 \times 6 = 156$. Since 31 is the predominant unit, the first explanation is more probable.

The singular point is that the lines in the MS. are shorter than any of these figures, the average in those which I glanced at being 22–4 letters. This is contrary to the usual result of such an analysis. We generally find evidence of shorter lines in previous MSS. The solution appears to be provided by ff. 56–63, where long lines are used. Apparently the scribe was working with a model written in long lines, which he put into two columns, except in the eighth quaternion. Behind the model there were previous ancestors in long lines. (Cf. p. 341.)

Breslau R. 169, cent. vii/viii (Uncial).
Gospels (Old Latin).

My knowledge of this MS., generally known as cod. Rehdigeranus, is derived from the transcript published by H. J. Vogels, with an excellent introduction (Namur, 1913). It now consists of 296 folios, but originally contained at least 45 quaternions. The MS. (*R*) is written in two columns, with 20 lines to the page arranged in paragraphs. Vogels says: '*Die Zahl der auf die Zeile entfallenden Buchstaben ist wegen der stichischen Schreibung sehr verschieden und schwankt zwischen* 3 *und* 17.' The contents of some columns which I had occasion to count are:

f. 15, col. 2 = 240.
f. 183, col. 2 = 238.
f. 207^{v}, col. 1 = 243.
col. 2 = 257.
f. 268, col. 1 = 255.

It will be seen, therefore, that in spite of irregularities the contents of the columns are fairly uniform and yield an average of about 12 letters to a line.

The special interest of *R* lies in the fact that it is an exact copy of its model, line by line and page by page. Vogels points out various proofs of this. The most striking fact is that on f. 208^{v} the scribe originally repeated what he had written on 207^{v}, dividing the lines exactly as before. Haase says: '*inveni antea per errorem totam paginam versi folii* 207 *servatis lineis eisdem scriptam iterum fuisse.*' The scribe then rubbed out what he had written and substituted the correct passage.

On one occasion, f. 183^{v}, the first line of col. 2 was left vacant, apparently by accident. The result is that the lines become longer at the end of the page, so that the next page may begin at the proper place.

There are also indications which show that sometimes at least the scribe worked simultaneously on both columns, instead of first completing one column. Thus on one occasion, f. 70^{v}, he began too high up in both columns and then erased what he had written, rewriting it lower down. Other evidence is given by the colour of the ink. Thus f. 238^{v}, lines 1–9 in col. 1 and 1–10 in col. 2 are in ordinary ink, but the rest of both columns is written in unusually dark ink. So on f. 194^{r} the scribe wrote lines 1–10 in col. 1 and 1–13 in col. 2 with the same pen, while the rest of both columns is written with a fresh one.

It is, therefore, clear that the line divisions in *R* were also found in the model. We can, therefore, check all the blunders of the writer. I give one example:

f. 26: nunc regnum
caelorum

For *caelorum* the scribe originally wrote *caeluc*, his eye having been caught by *nunc* in the previous line.

This method of copying both columns together was well calculated to prevent omissions, but these occurred from time to time. On such occasions the practice of the scribe was to erase what he had written and to rewrite the whole passage. Thus on f. 193 seven lines are rewritten because the words *propter me* had been omitted. Haase says: 'maluit librarius tot lineas delere et iterum scribere quam duas voces omissas vel in margine vel inter lineas adicere.'

Other examples are:

(10) f. 131: timebant enim
eum quoniam
uniuersa turba
admirabatur.

The scribe omitted l. 2 and then rewrote ll. 2–4.

f. 178: omnis iudea et
hierusalem
et maritima
et trans fretum et
tyri et sidonis

The scribe omitted l. 3 and then rewrote ll. 3–5.

(13) f. 162: inluminare his
qui in tenebris
et umbra mor
tis sedent ad di
rigendos pedes

The scribe omitted l. 2 and then rewrote ll. 2–5.

(33) f. 219: minimo et in maiore fidelis est et qui in *om.* R^1.

The most interesting error is f. 268 (John vi. 24):

Voluerunt ergo
accipere eum in
naui et statim
fuit nauis ad ter
ram in qua ibant
altera die turba
quae stabat trans
mare uiderunt
quoniam naui
cula alia non
erat ibi nisi una

ubi manducaue
runt panem
quem benedi
xerat dn̄s
altera die turba
quae stabat trans

et quia non fue
rat simul cum
discipulis suis
ih̄s in nauem
sed soli discipu
li eius alius uero
superuenerunt
naues a teberia
de iuxta locũ

Here the writer has glanced back from col. 2, l. 5, to col. 1, l. 6. He then struck out the passage repeated by error and rewrote correctly.

R appears to have inherited certain errors from its model, e. g.:

f. 2, *uidens autem* is written twice, both at the end of col. 1 and at the top of col. 2. I assign this error to a predecessor, since the passage is not rewritten, as is the case when a blunder has been made by *R*[1].

f. 73 (Matt. xxv. 35): hospės eram et
collegistis me
infirmus et ui
sitastis me
in carcere et ue
nistis ad me
Tunc responde
bunt ei iusti
dicentes
dñe quando te
uidimus esuriẽ
tem et pauimus
sitientem et de
dimus tibi potũ
ṇụḍụṣ ẹṭ ọpẹ
ṛụịṣṭịṣ ṃẹ

So *R*[1]: lines 15–16 are here out of place. They should come after l. 2, where they are added by a corrector.

Also, the second hand has supplied a considerable number of omissions. These cannot represent errors of *R*[1], since, if so, the pagination of *R* would have differed from that of the model. They are, therefore, passages omitted by an ancestor and supplied by *R*[2] from another MS.

They vary in character. Sometimes the sense is spoilt by the omission, e.g.:

f. 248 (Luke xxiv. 21): et nunc tertia
dies est hodie
quod haec omnia
mulieres quaedam
ex nostris ter
ruerunt nos

So R^1: m. 2 supplies *facta sunt sed et* after l. 3.

The majority, however, are passages which are self-contained, e.g.:

f. 280 (John ix. 37): qui
tecum loquitur
ipse est et pro
cedens adorauit
eum

So R^1: m. 2 supplies *at ille ait, credo, dñe* after *est* in l. 3.

A striking example is:

f. 241 (Luke xxii. 62): et egressus foras petrus fleuit amare.

These omissions of self-contained clauses are important in view of an objection raised to my analysis of variants in the Gospels, viz. that scribes would not be likely to omit complete κῶλα.[1]

I would draw particular attention to

f. 200 (Luke x. 38). Here R^1 gives:

et mulier quaedã
martha nomine
et maria quae
etiam sedens
secus pedes dñi

Here *et* in l. 3 is a conjecture, introduced after the omission of

excepit illum in domu sua et huic erat soror nomine (*add. m.* 2)

after l. 2, in order to distinguish Mary from Martha. It is struck out by m. 2.

I now give a complete list of these omissions, marking with a cross those which form separate clauses:

(10) f. 61: et abierunt
(11) f. 168: qui fuit maat
f. 284: duob: diebus
(12) f. 169: qui fuit melea
f. 280: et dixit ei ih̄s

[1] *Journal of Theological Studies* xvi (1915), p. 233.

(14) f. 248: *facta sunt sed et
f. 284: discipulis suis
(16) f. 169: qui fuit zorobabel. (R^2 gives *zorabababel.* If so, = 18)
(17) f. 85: et farisei ad pilatũ
f. 251: quid dicis de te ipso
f. 280: +at ille ait credo dñe
(19) f. 277: opera eius qui misit me
f. 282: sed ego pono eã a me ipso
(26) f. 168: qui fuit matthiae, qui fuit amos
(28) f. 270: +ego non ascendo ad diem festũ istũ
(30) f. 272: hic est uere propheta, alii dicebant
(32) f. 241: +et egressus foras petrus fleuit amare
(33) f. 274: +ego de supernis sũ. Vos de mundo hoc estis
(41) f. 200: excepit illũ in domu sua et huic erat soror nomine
(43) f. 265: +et scio quia uerũ est testimoniũ quod perhibet de me
(45) f. 223: edebant et bibebant emebant et uindebant plantabant
(46) f. 212: +uerũ tamen oportit me odie et cras et sequenti[1] ambulare
(48) f. 276: mihi. Qui est ex dõ uerba dĩ audit, propterea uos non auditis
(52) f. 293: +si dš clarificatus est in eo et dš clarificauit eũ in semetipso
(57) f. 269: +nemo enim in occulto quid facit et q:rit ipse in palã esse si hęc facis.
(79) f. 228: dñe mna tua fecit quinq: mnas et huic ait et tu esto supra quinq: ciuitates et alter uenit dicens
(92) f. 257: erat autẽ et iohannis baptizans in enon iuxta salim quia aquę multę erant illic et ueniebant et baptizabantur
(140) f. 246: et dies erat parasceues et sabbatũ inluciscebat. Subsecutae autẽ mulieres quae cũ ipso uenerant de galilea uiderunt monumentũ et quẽadmodum positum erat corpus eius
(203) f. 15: et non cecidit, fundata enim erat supra petram. Et omnis qui audit uerba mea haec et non facit ea similis erit uiro stulto qui ędificauit domum suam super arenã. Et discendit pluuia et uenerunt flumina et flauerunt uenti et inruerunt in domum illam.

Here the phenomena are normal. The shorter omissions exhibit great variety, then they arrange themselves as multiples of 10–11. Thus we have:

30–33, three exx.
41–6, four exx.
52–7, two exx.

It is probable that a considerable proportion of these omissions represents lines in an ancestor.

The longest and most interesting addition of the second hand is

[1] The Vulgate has *sequenti die.* Possibly *die* has been omitted here.

on f. 252 (John i. 29). Here two columns of 20 lines, containing respectively 223 and 264 letters, are added in the margins, with omission marks (*h̄p* and *h̄d*):

hic est de
quo dixi pos me
uenit uir qui
ante me fac
tus est quia
prior me erat
et ego nescie
bam eum sed
ut manifesta
retur ihl̄ prop
terea ueni ego
in aqua bapti
zans et tes
timonium peri
buit iohannes di
cens quia uidi
spm̄ discenden
tẽ quasi colũ
bam de caelo et
mansit super eũ

et ego nesciebã
eũ sed qui misit
me baptizare
in aqua ille mihi
dixit super quẽ
uideris spm̄ des
cendentem et
manentẽ super eũ
hic est qui bapti
zat in spũ scõ
et ego uidi et tes
timoniũ perhibui
quia hic est filius dī
altera die iterũ
stabat iohannes
et ex discipulis
eius duo. Et respi
ciens ihm̄ ambu
lantem dicit
ecce agnus dī

The previous folio in *R* (and therefore in its model) ends with *mundi*. The omission therefore is due to the fact that the writer passed from *mundi* to *dī*. Are we therefore to say that R^1 omitted a page of his model? The contents, viz. col. 1 = 223, col. 2 = 265 (average = 243), agree very well with the contents of a page in *R*. Thus 207ᵛ, col. 1, contains exactly 243 letters. Also, it is to be noticed that there are 20 lines to the column in the supplement, as in *R*. On the other hand it is difficult to see why the scribe did not deal with his omission in the same way as on f. 208ᵛ, viz. by striking out the passage which he had repeated and turning the leaf into a palimpsest. He must have perceived at once that his recto (or verso) no longer corresponded with that of his model. We must therefore consider the possibility that the page was omitted by the writer of a previous ancestor who was not so conscientious or eager to repair his omissions as the writer of *R*. I may here repeat what I have said elsewhere, when speaking of the Gospels [1]: 'I do not

[1] *Primitive Text*, p. 57.

suggest that all the omissions in any of the important MSS. are due to the negligence of a single scribe. It is more probable that they represent the sum-total of omissions made by a series of ancestors written in columns of similar breadth.'

I conclude with a brief note upon the omissions in the genealogy (Luke iii. 23 sqq.). Nothing can be simpler than the omissions of *R*, viz.:

25 qui fuit matthiae, qui fuit amos
26 qui fuit maat
27 qui fuit zorobabel
30 qui fuit melea

All these are due to ὁμ. They seem peculiar to *R*, and no one attaches the smallest importance to them. We must, however, recollect that all scribes were subject to the same infirmities and that such omissions were possible at all times. I do not propose to enter into the vexed question of the genealogies in Matt. i and Luke iii, complicated as it is by the division into three periods of fourteen generations, found in Matt. i. 17. I would merely refer to Matt. i. 8. Here the ordinary reading is:

Ἰωρὰμ δὲ ἐγέννησε τὸν Ὀζίαν

Here three ancestors are left out, viz. Ahaziah, Joash, and Amaziah. Jehoram is called the father of Uzziah (or Azariah), his great-great-grandson!

𝔖[c], *Diat.*, *Eth.*, and other sources give:

Ἰωρὰμ δὲ ἐγέννησε τὸν Ὀχοζίαν, Ὀχοζίας δὲ ἐγέννησεν τὸν Ἰωάς, Ἰωὰς δὲ ἐγέννησε τὸν Ἀμασίαν, Ἀμασίας δὲ ἐγέννησεν τὸν Ὀζίαν

The hypothesis of omission here is more simple than that of interpolation.

CHAPTER IV

Douce 140, circa 700.

Primasius on the Apocalypse.

TRAUBE says of this MS. (*D*) that it was 'probably written in S.W. England, perhaps in the seventh century'.[1] If this date is correct, it would appear to be the oldest authority for the writer. The commentary of Primasius was used by Bede, and most of the MSS. come from monasteries founded by Anglo-Saxon or Irish monks. It is, therefore, only natural that a valuable copy should be found in England.

The other MSS. mentioned by Haussleiter are:

A = Karlsruhe ccxii, cent. viii, from Reichenau.

C = Paris. 2185, cent. x, from Corbie.

F = Cassel, MS. Theol. fol. 24, cent. ix, from Fulda.

G = Paris. 13390, cent. ix, from Corbie.

The last of these MSS. has some extensive lacunae and must be derived from a mutilated ancestor.

Haussleiter was only concerned with the text of the Apocalypse, as quoted by Primasius, not with the commentary. He was furnished for these quotations with a collation of *D* by Dr. Sanday. For the text of the commentary we must go elsewhere.

According to Haussleiter, two *editiones principes* appeared in the same year (1544) at Bale and Paris. The Bale edition was founded on a Murbach MS., which agreed closely with *A*. The Paris edition appears to have been drawn from some MS. resembling *G*. Haussleiter considers it to be the fount of the *vulgata*, as published in successive editions of La Bigne's *Magna Bibliotheca Patrum* (Cologne, 1618), also in Migne's *Patrologia Latina*, vol. 68 (Paris, 1866).

The Bale edition is a scholarly production and gives a readable text. It is somewhat singular that it has never been reprinted,

[1] *Nomina Sacra*, p. 33.

while its rival, which omits long passages, without signifying a lacuna, and is full of gross errors, has passed through successive editions.

As a specimen of the lacunae I would refer to

ed. Bas. i 5r: serpentum morsu typice sanabatur et his similia quae si ad litterarum discussa tractantur ludicra pro tempore putabuntur

Five pages further on comes:

Ille est quod in titulo psalmi tricensimi tertii dicitur psalmus ipsi David commutavit vultum

Migne (823 B) here gives:

serpentium morsu liberavit typice mutavit David vultum *med. om.*

Dr. Sanday says of *D* '*textus non habet lacunas*'. He does not, however, indicate that *D* contains considerable blocks of text omitted by ed. Bas. as well as by Migne, which, so far as I know, have not yet been printed. While, therefore, ed. Bas. gives a longer text than Migne, *D* gives one which is longer still.

As *D* possesses great interest from many points of view, I add some further details.

In its present condition it has lost various folios, viz. seven ff. after f. 65; one folio + an entire quaternion after f. 83; one after f. 103; one + a quaternion after f. 136, and one after f. 144. The last folio (f. 148) is lost, but the contents are supplied on an extra leaf by a recent hand. A folio has been cut out after f. 118, but nothing is here lost. F. 75 is written on thin parchment, in a different hand from ff. 74 and 76, though of contemporary date. It is in a different formation from the rest of *D*, and appears to have been inserted to remedy an omission.

The number of lines to a page varies from 25–30, the normal number being 26. The change from one size to another sometimes corresponds with the beginning of a fresh quaternion written by a different scribe, but there is sometimes variety in pages of the same quaternion and even on the *recto* and *verso* of the same leaf. Thus 74r has 28 and 74v 27 lines. The inserted leaf, f. 75, has exceptionally only 24 lines. This irregularity seems to characterize MSS. of Primasius. Thus Haussleiter says that in *A* the lines vary from 21–6, and notices pages of 27, 30, and 36 lines in *F*.

The number of letters in a line also varies. I had occasion to copy out some sixteen pages of *D*, where it contains long passages omitted by Migne, or Migne + ed. Bas., and to count the number of letters. The figures are interesting since, although they vary greatly, viz. from 884 to 1108, it will be seen that certain sizes tend to reappear. I give them in order of magnitude, adding in brackets the number of lines to the page and the average number of letters to the line:

(884)	76ᵛ	(26)	avg. 34
(913)	76ʳ	(26)	avg. 35
	77ʳ	(26)	
(917)	74ʳ	(27)	avg. 34
(931)	78ʳ	(26)	avg. 36
(950)	74ʳ	(28)	avg. 34
(954)	73ᵛ	(28)	avg. 34
(959)	77ᵛ	(26)	avg. 37
(983)	23ʳ	(27)	avg. 36½
(1002)	16ᵛ	(27)	avg. 37
(1051)	36ʳ	(27)	avg. 39
(1073)	96ᵛ	(28)	avg. 38⅓
(1095)	36ᵛ	(27)	avg. 40
(1096)	95ᵛ	(28)	avg. 39
(1106)	96ʳ	(28)	avg. 39½
(1108)	95ʳ	(28)	avg. 39½

Here we have to notice that 913 occurs twice, also that there is a case of 917: afterwards we have the sequence 950, 954, 959, and again 1095, 1096, and 1106, 1108. The general average for the 16 pages is 1002 letters to a page and 37 to a line. It is to be noticed that f. 16ᵛ contains the exact figure 1002.

The contents of the inserted folio (75) are, *recto* = 690, *verso* = 663, which gives an average of 28 letters to a line (24 lines to a page).

The appearance of *D* suggests that, at any rate in some quaternions, the scribes reproduced the pagination, though not the distribution of lines found in the model. Thus words are often added at the foot of the page, e.g. 134ʳ *ut uinci tanto eius impetu*, 140ʳ *de uno fundamento xp̃o*, while still more frequently part of the last line in a page is left blank, e.g. 56ᵛ, 57ᵛ, 58. On 38ʳ the last line has been left blank after *arenae* has been erased, 38ᵛ begins with *arenae* and lines 1–3 are spaced out. There is an interesting dittography on f. 23ʳ. Here D^1 gave:

optionem dicimus et nomen ciuitatis dī mei
tionem dicimus et nomen ciuitatis dī mei

The second line was then erased. The inference is that the model had:

op
tionem dicimus et nomen ciuitatis dī mei

It would, therefore, appear probable that in the model the lines were a little shorter than in *D* (p. 43). The writers of *D*, or some of them, preserved the pagination, but not the lineation: hence the irregularities to which I have called attention arose.

The insular abbreviation for *autem* (ħ) is not employed except where there was reason for compression. I have only noticed it in the last line of a page where the script is contracted (75^v^, 77^v^, 132^v^), or where a correction is made in the margin (86^r^), or an omission is entered in the text *in ras.* (145^v^).

Nomina sacra are generally abbreviated. Thus *ds̄*, *dn̄s*, *xp̄s*, *sp̄s*, *sc̄s* are normal. There are, however, irregularities. Thus on f. 95^v^ we find *xp̄i de xp̄o in xp̄o cum xp̄o post xp̄m per cristum propter cristum*. So also on occasions the first hand wrote *deus* or *dominus* in full, and the abbreviations were inserted by a second hand. Such lapses were clearly considered to savour of profanity: thus on f. 87^r^, where *domini* occurs in the text, a large *ħ* in blacker ink is written in the margin to call attention to the offence.

Various critical marks are found, e. g. *z* (= ζήτει) is frequent. On f. 9^v^ *ð*^ (? = *dimissum*) is added in the margin to mark a corruption in the text, *arcanis* (m[1]) for *arcam* (m[2]). This appears to be the same symbol as that which is frequently employed in the two Leiden MSS., *A* and *B*, which contain the *de Natura Deorum*, etc. (p. 328). On f. 81^r^, where the first hand gives *quiac* for *quia*, the corrector adds *ð* in the margin. On f. 66^r^, where *potestas* has been omitted, a later hand adds *hð potestas*.

Quotations from the text of the Apocalypse were originally introduced by γ (? = γράφεται): a second hand has generally combined with this *K* (= κείμενον)[1]. The symbol γ̇, or γ̇γ̇, is regularly used to mark quotations in Brit. Mus. 31031, cent. viii (e. g. f. 29^v^ nine times). Haussleiter mentions that *K* is used in *F* to introduce the

[1] This symbol is frequently used in Greek MSS., cf. p. 418. In Latin MSS. *K* (= *Caput*) was often used to mark paragraphs, cf. pp. 221, 318.

lemmata. I would here mention a curious blunder in the *vulgata*, which seems due to a misunderstanding of this symbol.

ed. Bas. f 7[v]: accipite sapientiam sicut aurum et scientiam sicut argentum electum. So also *D*.

For *electum* La Bigne gives ⋊ *elimet*, and in the margin ⋊ *emite*. Migne (812 C) prints *sicut argentum Kelimet* [*Kemite*].

There are various indications which show that a number of ancestors have intervened between *D* and the autograph of Primasius, written in the sixth century. Thus on three occasions omission symbols are embedded in the text. One of these is a short passage, viz.:

f. 112[v] (Migne, 900 C: ed. Bas. G 7[r]):

malis nequior septempliciter inueniatur
ꝺ ut et quod dicimus planius delucescat inten
tum decet esse lectorem ħ

The natural conclusion is that the words *ut et . . . lectorem* (57) were omitted by one ancestor, put into the margin of another with the symbols ꝺ and ħ, and received into the text of another, with the omission labels still attached to them.

The other passages are longer, viz.:

8[v] (Migne, 779 D: ed. Bas. c 5[v]):
ꝺ smirna canticum . . . congruit dn̄ō ħ
145[v] (Migne, 932 D: ed. Bas. Q 3[v]):
ħ nam ut eiusdem . . . probitas memoratur +

The first of these is of special interest, since it is omitted both by Migne and by ed. Bas., while in *D* it has been inserted in the wrong place. The order of the Churches is Ephesus, Smyrna, Pergamus, Thyatira, Sardis, Philadelphia, Laodicea. Consequently, the interpretation of Smyrna should come before that of Pergamus, while in *D* it comes in the middle of the section about Pergamus, and is there introduced in the middle of a sentence, viz. after *utique* in the sentence:

discernenda utique fuerat humilitas.

Various attempts were made to remedy the dislocation by the use of letters, *A* and *B*: also by numerals. Thus D^1 wrote *B pergama* and afterwards *asmirna* (i. e. *A smirna*): then *B* and *a-* were struck out, and ·III·, ·II· entered in their place, also I in the previous page, referring to Ephesus. Finally, ·*b*· was added in the margin, referring to Pergama, and ·*a*· also in the margin before *Smyrna*.

Here the passage must have been omitted by one ancestor, added in another at the top or foot of the page with omission marks, received into another in the wrong place, in another *B* must have been placed before *Pergama* and *A* before *Smyrna*. There must, therefore, have been at least three intermediate MSS. between *D* and the archetype.

It is, therefore, clear that the text has passed through several halting-houses before it came to *D*. The problems involved are, therefore, by no means simple.

Omissions and dittographies of D^1 or *D*:

(24) f. 135v (Migne, 916 C):
et quae solueris super terrã *om.* D^1

(25) f. 8v (Migne, 799 D):
tenentis fidem in aliis autem *bis scr.*

(32) f. 146v (Migne, 933 A):
et uerbum erat apud dm̃ et ds̃ erat uerbum *om. D*, ed. Bas.

(34) f. 23r (Migne, 811 C):
-tionem dicimus et nomen ciuitatis dĩ mei *bis scr.*

(36) f. 37v (Migne, 823 C):
*et indignos uos iudicastis aeternae uitae *om. D*, ed. Bas.

(52) f. 85r (Migne, 879 A):
*illis inimicus suũ dare dicitur thronũ quos maxime possidens *om.* D^1

(60) f. 86r (Migne, 879 D):
quando dignitatem ei specialiter debitam sibi ausus fuerit assignare *om. D*

f. 146v:
*beati qui lauerunt stolas suas ut sit potestas eorum super lignum uitae *om.* D^1. This comes in a passage omitted by Migne, 933 A, also by ed. Bas. Q 3v.

(65) f. 104r (Migne, 894 B):
naturali errore praebente ac lutulentis desideriis implicatae adiecerunt *bis scr. D*

f. 140r (Migne, 927 D):
duodecĩ portas singulę ex singulis margaritis. Quod de uno fundamento xp̃o est *om.* D^1. The scribe first omitted the words and went on to *duodecim apostolis agni satis superque iam*, he then erased this and rewrote the whole passage, partly *in ras.* and partly in an extra line at the top of 140v.

(245) f. 139r (Migne, 926 B):
mensura hominis quae est angeli, angelum hic aeclesia saepe poni

aperta locorum frequentia protestatur et quoniã ex hominib: conquisita constat aeclesia et Cristi promissionibus sublimata angelorum aequalitatem sperat eiusque omnis intentio eorum societati suspirat propterea dicit *bis scr.*

To these may be added a passage where an error in *D* throws light on its past history.

f. 19ᵛ (Migne, 807 B). *D* has:

aeclesia inluminata monetur non
a se lumen habere sed ueri luminis participatio
ne radiari meruisse apertius demonstratur
talibus etiam dicitur fuistis aliquando tenebrae
nunc autem lux in dñõ [K] et angelo aeclesiae quae
est inluminata tyatirae.

Here *inluminata* is a repetition due to ὁμ. The words *inluminata monetur . . . aeclesiae quae est* consist of 181 letters.

The first point to notice in these figures is that the numbers 60 and 65 occur twice. Also, there seems to be a relation between them and other numbers, viz. 32–4, 181, 245.

We can now reconstitute the passage as it seems to have stood in a previous MS., viz.:

aeclesia
inluminata monetur non a se lumen ha (30)
bere sed ueri luminis participatio (30)
ne radiari meruisse apertius demon (30)
stratur talibus etiam dicitur fui (29)
stis aliquando tenebrae nunc autem (30)
lux in dñõ et angelo aeclesiae quae est (32)
tyatirae

The only figures in the list which do not admit of this explanation are 24, 25, 52. These may be due to chance, but the relation of 24–5 to 52 is to be noted.

In addition to these omissions and dittographies there is a passage which is out of place in *D*, viz.:

(805) ff. 39ʳ–39ᵛ (Migne, 823 D–824 B; ed. Bas. i 8ʳ–k 1):
(39ʳ) sextus sane modus quo uterque xp̃ĩ di
noscatur aduentus id est quae ad primum quae
loca referenda sint ad secundum aliud est enim
uenturum (*in fine pag.*)
(39ᵛ) cognoscere aliud primum a secundo secernere pri

mus sibi humiliationis uendicat loca sicuti est quod
moysis dicit prophetam uobis suscitabit dn̄s ex
fratribus uestris sicut me illum audietis, itemque
posthaec in terris uisus est et cum hominibus conuer
satus est, et iterum non est species ei neque decor
et uidemus eum et non erat aspectus, dispectū
et nouissimum uirorum, uirum dolorum, et post
paulolum, languores nostros ipse tulit et cetera.
et iterum sicut agnus ad occisionem ducitur et
sicut ouis q^{c}uoram tondente se sine uoce sic non ape
riet os suum, de secundo autem aduentu legimus.
ds̄ manefestus ueniet ds̄ noster et non silebit et
aspicient ad te quem confixerunt. malachias quoque
dicit accedam ad uos in iudicio et ero testis uelox
super maleficos et adulteris et periuris et qui
calumniantur mercidem mercinnaris et cetera.

This passage is placed by *D* after *sentiendum* (Migne, 825 D; ed. Bas. K 3^{v}).

(*A*) Migne (with *G*) omits three large blocks of text found in ed. Bas. and *D*, viz.:

(1) ff. 35^{v}–37^{r} (ed. Bas. i 5^{r}–7^{v}: *om.* Migne 823 B, after *typice*):
**sanabatur et his . . . David quando com-

(2) ff. 73^{v}–78^{v} (ed. Bas. s 6^{r}–t 6^{r}: *om.* Migne 859 B, after *revelaretur*):
*quarto enim . . . aculeis et omnis

(3) ff. 95^{r}–97^{r} (ed. Bas. C 8^{r}–D 4^{r}: *om.* Migne 887 B, after *de virginibus*):
*nullum est . . . dicitur evangelium

The length of these passages as expressed in lines of ed. Bas. is as follows:

(1) = 85 lines. To this, however, has to be added two passages found in *D*, but omitted by ed. Bas., viz.:

36^{v}: in quibus . . . comprehendi (276 letters)
37^{r}: et abissus . . . eius (36 letters)

i. e. 312 letters. The average content of a line in ed. Bas. is 28 letters, so the total passage, as given by *D*, would fill 85 + 11 lines = 96.

(2) This passage includes the inserted leaf, f. 75. It, therefore, falls into three parts, viz.:

(*a*) ff. 73^{v}–74^{v} (ed. Bas. s 6^{r}–8^{v}): quarto enim . . . propinquantes
(*b*) f. 75 (ed. Bas. s 8^{v}–t 1^{v}): in arboribus . . . fictum
(*c*) ff. 76^{r}–78^{v} (ed. Bas. t 1^{v}–6^{r}): Et datum . . . et omnis

Here (*a*) = 98 lines, ed. Bas.
(*b*) = 49 " " "
(*c*) = 189 " " "

The exact correspondence of 49 and 98 shows conclusively that f. 75 represents a leaf of an ancestor. It is to be noticed that (*c*) is a little shorter than would be expected (47 × 4 = 188). There must have been some slight irregularity here.

(3) = 180 lines, ed. Bas.

I now arrange these figures in order of magnitude:

(49) f. 75 = one folio.
(96) ff. 35^v–37^r } = two folios.
(98) ff. 73^v–74^v }
(180) ff. 95^r–97^v } = four folios.
(189) ff. 76^r–78^v }

I now proceed to consider the number of letters in these passages, as written in *D*:

f. 75 = 1353.
ff. 35^v–37^r = 2662.
ff. 73^v–74^v = 2752.
ff. 95^r–97^r = 4858.
ff. 76^r–78^v = 5262.

Here we may take 1353 as an example of a normal folio; or take the average between 1353 and 2662 (= 49 and 98 lines in ed. Bas.), in which case we get as result 1338; or we may take the average of all the figures, viz. 1302.

We may say, therefore, with some confidence that this ancestor contained 1302 to 1353 letters to the folio, i. e. 651–76 to the page. If so, a page corresponded to about 18 lines of *D*, and about 24½ lines in the Bale edition.

In addition to these long passages where folios have been lost, I have noticed the following short omissions, all of which are assisted by ὁμ.:

(24) 56^r (ed. Bas. n 5^v: *om.* Migne, 838 B):
et pro domino mori meruerunt

(35) 23^r (ed. Bas. f 4^v: *om.* Migne, 811 B):
in ipsorum loco gentes saluari probantur

(40) 41^r (ed. Bas. k 5^v: *om.* Migne, 827 A):
spm̄ seruitutis iterum in timore sed accepistis

(53) 61[r] (ed. Bas. K 5[r] : *om.* Migne, 842 B) :
et quaternitatis conternatae ut quater terni decus dipundius.

It is probable that there are many others.

(*B*) The Bale edition omits the following passages which are found in *D* and Migne :

(27) 67[r] (Migne, 853 D, ed. Bas. r 3[r]) :
qui (quia *Migne*) seruire memoratur in templo

(417) 57[v] (Migne, 839 D : ed. Bas. n 7[v]) :
*concussi ab ecclesia diuelluntur, propriȩ
autem aceruis fici fructib: comparantur
siue pro infidelitate quam conuersi in arcũ
prauum relicta malunt fide repetere
siue propter immaturitatem temporis
per quam contigit ut cum felicem
aeclesia eorũ concipiendo quaesierit ortum
infelici tamen euentu flebilem de eis patiatur
aborsus, [K] et caelum recessit ut liber cum euolui
tur. recte caelum id est aeclesiam ut euolutũ
et non inuolutum librum insinuat recessisse
quidquid enim fuerit inuolutum.

The following omission of ed. Bas., reported by Haussleiter, occurs in a passage where *D* has been mutilated, viz.:

(27) Migne, 865 B : ed. Bas. x 2[r] :
statim repletus est venter meus

I add the following passage where *D* gives correctly a longer reading, while Migne and ed. Bas. have different omissions :

f. 39[v] (Migne, 823 D : ed. Bas. i 8[r]) :
aliud est enim uenturum agnoscere, aliud primum a secundo secernere *D*
(28) aliud primum a secundo secernere *om.* ed. Bas.
(42) aliud est cernere *med*: *om.* Migne.

(*C*) I now come to passages omitted both by ed. Bas. and by Migne, but found in *D*. These, so far as I know, are at present unpublished. Two of them, viz. 37[r] (36) and 36[r] (276), belong to a passage which is wholly omitted by Migne (and *G*), viz. :

35[v]–37[r] : sanabatur et his . . . David quando com-

The Bale edition contains the passage, except for these two omissions, while *G* seems to be descended from a mutilated ancestor.

(28) 128^{v} (Migne, 912 A: ed. Bas. L 1^{v}, after *exhaurienda peccata*):
in suis autem membris frequenter *D*: *om. cett.*

(33) 41^{r} (Migne, 827 A: ed. Bas. k 5^{r}, after *gloria dei*):
*iustificati gratis per gratiam ipsius *D*: *om. cett.*

(36) 37^{r} (ed. Bas. i 7^{r}, after *adoratur in tribus*):
et abissus sicut uestimentum amictus eius *D*: *om.* ed. Bas. (*def.* Migne)

(63) 82^{v} (Migne, 862 B: ed. Bas. u 4^{r}, after *fumo et sulpure*):
ab his trib: pla
gis occisa est tertia pars hominum de igni et fu
mo et sulpure *D*: *om. cett.*

(97) 55^{r} (Migne, 838 A: ed. Bas. n 4^{r}, after *chrisma baptismatis*):
quod aperte in
euangelio dn̄s dicit pater quos dedisti mihi
costudiui et nemo ex eis peribit nisi filius per
ditionis *D*: *om. cett.*

(127) 23^{r} (Migne, 811 B: ed. Bas. f 4^{v}, after *in genere*):
*uerū
quia cuius uult miseretur quos sub alis suis sal
uandos congregare uoluerit congregat potens
est enim ds̄ inquid apostholus iterum inserere
illos *D*: *om. cett.*

(174) 44^{v} (Migne, 829 D: ed. Bas. l 4^{r}, after *praedicantur*):
*ipse scilicet qui de patre
coeternus inuisibiliter genitus de matre
mirabiliter nasci uoluit moriturus atque hȩc
ꝑ sp̄m sc̄m de caelo missum aeclesiae reuelauit
quam sibi sponsam misericorditer adquisiuit *D*: *om. cett.*

(276) 36^{v} (ed. Bas. i 6^{v}, after *in Christo et in ecclesia*):
*in quibus utrumque docet impleri cum
et terrenae hierusalem filios seruire dicit et abra
hae experto claruit temtata deuotio et de con
iugio loquens manente cristi aeclesiae quae mysti
rio dixit neque enim quisquam carnem suam odio ha
buit sed nutret et fouet eam sicut et cristus aecle
siam ut utraque his ostenderit comprȩhendi *D*: *om.* ed. Bas. (*def.* Migne)

(303) 54^{r} (Migne, 837 A: ed. Bas. n 2^{v}, after *sunt pretio*):
*portio sane, hereditatis
cristi quae in electorum plenitudine com
mendatur non inaniter hic tritici nomine
figuratur se enim dn̄s in euangelio desig
nabat dicens nisi granum tritici cadens
in terra mortuum fuerit ipsum solum ma
net si autem mortuum fuerit multum fruc

tum affert quod a parte potiore inferio
ra quoque aeclesiae membra in ordei menti
one cognosce *D*: *om. cett.*

(336) 107v (Migne, 897 A: ed. Bas. F 7v, after *veritate*
*iam quippe ante
quam septem fialarum faceret mentio
nem de sc̄orum persona et dignitate prę
miserat quod cantarent canticum mo
si serui dī et canticum agni dicentis
magna et mirabilia sunt opera tua
domine omnipotens uel cetera nam
et lenteamina eis mundae [1] candida
zonasque aureas sc̄orum pectoribus
adesse praemisit, in quorum compara
tione ranarum respuenda feculentia
paruolis etiã monstraretur *D*: *om. cett.*

(438) 8v (Migne, 779 D: ed. Bas. c 5v):

Here *D* has:
đ
utique
*smirna canticum eorum cum hoc consequen
ter libro canticum moysi serui dī dictum et in
aliis nouerimus generaliter frequentatũ
diuinae laudis canticum sanctis praecipue
deputati sicuti est cantare dn̄o canticum
nouum laus eius in aeclesia sc̄orum et exulta
te iusti in dn̄o rectos decet conlaudatio
in hoc etiam nomine quod interpretatum
dicitur canticum eorum hoc nos conuenit
intellegere quod eorum placeat canticum
dõ quibus sequentia concinunt demonstra
tur quia rectos decet conlaudatio quo
rum laus congruit dño h fuerat humilitas.

This passage, which is omitted in Migne and ed. Bas., is inserted in the wrong place in *D*, viz. in the middle of the sentence *utique fuerat humilitas*. It ought to come earlier, viz. before *Pergama interpretatum dicitur* (a few lines above).

The passage *Pergama* to *utique* is written thus in *D*:

·iii·
ꝑ pergama inter
praetatum dicitur diuidenti cornua eorum
v
uel dissicenti ballem: in sermone porro qui ad
eius angelum fecit duas hominum species demon
strauit in ipso tenentis fidem in aliis autem te

[1] munda et *m.* 2.

nentis fidem in aliis autem tenentium doctri
nam nicolait,um nec inmerito inter iustorum
et peccatorum cornua quod idem nomen resonat
diuidit nisi ut sicut legimus cornua peccatorum
confringantur et exaltentur cornua iusti
et dissicenti ballem discernenda utique.

(The "ar" is written above "nicolait,um"; the "v" is written above "ballem".)

This gives a total of 366 letters, if we exclude the dittography *in aliis autem tenentis fidem* (25). This may, however, be inherited from a previous MS., in which case the total becomes 391.

(496) 18[r] (Migne, 807 B: ed. Bas. e 4[r], after *veritas non est*):

sicut in singulis aeclesiis commonet
totum ut unitatis nexam uinculo significet uniuer
sam sic in ea conlatam donorum suorum declarat
largitatem ad hoc enim inluminatam maluit
erudiri ut ex suo primum nomine gratia se preuentã
agnoscens tamquam misericordiam consecuta ÷ ali
is quoque consulat a laqueis zizabil protinus retra
hendis quando quidem nec ipsi dicit fuisse parcen
dum cum ergo aeclesia inluminata monetur non
a se lumen habere sed ueri luminis participatio
ne radiari meruisse apertius demonstratur
talibus etiam dicitur, fuistis aliquando tenebrae
nunc autem lux in dn̄o

In l. 1 *D* has iiii before *sicut*.

After *dn̄o* comes:

K et angelo aeclesiae quae
est inluminata ecclesiae

The numeral iiii ought to come here, not before *sicut*. There has, therefore, been some previous dislocation.

(930) 91[v], 92[r] (Migne, 884 C: ed. Bas. C 3[r], after *insinuetur asperitas*):

aliter in sex dieb: omnia dm̄ opera
perfecisse diuina testatur auctoritas, idē
namque numerus suis constare partib: inue
nitur, id est sexta sui parte, tertia et dimedia
unum enim et duo et trea sex faciunt et quia
eorum quae in sex dieb: perfecta sunt finis prae
dicetur adfuturus et dicet in melius transfe
renda ignis tamen ardore, a beato petro ele
menta resoluenda dicuntur, non incongrue pu
to a sexto numero usque ad huius summam
numeri tamquam conditorum terminum sig

nificando finalem increscere et desiturum
eo usq: uenire futuramq: meliorationem
circa ipsius temporis suppletionem hoc nume
ro designari nam et a senario sexagenarius
surgit sicut a denario centenarius quasi quad
ratus qui ut solidetur ad mille usq: peruenit
sicut sexagenarius ad sexcentos et ut sibi initia
cum fine concordent adiecit subinde ipsum
senarium ut essent sexcenti sexaginta sex
ni
sic namque dicit uenit dies ḍọṃịṇị ut fur per
quam caeli ardentes soluentur et elementa ig
nis ardore coquentur ad meliorationem autem
dicit, nouos uero caelos et terram nouam secun
dum promissa ipsius expectamus in quibus ius
titia inhabitat

(1084) 145v–146v (Migne, 932 D: ed. Bas. Q 3v, after *manifestet*):

h̄ nã
ut eiusdem cum patre et filio doceatur
essentiae, et idem filii qui et patris
esse sp̃s declaretur profundioris adhuc
m̃
mystirii secreta cognosce, ḍẹụṃ sane abra
hae et totam nos debere accipere trini**tatẽ no**
uimus si lr huic nomini sempiternam uerita
tem adiungas personarum profecto pro
prietates induces ut dĩ abrahae nomine
solius patris uideatur significari persona
sicut et ille in danihele locus insinuat ubi
dicet et antiquus dierum sedit id est pater
sempiterna autem ueritas filius indubi
tanter agnoscitur qui dicit, ego sum uia
ueritas et uita, uerum ne sancti sp̃s omis
sa putetur esse persona ipsa eiusdem nu
meri redintegratione patri et filio ut
uere amborum sp̃s conuenienter occurrit
quid ei[1] profunda solus agnoscit aposṭholo
dicente sp̃s autem omnia scrutatur etiã
profunda dĩ ut autem fili quoque sp̃s demon
stretur subiunxit si quis autem sp̃m xp̃i
non habet hic non est eius quod ergo de nu
meris promisimus impleamus hoc modo

VIIII V LXX CC I II C I I XL VIII I V X IIII X LXX
ΘЄΟϹ ΑΒΡΑΑΜΗ Α·ЄΙ ΔΙΟ

[1] qui di *m.* 2.

cc i xxx viiii viii[1] v x i
C Α Λ Η Θ Ε Ι Α quod cum grae
cis litteris per numeros duxeris promis-
sam eiusdem numeri summam profecto
<[2] v c x cc
repperies quam in peristera Π Ε Ρ Ι C
ccc v c i
Τ Ε Ρ Α id est columba docuimus subsum
mari in cuius specie scm̃ spm̃ specialiter
legimus discendisse ∂ post fidem morum
probitas memoratur +

At the foot of the page is written:

∂ beati qui lauerunt stolas suas ut sit potestas eorum super lignum uitae (60)

(1968) 16r–17r (Migne, 806 c: ed. Bas. e 2v, after *inquit omnes*):

aliter dies decim to
tum huius uitae cognoscendum puto corricolũ
in quo fidelibus trina non potest deesse temta
tio, ubi temtatio est uita hominis super terrã
quamdiu diebus praetermeantibus et reme
antibus septim omne tempus uitae praeteri
tis euoluetur quam temtationem dño quoque
nostro tamquam capiti aeclesiae ih̃u xp̃o
diabolus permissus legitur intulisse haec
nihilominus aeclesiae xp̃i sub figurata perso
na mulieris agonis pugna spiritalis indicitur
ubi dñs serpenti dicit inimicitias ponam inter te
16v et mulierem illa tuum obseruabit capud et tu
insidiaberis calcaneo eius, in hoc igitur saeculo
quod septim dierum mobilitate peragetur eui
denter agnoscitur uariis temtationibus xp̃i
aeclesiam subiacere quae potissimum in his tri
bus uitiis obtenent principatum in adpetitu car
nalium uoluptatum et efrenata prohibitae
superfluetatis ingluuiaę unde in pane dño inimi
cus niteba||tur inludere tamquam secundo adę
eo quod inde primum mortis pocolum propinaue
rit quando uetita homini gustare persuasit
ut gastrimargiae primum reddens uitio cap
tiuatum ceteris deinde carnalibus desideriis
tenerit obnoxium alio autem priuatae gloriae
elatione temtatur ℵ pulsare permittetur
cum de pinna templi eum hortaretur iactari
praecipitem testimonium subrogans psalmi di

[1] This is an error for ix. [2] So *D* here: on the previous folio *D* has $\overset{\text{LXX}}{\Pi}$.

centis quoniam angelis suis mandauit de te et
cetera. sicut primo homini decipiendo sugesse
rat dicens eretis sicut dii scientes bonum et
malum ut in concessae diuinitatis adpe||titu
deiecisset incautum, tertia uero temtatio
audacter infertur in qua regnorum gloria
terrenorum et saecularium pompa diuitia
rum significatur da||mnanda cupiditas hac
ergo trina temtatione uitae huius tem
poribus quae diebus septim uoluuntur
17r adplecita dinarius numerus adimpletur prop
ter quod ita dicitur habebis tribulationem die
rum decim sequitur denique esto fidelis usque ad
mortem quod omni ecclesiae intellegi conuenit
dictum nam et apostholus huius docens intelli
gentiae formam cum de adam loqueretur et
diceret adam non est seductus, mulier autem
seducta facta est in praeuaricatione ad fi
guratam mox locutionem transiens aeclesi
am demonstrauit dicens, salua autem erit
per filiorum generationem si permanserit in
fide et dilectione et sanctificatione cum subri
etate haec autem non mulieri mortuae sed xp̄ī
euidenter aeclesiae conuenire nullus ignorat.

This long passage, preserved by *D* only, is given by it in the wrong place, viz. after *omnes* in the sentence (Migne, 806 C: ed. Bas. e 2v):

perdidisti inquit omnes qui fornicantur abs te.

It would give a good sense if placed before *esto fidelis* (Migne, 805 D: ed. Bas. e 1v).

The passages omitted by Migne and ed. Bas. do not afford an obvious clue, such as is furnished by the three large lacunae in Migne. I therefore submit a general list of all the passages referred to in the course of this discussion, in the hope that they may throw some light upon the transmission of the text. It must be borne in mind that there are several ancestors between *D* and the archetype: also that some of the omissions may be due purely to chance, assisted by ὁμ.

(24) 56r: et . . . maluerunt *D*, *ed. Bas.*: *om. Migne*
135r: et . . . terram *om. D*[1]
(25) 8v: tenentis . . . autem *bis scr. D*

(27) 67r : qui . . . templo *D*, *Migne*: *om. ed. Bas.*
Migne, 865 B: statim . . . meus *Migne*: *om. ed. Bas.* (*defic. D*)
(28) 39v : aliud . . . secernere *D*: *om. ed. Bas.*
128v : in . . . frequenter *D*: *om. Migne*, *ed. Bas.*
(32) 146v : et . . . verbum *Migne*: *om. D*, *ed. Bas.*
(33) 41r : iustificati . . . ipsius *om. Migne*
(34) 23r : -tionem . . . mei *bis scr. D*
(35) 23r : in ipsorum . . . probantur *om. Migne*
(36) 37r : et abyssus . . . eius *om. Migne*
37v : et indignos . . . vitae *Migne*: *om. D*, *ed. Bas.*
(40) 41r : spm̃ . . . accepistis *om. Migne*
(42) 39v : enim . . . secundo se- *om. Migne*
(52) 85v : illis . . . possidens *om. D*[1]
(53) 61r : et quaternitatis . . . dipundius *om. Migne*
(57) 112v : ∂ ut et . . . lectoremh (i.e. omitted by ancestor of *D*)
(60) 86r : quando . . . assignare *om. D*
146r : beati . . . vitae *om. D*[1]
(63) 82v : ab his . . . sulpure *D*: *om. Migne*, *ed. Bas.*
(65) 104r : naturali . . . adiecerunt *bis scr. D*
140r : duodecim . . . Christo est *om. D*[1]
(97) 55r : quod aperte . . . perditionis *D*: *om. Migne*, *ed. Bas.*
(127) 23r : verum . . . illos *D*: *om. Migne*, *ed. Bas.*
(174) 44v : ipse . . . adquisivit *D*: *om. Migne*, *ed. Bas.*
(181) 19v : *inluminata* repeated in *D*
(245) 139r : mensura . . . dicit *bis scr. D*
(276) 36v : in quibus . . . comprehendi *D*: *om. ed. Bas.* (*defic. Migne*)
(303) 54r : portio . . . cognosce *D*: *om. Migne*, *ed. Bas.*
(336) 107v : iam quippe . . . monstraretur *D*: *om. Migne*, *ed. Bas.*
(417) 57v : concussi . . . involutum *om. ed. Bas.*
(438) 8v : Smyrna . . . congruit domino *D*: *om. Migne*, *ed. Bas.* (out of place in *D*)
(496) 18r : sicut . . . in domino *D*: *om. Migne*, *ed. Bas.*
(806) 39r : sextus . . . cetera: out of place in *D*
(930) 91v : aliter . . . inhabitat *D*: *om. Migne*, *ed. Bas.*
(1084) 145v : nam ut . . . memoratur *D*: *om. Migne*, *ed. Bas.*
(1353) 75 : in arboribus . . . fictum *om. Migne*
(1968) 16r : aliter . . . ignorat *D*: *om. Migne*, *ed. Bas.* (out of place in *D*)
(2662) 35v–7r : sanabatur . . . quando com- *om. Migne*
(2752) 73v–4v : quarto enim . . . propinquantes *om. Migne*
(4858) 95r–7r : nullum est . . . evangelium *om. Migne*
(5262) 73v–8v : quarto enim . . . omnis *om. Migne*

I take the large numbers first.

(1) I have already dealt with 1353, 2662, 2752, 4858, 5262. Their equivalents in lines of the Bale edition are 49, 96, 98, 180,

189. They must represent 1, 2, 2, 4, 4 folios in one and the same ancestor. These omissions are peculiar to Migne (and *G*).

It is probable that some of the smaller numbers represent lines of the same ancestor. Thus 806 × 6 = 4806, cf. 4858. So also there appears to be a relation between 417 and 806.

(2) The largest number among the passages preserved by *D* only is 1968. If this is divided by 4, the result is 492, cf. 496 (f. 18^r^). If 492 is divided by 2, the result is 246, which is almost the exact length of the dittography (245) in *D* on f. 139^r^.

This dittography is unlike the others found in *D*. Whereas they have been erased, or partially so, it is enclosed in a rectangle by the first hand. It is, therefore, antecedently not improbable that it was already present in the model.

This series 245, 496, 1968 does not seem to be connected with the previous series 417, 806, 1353, 2662, 2752, 4858, 5262. It would therefore appear to represent lines in another ancestor.

In all probability the other passages preserved by *D* only belong to this second series.

It is to be recollected that some of these passages occur in the wrong place in *D*, viz. 438 (8^v), 806 (39^r), 1968 (16^r). Also, two of them, viz. 438 (8^v) and 1088 (145^v), preserve in *D* omission labels which show that they were at one time omitted by an ancestor of *D*. The probability, therefore, is that the omissions of ed. Bas. + Migne go back to a further stage in the tradition than those of Migne only.

It is tempting to suppose that 930 represents a folio in this more remote ancestor, and that 1968 represents two folios. The correspondence is not so exact as could be wished, but there is a possible explanation, viz. that the number of lines in a page of this ancestor varied as is the case with *D* and other MSS. of Primasius.

(3) If we look at the smaller numbers, we observe two units, viz. 27–8, followed by 54–7 and 32–3 followed by 60–5, 97, 127. We cannot be sure whether these are separate units or whether they are the limits of variation in the same MS. It will be seen that the larger figures ascend by what I may call a tricesimal system. Thus 31 × 16 = 496 (18^r), 31 × 26 = 806 (39^r), 31 × 30 = 930 (91^v). The fact that these successive numbers are exact multiples of the same unit is very remarkable. This tricesimal system seems to pervade the figures from whatever source they are drawn. Thus 32 × 3 = 96,

cf. 97; 32×4 = 128, cf. 128; 30×6 = 180, cf. 181; 30×8 = 240, cf. 245; 31×9 = 279, cf. 276; 30×10 = 300, cf. 303; 30×11 = 330, cf. 336; 30×14 = 420, cf. 417.

I can only conclude that the content of a line was much the same in more than one ancestor, though the number of lines in a page varied.

I conclude by drawing attention to passages where the text in Migne or Migne + ed. Bas. appears to have been doctored after an omission. Thus in the long omission mentioned at the beginning of this discussion the loss of two folios containing the passage *sanabatur . . . quando com-* left the reading:

serpentum morsu typice mutavit vultum.

For this Migne (823 B) has:

serpentium morsu liberavit, typice mutavit David vultum.

So in the second large lacuna the omission of the passage *nullum est evangelium*, due to the loss of four folios, left the reading:

praeceptum domini de virginibus praedicare

For this Migne (887 B) has:

praeceptum domini non habeo de virginibus praedicare

I have noticed a similar attempt to doctor a short omission, viz.:

f. 41r (Migne, 827 A: ed. Bas. k 5v):

sic apostholus utrumque discernit
cum dicit non enim accepistis spm̄ seruitutis
iterum in timore sed accepistis spm̄
adoptionis filiorum

So *D* and ed. Bas. The reference is to Rom. viii. 15:

οὐ γὰρ ἐλάβετε πνεῦμα δουλείας πάλιν εἰς φόβον, ἀλλ' ἐλάβετε πνεῦμα υἱοθεσίας.

Migne gives:

sic apostolus utrumque discernit cum dicit, vos enim accepistis spiritum adoptionis filiorum

Here *vos* is a conjecture for *non* after the omission of *spm̄ servitutis . . . accepistis*.

I came across one passage where Migne + ed. Bas. have an abridged text, viz.:

54^{v} (*Migne*, 837 C: ed. Bas. n 3^{r}):

quae una in tribus
quartis constare nuntiatur siue quia in
trina unitate credit siue quod trium professi
onum ordinibus grata uarietate distin
guitur uirginum uiduarum et coniugum, in
quibus nunc tribus quartis dari praedicet po
testatem hanc dixit aeclesiam quae et una
est et ex tribus quartis quadrata stabilita
te consistet cum ad unum capud reperitur
trina professio superaedificata inquid super
fundamentum aposthọlorum et propheta
rum, ipso summo angulari lapide xp̄ō ih̄u, hanc
uariis praedicet malorum cladib: exercen
dam a gentilitate simulata fraternita
te et heretica prauitate.

For this Migne and ed. Bas. give:

In qua nunc quartam dari praedixit potestatem. Hanc dicit ecclesiam qua ex parte consistit variis malorum gladiis exercendam

This abridgement seems to be an attempt to make a sense out of a mutilated text.

CHAPTER V

CICERONIAN PALIMPSESTS

de Re Publica (Vat. 5751).

A TRANSCRIPT of this famous palimpsest (*C*), together with an able introduction dealing with orthographical peculiarities, has been published by A. W. Van Buren in the Supplementary Papers of the American School in Rome, vol. ii (1908). The reproduction of the MS. in facsimile, which was undertaken by the Vatican Library some years ago, has not yet appeared. For practical purposes Van Buren's transcript is more helpful than a facsimile, since it can be read rapidly. The MS. is interesting not only on account of its date (cent. iv), but also because it is written in very narrow columns. It contains unmistakable evidence of having been copied from a model in very similar formation, and throws much light upon the errors which a scribe was likely to make when writing such very short lines. Since there is reason to believe that MSS. in very narrow columns have played an important part in the transmission of texts, this palimpsest deserves attentive study.

C is written in two columns with 15 lines to the page.

The columns vary a good deal in content. I took the trouble to count the letters in some 20 pages, selecting in the first place some in which there were very few corrections and abbreviations, and secondly others which appeared to contain considerably less than the pages which I first selected. The results were as follows. I give the numbers of the pages from Van Buren's transcript:

	Col. 1	Col. 2	Total
p. 24	152	152	304
p. 29	151	143	294
p. 31	144	153	297
p. 36	143	146	289
p. 50	159	153	312
p. 51	167	169	336

	Col. 1	Col. 2	Total
p. 62	151	145	296
p. 79	151	165	316
p. 80	152	151	303
p. 81	147	156	303
p. 92	164	163	327
p. 93	153	157	310
p. 112	151	135	286
p. 129	146	144	290
p. 142	154	147	301
p. 143	150	146	296
p. 152	166	174	340
p. 153	151	160	311
p. 205	157	154	311
p. 256	148	142	290
	3057	3055	6112

The average for these 20 pages works out at $305\frac{3}{5}$ for a page, $152\frac{17}{20}$ for a column, and $10\frac{1}{5}$ for a line.

It will be seen that the content of these columns varies from 135 to 174. The interesting point is that the same size recurs so frequently. Thus there are six examples of 151, three of 152, three of 153, and two of 154. So also there are three of 146 and two of 147. In the same way two pages contain 296 letters, two 303, and two 311. The scribe appears to adopt in some columns a unit of 9–10 letters and in others one of 10–11, and to maintain this unit throughout the column. Consequently, certain sizes, such as those which I have quoted, appear frequently, while others are not found.

The reader will observe the singular fact that the total for the two columns in these 20 pages is almost identical (3057 and 3055).

A full account of the abbreviations is given by Van Buren. The chief are *b·* = *-bus* and *q·* = *que*. Both of these are optional and most frequent at the end of a line. The abbreviations *res p.*, *p.r.*, *cons.* (sing.), *cos.* (plur.), *tr. pl.* are normal, but we find *rerum publicarum* (several cases), *rebus publicis*, *populi r.* (pp. 38, 278), *consul* (pp. 60, 83), *consules* (p. 186), *tribunis plebis* (p. 192). The abbreviation *mag.* (= *magistratus*) occurs on p. 119, and *s.c.* (= *senatus consultum*) on p. 12. The praenomina are generally abbreviated, but we find *Servius* (p. 250), *Spurius* (p. 30 *bis*, p. 210), *Quintus*

(p. 210), and *Tiberius* (p. 213). Numerals are sometimes written in figures, more frequently in full, and often both methods are combined.

The confusion between *b* and *v* is complete, e.g. 14 uelubis (= beluis), 24 bolscam, 27 bellet, 38 bouisse, 55 prouabiles, 57 iobis, 77 bis, 91 siui, 123 lauorib·, 151 pribatum, 172 insitiba, 175 inuecillis, uelli, 193 probabisse, laudabisse, &c.

Corrections are generally made by striking out letters or by supralineal dots. In order to simplify the work of the printers I have not attempted to reproduce the corrections, but use the familiar method of dots under the line for corrections of all kinds.

There is abundant evidence that the model of *C* contained a large number of alternative readings. I have noticed the following cases: 7 secututus segutus,[1] 9 non posset,[2] 13 erant, 42 habererent, 55 ex perpoliti (i. e. expoliti), 71 consiliao, 82 aut aput, 87 cultums, 93 assiduumos, 101 plebie, 120 sublata perta (i. e. perlata), 124 et si, 134 rebrum (i. e. reb.), 186 senatus enatus,[3] *ib.* anni annuam, 196 progeniae, 217 etsse (i. e. et se), 229 perubreuiter (i. e. perbreuiter), 234 appellabitur, 237 consilio que quae, 278 ac uetus ac uetusta.

Most of these are due to the correction of blunders in a previous ancestor. Others look like traditional variants, e. g.: 52 ut rhodii ut rhodii ut athenienses, 94 liticinibus, 108 et suffragiis, 168 ullae . . . peruerterunt, 271 potentatus, 261 conuenit.

Omissions of m. 1.

(8) p. 195 (i. 38): * tum demum
(9) p. 102 (i. 63): ** nam dictat- (a)
(10) p. 5 (ii. 56): obtinendam
(11) p. 30 (ii. 48): liberata iam (b)
(13) p. 83 (i. 10): fuissem consul

[1] This is wrongly quoted as an example of dittography by some writers.

[2] Immediately afterwards the passage is repeated by error. On the second occasion *C* gives *non posset set.*

[3] The corruption *sanatus* for *senatus* is common in *C*, e. g. pp. 46, 186, 191, 192, 237, 241, 281. Cf. *Dom.* 24 (saenatu *P*).

p. 72 (i. 25): intermenstruo
(24) p. 265 (i. 60): eam consilio sedari uolebat
(27) p. 217 (ii. 31): ** isque de imperio suo exemplo pom- (c)
p. 255 (ii. 45): ipse poenam sceleris sui summam (d)
(32) p. 106 (i. 43): servitutis si Athenienses quibusdam (e)
(33) p. 182 (i. 31): quo modo duo soles visi sint non quaerit.
(34) p. 8 (ii. 58): imperium tr. pl. sic illi contra vim regiam (f)
(38) p. 268 (i. 61): ** -co quid domi pluresne praesunt negotiis tuis (g)
(50) p. 228 (ii. 9): Thraciam, Italiam, Siciliam, Africam praeter unam Magnesiam.[1]

There are two other cases where it is not clear what the omission is, viz.:

p. 108 (ii. 39). C^2 adds above the line:

habeat quib· cent. quattor centuriis

The reading seems uncertain and the abbreviations cause some difficulty, since we cannot be sure what was in the model.

p. 70 (ii. 28):

regem istum Numam Pythagorae ipsius discipulum aut certe Pythagoreum fuisse.

C has:

regem istum
numam py
thagoraene ip
{ sius discipulum aut cer
{ te pythagoreum fuisse

The last two lines are written in a compressed hand and the page has an extra line. The presumption is that C^1 omitted *ipsius discipulum aut certe pythagoreum* (ὁμ.), and that the passage was then rewritten. If so, 35 letters were omitted by C^1.

I now add a few remarks on some of the omissions included in the table given above.

(*a*) p. 102:

indicat nam dictator.

C^1 gave:

indicator *med. om.*

Probably the model had:

indicat nam
dictator

[1] The omission mark ϟ is used in the margin to denote where the omission occurred, also at the foot of the page, where the supplement is given.

The scribe passed from the first to the second line.

(*b*) p. 30:

qui etiam liberata iam civitate

C^1 gave:

qui
etiam ciui
tate

This indicates in the model:

qui et
iam liberata (11)
iam ciuitate (11)

(*c*) p. 217:

comitiis curiatis creavit, isque de imperio suo exemplo Pompili populum consuluit.

C^1 gave:

commit
tis curiatis
craeui pilipo
pulum con
suluit.

C^2 inserts *t* over *i* in *craeui*, strikes out *pilipo*, inserts *po* before *-pulum*, and adds in an extra line:

isq· de imperio suo exemplo pompili.

The model here may be arranged either in two or three lines. I incline to three in view of the telescoped passage of nine letters, p. 102. If so, we may arrange:

creauit
isque de im
perio suo ex
emplo pom
pili populum
consuluit

C^1 passed from l. 1 to l. 5.

(*d*) p. 255:

et cum metueret ipse poenam sceleris sui summam, metui se volebat.

C^1 gave:

et cum
metueret u
tui se uolebat

Van Buren says that *u* in l. 2 is erased.

C^2 adds *ipse poenam sceleris sui summā* above the line and *me-* before *-tui.* I suspect that *u* is a relic of *me-*. It may, however, be meaningless, in which case the omission was *ipse . . . summam me-*. If so, the total of letters is 29, and the passage is telescoped.

(*e*) C^2 adds:

seruitutis si athenienses quib·dā.

If we take the abbreviations into account, the total is reduced to 30.

(*f*) p. 8 (and p. 191):

ut contra consulare imperium tr. pl., sic illi contra vim regiam constituti

C^1 gave:

ut
contra con
sularem cons
tituti

C^2 struck out *-sularem* and inserted:

sulare imperium tr. pl. sic illi contra vim regiam

Here *consularem* may be a blunder for *-lare*, and I have treated the passage accordingly. It is, however, possible that *m* is the last letter of *regiam*. The model may have had:

tra consulare
imperium tr.
pl. sic illi con
tra uim regiam
constituti

If so, the passage has been telescoped and the omission is one of 33 letters.

(*g*) p. 268:

ut uni dicto audiens esset. Quippe vilico. Quid domi? pluresne praesunt negotiis tuis? Immo vero unus inquit

C^1 appears to have written:

uni dicto au
diens esset
quippe uili t
immo uero
unus inquit.

C^2 added *-co* above the line after *uili* and apparently *-uis* after *t*.

He then struck out *tuis* and *immo vero* and rewrote the passage. Mai gives *praesunt negotiis tuis*, but *-sunt* is not legible. Van Buren gives as the addition of C^2:

quid domi pluresne prae
egot is tuis immo uero

but says in a note that *negotiis tuis* seems to have been written (by C^2). It is possible that *tuis* after *vili* may have been written by *m.* 1. If so, the omission was one of *-co quid . . . negotiis* (34).

I will here mention an omission of Nonius, viz. i. 16, *et in Siciliam* (12). In *C* the passage is written thus:

p. 34: post in ita
liam et in sici
liam conten
disse

It would seem likely that there was a similar arrangement in the MS. of Nonius. I do not wish to suggest any connexion between *C* and Nonius, as the material is so scanty. It may, however, be worth mentioning that in

i. 70: expositaque ad exemplum nostra re p.

C and Nonius both have the corruption *nostrae rei p.*

Dittographies.

(8) p. 97 (i. 15): sole quod
(10) p. 257 (i. 68): vel in agris
(15) p. 117 (i. 52): nulli cupiditati [1]
(18) p. 140 (i. 27): numquam se plus agere [2]
(19) p. 59 (i. 23): diligebam et in primis
p. 283 (ii. 24): qualiscumque is foret
(21) p. 253 (i. 65): ac totam rem p. substravit
(22) p. 94 (ii. 40): et is valebit in suffragio
p. 153 (i. 58): gentem ingenia quaerimus
(30) p. 189 (ii. 51): hoc regiae civitatis everterit sit.
(31) p. 88 (ii. 27): -discenda quaeque observanda essent
(36) p. 266 (i. 60): -fectum nihil vero inquit magis ergo non pro-
(37) p. 9 (ii. 70): sine iniuria non posset hoc verissimum esse
(41) p. 290 (ii. 5): -que facillimum ut in agrum Rutulorum aboriginum
49) p. 85 (i. 11): cogantur cum quod est multo proclivius nulla necessitate

[1] This passage is not repeated immediately, but after 53 letters.

[2] This passage is not repeated immediately, but after *quam nihil cum ageret* (18).

(57) p. 150 (i. 64): eadem voluntas in eorum posteris si regum si̧militudo permansisset

(74) p. 170 (i. 49): teneri potest cum par non sit condicio civium si enim pecunias aequari non placet si inge- [1] (*in fine pag.*)

Simple corruptions.

p. 26 (ii. 69). *C* has:

sic ex sum	∴		
mis et infimis		et mediis	(8)
et mediis ẹṭ		interiectis	
interiectis			

p. 169 (i. 49). *C* has:

cum lex sit	∴	cum lex	
ciuilis ṣịṭ		sit ciuilis	(10)

p. 198 (i. 18). *C* has:

quaesi	∴	quaesierat	
erat ex me		ex me scipio	(10)
scipio ẹx ṃẹ			

p. 88 (ii. 26). *C* has:

et cupi	∴	et cupiditate	(12)
ditate ẹṭ bellā		bellandi	
di			

p. 243 (i. 65). *C* has:

autem	∴	autem	
f̣ mare ullum		mare ullum aut	(12)
aut flamam		flammam	

The scribe began to write *flammam* from the next line.

p. 206 (iii. 13). *C* has:

ut cali	∴	calida et	(8)
da et frigida		frigida et	(9)
et c̣amara		amara	

The scribe repeated *c* from *calida*.

p. 220 (ii. 35). *C* has:

legem			
tulit princi	∴	legem tulit	(10)
pio ḷẹg̣ẹṃ		principio	(9)
ṭụḷịṭ			

The writer has repeated l. 1 after l. 2.

[1] The dittography is not immediate, but comes after 197 letters; cf. p. 135.

p. 46 (ii. 43). *C* has:

ut			
ut spartae ly	∴	ut spartae ly	(11)
curgi legib.		curgi legib.	(11)
ut			
ụṭ et sit aliquod		et sit aliquod	

Here *ut* is contrary to the sense (*quamvis in ea sit et senatus . . . et sit aliquod etiam populi ius*). It is to be noticed that here the lines of *C* seem to coincide with those of the model.

p. 288 (ii. 4). *C* has:

ụṭ bene meri	∴	bene meriti de	(12)
ti de reb. com		reb. communib.	(13)
munib. ut		ut	

The writer looked forward two lines.

pp. 221, 294 (i. 35). *C* has:

	∴	sit	
sit in illo gene		in illo gene	(10)
re melior ego		re melior ego	(11)
cum mihi sit		cum mihi sit	(10)
ịṇ unum opus		unum	

The writer looked back three lines.

pp. 130, 41 (ii. 60). *C* has:

post ṛẹṣ	∴	post	
ṃụḷṭịṣ ḍịc̣ẹ		ea xx. ex eo	(8)
ḍịṣ ea xx. ex		quod l. papi	(9)
eo quod l. pa		rius p. pina	(9)
pirius p. pina		rius censo	(9)
rius censo		res multis	
res multis		dicendis	
dicendis			

The writer looked forward four lines.

To these may be added:

p. 10 (ii. 70). *C* has:

finis			
disputandi	∴	disputandi	(10)
in eum diṣẽ		in eum diem	(9)
p̣ụṭạṇḍị fac		factus est	
tus est			

Here the writer when he had written *di-* in l. 2 went back to *-sputandi* in the previous line. He then changed *dis* to *diẽ*.

p. 16 (ii. 45). *C* has:

adque circu
itum a primo
discite adq̣.
c̣ọgnoscere

Probably here there were two variants, viz. *[ad] cognoscere*.[1] If so, *que* has been introduced from two lines above.

p. 270 (i. 19). *C* has:

omnis
os
que auidạẹ
ọṃṇịṣ sapiē
tiae

Here *avidos* seems to have been assimilated in case to *sapientiae* while *omnis* has been repeated.

p. 266 (i. 60):

nihil isto ani			
mo ṇịḥịḷ ịṭạọ	∴	nihil isto	(9)
ạṇịṃọ ạni		animo nihil	(10)
hil ita anima		ita animato	(10)
to homine		homine mise	(10)
miserius du		rius ducerem	(11)
cerem			

The writer, after writing *ita*, seems to have added *-o* from *animo* in the previous line. There is a further confusion between *nihil* and *ani-*.

The following passages exhibit larger figures:

p. 272 (ii. 14). *C* has:

patres populū	
que et suo et	(10)
ine	
taṇti noni et	(10)
lucumonis	(9)
qui romuli	(9)
socius in sabi	(12)
quẹ no	

Here *que* comes from l. 2. *C* seems to reproduce the line division of the model. If we credit the model with the same errors, viz. *tanti* (= *Tati*) and *-ine* s. l., the words *que et . . . sabi-* consist of 50 letters.

[1] Cf. Cic. *Mil.* 38 adcognovisset *E*.

p. 117 (i. 52). *C* has:

ip
se nulli cupi
ditati cum quas
ad res ciuis ins
tituit et uocat
eas omnis cō
plexus est in ul
la cupiditati
ipse

The words *cum quas . . . complexus est*, as written, consist of 52 letters. The error is due to the recurrence of *ipse*. Possibly *in ulla cupiditati* is a variant, which has been inserted in the wrong place.

pp. 157–8 (ii. 5). *C* has:

ad spem diutur
nitatis conde
rentur adq. ī
perii primum
quod essent
urbes mariti
mae non so
lum multis
periculis oppo
sitae sed etiā
caecitatis

Here *caecitatis* is an error for *caecis*, due to *-tatis* in l. 2. The words *-tatis . . . caeci-*, if written as in *C*, consist of 100 letters.

p. 72 (i. 25). *C* has:

certo illut
tempore fieri
et necessario
cum tota se
luna sub or
bem solis sub
iecisset itaq.
etsi non om
ni intermens
truo tamen
id fieri non
posse nisi cer
to tempore

Here *certo* has been repeated from l. 1. The intervening words *certo . . . nisi* as written consist of 124 letters.

p. 170 (i. 49). I here give both columns as they appear in *C*:

lum ius autē
legis aequale
quo iure so
cietas ciuiū
teneri potest
cum par nō
sit condicio
ciuium si enī
pecunias ae
quari non
placet si inge
nia omniū
paria esse nō
possunt iura
certe paria

debent esse
eorum inter
se qui sunt ci
ues in eadem
rep. quid est
enim ciuitas
ṇisi iuris so
cietas ciuiū
ṭẹṇẹṛị p̣ọṭẹṣṭ
c̣ụṃ p̣ạṛ ṇọṇ
ṣịṭ c̣ọṇḍịc̣ịọ
c̣ịụịụṃ ṣị ẹṇị̄
p̣ẹc̣ụṇịạṣ ạẹ
q̣ụạṛị ṇọṇ
p̣ḷạc̣ẹṭ ṣị ịṇg̣ẹ

We here observe that in l. 9 of col. 2 the writer went back to l. 5 in col. 1 and proceeded to repeat the passage. There is here a lacuna in *C* due to the loss of folios, so we cannot be sure how much more was repeated. The passage *teneri potest* (col. 1, l. 5) . . . *-cietas civium* (col. 2, l. 8) consists, as written, of 197 letters. It may be noted that the dittography of seven lines contains 73 letters (74, if *enim* in full).

p. 67 (ii. 20). Here again I give both columns. Before col. 1 should come *immor-* (p. 302).

talitate credi
tum cum iā
inueterata
uita hominū
ac tractata
esset et cogni
ta sed pro
fecto tanta
fuit in eo uis
ingenii atq.
uirtutis ut id
de romulo
proculo iulio
homini agraes
r
ti cederetur

quod multis
iam ante sae
clis nullo alio
de mortaliṭạ
ṭẹ homines
credidissent

Here the error in col. 2, l. 4, *mortalitate* for *mortali*, is due to the occurrence of *immortalitate* in col. 1, l. 1. We may compare the similar blunder *caecitatis* for *caecis* (p. 158). The passage *-tate creditum* (col. 1, l. 1) . . . *de mortali* (col. 2, l. 4) consists, as written, of 197 letters (I include the letter *r* sup. lin. in col. 1, l. 15).

Here we have a very remarkable coincidence, viz. that in these two passages, where there is a repetition after a considerable interval, the intervening words in each case consist of 197 letters.

It appears to be highly probable that 197 represents a column of the model, and that the scribe looked back from one column to another. (Cf. p. 52.) If so, the model would appear to have had 19–20 lines to the page, i. e. 4–5 more than *C*.

It is interesting to put together the largest figures which have emerged in the course of this analysis, viz.:

(49) p. 85 : dittography
(50) p. 228 : omission
(52) p. 272 : repetition (ọ̣ụẹ̣)
p. 117 : repetition
(57) p. 150 : dittography
(74) p. 170 : dittography
(100) p. 157 : repetition (-ṭạṭịṣ)
(124) p. 72 : repetition (ẹẹṛṭọ)
(197) p. 67 : intervening space
p. 170 : intervening space

On p. 170 I have included both the dittography of 74 letters and the intervening space (197).

The interesting points here are the three examples of 49–50 and their connexion with 100 and the two examples of 197.

I add a few suggestions on textual points.

i. 22 : Hanc sphaeram Gallus cum moveret, fiebat ut soli luna totidem conversionibus in aere illo quot diebus in ipso caelo succederet, ex quo et in [caelo] sphaera solis fieret eadem illa defectio et incideret luna tum in eam metam

Caelo here was struck out by Heinrich and Dobree. The model may have had

in ipso
caelo succede (12)
ret ex quo et in (12)
sphaera

i. 28: Quis enim putare vere potest plus egisse Dionysium tum cum omnia moliendo eripuerit civibus suis libertatem quam eius civem Archimedem, cum istam sphaeram, nihil cum agere videretur, [de qua modo dicebatur] effecerit?

So Heinrich and others. Steinacker proposed to place the bracketed words before *nihil*. An ancestor may have had:

de qua modo	(9)
dicebatur	(9)
nihil cum age	(11)
re uideretur	(11)

i. 49: multo iam id in regnis minus quorum, ut ait Ennius, nulla [regni] sancta societas nec fides est.

'*vel quoniam*' (i. e. for *quorum*) 'scribendum videtur, vel in sequenti versu omittenda vox *regni*' (Mai).

The model may have had

regnis minus	(11)
quorum ut ait	(11)
ennius nulla	(11)
sancta	

Regni may be a repetition from *regnis*, or a variant which has got into the wrong place.

i. 67: Ex quo fit ut etiam servi se liberius gerant, uxores eodem iure sint quo viri inque tanta libertate canes etiam et equi, aselli denique liberi sic incurrant ut iis de via decedendum sit.

So Madvig: *C* adds *sint* before *sic incurrant*. I am inclined to place *liberi sint* (10) before *aselli denique* (13). The model may have had

canes	
etiam et equi	
liberi sint	(10)
aselli deniq.	(12)
sic incurrant	

For the sense cf. *Deiot.* 34 'et quem nos liberi in summa populi Romani libertate nati'.

i. 71: Tum Laelius: 'Tuum vero', inquit, 'Scipio, ac debitum quidem munus'.

So Halm: *C* has *tuum* for *debitum*. I am not satisfied with the emendation, but *tuum* may have been repeated from the context and taken the place of *debitum* or some other word. The model may have had, e.g.,

tuum uero in (10)
quit scipio ac (12)
debitum

ii. 30: multa intelleges etiam aliunde sumpta meliora apud nos [multo] esse facta

So Halm: *C* has (p. 40)

aliunde sū
ta meliora aput
multo
nos esse fac
ta

I am inclined to think that C^2 has inserted *multo* in the wrong line, i.e. that it should come before *meliora* in l. 2.

Taur. A II. 2*, cent. iv.

In this volume Peyron has united palimpsest leaves containing fragments of Cicero. Most of these are similar in appearance and may have come from one MS., viz.:

(1) *Quinct.* 3 ff., *Caec.* 5 ff., *Pomp.* 1 f., *Clu.* 12 ff., *Cael.* 4 ff., *Pis.* 8 ff., *Mil.* 5 ff., *Tull.* 8 ff., *Scaur.* 5 ff., *in Clodium* 1 f.

There are also two stray leaves, viz.:

(2) *Verr.* 1 f. (3) *Ad Fam.* 1 f.

These are fragments of other MSS.

I take first the leaves which are similar in point of formation. They are written in two columns with 21 lines to the page. The average number of letters to the line is 18.

The contents of the first two folios of the *pro Quinctio* are as follows, if expressed in lines of the Teubner text:

Fol. i = §§ 50–53 sed bonorum . . . tu te conlegis- = 37½ lines
Fol. ii = §§ 66–70 -sentem sine . . . renoua- = 37 ,,

The verso of f. iii is illegible. The recto contains

§§ 92–93 minas quas . . . officium = 18½ lines.

If we allow 18½ lines for the verso, we may ascribe to it

§§ 93–94 fidem . . . tanta potest.

I now combine those parts of the speech which have been lost with those which survived, marking the latter with an asterisk.

1–50:	quae res . . . cohonestandas	$= 526\frac{1}{2}$ lines	= 14 ff.
	($37\frac{1}{2} \times 14 = 525$)		
*50–53:	sed bonorum . . . tu te collegis-	$= 37\frac{1}{2}$	= 1
53–66:	-ses non . . . Quinctium ab-	$= 152\frac{1}{2}$	= 4
	($37\frac{1}{2} \times 4 = 150$)		
*66–70:	-sentem sine . . . commemorando renova-	= 37	= 1
70–92:	-re cuius . . . illorum	= 284	= 8
	($37 \times 8 = 296$)		
*92–93:	minas quas . . . tanta potest	= 37	= 1
95–end:	miserum est . . . prosequatur	= 46	

It is to be noted that there is a lacuna in § 85 after *hoc dico.* Apparently about 12 lines of Teubner text are here lost. (284 + 12 = 296.) At the end of the speech there must have been a blank space.

I now give in a combined form the results in the other speeches:

Caec.	1–6:	si quantum . . . disceptatore do-	$= 77\frac{1}{2}$ lines	= 2 ff.
	*6–9:	-mestico diiudicatur . . . atrocitatem nostram	= 39	= 1
	9–13:	reprehendere . . . haec auctio	= 39	= 1
	*13–16:	hereditaria . . . Aebuti-	$= 36\frac{1}{2}$	= 1
	16–38:	-us quo testimonio . . . non perspicu-	= 282	= 8
		($36 \times 8 = 288$)		
	*38–41:	-um est ad . . . hoc interdicto	= 37	= 1
	41–47:	Aebutius non . . . quisquam post	$= 73\frac{1}{4}$	= 2
	*47–50:	hac possessionis . . . qui se prae-	$= 38\frac{1}{2}$	= 1
	50–62:	-cipitatos ex . . . implorare pos-	$= 152\frac{1}{4}$	= 4
		($38 \times 4 = 152$)		
	*62–65:	-ses quod homines . . . obtempera-	= 39	= 1
	65–end:	-ri non oportere . . . indicetis	= 506	= 13
		($39 \times 13 = 507$)		

Here the end of the speech appears to have coincided with the end of a page.

Pomp.	1–40:	quamquam mihi . . . quae ceteri	= 503 lines	= 13 ff.
	*40–43:	tollenda esse . . . quo homine	= 35	= 1
	43–end:	vos id quod . . . oportere	= 361	= 10
Clu.	*1–7:	animadverti . . . iudicium	$= 75\frac{1}{2}$ lines	= 2 ff.
	7–18:	quod in . . . nuper Larino	= 147	= 4
	*18–24:	huius opprimendi . . . ac minis	= 76	= 2
	24–32:	insequi . . . sustulisset	$= 115\frac{3}{4}$	= 3
		($38 \times 3 = 114$)		
	*32–38:	quanto . . . constituunt	= 75	= 2
	38–74:	atque ille . . . Habitus pa-	$= 517\frac{1}{2}$	= 14
		($37 \times 14 = 518$)		

Clu.	*74–78:	-tiebatur . . . nonnullis sus-	= 68 lines.	= 2 ff.
	78–92:	-picio . . . aliquid de Clu-	= 179	= 5
		(35 × 5 = 175)		
	*92–94:	-entio . . . Fausto tamen	= $37\frac{3}{4}$	= 1
	94–101:	illi iudices . . . viri boni	= $73\frac{1}{4}$	= 2
	*101–103:	suscepta . . . iudicio mul-	= 35	= 1
	103–129:	-ta est ab . . . civem sine	= 350	= 10
	*129–131:	ignominia . . . probavisse	= $35\frac{1}{2}$	= 1
	131–145:	-res enim . . . causam si-	= $213\frac{1}{2}$	= 6
		(35 × 6 = 210)		
	*145–147:	-ne lege . . . praescripto	= $35\frac{1}{2}$	= 1
	147–end:	fieri . . . veritati	= 759	= 20
		($37\frac{1}{2}$ × 20 = 750)		
Cael.	1–38:	si quis . . . fama quotus	= 520 lines	= 14 ff.
		(37 × 14 = 518)		
	*38–42:	quisque est . . . curam rei	= 72	= 2

The second folio here has lost a few lines, but it is not clear from Peyron's account what the mutilation is.

42–54:	domesticae . . . illius stu-	= $151\frac{1}{4}$ lines	= 4 ff.
	(38 × 4 = 152)		
*54–56:	-dis illis . . . futurum Caelio	= 37	= 1
56–66:	fuisse nisi . . . in causa nul-	= 187	= 5
	(37 × 5 = 185)		
*66–69:	-lus exitus . . . miramur si il-	= 38	= 1
69–end:	-lam commenticiam . . . capietis	= $147\frac{1}{2}$	= 4
	(37 × 4 = 148)		

Here again the end of the speech seems to coincide with the end of a folio.

Pis.	1–17:	iamne vides . . . tyrannus omit-	= 224 lines	= 6 ff.
		(38 × 6 = 228)		
	*17–23:	-to enim . . . aut te	= 79	= 2
	23–33:	fuisti Romae . . . omnes exsecra-	= 157	= 4
	*33–36:	-rentur male . . . esse visam	= $40\frac{3}{4}$	= 1
	36–47:	nullis consiliis . . . Macedoni-	= 160	= 4
	*47–50:	-am in quam . . . ille si non	= $42\frac{3}{4}$	= 1
	50–61:	acerrime fureret . . . nummus in	= 157	= 4
	*61–64:	-terea, mi Caesar . . . inflixerint	= $40\frac{3}{4}$	= 1

(The passage *-niam quidem . . . inflixerint* has been cut out.)

*64–67: num etiam . . . quicquam praeter = $40\frac{3}{4}$ = 1

(The folio ends at *autem nolite*, but I have added the amount which has been cut out.)

67–75: libidines . . . deberem = $119\frac{1}{2}$ = 3

*75–79:	quorum quidem . . . invitavit roga-	= 42 lines	= 1 f.
	(The words *Caesarem* . . . *roga-* have been cut out.)		
*79–82:	-vit non sum . . . montes rese-	= 41	= 1
82–end:	-dissent amnes . . . viderem	= 270	= 7
	(40 × 7 = 280)		

In this speech the unit is higher than previously, viz. about 40. There appears to have been a blank space of 10 or more lines at the end.

Mil. 1–29:	etsi vereor . . . partim occisi	= 363 lines	= 9 ff.
*29–32:	sunt partim . . . personis valeat	= 40½	= 1
32–33:	etsi boni . . . non debeo	= 34	= 1
*34–36:	fuerit occidi . . . iam illum na-	= 39¾	
36–72:	-tura ipsius . . . quia nimis	= 402½	= 10
*72–75:	amplecti plebem . . . si sibi pecu-	= 41	= 1
75–86:	-niam quantam . . . sacrarium	= 159	= 4
*86–88:	bonae deae . . . circumscripsisset ne	= 40½	= 1
88–92:	cum solebat . . . multa de cau-	= 39½	= 1
*92–95:	-sa extra . . . enim negat	= 42½	= 1
95–end:	ingratis civibus . . . elegit	= 124	= 3

Here the unit is much the same as in the *in Pisonem*. A noticeable exception is §§ 32–33 = 34. Peyron has shown that the missing leaf must have contained more than is found in the extant MSS. (p. 292).

Tull. 1–3:	ante sic . . . consului. Pri-		= 1 f.
	The leaf has been mutilated.		
7–11:	pecuniae paret . . . datum esset	= 36½ lines	= 1
24–28:	turbarunt. Audite . . . malo eius er-	= 35	= 1
28–32:	-go addit . . . nocte sine	= 39½	= 1
32–36:	vi sine . . . solum igitur	= 35¾	= 1
37–41:	ego intellego . . . dedit de cete-	= 36¼	= 1
41–46:	-ris damnis . . . nimiamque hominum	= 36¾	= 1
47–51:	boni debent . . . fugit ma-	= 37	= 1
53–56:	tamen verum . . . potest ut eum	= 37	= 1
Scaur. 2–7:	-tis suae . . . etiam facilius	= 36½	= 1
18–23:	quoniam habet . . . genus primum	= 36½	= 1
23–28:	ut inquisitum . . . odium popu-	= 36½	= 1
31–36:	aut eius qui . . . detraxerint	= 37	= 1
46–50:	-tuisse templo . . . incendio di-		= 1
	The leaf has been mutilated.		

The signature VIIII is found on the verso of the fourth folio of this speech, after *detraxerint* (§ 36).

in Clod. 19–24: lego quam . . . tamen ex = 37 lines = 1 f.

The following conspectus may be of interest. I give the contents of the MS. when perfect, except in the case of *Tull.*, *Scaur.*, and *in Clodium*, omitting *Quinct.* 95–end, where there was a vacant space, and two mutilated leaves in *Tull.* and *Scaur.*

		Teubner lines	folios	avg. for f.	
Quinct.	=	$1074\frac{1}{2}$	29	37	($37 \times 29 = 1073$)
Caec.	=	1320	35	38	($38 \times 35 = 1330$)
Pomp.	=	899	24	$37\frac{1}{2}$	($37\frac{1}{2} \times 24 = 900$)
Clu.	=	2793	76	37	($37 \times 76 = 2812$)
Cael.	=	$1152\frac{3}{4}$	31	37	($37 \times 31 = 1147$)
Pis.	=	1414	36	39	($39 \times 36 = 1404$)
Mil.	=	1326	33	40	($40 \times 33 = 1320$)
Tull.	=	$293\frac{3}{4}$	8	37	($37 \times 8 = 296$)
Scaur.	=	$146\frac{1}{2}$	4	$36\frac{1}{2}$	($36\frac{1}{2} \times 4 = 146$)
Clod.	=	37	1	37	

It will be seen that the average is remarkably constant except in *Pis.* and *Mil.*, where there is a slight rise. It is very probable that, with the possible exception of *Pis.* and *Mil.*, the speeches were united in one MS. It is also quite likely that towards the end of the MS. the scribe slightly contracted his hand. I have already noticed the quaternion mark VIIII at *Scaur.* 36.

The MS. (*T*) does not contain much evidence concerning its past history.

There are some interesting corruptions in the *pro Tullio*, which deserve attention, viz.:

§ 36: bona me hercule. Si hoc solum

T has:

hoc solum bona me her
cule si hoc solum

This indicates in a previous MS.:

bona me hercule si (15)
hoc solum

§ 53: tamen per vim factum esset, tamen in eo ipso loco qui tuus esset, non modo servos

For *per vim T* has *verum.* The passage is written thus:

tamen uerum factum
esset non modo seruos
tamen in eo ipso loco qui
tuus esset non modo ser
uos

This indicates (after *factum*):

esset
tamen in eo ipso lo (15)
co qui tuus esset (14)
non modo seruos

The repetition of *non modo servos* is due to ὁμ.

§ 33: ego non in una re sola, quod mihi satis est, neque in universa re solum sed

T has:

ego non in una re sola
quod mihi satis est neq.
in uniuersa re solum
quod mihi satis est sed

This indicates:

re sola
quod mihi satis est (16)
neque in uniuersa (15)
re solum sed

The writer looked back from *re solum* to *re sola* and repeated a line before he saw his mistake. He then went on at the right place, but did not correct the error.

§ 49: at primum istae ipsae leges quas recitas, ut mittam cetera, significant quam noluerint maiores nostri, nisi cum pernecesse esset, hominem occidi. Ista lex sacrata est.

T repeats *primum* before *ista lex*. This indicates:

primum istae ip (13)
sae leges quas re (14)
citas ut mittam ce (15)
tera significant (15)
quam noluerint ma (15)
iores nostri nisi (15)
cum pernecesse es (15)
set hominem occidi (16)
ista lex

The writer looked back from *ista lex* to *istae ipsae leges*.

§§ 29, 30: satis est planum facere, vel se a me ipso vi deiectum esse vel me consilium inisse ut vi deiceretur. Plus igitur datur Claudio, cum ita interdicitur, unde dolo malo meo vi deiectus sit, quam si daretur, unde a me vi deiectus esset. Nam in hoc posteriore, nisi ipse egomet deiecissem, vincerem sponsionem: in illo priore, ubi dolus malus additur, sive consilium inissem, sive ipse deiecissem.

Here the scribe made two errors, which he then corrected, viz.:

(1) For *unde dolo malo meo* he wrote *unde a me* from the immediate context.

(2) After writing *sive consilium inissem*, he looked back to *me consilium inisse*, and repeated *ut vi deiceretur*. He then struck this out and substituted *sive ipse deiecissem* above the line.

I suggest the following distribution of the passage in the model :

consilium inisse	(15)
ut ui deiceretur	(14)
plus igitur datur	(15)
claudio cum ita in	(15)
terdicitur unde do	(16)
lo malo meo ui deiec	(16)
tus sit quam si da	(14)
retur unde a me ui	(14)
deiectus esset nam	(16)
in hoc posteriore	(15)
nisi ipse egomet de	(16)
iecissem uincerem	(16)
sponsionem in illo	(16)
priore ubi dolus ma	(16)
lus additur siue	(14)
consilium inissem	(16)

When the writer came to l. 5, he looked forward from *unde* after *-tur* to *unde* in l. 8 after *-tur*. After copying l. 16, he looked back to l. 1 and repeated l. 2.

The words *consilium inisse . . . additur sive* consist of 228 letters ($15 \times 15 = 225$). It is quite likely that they occupied a column in the model. If so, the writer looked back from the top of col. 2 to the top of col. 1.

The evidence seems to show that in the *pro Tullio* the model of *T* was written in lines with an average of 15 letters.

It is somewhat singular that these instructive errors are confined to the *pro Tullio*. In the other speeches there is a dearth of such evidence.

I have shown that the folios combined by Peyron in *T* may have come from the same MS., though I make certain reservations in the case of the *in Pisonem* and *pro Milone*. It does not, however, follow that the contents of this MS. were derived from one ancestor.

The following omissions may be noticed:

(11) *Quinct.* 53: adfinitatis *om.* *T*
(12) *Clu.* 130: a tr. seditioso *om.* *T*
Pis. 33: profectionis *om.* *T*
(14) *Clu.* 129: et turpitudinem *om.* *T*
Cael. 55: percipite atque *om.* *T*
(19) *Clu.* 37: Asuvium appellat ipse *om.* T^1

The last of these is interesting. We have already seen that the average number of letters in a line of *T* is 18. The suspicion, therefore, arises that in the *pro Cluentio*, at any rate, it may have been copied from a model very similar to itself.

To these, probably, should be added:

(19) *Pis.* 48: partim permutationes
(23) 21: et flagitiorum impunitate

In the first of these most MSS. give:

cum partim eius praedae profundae libidines devorassent, partim nova quaedam et inaudita luxuries, partim etiam in illis locis ubi omnia diripuit emptiones, partim permutationes ad hunc Tusculani (-num) montem exstruendum

Here *V* (Bas. Vat. H. 25), cent. viii, has:

tim etiam in illis lo
cis ubi omnia diripu
it emptiones *partim*
mutationes ad hunc
tus*culani* || || || || ||
montem exstruen
dum

The words italicized are written *in rasura*, also there is an erasure after *Tusculani*. It appears probable that V^1 wrote *emptiones ad hunc*, omitting *partim permutationes* (ὁμ.). The corrector then struck out *ad hunc* and rewrote the passage *in ras.* and above the line.

As omissions are very frequent in sentences where *partim* . . . *partim* occurs, I am now inclined to think that the words *partim permutationes* represent a genuine tradition. Havet ingeniously corrects to *partim mutuationes*.[1]

[1] *Manuel*, p. 58.

In the second passage, § 21, the later MSS. have:

ex omni scelerum importunitate et flagitiorum impunitate.

The omission by *T* of the last three words seems due to ὁμ. If this view is correct, the relation of *Pis.* 48 to *Clu.* 37 is to be noted. There are also some transposition variants which may be added, viz.:

Caec. 41: est periculosum *T*: periculosum est *cett.*
Pis. 49: pretio mei capitis *TV*: mei capitis pretio *cett.*
Mil. 75: exstruere aedificium *T*: aedificium exstruere *cett.*
Cael. 39: Fabricios fuisse arbitror Camillos *T*: fuisse arbitror Camillos Fabricios *cett.*
Pis. 22: in quo cum illum saltatorium versaret orbem, ne tum quidem *T*: in quo ne tum quidem cum illum saltatorium versaret orbem *cett.*

The theory of these transposition variants will be found discussed in detail further on (pp. 255–8). Here I will only remark that such a case as *Caec.* 41 indicates in a previous MS.

mg. est periculosum (11)

So we may explain the variants in *Cael.* 39, *Pis.* 22 as due to

				in quo	
	fuisse arbi	(10)		cum illum sal	(11)
mg. fabricios	tror camillos	(12)		tatorium uer	(11)
	sed		*mg.* ne tum quidem	saret orbem	(10)

I now turn to the two leaves from the *Verrines* and the *Epp. ad Familiares.*

The first of these was taken from a MS. of Cyprian, formerly belonging to Bobbio. It has been mutilated, 13 lines only having been preserved. The *recto* contained:

Verr. i. 44: -que iter fecit . . . magistratum Sicyonium

After this the portion of the page which was cut away contained:

44–5: nummos poposcit . . . semivivum.

The part of the *verso* which was preserved contained:

45: reliquit . . . participem C. Verr-

The rest of the page was cut away.

This leaf, which Chatelain ascribes, though doubtfully, to the third century, was written not in columns, but in long lines. They vary a good deal in length, since paragraphs are used, and blank spaces are left at the end of a paragraph. The contents of the 13 lines preserved are as follows :

recto. 24, 23, 22, 9, 22, 17, 23, 21, 22, 23, 22, 13, 20 = 261.

verso. 8, 24, 24, 21, 20, 25, 12, 23, 22, 21, 23, 23, 22 = 268.

The lost portion of the *recto* contained 294 letters (*nummos . . . semivivum*). The leaf, therefore, when intact must have had 27–8 lines.

The interest of the leaf lies in the fact that it preserves a passage omitted in most MSS., viz.:

§ 45 : dictum est hoc . . . aestimatum.

The other leaf contained

Ad Fam. vi. 9. 1–10. 6 : hunc a puero . . . etiam polliceri.

The *verso* was deciphered by P. Krüger, after Peyron had pronounced it to be illegible.[1]

The leaf is written in long lines with 27 lines to the page. One line on the *recto* is occupied by the title to vi. 10, viz. CICERO TREBONIO SAL. DIC. There are, therefore, 26 lines of text, as compared with the *verso.*

The contents are :

recto (26 lines) = 967 letters.

verso (27 lines) = 1000 letters.

The average length of a line is 37 letters (37 × 26 = 962, 37 × 27 = 999).

This leaf is extremely interesting. Whereas it is usual to find in palimpsests passages omitted in later MSS., this fragment has a series of omissions. Also, there are indications that the text was doctored in places after omission.

Peyron, therefore, suggested that the fragment belonged to a shorter version of the Letters made by an epitomator who selected those passages which seemed interesting to him. This theory has been adopted by subsequent writers, and Krüger suggests that this epitome may have been made by Fronto, who speaks of making excerpts from Cicero's letters.

In order to put the facts before the eyes of the reader, I write out the contents of the *recto* :

hunc a puero quod et spem magnam mihi adfere
bat summae probitatis summaeq. eloquentiae

[1] *Hermes*, v (1871), pp. 146–9.

L 2

et uiuebat mecum coniunctissimae ñ solum
amicitiae officiis sed etiam studiis communib.
semper dilexi nullo ut cum homine coniuncti
us uiuerem uides relicum esse ut cum cogno
rim quid tu et de bonorum fortuna et de reip.
calamitatib. sentias nihil a te petam nisi ut ad eā
uoluntatem quam tua sponte erga caecinam
habiturus es tantus cumulus accedat commē
datione mea quanti me a te fieri intellego
CICERO TREBONIO SAL. DIC.
Ego quanti te faciam semperq. fecerim quantiq.
me a te fieri intellexerim sum mihi ipse testis
nam et consilium tuum uel casus potius diutius
in armis ciuilibus commorandi semper mihi mag
no dolori fuit et hic euentus quod tardius quā
est aecum et quam ego uellem reciperas fortu
nam et dignitatem tuam mihi ñ minori curae
est quam tibi semper fuerunt casus mei itaq.
si auctoritate et gratia tantum possem quantum
in ea r.p. de qua ita meritus sum posse deberem
tu quoq. esses qui fuisti cum omni gradu amplis
simo dignus tum certe ordinis tui facile princeps
sed quoniam eodem tempore eademq. de causa
nostrum uterq. cecidit nihil erit saltem quod
ñ pro te mihi susceptum maximum semper ac

The other MSS. here contain certain passages omitted by the palimpsest (*T*), viz.:

l. 6, after *viverem*:

nihil attinet me plura scribere, quam mihi necesse sit eius salutem et fortunas quibuscumque rebus possim tueri *add. codd.*

l. 7, after *cognorim*:

pluribus rebus *add. codd.*

l. 11, after *intellego*:

hoc mihi gratius facere nihil potes. uale. *add. codd.*

l. 20, after *itaque*:

et Postumuleno et Sestio et saepissime Attico nostro proximeque Theudae, liberto tuo, totum me patefeci et haec eis singulis saepe dixi, quacumque re possem, me tibi et liberis tuis satis facere cupere, idque tu ad tuos velim scribas, haec quidem certe quae in potestate mea sunt ut operam consilium rem fidem meam sibi ad omnes res paratam putent. *add. codd.*

. 26, after *cecidit*, in place of the words *nihil erit saltem*:

tibi et illa polliceor quae supra scripsi, quae sunt adhuc mea, et ea quae praeterea videor mihi ex aliqua parte retinere tamquam ex reliquiis pristinae dignitatis: neque enim ipse Caesar, ut multis rebus intellegere potui, est alienus a nobis et omnes fere familiarissimi eius casu devincti magnis meis veteribus officiis me diligenter observant et colunt. Itaque si qui mihi erit aditus de tuis fortunis, id est de tua incolumitate, in qua sunt omnia, agendi, quod quidem cotidie magis ex eorum sermonibus adducor ut sperem agam, per me ipse et moliar. Singula persequi non est necesse, universum studium meum et benevolentiam ad te defero. Sed magni mea interest hoc tuos omnis scire, quod tuis litteris fieri potest ut intellegant, omnia Ciceronis patere Trebiano. Hoc eo pertinet ut nihil existiment esse tam difficile. *add. codd.*

It is clear that the words *nihil erit saltem* are an attempt to mend the passage after this long omission or excision.

The *verso* of *T* differs notably from the *recto*, in that there is only one omission. This occurs in l. 10 after *versatum*. I therefore give the first ten lines only:

iucundum futurum sit antea misissem ad te
litteras si genus scribendi inuenirem tali enim
tempore aut consolari amicorum est aut polli
ceri consolatione ñ utebar quod ex multis au
diebam quam fortiter sapienterq. ferres in
iuriam temporum quamq. te uehementer con
solarentur conscientia factorum et consilio
rum tuorum quod quidem si facis magnum
fructum studiorum optimorum capis in quib.
te semper scio esse uersatum simul et illud tibi

Here the other MSS. add, after *versatum*:

idque ut facias etiam atque etiam te hortor.

There is no possible explanation except that of deliberate abridgement. The method followed is somewhat odd. Thus the passage omitted on *recto*, l. 6, is not self-contained, but requires *vides* to complete the construction. In l. 20 the abbreviator takes *itaque*, which is the first word in a sentence, and then performs a large cut. The attempt to botch the construction after the long omission in l. 26 is very impudent.

Krüger calls attention to a statement of Fronto, who says (ii. 5. 107, ed. Niebuhr):

memini me excerpsisse ex Ciceronis epistulis ea dumtaxat quibus inesset aliqua de eloquentia vel philosophia vel de re publica disputatio, praeterea si quid eleganti aut verbo notabili dictum videretur, excerpsi

It occurred to me as possible that the abbreviator went on the method of cutting out lines in his model, and making small alterations from time to time where the wound in the text was left manifest. I noticed at once a very singular circumstance, viz. *nihil attinet . . . tueri*, the first passage omitted = 94 letters; also the block of text which comes between the omission of *pluribus rebus* and *hoc mihi . . . vale*, viz. *quid tu et . . . intellego*, as printed by Mendelsohn, consists of 187 letters. That which is omitted in l. 20 after *itaque*, viz. *et Postumuleno . . . putent*, consists of 284 letters. Here we have the sequence :

94.
187 (94 × 2 = 188).
284 (94 × 3 = 282)

This is somewhat astonishing. Of course, 94 cannot be the unit. The model is not likely to have had longer lines than *T*, which has an average of 37 to the line.

I now exhibit the whole passage, marking with an asterisk those portions which are found in *T*. Those not marked are supplied from the other MSS.

There are certain differences in reading between *T* and the other MSS. As I do not wish to assist my argument by picking and choosing, I give the readings of *T* throughout, though by so doing the figure 187, given above, is reduced to 183 (reading *sentias* for *sentires*, and *es* for *esses*, with *T*). I assume only the ordinary official abbreviations (*res p.* &c.), since we cannot tell if there were any sporadic abbreviations, e.g. *Q.* (= *que*), *B.* (= *bus*), in those portions of the model which were omitted by the maker of the abridged text.

I begin with l. 6 of the *recto*, where the first omission occurs :

nihil attinet . . . possim tueri	=	94
* vides relicum esse ut cum cognorim	=	29
pluribus rebus	=	13
* quid tu et . . . fieri intellego	=	183
hoc mihi . . . potes. Vale [1]	=	34
* ego quanti . . . mei itaque	=	310
et Postumuleno . . . paratam putent	=	284
* si auctoritate . . . uterque cecidit	=	217
tibi et illa . . . tam difficile	=	676

[1] If the abbreviation *V.* (= *Vale*) was used, this = 31. Cf. Schmitz, *Commentarii Notarum Tironiarum*, Pl. 64.

* quod non pro . . . esse versatum[1]	=	399
idque ut . . . te hortor	=	36

I now place these figures in numerical order:

13	94	310
29	183	399
34 (31)	217	676
36	284	

Here $31 \times 3 = 93$, $31 \times 6 = 186$, $31 \times 7 = 217$, $31 \times 9 = 279$, $31 \times 10 = 310$, $31 \times 13 = 403$, $31 \times 22 = 682$.

Only one number is recalcitrant to this explanation, viz. 13. This comes between 29 and 183. The probability, therefore, is that the words *pluribus rebus* were already omitted by the model. If so, the whole passage from *vides relicum* . . . *fieri intellego* forms one block ($29 + 183 = 212$). The similarity of 212 to 217 is to be noted.

The unit is represented by 29, 34 (31), and 36. The last passage is rather long. It is to be noticed, however, that *-que* and *atque* both occur in it. If *Q.* was used for *-que*, the total would be reduced to 32. The length, therefore, is more apparent than real.

I now venture to write out the passage, as I conceive it to have stood in the model of *T*, enclosing in brackets the portions omitted by *T*. I begin with l. 6 of the *recto*:

uiuerem	
[nihil attinet me plura scribere quam	(31)
mihi necesse sit eius salutem et fortu	(32)
nas quibuscunque rebus possim tueri]	(31)
uides relicum esse[2] ut cum cognorim	(29)
quid tu et de bonorum fortuna et de rei	(31)
p. calamitatibus sentias[3] nihil a te pe	(31)
tam nisi ut ad eam uoluntatem quam tua	(31)
sponte erga caecinam habiturus es[4]	(29)
tantus cumulus accedat commendati	(30)
one mea quanti me a te fieri intellego	(31)
[hoc mihi gratius facere nihil potes, uale]	(34)
CICERO TREBONIO SAL. DIC.	

[1] I here read, with *T*, *susceptum maximum semper ac iucundum futurum sit*. The other MSS. give *susceptum iucundum sit futurum*. Krüger thinks that the words *maximum semper ac* are part of the botching. Since, however, they do not help out the construction, it seems to be more probable that they were present in the model of *T*.

[2] est *cett.* [3] sentires *cett.* [4] esses *cett.*

ego quanti te faciam semperque fece (30)
rim quantique[1] me a te fieri intellexe (31)
rim sum mihi ipse testis nam et consili (32)
um tuum uel casus potius diutius in ar (31)
mis ciuilibus commorandi semper mihi (32)
magno dolori fuit et hic euentus quod (31)
tardius quam est aecum et quam ego uel (31)
lem reciperas fortunam et dignitatem (32)
tuam mihi non minori curae est quam (29)
tibi semper fuerunt casus mei itaque (31)
[et postumuleno et sestio et saepissime (33)
attico nostro proximeque theudae li (31)
berto tuo totum me patefeci et haec eis (32)
singulis saepe dixi quacunque re pos (31)
sem me tibi et liberis tuis satis face (31)
re cupere idque tu ad tuos uelim scri (30)
bas haec quidem certe quae in potestate (33)
mea sunt ut operam consilium rem fidem (32)
meam sibi ad omnis res paratam putent] (31)
si auctoritate et gratia tantum pos (30)
sem quantum in ea re p. de qua ita meritus (32)
sum posse deberem tu quoque esses[2] qui (31)
fuisti cum omni gradu amplissimo dig (31)
nus[3] tum certe ordinis tui facile prin (31)
ceps sed quoniam eodem tempore eadem (31)
que de causa nostrum uterque cecidit (31)
[tibi et illa polliceor quae supra (28)
scripsi si quae sunt adhuc mea et ea quae (33)
praeterea uideor mihi ex aliqua parte (32)
retinere tamquam ex reliquiis pris (30)
tinae dignitatis neque enim ipse cae (31)
sar ut multis rebus intellegere po (29)
tui est alienus a nobis et omnes fere (30)
familiarissimi eius casu deuincti (30)
magnis meis ueteribus officiis me di (31)
ligenter obseruant et colunt itaque (31)
si qui mihi erit aditus de tuis fortu (30)
nis id est de tua incolumitate in qua (30)
sunt omnia agendi quod quidem cotidie (32)
magis ex eorum sermonibus adducor ut (31)
sperem agam per me ipse et moliar singu (32)
la persequi non est necesse uniuersum (32)
studium meum et beneuolentiam ad te (30)

[1] *om.* -que *cett.* [2] is esses *cett.* [3] dignissimus *cett.*

defero sed magni mea interest hoc tu (30)
os omnis scire quod tuis litteris fi (30)
eri potest ut intellegant omnia cice (31)
ronis patere trebiano hoc eo pertinet (32)
ut nihil existiment esse tam difficile] (33)
quod non pro te mihi susceptum maxi (29)
mum semper ac[1] iucundum futurum sit[2] an (31)
tea misissem ad te litteras si genus (30)
scribendi inuenirem tali enim tempo (31)
re aut consolari amicorum est aut pol (31)
liceri consolatione non utebar quod (31)
ex multis audiebam quam fortiter sa (30)
pienterque ferres iniuriam temporum (32)
quamque te uehementer consolaretur (31)
conscientia factorum et consiliorum (32)
tuorum quod quidem si facis magnum (29)
fructum studiorum optimorum capis (30)
in quibus te semper scio esse uersatum (32)
[idque ut facias etiam atque etiam te hortor] (36)

The last line becomes normal, if we attribute to the model:

idq. ut facias etiam atq. etiam te hortor (32)

Ambros. R. 57 sup., cent. v (*A*)

This palimpsest comes from Bobbio. It is written in three columns, with 24 lines to the page and an average of nearly 12 letters to the line. The contents of *A* are:

pro Scauro 6 ff.
pro Tullio 4 ff.
pro Flacco 1 f.
pro Caelio 1 f.

I have already (p. 13) given figures to show the regularity of writing in this MS. As expressed in Teubner lines, the contents of the folios in the *pro Scauro* and *pro Tullio* are as follows. I omit one folio, containing *Tull.* 8–14, since it has been badly mutilated:

Scaur.	8–13:	te dixi . . . flagitio defor-	$= 39\frac{1}{4}$
	13–19:	-matos habetis . . . disputem quid	$= 40\frac{1}{4}$
	19–25:	non habuisti . . . atque iniurias	$= 39\frac{1}{2}$
	29–34:	-litu Aetnam . . . quam ob rem	$= 40\frac{3}{4}$
	34–40:	se consule . . . hoc perfugi-	$= 41$
	40–45:	-um dolori . . . Scipionum int-	$= 41\frac{1}{2}$

[1] maximum semper ac *om. cett.* [2] sit futurum *cett.*

Tull. 4-8: ore putavit . . . facere cumque = $41\frac{1}{2}$
8-14: ea consuetudo . . . P. Fabius nu- = 39

The folio contained more than this, but has been damaged in § 11 after *datum esset.*

18-23: -minȩ eius . . . amici incomm- = 41

There can be no doubt that these leaves are taken from the same MS. The single leaf of the *pro Flacco* is in similar formation, three columns, with 24 lines to the page. The lines, however, are slightly shorter. The first column on the *recto* and the third column on the *verso* are imperfect, having lost 11 lines. The 13 lines which remain in both cases contain 145 letters (13 × 11 = 143). If we allow 11 letters for each of the lost lines (11 × 11 = 121), the total for each of the mutilated columns is 266. The total contents of the folio, after this addition, are as follows:

	Col. 1	Col. 2	Col. 3		
recto	266	264	266	= 796	= 1577
verso	266	249	266	= 781	

The average length of line for the whole folio is 11 letters, nearly (144 × 11 = 1584).

This compares with an average of 844 letters to a page (i. e. 1688 to a folio) in the *pro Scauro* and *pro Tullio.* As expressed in Teubner lines, if we make allowance for the lost lines, the equivalent is $37\frac{3}{4}$. It is, therefore, possible that this leaf comes from another source.

The leaf from the *pro Caelio* is said to contain:

§§ 71-75: C. Aeserni . . . et infelici

A photograph is given by Chatelain (Pl. xxix), but he describes the leaf as *malheureusement presque illisible*, and so I find it. The passage in question = $46\frac{1}{2}$ lines of Teubner text. The difference between this and the preceding figures, viz. 39–$41\frac{1}{2}$ for the *pro Scauro* and *pro Tullio*, and $37\frac{3}{4}$ for the single leaf of the *pro Flacco*, seems to show that this was taken from a separate MS.

In the *pro Scauro*, *A* on two occasions omits words found in *T*, viz.:

(9) § 23: ac facetum
(11) § 24: et discendam

These omissions suggest that *A* is derived from a MS. very like itself. If so, we may explain a corruption in

Scaur. 34: qui sive patricius sive plebeius esset—nondum enim certum constituerat—cum hoc sibi contentionem fore putabat.

So *T* and Asconius, except that Asconius has *constitutum erat* and *cum illo.*

A has:

Qui siue patrici
us siue plebeius
esset non enim
certum consti
tuerat cum hoc
sibi certum cō
tentionem fo
re putabat

Here *certum* is repeated from the context before *con-* (ὁμ.).

The model may have had:

enim	
certum con	(9)
stituerat	(9)
cum hoc sibi	(10)
contentionem	

In *Scaur.* 43, *A*, our sole authority, gives:

qua re cum integri nihil fuerit in hac gente plena, quam valde eam putamus tot transfusionibus coacuisse?

The reference is to the mixed descent of the Sardinians. I have inserted *pestilentiae* before *plena.* If so, we may attribute to the model:

in hac gente	
pestilentiae	(12)
plena	

I recently noticed an interesting parallel in *Fam.* vii. 24 1. Here Cicero, speaking of the Sardinian Tigellius, calls him *hominem pestilentiorem patria sua.*

I finally record certain transposition variants in *A* and the other MSS. which seem to go back to an ancestor in narrow columns, viz.:

Scaur. 23: iacere fundamentum *A*: fundamentum iacere *T*
32: in gratiam reditum *A*: reditum in gratiam *T*
Cael. 71: crimen quaestionis *AΣ*: quaestionis crimen *cett.*
disciplinae dedita *AΣ*: dedita disciplinis *cett.*
studiis aequalium *AΣ*: aequalium studiis *cett.*

These are the only instances which I have noticed, and their similarity is remarkable.

I reserve the palimpsest of the *Verrines* (Vat. Reg. 2077) for treatment together with the MSS. of these speeches.

Vat. 5750.

Scholiasta Bobiensis.

The remains of the *Scholiasta Bobiensis* have been preserved in two palimpsests, viz. Vat. 5750, Ambros. E. 147 sup.

The first of these has been reproduced in facsimile. The upper writing contains the Acts of the Council of Calchedon and Letters of Leo the Great. Underneath are Fronto, the *Scholiasta* and various other works.

The scholia are written in two columns, with 25 lines to the page and an average of 16 letters to the line. There are a large number of quaternion markings on the leaves, e.g. *Q* lxx on p. 189 of Ambr. E. 147, and Hildebrand says that, when perfect, the volume contained 73 quaternions. It must, therefore, have been very bulky.

There is one passage where words omitted by the first hand are added at the foot of the page, with omission symbols. This is

Vat. 15: servasse enim de caelo tunc videntur Domitius Calvinus et Q. Ancharius et C. Fannius: [ius] autem non erat aliquid cum populo agi eo tempore quo de caelo servaretur.

Here *ius* or *fas* is supplied by editors.

The MS. (*C*) has, after *videntur*,[1]

domitius caluinus et
q. ancharius et c. quid
cum populo agi eo tem
pore

C[2] puts *hd* over *c.*, and at the foot adds:

(22) fannius autem non erat ali *hs*

Hildebrand considers that this represents a line of the model, '*lineam cuius oblitus erat librarius . . . addidit*'. If so, it is to be noted that the line in the model was longer than in the copy, which, although possible, is not usual.

C contains a large amount of evidence in the shape of repetitions and dittographies, which seem to indicate that the unit was 11–12

[1] Cf. p. 27 of facsimile.

letters. If so, the passage omitted by C^1 in Vat. 15 represents not one line, but two. The instances which I have noted are as follows. The references are to the pages and lines of the Teubner text.

I take first simple dittographies, viz.:

(12) 135. 5: cum inrisione *bis scr.*
(49) 91. 4: tamen statim cum ipso corpore alii vero interiecto quodam *bis scr.*
(64) 95. 20: Claudia de bonis Ptolomaei publicandis M. Cato ut consenserit in legationem *bis scr.*

Here $12 \times 4 = 48$, $12 \times 5 = 60$.

I take next repetitions of a short word, or part of a word, after an interval, viz.:

(13) 141. 15: *fuisse* repeated after *fuisse denique*
(15) 142. 29: *Ciceronis* repeated after *Ciceronis ipsius*
(21) 136. 3: *contra* repeated after *contra dicente scilicet*
(25) 74. 8: *su* repeated after *supra in illarum quaestionum*

This indicates in the model:

supra in illa (11)
rum quaestionum (14)

In other cases the passage repeated is longer, viz.:

147. 1:

creber fuisti ut haec immodica

C^1 repeats *creber fuisti* (12) after *immodica*. This indicates:

creber fuisti (12)
ut haec immodica (14)

125. 27:

comparandum ut apud iudices editicios

C^1 repeats *comparandum* (11) after *editicios*. This indicates:

comparandum (11)
ut apud iudi (10)
ces editicios (12)

80. 10:

hoc ratiocinationibus validis implet subnectens ad hunc modum, nam quid de Cyro nuntiaret?

C^1 repeats *hoc ratiocinationibus* (20) after *nuntiaret*. This indicates:

hoc ratioci (10)
nationibus (10)
ualidis implet (13)

subnectens	(10)
ad hunc modum	(11)
nam quid de cy	(11)
ro nuntiaret	(11)

105. 25:

dicit ducentos bestiarios, id est venatores, sine dubio volens intellegi omnem

C^1 repeats *dicit ducentos bestiarios* (23) after *omnem*. This indicates:

dicit ducentos	(13)
bestiarios	(10)
id est uena	(9)
tores sine du	(11)
bio uolens in	(11)
tellegi omnem	(12)

125. 21:

Cn. Plancio dixit qui reus de sodaliciis petitus est lege Licinia quam M. Licinius Crassus

C^1 repeats *Cn. Plancio . . . sodaliciis* (33) after *Crassus*. This indicates:

cn. plancio di	(11)
xit qui reus de	(12)
sodaliciis	(10)
petitus est	(10)
lege licini	(10)
a quam m. lici	(10)
nius crassus	(11)

133. 8:

damnorum quibus fuerant hostili incursione vexati, adfuit igitur Caesar causae publicanorum eorumque desideriis

C^1 repeats *quibus . . . Caesar* (54) after *eorum*. This indicates:

damnorum	
quibus fuerant	(13)
hostili in	(9)
cursione ue	(10)
xati adfuit	(10)
igitur caesar	(12)
causae publi	(11)
canorum eorum	(12)
que desideri	(11)
is	

The writer's eye passed from *eorum* to *damnorum*. He discovered his error after writing five lines, and then stopped before completing the dittography. An attempt at correction has been made by commas above the line, but the first of these is put in the wrong place, viz. after *hostili* instead of after *eorum*.

This interesting series of corruptions shows how, when we have only one MS. of an author, the dittography may step into the place of the omission, and yield valuable information.

I now come to the upper writing, viz. the letters of Leo the Great and the Acts of the Council of Calchedon. Here also the first writer omitted passages which are added by a corrector with omission marks (*hd* and *hs*).

Leo Magnus (Migne, vol. liv).

(31) p. 34 (Migne, 777 B):
misericordiae dī ad satisfactionem

(32) p. 42 (805 B):
ut creator intellegatur non valebunt

(50) p. 43 (807 A):
unus ih̄s xp̄s et unus dī hominisque sit filius si caro et anima

(124) p. 49 (789 C):
et quidquid nostris temporib: contra impugnatores catholicae ueritatis industria sacerdotalis obtinuit ad uestram maxime gloriam redundabit.

Here $31 \times 4 = 124$. The omission of 50 letters seems due to chance, assisted by ὁμ.

Concilium Calchedonis (Mansi, vi, vii).

(16) p. 130 (Mansi, vi. 618 A):
*interloquutus sum

(28) p. 110 (vi. 590 C):
inimicos flauiani foris mittite

(32) p. 143 (vi. 634 A):
teneant quae in nicea constituta sunt

(41) p. 90 (vii. 471 A):
dignitate persistere, mortem uero carne gustare

(58) p. 13 (vi. 542 A):
in nouissimis autem dieb. eundem propter nos et propter nr̄am salutem

(63) p. 205 (vi. 715 D):
quae dicta sunt a sc̄is patrib. in nicea uel in ephesum congregatis et omnib.

(65) p. 82 (vii. 459 D):
et homo factus est quod discindit quidem spont[anea] uoluntate incarnatus est

(72) p. 258 (vi. 786 B):
non dixit nobis hominibus et ubi uultis iuro quia dixerat consubstantialis matri est

(79) p. 98 (vi. 570 B):
paulo mariamme secundae syriae eusebio seleucoboli eutychiano epyfaniae secundae syriae

(84) p. 102 (vi. 578 B):
heliodori ep̄i amathuntis et proecii ep̄i arsinoe epafrodito ag̃u et didimi lapitii dionisio dīac ag̃u

I also noticed an addition above the line without an omission mark, viz.:

(29) p. 98 (vi. 570 B):
tiranno germanicopolis isauriae

Here we have two sequences, viz.:

28–29, 58, 84.

16, 32, 63–65.

A possible explanation seems to be that the MS. is descended from an ancestor written in double columns, one of which contained an average of 14 and the other an average of 16 letters.[1]

If so, the following multiples account for all the numbers:

$14 \times 2 = 28$, $14 \times 3 = 42$, $14 \times 4 = 56$, $14 \times 5 = 70$, $14 \times 6 = 84$, $16 \times 2 = 32$, $16 \times 4 = 64$, $16 \times 5 = 80$.

There is also a very curious dittography of unusual length.

On p. 236 a second hand has added at the top of the page:

hic pertransi usque ubi adnotationem uidis quia reiterata est scribtura.

Mansi, vi. 759 D, has:

Macedonius vir spectabilis, tribunus, notarius et referendarius dixit: Eutyches reverendissimus archimandrita

Also, 762 C:

Macedonius spectabilis tribunus, notarius et referendarius dixit: Piissimus dominus noster.

[1] I offer this suggestion with considerable reserve, since the evidence in the shape of short omissions is scanty.

The writer of this MS., when copying the last passage, after having got so far as *Macedonius ṽs* (= *vir spectabilis*) *tribunus notarius et referendarius*, looked back to the previous passage and went on with *Eutyches rẽu archimandrita.*

He then rewrote the whole passage from 759 D to 762 C without discovering his error.

CHAPTER VI

CICERO, *PHILIPPICS*

THE chief MS. for Cicero's *Philippics* is Bas. Vat. H. 25 (*V*). In its present state this consists of 80 folios, which are distributed thus:

1^r–8^v: *in Pisonem*, §§ 32–74.
9^r–11^v: *pro Flacco*, §§ 39–54.
11^v–17^v: *pro Fonteio*, §§ 11–49.
18^r–80^v: *Philippics*, i–xiii. 10.

V has suffered various mutilations. A quaternion has been lost before *Pis.* 33, and four quaternions, as is shown by subsequent signatures, have perished after *Pis.* 74. It follows, therefore, that f. 9, on which *Flacc.* 39 begins, was originally f. 49 in *V*, when complete. There is no loss between the *pro Fonteio* and *Philippics.*

Flacc. 54 ends on f. 11^v, col. 2, l. 20, and is followed without a break by the extant fragment of the *pro Fonteio.* The title *Pro Fonteio* is written at the top of the page above the fragment of the *pro Flacco*, while the fragment of the *pro Fonteio* has no title. A late hand (cent. xvi) has corrected *Pro Fonteio* to *Pro Val. Flacco*, and inserted *Pro Fonteio* in the margin of f. 11, col. 2, l. 20. It appears that the two speeches were confused, owing to a dislocation of folios in an ancestor, assisted by the similarity of the subject matter. In the case of the *pro Fonteio* we may be sure that the fragment preserved represents folios of the ancestor: in that of the *pro Flacco* we have no such guarantee, since we cannot tell what came before f. 9.

In this connexion the *excerpta Cusana* are of considerable interest. They are contained in a MS. belonging to the Hospital at Cues, cod. C 14, cent. xii. They consist of extracts from Cic. *in Pisonem*, *pro Fonteio*, *pro Flacco*, *Philippics*, also from some non-Ciceronian works. The MS. from which they are drawn appears to have contained the same speeches as *V*. Also the readings of *Cus.* show striking agreements with *V* in the *Philippics*, as against all other MSS. In the *pro Fonteio* and *pro Flacco* the excerpts preserve a number of passages not known from any other source. The inference is that they come from parts of these speeches which, when *V* was perfect, were contained in the missing leaves before *Flacc.* 39. The interesting point is that in *Cus.* extracts from the *pro Fonteio* precede and follow those from the *pro Flacco*. If we combine this evidence with the title PRO FONTEIO given to the fragment of the *pro Flacco* in *V*, the conclusion that the two speeches were mixed up seems to follow.

The quaternion which contains *Pis.* 33–74 corresponds to 598 lines of Teubner text. This gives an average of about 75 Teubner lines to a folio of *V*. The previous part of the speech, §§ 1–32, as given in the other MSS., occupies only 445 lines. This would only suffice for about six folios of *V* (75 × 6 = 450). It follows, therefore, that *V* at one time contained the equivalent to about 150 Teubner lines more than now appears in our texts. As a matter of fact the beginning of the speech is defective, and various Cusan excerpts, as well as quotations of Asconius and other authorities, are placed here by editors.

The rest of the *in Pisonem*, §§ 74–end, occupies 445 lines in the Teubner text. This would suffice to cover six folios of *V* (75 × 6 = 450). We may, therefore, infer that in *V*, when complete, the *Pisoniana* occupied ff. 1–22, and that the missing folios, 23–48, were occupied by portions of the *pro Fonteio* and *pro Flacco*.

V is a composite MS. The first quaternion is written in a semi-uncial hand of the eighth century: the rest of the MS. is written in Caroline minuscule, and belongs to the ninth century. We cannot tell whether the lost quaternions were written in semiuncial or in minuscule. It would appear probable that the rest of the *Pisoniana* was written by the same scribe as §§ 33–74.

In spite of its composite character, *V* exhibits the same formation throughout, being written in three columns with 30 lines to the page. This is a fact which calls for particular notice.

The use of three columns is a mark of antiquity. We are told by various authorities that a tricolumnar arrangement was not employed by scribes after the sixth century, except in certain ecclesiastical works, e. g. Psalters and Bibles. Three columns are used in Laud. Lat. 33 (Psalter from St. Kilian's), cent. x, and in Harl. 5786 (Psalter), cent. xii, also in Brit. Mus. 24142 (Bible of

Theodulphus), cent. ix, while a Paris Psalter, *Nouv. Acq.* 2195, cent. xii, is written in four columns. In the case of other works, three columns are rare after the sixth century. The British Museum possesses an example in Egerton 1934, Isidorus, cent. viii/ix. Traube says *kurz ist die Reihe der dreispaltigen Klassiker.*[1] He mentions, in addition to *V*, a ninth-century palimpsest of Quintilian's *Declamationes* (Paris. 7900 A). I have published a Bodleian leaf (Laud. Lat. 29) of the ninth century containing a fragment of Cic. *Tusc.* (iv. 114–20), written in three columns.[2] *V*, however, seems to be the only more or less complete MS. now extant of a classical author written at this date (cent. viii/ix) in this formation.[3]

It was the opinion of Traube that the writer of *V* was imitating the formation of an ancient model (*einen viel älteren Codex in der Schrift und vielleicht auch sonst in der Einrichtung nur nachahmt*), and the correctness of this diagnosis seems obvious. It is also *prima facie* probable that such imitation could take place more than once. This consideration seems to explain the composite character of *V*. Let us suppose that an ancient MS. in three columns was reproduced more than once in the same formation. One of these copies, made in the eighth century, became the model for another copy, made in the ninth. By some accident a part of the model was bound up with the new copy.

If this conjecture is well founded, it is worth while to examine ff. 1–8 with some care. The methods of the writer responsible for the rest of *V* can be controlled, if we actually possess a quaternion of his model.

The contents of folios 1–8 are as follows:

1^{r} (§§ 32–4): *col.* 1 tamen misericordia . . . sapienti op-, *col.* 2 -tabilius . . . post obitum, *col.* 3 occasumque . . . servandi

1^{v} (§§ 34–7): *col.* 1 causa Romam . . . fratrem, *col.* 2 inimici mei . . . vestrorum, *col.* 3 propinquorum . . . conscripserat.

2^{r} (§§ 37–40): *col.* 1 aerarium . . . attingitur ut, *col.* 2 semper . . . afflixeras, *col.* 3 quem deleveras . . . an so-

2^{v} (§§ 40–2): *col.* 1 -ciorum direptio . . . auderet, *col.* 2 a senatu . . . laceratione quam, *col.* 3 afficior . . . esse umquam.

3^{r} (§§ 42–4): *col.* 1 vir bonus . . . saepe feci, *col.* 2 in quo . . . quae cruces, *col.* 3 esse duos . . . litterae

[1] *Pal. Forschungen*, iv, p. 28.

[2] *Mélanges Chatelain*, pp. 169–73.

[3] Guarino's ancient MS. of Pliny's letters, now lost, was written in three columns. Cf. Sabbadini *Codici posseduti* etc. *da Guarino*, p. 60.

3^v (§§ 44–7): *col.* 1 recitatae . . . se civem, *col.* 2 esse meminerit . . . in scena, *col.* 3 videtis . . . reliquisse

4^r (§§ 47–50): *col.* 1 mitto de . . . praeda quam ex, *col.* 2 fortunis . . . tantos ha-, *col.* 3 -beret . . . gravissimae sunt

4^v (§§ 50–2): *col.* 1 furore . . . vetarent, *col.* 2 sed quoniam . . . immortali-, *col.* 3 -um festi . . . expilaras

5^r (§§ 52–5): *col.* 1 quam incenderas . . . Macedonia, *col.* 2 nobilis . . . a porta, *col.* 3 cum lictoribus . . . Macedonicus

5^v (§§ 55–7): *col.* 1 imperator . . . pestis, *col.* 2 o labes . . . etiam recu-, *col.* 3 -santem . . . cumque omnium

6^r (§§ 57–9): *col.* 1 tuorum . . . a senatu, *col.* 2 P. Servili . . . cupiditate, *col.* 3 iusti et . . . facies fidem

6^v (§§ 59–62): *col.* 1 scilicet cum . . . Macedonicam, *col.* 2 lauream . . . manu, *col.* 3 perfricans . . . alteri illum

7^r (§§ 62–5): *col.* 1 honorem collega . . . ferreum, *col.* 2 senatus . . . nominis sui, *col.* 3 videre . . . philosophi

7^v (§§ 65–8): *col.* 1 manus tibi . . . scitote esse, *col.* 2 luxuriosius . . . in lectis, *col.* 3 saepe plures . . . ut prorsus.

8^r (§§ 68–71): *col.* 1 una viveret . . . distinguere, *col.* 2 et dividere . . . assen-, *col.* 3 -tatorem et . . . qui scripsit

8^v (§§ 71–4): *col.* 1 detrahi nihil . . . versus tui, *col.* 2 nimis negare . . . nec arma, *col.* 3 scutum aut . . . oratione hoc.

The contents, if we allow the usual official abbreviations, are as follows:

	Col. 1	Col. 2	Col. 3		Total
1^r	546	481	511	=	1538
1^v	509	528	537	=	1574
2^r	529	495	514	=	1538
2^v	531	515	488	=	1534
3^r	516	505	476	=	1497
3^v	483	508	450	=	1441
4^r	537	489	446	=	1472
4^v	506	477	467	=	1450
5^r	506	450	520	=	1476
5^v	538	494	499	=	1531
6^r	528	536	548	=	1612
6^v	584	561	530	=	1675
7^r	601	564	547	=	1712
7^v	546	561	524	=	1631
8^r	593	581	562	=	1736
8^v	589	576	565	=	1730
	8642	8321	8184	=	25147

This gives an average content of about 3,144 letters to a folio, 1,572 to a page, 524 to a column, and 17½ to a line.

It is to be noticed that col. 1 tends to squeeze cols. 2 and 3, especially 3. The averages are: col. 1 = 540, col. 2 = 520, and col. 3 = 511. The average numbers of letters to the line are, in col. 1, 18; in col. 2, 17⅓; in col. 3, 17.

As actually written in *V*, the number of letters is slightly less. Chatelain (Pl. 26) has a reproduction of f. 3^{r}, and I possess a photograph of f. 4^{r}. These give the following results:

	Col. 1	Col. 2	Col. 3		
3^{r}	509	498	471	=	1478
4^{r}	534	468	436	=	1438

i. e. 53 letters less than if only official abbreviations are allowed. If we extend this allowance to the other leaves, which have not been reproduced, we shall have to deduct 424 letters from the total. This would yield about 3,090 for a folio, 1,545 for a page, 515 for a column, and 17 for a line.

The hypothesis which I have advanced appears to receive confirmation from a passage in *Phil.* xi, §§ 18 and 20, viz.:

§ 18: Ita populus Romanus consuli potius Crasso quam privato Africano bellum gerendum dedit.

§ 20: Otioso vero et nihil agenti privato, obsecro te, L. Caesar, cum peritissimo homine mihi res est, quando imperium senatus dedit?

After this comes:

sed de hoc quidem bactenus . . . consul designatus.

In § 18 V^1 adds after the first *dedit* the passage *sed de hoc . . . designatus*, which should come after the second. The words are then struck out by the original scribe, and occur in § 20 in their proper place.

It is to be noticed that the passage as given by V^1 in § 18 is grossly corrupt, while in § 20 it is fairly correct. I add the two versions side by side, marking the first *A*, and the second *B*.

(*A*) bellum
gerendũ dedit. Sed de hoc di
quidem actenus ne refragari ho
mini aceme optime frito amicissi
mo uidear et si quis potest refra
gari non modo non petenti uerba

(*B*) senatus dedit
sed de hoc quidem actenus
ne refragari homini ami
cissimo ac de me optime
merito uidear si quis si quis
potest refragrari non modo

etiam recusati. illa uero hic
aliena consulũ dignitatẽ alie
natem dorũ grauitates senten
tiae tot cos. dolabellae ꝓsequen
di causa si et suria sortiantur
dicã curi nutili. Rp. sed prius
quã turpe cosue pete cum cos. de
signatus

non petenti uerum etiam recu
santi. illa uero p. c.
aliena consulũ dignitate
aliena tẽporum grauitate
sententia est ut consul dolabellae
persequendi causa asiã et suri
am sortiant̃. dicã cur inutile
republicae sed prius quã turpe
consulibus sit uide||||
Cum consul designatus

The corruption of *A* may be seen from e.g. l. 4, *aceme optime frito* (where the confusion of *F* and *E* goes back to a MS. in rustic capitals); l. 6, *uerba etiam recusati*; l. 8, *alienatem dorũ grauitates*; l. 12, *curi nutili*, &c. It is to be noticed that the words *ac de me optime merito* (18), or *aceme optime frito* (16), are out of place in *A*. Apparently they had been omitted and were then inserted too soon.

The natural inference is that *A* represents an alternative version for *B*, probably an older version, which V^1 inserted after the first *dedit* in § 18. The error would be simplified, if *dedit* in §§ 18 and 20 occupied the same place on two pages (cf. p. 52).

If so, we should expect the intervening passage, viz.:

§§ 18–20: De Cn. Pompeii imperiis . . . senatus dedit,

to represent a page of the model from which *V* was copied.

This passage, if we allow the official abbreviations, consists of 1,584 letters. If we suppose that the model, like *V*, was written in three columns with 30 lines to the page, this gives us 528 letters to a column and 17½ letters to a line. We have previously found that in ff. 1–8 the averages were 1,572 to a page, 524 to a column, and 17½ to a line. The correspondence could hardly be more exact. I, therefore, regard the hypothesis as verified.

I have previously pointed out that in *A* the words *aceme optime frito* (16) are out of place. It is interesting to notice that in § 20 *V* goes on:

obsidea
tur cũ in eo liberando salus sit
posita rei publicę sed priusquam
turpe

Here the words *sed priusquam turpe* (17) have been repeated by V^1 from four lines above.

Apart from the first quaternion, *V* is written in Caroline minuscule. The script varies a good deal in character. In the first *Philippics* it is large, and the lines contain little more than is the case in ff. 1–8. In *Phil.* ii. there are some very short lines, e. g. of 15–16 letters. The hand, however, gradually contracts, and towards the end of the MS. this contraction becomes very marked. This may be illustrated by the following figures:

	Col. 1	Col. 2	Col. 3		Total
37v	597	516	512	=	1625
38r	559	519	563	=	1641
60r	628	566	593	=	1787
62v	698	597	583	=	1878
78v	669	657	667	=	1993
79r	764	661	690	=	2115
80r	810	686	743	=	2239

These exhibit a rise in the average content of a line from 18 up to nearly 25. It will be noticed that col. 1 is generally broader than the others.

These figures represent the number of letters actually written in pages of which I possess photographs. If only official abbreviations were allowed, the totals would be larger, particularly towards the end of the MS.

I think it probable that the text of the *Philippics*, as given in *V*, was transmitted through more than one intermediate ancestor written in three columns. Since, however, it is impossible to distinguish between these, I shall use the letter *U* to denote both the model and its tricolumnar ancestor or ancestors.

The interest of *V* is due to its freedom from sophistication. Although written in a Caroline hand, it shows no trace of Caroline learning. The scribe was an ignoramus, who wrote without understanding and reproduced nonsense with fidelity. The result is that *V* gives a more faithful text than is found in any other MS. of Cicero's orations, all of which have passed through the hands of Caroline revisers. It gives precious information concerning the state of the documents before they were emended by ninth-century scholars.

I proceed, therefore, to give some further account of *V*.

(1) Orthography.

An initial *i* is common before *s*, e. g. isceleratorum (ii. 20), iscio

(ii. 41), istatim (ii. 44), ispecies (ii. 68), ispem (ii. 77), iscorta (ii. 105); so also before other words, e.g. inefarios (i. 5).

Occasionally *a* and *e* are prefixed to words, e.g. adefendetur (i. 19), apotius (i. 20), afiliam (ii. 99), asuscepimus (x. 14), acuius (xi. 6), esentire (ii. 24), enemo (ii. 36), euxoris (iii. 4), eprodideritis (x. 7).

The spelling *quum* is frequent, e.g. v. 36, 47, 48.

There is complete confusion between *b* and *v*. The corrector was as uncertain on this point as the scribe; thus viii. 6:

verba nec bellica] uerua nec bellica V^1: berua nec uellica V^2.

Vowels are frequently confused; thus *e* is written for *a*, e.g. ii. 78 *audecem*, viii. 17 *feveo*; or for *i*, e.g. vii. 19 *perspecua*, xi. 13 *rediculum*, ib. 18 *eta*; so *a* for *i*, e.g. *daripere*, xi. 4, and *o* for *e*, e.g. xii. 13 *comcodere* (= *concedere*).

Letters are often omitted, e.g. i. 31 *Dola* = *Dolabella*, ii. 37 *mnens* = *manens*, 61 *near* = *negare*, and still more frequently transposed, e.g. ii. 40 *agrumento* = *argumento*, 48 *su aegra* = *sua erga*, 49 *gatria* = *gratia*, 56 *de ea ealgelem* = *de alea lege*, v. 14 *thaheniensium* = *Atheniensium*, 29 *sinsi* = *nisi*, 46 *suma* = *suam*.

(2) Abbreviations.

A vertical stroke is frequently used for *-m* final, also for other abbreviations, e.g. *clarissimorù hominù* (viii 7), *cù uinus* (ii. 106), *nr̍is bellù* (ix. 4), *nà cũ* (ib.), *ȯsederit* = *obsederit* (vii. 15); also for a transposition mark, i. 24 *àès* = *eas*.

Praenomina and official abbreviations have a tendency to disappear. Thus *Marcus* is nearly always written for *M.*, so *populus Romanus* and *res publica* for *p. R.* and *r. p* (cf. Halm on vi. 16). Various errors show that the full forms are recent, e.g. v. 28 marcus antoni, viii. 21 domitius bruti, 27 ex domitio bruti exercitu (cf. xi. 17 at quo domiti = ad quod), xi. 20 populoque romanum, xii. 20 populi romano, v. 21 populŏ romanŏ; so xii. 20 populo romano = praetores (PR.).

The abbreviation *P. C.* is found from time to time, e.g. x. 8, xii. 19, so *c. u.* = *clarissimus vir*,[1] e.g. ix. 3; so xi. 6 *cre* = *civium Romanorum*. Cf. i. 20 *iud.* V^1: *iudices* V^2.

Among rarer abbreviations may be mentioned xi. 20 *senatui dico populoque Romano*] *senatui l. populoque romanum V*, where *l* appears

[1] Cf. xiii. 50 *u. c.* in *D* = *viri clarissimi*.

to stand for *d* (= *dico*), v. 39 *sapientia etiam*, where *etiam* appears to represent *et mīā*, i. e. *et misericordia*.

(3) Double readings.

These are very frequent, e. g. i. 7 ueritus, uertus, 17 multais, ii. 8 ipsũo, 23 coniunctionise, 43 quods, 45 confirmauiat, 50 alienis alieni, 86 uixereas, 99 frequentissimeo, 104 hastaea, 114 mortali inmortali, 116 magmultis, iii. 1 postulabatuit, 7 commodoa, 12 consilium oiudicat, 16 traxit tarxerat, 19 pertitnenat, 22 intellegitat, 36 patefaciunt fecerunt, iv. 5 possiumus, ix. 6 uestraea, xi. 12 nequec, *etc., etc.*

Some strange corruptions are due to various readings, which have been introduced in the wrong place, e. g. ii. 39 *plena curae*. Here *V* gives *pl*^{a}*ena curae*. There appears to have been a variant *plana*. V^2 inserts *a* above *n* instead of above *e*. So i. 13 editors read with *V fuerit ille Brutus*, while *L.* is added before *Brutus* by *D.* As a matter of fact *V* has *bru*^{ui}*tus*. Here *ui* = *Lu.* (i. e. *Lucius*), which has been inserted out of place.

(4) Critical signs.

The omission mark *hs* (= *hic supple*) has been incorporated in the text i. 11. The rare symbol *h.m.* (= *hic minus*) is used in the margin in v. 4 *h.m. quam senatus, si quidem legiones*, and is incorporated in the text vii. 6 *h.m. pagate*. Marginal supplements are frequently introduced by *h*. In vii. 11 *ad bellum proficiscerentur, quod erat bellum V* inserts *R.* before *proficiscerentur*. Here *R.* = *require*, a critical note due to the fact that after *quod* there is a long insertion taken from § 6. In ii. 110 for *cessas V* gives *ca*^{r}*esas*, which seems to be a misinterpretation of the same sign. In this connexion I would mention a mistake made by the second hand at the end of viii. Here V^1 gives the subscriptio *M. Tulli Ciceronis Philippicarum liber viii explicit*; V^2 inserts after *Ciceronis* the sign *đ* (= *deest*), and adds below *đ* FELIX NAVIGAT. This appears to = *feliciter*; it will be noticed that the insertion is out of place.

The writer of *V* was capable of anything. Among the more remarkable corruptions may be mentioned ii. 69 ille vir, patres conscripti, sicuti scitis, cum foris clarus] illeur po. scutis scitet cu floris clarus *V*. 86 ut facile servires a nobis] ut facilies aruspres a nouis *V*. vi. 17 Quirites] quosplus *V*. vii. 10 pecunias] pepo V^1.

viii. 13 honesta] omneista *V*. x. 17 omnia verentur] omni haberentur *V*. xi. 2 nostris] contris *V*. *ib.* 9 quo maior vis est] quomairuissest *V*. No glimmer of intelligence is seen except when a little knowledge of ecclesiastical Latin leads him astray,[1] e.g.:

xiii. 6: seiungamus tamen] seiungamus amen *V*
v. 34: auctoritatemque vestram] auctoritatemque bestiaram *V*

The first hand made a few corrections. Thus i. 8 *senatum frequentem* appears to be inserted by him, possibly also § 12 *audientibus cum fabris se*, § 18 *nempe*. He corrects in § 21 popular*es* to popular*is*, and in § 27 oporteb*a*t to oporteb*i*t by means of *i* longa inserted through *e* and *a*. The repeated passage in xi. 18 is struck out by the first hand. A note on ii. 24 *Nota Prisc̃.* (i.e. Priscian, viii. 27 and 42) appears to have been in the model.

Various correctors have been at work. The earliest uses blacker ink and writes a somewhat clumsy hand. On various occasions he struck out the reading of the scribe and rewrote the word. Thus in ii. 50 V^1 seems to have written *omnium malorum reperietis*, omitting *principium natum* (after *malorum*). The corrector, instead of making a marginal addition, rewrote the passage. So i. 2 *-ris commentaris reperiebatur summa*. ii. 53 *sublatum circumscriptus*: also single words written *in ras.*, e.g. ii. 62 *tradere*. 95 *sententia*. He also adds words, e.g. i. 6 *timebant* (over *caverant*). ii. 1 *L.* before *Catilina*, *P.* before *Clodius*. § 3 *cum omnes*. § 70 *st* (= *est*) after *opera tua*. Two hands seem to belong to the tenth century. One writer, who uses an 'open' *a*, is responsible for various supplements, e.g. ii. 79 *qui tum . . . in Dolabella*. vii. 3 *-ne sic . . . nequam est*. § 25 *plena discordiarum*. ix. 2 *quam in Ser. Sulpicio re-*. *ib. non morbus . . . retardauit*. x. 5 *nisi . . . nossem*. § 20 *libertate fugienda*. § 23 *senatus libertatem*. xi. 5 *atque laniatum*. xiii. 2 *hominum . . . potuisset*. § 5 *quas in eos*. The other adds i. 7 *nec ita . . . proiectus*. § 11 *de hesterna . . . erat causae cur*, and possibly § 30 *urbe . . . liberata*.

Other additions seem due to a corrector of the eleventh century, e.g i. 27 *quam . . . habui*. § 29 *qui . . . carissimus*. ii. 118 *contempsi . . . tuos*. *ib. adeptus . . . unum ut*. iii. 15 *non . . . Aricinum*. § 23 *subito*.

[1] For a similar substitution in *t*, cf. xiii. 18 *ad caelum* (= *caedem*) *optimi cuiusque*.

A still later corrector, probably belonging to the twelfth century, is responsible for vii. 5 *aetate illius . . . sed etiam*, also for a note on the dislocation after xi. 17, viz. *Transi ad istam notam* ⚹ *abhinc usque ad sequentem notam* ψ *ex* xii *libro scias*. (Cf. p. 194.)

All other MSS. of the *Philippics*, if written before about 1430, belong to a family known as *D*. Shortly before this date *V* was collated by Poggio, and supplements taken from it were incorporated in various MSS. These, however, do not concern us.

The *D* family all exhibit the same omissions. The chief of these are:

ii. 93–6: sunt ea quidem . . . acta defendimus
v. 31–vi. 18: -onem nullam . . . interfui nullam
x. 8–10: populus Romanus . . . Italia omnis in-

The length of these in lines of the Teubner text is as follows:

ii. 93–6 = 34 lines
v. 31–vi. 18 = 527 lines
x. 8–10 = 33 lines

Here it is to be noticed that 33 × 16 = 528. The conclusion is that 33–4 = a folio, and that in v. 31–vi. 18 two quaternions have been lost. I must point out that something should be added to 527 for the *subscriptio* to *Phil.* v and the title to *Phil.* vi.

I cannot give the number of letters in v. 31–vi. 18, since the passage is too long. If we allow the usual official abbreviations, the totals for ii. 93–6 and x. 8–10 are 1,423 and 1,419 respectively. It cannot be doubted that these omissions go back to one MS.

The next point to consider is the relation of *D* to *V*.

It must be premised that some of the *D* family are little inferior to *V* in antiquity, also that several of the *D* readings are supported by ancient quotations, e.g. by Aulus Gellius. Such agreements, however, do not prove that the *D* family in its present form goes back to so distant a period, but merely that in the time of Aulus Gellius there were ancient variants, such as we find in the *de Re Publica* palimpsest and in the Greek papyri. There is, however, no reason to doubt that the *D* text with its characteristic dislocations may go back to a very early date.

It is generally agreed that *V* and *D* both go back to the same archetype.[1] This is shown by *proprii errore s*common to them, e.g.:

[1] Cf. Lutz, *Quaest. Crit. in Philippicas*, p. 26.

i. 5 sui similibus] suis similibus 21 at res popularis] ad res populares iii. 3 ne optantibus quidem] nec optantibus quidem v. 10 eae] ae *V*: a *t*: oeae *s*: hae *b* viii. 28 usi] i *Vt*: hi *b*: si *ex* sed *s*: *om. n.* ix. 15 grati simus] gratissimus xi. 6 cuius] acuius *ib.* efficta] effecta 19 committis] comitiis xii. 22 exitum] exitus

Also, they frequently have the same gloss, though in a different place, e.g.:

ii. 69 conclavibus popinae] conclavibus popinae triclinis *V*: tricliniis popinae *D*

For further information concerning the past history of *V* and *D* we must turn to the omissions. I therefore give a complete list, so as to provide the reader with all the data. Where the omission may be explained by ὁμοιότης of any kind I affix no mark, where there is no such explanation I affix an asterisk, and where the passage has been telescoped I use two asterisks.

I take, first, omissions of *V* or of V^1:

(13) xi. 5: atque laniatum *om.* V^1
(14) iv. 6: fidelissimorum *om.* V^1
viii. 33: *primo quoque die *om.* *V*
(15) i. 33: *quam diligi malis *om.* *V*
v. 24: et fortissimorum *om.* V^1
(16) ii. 20: *operis subsicivis *om.* *V*
79: *induxit ut peteret *om.* *V*
(17) i. 8: *senatum frequentem *om.* V^1 (*suppl. m.* 1)
ii. 24: gravitatis alterum *om.* V^1
76: turpius vidi nullum *om.* *V*
ii. 118: **-quando rem p. M. Antoni *om.* *V*
vii. 25: plena discordiarum *om.* V^1
viii. 9: homines agrestes si *om.* *V*
x. 20: libertate fugienda *om.* V^1
23: senatus libertatem *om.* V^1
(18) ii. 116: quid multa? attulerat *om.* V^1
(19) i. 29: *qui es mihi carissimus *om.* V^1
ii. 8: *Seio et Tironi Numisio *om.* *V*
viii. 3: non sit tumultus autem *om.* *V*
ix. 2: ** quam in Ser. Sulpicio re- *om.* V^1
3: patres conscripti sic *om.* V^1
(20) i. 27: *quam in re p. semper habui *om.* V^1
(22) i. 12: *audientibus cum fabris se *om.* V^1
ii. 49: *rem illam referri malebam *om.* *V*
53: *sublatum circumscriptus *om.* V^1
(23) ii. 52: neque maiores natu monendo *om.* *V*
(24) ii. 35: officina agrorum oppidorum *om.* *V*

iii. 25: nullam se habere provinciam *om.* V^1
(25) ii. 72: ego leges perniciosas rogavi *om.* *V*
iii. 15: non contemnit is qui Aricinum *om.* V^1
xi. 13: quorum alter commentatus est *om.* *V*
(26) ii. 71: * quid fuit causae cur in Africam *om.* *V*
xiii. 5: * per deos immortales, quas in eos *om.* V^1
(27) i. 7: ** nec ita multum provectus reiect- *om.* V^1
v. 4: quam senatus si quidem legiones *om.* V^1
(28) vii. 14: ** nisi paruerit huic ordini quid re- *om.* *V*
(29) x. 21: legio fregit IV[1] afflixit sic a suis *om.* V^1
(30) xii. 16: ** -cear in quo ne si dissensero quidem a *om.* *V*
(31) ii. 118: ** contempsi Catilinae gladios non per- *om.* *V*
ix. 2: non morbus ingravescens retardavit *om.* V^1
(32) i. 30: *urbe incendio et caedis metu liberata *om.* V^1
(33) xi. 10: cuius sanguinem non bibere censetis, in *om.* *V*
(36) xiii. 2: hominum in re p. sanitas remanere potuisset *om.* V^1
(37) vii. 3: * irritatum Antonium non oportuit nequam est *om.* V^1
(43) ii. 119: * adeptus sum quasque gessi. Duo modo haec opto, unum ut *om.* V^1
(84) ii. 79: qui tum est impulsus inductus elusus. Qua in re quanta fuerit uterque vestrum perfidia in Dolabellam *om.* V^1
(112) i. 11: M. Antoni . . . die hesterno *om.* V^1
(280) vii. 6: ** -te usus consuetudo . . . dico sed *om.* *V*
The words are omitted *loco suo* and inserted subsequently in § 11.

Here various points attract attention, viz.:

(1) The numerous omissions of 17 letters. These appear to represent lines of *U*.

(2) Among them is a telescoped passage, ii. 118. There is also a telescoped passage of 19 letters, ix. 2. With an average of 17, variations from 15 to 19 are to be expected.

(3) There are also telescoped passages of 27, 28, 30, and 31 letters.

(4) The number 28 appears in the three largest omissions, viz.: $28 \times 3 = 84$, $28 \times 4 = 112$, $28 \times 10 = 280$.

The question arises whether 27–31 represent a new unit or two shorter lines. Two lines of 17 letters should contain about 34 letters, but it might be held that we are here concerned with a more remote ancestor written in narrower columns. If so, however, we should expect to find more omissions below 17. For further light we must turn to *D*.

[1] I write IV, since Roman numerals seem to have been used in the archetype. Cf. Halm on iii. 39, v. 53, xi. 37.

Omissions of *D*:

(13) viii. 22: deserti inquam
xi. 20: Martia et legio
xiii. 2: sive simulabat
(14) i. 30: *praeter ceteros
v. 3: et severissimum
13: *quod maximum est
vii. 2: leges imponeret
6: *fuisse fautorem
xi. 11: propter eximiam
(15) v. 29: *timeam et cogitem
(16) ii. 105: quae cogitabantur
viii. 28: et tu acta Caesaris
xi. 17: quam Punico tertio
(17) i. 3: *nullae respondebat
(18) xi. 20: C. Caesarem. Imperium C.
(22) ii. 64: *cum omnia metu tenerentur
v. 27: ad nostrum civem mittimus
(23) vii. 18: fecerit, hunc praedae causa
(24) i. 2: *nisi quod erat notum omnibus
(28) vii. 14: multo postea gravius urguebamur
xii. 16: si accipiendam, cur non rogamur si
(30) v. 20: ** habebat possessor quantum relique-
(31) iv. 15: ** esse Catilinae gloriari solet scele-
(32) i. 30: *urbe incendio et caedis metu liberata
(34) iv. 7: Brutorum genus et nomen ad libertatem P. R.
vii. 15: firmissimam oppugnarit, imperatorem P. R.
(36) viii. 33: *si quis eorum qui cum M. Antonio sunt fecerit
(38) i. 33: in te sordidum, nihil humile cognovi. Quamquam
(67) ii. 62: tum sibi non hanc quam nunc male tuetur, sed M. Pisonis domum ubi habitaret legerat
(73) ii. 9: solum sed etiam amentiae. Quod enim verbum in istis litteris non est plenum humanitatis
(143) ii. 3: *sed hoc idcirco commemoratum a te puto ut[1] te infimo ordini commendares, cum omnes recordarentur libertini generum et liberos tuos nepotes Q. Fadi, libertini hominis, fuisse
(1419) x. 8–10: ** populus Romanus . . . omnis in-
(1423) ii. 93–6: *sunt ea . . . defendimus

Also, the long passage v. 31–vi. 18.

Here we have two telescoped lines of 30 and 31 letters. It will also be noticed that there are two omissions of 28.

I have already referred to the long omissions in x. 8–10, ii. 93–6,

[1] *V* has *uit*. Halm reads *uti*.

v. 31–vi. 18 as corresponding to 33, 34, and 527 lines of Teubner text (p. 172).

The omission of 143 letters admits of more than one explanation. The figure is almost twice the one which precedes it, 73, which may $= 36 \times 2$, or 24×3. On the other hand $28 \times 5 = 140$. It seems rather to be connected with the figures which follow, viz. 1,419 and 1,423.

The question now arises whether the telescoped passages of 30 and 31 in *D* are to be connected with those of 27, 28, 30, and 31 in *V*.

There are two passages in which omissions of *V* and *D* occur in close proximity, viz.:

vii. 14: ** nisi paruerit huic ordini quid re- (28) *om. V*
ib.: multo postea gravius urguebamur[1] (28) *om. D*

The intervening letters number 368 ($28 \times 13 = 364$).

Here we seem to be on the track of the common ancestor (*P*), which appears to have had:

paratum illi exitium	
nisi paruerit huic ordini quid re	(28)
fert tamen opinio est grauis mis	(27)
sos enim legatos omnes uident decre	(30)
ti nostri non omnes uerba nouerunt	(29)
retinenda est igitur nobis con	(26)
stantia grauitas perseuerantia	(28)
repetenda uetus illa seueritas si	(29)
quidem auctoritas senatus decus	(28)
honestatem laudem dignitatemque	(29)
desiderat quibus rebus hic ordo ca	(29)
ruit nimium diu sed erat tunc excu	(28)
satio oppressis misera illa quidem	(30)
sed tamen iusta nunc nulla est li	(27)
berati regio dominatu uidebamur	(28)
multo postea grauius urguebamur	(28)
armis domesticis.	

l. 2 *om. V* l. 16 *om. D* (ὁμ.)

xii. 16: si accipiendam cur non rogamur si (28) *om. D* (*suo loco*)
ib.: **-cear in quo ne si dissensero quidem a (30) *om. V*

In this case the writer seems to have passed from *-cear* to *ceteris* in the line below.

[1] So *V*, not *urge-*.

P seems to have had:

si accipiendam cur non rogamur si (28)
postulandam quid timemus in hac (27)
ego legatione sim aut ad id consili (29)
um admiscear in quo ne si dissense (28)
ro quidem a ceteris

l. 1 *om. D* (*suo loco*) ll. 4–5 admisceteris (*med. om.*) *V*

Interesting evidence is also afforded by ii. 93–6 *sunt ea . . . defendimus.*

Here *D* omits the whole passage, going on immediately to § 97:

Quid ego de commentariis infinitis, quid de innumerabilibus chirographis loquar?

V in § 97 has:

Quid ego de commentariis
infinitis quid de innu
merabilibus cyrographis
loquar

but in § 93, before *sunt ea*, inserts:

Quid ego de cōmenta
ris caesaris infinitos
quidennumerabilibus
cyrigraphis caesaris lo
quar.

This looks like a corrupt version of the passage, which has been inserted a folio too soon (cf. p. 166 on xi. 18–20) in an ancestor of *V*. If we suppose that there was a loose folio in *P* here, the addition of the variant in *V* and the omission of the leaf by *D* are at once explicable.

There are other proofs which will be mentioned later on in the discussion. The evidence already adduced seems to show that *V* and *D* are derived from a common ancestor with an average line of about 28 letters. This ancestor must be prior to the parent of *V* first arranged in three columns.

Here I would call attention to de Ricci's fragment of the *pro Plancio*, cent. v, to which reference has already been made. This exhibits with exactitude the formation revealed by this analysis, viz. 28 letters to the line.

Before I discuss further the relation of *V* and *D* to *P*, it will be best to clear the way by dealing with some corruptions peculiar to

V, which appear to have been inherited from one or more ancestors in three columns (*U*). Most of them are simple cases, e.g. repetitions from the context and variants which have got into the wrong place. I give first the reading of *V*, and then that which I attribute to *U*. The passages are arranged in order of length.

ii. 68. *V* has: os impurissimum ostenim
portumnissimum dere
U (?): os
impurissimum osten (17) *mg.* importunissimum
dere

viii. 9. *V* has: inuitus
dico ha sed dicendum est ista
caesaris
U (?): inuitus dico
sed dicendum est ista (18) *mg.* ha
caesaris

Halm says 'apparet correctionem *ha,* quae post *dico* legitur, ex margine in alienum locum illatum esse.'

ii. 69. *V* has: pro conclavibus popinae triclinis
U (?): pro
conclauibus popinae (18) *mg.* triclinis

viii. 7. *V* has: ut clarissimi
morú hominú clarudeissi
mā p oeniretur necem
U (?): ut
clarissimorum hominū (19)
crudelissimam poeni (18)
retur necem

The writer of *V* looked back from l. 2 to l. 1 and conflated the two adjectives.

iii. 31. *V* has: imperator quas effecerit
strages imperatori ubicūq:
posuit uestigium
U (?): imperator *mg.* imperatori
quas effecerit strages (20)
ubicumque

ii. 74. *V* has: dicebatur esse
cum inte inuehens sic

ad quo caesar in senatu
in
aperte inte inte uehens
quaestus est

U (?): dicebatur esse cum
sica de quo caesar in (17)
senatu aperte in te (16) *mg.* in te inuehens
uehens

iii. 17. *V* has: cõpellat edicto nescenti
tamen **s** commendationem
esse con pellationem **ã**

U (?): edicto nescit tamen
commendationem es (16)
se compellationem ^ (16) *mg.* ^ suam

In *V s* and *ã* are additions by the second hand. This is a remarkable instance of a phenomenon not infrequent in *V*, viz. that a word is bisected and the *disiecta membra* are scattered.

xi. 1. *V* has: enim quam arma coepert
a in hiis qui contra patriã
is scelerata arma coeperunt
inesset immanitas.

Here *arma coeper* is a *v. l.* for *arma coeperunt*, which has got into the text between *quam* and *ta*, i. e. *quanta*.

U (?): enim quan
ta in hiis qui contra (17)
patriam iscelerata (17)
arma coeperunt *mg.* arma coeper.

v. 24. *V*[1] gives: circumsedem utinam
ṇịạ̃ firmissimam et splen
didissimam populi roma
ni coloniam.

U (?): mutinam
firmissimam et splen (18)
didissimam P. R. colo (16)
niam

The copyist looked forward two lines.

viii. 22. *V* has: mihi quidem ạṃịṣ
ṣị ṣụṇṭ nullum quãuis de
illo ad quem missi sunt be
ne existiment

U (?): mihi quidem
nullum quamuis de il (17)
lo ad quem missi sunt (17) *mg.* amissi sunt

iii. 21. *V* has: nec poterat aliter .ci. aliteri de
aduersaris iudicari ducibus si
igur Caesar hostis.

Here *aliteri* is a *duplex lectio* for *aliter*, and *igur* a slip for *igitur*. For *Caesar* the reading of *D* is *C. Caesar*, and I take *.ci.* in l. 1 to represent *C.*

U (?): aliter *mg.* aliteri
de aduersaris iudica (18)
ri ducibus, si igitur (17)
mg. ∧ C. ∧ Caesar hostis

ii. 75. *V* has: cum
peterent armis ii quo
rum erant legibus est
in rebus iniquissimis
rum erant legibus quid
potest esse equi

Here *est* (l. 3) = *etsi.*

U (?): cum
peterent armis ii quo
rum erant legibus est (18)
in rebus iniquissimis (19)
quid potest esse aequi

V repeats *rum erant legibus* after *iniquissimis.*

I would here mention a dittography of 37 letters in *V*, viz.:

ii. 115: ne metus quidem a foedissimis factis potest *bis scr.*

This seems to represent two lines of *U.*

ii. 54. *V* has: consules ex italiae
expul ịṃp̣ẹṛị p̣ọp̣ụḷị
ni cum
ṛọṃạ sos que iis CN.
pompeium quod imperi
decus ac lumen fuit.

Here *imperi populi roma* is a *v. l.* for *imperi* in l. 4, which has been sandwiched between the two parts of *expulsos.*

U (?): ex italia expul
sos·cumque iis CN (14)
pompeium quod imperi (18) *mg.* imperi populi roma
decus ac lumen fuit

iii. 8. *V* has: neque enim tarquinio
expulso maioribus nr̃is
tam fuit optata libertas
quam est depluso maio
ribus nr̃is tam antonio
retinenda

U (?): neque enim
tarquinio expulso
maioribus nr̃is tam (16)
fuit optata liber (15)
tas quam est depulso (17)
antonio retinenda

The repetition of *maioribus nostris tam* is due to ὁμ. (*expulso* . . . *depulso*).

ii. 39. Here *U* seems to have had:

quid
de me senserit sciunt (18)
qui eum de pharsalia (17)
fuga paphum persecu (17)
ti sunt numquam ab eo (17)
mentio de me

V has *quid ment de me senserit*. The writer looked forward five lines, the error being due to ὁμ. (*de me*).

vi. 3. *V* has: discessio facta non
esset tamen praeter pau
cos ḥọṃịṇẹṣ omnes mihi
adsensuri uiderentur
|||| hodierno autem dieṣ
ṇọṇ ẹṣṭ pene
scio quaeis obiectarem
missior senatus fuit.

Here *non est* in l. 6 is a *v. l.* for *non esset* (l. 1), which has been sandwiched between *s* and *pe*, i.e. *spe*. (The passage as printed by editors is *spe nescio qua eis obiecta remissior*.)

U (?): discessio facta
non esset tamen prae (17) *mg.* non est
ter paucos omnes mihi (18)
adsensuri uiderentur (19)
hodierno autem dies (17)
pene scio quaeis obiec
ta remissior

ii. 30. *V* has: ergo ego isceleratus
appelloratho quem tu
suspicatum aliquid sus
picaris ille qui stillantẽ
prae se pugionem tulit is
autenoris causa nomi
natur.

Here we have to notice the corruptions *appelloratho* (= *appellor a te*) in l. 2 and *autenoris* (=*a te honoris*) in l. 6.

U (?): ergo ego isce
leratus appellor a te (18)
quem tu suspicatum ali (19)
quid suspicaris ille (18)
qui stillantẽ prae se (18)
pugionem tulit is a te ^ (18) *mg.* ^ ho
noris causa nominatur

The marginal addition *ho-* was added to *a te* in l. 2 instead of to *a te* in l. 6.

ix. 3. *V* has: nisi seruilio cui
respondendum putarẽ qui
hunc honorẽ statue nemi
ni tribuendũ censuit nisi ei
p. qui ferro esset

Halm says 'videtur hoc *p* ad *Servilio* pertinere et ex margine falso loco hic suppletum esse'. For *cui* in l. 1 editors read *clarissimo viro* (i. e. *c. u.*)

U (?): nisi *mg.* p.
seruilio cui responden (20)
dum putarẽ qui hunc ho (18)
norẽ statue nemini tri (19)
buendũ censuit nisi ei (19)
qui ferro esset

Here *p* was inserted after *nisi ei* in l. 5 instead of after *nisi* in l. 1.

ii. 58. *V* has: uehebatur
in essedo TR. pl. litores lau
reati antecedebant inte
quos aperta lectica mima
portabatur in esse dot
R. pl. lictores laureati

antecedebant inter quos q̃·
ex oppidis

Here the corruption is due to the variants *in essedo tr. pl.* and *in esse dot R. pl.*

U (?): uehebatur
mg. in esse dot R. pl.
in essedo TR. PL. lic (15)
tores laureati an (15)
tecedebant inter (15)
quos aperta lecti (15)
ca mima portabatur (16)
quam ex oppidis

The variant was inserted after *portabatur*, and the words *lictores . . . inter quos* were repeated.

ii. 56: Hominem omnium nequissimum] *V* inserts *in eodem vero* before *hominem.* Halm says 'aberravit scriba ad v. 23'.

U (?): hominẽ omniũ nequis (17)
simũ qui non dubitaret (19)
uel in foro alea ludere (19)
lege quae est de alea (17)
condemnatũ qui in inte (19
grũ restituit is non a (18)
pertissime studiũ su (18)
um ipse profitetur (16)
In eodem uero

The scribe looked forward nine lines.

ix. 4. *V* has: nemo ṛũṃạx̣ịṃẹ
q̣· ụṭ ṇẹp̣ọṭẹṇṣ ṛẹg̣ịṣ ạṇṭịọc̣ḥị ẹịụṣ
q̣ụị c̣ũ ṃạịọṛịḅụṣ ṇr̃ịṣ ḅẹḷḷú g̣ẹṣṣẹṛạṭ
uirtutem non honorabat.
At ea fuit legatio octaui in qua
periculi suspicio non subesset ná
cũ esset missus a senatu ad animos
regum respiciendos liberorum
q· populorũ maximeq· ut nepotẽ
regis antiochi eius qui cum ma
ioribus nr̃is bellum gesserat
classes habere

Here the words struck out after *nemo* occur subsequently *suo loco.*

U (?): nemo
uirtutem non honora (17)
bat at ea fuit legatio (18)

octaui in qua pericu (17)
li suspicio non subes (18)
set nam cum esset mis (17)
sus a senatu ad animos (18)
regum respiciendos (17)
liberorumque populo (18)
rũ maximeq· ut nepotẽ (17)
regis antiochi eius (17)
qui cum maioribus nos (18)
tris bellũ gesserat (17)

The writer of *V* omitted lines 2–9; then, after copying lines 10–13, he discovered his mistake and rewrote the whole passage.

The two most singular combinations of variants are in:

(a) viii. 5: D. Brutus oppugnatur: non est bellum. Mutina obsidetur: ne hoc quidem bellum est.

V has: domitius brutus oppug
natur. non est bellum. mutine
dominaretur seturna opside
turne hoc quidem bellũ est

Halm says 'quid lateat plane ignoratur. Vide tamen ne verba inepta ex loco inferiore p. 1329. 9 huc invecta sint.' The reference is to § 7:

rursus cum Mario et Carbone Sulla, ne dominarentur indigni

Halm does not attempt to explain *seturna*. Müller (with Lehmann) reads *Mutina vetus et firma colonia obsidetur*, a very bold alteration.

It is to be noticed that in § 7 *V* reads *dominarentur* correctly, while in § 5 it has *dominaretur*. The natural inference is that a *v. l.* has migrated from the margin in § 7 to the text in § 5. With regard to the strange word *seturna*, I would point out that *V* has incorrectly *Mutine* for *Mutina*. It looks as if *-na*, a correction, had been conflated with the termination of *obsidetur*. If so, *U* may have had:

mutine obsidetur ne *mg.* na
hoc quidem

the correction being placed over the wrong *-ne*.

Since I shall have to refer subsequently to this passage, I will here mention that the intervening words between *Mutina* and *dominarentur* occupy 27½ lines of Teubner text and consist of 1,166 letters (i. e. allowing official abbreviations).

(b) vi. 10.

Here we are wholly dependent on *V*, which gives:

ris quamtius plancius
uidete quan decertum est
ut exercitum citra flu
men rubiconem qui fi
nis est galliae educeret
dum ne propius urbem
romam ducenta milia
admoueret huic denun
tiationi ille pareat tum
exiluerit adulescens no
bilis
Plancum qui

The words *uidete quan decertum est* have been inserted by m. 2 either in a lacuna or over an erasure. The passage which has been struck out, *ut exercitum . . . pareat*, comes from § 5, where *V* has:

ante decretum est ut exercitum citra $\overset{\text{flu}}{\text{mẽ}}$ (rubiconem *add. in mg.*) qui finis est Galliae educeret dum ne plus urbem Roman $\overset{\text{CC}}{\text{mil.}}$ admoueret huic denuntiationi ille pareat

In § 10 *decertum est* obviously = *decretum est.* The words *uidete quan* are omitted by editors without comment.

With regard to *uidete quan*, it is to be remembered that in § 5 *decretum* is preceded by *ante.* I recognize the two parts of this, viz. *an-* *-te*, in *-te an-*. These have been combined with *uide* and *qu-*. What do these stand for? The answer must, I think, be *quidem.* If so, *quidem* is out of place. A proper place for it would be after *Plancum* in l. 12, viz. 'Plancum *quidem*, qui . . . ita maestus rediit ut retractus non reversus videretur, sic contemnit tamquam si illi aqua et igni interdictum sit'. In my edition of 1900 I had proposed to insert *quidem* at this place.

As there are several variants between the passages in §§ 5 and 10, it seems probable that an alternative version was by error copied on the wrong folio of an ancestor, not necessarily the immediate model. This suggestion will be discussed later on. Here I will only mention that the intervening passage, viz. §§ 5–10 *ille se fluvio . . . quam T. Plancus* occupies 54¼ lines of Teubner text.

I now turn to *P*, the common ancestor of *V* and *D*. I will first repeat the telescoped passages in *V* and *D* which bear witness to it, viz.:

(27) i. 7: nec ita multum provectus reiect- *om.* V^1
(28) vii. 14: nisi paruerit huic ordini quid re- *om.* *V*
(30) v. 20: habebat possessor quantum relique- *om.* *D*
xii. 16: -cear in quo ne si dissensero quidem a *om.* *V*
(31) ii. 118: contempsi Catilinae gladios non per- *om.* V^1
iv. 15: esse Catilinae gloriari solet scele- *om.* *D*

The regularity with which 28 appears as the unit in the larger omissions and corruptions suggests that some lines were shorter, e. g. 25–6. We may, therefore, not unreasonably suppose that the following omissions may represent single lines of *P*.

(25) ii. 72: ego leges perniciosas rogavi *om.* *V*
iii. 15: non contemnit is qui Aricinum *om.* V^1
xi. 13: quorum alter commentatus est *om.* *V*
(26) ii. 71: *quid fuit causae cur in Africam *om.* *V*
xiii. 5: *per deos immortales quas in eos *om.* V^1
(27) v. 4: quam senatus si quidem legiones *om.* V^1
(28) vii. 14: multo postea gravius urguebamur *om.* *D*
xii. 16: si accipiendam, cur non rogamur si *om.* *D*
(29) x. 21: legio fregit IV affixit sic a suis *om.* V^1
(31) ix. 2: non morbus ingravescens retardavit[1] *om.* V^1

In the last passage Halm records V^2 as adding *cum* after *retardavit*, but this is not supported by my notes.

The most interesting of these passages is v. 4. Here *V* gives:

honestiora decreta
esse legiones h̄ decre
uerunt senatum de
fendere

and in the margin:

h̄ m. quã senatus si quidem legiones

Here *h. m.* (= *hic minus*) is a rare omission-symbol, which occurs elsewhere in *V*, viz. vii. 6 (cf. p. 34).

As a matter of fact what V^1 has omitted here is *legionum quam*

[1] Halm says '*non morbus ingravescens retardavit cum*, quae V^1 *om.*, supplevit m. 2'. According to my notes, *V* has:

n̄ morb' (*m.* 2, *sup. lin.*)
non asperitatis uiarumq· ịaṃ.
ingrauescens retardauit (*m.* 2, *sup. lin.*)
ad congressum conloquiũq· ei',

i. e. *cum* is not added by V^2.

senatus si quidem, not *quam senatus si quidem legiones*. Also, the omission-symbol is out of place. It should come after *esse*.

It will be convenient to put together at this point some passages where variants of *V* or *D* appear to be due to their derivation from an ancestor written in lines of this length.

ii. 85: unus inventus es qui cum auctor regni esses eumque quem collegam habebas dominum habere velles

Here *regni* is added by *D* after *collegam*.

P (?): cum auctor
regni esses eumque quem collegam (28)
habebas

Regni was repeated from the previous line.

§ 110: An supplicationes addendo diem contaminari passus es, pulvinaria noluisti?

So *D*: *V* adds *contaminari* after *pulvinaria*.

P (?): addendo diem
contaminari passus es, puluinaria (29)
noluisti

Here the same explanation applies.

§ 115: non intellegis qui isto modo iudicia non timeat, ei quid timendum sit

Here *V* has:

non intel
e
legeṛịs qui isto modo iudi
cia non timeat ẹṭ quid ti
mendum sit

In *D ei* is added after *intellegis*, while *et* (i. e. *ei*) is omitted before *quid*.

P (?): non intellegis
qui isto modo iudicia non timeat ^ (27) *mg.* ei

iii. 36: sunt impii cives, sed pro caritate rei publicae nimium multi, contra multitudinem bene sentientium admodum pauci

So *V.*: sed *om. D.*

The proper place for *sed* is before *contra*.

P (?): sunt impii ciues
pro caritate rei p. nimium multi (26) *mg.* sed
contra multitudinem

iv. 4: quod autem praesidium erat salutis libertatisque vestrae, si C. Caesaris fortissimorum sui patris militum exercitus non fuisset?

So *V*: suique *D*.

Here *-que* may = *Quirites* ($\tilde{Q}$), which has got into the wrong place. It would come in admirably after *vestrae*.

P (?): libertatisque uestrae *mg.* Q̃.
si C. Caesaris fortissimorum sui (27)
patris militum

vii. 4: aduersarium multitudinis temeritati haec fecit aduersatum praeclarissima causa popularem *V*

aduersatum multitudinis temeritati haec fecit praeclarissima causa popularem *D*

P (?): aduersarium *mg.* aduersatum
multitudinis temeritati haec fecit (31)
praeclarissima causa popularem

viii. 32: diutiusque seruitutem perpessi quam captiui frugi et diligentes solent *D*

V adds *serui* after *captiui*.

P (?): diutiusque
seruitutem perpessi quam captiui (29)
frugi et diligentes solent

V repeats *serui* from the previous line.

ix. 2: cumque iam ad congressum colloquiumque eius peruenisset ad quem erat missus in ipsa cura ac meditatione obeundi sui muneris excessit e uita *D*

V has: ad congressũ conloquiũq· ei'
in ipsa cura ac mediaue p
uenisset ad quẽ erat missus
in ipsa cura ac meditatio
ne

P (?): peruenisset ad quem erat missus (27) *mg.* in ipsa cura
in ipsa cura ac meditatione ac mediaue

ib. § 4: quorum statuae steterunt usque ad meam memoriam in rostris *V*

In *D* the words *in rostris* come before *steterunt*.

P (?): quorum statuae
steterunt usque ad meam memoriam (28) *mg.* in rostris.

xi. 26: non ut ex ea acie respectum haberemus, sed ut ipsa acies subsidium haberet transmarinum *D* (*defic. V*)

Editors mark *ea* as corrupt: it would come better before *ipsa*.

P (?): non ut ex
acie respectum haberemus sed ut (27) *mg.* ea
ipsa acies subsidium haberet

We also find multiples of 28, e.g.:

(*a*) $28 \times 2 = 56$.

v. 30: quo die primum convocati sumus, cum designati consules non adessent, ieci sententia mea maximo vestro consensu fundamenta rei publicae

So *D* and edd.: *V* has:

con
uocati sumus cũ designati
consules non adessent ieci
sententia mea maximo
úro consensu adfuissem
cum fundamenta reipub
licae

Halm says of *adfuissem cum* 'manifestum est glossema, saltem nescimus quid lateat'. The words appear to stand for *adfui ipse cum*, the error being due to the vulgar spelling *isse* for *ipse*.

The sense required is *adfui ipse cum designati consules non adessent.* Cf. *Sull.* 81 non adfuit alio in iudicio cum adessent ceteri; *Phil.* i. 36 cum adesse ipsis propter vim armorum non licebat, aderant tamen; iii. 19 edixit ut adesset senatus . . . eo die ipse non adfuit, &c., &c.

The words *adfui ipse* or *adfui ipse cum* appear to have been first omitted and then inserted in the margin of *P*, e.g.:

conuocati sumus *mg.* adfuissem cum
designati cos. non adessent ieci sen (30)
tentia mea maximo uestro consensu (29)
fundamenta rei p.

ix. 14: sed statuae intereunt tempestate vi vetustate, sepulcrorum autem sanctitas in ipso solo est quod nulla vi moveri neque deleri potest

The first *vi* is omitted by V^1: V^2 gives *uel,* while in *D* we have the variants ·*u*·, ·*ui*·, *ui.* There seem to have been *duplices lectiones,* viz. *ui* and *uel.*

P (?): tempestate
uetustate sepulcrorum autem sanc (29)
titas in ipso solo est quod nulla ui (29) *mg.* uel
moueri

x. 15: etsi est enim Brutorum commune factum et laudis societas aequa, Decimo tamen iratiores erant qui id factum dolebant, quo minus ab eo rem illam dicebant fieri debuisse.

Here *eo* seems to be required with *iratiores*, to correspond with *quo minus* (Naugerius).

V has *cō* before *Brutorum*. This may be a corruption for *eo*, which has got out of place.

P (?): etsi est enim
brutorum commune factum et lau (26)
dis societas aequa decimo tamen (27) *mg.* eo
iratiores

(*b*) 28 × 3 = 84.

To this I should refer the omission of *V* in ii. 79:

qui tum est impulsus inductus elusus. Qua in re quanta fuerit uterque vestrum perfidia in Dolabellam (84).

Before I had recollated *V*, I had arranged the reading of its ancestor thus:

nihil queror de dolabella
qui tum est impulsus indictus elu (28)
sus qua in re quanta fuerit uterque (29)
uestrum perfidia in dolabellam (27)

I afterwards found that V^2 arranges the supplement at the foot of the page in three lines, thus:

qui tũ est impulsus inductus elusus
qua in re quam fuerit utterq;
uestrum perfidia in dolabella

The coincidence in the arrangement is striking.

There is an interesting dislocation in ii. 27. I write the passage as I imagine it to have stood in *P*:

Cn. domitium non patris interitus (28)
c. u. non auunculi mors non spoliatio (29)
dignitatis ad reciperandam liber (29)
tatem sed mea auctoritas excitauit (30)
an C. trebonio ego persuasi cui ne (27)
suadere quidem ausus essem quo et (28)
iam maiorem ei res p. gratiam debet (28)

I write *c. u.* (= *clarissimi uiri*) in l. 2, since this seems to have been used in the archetype (cf. ix. 3 *cui* V^1: *c. u.* V^2: *cum t*: *om. cett.*).

Here lines 5–7 *an C. . . . debet* (83) are placed before lines 1–4 *Cn. domitium . . . excitauit* (116) in *V*.

ii. 94. Here *V*, our sole authority (*defic. D*), gives:

quidquam aequi
boni imperauit aput
mortuum factũ ẽ grat̃
compellerat hospitẽ
praesens computarat
pecuniam impetrarat

Here it is usual to read *impetravit* in l. 2 and *imperarat* in l. 6 (so Poggio). It seems more likely that *impetrarat* is a *v. l.* for *imperavit* (or *impetravit*), which has got into the wrong place.

P (?): quidquam aequi boni
imperauit aput mortuum factus (26) *mg*. impetrarat
est gratus compellarat hospitem (28)
praesens computarat pecuniam (26)

For *gratus*, in all probability. *gratiosus* (Ubaldinus) should be read.

xiv. 14: quemquamne fuisse tam sceleratum qui hoc fingeret, tam furiosum qui crederet? Unde igitur ista suspicio vel potius unde iste sermo? Cum, ut scitis, hoc triduo vel quadriduo

Here, for *furiosum*, *t*, the best member of *D* (*defic. V*), gives *fuit*. Later on, *t* inserts *fusum* (so *b*, *susum*) after *triduo vel*. This appears to be a variant for *furiosum*, which has got into the wrong place.

P (?): tam sceleratum qui hoc fingeret, tam
fuit qui crederet unde igitur is (27) *mg*. fusum
ta suspicio uel potius unde iste (27)
sermo cum ut scitis hoc triduo uel (28)
quadriduo

xiii. 19: eoque ipso die innumerabilia senatus consulta fecit quae quidem omnia citius delata quam scripta sunt (87)

These words present great difficulty in their present context, since Cicero is speaking of Antony's headlong flight from Rome. Possibly there has been a dislocation of three lines in *P*. The passage would come in suitably after *polliceretur* (supr.).

(*c*) $28 \times 4 = 112$.

i. 11: priusquam de re publica dicere incipio, pauca querar de hesterna M. Antoni iniuria, cui sum amicus, idque me non nullo eius officio debere esse prae me semper tuli. Quid tandem erat causae cur in senatum hesterno die tam acerbe cogerer *D*

priusquam de re publica dicere incipio pauca quaerar hs de hesterna in senatum tam acerbe cogerer (*med. om.*) *V*

Here *hs*, the common symbol for an omission, has got into the text. V^2 supplies at the foot of the page the ordinary reading, as given by *D*. Halm, however, points out that the collocation of words at the end of the sentence must have been different in the ancestor of *V*, viz. *cur die hesterno in senatum*, not *cur in senatum hesterno die*. The omission is due to ὁμ.

P (?): de hesterna
M. antoni iniuria cui sum amicus id (28)
que me non nullo eius officio debe (28)
re esse prae me semper tuli quid tan (29)
dem erat causae cur die hesterno (27)
in senatum tam acerbe cogerer

There are here three stages in the process of corruption, viz.:

(1) lines 2–5 were omitted;

(2) the correction with the sign *hs* was written in the margin;

(3) it was inserted in the text in the wrong place, viz. before *de hesterna*, instead of after these words.

It is therefore likely that the original omission goes back to *P*.

(*d*) $28 \times 5 = 140$.

ii. 3: sed hoc idcirco commemoratum a te puto, ut te infimo ordini commendares, cum omnes recordarentur libertini generum et liberos tuos nepotes Q. Fadi, libertini hominis, fuisse (143) *om. D*

I am inclined to refer this omission of *D* back to *P*. The relation of this, the largest omission of *D* (apart from the three large lacunae) to 280, the longest omission of *V* (vii. 6), should be noticed.

We may also compare:

i. 36: populi quidem Romani iudicia multa ambo habetis quibus vos non satis moveri permoleste fero

Here *vos non* is a correction made by Poggio. *V* has *uobis* without *non*, while both words are omitted by *D*.

Shortly afterwards, for *quid duobus tribunis pl. qui vobis adversantur*, *V* gives:

qud ii. T.R. P. quiuobis
ụọ[1] aduersantur

[1] Halm erroneously quotes *V* as reading *vobis non*.

Here *uo* may = *vos*, a correction for *vobis* after *quibus*, which got into the text of *V* after the second *vobis*, while *D* omitted the corruption. The words *vobis satis . . . tr. pl. qui* = 140 letters.

P (?):

	quibus		
	uobis satis moueri permoleste fe	(28)	*mg.* uos
	ro quid enim gladiatoribus clamo	(28)	
	res innumerabilium ciuium quid	(27)	
	populi uersus quid pompei statuae	(29)	
	plausus infiniti quid .ii. tr. pl. qui	(28)	
	uobis aduersantur		

(*e*) 28 × 10 = 280.

vii. 6: usus, consuetudo . . . esse dico sed *om. V.*

For the sake of clearness I write the passage as I conceive it to have stood in *P*:

ab ineunte illius aeta	
te usus consuetudo studiorum eti	(28)
am honestissimorum societas simi	(29)
litudoque deuinxit eiusdemque	(27)
cura incredibilis in asperrimis	(28)
belli ciuilis periculis perspec	(28)
ta docuit non modo salutis sed eti	(28)
am dignitatis meae fuisse fauto	(27)
rem tamen eundem ut dixi nisi talis	(29)
cons. esset negare esse cons. aude	(27)
rem idem non modo cons. esse dico sed	(29) = 280
memoria mea praestantissimum	

For this *V* gives:

ab ineunte illius
h. m. pagate memoria mea
praestantissimum

Here *h. m.* is the omission mark, previously noted on v. 4 (see p. 186). I would suggest that *pag.* = *pagina*. If so, the passage should contain a clue to the pagination of some intermediate ancestor. It is to be observed that the omission mark is again out of place. It should come before *memoria*.

V, therefore, has here omitted lines 2–11 of *P*. A later hand (cent. xii) has added at the foot of the page the passage as found in *D*, viz. l. 1 *aetate illius*, 6–7 *perspexi non modo*, l. 11 *sed etiam*. This supplement is obviously drawn from a different source.

The missing passage occurs later on in the text of *V*, § 11 *ad bellum proficiscerentur quod erat bellum* between *quod* and *erat bellum*. Before *proficiscerentur V* has the letter *.R.*, for which Halm conjectured *Roma*. I interpret it as ℞ (i. e. *require*), a critical mark which has got into the text. As given by *V* in § 11, the passage runs as follows:

ad bellum .R.
proficiscerentur quod [te
usus consuetudo studio
rum societas similitudoq.
deuinxit eiusdemq. cura
incredibilis in asperum (with v over "incredibilis" and r over "asperum")
is belli ciuilis periculis p̣
specta docuit non modo sa
lutis sed etiam dignitatis
meae fuisse factorẽ tamen
eundem ut dixi nisi talis
esset consul negare esse
consulem auderem idem
non modo consulem esse
dico sed] erat bellũ

The natural inference here is that ten lines of *P* were originally omitted and subsequently entered on the wrong page of an intermediate MS. I will, therefore, mention that the intervening passage, viz. §§ 6–11 *memoria mea . . . proficiscerentur quod* = 54½ lines of Teubner text, and contains 2,270 letters.

So far we have been concerned with the number of letters in a line of *P*. The next point to inquire into is the number of lines to a page. Here we have two clues, viz. (*a*) the dislocations in *V* after xi. 17 (cf. p. 172) and (*b*) the mutilations in *D*.

The first point to consider is whether these represent leaves of the same MS., or whether they are separate phenomena. The first hypothesis has the merit of simplicity, since then one explanation, viz. that of loose leaves in *P*, will apply. The evidence is as follows. I take (*a*) first.

The displaced blocks are

xii. 12–23: -sumus iudicare . . . nec corpo-
xiii. 1–10: a principio . . . rem acerbam

The first of these occupies 140 lines of Teubner text and the second 139¾. Their respective content in letters is 5,828 and 5,826. They are, therefore, identical.

If we divide 5,826 by 28, the result is 208 (28 × 208 = 5824). This gives a very satisfactory solution, viz. that four folios, i.e. eight pages of 26 lines (8 × 26 = 208) have been displaced. If so, the average content of a folio was 1,456 letters.

The lacunae in *D* at ii. 93–6, x. 8–10 correspond to 34 and 33 lines of Teubner. As given in *V*, the passages contain respectively 1,423 and 1,419 letters. They are, therefore, some 33–7 letters short of 1,456.

Here it must be remembered that, whereas in xii. 12–23, xiii. 1–10 we have the evidence of both *V* and *D*, in ii. 93–6 and x. 8–10 we have that of *V* only. It is possible, therefore, that *V* may have omitted a few words in each case. On the whole, I am inclined to refer both the dislocations of *V* and the omissions of *D* to the same cause.

So far I have dealt with *U*, the immediate ancestor of *V*, and *P*, the common ancestor of *U* and *D*. I have already said that *U* is a composite term, since there must have been intermediate ancestors in three columns. Their existence is shown by such complicated errors, as e.g. i. 11 *hs de hesterna* and vii. 6 *h. m. pagate.* I do not pretend to disentangle the complicated skein, but would only indicate three passages already discussed, which seem to throw light on the pagination of some intermediate MS. These are:

viii. 5: dominaretur seturna (*ex* § 7)
vi. 10: videte quan decertum . . . ille pareat (*ex* § 5)
vii. 11: -te usus . . . dico sed (*ex* § 6)

It is to be noted that the intermediate passages between vi. 5–10, viz. *ille se fluvio . . . quam T. Plancus*, and vii. 6–11, viz. *memoria mea . . . proficiscerentur quod* occupy respectively 54¼ and 54½ lines of Teubner text. Also, in viii. 5–7 the intermediate passage, viz. *obsidetur . . . Sulla ne*, occupies 27½ lines of Teubner. The relation between 27½, 54¼, and 54½ is very significant. The content of the intermediate passages as given in letters is 1,166 (viii. 5–7), 2,236 (vi. 5–10), and 2,270 (vii. 6–11). There does not seem to be any connexion between these and the other figures which I have discussed.

So far we have been enabled by the help of *V* and *D* to reconstitute their common ancestor (*P*). It remains to ask, if *P* contains any evidence which casts light on its antecedents.

There is, I think, considerable evidence to show that *P* was derived from an ancestor very similar to itself, so far as the length of line is concerned. I will call this ancestor *Q*.

I would draw attention to the following corruptions, some of which are rather complicated:

iii. 12: cum autem omnis servitus est (est omn. ser. *V*) misera, tum vero intolerabilis est servire impuro

So *VD*: except *c* (*intolerabile si*): most editors adopt *intolerabile est*, a conjecture of Poggio. The construction *cum . . . est* is very odd; we should expect *cum . . . sit*. The corruption *intolerabilis* seems due to the corruption *intolerabile si*, which is preserved by *c*, where *si* may stand either for *st* (i. e. *est*) or for *sit*.

This points to an original reading:

cum autem omnis seruitus sit
misera tum uero intolerabile est (28) *mg.* si

viii. 30: summa laus consularium vigilare, cogitare, adesse animo, semper aliquid pro re publica aut cogitare aut facere aut dicere.

So *V*: aut cogitare *om. D.*

'ut saepe in V factum invenimus, ex proxime sequentibus verbum a scriba praeceptum est, quod deinde in codd. dett. a suo loco detrusum est' Halm.

Here the proper place for *cogitare* is before *aut facere*, where it is omitted in *D*; in both *V* and *D*, however, it is found before *adesse*. The mistake, therefore, must be prior to *P*. It is possible either that *aut cogitare* was added in the margin of *Q* or that *cogitare* was a variant for *aut cogitare*. The words:

adesse animo, semper aliquid pro re p. = 30 letters.

I now turn to a very puzzling passage, v. 12.

Here *V* has:

qui
bus rebus tanta pecunia
unam in domo coacerua
ta est ut si hoc genus pene
in unum redigatur non
sit pecunia rei publicae
defutura

Pene in l. 4 is omitted by *D*: it may be a senseless variant for *pecunia* in line 2 or 6. The emendations *pecuniae* and *rapinae* have been suggested.

The reading of *V* seems to show that there was a confusion between *una in domo* (*D*) and *unam in domum* (Garatoni). If so, *unum* may be a variant which had got into the wrong place. This mistake must have been already present in *P*. If *unum* is struck out we are left with *in redigatur*. This indicates a very simple correction, viz. *iure redigatur*, which produces an excellent rhythm for the colon, while all the other emendations give the hexameter ending.

I therefore suggest that *Q* had:

una in *mg.* unum
domo coaceruata est ut si hoc genus in (31)
redigatur

The existence of this more remote ancestor throws light upon the mysterious passage i. 30 *urbe incendio et caedis metu liberata* (32), which rests on the authority of V^2 only (*om.* V^1D). It may represent a line of *Q*. As written by V^2, it is *urbe incendio et tedis metu liberat* (30). We may also notice that in v. 53, where there is a lacuna in *V* (*defic. D*), Garatoni's supplement *auctoritatem secuti libertatem P. R.* = 30 letters.

iv. 13: hanc retinete, quaeso, quam vobis tamquam hereditatem maiores vestri reliquerunt. Quamquam alia omnia falsa, incerta sint, caduca, mobilia: virtus est una altissimis defixa radicibus

So *V*: some members of *D* give *Quirites quaeso quam*, others *quaeso qr. p. r. quam*. The confusion between *Quirites* ($\tilde{Q}$) and *quam* is constant.

The subjunctive *sint* is unusual with *quamquam* (*sunt D*). Madvig strikes out *quamquam*, while Halm reads *nam cum* with P. R. Müller.

The variants point to an original reading:

hanc retinete quaeso
qũi[1] quam uobis tamquam heredita (27) *mg.* quamquam
tem maiores uestri reliquerunt (27)
alia omnia falsa

xi. 7: est enim sapientis quicquid homini accidere possit, id praemeditari ferendum modice esse, si evenerit. Maioris omnino est consili providere ne quid tale accidat, animi non minoris fortiter ferre, si evenerit *VD*

The first *si evenerit*, which has been struck out by various editors, is defended by the clausula, the second can be removed without

[1] = Quirites.

injury to the rhythm (Zielinski). The repetition may be due to the following arrangement in *Q*:

si euenerit maioris omnino est con	(29)
sili prouidere ne quid tale accidat	(30)
animi non minoris fortiter ferre	(28)

i. 31: quanto metu veterani, quanta sollicitudine civitas tum a te liberata est

The veterans were not in any danger, but they were a menace to the republican party. Various emendations have been made. The best sense is given by *senatus* (Ernesti), but there is no similarity between this word and *veterani*.[1]

As a matter of fact the reading is somewhat doubtful. I noticed in *V* that the first hand wrote *veteranis*. In *D* besides *ueterani* I find *ueteri*, *ueter*, *uetera*^{ni}. The reading, therefore, is doubtful. In view of preceding passages, we are led to ask if some corruption has been introduced from the context. Shortly above we have the passage (§ 30) *se beneficio nouo memoriam ueteris doloris abiecisse*.

Such variants as *ueterē*, *ueterēs* are common, e.g. in the palimpsest of the *de Re Publica*, p. 228, col. 2 (Van Buren). It occurred to me that the various corruptions here might be variants for the preceding *ueteris* in § 30. The words *ueteris . . . metu* consist of 300 letters (28 × 11 = 308). This indicates the following arrangement in *Q*. I postulate some original error, e.g. *ueteres* for *ueteris*.

memoriam	
ueteris doloris abiecisse hanc	(27)
tu P. dolabella magno loquor cum	(26)
dolore hanc tu inquam potuisti ae	(28)
quo animo tantam dignitatem de	(26)
ponere tu autem M. antoni absentem	(28)
enim appello unum illum diem quo	(27)
in aede telluris senatus fuit non	(28)
omnibus his mensibus quibus te qui	(29)
dam multum a me dissentientes be	(27)
atum putant anteponis quae fuit	(27)
oratio de concordia quanto metu	(27)

xi. 14: T. Annium Cimbrum, Lysidici filium, Lysidicum ipsum Graeco verbo, quoniam omnia iura dissolvit.

Graeco uerbo *V*: in Graeco uerbo *D*, *del.* Manutius

The gloss here must have been present in *P*.

Shortly afterwards for *gravem* (§ 15) *V* has a singular corruption,

[1] *Senatus* may have dropped out after *metu*.

viz. *grecauem*. This seems due to a survival of the original gloss, viz. *graec.* or *grec.*, which was afterwards expanded into *Graeco uerbo* and received into the text. Cf. *Nat. D.* i. 85 *sententiis quas appellatis* κυρίας δόξας. Here Harl. 2622 has *G̃R* in the margin, while *C* gives *sententiis G̅R̅ quas appellatis cyrias doxas.*

Here the intervening words *quoniam omnia . . . dixit enim severam* consist of 395 letters (28 × 14 = 392). This indicates the following distribution in *Q*:

lysidicum ipsum		*mg*. grec.
quoniam omnia iura dissoluit nisi	(29)	
forte iure germanum cimber occidit	(30)	
cum hanc et huius generis copiam	(27)	
tantam habeat antonius quod sce	(27)	
lus omittet cum dolabella tantis	(28)	
se obstrinxerit parricidiis nequa	(30)	
quam pari latronum manu et copia	(27)	
quapropter ut inuitus saepe dis	(27)	
sensi a Q. fufio ita sum eius senten	(28)	
tiae libenter assensus ex quo iu	(27)	
dicare debetis me non cum homine so	(29)	
lere sed cum causa dissidere itaque	(30)	
non adsentior solum sed etiam gra	(28)	
tias ago fufio dixit enim seueram	(28)	
grauem re p. dignam sententiam		

The gloss *grec.* was combined with *grauem*.

I now come to two very singular cases:

ii. 106. *V* has: incredibile dictum sed cū
uinus inter omnis consta
bat neminem esse resalu
tatum

For the corrupt words *cū uinus* we find in *D* other corruptions, viz. *et sermulcinus, et simul unũ cinus, simul.* Madvig conjectured *sum vicinus.*

It cannot, I think, be doubted that Madvig was on the right track, but his correction gives a strange sense, viz. 'it is an astonishing story, but I am a neighbour.' We should expect, 'but I heard it from neighbours.'

It occurred to me that *cū uinus* might stand not for *sum uicinus* but for *u*^ci^*nus*. In view of previous experience I looked to see if *vicinus* is found in the context. In § 104 we have *quivis amicus, vicinus, procurator arcebit.*

The words *vicinus hospes . . . dictum sed* consist of 953 letters ($28 \times 34 = 952$).

xiv. 13. Here we have *D* only, as *V* has been mutilated. I will give the reading of *t*, viz.:

> etiam in eos qui omnis suas curas in rei publicae salute defigunt impetus crimen quaeretur?

The other members of *D* add *invidia* after *crimen*, and the omission of this word by *t* seems due to accident.

The important point is that for *impetus* (*bt*) we have the variants *impeius* (*s*) and *in peius* (*cett.*). As *impetus* is here corrupt, we have to seek for an explanation in the context. The word occurs in § 15:

> tum in me impetus conductorum hominum quasi in tyrannum parabatur

The hypothesis presents itself that in § 15 there was a variant *impeius* which has got into the text in § 13.

The intervening words, viz. *crimen invidia . . . in me impetus*, consist of 951 letters. The agreement between 953 and 951 is most remarkable. The natural explanation is that both here and in ii. 104–6 a variant has been entered by error on the wrong folio. If so, *Q* contained 34 lines to a folio, i.e. 17 to a page.

I have previously remarked that de Ricci's fragment of the *pro Plancio* contains an average of 27–8 letters to the line. It also has 17 lines to the page. The formation of *Q*, therefore, as revealed by this analysis, appears to have been identical with that of this fragment.

De Ricci's fragment contains on the recto 444 letters, but there are two short lines, viz. one of 19 letters, and one, at the end of a paragraph, of 4 letters only. The verso, which has only one short line, of 22 letters, contains 474 letters. If we take 474 as normal and multiply by 2, the result is 948.

I think it worth while to write out these two passages as I conceive them to have stood in *Q*.

ii. 104–6:

mg. ci uinus

uicinus hospes procurator arce	(27)	madebant parietes ingenui pueri	(28)
bit at quam multos dies in ea uilla	(28)	cum meritoriis scorta inter matres	(30)
turpissime es perbacchatus ab ho	(28)	familias uersabantur casino salu	(29)
ra tertia bibebatur ludebatur uo	(28)	tatum ueniebant aquino interamna	(29)
mebatur o tecta ipsa misera quam	(27)	admissus est nemo iure id quidem in	(29)
dispari domino quamquam quo modo	(28)	homine enim turpissimo obsolefi	(28)
iste dominus sed tamen quam ab dis	(28)	ebant dignitatis insignia cum in	(28)
pari tenebantur studiorum enim su	(29)	de romam proficiscens ad aquinum	(28)

orum M. uarro uoluit illud non libi	(28)	accederet obuiam ei processit ut	(28)
dinum deuersorium quae in illa uil	(29)	est frequens municipium magna sa	(28)
la antea dicebantur quae cogita	(27)	ne multitudo at iste operta lecti	(28)
bantur quae litteris mandabantur	(29)	ca latus per oppidum est ut mortu	(27)
iura P. R. monimenta maiorum omnis	(27)	us stulte aquinates sed tamen in	(27)
sapientiae ratio omnisque doctri	(29)	uia habitabant quid anagnini qui	(28)
nae at uero te inquilino non enim do	(29)	cum essent deuii descenderunt	(26)
mino personabant omnia uocibus	(27)	ut istum tamquam si esset cons. sa	(27)
ebriorum natabant pauimenta uino	(29)	lutarent incredibile dictum sed	(28)
	= 477		= 476

xiv. 13–15:

crimen inuidia quaeretur scitis	(28)	unde iste sermo cum ut scitis hoc	(27)
enim per hos dies creberrimum fu	(27)	triduo uel quadriduo tristis a mu	(28)
isse sermonem me parilibus qui di	(28)	tina fama manaret inflati laeti	(27)
es hodie est cum fascibus descen	(27)	tia atque insolentia impii ciues	(28)
surum in aliquem credo hoc gladia	(28)	unum se in locum ad illam curiam ui[3]	(28)
torem aut latronem aut catilinam	(28)	ris potius suis quam rei p. infeli	(27)
esse consulatum[1] non in eum qui ne	(27)	cem congregabant ibi cum consilia	(29)
quid tale in re p. fieri posset effe	(28)	inirent de caede nostra partiren	(28)
cerit an ut ego qui catilinam haec	(28)	turque inter se qui capitolium qui	(29)
molientem sustulerim euerterim	(28)	hostia qui urbis portas occupa	(26)
afflixerim ipse extiterim[2] repen	(28)	rent ad me concursum futurum ciui	(28)
te catilina quibus auspiciis istos	(30)	tatis putabant quod ut cum inuidi	(28)
fasces augur acciperem quatenus	(28)	a mea fieret et cum uitae etiam pe	(27)
haberem cui traderem quemquamne	(28)	riculo famam istam fascium dissi	(28)
fuisse tam sceleratum qui hoc fin	(28)	pauerunt fasces ipsi ad me delatu	(28)
geret tam furiosum qui crederet un	(29)	ri fuerunt quod cum esset quasi mea	(29)
de igitur ista suspicio uel potius	(29)	uoluntate factum tum in me impetus	(29) *mg.* impcius
	= 477		= 474

I now turn to the *D* family. Various MSS. belonging to *D* were used by Halm, the most important of which is:

t = Tegernseensis, now Monacensis 18787, cent. x/xi.

In my edition of 1900 I also used:

c = Paris. 5802, cent. xiii, 6602, cent. xiii, Berol. Phil. 201, cent. xii.

n = Voss. Lat. O. 2, cent. x.

l = Brit. Mus. Regius 15 A. xiv, cent. xi.

Since then I have collated various other MSS., the most important of which is:

s = Vatic. 3228, cent. x.

The MSS. which I term *c* contain *Phil.* i–iv only. They agree with the readings quoted by Ferrarius from his *codex Colotianus*, a MS. belonging to A. Colocci. I term the group *familia Colotiana*. In *Phil.* i–iv *c* frequently agrees with *V* as against the other

[1] so *t*. [2] so *codd.* [3] so *t*.

members of *D*. An interesting feature in this group of MSS. is that they are derived from an ancestor written in insular script. This is shown by the corruptions for *autem*, due to misunderstanding of the insular sign *h*. In the two Paris MSS. *autem* is continually corrupted to *hoc*, *haec*, *huius*, or confused with *enim* (ꞁꞁ). In the Berlin MS., wherever the first hand gives *h*, a corrector adds ꞁꞁ above it, and then above this writes *enim* in full.[1]

Vat. 3228 (*s*) is the MS. which Ferrarius calls *codex Scalae*. It occupies the next place in the Vatican library to another MS. used by Ferrarius, Vat. 3227, which he termed his *Langobardicus*, a twelfth-century MS. It is singular that *s* should have remained neglected until now, since Vat. 3227 (*v*), which is inferior to it in age and value, was collated in *Phil.* xiv by E. Freiburg for Halm.

Though inferior to *t* in value, *s* is equal or superior to it in antiquity. The script of *s* varies in character. It is mainly Caroline, but in places the scribe seems to be imitating an old French model. A number of critical marks are used, the most frequent being *r̃* (= *require*), which is sometimes combined with *t̃* or *at̃*, e.g.:

viii. 28: usi] sed *s*: *sup. lin.* r̃ t̃ si
xii. 27: tuti] ut *s*: *mg.* r̃ at̃ si hic

The omission signs are *hd*, *hh*.

There are great similarities between *s* and *t*, e.g.:

i. 10: praesentes] praesentes dixit pro populo praesentes *t*: sequens dixit pro populo praesentes *s* (above "dixit": t̃ cū p̃sens)

x. 15: Brutorum commune factum et laudis societas aequa, Decimo tamen iratiores *V*: Brutorum actiones *st* (*med. om.*)

xi. 13: emptor tamen in ea auctione] emptoriaamenea auctione *t*: emptori à à *s*

There is no doubt that the form of the text found in *t* is prior to that of *s*. On the other hand *s* appears to be an ancestor of *l*.

On various occasions marginal notes in *s* have been incorporated in the text by *l*. Thus xiii. 8 *s* has:

pignorib.
magnis multisq: itineribus m. lepidū r. p. obligatū tenet. sūma nobi
ei'
Bonitas. M. lep̄. litas om̄is honor ⁖ amplissimū sacerdotiū. plurima urbis orna m̄
ta

[1] *Class. Rev.*, xiv (1900), p. 41.

Here *l* has:

plurima bonitas M. lepidi urbis ornamenta

Other cases are xi. 8 *crudelitas Dolabellae*, 33 *laus Deiotari regis*.
Also variants in *s* are conflated by *l*, e.g.:

i. 21: populi Romani] publicae rei *s*, *sup. lin.* populi romani: populi romani plubice rei *l*

ii. 59: tu quaesisti] tu que sis te *s*, *sup. lin.* ꝉ dedisti: ꝉ dedisti tum que siste *l*

In the following case a conjecture in *s* is adopted by *l*:

x. 14: Italia] fatalia *s*, *sup. lin. puto* Italia: puto Italia *l*

The strongest evidence is yielded by an omission of *l*, viz.:

vii. 1: parvis de rebus sed fortasse necessariis consulimur, patres conscripti *om. l*

In *s* after the end of *Phil.* vi the words PARVIS DE REBVS are written at the end of a line in capitals, while the rest of the passage (*sed . . . consulimur p. c.*) is entered in minuscule in the blank part of the line before PARVIS. Here the scribe of *l* seems to have left out a line.

I did not notice in my examination of *s*, which was somewhat hurried, any other omission of a line by *l*, except possibly iii. 24. Here *s* has:

legione quarta mente cecidit et fugere festinans s. c. de sup
plicatione ꝑ discessionem fecit

l omits *quarta . . . supplicatione* (ὁμ.):

Also, ii. 54: O miserum te si haec intellegis, miseriorem si non intellegis hoc litteris mandari, hoc memoriae prodi

Here *s* omits *miseriorem . . . intellegis*, while *l* omits the entire passage. In *s prodi* comes exactly under *constitisse* (in the middle of a line), this being the word which precedes *O miserum*.

On the other hand *l* is not a direct copy of *s*. The omissions of *l* are very frequent and exhibit regular units. I did not, however, find any explanation of them in *s*, except in the few cases I have mentioned. Also *l* has some large omissions. The two chief cases are:

viii. 9–15: illud est . . . ego Catilinam
ix. 8–14: sarciamus . . . quidem nostri

Here viii. 9–15 = 76 lines of Teubner text, while ix. 8–14 = 77½. It is clear that folios of an ancestor have changed places.

There is a shorter omission, which has been repaired by a fly-sheet, viz.:

ii. 108–10: memineramus . . . ignores.

This = 33 Teubner lines. There is no connexion between this and the preceding figures.

There is also a long dislocation, viz.:

iii. 3–18: quo enim . . . imitari velit.

This is placed after iv. 15 *industria inferior*.

Here iii. 3–18 = 210 Teubner lines. Here 30 × 7 = 210.

There appears to be a connexion between this and ii. 108–10.

The probability is that the omission in ii. 108–10, which is supplied on the fly-sheet, represents a page or folio in the model of *l*, while the omissions in viii. 9–15, ix. 8–14 represent similar divisions in a more remote ancestor. In neither case does *s* throw any light. We must, therefore, allow two intermediate ancestors between *s* and *l*.

This conclusion is interesting, since *l* is not much later than *s*. It shows how frequently MSS. were copied at this period, and how careful we must be before saying that one MS. is a direct copy of another.

It would be in some ways not without interest to trace the pedigree of the MSS. which compose the *D* group, but the practical results would be small, since they are all derived from one fountain-head and that less pure than *V*. I have not, therefore, thought it worth while to pursue the inquiry, except in the case of *t*, which, where *V* is not extant, is our most valuable MS.

The contents of *t* are: *Philippics*, *pro lege Manilia*, *pro Milone*, *pro Sulla*, *pro Plancio*, *pro Caecina*, *pro Marcello*.

It is written in long lines, with an average of about 75 letters to the line, without allowance for abbreviations. A plate is given by Chatelain (Pl. xxvii. 1).

In the *Philippics* the omissions of *t* recorded by Halm are as follows:

(11) xiii. 32: *subornastis
(12) ii. 34: *hoc consilium
iii. 35: *nostis amicos
viii. 4: *auctoritatem
(14) xiii. 30: in praetereundo

(15) xiii. 46: Brutum obsideant
(19) xii. 29: **credunt improbis cred-[1]
(21) ix. 6: **-que coniugis diligentia
(22) xi. 37: **-audio ego etiam veteranos
(26) viii. 1: filio fecit et ut luctu sororis
(28) ii. 105: omnia vocibus ebriorum natabant
(42) x. 15: **commune factum et laudis societas aequa D. tamen ir-[2]
iii. 6: *quod profecto non fecisset, si eum cons. iudicasset
(45) xiv. 20: principem revocandae libertatis fuisse me ex Kal. Ian.
(56) xiv. 1: *quam avidissime civitas exspectat allata, laetitia frui satis est
(59) ii. 82: vocatur, renuntiatur: deinde, ut adsolet, suffragia: tum secunda classis
(66) xiii. 32: natus hostis Antonius qui tanto opere eam civitatem oderit quam scit huic rei p.
44: quamquam enim prima praesidia utiliora rei p. sint, tamen extrema sunt gratiora
(68) viii. 15: *aliquod potius quam totum corpus intereat, sic in rei p. corpore, ut totum salvum sit
(74) xiii. 24: **ut faciebas, cum in gremiis mimarum mentum mentemque deponeres. Et te, o puer—Puerum appell-
(76) x. 14: maximeque noster est Brutus semperque noster cum sua excellentissima virtute rei p. natus
(77) iii. 39: *legio Martia Albae constiterit in municipio fidelissimo et fortissimo seseque ad senatus
(78) iii. 11: neglectisque sacrificiis sollemnibus ante lucem vota ea quae numquam solveret nuncupavit[3]
viii. 33: dignum esse videatur uti C. Pansa A. Hirtius cons. aaue[4] si iis videbitur de eius honore praemiove
(79) i. 18: *ecquid est quod tam proprie dici possit actum eius qui togatus in re p. cum potestate imperioque
(84) i. 17: *quae tamen multo plura illo mortuo reperta sunt quam a vivo beneficia per omnes annos tributa et data
(86) ii. 25: cuius autem qui in eo numero fuisset nomen est occultatum? occultatum dico? Cuius non statim divulgatum?
(89) v. 20: suum in illa gladiatoria pugna multum profuderat. Hic pecunias vestras aestimabat, possessiones notabat
(91) x. 26: *si qua opus sit quae publica sit et exigi possit, utatur, exigat, pecuniasque a quibus videatur, ad rem militarem

[1] Here other MSS. have *sed credunt improbis, credunt turbulentis*: *t* gives *sed ut turbulentis* (*med. om.*). I take *ut* to represent *-ũt*, i. e. the last syllable in *credunt*.

[2] For *iratiores t* has *actiones*. This appears to be a correction for *-atiores*.

[3] For this passage *t* has the single word *vota*. This seems to have been inserted by conjecture. I, therefore, treat the passage as a single omission.

[4] = *alter ambove*. So *V* here and v. 53, and *Vt* in ix. 16.

(101) xiii. 24: *ornatum sed illa ornamenta in virtute et industria posita lucent. Tu vero qui te ab eodem Caesare ornatum negare non potes

(116) xiii. 46: *quid de Pansa et Hirtio loquar? Caesar, singulari pietate adulescens, poteritne se tenere quin D. Bruti sanguine poenas patrias persequatur?

(160) viii. 30: *nam illud quidem non adducor ut credam esse quosdam qui invideant alicuius constantiae, qui labori eius, qui eius perpetuam in re p. adiuvanda voluntatem et senatui et P. R. probari moleste ferant

This list is unusually interesting. In the first place we have to notice the three telescoped passages of 19–22 letters, and the telescoped passage of 42 letters. Here a unit emerges which cannot be denied.

The next point which we have to notice is the telescoped passage of 74 letters in xiii. 24. There is no connexion between this and the previous passages. Also, we must observe the unusually large number of omissions ranging from 74–9 letters, viz, six examples, two of which contain the same number (78).

These facts are interesting, since this is about the content of a line in *t*, apart from abbreviations. If these were not employed, a line in *t* would contain somewhat more. The suspicion arises that *t* was copied from a MS. very like itself and that these omissions represent lines in the model. If so, we should expect to find similar phenomena elsewhere in the MS. I, therefore, give a list of all omissions over 70 letters elsewhere in the MS. as recorded by editors:

(70) *Mil.* 21: amicos meos neque enim hoc cogitavit vir iustissimus neque in bonis viris legendis

(71) *Planc.* 76: oppugnator, ut inimici mei putarant, sed etiam defensor fuisset, huius in periculo non

(77) *Planc.* 72: *familiaritatis, vicinitatis, patris amicitiae, quae si non essent, vererer, credo, ne turpiter

(81) *Caec.* 88: restitues, sive ex hoc loco deiecisti, restitue in hunc locum: sive ab hoc loco, restitue in eum locum

Planc. 62: **magistratus quasi rei p. vilicos in quibus si qua praeterea est ars, facile patitur, sin minus, virtu-

(87) *Mil.* 12: **amentiam perditorum. Hanc vero quaestionem, etsi non est iniqua, numquam tamen senatus constituendam pu-

(152) *Caec.* 91: ostendo si sine armatis coactisve hominibus deiectus quispiam sit, eum qui fateatur se deiecisse, vincere sponsionem, si ostendat eum non possedisse. Neque deiici nisi qui possideat

To these may be added a dittography:

(80) *Sull.* 34: pro salute rei p. suscepi atque gessi. L. ille Torquatus, cum esset meus contubernalis in consulatu *bis scr.*

The significance of these figures will be seen when I mention that apart from *Mil.* 50, where an omission of 55 letters is shared by *E*, the only omissions of 50–70 letters in *t* recorded by editors are *Planc.* 67 *rebus ... valuit* (57) and *Caec.* 24 **sed ideo ... alienum* (67).

In this list it is to be noticed that there are two telescoped passages; also that the number 81 occurs twice.

I now proceed to combine the evidence, affixing asterisks to the telescoped passages:

(70) *Mil.* 21	(80) *Sull.* 34
(71) *Planc.* 76	(81) *Caec.* 88, **Planc.* 62
(74) **Phil.* xiii. 24	(84) *Phil.* i. 17
(76) *Phil.* x. 14	(86) *Phil.* ii. 25
(77) *Planc.* 72, *Phil.* iii. 39	(87) **Mil.* 12
(78) *Phil.* iii. 11, viii. 33	(152) *Caec.* 91
(79) *Phil.* i. 18	(160) *Phil.* viii. 30

The favourite numbers are 77–81. There is considerable irregularity among the other numbers, due, in all probability, to the use of abbreviations in the model. The relation of the largest number, 160, to the dittography of 80, and the two cases of 81, one of which is telescoped, is to be noted.

In view of the cumulative evidence I have no doubt that these omissions represent lines in the model of *t*.

So far two units are yielded by the omissions, viz. 19–22 and 77–81. It is obvious that some of the larger omissions, e.g. 101 and 115, may be multiples of the small unit. I hesitate to say more, since 101 and 115 may be connected with 56 and 59, and these again with 26 and 28. If so, there may be another intermediate ancestor or these omissions may go back to an earlier stage.

The following corruptions in *t* may be taken in connexion with the ancestor in lines of 19–22 letters:

ii. 18: vitricum tuum fuisse in tanto scelere fatebare

In *t fuisse* comes after *fatebare*. This suggests the arrangement:

uitricum tuum	*mg.* fuisse
in tanto scelere fatebare	(22)

xi. 6: ille pervenisse videtur quoad progredi potuerit

In *t* the words *pervenisse videtur* come after *potuerit.* This suggests:

ille *mg.* peruenisse uidetur
quoad progredi potuerit (21)

xiii. 42: mihi quidem constat nec meam contumeliam

After *meam t* repeats *quidem.* This suggests:

mihi
quidem constat nec meam (20)
contumeliam

I now turn to *s* and *n.* They are closely connected with each other, also with *a* (Bamberg. M. iv. 5), cent. xiii, a MS. used by Halm.

The following dittographies are interesting:

(27) v. 13: quis nouit aut quis nosse potuit *bis scr. s.*
(28) ii. 67: tam distantibus in locis positas *bis scr. s.*
(38) iii. 13: potestatem nobis de tota re p. fecisse dicendi *bis scr. s.*
viii. 5: enim tempus nondum uenerat belli aũt (so *sn*) gerendi *bis scr. sn.* In the margin of *s* is r̄ (= *require*).
(52) x. 14: nec hoc cadere uerbum in tantam uirtutis praestantiam potest *bis scr. n.*
(73) xii. 3: quod uidebam equidem, sed quasi per caliginem: praestrinxerat aciem animi D. Bruti salus *bis scr. s.*

Here there are two series, viz.:

27, 28, 52
38 (*bis*), 73

The first of these dittographies is instructive. The repetition takes place after the intervening words *nam Lysiaden Atheniensem* (22). It seems likely that these words were inserted in the margin, after previous omission, and that the scribe when inserting them lost his place and wrote a line of his model twice.

In iii. 13 also the dittography is not immediate, but comes after *cum enim . . . praesidio* (37). Here it is clear that the intermediate ancestor had:

potestatem nobis de tota re p. fecisse dicendi (38)
cum enim tuto senatum haberi sine praesidio (37)

In viii. 5 the dittography is a little complicated. The passage as given by other members of *D* is:

decernendi enim tempus nondum venerat: belli autem gerendi tempus si praetermisisset

In *sn* we find:

decernendi enim tempus nondum uenerat belli aũt gerendi enim tempus nondum uenerat belli aũt gerendi tempus si praetermisisset

This indicates:

decernendi enim tempus nondum uenerat belli (38)
aũt gerendi tempus si praetermisisset

The writer looked back from *-endi* to *-endi* and repeated *enim . . . belli*, before he realized his error.

In connexion with the dittographies of 27, 28, 52 letters the following omissions are interesting:

(29) vii. 27: *bellum indixerit sed uos moneo PR̃T s^2 *in mg.*
xiv. 18: sententiis vinci non possum bonis *om. s*
Cf. xiv. 33: neque oblivione eorum qui nunc sunt nec reticentia posterorum

Here s^1 repeats *eorum* for *posterorum*. This suggests:

eorum qui nunc sunt nec reticentia (29)
posterorum

There is an interesting dislocation in xi. 9, which may be due to this ancestor. Here we have:

nam quo maior vis est animi quam corporis, hoc sunt graviora ea quae concipiuntur animo quam illa quae corpore

Here *snl* and Halm's MS. *a* omit the words *quam corporis . . . animo* (50) in their proper place and insert them later on after *sine Trebonii maxima contumelia.* The intervening passage *quam illa . . . contumelia* consists of 450 letters. Here 50 × 9 = 450. We may compare the following omissions:

(25) ii. 54: miseriorem si non intellegis *om. s*
(50) iii. 2: fuissent eo die quo primum ex urbe fugit Antonius, aut eae non *om. s*

In connexion with the dittographies of 38 and 73 letters I mention the following omissions:

(35) xi. 27: iam nobis notus esset exercitus alterius *om.* s^1
(36) x. 7: eos qui diadema imposuerint conservandos *om. s*
xii. 18: sic me iniquum eierabant, de me querebantur *om. sn*
(39) viii. 8: et discordia civium sed in maxima consensione *om.* s^1
(76) xiii. 47: bene me novit, quod venias, proposito praesertim exemplo Dolabellae. Sanctiore erunt, credo *om. s*

It is probable that *s* and *n* contain much further evidence, but my inspection of *s* was hurried, while at the time when I used *n* my attention was not directed to such points and my notes are defective.

I now come to *c*, the *familia Colotiana* (p. 201). In this I have only noticed two omissions common to the family, viz.:

(68) i. 24: civitas data non solum singulis sed nationibus et provinciis universis a mortuo

(173) iii. 27: etenim in contione dixerat se custodem fore urbis, usque ad Kal. Martias ad urbem exercitum habiturum. O praeclarum custodem ovium, ut aiunt, lupum. Custosne urbis an direptor et vexator esset Antonius. Et quidem

The unit here appears to be 34 ($34 \times 2 = 68$, $34 \times 5 = 170$).

There are also two omissions, not shared by Berol. Phil. 201, which throw light upon a common ancestor of the two Paris. MSS., viz.:

(83) ii. 84: *fecit. Quae potest esse turpitudinis tantae defensio? Cupio audire ut videam ubi rhetoris sit tanta *om.* Par. 6602 (*m.* 1)

iii. 16: atque optimae pater M. Atius Balbus, in primis honestus, praetorius fuit: tuae coniugis, bonae feminae *om.* Par. 5802, 6602

These are the only two cases which I have noted, and their agreement is remarkable.

I now sum up the results indicated by this analysis. We have seen that the *D* family is derived from the same archetype as *V*, i. e. a MS. with an average of about 28 letters to a line. The telescoped passages, v. 20 and iv. 15, bear witness to this stage, and probably other omissions (vii. 14, xii. 16) go back to this ancestor. The most authoritative member of *D* is *t*. In this we find clear indications of an ancestor with 19–22 letters to the line, the evidence being given by three telescoped passages of this length (ix. 6, xi. 37, xii. 29), also one of 42 letters (x. 15).

In *s* and *n* there are indications of an immediate ancestor with an average of 37–8 letters to the line, preceded by one with an average of 27–9. There is slighter evidence (v. 13), which may show that this was preceded by a MS. with an average of 22 letters to the line. This, it is to be noticed, is the length of a line in the ancestor of *t*.

It seems likely that this MS. in 19–22 letters was the common ancestor of *D.* If so, we may refer to it the following omissions of *D*:

(22) ii. 64: *cum omnia metu tenerentur
v. 27: ad nostrum civem mittimus
(23) vii. 18: fecerit, hunc praedae causa
(24) i. 2: *nisi quod erat notum omnibus

If in the last passage we write *omnib.*, the number is reduced to 22. I pass over the higher numbers, in which more than one explanation is possible. Such an ancestor would, without doubt, be written in two columns.

CHAPTER VII

VERRINES

THE well-known palimpsest of the *Verrines*, Vat. Reg. 2077 (*V*), is ascribed to the fourth century. It is written in two columns, with 20 lines to the page.

Chatelain (Pl. 32) gives a facsimile of f. 88[r], containing *Verr.* ii. 113–15, *de publico . . . flagitiorum*. The contents of this, as written, are col. i = 378, col. ii = 371 letters, total = 749. In col. ii there is one exceptionally short line of seven letters at the end of a paragraph. We learn from Mai, who records the contents of the various pages, that the *verso* of f. 88 contains §§ 115–16, *crudelitatisque . . . non de Sthe-*. This passage, as printed, consists of 719 letters, but probably, as written, there would be a few abbreviations. It contains, therefore, a little less than the *recto*.

The total contents of the folio are 749 + 719 = 1468. The average number of letters to the line is 19 for the *recto* and 18 for the *verso*.

As expressed in Teubner lines the contents are *recto* = 18, *verso* = 17, total = 35.

V in its present form consists of 101 ff. It possesses various quaternion markings, the last of which, *Q*. xxxxii, occurs at v. 120. When complete it must have contained at least 45 quaternions. In view of these signatures I endeavoured to reconstitute the MS. in its original form. I found at once that the unit of 35 Teubner lines to a folio is remarkably constant. On the other hand the investigation is made difficult by various circumstances.

The scribe who superimposed the second work (Prosper's continuation of Jerome) upon the *Verrines* took scattered leaves at random from a heap. Thus f. 1 of the palimpsest, as it now stands, contains *Verr.* v. 70–1, and f. 2 contains i. 106–7. Also many folios are legible on one side only. Mai frequently remarks of a page *non legitur* or *oblitterata est*, or *funditus eluta*. In such cases editors give, as contained in *V*, only what is printed by Mai, without mentioning the illegible page. Since, however, it is very inconvenient to deal with occasional pages among the folios, I have in such cases allowed 17½ lines for the illegible page. A more serious complication is caused by the fact that a number of pages in *V* were left blank by the writer of the *Verrines*. On this subject Mai is quite explicit, and not infrequently points out that there is no gap, but that after a blank *recto* or *verso* the text is resumed without any lacuna. He says (p. 402):

Cur autem Verrinarum amanuensis reliquerit has aliasque paginas vacuas divinare vix queo. Dicerem ob membranarum asperitatem nisi hae mihi laeves esse viderentur: id quod tamen postea a rescribente fortasse curatum est.

As I have not myself seen *V*, I can only quote this statement.

In the following tabulation I combine the portions of the speech surviving in *V* with those which have been lost, marking the first with an asterisk and adding the folios of the MS. in its present form on which they are found. Where a page is illegible, I allow 17½ lines for its contents. In such cases the content which I ascribe to the folio will differ by this amount from that usually ascribed to *V*. Where Mai states that a page is blank, I record the fact.

The first passage preserved by *V* is i. 105–14. The previous part of the speech, viz. *Verr.* i–105, which is lost, = 1,392 Teubner lines. I will merely remark that 35 × 40 = 1400. Allowance has to be made for the title. The rest of *Verr.* i is distributed as follows:

		Teub. lines
*105–114 =	ff. 19 (19[v] blank), 2, 5, 11 docet . . . satis	= 121½
114–119	est ostendere . . . iniuriae	= 71
*119–130 =	ff. 14, 4, 7, 22 (22[v] blank), 89 (89[r] blank), videbantur . . . locavissent	= 140½
130–136	neque potuissent . . . dominata est	= 71
*137–139 =	f. 79 venit ad . . . deferre	= 35¾
139–142	tamen de . . . consuetudo in	= 35¾
*142–148 =	ff. 101, 96 bonis . . . existimationem con-	= 71¾
148–150	-tempserit . . . Haboni	= 36½
*150–153 =	f. 86 tabulae . . . illorum	= 33¾
153–158	solitudo . . . sodalem suum	= 72
*158–end =	f. 92 Q. Curtium . . . subsortiebatur	= 4½

Here only the first and the last figures call for comment. As f. 19[v] is blank, 121½ = 3 ff. + 1 page. If we add 17½ for the blank page, the result is 139 (35 × 4 = 140). As there are two blank pages in the next passage, 119–30, the number comes out right. With regard to the last passage, Mai nowhere else mentions f. 92, and *Verr.* ii begins on f. 97. The inference, therefore, is that the rest of the *recto* and the whole of the *verso* were blank.

If we add $17\frac{1}{2}$ to $121\frac{1}{2}$ and leave out of sight f. 92 ($4\frac{1}{2}$), the total for 20 ff. is 707 ($35 \times 20 = 700$).

Verrine ii falls into the following parts:

*1–3	= f. 97 (*verso* illeg.) multa . . . pulcherrimis (?)	= 34
3–21	exornavit . . . Erycinae esse	= 212
*21–24	= f. 100 (*recto* illeg.) multatum (?) . . . Venerius ho-	= $35\frac{1}{2}$
24–32	-mo qui e . . . civi	= 115
*32–35	= f. 49 (*verso* illeg.) Romano . . . vestis	= 37
35–40	pretiosorum . . . iudicii	= 73
*40–43	= f. 56 (*recto* illeg.) metus (?) . . . hereditas	= $36\frac{3}{4}$
43–52	ea quae . . . videamur	= 141
*52–68	= ff. 52, 90, 84, 81, 91, 53 (52^r illeg.) nam me (?) . . . innocens	= 213
68–83	et quod . . . studiose ut	= $208\frac{1}{2}$
*83–87	= f. 95 dixi . . . putant	= 34
87–100	artificio . . . postremo me	= 174
*100–102	= f. 93 ipsum apud . . . Romae cum ac-	= 34
102–113	-ta res . . . sacro nihil	= 141
*113–116	= f. 88 de publico . . . non de Sthe-	= 35
116–119	-ni bonis . . . remque hanc	= $35\frac{1}{2}$
*119–121	= f. 82 (*recto* illeg.) totam (?) . . . dandarum	= $36\frac{3}{4}$
121–124	ab senatu . . . erat legibus	= $36\frac{1}{2}$
*124–127	= f. 80 ut is . . . erat ut	= 35
127–138	quot essent . . . magistratus	= $141\frac{3}{4}$
*138–140	= f. 85 adepti . . . iudicent	= $34\frac{1}{2}$
140–142	si tibi . . . statuarum	= 35
*142–145	= f. 83 (*verso* illeg.) nomine . . . considerate (?)	= 35
145–152	Syracusana . . . possit quem	= $105\frac{1}{2}$
*152–156	= ff. 50, 55 voles . . . vobis	= $70\frac{3}{4}$
156–166	planissimeque . . . togatorum enim	= $139\frac{1}{2}$
*166–169	= f. 51 causa . . . posset	= $36\frac{1}{2}$
169–188	ego mea . . . arator	= $244\frac{1}{2}$
*188–191	= f. 54 an pecuarius . . . dilucide quod	= 35
191–end	copiose . . . existimarentur	= $24\frac{1}{2}$

Here there appears to have been a vacant space at the end of the speech. Allowance must be made for the subscriptio.

I add the following multiples of 35:

$$35 \times 3 = 105,\ 35 \times 4 = 140,\ 35 \times 5 = 175,\ 35 \times 6 = 210,\ 35 \times 7 = 245.$$

It will be seen that all the numbers here are quite normal, except

115 (§§ 24–32), where the unit rises to 38. The writer appears to have contracted his hand very slightly here and in the following folio (= 37).

Verrine iii.

*iii. 1–3	= f. 87 omnes etiam . . . teneremus (?), *verso* illeg.	= 34½
3–20	numquam . . . tradidit	= 212¼
*20–29	= ff. 94, 61, 57, 63 ut neque . . . neque tamen	= 142½
30–40	ullum . . . amentissime	= 140½
*40–47	= ff. 58, 64, 60 (*verso* blank), 31 (*recto* blank) vendidisti . . . annonae cari-	= 109
47–52	non vererere . . . diripi	= 74
*52–62	= ff. 25, 34, 39, 32 profecto . . . convivio	= 144
62–66	cum interea . . . fugitivorum	= 72
*66–70	= ff. 26 (*recto* blank), 40 (*recto* blank), 35 insolentia . . . virgis te	= 71½
70–74	ad necem . . . fidelitate	= 68½
*74–78	= ff. 30, 27 tantus dolor . . . ventum	= 66½
78–83	est coguntur . . . quae cum	= 68¼
*83–88	= ff. 38, 33 (33^{v} illeg.) de populi . . . magnis (?)	= 68
88–128	decumis ut . . . sapientiaque	= 604½
*128–130	= f. 44 (*recto* illeg.) opus (?) . . . decumani	= 37
130–137	palam et . . . suam sibi	= 110
*138–144	= ff. 66, 69 totam . . . aratorum	= 74½
144–151	fugae . . . emere	= 110
*152–157	= ff. 45 (*verso* blank), 48 (*recto* blank), 43, 42 tenetur . . . videtis ut	= 113
157–168	moneat . . . fecit umquam	= 152
*168–177	= ff. 47, 46, 41, 65 quis denique . . . vidimus	= 148½
177–182	huic ab . . . labefactari atque	= 75½
*182–186	= ff. 68, 67 oppugnari . . . praedonum	= 70
186–190	incendiis . . . innocentissimos	= 75½
*190–196	= ff. 70, 78 meminimus . . . hoc quid	= 75½
196–199	est venit . . . nummos vero	= 40¾
*199–209	= ff. 74, 59, 62, 75 ut det . . . auctoritas	= 144
209–212	et tanta . . . provinciam	= 38½
*212–214	= ff. 71 (*recto* blank), 72 (*recto* blank) adflictam . . . in illo	= 36½
214–220	laudis . . . severitas iudicis	= 70
*220–225	= ff. 76, 73 quotus erit . . . tanti	= 85
225–228	ut homines . . . pati	= 43½
*228-end	= f. 77 nullo modo . . . revertantur	= 6¾

In connexion with the end of *Verr.* iii we must take the beginning of *Verr.* iv. The first extract given by Mai is § 6, *hospes esset*, &c. This comes on the *verso* of f. 36, the *recto* of which is illegible. If we allow 17½ lines for the *recto*, the *verso* will begin with § 5, *verum ut.* The previous sections 1–4 occupy 54 lines of Teubner, i. e. 1 folio + 1 page. Probably 77^{v} and the *recto* of another folio were blank.

The character of the script seems to vary more in *Verr.* iii than elsewhere. In §§ 70–88 the unit sinks to 33–4 lines, then it rises to 37 in §§ 128–82 (37 × 3 = 111, 37 × 4 = 148). There are three exceptional figures, viz. 40¾ (§§ 196–9), 43½ (§§ 225–8), 85 (§§ 220–5). The first of these contains a dialogue, which is spaced out by Müller, so its length is somewhat less than it appears. For the other two there is no such explanation, and, as 85 = two existing folios, it is clear that the writer contracted his hand here, with the result that for these two folios and the one which came after them the unit becomes 43.

The large figure 604½ (§§ 88–128) presents some difficulty, since it comes between the smaller unit, 33–4, which is clearly visible in §§ 70–88, and a larger unit, 37, which is equally visible after § 128. I, therefore, leave it for the moment, merely remarking that 35 × 17 = 595.

There is a great gap in *Verrines* iv–v, extending from iv. 19–v. 70. The distribution of these speeches is as follows:

iv. 1–4	venio . . . attigit	=	54
*5–19	= ff. 36 (*recto* illeg.), 28, 98, 99, 29, 37 verum (?) . . . onerariam	=	208½
19–v. 70	navem maximam . . . homines maxime	=	3001
*v. 70–72	= f. 1 (*recto* illeg.) mediterraneos (?) . . . crudelissimoque	=	35
72–80	cruciatu . . . provinciae praesi-	=	109
*80–85	= ff. 12, 13 -dio verum . . . inter tu-	=	72½
85–94	-am libidinem . . . ex Timarchide	=	106
*94–99	= ff. 8 (*recto* blank), 24 (*recto* blank), 23 sagum . . . aratorum-	=	71
99–104	-ne liberos . . . in eum disso-	=	69½
*104–109	-lutus qui . . . reliquisses	=	70½
109–114	filium tecum . . . quia legatus	=	73
*114–136	= ff. 18, 17, 21, 3, 9, 16, 6, 20 isto praetore . . . cum tibi	=	292
136–end	maritimum . . . necesse sit	=	763½

Here the large figure, 3,001, comes out very satisfactorily (35 × 86 = 3010). We cannot expect so much accuracy in the case of 763½, since it includes the end of the *Verrines*, but here also the unit works well (35 × 22 = 770).

Verr. iv, v together occupy 4,935½ lines of Teubner text, = 140 ff. + 1 page. The extra page comes at the beginning of *Verr.* iv, where either the beginning of the speech was on the *verso* of f. 77 or there were two blank pages.

If we subtract 17½ lines for the odd page, the result is 4,918 lines for 140 folios. Here again the unit 35 holds good (35 × 140 = 4900).

In the preceding tables I have noted 28 cases of single folios. Out of these 25 contain 33–7 lines of Teubner. The others are 38½ (iii. 209–12), 40¾ (iii. 196–9), 43½ (iii. 225–8). The last is highly exceptional.

There are 25 examples of two folios. Out of these 19 contain 70–5 lines. There are five examples of 66½–9½, and one exceptional case of 85 (iii. 220), which comes just before the exceptional unit 43½.

For three folios there are eight examples ranging from 105½–15. For four folios there are 12 examples. Of these ten contain 139–44 lines. The others are 148½ (iii. 168–77), and 152 (iii. 157–68).

There are five examples of six folios (35 × 6 = 210), for which the numbers are:

(208½) ii. 68–83, iv. 5–19
(212) ii. 3–21, iii. 3–20
(213) ii. 52–68

The remaining numbers are:

174 (35 × 5 = 175)
244½ (35 × 7 = 245)
292 (35 × 8 = 280)
604½
763½ (35 × 22 = 770)
1392 (35 × 40 = 1400)
3001 (35 × 86 = 3010)

I have left blank here the somewhat puzzling figure 604½, where there is some uncertainty as to the unit. We may explain it as 35 × 17 = 595, which is sufficiently near, or it may represent 18 folios of a smaller unit (33½ × 18 = 603). If we take the preceding number 292 and multiply by 2, the result is 584. If we subtract 17½ from 604½, the result is 587. The probable solution, therefore, is that 604½ = 16 folios + a page, i. e. one side of a folio in *V* was blank. This is an interesting example of the way in which the large figures hang together and explain each other.

I now return to the contents of *Verrine* iii. The whole speech, if we exclude §§ 228–end, occupies 3,376 lines of Teubner. This corresponds to 92 folios of $V+1$ page. If we deduct 18 for the extra page, the result is $3358 \div 92$. This gives an average of exactly $36\frac{1}{2}$ for this speech, as against 35 elsewhere.

The whole of *Verrines* i–v, if we exclude the short folios at the end of i, ii, iii, amounts to the following total:

i. 1–158	= 2081 lines	=	$59\frac{1}{2}$ folios
ii. 1–191	= 2545 ,,	=	72 ,,
iii. 1–228	= 3375 ,,	=	$92\frac{1}{2}$,,
iv–v	= 4935 ,,	=	$140\frac{1}{2}$,,
	12936		$364\frac{1}{2}$

The general average for a folio is $35\frac{1}{2}$ ($35\frac{1}{2} \times 364\frac{1}{2} = 12939\frac{3}{4}$). It is somewhat remarkable to find such regularity in the case of so large a MS.

I now proceed to consider the quaternion marks in *V*. There are eight of these, viz. at:

iii. 46 (f. 60^v): *Q*. xxi, after *arationes sed etiam*
67 (f. 26^v): *Q*. xxii, after *decumas ei quem*
88 (f. 33^v): *Q*. xxiii, after *ita magnis*
153 (f. 48^v): *Q*. xxvi, after *inquam Metellum*
175 (f. 41^v): *Q*. xxvii, after *gesta esse iudices*
213 (f. 72^v): *Q*. xxviiii, after *sociorum salutem*
v. 94 (f. 24^v): *Q*. xxxxi, after *provincia verum*
120 (f. 17^v): *Q*. xxxxii, after *cum Timarchide*

I will take first a case about which there is no trouble, viz. iii. 175–213, *cognoscite et ex . . . sociorum sàlutem.*

This passage should occupy *QQ*. xxviii, xxix. It is distributed thus:

*175–7 (f. 65): cognoscite . . . vidimus	= 35 lines	= 1 f.
177–82: huic ab aerario . . . labefactari atque	= $75\frac{1}{2}$,,	= 2 ff.
*182–6 (ff. 68, 67): oppugnari . . . praedonum	= 70 ,,	= 2 ,,
186–90: incendiis . . . innocentissimos	= $75\frac{1}{2}$,,	= 2 ,,
*190–6 (ff. 70, 78): meminimus . . . hoc quid	= $75\frac{1}{2}$,,	= 2 ,,
196–9: est. Venit . . . nummos vero	= $40\frac{3}{4}$,,	= 1 f.
*199–209 (ff. 74, 59, 62, 75): ut det . . . auctoritas	= 144 ,,	= 4 ff.
209–12: et tanta . . . tu provinciam	= $38\frac{1}{2}$,,	= 1 f.
*212–13 (f. 71, *recto* blank): adflictam . . . salutem	= 18 ,,	= 1 ,,
		16

Here there is no irregularity, except that f. 71^r is blank.

Elsewhere there are difficulties. I take first the content of *Q.* xxii.

Mai states on iii. 46, *arationes sed etiam sedes*:

'*Q.* xxi in calce p. vacuae 120 (= f. 60^v). Ergo p. 61 (= f. 31^r) incipit *Q.* xxii' (i.e. with *sedes*).

He also reports *Q.* xxii as coming at § 67 (on f. 26^v) after *decumas ei quem*.

The intervening space is distributed thus:

*46–7 (f. 31, *recto* blank): sedes . . . annonae cari-	= 17 lines	= 1 folio	
47–52: -tatem non vererere . . . diripi	= 74 "	= 2 "	
*52–62 (ff. 25, 34, 39, 32): profecto . . . convivio	= 144 "	= 4 "	
62–6: cum interea . . . fugitivorum	= 72 "	= 2 "	
*66–8 (f. 26, *recto* blank): insolentia . . . quem	= 17¼ "	= 1 "	
		10	

Here the gathering consists of 10 folios, with two blank pages.

The next signature, *Q.* xxiii, comes at § 88 (on f. 33^v) after *ita magnis*. The intervening space is distributed thus:

*68–70 (ff. 40, *recto* blank, 35): ad modum . . . virgis te	= 54¼ lines	= 2 folios
70–4: ad necem . . . fidelitate	= 68½ "	= 2 "
*74–8 (ff. 30, 27): tantus . . . ventum	= 66½ "	= 2 "
78–83: est coguntur . . . quae cum	= 68¼ "	= 2 "
*83–8 (ff. 38, 33): de populi . . . magnis	= 68 "	= 2 "
		10

Here again we have 10 folios, with one blank page.

The next signature, *Q.* xxvi, comes at § 153 (f. 48^v), after *inquam Metellum*. Here we have to account for *QQ.* xxiv, xxv, xxvi. The intervening space is distributed thus:

88–128: decumis . . . sapientiaque I have already discussed this passage and given reasons for supposing that one page was blank.	= 604 lines	= 17 folios
*128–30 (f. 44): opus est . . . decumani	= 37 "	= 1 "
130–7: palam et . . . suam sibi	= 110 "	= 3 "
*138–44 (ff. 66, 69): totam iniquam . . . aratorum	= 74½ "	= 2 "
144–51: fugae, calamitates . . . voluerit emere	= 110 "	= 3 "
*152–3 (f. 45, *verso* blank): tenetur . . . Metellum	= 19 "	= 1 "
		27

The probability is that there were other blank pages.

The next signature, *Q.* xxvii, comes at § 175 (f. 41^{v}), after *esse, iudices.* The intervening space is distributed thus:

*153–7 (ff. 48, *recto* blank, 43, 42): sed hoc . . . videtis ut	= 94 lines	= 3 folios
157–68: moneat Apronium . . . fecit umquam	= 152 ,,	= 4 ,,
*168–75 (ff. 47, 46, 41): quis denique . . . esse iudices	= $113\frac{3}{4}$,,	= 3 ,,
		10

Here again we have 10 folios, with one blank page.

I have already dealt with the next signature, *Q.* xxix, which occurs at § 213, *sociorum salutem.* Here we have the normal number of 16 folios for two quaternions, one page being blank.

The next signature, *Q.* xxxxi, comes at v. 94 (f. 24^{v}), after *provincia verum.* The intervening space is distributed thus:

*iii. 213–14 (f. 72, *recto* blank): multa contra . . . in illo	= $18\frac{1}{2}$ lines	= 1 folio
214–20: laudis causam . . . severitas iudicis	= 70 ,,	= 2 ,,
*220–5 (ff. 76, 73): quotus erit . . . aestimavit tanti	= 85 ,,	= 2 ,,
225–8: ut homines . . . quae pati	= $43\frac{1}{2}$,,	= 1 ,,
*228–end (f. 77): nullo modo . . . revertantur	= $6\frac{3}{4}$,,	= 1 ,,
The rest of this folio appears to have been blank.		
iv. 1–4: venio nunc . . . attigit	= 54 ,,	= 2 ,,
There must have been a blank page here.		
*5–19 (ff. 36, 28, 98, 99, 37): verum ut . . . onerariam	= $208\frac{1}{2}$,,	= 6 ,,
19–v. 70: navem maximam . . . homines maxime	= 3001 ,,	= 86 ,,
*v. 70–2 (f. 1): mediterraneos . . . crudelissimoque	= 35 ,,	= 1 ,,
72–80: cruciatu dicam . . . provinciae praesi-	= 109 ,,	= 3 ,,
*80–5 (ff. 12, 13): -dio verum . . . inter tu-	= $72\frac{1}{2}$,,	= 2 ,,
85–94: -am libidinem . . . ex Timarchide	= 106 ,,	= 3 ,,
*94 (f. 8, *recto* blank): sagum sumit . . . provincia verum	= $18\frac{1}{4}$,,	= 1 ,,
		111

Here we have 111 folios to represent the twelve gatherings xxx–xli. The probability is that there were a number of blank pages in the long gap iv. 19–v. 70.

The last signature is at v. 120 (f. 17^{v}), after *cum Timarchide.* The intervening space is distributed thus:

*94–9 (ff. 24, *recto* blank, 23): etiam hac . . . aratorum	= 53 lines	= 2 folios
99–104: -ne liberos . . . in eum disso-	= $69\frac{1}{2}$,,	= 2 ,,
*104–9 (ff. 10, 15): -lutus qui . . . reliquisses	= $70\frac{1}{2}$,,	= 2 ,,
109–14: filium tecum . . . quia legatus	= 73 ,,	= 2 ,,
*114–20 (ff. 18, 17): isto praetore . . . cum Timarchide	= $68\frac{3}{4}$,,	= 2 ,,
		10

Here again we have 10 folios, with one blank page.

V, like the palimpsest of the *de Re Publica*, contains a number of double readings. I instance the following:

i. 111 in isdem causam sis (= causam with "sis" written above), ii. 84 facile tacite, 100 quod cum, 143 et eamque, 154 enim nimirum, 169 apud aduersus, iii. 70 aduersuṃs, 155 primum plurimum, v. 72 sua uoluntateme, 83 autem aut, 107 poṣṣẹtuit, 120 in e carcere, 129 sororesque uxoresque, 135 subito suppeditatam, 136 possẹṭs

In iii. 77 *V* has *peruagatum et peruulgatum*, where other MSS. have *peruulgatum* only. Since elsewhere (iii. 129, iv. 64) *peruagatum* and *peruulgatum* are variants, it appears probable that here two readings have been combined. In v. 72 supponere coepit cives Romanos quos in carcerem antea coniecerat *V* adds *ceruos* after *quos*. This appears to be a corruption for *c. r^os^*, i.e. *cives Romanos*. The abbreviation *c. r.* is frequently found in the MSS. and was doubtless used in the archetype. In § 73 *V* has *ameonis* for *Romanis*. This seems due to *R^omanis.^*

The spelling *saenatus* (= *senatus*), which is frequent in the *de Re Publica* palimpsest, occurs in *V*, in iii. 170. It is to be noted that the abbreviation *R* = *recita* is normal in *V*. On one occasion, v. 126, we find *KP* = *caput*.

With regard to the character of the text found in *V*, different views have been held. Meusel, in a well-known dissertation, has attempted to show that it is inferior to that of *R* (= Paris. 7774 *A*), but his arguments are based upon a misconception. He ignores the fact that *R* is a MS. of the Caroline period, which has undergone revision. *V*, on the other hand, teems with obvious corruptions. It is easy to show that *R* is more 'correct'; its 'correctness', however, does not prove its *fides*. Peterson says, 'Meusel's laborious enumeration of differences between *V* and *R* in the minutiae of spelling, &c., has tended to obscure the real issue as to the comparative value of *V* where it differs vitally from the other MSS.'[1] He points out elsewhere[2] that Quintilian, in his quotations from *Verr.* v. 117–18, 'seems to have had the *Vp* tradition before him throughout the passage'. The most striking case is in § 118, where we have the following variants:

cibum vestitumque Quintil. ix. 4. 71: tibi cibum vestitumque *V*: cibum tibi *R*, *cett.*

[1] *The Vatican Codex of Cicero's Verrines*, *Am. J. Ph.*, xxvi, p. 409.

[2] *Variants in Cicero's Verrines*, *Am. J. Ph.*, xxviii, p. 132.

Peterson's general conclusion is that 'the common text from which the various MSS. have been derived is to be found in its most ancient form in *V*', and this verdict appears to me in every way rational.

I now proceed to consider the antecedents of *V* in the usual way.

Omissions of *V*:

(9) v. 72: capitibus (*om.* V^1)

83: ubi legati

98: portusque

116: Cleomenes

(10) iii. 22: cogitate ac (*O*)

45: et iniuriis (*O*)

156: ludibundos

171: ac rationem

v. 81: exceptione

(11) iii. 171: suum probare (*p*)

(12) ii. 63: alia Panhormi (O^1)

iii. 172: **-lia frumentum

186: nobilissimos (*O*)

v. 71: et flagitaret

133: ornatarumque

(14) iii. 228: non pertulerunt

(16) i. 121: et iniquitatem tum

iii. 56: non quantum vellet (*om.* V^1)

(17) iii. 52: ac locupletissimos (*p*)

53: ac diligentissimos

(20) ii. 167: aut quo modo existiment

(22) iii. 56: honestissimae civitatis

156: ludibundi quae volebatis

(24) i. 158: *erepta esset facultas eorum

(26) i. 106: *cum intellegam legem Voconiam

(31) iii. 85: *R. testimonium publicum Liparensium

(44) iii. 200: addite nunc eodem istius edicta instituta iniurias

(222) v. 131–2: * te illo tempore ipso superioribusque diebus omnibus in litore cum mulierculis perpotasse dico: harum rerum omnium auctores testesque produco. Num tibi insultare in calamitate, num intercludere perfugia fortunae, num casus bellicos exprobrare aut obicere videor

The most significant of these omissions is the telescoped passage iii. 172. Here a previous MS. seems to have had:

in sici
lia frumentum (12)
aut

V has *in sici aut* (med. om.).

It is interesting to notice that Mai explains the omission as due to the loss of a line. He says:

'cod. *in Sici aut.* Amanuensis enim praetermisit versiculum'

The omission in v. 81 is also interesting. Here a previous MS. seems to have had:

et
si recte sine
exceptione (10)
dixeram

The omission of *exceptione* is due to ὁμ.

Most of the omissions consist of 9–12 letters (15 exx.). Multiples of this unit appear in 20–4 (4 exx.), 31, 44. It is to be noticed that the largest figure, 222, is almost exactly a multiple of the next largest, 44 ($44 \times 5 = 220$).

There is also some significant evidence furnished by corruptions, e.g.:

(11) ii. 64: epistulas complures attulerat, in his unam domo

V^1 has *at* before *domo*. This seems to indicate:

complu
res attulerat
in his unam do (11)
mo

The copyist looked up to the preceding line and wrote *-at* for *do*.

(11) iii. 77: mulieris spoliatum iri, liciti

For *liciti* *V* has *policiti*. This indicates:

mulieris
[1] poliatum iri (11)
liciti

(11) iii. 175: nihil fictum, nihil ad tempus

V inserts *a te* before *fictum*. This indicates:

nihil
fictum nihil (11)
ad tempus

A te appears to be an anticipation of *ad te-*. The error is due to ὁμ.

[1] I assume an omission of *s-* after *-ris*.

(12) iii. 183: eorum hominum fidei tabulae . . . committuntur

V repeats *hominum* after *fidei*. This indicates:

eorum
hominum fidei (12)
tabulae

(12) v. 133: dicit sese in terram esse egressum

For *sese* *V* has *esse*. This indicates:

dicit
sese in terram (12)
esse egressum

(19) v. 98: quae est urbs Syracusis suo nomine ac moenibus, quo in loco

V has *suo* for *quo*. This indicates:

Syracusis
suo nomine (9)
ac moenibus (10)
quo in loco

The mistake is due to ὁμ.

(21) ii. 155: quo confugies? ubi nitere? modo . . . abalienasti

V repeats *quo* before *modo*. This indicates:

quo confugi (10)
es ubi nitere (11)
modo

(21) v. 126: nemo istorum dissimulat, nemo laborat

Here *V* has *eistorum* and *elaborat*. The corruptions seem due to the variant *enemo* (bis) for *nemo*. Cf. *Phil.* ii. 36 nemo] enemo *V*: so also ii. 24 esentire *V*, iii. 4 euxoris *V*, x. 7 eprodideritis *V*. If so, a previous MS. may have had:

mg. e nemo
istorum dis (10)
mg. e simulat nemo (11)
laborat

(22) v. 121: quin ita calamitatem illam putaret illorum ut fortunam tamen non alienam . . . arbitraretur

Here *V* repeats *putaret* before *tamen*. This indicates:

illam	
putaret illoꝝ	(12)
ut fortunam	(10)
tamen	

The repetition is due to ὁμ.

(30) ii. 1: suscepi enim causam totius ordinis, suscepi causam rei publicae

V repeats *enim* in the second clause after *suscepi*. This indicates:

suscepi	
enim causam	(10)
totius ordi	(10)
nis suscepi	(10)
causam	

(40) v. 130: satis illorum voluntati qui a me hoc petiverunt factum esse arbitrabor

Here V repeats *satis* before *factum*. This indicates:

satis illo	(9)
rum uolunta	(10)
ti qui a me hoc	(11)
petiuerunt	(10)
factum	

(62) iii. 171: quod omnis frumenti copia decumarum nomine penes istum esset redacta, solitum esse istum pecuniam cogere.

V gives *quod omnis frumenti pecunia decumanorum*, &c. Here *decumanorum* is a slip for *decumarum*, while *pecunia* looks like a variant for *pecuniam*, which has got into the wrong place. This may indicate:

	frumenti	
	copia decu	(9)
	marum nomine	(11)
	penes istum	(10)
	esset redac	(10)
	ta solitum es	(11)
mg. pecunia	se istum pecu	(11)
	niam cogere	

The variant may have been transferred through ὁμ. (*decu-*, *pecu-*).

(81) iii. 69: summittebat iste Timarchidem qui moneret eos, si saperent, ut transigerent. Pernegabant. Quid ergo? In singulos HS quinquagenis milibus damnari mavultis

V inserts *septu* before *mavultis.* This corruption may be due to a conflation of two variants, viz. *sep-* for *sap*(*erent*), and *tu* for *ut*. This indicates:

mg. sep	si saperent	(10)
mg. tu	ut transige	(10)
	rent pernega	(11)
	bant quid er	(10)
	go in singu	(9)
	los HS quin	(9)
	quagenis mili	(12)
	bus damnari	(10)
	mauultis	

To these I would add:

ii. 116: ardebat amore illius hospitae propter quam hospiti iura violarat. Hoc non solum sciri verum etiam commemorari semper volebat. Itaque ex illa ipsa re quam accusante Agathino gesserat Veneri potissimum deberi praemium statuit

Here for *Veneri potissimum V* gives *hostissimum Veneri.* The corruption *hostissimum* appears to be a conflation of *hos-* from *hospitae*, or *hospiti* with [*po*]*tissimum.* Apparently the writer looked back. The variety in the collocation may indicate a previous omission of *potissimum* (10).

I would call attention to the fact that the long omission of 222 letters is not explained by ὁμ. It seems not unlikely that the scribe skipped a column in his model. If so, this would seem to have contained 20 or 21 lines to the page.

Before I proceed to the minuscule MSS., I must mention that the Turin palimpsest A. ii. 2 contained a single leaf from a MS. of the *Verrines.* The interest of the leaf is due to the fact that it contains a passage found in *p*, but omitted by *DΨ*, viz.:

(54) i. 45: dictum est hoc in Cn. Dolabellae iudicio. Dictum? etiam aestimatum

The omission is due to ὁμ.

I also mention here, for the sake of completeness, a fragment from a papyrus book, containing *Verr.* i. 60–1, published in *Papiri Greci e Latini* (pp. 43–7), cent. vi. This is written in lines averaging 36 letters to the line. It does not throw any light upon the text.

I now turn to *R* = Paris. 7774 *A*, cent. ix. This MS. is written in two columns, with 21 lines to a page. The contents of a page (f. 80^{v}) reproduced by Chatelain (Pl. 31) are:

Col. i = 517 letters, avg. 24½ to line.
„ ii = 464 „ „ 22 „

Another page (f. 92^{v}) is reproduced by E. Thomas in his edition of *Verr.* iv, v. In this:

Col. i = 498 letters.
„ ii = 454 „

In both pages col. ii contains less than col. i.

Various indications show that *R* is not far removed from a MS. written in capitals. Thus we find in it stray capitals,[1] e. g.:

iv. 67: querimonia. M = querimoniam
74: L. N. suls = in suis
81: de L. N. de = deinde
97: fano P = fanorum

The confusion of *E* and *F*, due to the similarity of these letters in capitals, may be illustrated by:

iv. 52 electus = fletus; v. 27 rosae artus = rosa fartus; 72 forum = eorum; 177 prima faccionis = primae actionis.

Whereas *V* has a number of doublets in its text, only a few survive in *R*. I have noticed:

iv. 95: praetorisa (= praetoris^{a})
v. 126: peruenire se (= peruenire^{sse})
140: in ad corpora

It is probable that more occurred in the model, but were removed by Caroline revisers.

R in its present form contains *Verr.* iv–v only. It has, however, been mutilated, as is manifest from the signature *Q.* xxxv, which occurs on f. 80^{v} (Chatelain, Pl. 31). E. Thomas has pointed out that 200 folios must have perished before *Verr.* iv, and that 200 folios would exactly suffice for the previous speeches.[2]

[1] These stray capitals are found in the same places in *S*, also in Harl. 2682 (*H*), which has excerpts from *Verr.* iii, iv. If *S* and *H* are not derived from *R*, all three MSS. must have been drawn from a common ancestor written in minuscules.

[2] *Revue de Philologie*, 1885, p. 167. The same conclusion was reached independently by Peterson.

R is not alone, but belongs to a family in which it is the chief member. Some members of the group seem to be derived from *R*; others may be drawn from a *gemellus*. Peterson has drawn particular attention to

S = Paris. 7775, cent. xiii (mutilated).
D = Paris. 7823, cent. xv.

He considers *D* to have been derived from *S*, before *S* was mutilated, and *S* to be derived from a *gemellus* of *R*, which contained all the *Verrines*. It is, I think, not impossible that the parent of *S* was *R* itself before it was mutilated. In any case *S* and *D* appear to give the *R* tradition where *R* is no longer extant. As *S*, in addition to *Verr.* iv and v, only contains a fragment (i. 90–111), *D* is of real importance for the previous speeches.

Omissions of *R* + dittography:

(9) iv. 132: *religione
v. 42: praedonum
61: *civitatum
(10) iv. 66: *rex ad istum
103: reponendos
v. 40: imperium ac
56: **litterae re-
(11) v. 118: vestitumque
(12) iv. 23: aedificandam
25: et amplissima
80: monumentorum
140: conservandis
v. 81: iam continuos
95: stupri plenus
133: hoc Hennenses
(13) iv. 6: atque amicorum
144: adulteriisque
(14) v. 71: remouerat atque
76: quisquam omnium
174: quae ad iudicium
(15) v. 180: senectutem summa
(17) v. 47: princeps civitatis
(19) v. 102: id facere desistant et
152: et animo aequo videmus
(21) v. 75: nulla esset hic defensio
(22) v. 154: partim in vinclis necatos
(23) v. 133: feriri debere (oportere *V*) non ego metum

(24) iv. 54: atque hac tota de re audistis
(28) v. 172: vestram severitatem desiderant
(29) v. 51: tot annos post iure imperii nostri
(33) v. 125: et ex complexu matris ereptus innocens
(40) iv. 143: *Peducaeo. Dicit qui primi suaserint. Decernitur
v. 66: victoria dulcius, nullum est autem testimonium
(44) v. 136: tu in iudicium archipiratam domo producere ausus es
(46) iv. 70: Antiochum regem Syracusis: se illud scire ad istum esse
(50) iv. 142: *sese antea cum audissent ei negotium facessitum cumque eum (*add. m.* 2 *in lac.*)
(83) v. 110: *est destitutus. Quid erat autem quod quisquam diceret aut defenderet. Cleomenem nominare non licet (*add. m.* 2 *in lac.*)[1]
(102) iv. 35: quod verbo transigere possum. Ede mihi scriptum quid argenti in provincia Sicilia pararis, unde quidque aut quanti emeris.
(124) iv. 27: peripetasmata. Quaesivi an misisset: respondit id quod necesse erat, scilicet dicto audientem fuisse PR.: misisse. Rogavi, pervenissentne Agrigentum.
(215) v. 187: quarum sacra, sicut opiniones hominum ac religiones ferunt, longe maximis atque occultissimis caerimoniis continentur, a quibus initia vitae atque victus, morum, legum, mansuetudinis, humanitatis hominibus et civitatibus data ac dispertita esse dicuntur *bis scr.* (*e coll. mea*)
(318) iv. 151: *reliquerat, ademisset. Ac videte hominis impudentiam atque arrogantiam, iud., qui non solum Verria haec turpia ac ridicula ex Heraclii pecunia constituerit, verum etiam Marcellia tolli imperarit, ut ei sacra facerent quotannis cuius opera omnium annorum sacra deosque patrios amiserant; eius autem familiae dies festos tollerent, per quam ceteros quoque festos dies recuperarent.

This passage comes at the end of iv, after the words *calamitoso dies*. Halm says:

'*calamitoso dies R*, in quibus verbis in cod. folium desinit, ut reliqua verba desiderentur. Nec tamen videtur folium in cod. excidisse.'

There is also a long omission, viz.:

v. 162–71: *se commemoratione . . . amicos nostrae civitatis

The omitted passage occupies 141½ lines in the Teubner text. Here several folios of an ancestor must have been lost.

Before I go further I would refer to some remarks of Peterson concerning 'lacunae occurring in the *X* family', i. e. in *R*, *S*, *D*, &c.[2]

[1] This reading, which is not mentioned by Halm, is taken from my own collation.
[2] *Journal of Philology*, xxx, p. 174.

He says, 'Where these are found in *D*, it is probable that they had already existed in *S*, of which *D* is a copy; they may, in fact, be traceable to the lost archetype of *R* and *S*.' He refers to six omissions in iv–v, found in the preceding list, viz. v. 152 (19), v. 154 (22), v. 136 (44), iv. 142 (50), iv. 35 (102), iv. 27 (124), which are common to the family. He also quotes a similar lacuna found in *D* and its allies in *Div.* 65–6, where, in the absence of *R*, *D* becomes the chief representative of the family. The omitted passage is:

(317) dubitare quisquam potest quin honestius sit eorum causa apud quos quaestor fueris quam eum cuius quaestor fueris accusare. Clarissimi viri nostrae civitatis temporibus optimis hoc sibi amplissimum pulcherrimumque ducebant, ab hospitibus clientibusque suis, ab exteris nationibus, quae in amicitiam P. R. dicionemque essent, iniurias propulsare eorumque fortunas defendere

The agreement between 317 and 318 (iv. 151) is so striking that Peterson's diagnosis of *D* appears to be verified. It is also interesting to notice that 102 (iv. 35) + 215 (v. 187) = 317. This is a very singular fact.

I now turn to the shorter omissions. There is one telescoped passage, viz. v. 56. Here editors read with Zumpt:

litterae rerum decretarum

R has *eum decretarum*, so also *S*. This appears to indicate in the common ancestor:

litterae re (10)
rum

After omission of a line, *-rum* was changed to *eum*.

In this connexion I may mention:

v. 61: testimonia civitatum

Here *RS* have *testimonium*, without *civitatum*. This may indicate:

testimonia (10)
ciuitatum (9)

There are also some interesting corruptions which may go back to this early stage, viz.:

iv. 88: innocentem in hominem.

R has *innocentem* ^in^ *in hominem.* This indicates:

innocentem (10)
in hominem

v. 160: se Syracusis in lautumiis fuisse.

R has *lautumisse* for *lautumiis.* This indicates:

se Syracusis (11)
in lautumis (10)
fuisse

I would also mention, with some doubt:

v. 93: non enim sicut erat anper consuetudo praedonum adventum significabat ignis.

So R^1, *nuper* (for *anper*) R^2; antea *p.* It is possible that *anper* is a conflation of *añ* (= *ante*) and *per*, a variant for *prae-* (cf. v. 108 perditum *edd.*; praeditum *codd.*). If so, the corruption may go back to

sicut erat añ
consuetudo (10)
mg. per praedonum

The short omissions of *R* are curiously like those of *V.* Thus I have noted 15 omissions of 9–12 letters in *V*, and oddly enough 15 similar omissions in *R.* So *V* and *R* both have four omissions of 20–4, *V* has one of 31, and *R* one of 33, while both *VR* have one of 44. The evidence seems to suggest that both MSS. go back to an ancestor, not necessarily the same, written in lines of 9–12 letters.

It is necessary, when dealing with the longer omissions of *R*, to speak with caution, since it is highly improbable that *R* was copied directly from a MS. written in such narrow columns. It is likely that more than one intermediary ancestor has intervened. The following corruption is significant:

v. 173: sed mehercule vestra reique publicae causa, iudices, nolo in hoc delecto consilio tantum flagiti esse commissum, nolo eos iudices, quos ego probarim

R inserts *quos ego probarim* (15) after *causa iud.*, as well as in the proper place. The words *nolo in . . . eos iud.* consist of 60 letters (15 × 4 = 60). This suggests in an intermediate MS.:

causa iud.
nolo in hoc delecto (16)
consilio tantum (14)
flagiti esse com (14)
missum nolo eos iud. (16)
quos ego probarim

With this we may connect:

v. 94: verum habita est a multitudine ratio temporis, habita tumultus, habita etiam dignitatis

So *V*, *edd.*; *R*, after *habita etiam*, repeats *tumultus habita* (14). An ancestor may have had:

temporis habi
ta tumultus habita (16)
etiam dignitatis

The scribe, after writing *etiam*, looked back to the previous line.

The evidence is somewhat meagre, since *R* is, on the whole, carefully written, and its text has been purified of those errors which are especially useful for the purposes of this inquiry. It is, however, interesting to notice some singular points of resemblance in the chief corruptions which it contains, viz.:

(53) v. 18. Here *R* gives:

servos quos ipse de consilio belli faciendi causa consensisse iudicavit, eos sine consili sententia . . . liberavit.

In *p* we find *cum* for *de*, before *consilio*, which is obviously a correction. Lambinus more plausibly reads *de consilii sententia . . . sine consilio . . . liberavit.* E. Thomas remarks '*sententia* a dû être transposé.'

Since the transposition is shared by *p*, it probably goes back to a remote ancestor. We may, therefore, arrange thus, postulating an original omission of *sententia* (9):

mg. sententia de consili
belli facien (11)
di causa con (10)
sensisse iudi (12)
cauit eos si (10)
ne consilio (10) = 53

(56) v. 20: si maxime in culpa fuerit Apollonius, tamen in hominem honestissimae civitatis honestissimum tam graviter animadverti causa indicta non oportuisse

R has *maximae* after *honestissimae*. Thomas remarks, 'le mot a dû être transposé de la ligne précédente.' The words *maxime* . . . *honestissimae* consist of 56 letters. The resemblance to the previous passage is striking. I, therefore, venture to arrange as follows, supposing *maximae* to be a variant for *maxime*, which has got out of place in *R* :

	si	
mg. maximae	maxime in cul	(11)
	pa fuerit apol	(12)
	lonius tamen	(11)
	in hominem ho	(11)
	nestissimae	(11) = 56
	ciuitatis	

(103) v. 140: nullum fuit omnino civitatis isto praetore in hoc genere discrimen. Itaque iam consuetudine ad corpora civium Romanorum etiam sine istius nutu ferebatur manus ipsa lictoris. Num potes hoc negare?

For *negare R* has *genere*, the mistake being due to the occurrence of *hoc* before *genere* and *negare*.

The abbreviation *C. R.* for *civis Romanus* is frequent in the MSS., e.g. v. 72, *c. r.* = *cives Romani V*, ib. *ceruos* = *c. r*[os] (cf. p. 221), 73 *civem Romanum R* : *c. r.* δ, and must be ascribed to the archetype.

The words *genere* . . . *potes hoc* consist of 103 letters. This is interesting in view of the omission by *R* of 102 letters in iv. 35. Also, there seems to be a relation between 103 and 53 in v. 18.

The reason for the error becomes apparent if we arrange the passage thus:

hoc	
genere dis	(9)
crimen itaque	(12)
iam consuetu	(11)
dine ad corpo	(11)
ra c. r. etiam	(9)
sine istius	(10)
nutu fereba	(10)
tur manus ip	(10)
sa lictoris	(10)
num potes hoc	(11) = 103
negare	

(154) v. 152–3: tantum sibi auctoritatis in re publica suscepit ut . . . iis omnibus mortem acerbam crudelemque proponeret, si fortuna eos ad aliquam partem Siciliae detulisset. Ad Cn. Pompeium, clarissimum virum et fortissimum, permulti occiso Perperna ex illo Sertoriano numero militum confugerunt.

For *ex illo R* has the corruption *ex* [h]*is illo*; also, after *suscepit ut* . . . *R* has *his* for *iis*. It would appear that *is* (i. e. *iis*) and *his* are variants, and that *is* has got into the wrong place. The words *iis omnibus* . . . *Perperna ex* consist of 154 letters.

(156) v. 186: mater Idaea, quam . . . sic spoliatam reliquit ut nunc nomen modo Africani et vestigia violatae religionis maneant, monumenta victoriae fanique ornamenta non exstent: vosque omnium rerum forensium, consiliorum maximorum, legum iudiciorumque arbitri et testes

Here for *legum R* has *reliquum*. The eye of the copyist seems to have fallen on *reliquit* after *spoliatam*. Or, *reliquum* may be a variant for *reliquit*, which has got into the wrong place.

These figures, 53, 56, 103, 154, 156, hang together in a singular way. They become still more significant if combined with some evidence previously considered, viz. the omission of 102 letters by *R* in iv. 35, and of 318 letters (159 × 2 = 318) in iv. 151. Also, we have the omission of 317 letters by *D*, the representative of *R*, in *Div.* 65–6. Further, we have the interesting fact that the omission of 102 letters by *R* in iv. 35 + the dittography of 215 letters in v. 187 = 317. The numbers 154–156 appear to be connected with 317–18.

The conclusion seems to follow that 154–156 represents a column in the ultimate ancestor of *R*, and that the corruptions in v. 186, 153, are due to the fact that a variant has got into the wrong column.

It is interesting to observe that the palimpsest of the *de Re Publica* has columns of exactly this size. I have noticed the following examples:

(154) pp. 142, col. i; 205, col. ii
(156) p. 81, col. ii
(157) pp. 93, col. ii; 205, col. i
(159) p. 50, col. i

In order to illustrate the point I write out *de Re Publica*, p. 81, col. ii, side by side with *Verr.* v. 186, put into similar formation:

de Re Publ., p. 81, col. ii		*Verr.* v. 186	
tasse set a uita	(13)	reliquit ut	(10)
hominum ab	(9)	nunc nomen	(9)
horrentem	(9)	modo africa	(10)
et a maiorib.	(10)	ni et uestigia	(12)
reliqui disse	(12)	uiolatae re	(10)
ruerunt sine	(11)	ligionis ma	(10)
ullo certo ex	(11)	neant monu	(9)
emplari for	(10)	menta uicto	(10)
maque reip.	(9)	riae fanique	(11)
de generibus	(11)	ornamenta non	(12)
et de rationi	(11)	exstent uos	(10)
bus ciuitatū	(11)	que omnium re	(11)
tu mihi uide	(10)	rum forensi	(10)
ris utrumq.	(9)	um consilio	(10)
facturus es	(10)	rum maximorum	(12)
	156		156

The next column in the ultimate ancestor of *R* began with *legum*, for which *reliquum* has been substituted. (Cf. p. 136.) There is, therefore, good ground for believing that *R* is derived from a MS. which in point of formation was a *gemellus* of the *de Re Publica* palimpsest.

If this analysis is sound, it follows that *R* has omitted a page of its ancestor at the end of *Verr.* iv. This may be due to accident, or there may have been a blank page after *Verr.* iv, in which case a folio was lost.

I abstain from any speculations concerning the large lacuna in v. 162–71, since this may be due to an intermediate ancestor.

C = Holkham 387, cent. ix.

This MS. was formerly no. 498 in the Cluni catalogue,[1] where it is described as containing 'Cicero in Catillina et idem pro Quinto Ligario et pro rege Deiotaro et de publicis litteris et de actione idemque in Verrinis'. The portion of it which still exists contains parts of the *Catilinarians*, *pro Ligario*, *pro rege Deiotaro*, and *Verr.*

[1] Delisle, *Cabinet des MSS.*, ii. 478.

ii. 1, distributed among 39 folios. It is written in double columns, with 24 lines to the page in ff. 1–33 and 25 in ff. 34–9. I have counted the letters in the following pages:

	Col. 1	Col. 2		
(*Cat.*) 7ᵛ	528	555	=	1083, avg. 22½
(*Lig.*) 19ʳ	601	595	=	1196, avg. 25
(*Verr.*) 28ʳ	652	602	=	1254, avg. 26
(*Verr.*) 37ʳ	731	693	=	1424, avg. 28½

In the last passage there are 25 lines to the page.

It will be seen that the script gradually contracts in the course of the work.

The 39 folios fall into the following blocks. I add the number of lines which they occupy in the Teubner text:

(1) f. 1. *Cat.* i. 1–5: quousque . . . pridem = 60.
(2) ff. 2–8. *Cat.* i. 17–ii. 11: viderem . . . quacunque = 371. The subscription to i and the title to ii must also be taken into account.
(3) ff. 9–12. *Cat.* ii. 15–iii. 1: ne mihi . . . resti- = 209 + subscription + title.
(4) ff. 13–15. *Cat.* iii. 9–19: regem huius . . . urbis atque = 168.
(5) f. 16. *Cat.* iii. 23–6: ac miserrimo . . . fortuna = 54.
(6) ff. 17–18. *Cat.* iv. 8–15: constituta esse . . . studio = 119.
(7) ff. 19–20. *Lig.* 18–28: hoc victore . . . sed tum = 115.
(8) f. 21. *Lig.* 38–*Deiot.* 6: si illi . . . disceptante = 52 + subscription to *Lig.* and title to *Deiot.*
(9) ff. 22–7. *Deiot.* 15–43: finitimi . . . tuae = 351½ + subscription.
(10) ff. 28–33. *Verr.* ii. 1–30: multa . . . cohorte = 360 + title.
(11) f. 34. *Verr.* ii. 112–17: magnificentissime . . . cupidissimumque = 70¾.
(12) ff. 35–9. *Verr.* ii. 157–83: iam dudum . . . manifestum = 334.

Four quaternion marks preserve a record of the original foliation, viz. on fol. 4 q̄. i, on f. 11 q̄. ii, on f. 16 q̄. iii, on f. 34 q̄. x. In the last case two or more letters have been erased after x. It is, however, common in MSS. to find quaternion marks tampered with after a loss of leaves, and the erasure after x. may represent a correction which has subsequently been struck out, like so many other corrections in *C*. If the signature is correct, f. 34 must have been f. 80 when *C* was complete.

The content of these leaves is much the same until we come to f. 34. Thus:

(1) f. 1 = 60.
(2) ff. 2–8 = 371 ÷ 7, avg. 53. The subscription and title must be taken into account.

(3) ff. 9–12 = 209÷4, avg. 52¼ + subscription and title.
(4) ff. 13–15 = 168÷3, avg. 56.
(5) f. 16 = 54.
(6) ff. 17–18 = 119÷2, avg. 59½.
(7) ff. 19–20 = 115÷2, avg. 57½.
(8) f. 21 = 52 + subscription and title.
(9) ff. 22–7 = 351½÷6, avg. 58½ + subscription.
(10) ff. 28–33 = 360÷6, avg. 60 + title.
(11) f. 34 = 70¾.
(12) ff. 35–9 = 334÷5, avg. 67 (nearly).

If we take those blocks where we have not to make allowances for a subscription or title, the averages for folios 1–28 works out at 57.

I now take those parts of the speeches which have been lost, viz.:

Cat. i. 5–17: factum . . . offensum = 159½, i.e. 3 ff., avg. 53.
ii. 11–15: ratione . . . timeo = 56, i.e. 1 folio.
iii. 1–9: -tutam . . . ad quem = 106, i.e. 2 ff., avg. 53.
19–23: imperii occasum . . . crudelissimo = 57, i.e. 1 folio.
26–iv. 8: atque condicio . . . impiis = 165, i.e. 3 ff., avg. 55.
iv. 15–end: qua virtute . . . possit = 145 }
Lig. 1–18: novum . . . quamquam = 186 } = 331, i.e. 6 ff., avg. 55 + subscription to *Cat.* iv and title of *Lig.*
28–38: sero erat . . . admonebo = 116, i.e. 2 ff., avg. 58.
Deiot. 6–15: te quantam . . . multi erant = 114, i.e. 2 ff., avg. 57.
Verr. ii. 30–112: cognoscere . . . amplissime = 1106, i.e. 18 ff., avg. 61½.

The average for the last passage is higher than for the preceding speeches, but agrees closely with the passage which comes before it, viz. 360÷6 = 60 (+ title).

The rest of *Verr.* ii comes after f. 34, where the lines are longer and there is an extra line to the page, with the result that the unit rises to 71.

Verr. ii. 117–57: cognosce . . . cupierint = 570, i.e. 8 ff., avg. 71¼.
183–end: erit de . . . revertuntur = 3520, i.e. 50 ff., avg. 70½ (nearly).

It thus appears that 96 leaves of *C* have perished.

The quaternion markings on ff. 4, 11, 16 show that there was a blank leaf at the beginning of *C*. This is most easily seen from the signature q̃. iii on f. 16, containing *Cat.* iii. 23–6 *ac miserrimo . . . fortuna*, since this is a separate fragment, while q̃. i and q̃. ii come each in the middle of a block. The contents of *C* up to and including *Cat.* iii. 23–6 were as follows. I mark with an asterisk those leaves which are still extant:

*i. 1–5	=	1 f.
5–17	=	3 ff.
*17–ii. 11	=	7 ff.
ii. 11–15	=	1 f.
*15–iii. 1	=	4 ff.
iii. 1–9	=	2 ff.
*9–19	=	3 ff.
19–23	=	1 f.
*23–6	=	1 f.
		23

An extra leaf is required to make the signature q̃. iii correct.

The total content of the MS., therefore, apart from the question of further loss after the *Catilinariae*, was 1 + 39 + 96 = 136, i.e. 17 quaternions.

I now come to the signature q̃. x on f. 34 (*Verr.* ii. 112–17).

We have found that *Cat.* i. 1–iii. 26 occupied 24 ff. After this point, up to and including f. 34, we have:

Cat.	iii. 26–iv. 8	=	3 ff.
	*iv. 8–15	=	2 ff.
	15–end	=	6 ff.
Lig.	1–18		
	*18–28	=	2 ff.
	28–38	=	2 ff.
	*38–*Deiot.* 6	=	1 f.
Deiot.	6–15	=	2 ff.
	*15–43	=	6 ff.
Verr.	ii. 1–30	=	6 ff.
	30–112	=	18 ff.
	*112–17	=	1 f.
			49

Here 24 + 49 = 73. We are, therefore, 7 ff. short, if *Verr.* ii. 112–17 is to be on f. 80.

In view of the relation of *C* to other MSS. which contain the *pro Marcello* as well as the *pro Ligario* and *pro rege Deiotaro*, the question whether *C* originally contained the *pro Marcello* is one of considerable importance. It remains, therefore, to see whether the *pro Marcello* will fit into the gap.

The *pro Marcello* occupies 359 lines in the Teubner text, to which an addition has to be made for the title and subscription, also for a possible blank space. If we divide 359 by 7, the result is $51\frac{2}{7}$. If we allow 12 lines extra, a very moderate estimate, we have 371, which, divided by 7, gives 53. The conclusion is that the *pro Marcello* would suffice to make the signature $\tilde{q}$. x to f. 34 correct.

The probability, therefore, is that *C* originally contained the *pro Marcello*, but that this was lost before the twelfth century, when the old Cluni catalogue was made. This supposition would account for the silence of the catalogue concerning the *pro Marcello*, also for the attempt to correct the signature $\tilde{q}$. x.

If this view is correct, the total contents of *C* up to *Verr.* ii. 117 were ten quaternions, i.e. 80 ff.

After this we have:

Verr. ii. 117–57	=	8 ff.
* 157–83	=	5 ff.
183-end	=	50 ff.
		63

This gives a total of 143 ff. for the contents of *C* before it was mutilated. As 144 ff. = 18 quaternions, there must have been one folio or a portion of one folio blank at the end of the volume.

The contents of *C*, when intact, appear to have been distributed thus:

f. 1	blank
* f. 2	*Cat.* i. 1–5
ff. 3–5	5–17
* ff. 6–12	17–ii. 11
f. 13	ii. 11–15
* ff. 14–17	15–iii. 1
ff. 18–19	iii. 1–9
* ff. 20–2	9–19
f. 23	19–23
* f. 24 ($\tilde{q}$. iii)	23–6
ff. 25–7	26–iv. 8
* ff. 28–9	iv. 8–15
ff. 30–42	15-end + *Marc.* + *Lig.* 1–18
* ff. 43–4	*Lig.* 18–28
ff. 45–6	28–38
* f. 47	38–*Deiot.* 6
ff. 48–9	*Deiot.* 6–15

* ff. 50–5	*Deiot.* 15–43
* ff. 56–61	*Verr.* ii. 1–30
ff. 62–79	30–112
* f. 80 ($\tilde{q}$. x)	112–17
ff. 81–8	117–57
* ff. 89–93	157–83
ff. 94–143	183–end

I now proceed to discuss the antecedents of *C* (*c*) in the *Verrines* (*c* = variants quoted from *C* before it was mutilated).

I give first a list of omissions. It is to be noticed that in three cases (ii. 22, 26, 27) the missing passage is added by the second hand. There is also one dittography.

(10) ii. 26: HS CCC milia *om. C*
165: est quantum *om. C*
176–7: ** daret satis- *om. C*
179: nullius vim *om. C*
(11) ii. 28: abstinentes *om. c*
40: deterrime et *om. c*
50: ex aere facta *om. c*
54: hereditatem *om. c*
156: quam multi et *om. c*
(12) ii. 11: tantis opibus *om. C*
113: nihil ex sacro *om. C*
168: ab aratoribus *om. C*
176: quid sociorum *om. C*
186: male gestarum *om. c*
(13) ii. 114: legati laedant *om. C*
(14) ii. 23: ac pudentissimi *om. C*
169: familiaritatem *om. C*
(15) ii. 7: summa parsimonia *om. C*
17: sive pecuariorum *om. C*
42: atque obsecraret *om. c*
(17) ii. 13: causas satis iustas *bis scr.*
26: Verres cognoscebat *om.* C^1
(18) ii. 22: licebat Venerem quod *om.* C^1
40: et in iudiciis maxime *om. c*
(22) ii. 70: * quid sibi esset faciendum *om. c*
(32) iii. 167: adlatarum libris Romae in litterarum *om. c*
(39) ii. 45: * sed ad communem litium aestimationem venisse *om. c*
(80) ii. 2: nostram venissent numquam postea deficerent, pleraeque autem et maxime inlustres in amicitia *om. C*
(82) ii. 24: satisne vobis magnam pecuniam Venerius homo qui e Chelidonis sinu in provinciam profectus esset *om. C in lac.*

(88) ii. 23: dixit hoc idem M. Lucullus se de his Dionis incommodis pro hospitio quod sibi cum eo esset iam ante cognosse *om. C in lac.*

(93) ii. 27: nocens adducetur qui ista defensione non possit uti: etenim cum Verres utatur, quis erit umquam posthac reus tam *om.* C^1

This omission requires some explanation. In *C nocens* is added in the margin immediately after *quis reus tam*, which comes at the end of the line. After *nocens* there is an omission mark, and at the foot of the page is added in smaller characters, *adducetur* . . . *reus tam*.

In *O*, a MS. to be discussed shortly, the text has

quis reus tam nocens . . . posthac reus tam

but in the margin the words *tam convictus* (12) are added before *tam nocens*, and Müller, with most editors, accepts the addition. Peterson thinks that it comes from

i. 10: reus tam nocens, tam perditus, tam convictus.

To me the parallel passage appears to support *tam convictus*. If we add these words, the total here omitted by the scribe = 105 letters.

The first point to notice here is the large number of small omissions, 10–12 letters (14 examples). I have marked one of these as a telescoped passage, viz.:

ii. 176–7: misisse l. Canuleium qui in portu operas daret. Satisne magnum crimen hoc videtur.

Here *C* after *portu* gives *operas ne magnum*, &c. (*med. om.*).

The number of short omissions in *C* and the other chief MSS. of the *Verrines* justifies the assumption that this goes back to a MS. which had:

operas
daret satis (10)
ne

There are clear indications of an intermediate MS., which may have been the model. In addition to the long passage in i. 10 there are two marginal additions, viz.:

(17) ii. 22: licebat uenerẽ quod
26: uerres cognoscebat

As written in the MS. ii. 22 is of exactly the same length as ii. 26.

There is also one dittography, viz.:

(17) ii. 13: causas satis iustas *bis scr.*

I notice also that in § 177, after *iuris iurandi*, Peterson mentions an erasure 'sedecim fere litterarum'. This was most probably another dittography.

The only other marginal addition is in ii. 27. It is most natural to connect this with ii. 22, 26. If we take this as 93 letters, there is no explanation except ὁμ. If, however, we add *tam convictus*, the total is 105, which yields a satisfactory result (17 × 6 = 102).

The other large omissions, 80, 82, 88, are strikingly similar. The first of these is peculiar to *C*, the missing words having been recovered in *O*; the other two are shared by *O*. The probability is that all three represent lines in the same MS.

The passages omitted in ii. 23 and 24 are represented in *C* by two lacunae which occur on the same page, 32ᵛ.

In col. i lines 7–10 are left blank. In col. ii the first hand wrote:

in hoc crimine eripuit non is
tius innocentia sed legis excep
tio

He left the rest of l. 3 blank, also ll. 4–6. A second hand completed l. 3 by adding in darker ink:

℞. TESTIMONIV̄ IVCVLLI CHIOREDIONIS = recita testimonium Luculli, Chlori, Dionis.

The correspondence between 88 and 82 suggests that the columns of the model were damaged at the same place. The omissions, therefore, seem not to go back to the remote ancestor revealed by the short omissions, but to represent lines either in the model or in an intermediate MS. It is quite possible that the model of *C* was written in longer lines than those formed by an average of 17 letters. Since, however, this is the only other unit disclosed by the omissions, I venture to arrange ii. 23 and 24 on the hypothesis that this is the ancestor concerned.

col. i		col. ii	
dixit hoc idem M. lucul	(18)	satisne nobis magnam	(18)
lus se de his dionis	(16)	pecuniam uenerius	(16)
incommodis pro hospi	(18)	homo qui e chelido	(15)

col i

tio quod sibi cum eo es (18)
set iam ante cognosse (18)
quid lucullus qui tum (18)
in macedonia fuit me (17)
lius haec cognouit (16)
quam tu hortensi qui (17)
romae fuisti ad quem (17)
dio confugit qui de (16)
dionis iniuriis gra (17)
uissime per litteras (18)
cum uerre questus es (17)
noua tibi haec sunt in (18)
opinata nunc primum (17)
aures hoc tuae crimen (18)
accipiunt nihil ex di (18)
one nihil ex socru tua (18)
femina primaria ser (17)
uilia uetere dionis (17)
hospita audisti non (17)
ne multa mei testes (16)
quae tu scis nesciunt (18)
nonne te mihi testem in (19)
hoc crimine eripuit (17)
non istius innocenti (18)
a sed legis exceptio (17)

col. ii

nis sinu in prouinci (17)
am profectus esset (16)

C omits ll. 1–5, *dixit hoc . . . cognosse* (88) and *satisne . . . esset* (82), leaving a lacuna in both places.

References to official documents are frequently omitted by the MSS., and I am inclined to think that they must have been often written in the margin. In this case it is to be noticed that the words

℞ TESTIMONIV̄ IVCVLLI CHIOREDIONIS

are written in capitals.

I have, therefore, not included them in this reconstruction.

I would draw attention to the following corruptions:

ii. 10: quae non postulata, sed in istum crimina viderentur esse.

In *C quae* is repeated above the line after *crimina*. This may be due to the following arrangement in a previous MS.:

quae non postulata (16)
sed in istum crimina (17)
uiderentur esse

ii. 22. Here *C* has:

qui ery
cum montem obtinebat petit nae
uius turpio quidam istius excur
sor et emissarius homo omnium
ex illo conuentu quadruplatorũ
deterrimus a sacerdote PR. con
demnatus iniuriarum etenim
erat eiusmodi causa ut ipse ery
cum quaereret.

Here *erycum* in ll. 8–9 is an error for *cum*, introduced from *erycum* in ll. 1–2. The error may be explained by the following arrangement in a previous MS.:

qui
erycum montem obtine (18)
bat petit naeuius tur (18)
pio quidam istius ex (17)
cursor et emissarius (18)
homo omnium ex illo con (19)
uentu quadruplatorum (19)
deterrimus a sacerdo (18)
te PR. condemnatus iniu (19)
riarum etenim erat ei (18)
us modi causa ut ipse (17)
cum quaereret

Flor. Bad. 2618 (79), cent. xv.

This MS. (*O*), also known as Lag. 42, from Lagomarsini, a learned Jesuit who collated the Florentine MSS. of Cicero, is of great importance for *Verr.* ii, iii, in spite of its late date, since it represents the tradition of *C*, where this is defective.

It is bound up with another MS. which contains the Invectives ascribed to Cicero and Sallust, the *Catilinariae* and *Caesarianae*, also sundry humanistic works, e.g. a poem of Petrarch on Coluccio and epigrams on Dante and other distinguished Florentines. *O* contains all the *Verrines*, but its appearance suggests that *Verr.* ii, iii, which are in a fairly good hand, resembling that of Wolfenbüttel 205 (p. 18), are taken from a separate source. The rest of the MS., which is vulgar in character, is written in a very illegible cursive. On the first page there is a partially erased library mark *iste liber est* || || || || ||.

The connexion between *C* and *O* is of the closest character. I illustrate by a single example:

ii. 163: dilexerit ea.

For *ea* *C* has *F. A.*,[1] while *O* has *f. a.* This *proprius error* is due to the confusion of F and E, which is frequent in capital script. As a rule *O* follows the second hand in *C*, e.g. ii. 9 iniur^{i}s *C*: iniuriis *O*; sometimes, however, it adopts the reading of C^1, e.g. ii. 1 venerit C^1O: veniret C^2. In a considerable number of cases where *O* has a variant, a correction in *C* has been erased and cannot now be read. The regularity with which this phenomenon occurs shows that the erased correction must have been similar to the reading of *O*.

Peterson holds that *O* is a direct copy of *C*. I cannot follow him here. What appears to me a fatal difficulty is that *C* omits a passage which is found in *O*, viz.:

(80) ii. 2: nostram venissent numquam postea deficerent, pleraeque autem et maxime illustres in amicitia.

In the model of *O* these words must have been added in the margin, or elsewhere.

A further objection is that, according to Peterson's statement, with which I agree, the erasures in *C* took place at an early date. They cannot, therefore, have been legible in the fifteenth century when *O* was written. I therefore conclude that there was an intermediate ancestor between *C* and *O*.

I now give a list of omissions in *O*, marking the agreement of *C*, where the MS. is extant, or of *c*, where we have quotations from sixteenth-century scholars. The present contents of *C*, it is to be remembered, are ii. 1–30, 112–17, 157–83.

I would mention that *O* was recollated for Müller by A. Reifferscheid, who corrected a number of misstatements made by previous collators. It is therefore necessary to consult his notes as well as the collation and supplement (pp. 451–60) in Baiter-Halm.

(9) ii. 49: summa cura
ib.: * suae famae
145: * ut putetis
iii. 13: civitates

[1] Peterson quotes the reading of *C* as *E. A.* When, however, I recently recollated the MS., I had no doubt that it has *F. A.*

iii. 138: * senatores
154: invenimus
(10) ii. 45: * hereditate
86: * recuperare
137: * XXXIX milia
165: est quantum (*C*)
179: nullius vim (*C*)
iii. 47: * vehementer
125: familiarem
156: et contemni
187: * in contione
188: iste hordei
(11) ii. 26: * HS CCCC milia (*C*)
28: * abstinentes (*c*)
31: * eiusdem modi
39: quis vestrum
40: deterrime et (*c*)
50: Syracusanos
ib.: ex aere facta
54: * hereditatem (*c*)
152: rogato et eum
156: quam multi et (*c*)
iii. 133: * satis facere
144: * ea dictitare
204: sed ita fieri
(12) ii. 62: * in provinciam[1]
63: alia Panhormi
113: nihil ex sacro (*C*)
168: ab aratoribus (*C*)
176: quid sociorum (*C*)
iii. 1: continentiae (*c*)
30: ac turpissimo
64: * esse versatum
97: et fortissimo
178: Carbonem et in
186: male gestarum (*c*)
220: eripiendarum
226: * et si aratorum
(13) ii. 57: * qua in re ipsius
74: non solum mente
114: legati laedant (*C*)
iii. 26: * professionem R.
132: ignorabas haec

[1] For *in provinciam O* has *hinc.* This may possibly represent an omission mark *h̄* which has been received into the text.

iii. 169: * fenore accepto
(14) ii. 23: ac pudentissimi (_C_)
53: nisi ei venisset
57: ob tuum decretum
150: * datur id accipio
iii. 60: summa industria
190: ac difficillima
(15) ii. 17: sive pecuariorum
42: atque obsecraret (_c_)
iii. 60: asservatum neque
75: hominum summorum
92: contra omnia iura
(16) ii. 50: Syracusanis locum
78: et trades cui uoles
97: neque humanitatis
iii. 128: epistula L. Metelli
168: et recte non putant
172: * quod numquam antea
217: improbe factum est
(17) iii. 151: quod iam addixisses
(18) ii. 40: et in iudiciis maxime (_c_)
83: sed etiam habitasset
(19) iii. 3: atque eloquentissimo
(20) iii. 211: * ratione innumerabilem
224: vestro, minore periculo
Cf. iii. 24: idem habuit in edicto se _bis scr._
(21) ii. 76: minus ad vitae discrimen
iii. 131: ** terror in auribus animis-
(22) ii. 38: ab institutis superiorum
70: * quid tibi esset faciendum (_c_)
iii. 215: tempore magnum videretur
(23) iii. 205: non ex iure non ex aequitate
207: neque tam longinquus neque
(24) iii. 59: mitto vincla, mitto carcerem
208: publice testimonium dicere
(25) ii. 63: gerere quam istius praeturam
80: iuratus dicit pecuniam datam
iii. 133: non perseveras, non perquiris
157: * ea monet alienum hominem quae
(26) iii. 204: * bonis everti aratores et id non
(27) iii. 79: atque hoc agebat in cubiculo, iud.
83: * lex decumis vendundis C. Verre PR. (_add. m._ 1 _in mg._)
179: in medimnum iterum P. R. a quo HS. XXI
(28) iii. 109: ** quod ipsi Leontini publice non sa-[1]
iii. 125: tamen incolumis numerus manebat

[1] Cf. Müller, p. lxxv.

(30) ii. 1: enim causam totius ordinis suscepi
iii. 96: senatorem ut hoc amplissimum nomen (*c*?)
190: * secuti sunt avariores magistratus
226: atque opportunissimam provinciam
(31) ii. 139: retinere si salvus ipse in provincia
iii. 161: non modo tibi voluptati sed etiam qui
(32) iii. 167: allatarum libris Romae in litterarum (*c*)
223: hoc ad commodum senatorium pertinere
(34) iii 228: etiamne frumentum pro empto gratis dare
(35) iii. 117: * C. Norbani decumae venditae agri Leontini
202: est pecunia, Verres, una qua frumentum tibi
(36) iii. 74: * R., litterae publicae, testimonium publicum
123: se lege Hieronica vendidisse quid scribit
(39) ii. 45: * sed ad communem litium aestimationem venisse (*c*)
iii. 164: pecuniam domum tuam avertisse. Etenim sic hanc
(40) iii. 114: quaterna etiam quina exigerentur, multis autem[1]
(41) iii. 128: in reliquum tamen tempus vectigalibus prospexi
(45) iii. 116: CCXVI quanti decumae venierunt, reliqua sunt tritici
(48) iii. 167: * litterae missae P. Vettii, P. Servilii, C. Antistii magistrorum
iii. 124: * ut aratores qui reliqui erant quam plurimum sererent qui
(54) iii. 85: testimonium publicum. Quo modo solutum sit ex litteris publicis
126: * tamen pro eo ut temporis difficultas aratorumque penuria tulit
(57) ii. 21: quid? tum nemo molestus Dioni fuerat? Non plus quam Liguri C. Sacerdote
(58) iii. 148: atque aliorum quidem agrorum pro portione magno decumas vendidisse
(60) ii. 55: antequam mentio denique controversiae facta esset ulla, discessisset
(69) iii. 220: aequitatis et legis transieritis, scitote vos nullum ceteris in aestimando finem
(82) ii. 24: * satisne vobis magnam pecuniam Venerius homo qui e Chelidonis sinu in provinciam profectus esset (*C*)
(88) ii. 23: * dixit hoc idem M. Lucullus, se de his Dionis incommodis pro hospitio quod sibi cum eo esset iam ante cognosse (*C*)
iii. 99: * tabulae Thermitanorum et testimonium. Imacharensis iam omni frumento ablato, iam omnibus iniuriis tuis

We have here to notice:

(1) The large number of small omissions, viz.:

(9) 6 exx.	(11) 13 exx.
(10) 10 exx.	(12) 13 exx.

Six of these occur in the sections preserved in *C*, and in all cases *C* agrees with *O*. Also we have six agreements of *cO*, where *C* is no longer extant. The probability, therefore, is that a large majority

[1] Cf. Müller, p. lxxvi.

of these short omissions were already present in *C*, and were inherited by *C* from a remote ancestor. *O*, therefore, exhibits the same phenomenon as *VCR*, viz. a striking number of short omissions.

(2) *O* also agrees with *C*, in the larger omissions, viz. (82) ii. 24, and (88) ii. 23. Also, it has an omission of 88 letters in iii. 99, which in all probability goes back to *C*. Further, it is to be noticed that the passage omitted by *C* in ii. 2 *nostram . . . amicitia*, but found in *O*, consists of 80 letters.

The agreement of *CO*, therefore, apart from ii. 2, where *O* has recovered—through a corrector—a passage lost by *C*, is complete.

We have next to consider the telescoped passages, iii. 131 and 109. I do not attach much importance to:

iii. 131: cum tui nominis terror in auribus animisque aratorum versaretur

where *O* gives

cum tui nominis que aratorum versaretur *med. om.* (21)

since *que* might easily be detached from *animis*.

The other example is more striking, viz.:

iii. 109: propter hanc causam quod ipsi Leontini non sane multum

Here, according to Reifferscheid's collation, *O* has:

propter hanc causam ne multum (*med. om.*)

This indicates in a previous MS.:

propter hanc causã
quod ipsi leontini publice non sa (28)
ne multum

The omission is assisted by ὁμ.

The question now arises as to whether any omissions of *O* represent lines in *C*. This is a subject which has been already raised by Peterson, who has pointed out that various omissions of *O* are 'of the average length of a line in *C*'.[1] The instances which he gives are to be found in the preceding list, viz.:

(21) iii. 131	(28) iii. 109, 125
(25) iii. 133, 157	(30) iii. 190, 226
(26) iii. 204	

He does not give the number of letters, but speaks generally of average length.

[1] *Class Rev.*, xvi (1902), pp. 402–3; *J. Phil.*, xxx, p. 195.

It is of interest here to consider more closely the formation of *C*. I have already (p. 236) given the figures for two pages of *C*, viz. 28ʳ and 37ʳ. In the first of these, which contains the beginning of *Verr.* ii, the average number of letters to the line is 26.

The separate figures are:

(col. i) 26, 28, 29, 30, 29, 26, 28, 30, 26, 28, 23, 28, 25, 28, 26, 28, 26, 31, 27, 25, 24, 26, 25, 30
(col. ii) 24, 25, 26, 28, 30, 21, 27, 25, 23, 23, 24, 24, 26, 24, 25, 23, 26, 22, 24, 25, 23, 28, 29, 27

F. 37ʳ contains ii. 166–9. This comes after a slight contraction in the hand has set in. The figures are:

(col. i) 28, 28, 28, 31, 29, 30, 30, 30, 27, 33, 27, 30, 31, 28, 29, 29, 30, 30, 28, 32, 31, 29, 30, 25, 28
(col. ii) 31, 25, 27, 27, 28, 24, 28, 29, 25, 25, 29, 30, 27, 28, 30, 28, 29, 27, 29, 25, 29, 27, 30, 29, 27

The average for the page is 28½.

The extreme limits of variation are, on f. 28ʳ, 21 (one ex.)—31 (one ex.), and, on f. 37ʳ, 24 (one ex.)—33 (one ex.). I do not wish to avail myself of exceptionally short or long lines, but would merely remark that if *O* is derived from *C*, we should expect to find a bulge in the curve of omissions at 25–30. As a matter of fact we find no less than 14 examples, one of which is a telescoped passage.

We also find five examples of 54–60 letters, which may well represent 27–30 × 2.

Only one of the omissions of 25–30 letters occurs in those sections for which we now possess *C*, viz.:

(30) ii. 1: enim causam totius ordinis suscepi

The passage is written thus in *C*:

amplexus animo
sum aliquanto amplius suscepi (26)
enim causam totius ordinis susce (28)
pi causam

Here it is not an exact line of *C*, which is omitted by *O*, but it is easy to see how a scribe after writing *suscepi* might pass on to *causam* after the second *suscepi*. I may illustrate from my own experience in connexion with this particular passage.

When I was counting the figures for this column, I found that

I was a line short. I discovered on examination that I had omitted the line *enim . . . susce-*, having fallen a victim to ὁμ.

It may now be asked if there are any traces of an intermediate MS. between *C* and *O*. If we look at the list of omissions we find, after the four omissions of 30 letters, nine omissions of 31–6 letters. I would not lay much stress on two of these, iii. 117 and iii. 74, since these are titles of documents, which may have been transmitted in the margin.

It is, I think, somewhat remarkable that the bulge in the curve is so prominent at the figure 30. Many lines of this length are found in *C* on ff. 28^r and 37^r, but the averages for these pages are 26 and 28½. I would suggest that *C* was followed by a MS. very like *C*, but with slightly longer lines. If so, this MS. may have contributed to the omissions of 30 letters and be responsible for some of those which follow (31–6).

In conclusion, I would draw attention to two corruptions in *O*, one of which is striking, viz.:

(151) ii. 151: concedas, quod tibi honestissimum est, aratores tibi ad statuam honoris tui causa voluntate sua contulisse. Da mihi hoc, iam tibi maximam partem defensionis praecideris, non enim poteris aratores tibi iratos esse atque inimicos dicere.

O has *honestis* for *iratos*. Müller says 'aberratum videtur esse ad *honestissimum*.'

We may attribute the following distribution, either to *C* or to the intervening MS.:

quod tibi	
honestissimum est aratores tibi ad	(30)
statuam honoris tui causa uolunta	(29)
te sua contulisse. Da mihi hoc iam tibi	(31)
maximam partem defensionis praeci	(30)
deris non enim poteris aratores tibi	(31)
iratos esse	

The error is due to ὁμ.

The other case is:

(93) ii. 181: quod in publicanorum causis vel plurimum aetatis meae versor vehementerque illum ordinem observo, satis commode mihi videor eorum consuetudinem . . . cognosse.

O has *cons* for *causis*. The analogy of the preceding passage suggests that the writer looked forward to *cons[uetudinem]*. If so, a previous MS. may have had:

publicanorum
causis uel plurimum aetatis meae uer (31)
sor uehementerque illum ordinem ob (30)
seruo satis commode mihi uideor eorum (32)
consuetudinem.

Paris. 7776 (*p*), cent. xi.

This MS. is written in long lines with 27 lines to the page, and an average of about 62 letters to the line. Its *fides* is inferior to that of *C* (*O*) and *R*, but on one occasion, at least, it preserves a passage omitted by other MSS., viz.:

(12) i. 130: * sic abusus est *p*: *om. cett.*

This may well have formed a line in the common archetype. While the first-class MSS. contain only portions of the *Verrines*, the whole *corpus* is found in *p*.

A number of additions are made by the second hand. Some of these are placed in the margin, others are entered in a lacuna left by the first writer. The second class differs from the first in that there is no numerical relation between the additions and ὁμ. is hardly ever present. It follows that they have nothing to do with the lineation of ancestors, but are merely passages which were illegible in the model. I therefore confine myself to the marginalia.

The following passages are added by p^2 *in mg.* (or *sup. lin.*):

(10) ii. 61: occasionem
(11) iii. 63: * et domestico
(16) iii. 168: et recte non putant (*om. O*)
(17) i. 74: quod iste iussisset
ii. 192: neque committebant
(18) *Div.* 25: et ita tamen mutandam
iii. 184: hoc quamquam denique
(19) i. 8: * non id solum quaeritur
28: * stragulae quod fuerit
137: talis viros quo dolore
iii. 79: emerat. Hic est Docimus
177: sed nunc demum tenetur
(21) i. 119: quam diu fuit designatus
iii. 222: * cupias tibi licere, atqui

(22) ii. 93 : si tantulum morae fuisset
iii. 210 : * et iudicia severa fiebant
(23) i. 158 : curando ne litura appareat (*add. m.* 1)
iv. 8 : nihil cuiquam relinqueret
(26) iv. 150 : negare non poterunt frumentum
(31) ii. 108 : ut sibi ipse peracutus esse videatur
iii. 12 : * ac sustinemur. Haec causa tripertita
iv. 18 : ecqui pudor est, ecqua religio, Verres
(33) ii. 180 : quaeram decretumne sit. Cum id invenero
(34) *Div.* 8 : vim gravitatemque requirit. Iudiciorum
iv. 52 : scuta si quando conquiruntur a privatis
53 : * obscurissime per magistratum solebant
(38) i. 27 : Hortensi quod saepe experti in dicendo sumus
(39) v. 70 : a navigando rebusque maritimis remotissimos
(45) iv. 86 : praeditum divaricari ac deligari iubet. Quo cruciatu
(51) i. 16 : non quantam habere poteram istorum studio quos iste vexarat
(71) i. 12 : confessum esse duces praedonum a se securi non esse percussos, se iam tum esse veritum
(73) iii. 62 : quid est, Lolli, inquit, tu nisi malo coactus recte facere nescis. Homo quid ageret, taceret

To these must be added omissions of *p*, which have not been supplied by the corrector, viz. :

(24) i. 87 : ** -nio quod in Hispania est ad Si-
(25) iv. 134 : adductam civitatem et pretio
(34) iii. 41 : et iis tacitus os tuum praebere malueris
(88) iii. 140 : vituperationem, dictitarat homo improbus atque impurus, Apronius, socium esse PR., venerat res in iudicium

I have not included in this list omissions which *p* shares with most other MSS., e. g.

(9) ii. 29 : et honesti *CO*, *om. p*, *cett.*
(10) iii. 158 : in aratorem *cO*, *om. p*, *cett.*
174 : Siciliense *cO*, *om. p*, *cett.*
(11) iii. 137 : teneo inquam *cO*, *om. p*, *cett.*
(12) ii. 188 : an negotiator *cO*, *om. p*, *cett.*

These appear to go back to an earlier stage in the tradition. When we are dealing with a comparatively late and sophisticated MS., such as *p*, we must expect to find the skein somewhat tangled.

The omissions of p^1 differ from those which we have hitherto considered in the case of *VRCO*, in that only two of them are of 10–11 letters. One of them is a remarkable case, viz. ii. 61. Here Müller, followed by Peterson, reads with VOp^1 :

iste amplam nactus

explaining *amplam* as = 'handle', from Servius on *Aen.* vii. 796, who explains the name Labicus as 'ἀπὸ τῆς λαβῆς quam Latine *amplam* vocamus'. The word is used in a literal sense by Ammianus xxi. 2, 1, *ampla remanserat sola quam retinens valida manu stringebat.* Müller confesses 'voc. *ampla* iam Ciceronis aetate in usu fuisse mirum videtur.'

Here p^2 adds *occasionem* (10), while some inferior MSS. give *occasionem calumniae*, a reading which is printed by editors before Müller and gives an excellent sense.

I find it very difficult to believe that Cicero used this strange word. In view of i. 130, where p preserves the words *sic abusus est* (12), I prefer to consider *occasionem* as a line of the distant archetype, which has been preserved as a variant by p^2. If so, the archetype had:

iste amplam
occasionem (10)

The omission is due to ὁμ.

There is a curious error in p, which may go back to an early stage, viz.:

v. 141: reciperatores se de cohorte sua dicebat daturum

Here p inserts *sed ego* before *reciperatores.* Peterson points out that this is a variant for *se de co-*. This indicates in a previous MS. the arrangement:

reciperatores (13)
mg. sed ego se de cohorte

The variant was inserted a line higher up.

The noticeable points in the omissions of p^1 (and p) are:

(1) The telescoped passage i. 87. This must represent a line, or two lines of an ancestor. I formerly[1] adopted the second explanation, but now prefer the first, since there are so few omissions of 10–12 letters in the list. I therefore ascribe to an intermediate ancestor the reading:

usque ab dia
nio quod in hispania est ad si (24)
nopam

(2) There are two striking bulges in the curve of omissions, viz. at 19 (5 exx.) and 34 (3 exx.). It is difficult to draw any conclusion

[1] *Primitive Text*, p. 3.

concerning the first of these. They may throw light on a separate ancestor, but they may be connected with the same MS. as that revealed by the telescoped passage. The omissions of 34 are more remarkable, especially as they are preceded by three of 31 and one of 33, and followed by one of 38 and one of 39.

It is not likely that *p*, which contains an average of over 60 letters to the line, was copied directly from a MS. with e.g. 24 letters (or less) to the line. On the other hand, it is quite possible that its model may have contained about 34 letters to the line. This unit, therefore, seems very suitable.

Here some light is to be derived from the fact that two omissions of 34 letters are in close proximity to each other, viz.:

iv. 52 : scuta si quando conquiruntur a privatis
53 : obscurissime per magistratum solebant

The intervening passage consists of 384 letters, which appears to represent 11 lines of the model (35 × 11 = 385). I therefore venture to arrange the model thus:

scuta si quando conquiruntur a priuatis (34)
in bello ac tumultu tamen homines inuiti (34)
dant etsi ad salutem communem dari senti (34)
unt ne quem putetis sine maximo dolore argen (37)
tum caelatum domo quod alter eriperet pro (35)
tulisse omnia deferuntur cibyratae fra (34)
tres uocantur pauca improbant quae proba (35)
rant iis crustae aut emblemata detraheban (36)
tur sic haluntini excussis deliciis cum ar (36)
gento puro domum reuertuntur quod umquam (35)
iud. huiusce euerriculum ulla in prouin (33)
cia fuit auertere aliquid de publico quam (35)
obscurissime per magistratum solebant (34)

The writer of *p* omitted ll. 1 and 13.

The last point which I have to notice is the similarity between the two large omissions, viz. 71 and 73. These admit of more than one explanation, viz. 24 × 3 = 72, or 36 × 2 = 72.

I now proceed to consider a subject to which attention has been called by Peterson in a valuable paper upon 'Transposition Variants in the *Verrines*'.[1] In this he points out the large number of cases in which the collocation of words differs in various MSS., and suggests

[1] *Am. J. Phil.*, xxviii. 2.

two explanations, viz. (1) that the variety is due to omission followed by insertion in the wrong place, (2) that the scribes altered the order on subjective grounds, e.g. to produce rhythms. I do not believe in the second explanation, since scribes were far too ignorant to think of such considerations. His first suggestion, however, entirely accords with my own observations both in the *Verrines* and elsewhere.

I add a list of those passages which appear to me instructive:

i. 114: iniquissimi hominis *V*: hominis iniquissimi *cett.*
125: non dicam pecuniam *V*: pecuniam non dicam *cett.*
151: praetextatum venisse *V*: venisse praetextatum *cett.*
ii. 7: vos propinquos *CO*: propinquos vos *cett.*
15: negotiantur in Sicilia *CO*: in Sicilia negotiantur *cett.*
17: in re umquam ulla *CO*: ulla in re umquam *cett.*
26: obtinebant causas *CO*: causas obtinebant *cett.*
36: ex testamento negent *O*: negent ex testamento *cett.*
54: amicorum suorum *V*: amicorum *cO*: suorum amicorum *dett.*
56: male acceptos ab se *V*: ab se male acceptos *cett.*
60: eius existimatione *O*: existimatione eius *V*, *cett.*
64: mecum decedere *VO*: decedere mecum *cett.*
70: iudicium dimittitur *Op*: dimittitur iudicium *cett.*
72: antea adfuerant *O*: adfuerant antea *cett.*
77: si ex hoc iudicio *O*: ex hoc iudicio si *cett.*
85: iste cupiditate *VO*: cupiditate iste *cett.*
94: pronuntiat de sella ac tribunali *O*: de sella ac tribunali pronuntiat *cett.*
131: isto PR. in Sicilia *Op*: in Sicilia isto PR. *cett.*
155: laudarent publice *V*: publice laudarent *cett.*
156: necessario tibi *O*: tibi necessario *cett.*
163: Centuripinos reponere *CO*: reponere Centuripinos *cett.*
168: tu auctoritate *VCO*: auctoritate tu *p*, *cett.*
181: videbitis teneri *CO*: teneri videbitis *cett.*
191: litteras primas *V*: primas litteras *cett.*
iii. 3: consilio confirmato *O*: confirmato consilio *cett.*
14: sapientiam maiorum *O*: maiorum sapientiam *cett.*
23: saltare in convivio *O*: in convivio saltare *cett.*
26: rusticarum rerum *O*: rerum rusticarum *cett.*
28: aiebat omnis esse *V*: esse aiebat omnis esse *O*: omnis dicebat esse *p*
29: decumanum putatis *O*: putatis decumanum *cett.*
32: in octuplum daturum *O*: daturum in octuplum *cett.*
33: mentionem iudicii *O*: iudicii mentionem *cett.*
40: decumas vendidisti *cO*: vendidisti decumas *V*, *cett.*
42: pro his decumis pecunia *VO*: pecunia pro his decumis *cett.*
44: civitates Siciliae *V*: Siciliae civitates *cett.*

48: frumentariae rei *O*: rei frumentariae *cett.*
51: illa locatione *O*: locatione illa *cett.*
55: se accepturum *VO*: accepturum se *cett.*
58: iniurias eorum *V*: eorum iniurias *cett.*
63: contumeliis iniuriisque *O*: iniuriis contumeliisque *cett.*
65: fortunarum tuarum *O*: tuarum fortunarum *cett.*
66: tractatae quem ad modum *V*: quem ad modum tractatae *cett.*
67: praesertim magno *O*: magno praesertim *cett.*
70: tamen in consilio *O*: in consilio tamen *cett.*
75: lucri dare ei *O*: ei lucro dare *cett.*
97: arationes haberet *O*: haberet arationes *cett.*
99: esse videatur praeda *O*: praeda esse videatur *cett.*
104: in Sicilia nullum *O*: nullum in Sicilia *cett.*
124: perditamque provinciam miseram *O*: provinciam miseram perditamque *cett.*
156: domestica coniectura *O*: coniectura domestica *V*, *cett.*
157: socium in decumis *O*: in decumis socium *cett.*
167: litteras in Siciliam *O*: in Siciliam litteras *cett.*
168: usura publicanos *VO*: publicanos usura *cett.*
171: Timarchidi et Volcatio *V*: Volcatio Timarchidi *cett.*
182: pecuniam civitatibus *V*: civitatibus pecuniam *cett.*
184: moleste ferunt esse *V*: esse moleste ferunt *cett.*
esse aliquos ibi *V*: ibi esse aliquos *cett.*
terdecies uno nomine *VO*: uno nomine terdecies *cett.*
190: ad portandum loca *cO*: loca ad portandum *cett.*
217: vestram defensionem *O*: defensionem vestram *cett.*
v. 72: involutis e carcere capitibus *V*: capitibus obvolutis e carcere *cett.*
82: vir Cleomenes *V*: Cleomenes vir *cett.*
97: parvis myoparonibus *V*: myoparonibus parvis *cett.*
108: catenis aspiciunt *V*: aspiciunt catenis *cett.*
121: neque illis neque tibi *V*: neque tibi neque illis *R*: neque tibi *dett.*
126: non aurum non argentum *V*: non argentum non aurum *cett.*
132: calamitates quidem *V*: quidem calamitatis *cett.*
186: praesidium propugnaculumque *V*: propugnaculum praesidiumque *cett.*

The absence of instances from iv is due to the fact that only a small part of this speech in preserved in *V*, and that in a somewhat illegible condition, while *CcO* only contained ii and iii.

Several of these transpositions are due to simple inversion of words similar in length. This is easy at all times, but especially so when very narrow columns were used. Thus in iii. 156, if a MS. had

coniectura (10)
domestica (9)

it is easy to see how the words would come to be inverted.

In most cases, however, the variety seems due to a previous omission. Peterson mentions an interesting example[1]

ii. 153: iniurias acceperit

Here p^1 omits *iniurias*, which was added above by the corrector. Another MS. which is derived from it (*q*) has in consequence *acceperit iniurias*.

In several cases the previous omission is manifest, e.g.:

iii. 124: provinciam miseram perditamque offendisti

O gives *perditamque provinciam miseram*. It is clear here that *perditamque* (11) was first omitted and then added in the margin of a subsequent MS., which had:

provinciam miseram (17)
mg. perditamque offendisti

iii. 99: praeda esse videatur

O has *esse videatur praeda*. Peterson[2] calls this a 'scholarly correction made by the copyist of *O*'. As the collocation in *O* is a violation of Cicero's favourite rhythm, I prefer to explain it as a mechanical error going back to a MS. which had:

mg. praeda esse uideatur (12)

I would call attention to two cases where evidence of the omission survives, viz.:

ii. 54: amicorum suorum *V*: amicorum *cO*: suorum amicorum *dett.*
v. 121: neque illis neque tibi *V*: neque tibi *dett.*: neque tibi neque illis *R*.

In view of these facts the bulk of these variants carry their interpretation on their face. I take as typical examples:

iii. 48: frumentariae rei *O*: rei frumentariae *cett.*
55: se accepturum *VO*: accepturum se *cett.*

These clearly go back to:

mg. rei frumentariae (12)
mg. se accepturum (10)

These transposition variants register the formation of intermediate MSS. as well as of the distant ancestor. I take as an example the reading of *O* in ii. 94, which seems due to:

mg. pronuntiat de sella ac tribunali (18)

The similarity of this passage to iii. 124 should be noted.

[1] *Am. J. Phil.*, xxvi. 4, p. 422.
[2] Ibid., xxviii. 2, p. 144.

I now put together in a tabulated form the chief contributions of the principal MSS. to the text of these speeches. Where *V* is not quoted, it is deficient :

(9) ii. 29 : et honesti *CO* : *om. cett.*
iii. 48 : bene de re p. *cO* : *om. cett.*
74 : civitates *VO* : *om. cett.*
(10) i. 107 : * reprehendi *V* : *om. cett.*
143 : addiderunt *V* : *om. cett.*
ii. 61 : occasionem p^2 : *om. V, cett.*
66 : * ad praesens *V* : *om. cett.*
iii. 74 : iniuriis et *V* : *om. cett.*
158 : * in aratorem *cO* : *om. cett.*
174 : Siciliense *cO* : *om. cett.*
(11) ii. 86 : * et sua sponte *V* : *om. cett.*
iii. 29 : ac multo plus *VcO* : *om. cett.*
137 : teneo inquam *cO* : *om. cett.*
iv. 32 : * poposcerant *R* : *om. p*δ
v. 97 : Syracusanum (-norum *R*) *VR* : *om. cett.*
118 : vestitumque *V, Quintil.* : *om. cett.*
(12) i. 130 : * sic abusus est *p* : *om. cett.*
ii. 86 : et aequitatem *VO* : *om. cett.*
102 : * ornatissimus *VO* : *om. cett.*
188 : an negotiator *cO* : *om. cett.*
iii. 179 : * per triennium *cO* : *om. cett.*
v. 46 : turpe numquam *R* : *om. cett.*
81 : iam continuos *V* : *om. cett.*
95 : stupri plenus *V* : *om. cett.*
(13) iii. 16 : et clarissimos *cO* : *om. cett.*
199 : quos non exarat (-ararat *V*) *VCO* : *om. cett.*
iv. 6 : atque amicorum *V* : *om. cett.*
(14) iii. 66 : * rex fugitivorum *cO* : *om. cett.*
220 : denis non licere *VcO* : *om. cett.*
(17) ii. 135 : omnium necessarios *cO* : *om. cett.*
iii. 52 : ac locupletissimos *cO* : *om. V cett.*
64 : in tanta impudentia *cO* : *om. cett.*
200 : ex vestris impensis *V* : *om. cett.*
(18) iii. 48 : in tanta improbitate *cO* : *om. cett.*
161 : ad tua flagitia neque *cO* : *om. cett.*
(20) ii. 130 : qui consequitur mensem *cO* : *om. cett.*
135 : quid cuique accidisset *cO* : *om. cett.*
167 : aut quo modo existiment *CO* : *om. V, cett.*
(21) iii. 205 : non ex eo quod oportuerit *cO* : *om. cett.*
(22) i. 146 : facito. Quid est suo cuique *V* : *om. cett.*
(24) ii. 175 : iudicio condemnarunt horum *CO* : *om. cett.*

iii. 70 : atque adeo cum damnatus eris *V*: *om. cett.*
(25) iii. 171 : cum suum frumentum (*om. cO*) probasset *VcO*: *om. cett.*
(33) v. 125 : et ex complexu matris ereptus innocens *Vp*: *om. R*, *alii*
(34) *Div.* 8 : vim gravitatemque requirit. Iudiciorum p^2: *om.* Dp^1, *alii*
(40) i. 9 : cum praedonum duces accepta pecunia dimiserit *p*: *om. DΨ*
(53) iii. 221 : aestimare. Permissum est : stultissimus quisque posthac minimo *VO*: *om. cett.*
(54) i. 45 : dictum est hoc in Cn. Dolabellae iudicio. Dictum? etiam aestimatum *T* (= *pal. Taur.*), *p*: *om. cett.*
(56) ii. 162 : decreta Centuripinorum quae de statuis erant facta non tolluntur *CO*: *om. cett.*
(58) iii. 148 : atque aliorum quidem agrorum pro portione magno decumas vendidisse *c*: *om. cett.*
(63) ii. 110 : quem hominem absentem de litteris corruptis causa incognita condemnasti *cO* : *om. cett.*

Two passages which I have included in this list require some comment, viz. ii. 66, 86.

In ii. 66 the reading of the other MSS. is:

iste poenis compromissisque interpositis HS CCCC extorquenda curavit

V has *ad praesens* after *iste*. The phrase *in praesens* is used by Cicero in *Cat.* i. 22, while *ad praesens* occurs in Tac., Pliny, Suetonius. Whether we read *ad* or *in* here, the words give a good sense, i. e. as a 'bird in the hand', or as an instalment, apart from future exactions. We may compare:

ii. 54 : qui statim quod praesens esset (so *O*, praesensisset *V*, *cett.*) iubet cuidam amicorum suorum numerari HS LXXX

I therefore incline to look on *ad* (*in*) *praesens* as genuine here, though possibly out of place. The words might come in better before *extorquenda*.

ii. 86. Here the other MSS. give:

Scipio, qui hoc dignum populo Romano arbitraretur, bello confecto socios sua per nostram victoriam recuperare. Siculis omnibus Karthagine capta quae potuit restituenda curavit

For *sua V* has *et sua sponte*. It seems to me more probable that *sua sponte* is a genuine fragment which is out of place in *V*, than that it is due to invention. The words would give an excellent sense if used of Scipio. I should prefer to insert them after *recu-*

perare, regarding *et* as a repetition of *-e*, or as due to a variant *recuperaret*.

The converging evidence so far considered shows that the MSS. of the *Verrines* are drawn from ancestors, or from one ancestor, written in very narrow columns similar to those found in the palimpsest of the *de Re Publica*. The final question now remains whether we are dealing with a single archetype. This can only be proved by *proprii errores*, or minute flaws, pervading all the MSS.

I take first the other MSS., apart from *V*, since the case of *V* is not so clear.

We have to notice in the first place certain lacunae. I give the passages, enclosing in brackets the additions which have been made by editors, to my mind necessarily:

A. P. i. 1: opinio . . . quae non modo [apud nos sed] apud exteras nationes omnium sermone percrebruit

I here adopt the supplement which Peterson takes from Harl. 5428, a MS. written in A. D. 1470. Other editors supply in different ways.

iii. 93: pro decuma, cum pulsatus a Venerio esset, decidit HS $\overline{\text{XVI}}$ et [medimnis] DCLIIII

113: quod si fieri non poterat ut plus quam X medimna ex iugero exararent, medimnum [autem] ex iugero decumano dari oportebat, cum ager, id quod perraro evenit, cum decumo extulisset, quae erat ratio decumanis

iv. 133: nulla umquam civitas tota Asia et Graecia signum ullum, tabulam pictam [ullam], ullum denique ornamentum urbis sua voluntate cuiquam vendidit

v. 12: atque haec sicubi [facta sunt], ita facta sunt ut homines . . . levarentur

Here *ita* is preserved by *p*, but omitted by *R*.

141: cogere eum coepit, cum ageret nemo, [nemo] postularet, sponsionem . . . facere

The following minute flaws are significant:

Div. i. 1: defenderim . . . laeserim] defenderem . . . laeserim *codd.*

50: ad columnam Maeniam] a columna aenea (*vel simil.*) *codd.*

Verr. i. 35: relictionem] reiectionem *codd.*

104: P. Annius] C. Annius *codd.* The praenomen is given as P. in i. 107, ii. 21.

141: vafrum] fabrum (= favrum) pseudo-Ascon.: verum *p*: tectum *cett.*

ii. 17: si cuiquam] sive cuiquam *codd.*

175: venient . . . dicent] veniunt (-iant) . . . dicent *codd.*

iii. 96 : senatorem] senatorum *codd.*
iv. 12 : iuvat] iuvant *codd.* (*V* illegible)
38 : versatae] versata *codd.*
46 : peraeque] per ea quae *codd.*
97 : grandis simili in] grandissimi hii in (*vel simil.*) *codd.*
128 : parinum *codd.* : *varie emendatum.*
v. 15 : Imacharensi] macharensi *codd.*
27 : astro] austro *codd.*
81 : cupiditatem] cupiditate *codd.* (*V*)

I also draw attention to the following corruptions:

A. P. 26 : in eo esse haec commoda : primum M. Metellum amicissimum, deinde Hortensium cõs. non solum sed etiam Q. Metellum

Here *Hortensium* is out of place. The simplest method of treatment is to place the word after *solum* (so Müller). This suggests in a common ancestor:

deinde
cõs non solum (11)
Hortensium (10)
sed

iii. 67 : homines et satis fortes et plane frugi

So *V*, except that it has *sed plane* for *et plane*. The other MSS. repeat *satis* before *plane*. This may indicate in a common ancestor:

et
satis fortes et (13)
plane

iv. 144 : atque etiam hoc me docent eiusmodi senatus consultum fecisse laudationis ut omnes intellegere possent non laudationem sed potius irrisionem esse illam

So *R*, *sese fecisse laudationes p.* Various methods have here been adopted by editors. I look on *laudationis* (*-es*) as a variant for *laudationem*, which has got into the wrong place. If so, a common ancestor may have had:

fecisse
ut omnes in (9)
tellegere (9)
possent non (10)
mg. laudationes laudationem (11)
sed

The insertion of *sese* in *p* seems due to correction. It is more probable that the original reading was *fecisse se*. If so, this may be added to the minute flaws.

v. 56 : litterae rerum decretarum

I have already referred to this passage (p. 230). *RS* give *cum decretarum*, which indicates in a common ancestor:

litterae re (10)
rum decretaꝝ (11)

Here *pδ*, obviously by conjecture, give *et rerum decretarum tritici empti*.

To these should probably be added :

iii. 117 : CCXVI decumas agri Leontini vendidisti ; si ex lege, magno ; si ut lex esset libido tua, parvo ; si ut quae dimidiae essent decumae vocarentur, parvo vendidisti

Madvig here strikes out *parvo* after *tua*, as introduced from *parvo* before *vendidisti*.

The cumulative evidence appears to prove definitely the common origin of all MSS. except *V*. It is to be noticed that *V* is deficient in all the passages previously considered except iii. 67, iv. 12, v. 81.

The evidence concerning *V* is much more scanty. In one place it shares what appears to be a lacuna with all other MSS., viz. :

ii. 167 : an hoc dicere audebis utrum de te aratores, [utrum negotiatores], utrum denique Siculi universi bene existiment

The words *utrum negotiatores* were introduced by Garatoni from § 168, *ab negotiatoribus, ab aratoribus, a communi Siciliae . . . aratorum, negotiatorum, Siculorumque omnium testimonia*. It is difficult to suppose that something has not dropped out in view of *denique*. If so, this lacuna, common to *V*, *cett*., is very significant.

Other points of contact are :

ii. 54 : praesens esset *O* : praesensisset *V*, *cett*. Here the reading of *O* may be due to a correction.
iii. 60 : a Q. Apronio] quo Apronio *V* : atque Apronio *cett*.
v. 94 : acta commemorabatur] acta commemorabantur *V*, *cett*.
108 : perditum] praeditum *V*, *cett*.

I would call attention to :

ii. 121 : quicumque senator voluerat fieri, quamvis puer, quamvis indignus quamvis ex eo loco ex quo non liceret, si is pretio apud istum idoneus (so *c* : idoneus et *V* : fieret idoneus *p*) vinceret, factum esse semper

Editors generally read *idoneos*, with Garatoni. I incline to consider *idoneus* a variant for *indignus*, due to the confusion of *O* and ỏ (*D*) in uncials. In Livy xxxi. 3 the Vienna MS. has *inoindignarentur* for *indignarentur*, and Heraeus remarks 'in archetypo fuit *inoignarentur*.' It is possible that the archetype of *V cett.* here had:

	quamuis
mg. inoignus	indignus quã
	uis ex eo loco
	quo non lice
	ret si is pre
	tio apud istũ
	uinceret

I conclude by drawing notice to two passages, viz.:

iii. 74: iniuriis et incommodis civitates

Here the tradition is as follows:

iniuriis et *V*: *om. cett.*
civitates *VO*: *om. cett.*

This suggests in the archetype:

iniuriis et	(10)
incommodis	(10)
ciuitates	(9)

In another place (v. 81), a passage found in *V* only, viz. *iam continuos* (12), is followed shortly afterwards by a word *exceptione* (10), omitted by *V* only. The intermediate passage, *PR. P. R. . . . sine*, consists of 133 letters. This suggests the following distribution:

dies aestiuos	(12)
iam continuos	(12)
pr. p. r. custos	(10)
defensorque	(11)
provinciae	(10)
sic uixit ut	(10)
muliebria	(9)
cotidie con	(10)
uiuia essent	(11)
uir accumbe	(10)
ret nemo prae	(11)
ter ipsum et	(10)

praetextatum (12)
filium etsi (10)
recte sine (9)
exceptione (10)

V omits l. 16, while l. 2 is omitted by the other MSS., both omissions being due to *ὁμ.*

It appears, therefore, that there are some grounds for referring *V* to the same ancestor, though on this subject I speak with reserve.

CHAPTER VIII

ORATT. POST REDITUM (SEN., QUIR., DOM., HAR. RESP.), PRO SESTIO, IN VATINIUM, PRO CAELIO, DE PROVINCIIS CONSULARIBUS, PRO BALBO

THIS collection is contained in

Paris. 7794, cent. ix (*P*).

There are also some later MSS., the most important of which seem to be

Gemblacensis 5345, cent. xii (*G*).
Erfurtensis, now Berol. 252, cent. xii/xiii (*E*).
Harleianus 4937, cent. xii (*H*).

The relation of these MSS. to *P* is a matter of controversy. Halm held that they are derived from *P*, which, therefore, is to be considered the sole fount of information, while Klotz has recently argued in favour of the view that they are drawn from an independent copy of the archetype.[1]

Fresh information has recently come to light concerning one speech in this sylloge, viz. the *Caeliana*. For this we also have Σ = marginalia in Paris. 14749, taken from Clun. 496 at the beginning of the fifteenth century.

A considerable portion of the speech is contained in an Oxyrhynchus papyrus, no. 1251, cent. v.

Madvig showed that *P* was the best MS. then known for the *pro Caelio* and the other speeches which it contains. He made a number of brilliant corrections based on *P*, as opposed to the later MSS. He also drew attention to certain passages, generally printed, which were not found either in *P* or in any other MS. then known, although they occur in a late fifteenth-century MS., Monacensis

[1] *Rhein. Mus.* lxvii (1912), pp. 358–90.

15734 (*s*), afterwards used by Halm. These he denounced as Italian interpolations. The chief passage is in *Cael.* 24, where after *Titus Caiusque* the vulgate had:

Coponii qui ex omnibus maxime Dionis mortem doluerunt

Madvig said:

'confiteor me nescire unde homo audacissimus qui ineunte seculo XVI post primas editiones cum codd. conspirantes haec ita interpolavit, ut vulgo eduntur, *Coponios* illos fuisse rescierit, de quo neminem interpretum ne verbo quidem admonere video. Edendus est igitur necessario locus hoc tristi aspectu: *Titus Caiusque* ** † *omni cum doctrina homo atque humanitatis.*'

In another passage, *Cael.* 50, where the vulgate had *et huic et ceteris magnam ad se defendendum facultatem dabit*, while *PGE*, etc., have *et huic defendendum facultatem dabit*, he calls the addition *interpolationem ineptissimam et soloecam.*

One of these supplements deserves especial attention, viz.:

Cael. 49: ut non solum meretrix [sed etiam proterva meretrix] procaxque videatur

The words give an admirable sense and are defended by δμ.

Halm continued in the same track, but went further. While Madvig banished the 'Italian interpolations', Halm threw doubts upon the additions made by P^2. There are a large number of these throughout these speeches. Except in the case of the *de Prov. Cons.*, where he stayed his hand, Halm tarred them all with the same brush. He thus reached the result beloved by some critics, viz. that safety was only to be found in the first hand of the 'best' MS. It is only fair to add that Halm's method was not adopted by subsequent scholars, notably by Hertz, Müller, and more recently Peterson.

When the marginalia in Σ came to light, they confirmed some 25 conjectures made by various scholars. Madvig took the lion's share in these, with no less than six successful emendations. Three of these, which are consecutive in Madvig's dissertation, occur in a single page of Σ, one of them being an insertion of three words *e coni.* (*Cael.* 45). While, however, Σ indicates Madvig's extraordinary skill as an emender, it shows that in one important respect he was wholly wrong. The passages which he attributed to Italian conjecture occur in Σ side by side with his own emendations.

They are, therefore, brought back from the fifteenth century to the eighth. So also the additions of P^2, rejected by Halm, are confirmed *en bloc* by Σ, though sometimes given in a more correct version.

The testimony of the papyrus is of exceptional interest. Its agreements are about equally distributed between Σ and *P*. Among its agreements with *P* is one which gives a reading clearly inferior, viz.:

§ 37: dissice Σ (*Puteanus*): disce *Ox.* 1251, *P cett.*

This is a good example of an ancient corruption.

On three occasions *Ox.* agrees with *GE* or P^2GE against *P* or P^1, viz.:

§ 35 acta *Ox. GE*: actas *P*: § 35 effregit *Ox.* P^2GE: et fregit P^1: § 45 disputo *Ox.* P^2GE: disputato P^1: disputavi Σ.

There is one noteworthy agreement with *E*, viz.:

§ 30 deprecari vacationem *P*: deprecationem *G*: de praevaricatione *Ox. E.*

For the purposes of this discussion the three most important passages are:

Cael. 29: et copiose *Ox.* Σ: *om. PGE*

Cael. 35: facis, quae dicis, quae insimulas, quae moliris, quae arguis *Ox.* Σ: *om.* P^1 *in lac.*: facis, quae dicis, quae in sororem tuam moliris, quae argumenta P^2GE. Halm says of this 'supplement' found in P^2GE: 'Hoc ipsum supplementum homines Itali, ut est in cod. *S*, sic emendare conati sunt *si ea quae* [*facis, quae dicis, quae insimulas, quae moliris, quae arguis*], quo panno intolerabili etiam nunc editiones foedatae sunt'

Cael. 49: ut non solum meretrix sed etiam proterva meretrix procaxque videatur [1]

The papyrus is here much mutilated, but the editors, arguing from the space between letters which have been preserved, say 'the agreement of the papyrus in adding *sed etiam . . . meretrix* after *non solum meretrix* seems probable.'

These are the only cases where the papyrus contains passages disputed on the ground of omission by *P* or P^1, and on all occasions its evidence is in their favour.

I now proceed to say a few words about *P*.

P is a large MS. written in two columns. The number of lines

[1] Halm says 'lectio non ex cod. aliquo integriore deducta est, sed pro supplemento prudentis alicuius Itali habenda.'

to the page varies. In a page reproduced by Chatelain (Pl. xxiii) there are 37 lines in each column. I noticed that f. 18^r has 37 lines in col. 1 and 36 in col. 2, while f. 18^v has 36 lines in col. 1 and 38 in col. 2. The *recto* of f. 20 has 40 lines in both columns, and the *verso* has 43 lines in both columns. There is also considerable variety in the content of lines. The average appears to be about 34 letters.

When turning over the leaves of *P* I noticed several dittographies, viz.:

(30) *Dom.* 100: video me plane ac sentio restitutum
(31) *Sest.* 55: dicam immo vero etiam approbantibus
(32) *Quir.* 21: invidos virtuti et gloriae serviendo
(34) *Prov. Cons.* 20: videmus et vere ut dicam paene confectum
Sest. 18: equites R. minabatur senatui venditabat
(35) *Sest.* 6: optimis factus esset, reliquis honoribus
(37) *Cael.* 61: si apud Caelium mulieris servus visus esset
Vat. 6: vivendo consecutum esse quae tu impudenter

The evidence furnished by these eight dittographies, all of which consist of 30–7 letters, suggests that this was the length of a line in the model. If so, this was a MS. very much like *P* in formation.

One of the dittographies requires some explanation, viz.:

Sest. 6: cum tr. pl. primus inter homines nobilissimos temporibus optimis factus esset, reliquis honoribus non tam uti voluit quam dignus videri

After *nobilissimos P* has:

temporibus
s
optumis factum esset reliquis hominibus
optumis tactum esset reliquis
hominibus optumis tactum esset reliquis
honoribus

The model seems to have had:

optumis factus esset reliquis hominibus

with a marginal variant:

optumis tactum esset reliquis honoribus.

In connexion with these dittographies I would mention the following omissions of P^1:

(30) *Quir.* 6: aut Metellarum liberi pro Q. Metelli
Sest. 107: sententiam eius auctoritate neque
(32) *Cael.* 72: et cum vestra auctoritate coniunctum

The probability is that these also represent lines in the model. I abstain for the present from discussing possible multiples.

The majority of the additions made by P^2 exhibit a smaller unit, viz. 21–4. The conclusion which I reached at the commencement of this inquiry was that this unit represents a line in a previous MS., coming before the model, in which the columns varied slightly in breadth. I afterwards read a paper by A. Klotz, in which I find a notable anticipation of the method which I have followed.[1]

Klotz is arguing that *GE* are derived not from *P*, but from a common archetype, which had about 22 letters to a line. He refers to:

Cael. 38: filii causa est expeditissima. Quid enim esset in quo se non facile defenderet? Nihil iam in istam mulierem dico, sed si esset aliqua dissimilis istius

Here G^1 omits *filii . . . defenderet* (65), while *E* omits *se non . . . aliqua* (64). This indicates in the archetype:

filii causa est expeditis	(22)
sima quid enim esset in quo	(22)
se non facile defenderet	(21)
nihil iam in istam mulie	(20)
rem dico sed si esset aliqua	(23)

G^1 omits ll. 1–3, while *E* omits ll. 3–5.

Klotz points out that the ancestor thus revealed is not *P*, which is written in longer lines. He also holds that it must have been written in insular script on account of the corruptions for *autem* (h̶) which occur in *GE*.[2]

I had myself accepted the usual theory that *GE* are derived from *P*, and was somewhat incredulous at first about Klotz's conclusion. More recently, after further analysis, I am convinced that he is right, and I regard *GE* as drawn from an independent copy of the archetype. The point is of some importance, since, if *GE* are not derived from *P*, their omissions must be considered together with those of *P*:

I therefore proceed to deal with this point first.

There is a dislocation in the *pro Caelio* which is common to *PGE*, viz. §§ 17–27 *accommodavistis . . . convivium* come after §§ 27–36 *renuerit . . . timiditatem*. The error is rectified in *P* by a corrector,

[1] *Rhein. Mus.* lxvii (1912), p. 368.

[2] Halm on *Vat.* 41; cf. *Sest.* 21.

who at § 27 inserts in the margin the note *hic repete quod dimisisti.* In Harl. 4927 (*H*) the two passages are given in their proper order.

The length of these passages in Teubner lines is as follows:

§§ 17–27 = 137 lines.
§§ 27–36 = 130 lines.

It cannot be doubted that the dislocation is due to the transposition of folios in a previous MS., although the agreement is not so close as is usually the case. It is to be noticed that *P* has a considerable omission in § 24. It is possible that there was here some irregularity in the archetype, e.g. something may have been written in the margin.

I now come to a dislocation peculiar to *GE*, viz.:

Har. Resp. 46: quid enim faciat aliud? illos homines sapientissimos gravissimosque miror, primum quod quemquam clarum hominem atque optime de re p. (110)

These words are omitted *suo loco* by *GE* and inserted subsequently in § 50:

etiamne in sinu atque in deliciis quidem optimi viri viperam illam venenatam ac pestiferam habere potuerunt?

Here they come after *viperam illam*, destroying the sense. The natural inference in such a case is that an omitted passage has been accidentally inserted on the wrong page or folio. The intervening passage, viz. §§ 46–50, *saepe meritum . . . viperam illam*, occupies 64 lines of Teubner text. The relation of 64 to 130 (*Cael.* 27–36) is striking.

To these I add a minor transposition common to *PGE*, viz.:

Har. Resp. 18: sed quoniam mea causa expedita est, videamus nunc quid haruspices dicant. Ego enim fateor me et magnitudine ostenti et gravitate responsi et una atque constanti haruspicum *voce*[1] vehementer esse commotum

This passage is omitted *loco suo* by *PGE* and inserted in § 17 before *quamquam si me.* The intervening passage, §§ 17–18, *quamquam si me . . . respondeat admoneri*, occupies 16½ lines of Teubner text.

I now arrange these transpositions in order of length:

Har. Resp. 17–18 = 16½ lines.
46–50 = 64 „
Cael. 27–36 = 130 „

[1] So edd., *om. codd.*

The relation of these figures to each other is very significant. It is to be noticed that one of them (64) is peculiar to *GE*, while the other two are common to *PGE*. The inference appears to be that *P* and *GE* are descended from the same archetype, but that *GE* are not copied from *P*.

There is also some other evidence. In *Vat.* 4–5 editors print:

renovatus ille tuus in to **** veterem meum amicum.

Here there is a lacuna after *in to-*.

It is always likely that a new speech began at the top of a page. I thought it worth while, therefore, to count the number of lines in §§ 1–4, *si tantum . . . tuus in to-*.

The passage occupies 48 Teubner lines. Here also we find the same unit ($16 \times 3 = 48$).

There remains one other indication, which I think worth mentioning, though without the same confidence. We have seen that there is a lacuna in *Vat.* § 4. Shortly afterwards we have in § 6 *sanguinem principum civitatis exsorbere*. Halm notes:

'*prin P* in extremo versu, quattuor litterae deletae sunt, hinc voc. in cod. Bern. et aliis omnino deest.'

Peterson says that *H* has *principum*. I do not find the readings of *GE* expressly recorded.

The occurrence of this flaw shortly after the lacuna in § 4 is suggestive. It is possible that the word *principum* came at some division of the archetype, e.g. at the foot of a page. As a matter of fact, §§ 5–6, *veterem meum . . . principum*, occupy 32¼ lines of Teubner. This is a very singular agreement. If we accept this last case, which I mention with considerable reserve, we have the following figures: 16½, 32¼, 48, 64, 130.

The most natural interpretation to put on them is, that 16 = a column, 32 = a page, 64 = a folio, and 130 = two folios in the archetype.

As I have also taken the trouble to count the letters in the passages discussed, I add these results also:

Har. Resp. 17–18	= 686	letters.
Vat. 5–6	= 1324	„
Vat. 1–4	= 2019	„
Har. Resp. 46–50	= 2737	„
Cael. 27–36	= 5506	„

If we take 686 letters as representing a column and divide by 22, we get as a result 31 lines to a page ($22 \times 31 = 682$). I assume that the archetype was written in two columns.

After this preliminary discussion I proceed to consider the omissions of the various MSS.

We have already seen that the model of *P* was a MS. very like itself. There is, therefore, an intermediate ancestor between *P* and the archetype. It is *prima facie* possible that one or more intermediate ancestor has intervened between *GE* and the archetype. We must, therefore, expect to find more than one unit in the omissions.

I now give a complete list of omissions and dittographies, apart from those which have been already mentioned (in *P*):

(14) *Har. Resp.* 5: odio dignitatis *om. P*
51: quam in universo *om. P*[1]
(15) *Cael.* 24: *Caelio existimet *om. GE*
Prov. Cons. 6: *sed quia nunc sine *om. P*[1]
(16) *Sest.* 118: aut non exprimeret *om. P*[1]
(17) *Dom.* 86: et M. Furius Camillus *om. P*[1]
Sest. 132: **hominem et a caede ab- *om. P*[1]
(18) *Sest.* 100: res p. quam defenditur *om. G*
110: iuvabant anagnostae *om. P*[1]
Vat. 18: *esset etiam tum in re p. *om. GE*
(19) *Dom.* 132: quodam atque inaudito *om. P*[1]
Har. Resp. 26: istius modi patruus is *om. P*[1]
Cael. 50: *et ceteris magnam ad se Σ: *om. PGE*
Prov. Cons. 29: **-que illarum humanitas *om. P*[1]
(20) *Dom.* 17: **meo consilio auctorita- *om. P*[1]
Sest. 48: laudis partim vitandae *om. P*[1]
(21) *Quir.* 9: auctores hortatoresque *om. GE*
Sest. 129: de caelo servaret ne quis *om. G*
Cael. 66: cur non comprehenderint *om. P*
Vat. 12: terreres conscendentes *om. P*[1]
28: ** inimico suo contionem re- *om. P*[1]
(22) *Sest.* 17: si ora ipsa oculis vestris *om. G*[1]
57: honorem istum consecutus *om. P*[1]
Cael. 3: splendidus ipse aut parum *om. G*
(23) *Dom.* 97: quibus aequo animo carerem *om. G*
132: *tamen instituto ceterorum *om. P*[1]
Sest. 58: huius imperii Mithridatem *G*: *om. PE, cett.*
ib.: a se regem quam constrictum *bis scr. P*
Cael. 8: atque etiam isti dignitati *om. P*

Vat. 16 : quos privatos esse dicebas *om.* P^1

(24) *Cael.* 49 : sed etiam proterva meretrix Σ : *om. PGE*
Prov. Cons. 36 : *disciplinaque maiorum quam *om. GE*

(25) *Vat.* 36 : sibi P. R. appetivit qui numquam *om.* P^1

(27) *Sen.* 1 : *qua nihil potest esse iucundius *om.* P^1

(28) *Sen.* 23 : *amicitias igni perspectas tuear *om. G*

(33) *Har. Resp.* 26 : istius modi Megalesia fecit pater tuus *om. G*

(38) *Cael.* 52 : quam ad rem aurum tum iret an non dixerit. Si non *om.* P^1

(41) *Sen.* 2 : ne aperte incommoda patriae lugeretis ediceret *om.* P^1

(43) *Balb.* 47 : quoniam re non potest ut conspiciatis eum mentibus *bis scr. P*

(46) *Cael.* 24 : *Coponii qui ex omnibus maxime Dionis mortem doluerunt Σ : *om. PGE*

(48) *Cael.* 35 : *facis, quae dicis, quae insimulas, quae moliris, quae arguis Σ. *pap. Ox.* 1251, *et sic fere* P^2*GE* : *om.* P^1

(49) *Vat.* 10 : atque infimo conferam de te ipso homine et arrogantissimo *om.* P^1
Balb. 31 : *iuris habeat necesse est ne quis invitus civitate mutetur *om.* P^1

(55) *Vat.* 7 : etsi ego te perditorem et vexatorem rei p. fero, tu me conservatorem *bis scr. P*

(63) *Quir.* 23 : qui reddidit non habet, gratiam et qui rettulit habet et qui habet dissolvit *om. P* (*add. m. rec.*)

(64) *Har. Resp.* 47 : Caesaris in quo fallebat sed eum nemo redarguebat nisi eum inquam exercitum *om.* P^1
Cael. 38 : *se non facile defenderet. Nihil iam in istam mulierem dico, sed si esset aliqua *om. E*

(65) *Cael.* 38 : *filii causa est expeditissima. Quid enim esset in quo se non facile defenderet *om.* G^1

(66) *Cael.* 2 : cui utrum vellet liceret nec cum descendisset quicquam habiturum spei fuisse *om. G*

(79) *Cael.* 67 : *conspectus, lux denique longe alia est solis ac lychnorum. Quam ob rem excutiemus omnes istorum *om. E*

(81) *Sest.* 131 : legatorum undique missorum celebrabantur, ad urbem accessus incredibili hominum multitudine *om. G*

(83) *Sest.* 93 : amplectatur, qui bonis viris deserviat, qui solidam laudem veramque quaerat. Cum dicat duo illa rei p. *om.* P^1

(89) *Cael.* 58 : servos familiares esse dominae sciebat. Sin ei tanta consuetudo quanta a vobis inducitur non erat, quae cum *om. E*

(95) *Prov. Cons.* 35 : nondum satis fecerit et malit tamen tardius ad suorum laborum fructus pervenire quam non explere susceptum rei p. *om.* P^1

(103) *Balb.* 8 : *sic agere iud. non esse fas dubitari quin quod Cn. Pompeium fecisse constet, id non solum decuisse sed etiam debuisse fateamur *om.* P^1 (If *iudices*, = 107)

(106) *Balb.* 7 : huius crimen? Minime, nisi honos ignominia putanda est. Cuius igitur? Re vera nullius, actione accusatoris eius unius qui donavit *om. E*
Cael. 24 : *qui cum doctrinae studio atque humanitatis, tum etiam hospitio

Dionis tenebantur. Habitabat apud Titum, ut audistis, Dio: erat ei Σ, *sic fere* P^2GE: *om.* P^1

(111) *Har. Resp.* 46: quid enim faciat aliud? illos homines sapientissimos gravissimosque miror, primum quod quemquam clarum hominem atque optime de re p. *om. GE* (*suo loco*)

(132) *Cael.* 38: *se nulla cupiditate inductum de via decessisse. Quid signi? nulli sumptus, nulla iactura, nulla versura. At fuit fama. Quotus quisque istam effugere potest in tam *om.* P^1

I give this passage as written by P^2. The Turin palimpsest (*T*) adds *est qui* before *istam* and Σ adds *praesertim* before *effugere*.

(152) This figure represents the total omission of *P* and P^1 in *Cael.* 24, viz. *Coponii . . . doluerunt* (46) *om.* P + *qui cum . . . erat ei* (106) *om.* P^1

(159) *Cael.* 16: et de criminibus istis sodalium ac sequestrium, quoniam huc incidi, similiter respondendum putem. Numquam enim tam Caelius amens fuisset ut, si se isto infinito ambitu commaculasset, ambitus *om. GE*

(305) In addition to the previous omission of 159 letters in *Cael.* 16, *E* also omits:
alterum accusaret, neque eius facti in altero suspicionem quaereret cuius ipse sibi perpetuam licentiam optaret, nec si sibi semel periculum ambitus subeundum putaret, ipse (146).

Halm says that *E* omits 'usque ad *ipse*, v. 11', i.e. before *sibi perpetuam*. According, however, to Wunder's collation of *E*, it omits down to *putaret ipse*.

Here 159 + 146 = 305.

In this list there are four telescoped passages, all of them peculiar to P^1: viz. *Sest.* 132 (17), *Prov. Cons.* 29 (19), *Dom.* 17 (20), *Vat.* 28 (21). The bulges in the curve of omissions are at 21 (5 examples) and 23 (5 omissions and one dittography). There is a marked similarity between the omissions of *PGE*. Thus among the omissions of 21 letters, one is peculiar to *G*, one is shared by *GE*, and three, one of which is a telescoped passage, are peculiar to *P*.

The most interesting of the shorter omissions are *Cael.* 50, where Σ preserves 19 letters omitted by *PGE*, and *Sest.* 58, where *G* preserves 23 letters omitted by other MSS. (*sil.* Σ).

These figures point to an archetype written in two columns, one of which was slightly narrower than the other.

There are six omissions of 41–9 letters, the most important being *Cael.* 24, where Σ preserves 46 letters omitted by *PGE*. It can hardly be doubted that *PGE* have here omitted two lines of the archetype. Probably several of the other omissions are due to the same cause.

The omissions of 63 and 64 letters by *P* in *Quir.* 23, *Har. Resp.* 47 may be explained as representing either three lines of the archetype or two lines of the immediate model. There is not, however, any similar doubt in *Cael.* 38, where G^1 omits 65 and *E* omits 64 letters. Here both MSS. omit *se non facile defenderet* (21), while G^1 omits 44 letters before these words and *E* omits 43 letters after them. Here the unit 21–2 is clearly visible.

The following multiples of 22 throw light upon the higher numbers:

22 × 4 = 88	22 × 7 = 154
22 × 5 = 110	22 × 14 = 308
22 × 6 = 132	

For 110 we may compare 111 (*Har. Resp.* 46), also 106 (*Balb.* 7, *Cael.* 24): 132 is found in *Cael.* 38, while for 154 we may compare 152 in *Cael.* 25. For 88 we may compare 89 (*Cael.* 58), and for 308 we have 305 in *Cael.* 16. The relation of 152 to 305 is to be noticed.

As the numbers grow large the average asserts itself and becomes unmistakable.

Some of these passages are not far removed from each other. In such cases further evidence is yielded by the intervening words. A simple instance is *Cael.* 2–3. Here *G* has two omissions, viz. in § 2 *cui . . . fuisse* (66), and in § 3 *splendidus . . . parum* (22). The intermediate passage *nisi alicuius . . . aut parum* consists of 534 letters (22 × 24 = 528).

We may compare *Sest.* 58. Here all MSS. except *G* omit *huius imperii Mithridatem* (23), while the words *a se regem quam constrictum* (23) are written twice in *P*. The average here appears to be 23. The intervening passage *pulsum Ponto . . . constitutum* consists of 342 letters (23 × 15 = 345). We may, therefore, arrange thus:

huius imperii mithridatem	(23)
pulsum ponto opibus suis re	(23)
gnoque defendit et ab L. lucul	(24)
lo summo uiro atque impera	(22)
tore pulsus animo tamen hos	(23)
tili cum reliquis suis copi	(23)
is in pristina mente mansit	(23)

hunc CN. pompeius cum in suis (23)
castris supplicem abiectum (24)
uidisset erexit atque in (21)
signe regium quod ille de suo (24)
capite abiecerat reposuit (23)
et certis rebus imperatis (22)
regnare iussit nec minus et (23)
sibi et huic imperio glori (22)
osum putauit constitutum (22)
a se regem quam constrictum (23)

l. 1 *G*, *om. cett.* l. 17 *bis scr. P*

Balb. 7–8. Here *E* omits 106 letters in § 7, while P^1 omits 103 in § 8. The intervening passage *qui si adductus . . . nunc cuncter* consists of 440 letters (22 × 20 = 440). I should mention that the word *iudices* occurs once in the passage omitted by P^1 and once in the intermediate passage. If this is written in full, the totals are 107 and 444.

Certain corruptions may also be noticed:

(21) *Balb.* 37: potest esse ulla denique maiestas

GE have *potestas* for *maiestas*. This seems due to the arrangement:

potest esse ulla denique (21)
maiestas

The writer looked back to *potest* in the previous line and combined it with the end of *maiestas*.

(25) *Sest.* 42: non mihi vestrum studium sed meum prope vestro defuisse

P has:

non michi uestrũ studium ṣẹḍ
ṃẹụṃ p̣ṛọp̣ẹ ụẹṣṭṛũ ṣṭụḍịụṃ sed meum prope
uestro defuisse

This indicates:

non mihi uestrum
studium sed meum prope uestro (25)
defuisse

When the writer got to *vestro* he looked back to *vestrum* and repeated the intervening words.

(42) *Vat.* 26: ecquosnam alios posset nominare? Inculcarisne ut C. Pisonem, generum meum, nominaret

G inserts *inconculcarisne* (i. e. ^{in} *conculcarisne*) after *nominaret.* This looks like a variant which has got into the wrong place. If so, a previous MS. seems to have had :

	nominare	
mg. inconculcarisne	inculcarisne ut C. pisonem	(22)
	generum meum nominaret	(20)

(87) *Sest.* 58 : cum Armeniorum rege Tigrane grave bellum diuturnumque gessimus, cum ille iniuriis in socios nostros inferendis bello prope nos lacessisset. Hic et ipse per se vehemens fuit.

P after *bellum* adds *aut per ipsi*, which Halm emends to *nuper ipsi.* I incline to think that *aut per ipsi* is a variant for *et ipse per*. If so, the archetype may have had :

	graue bellum	
	diuturnumque gessimus cum	(23)
	ille iniuriis in socios	(20)
	nostros inferendis bello	(22)
	prope nos lacessisset hic	(22)
mg. aut per ipsi	et ipse per se	

(169) *Cael.* 42 : ergo haec deserta via et inculta atque interclusa iam frondibus et virgultis relinquatur: detur aliqui ludus aetati, sit adulescentia liberior: non omnia voluptatibus denegentur, non semper superet vera illa et derecta ratio.

Σ repeats *via et* after *derecta* (ὁμ.). The intermediate words *via et* . . . *derecta* contain 169 letters. The relation of 169 to 87, 42, 21 suggests that the archetype may have had :

deserta	
uia et inculta atque inter	(22)
clusa iam frondibus et uir	(22)
gultis relinquatur detur	(22)
aliqui ludus aetati sit	(20)
adulescentia liberior	(20)
non omnia uoluptatibus	(20)
denegentur non semper su	(21)
peret uera illa et derecta	(22)
ratio	

There are certain corruptions common to all our MSS., which appear to have been already present in what I have called the archetype. I would call attention to two passages omitted by the MSS. and preserved elsewhere, viz. :

(17) *Cael.* 27 : qui in hortis fuerit *Donatus* : *om. codd.*

(37) *Sest.* 8 : P. Sestius cum esset cum collega meo senserit *Schol. Bob.* : *om. codd.*

These omissions suggest a line of 17–18 letters in a previous MS. We may compare:

(17) *Har. Resp.* 23: si terram non tenuit aut tensam si lorum omisit aut si aedilis verbo aut simpuvio aberravit

So the MSS. It is clear that *terram* is a variant for *tensam*. Editors read:

si tensam non tenuit, si lorum omisit

This suggests in a previous MS. the arrangement:

	si	
mg. tensam	terram non tenuit si	(17)
	lorum	

The insertion of *aut* is a further corruption.

(36) *Dom.* 24: quas C. Gracchus . . . ut necesse esset quotannis constitui per senatum decreta lege sanxit, eas lege Sempronia per senatum decretas rescidisti

So the MSS. Editors cut out *decreta* before *lege*. Halm says:

'aberraverat scilicet librarii oculus a priore v. *senatum* ad posterius.'

This suggests the following arrangement:

per senatum	
lege sanxit eas lege	(17)
sempronia per senatum	(19)
decretas	

(50) *Sest.* 85: divini hominis, dicam enim quod sentio et quod mecum sentiunt omnes, divini.

Various emendations have been made. Mommsen removes *divini* before *hominis*. If this is right, a previous MS. may have had:

hominis dicam enim	(16)
quod sentio et quod me	(18)
cum sentiunt omnes	(16)
diuini	

I now recall attention to *Har. Resp.* 18.

Here the words *sed quoniam . . . esse commotum* are out of place in all our MSS. The transposition, therefore, seems prior to the common ancestor.

The missing passage is inserted higher up in § 17. The distance between this and the proper place is equivalent to 16½ Teubner lines. I have already shown (p. 272) that 16 Teubner lines is the unit which represents a column in the common ancestor. The conclusion follows that the passage was omitted by the common ancestor, and inserted at the top of a column instead of at the foot. If so, it may represent lines in a previous MS.

The passage in question, as given by the MSS., consists of 166 letters, but *voce*, which is supplied by editors after *haruspicum*, has clearly dropped out. If we add *voce*, the total is 170. This would exactly = 10 lines of 17 letters.

I conclude with a reference to a *locus vexatissimus*, viz.:

Sest. 110: nihil saneatę (sane atte *G*) iuvabant anagnostae

In § 111 we have:

illo ore inimicos est meos saviatus

I suggest that *saneatę* = *sauiat' ē*, i. e. *saviatus est*, a variant for *est . . . saviatus*.

The intermediate passage *iuvabant anagnostae . . . est meos* consists of 576 letters (17 × 34 = 578).

I now recall attention for a moment to the four telescoped passages in *P*, consisting of 17, 19, 20, 21 letters. The first of these is a little shorter than the normal content in the archetype (20–3 letters). It may, of course, represent a short line, but it is possible that the omission took place at a previous stage in the transmission.

CHAPTER IX

PRO FONTEIO, PRO FLACCO, PRO CLUENTIO, PRO MILONE, IN CATILINAM, CAESARIANAE

OUR knowledge of the *pro Fonteio* is derived from two sources, viz.:

(1) Three leaves in a palimpsest, Vat. Palat. xxiv, which contains:

§§ 1–2: oportuisse . . . Aquiliense por-
§ 3: -cite . . . arca e ra-
§§ 4–5: deorum . . . qualis

The contents of these leaves correspond to $22\frac{1}{2}$, $22\frac{3}{4}$, $22\frac{3}{4}$ lines of Teubner text.

(2) Basil. Vat. H. 25 (*V*), ff. 11^{v}–17^{v}.

This contains the body of the speech, as now known to us, viz.:

§§ 11–49: hoc praetore . . . valuisse videantur.

I have already pointed out (p. 163) that other portions of the speech must have come in *V* before the fragment of the *pro Flacco* (§§ 39–54); also that *Font.* 11–49 must represent a certain number of folios in a previous MS. These sections occupy 542 lines of Teubner text.

For the *pro Flacco* we are mainly dependent on fifteenth-century MSS. They are clearly descended from a single ancestor, which appears to be connected with France. The chief representative of the family is Paris. 14749 (Σ). In all these MSS. there are lacunae at §§ 5, 47, and 75.

Our other sources are:

Ambr. R. 57 sup. (*A*).

This palimpsest contains a single leaf, reproduced in facsimile by Peyron. It is generally termed the Milan fragment. It supplies a passage not found in any other MS., which is placed by editors in the lacuna after § 5.

Basil. Vat. H. 25 (*V*), ff. 9v–11v. This contains:

§§ 39–54: litterarum si . . . est egentium.

V here has a passage, §§ 47–53 *pecuniam Fufiis . . . in re sit*, which is omitted by Σ *cett.*

To these must be added the *fragmentum Peutingerianum.* This was printed in the *ed. Crat.* (1528) by the well-known scholar, Conrad Peutinger, of Augsburg (1465–1547), who states that he obtained it from Rorarius of Frejus. His words are:

'Cum superioribus diebus Hieronymus Rorarius Foroiuliensis, non vulgaris eruditionis, apud nos in prandio fuisset et nomismata sua vetusta nobis ostendisset, dedit etiam versus octo vel paulo plus supra quinquaginta, quibus oratio haec Ciceroniana pro Flacco hactenus formis excusa deficiebat, quos addere curavimus.'

This supplement fills the gap in Σ *cett.* at § 75, by inserting:

§§ 75–83: primum ut in . . . esse caetera

The fate of Peutinger's fragment is wrapped in mystery. Other scholars, notably H. Stephanus, professed to have a *codex* for §§ 75–83, which did not entirely agree with that of Peutinger, but their statements are regarded with incredulity. Our sole authority appears to be the edition of Cratander. I may add that the fragment, which is very corrupt, is clearly genuine.

The question now arises whether there is any connexion between the two lacunae, viz. at § 47 and § 75.

The length in Teubner lines of the passages omitted by Σ *cett.* is as follows:

§§ 47–53: pecuniam Fufiis . . . in re sit = 93½ lines.
§§ 75–83: primum ut in . . . esse caetera = 91½ lines.

The agreement is striking. In order to obtain further light, it is necessary to consider the intervening block of text between the two lacunae, viz.:

§§ 53–75: ut quam ob . . . Castricium mortuum.

This occupies 276½ lines of Teubner text. We have now the series:

§§ 47–53 = 93½ lines.
§§ 53–75 = 276½
§§ 75–83 = 91½

Here $92 \times 3 = 276$.

The significance of these figures cannot be disputed. The natural and simple solution is that 91½–93½ represents a folio in an ancestor, and that on two occasions a folio has been lost. The unit is a large one, and its size suggests that the ancestor in question was not of great antiquity.

I now turn to the lacuna in § 5. If this was due to loss of leaves in the same ancestor, we should expect §§ 6–47 *hunc igitur virum . . . respondit se omnem* to show a multiple of 91½–93½. If, however, the lacuna there had already taken place, then we should expect §§ 1–47 to show the operation of this unit, that is, if the speech, as is generally the case, began at the top of a page.

Here §§ 6–47 = 591½ Teubner lines. The unit does not here work (92 to 94 × 6 = 552 to 564).

§§ 1–47 = 663. This gives a better result (94 × 7 = 658).

The conclusion, therefore, is that the lacuna at § 5 goes back to a previous stage in the history of the text.

So far we are on firm ground. I now come to a very curious point. The fragment of the *pro Flacco*, preserved by *V*, begins on f. 9^v of that MS. in its present condition at the top of the page, after the loss of four quaternions, with § 39 *litterarum si.* It ends on f. 11^v, col. 2, l. 20, and is immediately succeeded by the fragment of the *Fonteiana*, without break or title. The portion of the *Fonteiana* preserved by *V* (§§ 11–49) occupies 542 lines of Teubner text. It must clearly represent folios of a previous MS.

I now turn to that part of the *pro Flacco* which comes before § 39 *litterarum si.* We know that there is a lacuna at § 5, but we do not know if *V* contained here anything more than the fifteenth-century MSS. As given by them, the contents of §§ 1–39 (*Cum in maximis . . . et corruptarum*) are as follows:

§§ 1–5 = 72½ lines.
§§ 6–39 = 469½ „

542

It is to be noticed that this is the exact length of the *Fonteiana*, as preserved in *V*.

This is a very surprising result. It may, of course, be due to accident, but the chances against such an accident are enormous. The natural inference seems to be that in an ancestor of *V* both *Flacc.*

1–39 and *Font.* 11–49 formed blocks of text which occupied the same number of folios. If so, this ancestor already had the lacuna at § 5.

It seems odd that § 39 *litterarum si,* which comes immediately after the 542 lines of Teubner text contained in §§ 1–39 (*Cum in . . . et corruptarum*), should occur at the top of a page in *V*, but, as we cannot tell what the lost leaves contained, we are necessarily in the dark. The evidence seems to show that the speeches *pro Flacco* and *pro Fonteio* were dislocated and confused.

For the convenience of the reader I add that the whole of the fragment of the *pro Flacco* contained in *V*, viz. §§ 39–54 *litterarum si . . . est egentium*, occupies 224 lines of Teubner text.

If the theory that §§ 39–54 represent a block of text in an ancestor is well grounded, then 224, as well as 542, must represent a number of folios in that ancestor. Both figures may be explained as multiples of 45 (45 × 5 = 225, 45 × 12 = 540).

The evidence appears to show that the lacuna at § 5 is very ancient. The Milan fragment seems to belong to this part of the speech; also certain passages quoted by the *Scholiasta Bobiensis.*

pro Cluentio.

Our knowledge of the speech *pro Cluentio* is derived from two sources, viz.:

M = Laur. li. 10, cent. xi.

Σ = Paris. 14749 (marginalia and supplements).

M contains Varro *de lingua Latina* and the *Auctor ad Herennium*, in addition to the *Cluentiana*. It is written in the Beneventan script, apparently at Monte Cassino. It is said to belong to the end of the eleventh century. If so, it was probably written shortly after the abbacy of Desiderius (1058–87).[1]

M is descended from a mutilated MS. with lacunae at §§ 102, 127, 149, 176. It has also lost the end of the speech, which terminates abruptly at the end of a page (f. 49^{v}), with the words *atque his rebus* (§ 192).

The lacunae which occur in the body of the speech are also found

[1] E. A. Loew, *The Beneventan Script*, pp. 11, 17, 70.

in a number of later MSS. (μ), which appear to be derived from *M*. These MSS. also have lost the end of the speech, but many of them end a few lines further on in the same section at the words *aut ne forte ma-*. The natural inference is that the ancestor of *M* also ended here, and that *M* has been mutilated after f. 49v.

Paris. 14749 is itself copied in this speech from an ordinary MS. of the μ family. It contains, however, a quantity of marginalia, four supplements inserted on fly-leaves, while the end of the speech, after § 192 *aut ne forte ma-*, is added by the writer of the supplements.

The marginalia and supplements were taken from the old Cluni MS., no 496, before this came into the hands of Poggio. It was from this source that the portions of the speech omitted by *M*μ were recovered.

I now give the length of the Cluni supplements expressed in Teubner lines:

§§ 102–107:	in tota . . . ornamenta	= 84½ lines.
§§ 127–132:	subscripserunt quis . . . standum	= 88½ „
§§ 149–154:	dicenda est . . . accusatur	= 90 „
§§ 176–182:	quemdam quasi . . . honestissi-	= 89 „

The intervening blocks of text preserved by *M*μ show the operation of the same unit, viz.:

§§ 107–127:	non quaerunt . . . de iudicio corrupto	= 259 lines
§§ 132–149:	non putavit . . . haec causa sola	= 269 „
§§ 154–176:	quae tum . . . medico Stratonem	= 270 „

Here the two last figures are practically identical, while the first exhibits a rather smaller unit ($86 \times 3 = 258$). It is to be noticed that there is a similar reduction in the Cluni supplement which immediately precedes this block, viz. §§ 102–7 = 84½. There is known to be a lacuna in § 103 where editors supply a few words after *ob rem iudicandam*. The correspondence of 84½ with 259 shows that the loss here is not great.

It has already been shown that the common ancestor of *M*μ must have ended at § 192 *aut ne forte ma-*, not a few lines higher in the same section where *M* itself ends at the foot of a page. We should therefore expect §§ 182–92 *-morum sententia . . . ne forte ma-* to exhibit some relation to the unit previously disclosed. This passage occupies 131 lines in the Teubner text. Here $88 + 44 = 132$.

The question now arises whether 88 represents a folio or two folios. The first explanation seems most probable, since it does not seem likely that two folios would be omitted on four separate occasions. If so, §§ 182–92 must represent a folio and a page. It is simple to suppose that the speech was damaged towards the end, and that the verso of a folio was illegible.

I now exhibit the whole of the speech down to § 192, marking with an asterisk the portions omitted by *Mμ*:

§§ 1–102	= 1372	(85 × 16 = 1360)
*§§ 102–107	= 84½	
§§ 107–127	= 259	(86 × 3 = 258)
*§§ 127–132	= 88½	
§§ 132–149	= 269	(90 × 3 = 270)
*§§ 149–154	= 90	
§§ 154–176	= 270	(90 × 3 = 270)
*§§ 176–182	= 89	
§§ 182–192	= 131	(88 + 44 = 132)

It is to be noticed that §§ 1–102 appear to have occupied two quaternions. The missing folios were ff. 17, 21, 25, 29. The remainder of the speech §§ 192–202 occupies 142 lines of Teubner text, which represents, roughly speaking, one folio + a page in the ancestor of *M*.

It now remains to ask if there is any evidence to show the length of line in this ancestor.

Apart from four doubtful passages where *M* omits one or two words found in Σ, viz. § 47 *comparatur*, § 116 *maiestatis*, § 94 *illi iudices*, § 86 *habebat simultates*, the only cases which I have noticed are:

(55) § 136: rogaretur, aliam non diceret atque ei dixerunt quorum sententiis

(56) § 141: Albanum poscebat, in Tiburti cum adsedissemus ego et Brutus filius[1]

(67) § 107: M. Iuventius Pedo fuit ex vetere illa iudicum disciplina, qualis L. Caulius Mergus

Here Σ^1 gives *iudicium* (68), and Σ^2 *iudiciorum* (70).

(93) § 57: nisi forte hoc causae est quod medici nihil praeter artificium, oratores etiam auctoritatem praestare debent

The coincidence between 55 and 56 is striking, and suggests that the passages represent lines in the model of *M*.

[1] So Σ. Cicero, *de Oratore* ii. 224, has *in Tiburti forte adsedimus ego et Brutus filius.*

I have counted the letters in §§ 149–54 (90 lines), a passage which I selected on account of its relation to §§ 154–76 (270 lines), and find the total to be 3,780. This is an exact multiple of 54 (54 × 70). If then §§ 149–54 represent a folio in the model of *M*, it seems to have contained 35 lines to a page, with an average of 54 letters to the line. This appears to be a very probable formation.

I may add that *M* is written in long lines with about 70 letters to the line.

It may be worth while to add here some evidence concerning the model from which the text in Paris. 14749 (σ), as distinguished from the marginalia and supplements (Σ), was copied.

The omissions of σ are as follows: [1]

(38) § 191: sed etiam cogitavit quibus eum rebus armaret

(73) § 55: *venenum id quod Habito daretur esse quaesitum? Quae porro tenuissima suspicio collata

(75) § 72: *ex eius sermone speculae degustarat. Unus et alter dies intercesserat cum res parum certa

§ 190: *illa sibi ad confirmandas inimicitias adfinitatis coniunctiones pignori fore putavit

(78) § 172: est usus, potius etiam simultas. Eine igitur quem sibi offensorem (*sic*), Oppianico familiarissimum

(81) § 175: *ibi primum in morbum incidit ac satis vehementer diuque egrotavit cum esset una Sassia et Statio

The fact that two passages of 75 letters are omitted is very striking. Also, the omissions of 73, 78, 81 letters are very similar. I am inclined to think that the model of σ contained 70–80 letters to the line, in which case it was very much like *M*. It is to be noticed that there is an omission of 38 letters, and it is tempting to take this as the unit. It is not, however, likely that two lines would be omitted on five occasions and a single line only once.

We have now to ask if there is any evidence as to the length of a line in the Cluni MS. itself.

It is interesting to notice that the writer of the supplements which have been stitched into the MS., in order to repair the omissions of *M*μ at §§ 102, 127, 149, 176, appears on various occasions to have begun or ended at the wrong place. I will take the passages in order.

[1] I give the passages as added by the second hand in σ.

§§ 102–7. *Mμ* here give:

quod nos (§ 102) non quaerunt (§ 107) *om. med.*

The writer of the supplement, after adding the missing passage, viz. *in tota causa . . . verborum ornamenta*, instead of stopping at *non quaerunt*, went on with a passage already contained by σ, viz.:

qualis uir M. Iuuentius pede fuit ex uetere illa iudici[or]um disciplina, qualis L. caulius mergus, M. basilus, C. Laudinus qui omnes in iudiciis publicis iam tum florente (138)

§§ 127–32. *Mμ* have:

de iudicio corrupto (§ 127) non putavit (§ 132) *om. med.*

The writer of the supplement here should have begun with *subscripserint quis est* after *corrupto.* Instead of doing so, however, he began too soon, in § 126 after *causa cognita statuisse*, and repeated a long passage already found in the text of σ, written thus:

dicent. Quod si ita fecissent, tamen id non ita fixum esse deberet ut conuelli non liceret. Non utar exemplorum copia, quae summa est, non rem ueterem, non hominem potentem aliquem aut gratiosum proferam. Nuper hominem tenuem, scribam aedilitium, Decimum Macrinium cum defendissem aput M. Iunium Q. Puplicium pretores et M. Pretorium C. Flaminium aediles curules, persuasi ut scribam iurati legerent eum quem eidem isti censores aerarium reliquisse subscripserunt. Cum enim in hominem nulla culpa inueniretur, quid ille meruisset, non quid de eo statutum esset, querendum esse dixerunt. Nam hec quidem quae de iudicio corrupto (513)

After this the supplement proper begins with *subscripserint quis est.* This is a very remarkable repetition. We cannot but suspect that the writer, instead of beginning at a particular place in one column, began at the same place in another.

At the end of this supplement the writer did not stop at *opinione standum* (§ 132), but went on with a passage already found in the text (σ), viz.:

quid est quam ob rem quisquam (24)

§§ 149–54. *Mμ* have:

causa sola (§ 149) Habitus accusatur (§ 154) *om. med.*

The supplement here begins, not with *dicenda est*, which should come after *sola*, but with *non enim mihi hec causa sola* (23), a passage already written in the text of σ.

§§ 176–82. *M* has: *medico Stratonem* (§ 176) *morum sententia* (§ 182) *om. med.*

Here *morum* is a relic of *honestissimorum*. It would appear that the model of *M* had *virorum honestissimorum*, not *honestissimorum virorum*.

The supplement begins correctly, but instead of stopping at *honestissimorum virorum*, goes on with *sententia constitutum esse* (24), a passage already given by σ.

I now put together the figures for these repetitions, viz.:

(23) § 149: non . . . sola
(24) § 132: quid . . . quisquam
§ 182: sententia . . . esse
(138) § 107: qualis . . . florente
(511) § 126: dicent . . . corrupto

Here 23 × 6 = 138, 23 × 22 = 506.

There is other evidence furnished by corruptions in the speeches *pro Sex. Roscio* and *pro Murena*, which were copied directly from Clun. 496.

Rosc. 72: ita moriuntur ut eorum ossa terra non tangat, ita iactantur fluctibus ut numquam abluantur.

Σ has: ita moriuntur ut eorum ossa terra non tangat ita iactantur [ut eorum ossa terra non tangat, ita iactantur] fluctibus ut numquam abluantur.

This suggests in the exemplar:

ita moriuntur
ut eorum ossa terra non tangat (25)
ita iactantur

The writer looked back from *iactantur* to *moriuntur*, and he repeated the intervening passage.

§ 101: eiusmodi ut libentibus animis ad eius testimonium vestrum ius iurandum accommodetis

Σ has: eiusmodi ut libentibus animis ad eius [modi ut libentius animis ad eius] testimonium etc.

This seems to indicate:

eius
modi ut libentibus animis ad (24)
eius testimonium

The writer looked back from *eius* to *eius*.

Mur. 86: confectus morbo, lacrimis ac maerore perditus

Σ^1 has a lacuna of 22 letters between *confectus* and *perditus*. The second hand adds in the margin :

lacrimis ac memore perditus (24)

This may represent a line of the exemplar.

The earliest Italian copy of which we know is Laur. 48. 10 (*A*). This was written by Joh. Arretinus, a Florentine calligrapher, in 1416, immediately after the arrival of Clun. 496 in Italy. I have only noticed one omission of any importance in *A*, viz. *Rosc.* 106 : *ac se in Chrysogoni fidem et clientelam contulerunt* (44). It is possible that this represents two lines of the model.

A ends suddenly at *Rosc.* 106 :

homines sapientes et ista aucto-

The rest of § 106, viz. :

-ritate et potestate praeditos . . . ex animis amittimus

consists of 534 letters (allowing for official abbreviations).

The similarity of this omission to the repetition of 511 letters by the French writer of the supplement at *Clu.* 127 is striking.

We know from the evidence of F. Barbaro that the Cluniacensis was extremely illegible, and it is possible that Joh. Arretinus gave up the end of the speech in despair. It must have been deciphered soon afterwards, since it appears in another MS. (Perusinus *E.* 71), which was written in the following year.

There is other evidence which may be used in this matter, viz. that given by the excerpts of Bartolommeo (Laur. liv. 5). I have noted in my published collation of these where in his excerpt he omits something. The evidence has to be used with caution, since he may have purposely omitted something which did not interest him.

I attach no importance to some short omissions, viz. :

(13) *Clu.* 30 : huiusce causae
(14) *Rosc.* 21 : vel nobilissima
(15) *Clu.* 18 : nihil mali timuit
(16) *Mur.* 19 : ius civile didicit
(17) *Mur.* 68 : consulatum petenti

The other cases are :

(19) *Clu.* 41 : qui gener eius fuisset
(22) *Mil.* 54 : uter nihil mali cogitaret
(23) *Clu.* 8 : *sicut facere instituistis

[1] *Vetus Cluniacensis of Poggio*, p. vi.

(24) *Clu.* 40 : *simul atque introductus est
(26) *Cael.* 12 : *sicuti meminisse vos arbitror
Mur. 70 : si interdum ad forum deducimur
(34) *Rosc.* 31 : *quae ad causam pertinere arbitror omnia
(38) *Clu.* 41 : *cum id multis locis fecisset post mortem eius
(46) *Mur.* 17 : *qui non modo Curiis, Catonibus, Pompeiis, antiquis illis
(48) *Mur.* 5 : *ipsi iam pridem tulerim de civium periculis defendendis.

The two last of these omissions are most important, since they destroy the sense of the passage. Also *Mur.* 17 contains information which Bartolommeo would find interesting. The relation of 46–8 to 22–4 is to be noticed.

It is to be observed that the cases of 19 and 38 occur in the same section of the *pro Cluentio.* They are only separated by the words *digito legata delevit et* (21). This is a somewhat remarkable fact, which seems to suggest that Clun. 496 had:

qui gener eius fuisset (19)
digito legata deleuit et (21)
cum id multis locis fe (18)
cisset post mortem eius (20)

If so, the breadth of the columns must have varied in places, as the rest of the evidence is in favour of a larger unit.

I have noticed a corruption in *B*, to which I should attach more importance than to the omissions, except *Mur.* 5 and 17, viz.:

Clu. 36 : ratio excogitata Larini est, res translata Romam (Romae Σ*B*).

B has *excogitata* for *translata.* This should indicate in the MS. before Bartolommeo:

ratio
excogitata larini est res (22)
translata

His eye was caught by the beginning of the previous line (ὁμ.). The combined evidence, therefore, appears to converge in one direction.

pro Milone.

Our authorities for the *pro Milone* are:

Taur. A. ii. 2*, cent. iv. This palimpsest has already been described (p. 138). In this speech it is called *P* by editors, in order to distinguish it from the Tegernseensis (*T*). Five leaves have been preserved containing §§ 29–32, 34–6, 72–5, 86–8, 92–5.

Paris. 14749 (Σ), marginalia taken from Clun. 496. These are reinforced by excerpts made from the Cluniacensis by Bartolommeo da Montepolitiano (*B*), who was with Poggio at the time of the discovery.

Harl. 2682 (*H*), cent. xi. The readings of this MS., which formerly belonged to Cologne Cathedral, generally agree with Σ*B*.

Tegernseensis (*T*), cent. xi, now Monacensis 18787.

Erfurtensis (*E*), cent. xii/xiii, now Berol. Lat. Fol. 252.

There are also a number of Italian MSS., the oldest of which is Laur. S. Crucis. xxiii, Sin. 3 (*a*), cent. xiv. This is copied from a MS. which belonged to Lapo da Castiglioncho, a friend of Petrarch.

There is a long lacuna in *H*, extending from § 18, *cruentata*, to § 37, *paene in-*. As the marginalia in Σ stop at § 18 and begin again at § 37, while Bartolommeo made no excerpts for the intermediate sections, it is clear that the lacuna was shared by Clun. 496. In *H* it is indicated by the critical sign *RQ̃* (= *require*), which has been received into the text before *cruentata*.

Within this long lacuna there is a minor lacuna common to all the MSS. except the palimpsest, viz.:

§ 34: -fuerit occidi . . . qui sibi solutam.

This passage begins at the top of col. 1 in the second folio of *P* and ends in l. 2 of the second column. A facsimile of the leaf is given by Peyron.[1] There is a lacuna between *-fuerit occidi* and § 33, which in *TEa*, &c., ends with *certe non debeo*.

There is a missing leaf of *P* between that which contains §§ 29–32, and the one which begins with *fuerit occidi*. Peyron pointed out that this missing leaf contained more than is given by the other MSS., viz. § 32, *etsi boni* . . . 33, *non debeo*. He estimated the amount lost as about equal to five lines of the edition (ed. Pat. 1754) employed by him. The contents of the five folios of *P* which were preserved occupy respectively 40½, 39¾, 40½, 42½ lines of Teubner, and the intervening blocks of the speech show the operation of a similar unit. Here, however, *TE cett.* (*defic.* Σ*H*) only contain enough to fill 34 lines of Teubner text. If we take 39¾–42½ as the limits of variation for a folio of *P*, it follows that the missing leaf must have

[1] *Ciceronis orationum fragmenta*, pp. 221–2.

contained from $5\frac{3}{4}$–$8\frac{1}{2}$ more lines of Teubner text than is given by *TE cett.*

Peyron filled the manifest lacuna before *-fuerit* by inserting *audistis*, *iudices*, *quantum Clodi* before it. He also inserted higher up in the same section after *deferre posses* two fragments quoted by Quintil. ix. 2. 54 and the *Scholiasta Bobiensis*, p. 176, ed. Hildebrand.

It seems arbitrary to assume two lacunae, when one is manifest, and Peyron's additions disturb the construction. It is now recognized that they come not from the written speech, but from that actually delivered, which, as Asconius tells us, was extant in his time, having been taken down by the shorthand writers.

I now proceed to consider the long lacuna characteristic of the Cluniacensis and *H*. It is natural to connect this with the shorter lacuna in *TE cett.* If this is so, it follows that in the common ancestor of our MSS., apart from *P*, the whole passage omitted by Σ*H* formed a certain number of folios, and that a folio ended at § 33, *non debeo.*

The first point, therefore, to ask is if there is any relation between the passages omitted by Σ*H*, but found in *TE*, before and after *debeo.*

The results as expressed in Teubner lines are:

§§ 18–33: cruentata . . . non debeo = 210 lines
§§ 34–37: P. Clodi . . . -terfici = 42 „

Here $42 \times 5 = 210$. So far we have no information as to whether the unit is 42 or 21.

The question now comes as to what has been lost by *TE cett.* after *debeo.* In the first place we have the passage preserved by *P* only, viz.:

§ 34: -fuerit occidi . . . qui sibi solutam.

This occupies 11 lines of Teubner text. To this we have to add the lost passage after *debeo*, the existence of which is inferred by Peyron from *P*. We have seen that this must have contained from $5\frac{3}{4}$–$8\frac{1}{2}$ lines of Teubner text. If we take the largest figure we have now $11 + 8\frac{1}{2} = 19\frac{1}{2}$. There is no relation between this and 42, but it is only $1\frac{1}{2}$ lines short of 21.

It is to be remembered that for § 34, *-fuerit . . . sibi solutam*, we have the evidence of *P* only, and it is possible that *P* may have omitted something which was preserved by the ancestor of the other

MSS. A place where the grammar appears to halt is after *admitteret* in the sentence:

> Quid Milonis intererat interfici Clodium? quid erat cur Milo non dicam admitteret, sed optaret?

It seems probable that the unit is 21, not 42. If so, *TE cett.* omit one folio of the common ancestor after § 33, while Σ*H* omit 10+1+2 = 13 ff.

It now remains to estimate the number of letters contained by a page of the common ancestor of Σ*HTE*, &c.

§§ 34–7, *P. Clodi . . . -terfici*, if we allow for a few official abbreviations, contain 1,748 letters. If these sections represent two folios, we have the following figures:

874 letters = one folio
437 letters = one page.

If the MS. was written in two columns, this gives 218 letters to the column. Such a MS. is likely to have been of great antiquity.

I have so far restricted myself to the mutilations in the text of the speeches *pro Fonteio*, *pro Flacco*, *pro Cluentio*, and *pro Milone*. I now mention some other points of interest connected with these orations.

The first point concerns the other contents of *V*, apart from the *Philippics*, viz. in *Pisonem*, *pro Fonteio*, *pro Flacco*. The internal evidence in their case shows different results from those furnished by the *Philippics*.

I take first the *Pisoniana*. In this *V* omits the following passages found in the other MSS.:

(11) § 43: conscientia
§ 46: constitutas
§ 49: periculoque
(33) § 55: admoniti et rogati. Togulae lictoribus

To these should possibly be added:

(12) § 33: in provinciam V^2: *om.* V^1, *cett.*

In this connexion a variant furnished by the *excerpta Cusana* deserves mention.

§ 60: quid tandem habet iste currus, quid vincti ante currum duces?

Here *Cus.* has *triumphalis* (11) before *currus*.

It is interesting to compare with these two other passages where the later MSS. omit passages contained by *V*, viz.:

(11) § 70: omnia stupra
(12) § 48: cum iam egeret

In the second case *V* is supported by the Turin palimpsest (*T*).[1] The conclusion suggested by these omissions is that all our MSS., including *V*, are derived from an archetype containing about 11 letters to a line.

I have not included in this list a passage which needs some explanation, viz. § 48. Here the later MSS. give:

> cum partim eius praedae profundae libidines devorassent, partim nova quaedam et inaudita luxuries, partim etiam in illis locis ubi omnia diripuit emptiones, partim permutationes ad hunc Tusculanum (-ni *TV*) montem exstruendum.
>
> partim permutationes (19) *om. T.*

In *V partim* after *emptiones* is written *in rasura*, while in the next line the last four letters of *Tusculani* have been corrected in darker ink and the rest of the line is left blank. A second, but contemporary hand, has inserted above *Tusculani* in darker ink an additional line, *mutationes ad hunc* (16). The natural interpretation is that the first hand wrote *emptiones ad hunc Tusculanum*, and that the corrector erased *hunc*, over which he wrote *partim*. He then added *mutationes hunc* above the line and altered *Tusculanum* to *Tusculani*. It is to be noticed that in the first quaternion of *V* the average content of a line in col. 2 is 17 letters. It is therefore possible that V^1 omitted a line of an ancestor written in the same formation, the mistake being due to ὁμ.

Omissions are especially frequent in the case of repetitions such as *partim . . . partim* (e.g. *Rull.* ii. 36), and the omission by TV^1 seems due to accident. M. Havet very ingeniously emends to *partim mutuationes*.[2]

In this connexion I would mention another passage:

§ 21: ex omni scelerum importunitate et flagitiorum impunitate conceptum.

So the later MSS. *T* omits *et flagitiorum impunitate* (23). *V* is not

[1] This is generally called *P* by editors in this speech.
[2] *Manuel de critique verbale*, § 220.

extant for this portion of the speech. *T* may have omitted two lines of the archetype, the omission being due to ὁμ.

The following variety in collocation is interesting:

§ 70: omnia cenarum conviviorumque genera

So *V*: the later MSS. have *genera conviviorum*. It seems likely that *conviviorum* was omitted (ὁμ.) and inserted after *genera*, *-que* being omitted. This passage comes immediately after *omnia stupra* (so *V*: *om. cett.*). The archetype may have had:

omnia stupra	(11)
omnia cenarum	(12)
conuiuiorum	(11)
que genera	

I have noticed other transposition variants which point in the same direction, viz.:

§ 47: sanctissimo et gravissimo *V*: gravissimo et sanctissimo *cett.*

Here either *sanctissimo* (11) or *gravissimo* (10) appears to have been inserted in the wrong place after omission.

§ 70: non ut improbum, non ut audacem, non ut impurum *V*
non ut impurum, non ut improbum, non ut audacem *cett.*

The variants appear to go back to an ancestor which had:

non ut improbum	(13)
non ut audacem	(12)
non ut impurum	(12)

§ 64: infimo ac despicatissimo sis antelaturus *V*
es infimo ac despicatissimo antelaturus *cett.*

Here *sis* is a mistake for *es*. Apparently *es* was omitted and *sis* inserted by conjecture. It is to be noticed that the words *infimo ac despicatissimo* consist of 22 letters (= 2 lines).

§ 65: ne acclametur times? Ne id quidem est curare philosophi. Manus tibi ne adferantur?

So *V*: the other MSS. place *times* after *adferantur*. The words *ne id . . . adferantur* contain 50 letters.

The following corruptions are interesting:

§ 70: ceteris studiis quae fere Epicureos neglegere dicunt *V*
studiis quae fere ceteros Epicureos neglegere dicunt *cett.*

Here *ceteros* appears to be a variant for *ceteris*, which has got into the text later on in the sentence. The words *ceteris . . . fere* contain 22 letters. The archetype may have had:

mg. ceteros | ceteris studi (12)
is quae fere (10)
Epicureos

§ 57: ut levitatis est inanem aucupari rumorem et omnis umbras etiam falsae gloriae consectari, sic est levis animi lucem splendoremque fugientis iustam gloriam . . . repudiare.

So *V*: the other MSS. place *levis* after *animi*. The word is struck out by editors with Lambinus. It looks like a variant for *levitatis*, which has got into the wrong place. The words *levitatis . . . sic est* consist of 80 letters.

§ 72: non illa tibi, inquit, invidia nocuit sed versus tui. Nimis magna poena te consule constituta est sive malo poetae sive libero. Scripsisti enim, cedant arma togae.

So *V*: the other MSS. add *versus* after *scripsisti enim*. This looks like an addition from *versus tui*. The words *versus tui . . . scripsisti enim*, if we write *cons.* for *consule*, consist of 81 letters. The agreement with § 57 is to be noticed.

The general conclusion is that, apart from § 48, where *V* may have omitted a line of a predecessor very like itself, the internal evidence is in favour of referring both *V* and the other MSS. to an archetype written in lines of about 11 letters.

In the case of the *pro Fonteio* there is little evidence, since we are wholly dependent on *V*. The following corruptions of *V* seem to point to a similar conclusion:

§ 32: omnes [in] equites R. qui in illa prouincia fuerunt *V*

This suggests in a previous MS.:

omnes
equites R. qui (11)
in illa

The scribe looked forward to the next line.

§ 25: fuit, fuit illis iudicibus divinum ac singulare iudicium, consilium, qui se non solum de reo [iudicium] sed etiam de accusatore, de teste iudicare arbitrabantur *V*

Here editors read *iudices* for *iudicium*, after *singulare*. The word has been repeated by error after *reo*. Probably there were variants, i. e. *iudicium* and *iudices*, in the model.

The words *iudicium* (*iudices*) . . . *de reo* consist of 35 (34) letters. The writer appears to have looked back three lines.

§ 23 : de clarissimis [dubitandum] nostrae ciuitatis uiris dubitandum non putauerunt *V*

Here *dubitandum* (10) is repeated before *nostrae civitatis viris* (21). This suggests in a previous MS. :

nostrae ciui (11)
tatis uiris (10)
dubitandum (10)

I would call attention to the following insertions made by editors where *V* has lost a word :

(10) § 17 : victoribus *suppl.* Niebuhr
(11) § 42 : fortissimis *suppl.* Orelli

I now come to the *pro Flacco.* Very little internal evidence is yielded by *V.* I have noticed the following corruptions :

§ 40 : cum tabulae illae ipsae, cuicuimodi sunt, proferuntur.

So editors with Schütz. For *cuicuimodi* V^2 gives *huiusmodi* (*in rasura*), while Σ, &c., have *cuiuscemodi.* It is to be observed that *V* inserts *cui* before *cum.* This looks like part of *cuicui-*, which has got into the wrong place. On the analogy of the *in Pisonem* and *pro Fonteio* we may suppose that *V* in this speech also was derived from a similar, or the same, ancestor. If so, this may have had :

cum tabulae (10)
illae ipsae (10)
mg. cui cuimodi

§ 46 : civem suum, cui debebat esse notissimus, percussit. Eius enim fide sumpsit a Fufiis

For *suum* *V* has *sume.* The corruption *sum* for *suum* is found elsewhere in *V.* The addition of *-e*, however, is odd. It is to be noticed that *V* gives *fides* for *fide.* In view of the parallel corruptions which *V* displays in the *Philippics*, it occurs to me that the *e* of *sume* represents a correction of *fides* (i. e. *fides* with *e* written above). The words *cui . . . fides* consist of 46 letters. A previous MS. may have had :

ciuem sum
cui debebat es (12)
se notissimus (12)
percussit ei (11)
us enim fides (11) *mg.* e

I have not observed any certain case where *V* omits. There is, however, one doubtful one, which is worth mentioning, viz.:

§ 47: habebat enim rhetor iste discipulos quosdam locupletis, quos dimidio redderet stultiores quam acceperat

So *V* and Arusianus (cent. iv–v A.D.). The other MSS. add:

ubi nihil possent (-int) discere nisi ignorantiam litterarum.

This addition is generally regarded as an interpolation. It is to be noticed that the clausula is excellent, but this may be due to accident.

The *Scholiasta Bobiensis*, after quoting in his lemma *habebat . . . acceperat*, adds the following scholium:

inludit personae rhetoris imperiti, hanc eruditionem discipulorum fuisse in eius schola dicens ut in ea nihil disceretur praeter ignorantiam litterarum

It appears to me that this note implies the presence of the incriminated words in the text before the scholiast. It is to be noticed that he uses the word *dicens*, not *significans*, or *innuens*.

The passage in question consists of 46 letters (cf. the corruption in § 46, *sume*), which would suffice for four lines of the previous MS. If it is genuine, *ubi* seems to be a corruption for *cum*.

I now turn to Σ and allied MSS. I have noticed the following omissions:

(15) § 72: et lectissimorum
(17) § 36: nullam constantiam
(18) § 18: imperio fuerit summo (*add. m.* 2)
§ 44: et conficientissima
(56) § 75: ipsi quidem dicunt. Vellem tantum habere me otii, ut possem recitare
(72) § 105: * est, nos qui iam progressi sumus hunc exitum nostrae temeritatis feremus. Sin hoc animo (*add. m.* 2)
(79) *ib.*: quid sentiatis. Huic, huic misero puero vestro ac liberorum vestrorum supplici, iud., hoc iudicio

In this family the speech *pro Quinctio* is closely connected with the *pro Flacco*. In Σ these two speeches, also the *pro Cluentio*, are written in a different hand, with longer lines than those employed in the previous part of the MS. It is therefore worth while to compare the omissions of Σ, &c., in the *pro Quinctio*. I have noticed the following cases:

(18) § 73: et complures fuerunt
(23) § 33: is posteriore loco diceret

(37) § 10: atque obsecrat ut multis iniuriis iactatam
(56) § 85: eum qui non latitaret, cui Romae domus uxor liberi procurator esset
(77) § 44: * quod peto, satis det. Actum iam potest esse, C. Aquili; iam tu potes liberatus discedere molestia (*add. m.* 2).
(79) § 85: ita possideto ut Quinctio vis ne adferatur. Quid? tu id quem ad modum observas? Mitto illud dicere (*add. m.* 2).
(85) § 92: nos nostram perfacile cuivis probaturos statuebamus; quod vitae ratio cum ratione vitae decerneret
(167) § 53: aut ad eorum aliquem qui consuluntur concurrisses? Cum ius amicitiae societatis adfinitatis ageretur, cum officii rationem atque existimationis duci conveniret, eo tempore tu non modo ad C. Aquilium

The relation between 85 and 167 deserves especial notice. In both speeches the occurrence of omissions of 70–80 letters is remarkable, especially those of 77 and 79 letters in *Quinct.* 85 and 44. It is especially significant that in three cases, *Flacc.* 72, *Quinct.* 44, 85, the passage omitted is added in the margin. The inference is that the writer omitted lines of his model. As in these speeches Σ contains 70–80 letters to a line, it would appear that it was copied from a MS. very similar to itself.

Further evidence is to be obtained from the *pro Cluentio.* I have already given a list of the passages omitted by the first hand in this MS. (p. 287). Apart from one shorter omission, we find the following figures: 73, 75 (*bis*), 78, 81.

I now combine these omissions in the three speeches:

(72) *Flacc.* 105 (*add. m.* 2)
(73) *Clu.* 55 (*add. m.* 2)
(75) *Clu.* 72 (*add. m.* 2)
190 (*add. m.* 2)
(77) *Quinct.* 44 (*add. m.* 2)
(78) *Clu.* 172 (*add. m.* 2)
(79) *Quinct.* 85 (*add. m.* 2), *Flacc.* 105
(81) *Clu.* 175 (*add. m.* 2)
(85) *Quinct.* 92
(167) *Quinct.* 53

There is no reason to suppose that the parent of the Σ family was a MS. of any antiquity. There can be no doubt that a number of abbreviations were employed in it. The general agreement, therefore, between these passages, when written in full, is striking.

It will be noticed that two of these omissions occur in immediate proximity to each other, viz. in *Flacc.* 105. The intervening words here consist of 44 letters. This is at first sight puzzling, but it is only necessary to write out the passage in order to see the solution. The parent MS. seems to have had:

est nos qui iam progressi sumus hunc exitum nostrae temeritatis feremus sin hoc animo (72)
quam plurimos esse uultis declarabitis hoc iudicio quid sentiatis huic huic misero puero (76)
uestro ac liberorum uestrorum supplici iud. hoc iudicio uiuendi praecepta dabitis

Σ omits l. 1, without ὁμ., and in ll. 2–3 writes *declarabitis hoc iudicio uiuendi praecepta dabitis* med. om. (ὁμ.).

The corrector repaired the first omission, but did not notice the second.

One further point deserves mention. It is to be observed that both in the *pro Flacco* and in the *pro Quinctio* there is an omission of 56 letters, coming before the longer omissions with which I have just dealt. This may be due to mere coincidence, but it is also possible that 56 = a line in a previous ancestor. The second view acquires considerable probability from:

Quinct. 85: ita possideto ut Quinctio vis ne adferatur. Quid? tu id quem ad modum observas? Mitto illud dicere, eum qui non latitaret, cui Romae domus, uxor, liberi, procurator esset, eum qui *etc.*

The whole of this passage was omitted by Σ[1]. The corrector added in the margin:

ita possideto . . . dicere (79)

but did not add

eum qui . . . esset (56)

The inference appears to be that the words *eum qui . . . esset* were already absent from the model.

I now return to the Cluniacensis. I have already collected evidence, chiefly based on the errors committed by the writer who inserted supplements in the *pro Cluentio*, to show that this was written in lines averaging 23–4 letters. I have noticed indications which seem to show that it was derived from an ancestor very like itself. In the *Cluentiana* this ancestor seems to be the parent of all the MSS. I quote the following cases:

Clu. 72: queritur se ab Oppianico destitutum et qui esset totus ex fraude et mendacio factus quique ea vitia quae ab natura habebat etiam artificio malitiae condivisset, pulchre adseverat sese ab Oppianico destitutum

So *Mμ*: as no variant is quoted in Σ, it is probable that Clun. had the same reading. Peterson strikes out *queritur se . . . destitutum.* It appears probable that the words *se . . . destitutum* (after *queritur*) are a repetition from the context (after *adseverat*).

The words in question consist of 23 letters, and the intervening passage, *et qui . . . adseverat se-*, consists of 139 letters. Here $23 \times 6 = 138$. This suggests the following arrangement in the common ancestor:

queritur
et qui esset totus ex fraude (23)
et mendacio factus quique ea (24)
uitia quae ab natura habebat (24)
etiam studio atque artifi (22)
cio quodam malitiae condi (22)
uisset pulchre adseuerat se (24)
se ab oppianico destitutum (23)

§ 84. The reading of $M\mu$ here is:

istam conciliationem gratiae Staienus tum recenti re cum faucibus premeretur excogitavit sive ut homines tum loquebantur a P. Cethego admonitus istam dedit conciliationis et gratiae fabulam.

Two variants are quoted in Σ, viz. *conciliationis gratiam* at the beginning of the sentence and *iutro* to be inserted before *dedit.*

The passage is undoubtedly corrupt, apart from the repetition *conciliationem gratiae* (*conciliationis gratiam*) and *conciliationis et gratiae.* An insertion which appears necessary is that of *est* (Kayser) after *admonitus.* At the beginning of the sentence *ita*, a word frequently confused with *ista*, seems to be required for *istam.* I previously considered *iutro* in Σ to stand for *ultro* and inserted *sive ultro* before *excogitavit.* I now incline to think that *iutro* = *intro*, and that *dedit* should be emended to *duxit* (i. e. *istam introduxit fabulam*).

The simplest explanation of the repetition is that a variant for *conciliationis et gratiae* has got into the context higher up. This suggests the following arrangement. I ignore the emendations which have been proposed, but add *iutro* from Σ:

istam
staienus tum recenti re cum (23)
faucibus premeretur exco (22)
gitauit siue ut homines tum (23)
loquebantur a P. cethego ad (22)

	monitus istam iutro dedit	(22)
mg. conciliationis	conciliationis et gratiae	(23)
gratiam	fabulam	

The similarity between this passage and § 72 should be noticed. In § 72 the passage *et qui . . . adseuerat se-* consists of 139 letters. Here the words *Staienus . . . gratiae* consist of 135. If we admit *est* after *admonitus*, the total would be 138.

I would also compare:

§ 137: ut id quod senatus decreverat ad illud invidiae praesens incendium restinguendum, id postea referendum ad populum non arbitrarentur.

So *M*μ: no variant is quoted from Σ, though in so small a point the argument from silence does not prove much.

Peterson strikes out *id* after *ut*. It seems more likely that *id* has been repeated before *postea*. If so, an ancestor may have had:

ut	
id quod senatus decreuerat	(23)
ad illud inuidiae praesens	(23)
incendium restinguendum	(22)
postea	

The scribe looked back three lines.

I add one more passage which occurs in one of the lacunae, where we have not the evidence of *M*μ:

§ 153: huiusce modi quaestionibus in iudicium vocarentur. Tunc (tum *edd.*) C. Flavius Pusio, Cn. Titinius, C. Maecenas, illa robora P. R. ceterique eiusce modi ordinis.

So Σ and the Italian copies. Editors read *eiusdem ordinis* with Klotz. It seems probable that *-ce modi* has been repeated from the context. An ancestor of Σ (and probably of *M*) may have had:

huius	
ce modi quaestionibus in iudi	(25)
cium uocarentur tunc C. flauius	(26)
pusio Cn. titinius C. maecenas	(24)
illa robora P. R. ceterique eius	(25)
ordinis	

The writer looked back from *eius* to *huius*.

I now call attention to the following passages in the *pro Murena*:

§ 58: saepe hoc maiores natu dicere audivi, hanc accusatoris eximiam vim, dignitatem, plurimum L. Cottae profuisse.

So Σ and all Italian copies with any claim to authority. Some late MSS. insert *et* after *vim*, while the *editio Romana* omits *vim*. It occurs to me that *vim* is a repetition from *-vi* in *audivi*. If so, a previous MS. may have had:

audi
ui hanc accusatoris eximiam (24)
dignitatem

§ 65: Nihil ignoveris. Immo aliquid, non omnia. Immo gratiae confeceris. Immo resistito gratiae.

So the MSS., except Lag. 9, which has *nihil omnino* for *immo* before *gratiae*. Editors read here *nihil*, and afterwards *causa feceris* for *confeceris*. A previous MS. may have had:

nihil gratiae confeceris (22)
immo resistito gratiae

If we credit it with *causa feceris*, the content of the line would be 24 letters.

§ 67: si mercede conducti obviam candidatis issent, si conducti sectarentur

So Σ: for *conducti*, after *mercede*, the Italian copies have *corrupti*. Neither word is necessary, as is shown by § 70, *at sectabantur multi. Doce mercede*. It seems probable that *conducti* was inserted from the context. An ancestor may have had:

si mercede
obuiam candidatis issent si (24)
conducti sectarentur

Before I quit this part of the subject I would refer to two passages in the *Cluentiana*, where there are indications of a remote ancestor written in narrow columns, viz.:

§ 176: cum essent animi servorum et spe et metu temptati ut aliquid in quaestione dicerent, tamen, ut arbitror, auctoritate advocatorum et vi tormentorum adducti in veritate manserunt.

This passage occurs in one of the lacunae, so we have not the evidence of $M\mu$. The statement that the slaves stuck to the truth on account of the cruelty of the torture is manifestly absurd, and the words were struck out by Halm and others. It has occurred to me as more probable that they should be transposed, i. e. after *et spe et metu*, and I observe from Orelli's note that this suggestion was previously made by Scheller.

The words *et vi tormentorum* consist of 15 letters, while the passage *temptati . . . advocatorum* contains 74 letters. Here 15 × 5 = 75. This suggests the arrangement :

et spe et metu	
et ui tormentorum	(15)
temptati ut ali	(13)
quid in quaestione	(16)
dicerent tamen ut	(15)
arbitror auctori	(15)
tate aduocatorum	(15)
adducti	

§ 130 : iudicia cum equestri ordine communicata, ut viderentur per hominum idoneorum ignominiam sua auctoritate illa iudicia [cum equestri ordine] reprehendisse

So Σ and the Italian copies. The passage occurs in one of the lacunae, so we have not the evidence of *Mμ*.

The Turin palimpsest omits *cum equestri ordine* after *iudicia*, also *illa* before it.

Apart from other possible corruptions, it is clear that the words *cum equestri ordine* (17) are repeated from the context. The intervening passage *communicata . . . illa iudicia* consists of 77 letters. This suggests the distribution :

iudicia	
cum equestri ordine	(17)
communicata ut ui	(15)
derentur per homi	(15)
num idoneorum igno	(16)
miniam sua auctori	(16)
tate illa iudicia	(15)
reprehendisse	

The writer looked back from *iudicia* to *iudicia*, and repeated a line.

The remaining speech with which I have dealt in this chapter is the *pro Milone*. I have found it somewhat barren of results for the purposes of this inquiry.

There is nothing to notice in the leaves of the Turin palimpsest except two transposition variants, viz. :

§ 74 : exstruere aedificium *P* : aedificium exstruere *cett.*
§ 31 : non illud iam in iudicium venit *P* : illud iam in iudicium venit non *cett.*

Here *aedificium* = 10, *illud . . . venit* = 23. I merely mention these on account of certain other transposition variants in this speech.

There remain Σ*HTEa*.

I take first *a* and the *dett.* generally.

Apart from certain omissions which they share with *T* or *TE*, they have the following which are peculiar to them :

(15) § 36 : iudiciumne timui (*om. a in lac.*)
(20) § 61 : commisit neque senatui
(23) § 48 : sed Milonem appropinquare
(30) § 44 : vos potestis dubitare quid fecerit
(57) § 12 : propter magna in r. p. merita mediocris in bonis causis auctoritas aut
(80) § 79 : * aut ipsum ab inferis excitare, utrum putatis potius facturum fuisse ? Etiam si propter amicitiam
(246) § 78 : nihil eorum vos visuros fuisse. In spem maximam et, quem ad modum confido, verissimam sumus adducti, hunc ipsum annum, hoc summo viro cons., compressa hominum licentia, cupiditatibus fractis, legibus et iudiciis constitutis, salutarem civitati fore. Num quis igitur est tam demens qui hoc P. Clodio vivo

The relation between 80 and 246 is to be noticed.

I now take *T*, marking agreements with *E* and δ (i. e. *a*, *cett.*):

(10) § 38 : * agnovisset
§ 102 : a quibus non (*E*)
§ 104 : non debitas
(11) § 28 : numquam fere
§ 30 : etiam beluis (*E*δ)
(13) § 105 : et fortissimum (δ)
(19) § 31 : de hoc igitur latum est
(55) § 50 : noctu occidisset. Insidioso et pleno latronum in loco occidisset (*E*δ)
(70) § 21 : amicos meos. Neque enim hoc cogitavit vir iustissimus neque in bonis viris legendis
(87) § 13 : ** amentiam perditorum. Hanc vero quaestionem etsi non est iniqua numquam tamen senatus constituendam pu-

It is to be noticed that the longest passage is telescoped. *T* itself is written in long lines with a number of abbreviations, and lines of 80 or more letters, if written in full without abbreviations, are common. I have noticed in the *Philippics* three omissions of 84–9 letters, also six of 74–9, one of which (xiii. 24) is a telescoped passage. There is also an omission of 77 letters in *Planc.* 72, and one of 152 in *Caec.* 91. The probability, therefore, is that in *Mil.* 13 *T* has omitted a line of its model.

Three omissions of *T* are common to *E*, the chief being in § 50 (55). No evidence in the shape of special omissions is furnished by *E*.

I now turn to *H* and the Cluniacensis. The closeness of their connexion may be seen from:

§ 8: aut C. Marius

Here *H* omits *aut C.* Σ inserts *h. d* as a variant from Clun. This shows either that Clun. had in the margin *hd̄ aut C.*, or that *hd̄* had been received into the text.

In connexion with this I would mention:

§ 67: armata est.

For *est* Σ has *sunt*, while *H* has *sunt R*. Here *R* = *require*.

There is a point of contact between Clun., *H*, and *E*, in that all three contain a mediaeval argument to the speech. This is given by Σ in a fly-sheet at the beginning of the MS., by *H* after the speech *de Imperio Cn. Pompei*, and by *E* before the *pro Milone*. It is to be noted that *E* generally reproduces the readings of the second hand in *H*.

There are a number of agreements between the text of *H*, or *H* + Clun., and that of Asconius and the *Scholiasta Bobiensis*, the most striking being in § 46, where *H*, with Asconius, omits *cuius . . . et Romae*.

Σ does not give any direct evidence as to omissions in Clun., but some is provided by the excerpts of Bartolommeo, which in this speech are unusually copious.

I now give a list of omissions in *H*, adding agreements or disagreements of *B*. Where *B* is not mentioned, the passage does not occur in the excerpts:

(11) § 57: occideritne *om. H*
§ 105: illam beatam *om. BH*
(12) § 86: sine lamentis *om. BH*
(13) § 42: fabulam falsam *B*, *cett.*: *om. H*
(14) § 48: non id nuntiasse *om. H*
§ 67: si Milonem times *om. H*
(15) § 79: * haec est quaestio [1] *om. H*

[1] This is very doubtful. *H* has *nempe . de interitu P. Clodi*: *TEδ* have *nempe haec est quaestio de interitu P. Clodi*. *H* seems to preserve the earliest form of a gloss.

(30) § 4: de bonis et fortibus viris, si umquam *om. BH*
(33) § 91: sustinetis furias insepulti? nisi vero *om. H*

I have not included in this list:

(63) § 46: cuius iam pridem testimonio Clodius eadem hora Interamnae fuerat et Romae

Here the omission is shared by Asconius in his *lemma*, while in his *scholium* he gives the information contained in these words. The frequency of the agreements between *H* and Asconius seems to show that the passage is an insertion.

There is only one passage which seems to throw any real light upon the relations of Clun., *H*, *TEδ*, viz.:

§ 50: noctu occidisset. Insidioso et pleno latronum in loco occidisset. Nemo ei neganti non credidisset.

So Σ. *H* repeats *nemo . . . credidisset* before *insidioso*, while *TEδ* omit *noctu occidisset . . . loco occidisset.* Of this omission Richter said, '*es scheint eine Zeile in der gemeinsamen Quelle von TE u. a. übersprungen zu sein*'.

Here the words *noctu occidisset . . . loco occidisset* consist of 55 letters, while the words *nemo . . . credidisset* consist of 27 letters. This is a striking fact and suggests in a previous MS. the arrangement:

noctu occidisset insidioso et	(26)
pleno latronum in loco occidisset	(29)
nemo ei neganti non credidisset	(27)

Here *TEδ* omit l. 3, while the writer of *H*, passing from *occidisset* to *occidisset*, has inserted the line out of place, as well as *loco suo.*

In connexion with this I would mention a passage which occurs shortly above (§ 47). Here the MSS. give:

Iacent suis testibus, hi qui Clodium negant eo die Romam nisi de Cyro audisset fuisse rediturum

Here Garatoni struck out *hi*, while *Richter* reads *eis.* I formerly struck out the whole clause as a scholium, but now feel doubts in view of the excellent clausula.

We have seen that various critical signs occur in the MSS., viz. *hđ* in Σ (§ 8), *RQ̃* in *H* (§ 18), also *R* in *H* (§ 67). In *E* the lacuna after *debeo* (§ 33) is marked by *dee̋* above the line. I, therefore, suggest that here *hi* may stand for *ħ*, the ordinary sign for omission. The words in question *qui . . . rediturum* consist of 59 letters, which is very like the omission of 55 letters by *TEδ* in § 50.

There is another passage in which a notorious corruption may be due to a similar cause, viz.:

§ 66: cum tamen si metuitur etiam nunc Milo

Many emendations have been made, into which I need not now enter. I would refer to *Mur.* 51. Here Σ has:

partim . . . quia nihil timebant, partim quia timebant. Cue

In the margin is: al. *que uel cur.* The Italian copies have *cum*, *cur*, *qui*, etc. These appear to me various corruptions for *q̃* or *que* (= *quaere*).[1] Probably *timebant* after *quia* has been substituted for *omnia.*

It is possible that *cum* here is due to a similar misunderstanding. If so, I would emend *tamen si* to *tametsi.* The paragraph would then end thus:

tametsi metuitur etiam nunc Milo

It is to be noticed that the words consist of 28 letters. It is possible that a line was omitted and *q̃* was written in the margin to mark the corruption. For this suggestion I would refer to:

Dom. 30: idemque cum dixisset, tum etiam pro salute mea populum Romanum obsecravit

Halm marks a lacuna between *idemque* and *dixisset*, saying '*cum* supra versum a vetere manu P habet atque videntur plura verba excidisse'. I do not agree with Halm's theory of the additions made in *P*, but the grammar seems odd. We should expect *idemque cum dixit, tum etiam.* It is possible that *cum* here is a corruption of *q̃*. In this case its position above the line would be natural.

I conclude this chapter by putting together some facts concerning the *Catilinariae* and *Caesarianae* (*pro Marcello*, *pro Ligario*, *pro rege Deiotaro*). The speeches were much read during the middle ages, as is shown by the large number of MSS. The criticism of the two groups is closely connected. They are generally found together, and in both there are three families of MSS., which Nohl, who is followed by recent editors, distinguishes as α, β, γ.

[1] The corruptions *que*, *quae*, *cur*, found in the MSS. of Lucretius at vi. 840, after a lacuna, are probably due to this symbol.

Three members of α contain both *Catilinariae* and *Caesarianae*, viz.:

C = Clun. 498, now Holkham. 387, cent. ix.

A = Ambros. C. 29 infr., cent. x.

V = Vossianus, Lat. O. 2, cent. xi.

To these must be added in the *Catilinarians*:

a = Laur. xlv, cent. xiii.

Also, in the *Caesarianae*:

H = Harl. 2682, cent. xi.

In this MS. there are two copies of these speeches. The second belongs to α, and the first to γ. *H* also contains the *Catilinarians*, but in these speeches its recension is mixed and I term it *h*.

The general superiority of the α group cannot be doubted, although occasional contributions are made by the other groups. Thus, to take a clear case:

> *Cat.* ii. 27: conivere possum γ, *Schol. Gronov.*, *Probus*, *Sacerdos*: consulere sibi possunt αβ

Here the true reading is preserved by γ only.

H. Reeder[1] has examined the quotations of Quintilian and the grammarians in order to fix by their aid the respective antiquity of α, β, γ in the *Caesarianae*. His conclusion is that the α text is in the main that used by Quintilian. He says:

> 'Quintiliani temporibus unam tantum recensionem praesto fuisse neque probabile esse alteram tunc exstitisse supra intelleximus.'

Priscian (cent. vi) generally agrees with α, but on three occasions with β. Among earlier writers he finds one agreement with β in Sacerdos, cent. iii (*Lig.* 21, *domi*) and one in Diomedes, cent. iv (*Lig.* 10, *acuit*). He therefore pronounces this family to be *satis vetusta*. He finds no support for γ in the ancient quotations and declares it to be unworthy of notice.

The line of argument which he adopts seems to me vitiated by the fact that very ancient MSS. contain double readings which represent traditional variants. Thus on Oxyrhynchus 16, cent. i, *Thuc.* iv. 36–41, the editors remark:

> 'The text is rendered particularly interesting by the presence of a considerable number of double readings. Of these the majority are certainly by the original

[1] *De codicibus in Ciceronis orationibus Caesarianis recte aestimandis.* Jena, 1906.

scribe, and may be explained either as traditional *variae lectiones*, or—though perhaps less probably—as the result of the use of more than one MS. by the copyist, who was careful in cases of disagreement to record alternatives.'

Ox. 1017, cent. ii/iii, Plato, *Phaedrus*, also contains a number of double readings, one of which supports a conjecture of Heindorf, while others appear in later MSS.

The evidence of the papyri is seldom in favour of one group of MSS. exclusively. I take as a typical example Ox. 463, cent. ii/iii, Xenophon, *Anabasis*. The editors remark:

'The peculiarity of the papyrus lies in the fact that it combines lections characteristic of both classes of MSS. Thus, while agreeing in several cases with the superior family against the inferior, it shows six instances of agreement with the inferior class against the superior where the latter is clearly wrong.'

The eclectic character of the papyri is also pointed out elsewhere, e.g. on Ox. 843, Plato, *Symposium*, cent. ii/iii; 844, Isocrates, cent. ii/iii; and especially 1251, Cicero, *pro Caelio*. Of this it is said:

'Its salient characteristic is its heterogeneousness. While sharing not seldom the excellences of Σ, it has side by side with these a number of distinctive P readings, some good, some bad, and occasionally carries back to the fifth century the tradition of still later authorities. The high antiquity of the bulk of the variants is the chief lesson of the papyrus.'

I have already called attention to the variants found in the palimpsest of the *de Re Publica* and the strange conflations of different readings, e.g. *quods* and *nequec*, given by *V* in the *Philippics*.

I do not, therefore, think that the agreements of Sacerdos and Diomedes with β on two occasions prove anything more than that these were ancient variants. I conceive the α text both here and in the *Catilinarians* to be on the whole that of Cicero, but I am willing to suppose that β and γ occasionally preserve the true reading. As examples where βγ or γ must be taken into account, I would give:

Marc. 2: conservatam ac restitutam βγ: conservatam α

Omissions of this kind are so frequent in the best MSS. that I now incline to follow βγ.

Lig. 14: cave credas, cave ignoscas, cave . . . te misereat γ: cave ignoscas, cave . . . te misereat αβ

Here again the explanation of omission through ὁμ. seems most likely.

A peculiarly instructive case is:

Cat. ii. 29: urbem pulcherrimam florentissimam potentissimamque γ: urbem pulcherrimam florentissimamque *A V* $\alpha\beta$

When *C*, the most important member of α, came to light, it was found to agree with γ, not with the other members of α.

I now turn to α. The following omissions are common to *A V* in the *Catilinarians* and *A VH* in the *Caesarianae*. The portions of these speeches extant in *C* are: *Cat.* i. 1–5, 17–ii. 11, 15–iii. 1, 9–19, 23–6, iv. 8–15; *Lig.* 18–28, 38—*Deiot.* 6, *Deiot.* 15–43.

Where we have the evidence of *C* I use the symbol *C*α:

(9) *Cat.* iii. 18: * nutu atque *C*α
Marc. 11: aliquando α
Lig. 28: praecipue α
Deiot. 18: est factum α (factum *C*)
(10) *Cat.* i. 7: * contra rem p. α
27: * diligenter *C*α
Deiot. 5: domesticos *C*α
(11) *Cat.* i. 23: * si id feceris *C*α
(12) *Cat.* i. 15: nihil moliris α
ii. 9: * esse fateatur *C*α
iv. 20: et contemptam α
(13) *Cat.* iv. 18: studio virtute α
Marc. 2: conservatam ac α
(15) *Cat.* iii. 3: et quam manifesta α
(17) *Cat.* ii. 11: intus insidiae sunt *C*α
(20) *Lig.* 12: artium atque optimarum α
Deiot. 27: amicitias res rationes *C*α
(23) *Cat.* iii. 25: conflagrare sed in hac urbe *C*α
(27) *Deiot.* 34: solus inquam es, C. Caesar, cuius in *C*α
(38) *Cat.* iv. 13: minueretur hic ad evertenda fundamenta rei p. *C*α
(62) *Cat.* i. 26: ad obsidendum stuprum verum etiam ad facinus obeundum, vigilare non solum *C*α

In this list the noteworthy point is the number of small omissions (9–12 letters), which reminds us of similar phenomena to be observed in the MSS. of the *Verrines*.

We have also omissions peculiar to one or more members of the family, viz.:

C^1 omits:

(15) *Cat.* ii. 25: pudicitia illinc
(23) *Deiot.* 42: cum e balineo exisses tecum
(56) *Cat.* i. 23: vix feram sermones hominum, vix molem istius invidiae, si in exilium

CA omit:

(10) *Cat.* iv. 10: et corporis
(12) *Deiot.* 38: tum non dubito
(17) *Deiot.* 25: tibi porro inimicus

A or *AH* omit:

(12) *Cat.* iv. 7: et miseriarum *A*
(18) *Lig.* 29: persequamini si rei p. *A*
(20) *Marc.* 25: si tibi soli viveres aut *AH*
Lig. 13: et nos iacentis ad pedes *A* (not *H*)
(38) *Cat.* i. 32: tantam in nobis consulibus[1] fore diligentiam A^1
(113) *Cat.* iii. 27: mentes enim hominum audacissimorum sceleratae ac nefariae ne vobis nocere possent ego providi, ne mihi noceant vestrum est providere *A*

C is defective in all of these cases, except *Cat.* i. 32, where it does not share the omission of A^1.

V omits:

(9) *Cat.* iii. 28: in nobis is
(16) *Cat.* iii. 21: * a nefariis civibus
(17) *Cat.* iv. 18: vobis aras Penatium
(18) *Cat.* iii. 2: restinximus idemque
(26) *Cat.* i. 19: et ad vindicandum fortissimum
(42) *Cat.* i. 16: assedisti partem istam subselliorum nudam atque
(46) *Cat.* i. 17: tam graviter atque offensum viderem, carere me aspectu
(152) *Cat.* i. 13: num dubitas id me imperante facere quod iam tua sponte faciebas? Exire ex urbe iubet cons. hostem. Interrogas me, num in exsilium? Non iubeo, sed, si me consulis, suadeo. Quid est enim, Catilina

There is only one omission peculiar to *H*, viz.:

(10) *Deiot.* 33: verberatos

I add one long omission of *a*, reported by Halm.

(117) *Cat.* ii. 19: arbitrantur. Quibus hoc praecipiendum videtur, unum scilicet et idem quod reliquis omnibus, ut desperent id quod conantur se consequi posse.

This is interesting in view of the omission of 113 letters by *A* in iii. 27, but in all probability the pedigree of *a* is somewhat tangled.

The omissions of *a* and of the MSS. which compose the family do

[1] I here write *consulibus* in full, since it is so given by *C* as well as by A^2. If *cons.*, = 32.

not give much information. For further light we must go to an interesting corruption which pervades the family:

> *Cat.* iii. 25 : atque illae tamen omnes dissensiones erant eius modi quae non ad delendam sed ad commutandam rem p. pertinerent: non illi nullam esse rem p. sed in ea quae esset se esse principes, neque hanc urbem conflagrare sed se in hac urbe florere voluerunt.

The simplest form of the corruption seems to be given by *V*, which after *principes* has *neque hanc urbem non florere voluerunt* (*med. om.*). This indicates the following arrangement in a previous MS. :

principes	
neque hanc urbem conflagrare	(25)
sed se in hac urbe florere	(21)
uoluerunt.	

V omits *-flagrare sed se in hac urbe* (22), with the consequential change of *con-* to *non*.

C has:

non illi nullam esse rem p. sed
in ea quae esset se esse principes
neque hanc urbem florere
se uoluerunt.

Here the words *conflagrare sed in hac urbe* (23) are omitted, and *se* is placed before *voluerunt*, where it spoils the rhythm.

A gives the whole passage thus:

> atque ille (*sic*) tamen omnes dissensiones erant eiusmodi florere si uoluerunt quae non ad delendam sed ad commutandam rem p. pertinerent. Non illi nullam esse rem p. sed in ea quae esset se esse principes neque hanc urbem.

Here we notice:

(1) that *A*, like *C*, omits *conflagrare . . . urbe*;

(2) that the model of *A*, like *C*, placed *se* before *voluerunt*;

(3) that in *A* the words *florere se* (*si*) *voluerunt* occur out of place. Apparently, they were in the margin of the model.

The last mistake should throw light on the model of *A*, as distinguished from the common ancestor of the family.

a has, after *principes*,

> conflagrare sed se in hac urbe neque hanc urbem florere uoluerunt.

Here the omitted words have been inserted before *neque hanc urbem*, instead of after *urbem*.

With this I would compare another passage:

Cat. i. 11: magna dis immortalibus habenda est atque huic ipsi Iovi Statori . . . gratia, quod hanc tam taetram, tam horribilem tamque infestam rei p. pestem totiens iam effugimus.

Here *A* inserts *terribilem* after *gratia*, while *V* has *terribilem* for *horribilem*. *C* is here mutilated.

The common ancestor of the group seems to have had:

gratia
quod hanc tam taetram tam (21)
mg. terribilem horribilem

The variant has got into *A* in the wrong place and supplanted *horribilem* in *V*.

These corruptions seem to show that the common ancestor of the group was written in lines of 21–3 letters. We may therefore attribute to this ancestor the following omissions of *a*, or members of *a*:

(20) *Lig.* 12: artium atque optimarum *om. a* (*defic. C*)
13: et nos iacentis ad pedes *om. A* (*defic. C*)
Deiot. 27: amicitias res rationes *om. Ca*
(23) *Deiot.* 42: cum e balineo exisses tecum *om.* C^1

as well as that of 23 in *Cat.* iii. 25.

I now return to the special corruption of *A* in *Cat.* iii. 25. Here the words *florere se* (*si*) *voluerunt* are out of place. The intervening passage consists of 114 letters. This is interesting in view of the fact that the two longest omissions of *A sol.*, apart from the other members of the group, contain 38 and 113 letters (38 × 3 = 114). I, therefore, arrange the model of *A* thus:

eiusmodi
quae non ad delendam sed ad commutandam rem p. (37)
pertinerent, non illi nullam esse rem p. sed in ea (39)
mg. florere si uoluerunt. quae esset se esse principes neque hanc urbem (38)

The marginal addition has got into the text three lines higher up.

I have not attempted to analyse *β* and *γ* with the same care. I have, however, made some observations upon three MSS. in the *Catilinarians* which may be of interest. These are:

h = Harl. 2682, cent. xi.
t = Monac. 19472, cent. xi.
u = Bruxell. 10060, cent. xi.

These have the following omissions.

I take first *h*:

(32) iii. 13: * inter sese aspiciebant ut non[1] ab aliis (*om. m.* 1)
(33) ii. 5: illum esse nobis quam hos qui exercitum (*om. m.* 1)
iii. 4: cum oculis maleficium ipsum videretis
(47) iv. 3: peste pereamus. Qua re patres c̃. incumbite ad salutem rei p. (*om. m.* 1)
I retain the official abbreviations, as given by *m.* 2.
(53) iv. 17: quaestus frequentia civium sustentatur, alitur otio, quorum si

Halm quotes from *t*:

(33) iv. 12: virginum atque puerorum ac vexationem
(46) iv. 5: deinde quod P. Lentulum se abdicare praetura coegistis
(47) ii. 15: sed cum sint homines qui illum cum profectus sit eiectum
iii. 6: ipsi comprehensi ad me, cum iam dilucesceret, deducuntur.
(54) iv. 13: * poenae crudeles in patriam quam ne severitate animadversionis

Also, from *u*:

(31) i. 29: virtute partam gloriam, non invidiam (*om. m.* 1)
iii. 19: * cum et simulacra deorum depulsa sunt
(46) iv. 29: ad modum iam antea vestra tecta vigiliis custodiisque
(53) iv. 9: * sed tamen meorum periculorum rationes utilitas rei p. vindicat[2]
(64) iv. 8: ** -re. Adiungit gravem poenam municipiis si quis eorum vincula ruperit, horribi-

The last case is very interesting, since the passage is mutilated at both ends. In view of the two omissions of 31, we may take 64 as 32 x 2. If so, the arrangement in a previous MS. must have been:

recusa
re adiungit grauem poenam municipiis (32)
si quis eorum uincula ruperit horribi (32)
les

These are, I think, the only omissions recorded from *tu* by Halm.

I now proceed to combine the evidence furnished by *htu*:

(31) i. 29 *om. u*[1]: iii. 19 *om. u*
(32) iii. 13 *om. h*[1]
(33) ii. 5 *om. h*[1]: iii. 4 *om. h*: iv. 12 *om. t*
(46) iv. 5 *om. t*: iv. 29 *om. t*
(47) iv. 3 *om. h*
(53) iv. 9 *om. u*: iv. 17 *om. h*[1]
(54) iv. 13 *om. t*
(64) iv. 8 *om. t*

[1] So *h*[2]: non iam *cett.*

[2] So the MSS. for *vincat.*

Here we have six examples of 31–3, together with one of 64, three examples of 46–7, three of 53–4, and nothing else.

More than one explanation can be offered, viz. (1) that the unit is 16 ($16 \times 2 = 32$, $16 \times 3 = 48$, $16 \times 4 = 64$). If so, we should expect examples of the unit as well as of the multiples. (2) that the figures refer to lines of different ancestors, viz. 31–3, 46–7, 53. The last two sets of figures might well refer to the same MS.

There must clearly be some close connexion between *htu*. The curious fact is that *h*, though its text is mixed, inclines to *α*, while *t* and *u* are prominent members of *γ*, containing the best variants preserved by that group.

I would here mention:

> *Cat.* iii. 20: fore ut ea consilia quae clam essent inita contra salutem urbis atque imperii inlustrarentur ut a senatu populoque Romano perspici possent. Atque illud signum collocandum consules illi locaverunt.

Halm proposes to insert *ita* before *inlustrarentur*. The word occurs in *u* before *collocandum*, also in another, and more ancient, member of *γ*, viz. Laur. L. 45 (*x*), cent. x. The words *inlustrarentur . . . signum* consist of 64 letters. This suggests in the common ancestor of *ux* the following arrangement:

	atque imperii	
mg. ita	inlustrarentur ut a senatu populoque	(32)
	R. perspici possent atque illud signum	(32)
	collocandum	

If so, *ita*, which appears to be genuine, was inserted two lines lower down.

I now call attention to two places where the *β* text appears to be clearly right, viz.:

> *Cat.* iv. 22: hostes alienigenae aut oppressi serviunt aut recepti in amicitiam beneficio se obligatos putant.

So *β*: *in amicitiam* (11) *om. αγ*.

> *Cat.* iv. 12: qui non dolore et (ac *β*) cruciatu nocentis suum dolorem cruciatumque lenierit.

So most members of *β*: *dolore . . . suum* (28) *om. αγ*.

The question now comes whether all our MSS. are to be referred back to a single archetype. There are a number of errors which are common either to all MSS. or to all except one, generally a late

MS., into which a correction seems to have been inserted by conjecture.

A striking case is:

Cat. iii. 25: atque illae tamen omnes dissensiones erant eius modi . . . atque illae tamen omnes dissensiones, quarum.

So all MSS. except *x* (Laur. L. 45), which omits *tamen omnes* in the first sentence. It seems impossible that Cicero can have repeated himself in this manner. Norden has recently in a very interesting paper suggested that Cicero intended to strike out one of the doublets, but that his correction was disregarded by the copyist.[1] I offer another explanation which will be found shortly.

Cat. ii. 4: Tongilium mihi eduxit quem amare in praetexta calumnia coeperat.

So all MSS. except *i* (a member of β), which omits *calumnia*. It is possible that *calumnia* is the note of a reader. I have suggested that it may be a corruption from *K* = *Kaput*, which occurs in the α family at i. 26. I have since noticed in Paris. 21242 the reading *in praetexta* ^{c}*alumnia*, which may support this view.

Cat. iv. 8: multas uno dolore animi atque corporis et omnis scelerum poenas ademisset.

So the MSS.: a word seems to be omitted after *corporis*, e.g. *aerumnas* (Halm) or *miserias*.

In the same speech, § 11, we have the following variants: *exsolvitis βh*: *defendetis lγ*: *eripiam i*, while the α family omit. The conclusion is that the variants are conjectures to replace the lost word.

§ 14: omnes adsunt omnium ordinum homines, omnium denique aetatum.

Putsche supplies *omnium generum* (13) after *homines*. The insertion seems necessary in view of *denique*.

§ 9: sed tamen meorum periculorum rationes utilitas rei publicae vincat.

So the *Schol. Gron.*: all MSS. have *vindicat*.

Lig. 13: quodne nos domi petimus precibus ac lacrimis.

So all MSS. except *cod.* (?) *Gruteri*, which omits *domi*. The word cannot be right, since Cicero is speaking of the present appeal in the senate house, not of that previously made *domi*.

§ 14: id a te in foro oppugnari et in tali miseria multorum perfugium misericordiae tollere.

[1] *Aus Ciceros Werkstatt*, pp. 6–10 (*Königl. Preuss. Akad.*, 1913, 1).

So all MSS. The combination of passive and active cannot be right.

Other examples are:

Cat. i. 13: infamiae (variously emended)
33: omnibus] ominibus *edd.* (1 *det.*)
ii. 5: ex Gallicanis] prae Gallicanis *edd.*
8: ne ullo] ne ullo quidem *edd.* (1 *det.*)
20: insperatis] in insperatis *edd.*
iii. 9: fastis αβ: libris γ] fatis *edd.*
14: Manlium] Annium *edd.*
iv. 12: quam] non quam *edd.* (numquam *Lactantius*)
17: nisi] immo *edd.* (2 *dett.*)
Marc. 2: et mihi et meae] et mihi meae *edd.*
3: in omnibus] omnibus *edd.*
12: adepta] adempta *edd. recc.*
Lig. 13: ignoscat] ignoscatur *edd.*
34: non noverit] noverit *edd.*

These errors are strongly in favour of descent from one archetype. There are various circumstances which suggest that this archetype was written in very narrow columns, such as those used in the *de Re Publica* palimpsest.

I have already called attention to the number of small omissions characteristic of α, viz. 11 cases of 9–12 letters.

It is to be noticed that whenever β or γ contribute something of their own, the addition consists of about this number of letters. The most striking case is:

Cat. iv. 22: in amicitiam (11) β: *om.* αγ

The chief additions of γ are:

Marc. 2: cum viderem (10)
8: tanta copia (10)
Lig. 14: cave ignoscas (12)

The theory that in certain cases β or γ have preserved lines of the archetype seems to be the simplest solution.

I would draw particular attention to Putsche's insertion of *omnium generum* (13) in *Cat.* iv. 14. This may represent a lost line of the archetype. I may also refer to a conjecture of my own in iv. 13:

cum sororis suae, feminae lectissimae, virum . . . vita privandum esse dixit, cum avum suum iussu consulis interfectum filiumque eius impuberem legatum a patre missum in carcere necatum esse dixit.

The statement required is not that they were executed, but that they were rightly executed. I, therefore, proposed to insert *e re p. necatos* (11) after *necatum.*

I now draw attention to some corruptions:

> *Cat.* ii. 5: ego illum exercitum prae Gallicanis legionibus . . . contemno.

The MSS. have *ex*, which cannot be right, for *prae*. The error may point to the arrangement:

illum
exercitum (9)
prae

The writer repeated *ex* from *exercitum.*

> *Cat.* iv. 9: meorum periculorum rationes utilitas rei p. vincat. Habemus enim a Caesare, sicut ipsius dignitas . . . postulabat.

For *vincat* the MSS. have *vindicat.* Here *-di-* may be introduced from *dignitas*. The words *-cat. Habemus . . . ipsius* consist of 33 letters. The archetype may have had:

uin
cat habemus e (11)
nim a caesare (11)
sicut ipsius (11)
dignitas

The writer looked forward from l. 2 to l. 5.

> *Cat.* i. 13: quae nota domesticae turpitudinis non inusta vitae tuae est? quod privatarum rerum dedecus non haeret infamiae?

So the MSS. The usual correction is *haeret in fama.* It appears to me likely that *infamiae* is a variant for *turpitudinis*, which has got into the wrong place. The words *turpitudinis . . . haeret* consist of 68 letters. The relation of 68 to 33 in the previous passage is to be noted.

I abstain from further guesses, and conclude by calling attention to three remarkable agreements, which seem to throw light upon some deep-seated corruptions. Two of them concern passages which have already been referred to, viz.:

> *Cat.* iii. 25: atque illae tamen omnes dissensiones.

These words occur at the beginning of two sentences, separated by an intermediate sentence (*non illi . . . voluerunt*). In my edition I have struck out *atque illae tamen omnes* (20) at the beginning of the first sentence. The intervening words between the first and the second occasion where the passage is found, viz. *dissensiones . . . voluerunt*, consist of 180 letters.

Lig. 13: quod nos [domi] petimus.

So the MSS. Shortly afterwards comes (§ 14):

si cum hoc domi faceremus, quod et fecimus, et, ut spero, non frustra fecimus, tu repente inruisses.

Domi before *petimus* seems to have been introduced from § 14. The intermediate words consist of 182 letters.

Deiot. 24: addit etiam illud equites non optimos misisse [ueteris] credo, Caesar, nihil ad tuum equitatum.

So $\alpha\beta$: *veteris om.* γ, *edd.*

In view of previous experiences, it struck me that *veteris* might be a variant which had got into the wrong place.

In § 23 we have:

non quaero quam veri simile sit.

For *veri simile sit* we have the following variants in α:

uerisiles it *C*: ueris si lesit *H*: simile sit ueri *A*.

The corruption *ueris* in *H* is especially noticeable; *ueri* is given by *A*, but the order has been changed. I think it probable that *ueteris* is a variant for *ueris* or *ueri*.

The words *veri simile . . . optimos misisse* consist of 358 letters.

If we compare these three passages we have the remarkable sequence:

Cat. iii. 25 = 180
Lig. 13 = 182
Deiot. 24 = 358

The inference which these figures suggest is that 180 represents a column in the archetype, and that the scribe has looked forward a column on two occasions, and two columns (i. e. a page) on another occasion. In order to make this clear, I write out the passages as I conceive them to have stood in the archetype:

(1) *Cat.* iii. 25:

dissensiones	(12)	atque illae	(10)
erant eius	(9)	tamen omnes	(10)
modi quae non	(11)	dissensiones	(12)
ad delendam	(10)		
sed ad commu	(10)		
tandam rem p.	(10)		
pertinerent	(11)		
non illi nul	(10)		
lam esse rem p.	(11)		
sed in ea quae	(11)		
esset se esse	(11)		
principes ne	(11)		
que hanc urbem	(12)		
conflagrare	(11)		
sed se in hac	(10)		
urbe florere	(11)		
uoluerunt	(9)		
	180		

The writer began to copy col. 2 before col. 1. The error was due to $\delta\mu$.

(2) *Lig.* 13:

petimus pre	(10)	domi facere	(10)
cibus lacri	(10)	mus	
mis strati ad	(11)		
pedes non tam	(11)		
nostrae cau	(10)		
sae fidentes	(11)		
quam huius hu	(11)		
manitati id	(10)		
ne impetremus	(12)		
oppugnabis	(10)		
et in nostrum	(11)		
fletum irrum	(11)		
pes et nos ia	(10)		
centes ad pe	(10)		
des supplicum	(12)		
uoce prohibe	(11)		
bis si cum hoc	(11)		
	182		

(3) *Deiot.* 23–4:

mg. ueteris	ueri simile	(10)	sam illam uic	(11)
	sit aut habu	(10)	tam esse ne	(9)
	isse regem	(9)	sciebat an cae	(12)
	quos mitteret	(12)	cilium istum	(11)
	aut eos quos	(10)	magnum homi	(10)
	misisset non	(11)	nem putabat	(10)
	paruisse aut	(11)	quem profecto	(12)
	qui dicto au	(10)	is qui optime	(11)
	dientes in	(9)	nostros homi	(11)
	tanta re non	(10)	nes nouit uel	(11)
	fuissent eos	(11)	quia non nos	(10)
	uinctos poti	(11)	set uel si nos	(11)
	us quam neca	(10)	set contemne	(11)
	tos sed tamen	(11)	ret addit eti	(11)
	cum ad caeci	(10)	am illud equi	(11)
	lium mitte	(9)	tes non opti	(10)
	bat utrum cau	(11)	mos misisse	(10)
		175		182

The next page would begin with:

credo, caesar
nihil ad tuum
equitatum.

The variant *ueteris* found its way into the text before *credo*.

CHAPTER X

DE NATURA DEORUM, DE DIVINATIONE, TIMAEUS, DE FATO, TOPICA, PARADOXA, LUCULLUS, DE LEGIBUS

Schwenke says of this collection :[1]

'Omnis memoria librorum *de Natura Deorum* ducitur a corpore operum Ciceronianorum maximam partem physicorum, quod olim integros libros *de Natura Deorum, de Divinatione, Timaeum, de Fato, Topica, Paradoxa, Lucullum, de Legibus* continebat. Eius corporis exstabat, ni fallor, in Gallia, exemplar iam minusculis litteris exaratum, quaternionibus non paucis singulisque membranis amissis mutilum, aliis suo loco motis perturbatum : ex hoc et ii codices fluxerunt qui quantum illius corporis restabat totum continent et ii qui libros *de Natura Deorum* aut solos aut cum aliis paucioribus atque selectis coniunctos exhibent.'

He enumerates the following MSS. :

A = Leid. Voss. fol. 84, cent. ix/x (Chat. Pl. 38 A). Of this MS. he says :

'Oriundus est codex *A* sine dubio e Gallia, monasterio aut ecclesiae ubi servabatur donatus a Rodulfo quodam episcopo, cuius sedem propter nominis frequentiam definire non potui.'

B = Leid. Voss. fol. 86, cent. x (Chat. Pl. 39). Schwenke says of *B* :

'Servabatur et hic procul dubio in Gallia, ut videtur, in eadem bibliotheca atque cod. *A*.'

C = Leid. Heins. 118, cent. xi (Chat. Pl. 38). *C* is written in Beneventan script. It appears to be a copy made for Desiderius, Abbot of Monte Cassino (1058–87).[2]

F = Flor. Marc. 257, cent. x (Chat. Pl. 37). *F* formerly belonged to the cathedral of Strassburg, to which it was given by Bishop Werinharius (1001–29).

[1] *Class. Rev.* iv (1890), p. 347.
[2] Loew, *The Beneventan Script*, p. 81.

M = Monacensis 528, cent. xi.

P = Vat. Palatinus 1519, cent. xi (Chat. Pl. 40).

V = Vindobonensis 189, cent. ix/x (Chat. 38).

A photographic facsimile of *C* was published by Messrs. Sijthoff of Leiden, in 1912, and one of *A* appeared in the same series in 1915.[1] Both of these have introductions by O. Plasberg.

The dates which I have given are those of Schwenke. Those of Chatelain are much the same except in the case of *P*, which he assigns to the ninth century. I recently asked the Rev. H. M. Bannister to look at the MS. in the Vatican library. He, after consultation with other experts, pronounced in favour of Schwenke's date.

It will be observed that Schwenke claims French provenance for *A* and *B*, as well as for the archetype. In view of his suggestion, the following entry in the twelfth-century catalogue of Bec[2] is interesting:

no. 77: Tullius de natura deorum libri iii, de divinatione libri ii, Timaeus Platonis ab eo translatus et de fato liber i, ad Ortensium liber i et de legibus libri iii[3]

We find among the books of Richard de Fournival in the thirteenth century:

no. 73: M. T. C. liber de natura deorum
74: eiusdem liber de divinatione et de fato casus
75: eiusdem liber Achademicarum disputationum. Item eiusdem liber de universalitate qui vocatur Thimeus Tullii. Eiusdem liber ad Hortensium qui inscribitur Luculus et interdum Hortensius.[4]

These are the only references to such a *corpus* in the mediaeval catalogues.

This list of MSS. must be reduced by the elimination of *F* and *M*. Schwenke says that *F* was copied from *B* in the *de Natura Deorum*. The proof for this statement is that on two occasions *F* omits a line of *B* (cf. p. 7). He also says that *F* was copied in the rest of its contents from *A*. His reason for making this statement appears to be that the other treatises are given in the order

[1] This chapter was written before the publication of *A*.

[2] Le Bec-Hellouin, near Pont-Audemer, in Normandy.

[3] Manitius, *Philologisches aus alten Bibliothekskatalogen*, p. 16.

[4] Ib., p. 17.

found in *A*, while in *B* there are extensive dislocations. He considers *M* to be a mixed MS., derived from *F*, or a *gemellus*, but corrected from *A*, or a copy of *A*.

We are thus left with *ABCPV* as our authorities.

A and *B* contain the entire *corpus*. In *A* the order is *Nat. D.*, *Div.*, *Tim.*, *Fat.*, *Top.*, *Parad.*, *Lucull.*, *Leg.*, and there can be no doubt that this was the order in the archetype. The dislocations in *B* will be described shortly. *P* and *V* are much mutilated. Schwenke holds that *V* once contained all the *corpus* except the *Topica*. It now contains *Nat. D.* ii. 16–86, 92–156, iii. 156–end; *Div.* i–ii. 14, ii. 48–142, 148–end; *Timaeus*, *Fat.*, *Parad.*, *Lucull.* 1–104.

P contains *N.D.* i. 27–75, ii. 16–58, 63–8, 162–end, iii. 6–end; *Div.* i. 1–51, 57–93, 100—ii. 150 (end).

C contains *N.D.*, *Div.*, *Leg.* It resembles *A* more closely than *B* and is inferior in value to *AB*.

It is indubitable that all our MSS. are descended from one archetype, which I will term *Q*. This is shown by certain lacunae, viz.:

N. D. iii. 13: ego autem a re rationes ***

So ACV^1: BV^2 add *requiro*. If this supplement is right,[1] only one word is missing.

ib. 65. Editors mark a lacuna before and after *videamus ea . . . fateare. Sed*

Div. i. 132: praeclare tu quidem inquam paratus ***

The end of the book is lost.

The *Timaeus* is fragmentary. There is a lacuna after § 2 *in percontatione consumpsimus*, another after § 28 *intellegentia continentur*, a third after § 48 *modo huc modo illuc*, and after § 52 *munere neque dabitur* the rest of the treatise is lost.

The *de Fato* is in a similar condition. The beginning and the end are lost. There is a lacuna at the end of § 4, after *considamus hic* * * *, and probably another, though only of a few words, after § 45 *ab his fatum abesse.*

The *Paradoxa* have a lacuna in § 27 after the words *sed dementem insanire.*

[1] It is possible that *requiro* is a correction founded on the critical note *R* (= *require*).

In the *de Legibus* there are clearly lacunae at:

ii. 53: sitque ea non ***
iii. 17: convertem lex in omnis est ***

Editors also mark losses, possibly of a few words, at i. 31, 35, 39, 57; ii. 28.

There is one large transposition found in all the MSS. This is in *N. D.* ii. 16, after *quid potius dixeris quam deum.* This passage is succeeded by §§ 86–156 *ex sese perfectiores . . . quae cum maxima,* then comes the missing block of text, §§ 16–86 *etenim si di . . . ferant aliquid.*

Here §§ 16–86 = 864 lines of Teubner text, while §§ 86–156 = 882 lines. The obvious inference is that quaternions of *Q* have changed places.

In the *Timaeus AD* (not *V*) have a common dislocation, viz. §§ 38–43 *sed quia . . . aptissimus* and §§ 44–8 *sed cum . . . modo illuc* have changed places. Here §§ 38–43 = 52 lines of Teubner text and §§ 44–8 = 54 lines. It is to be noticed that 54 × 16 = 864 (*N. D.* 16–86). It would, therefore, appear that 52–4 form a unit. If this represents a folio, then in the *Timaeus* two folios have changed places, while in *N. D.* two blocks, each consisting of two quaternions, have been transposed.

It will be noticed that *N. D.* ii. 86–156 is slightly longer than ii. 16–86, viz. 882 lines. Here 16 × 55 = 880. We must, therefore, also recognize 55 as a unit.

There is also a point common to *A* and *B*, viz. that the original scribe omitted *Top.* 1–3 *maiores res . . . etiam suavitate* and §§ 28–72 *divisionum autem . . . possimus hic.* The loss was repaired in *B* by the insertion of a fly-sheet containing §§ 1–3 and of three extra folios containing §§ 28–72. Pluygers had the temerity to remove these supplements from *B* and to insert them in *A*, where they are now found.

It may be remarked that this surgical operation was uncalled for. *B*[1] on f. 105 v., after writing *Top.* 28 *edictis magis-*, left the rest of the line blank. He then went on with §§ 73–4 *ergo argumenta . . . tum a corporibus.* This passage has been struck out by a corrector and rewritten *loco suo* after § 72, partly on the third of the inserted folios and partly at the top of the next page. The supplements, therefore, belong to *B*, not to *A*.

The important point is that both A^1 and B^1 omitted the two passages. Their length in Teubner lines is as follows:

§§ 1–3 = 27 lines.
§§ 28–72 = 430

Here $27 \times 2 = 54$. Cf. *Tim.* 44–8 (54) and 38–43 (52); also $54 \times 8 = 432$. The relation of this figure to *N. D.* 18–86 (864) is to be noted.

Lastly, I would call attention to *N. D.* i. 1–2. Here *A* and C^1 omit *esse debeat . . . dinumerare sententias.* The passage = $13\frac{1}{3}$ lines of Teubner text. We now have the following sequence:

($13\frac{1}{3}$) *N. D.* i. 1–2
(27) *Top.* 1–3
(52) *Tim.* 38–43
(54) *Tim.* 44–48
(430) *Top.* 28–72
(864) *N. D.* ii. 16–86
(882) *N. D.* ii. 86–156.

The inference which I draw is that $13\frac{1}{3}$ = a column of *Q*, 27 = a page, 52–4 = a folio, 430 = a quaternion, 864–82 = two quaternions. The reason why I take 52–4 to represent a folio will appear shortly.

I have put these striking results at the beginning of this inquiry in order to supply the reader with a clue. I will now ask him to follow me in patience through a somewhat tangled maze.

Before I go further it will be convenient to put together some tachygraphic symbols which occur in *A*. These are ∂″, ⊢ ∂″, ∂″ ⊢, which stand for *dimissum*, *hic dimissum*, *dimissum hic.* For the use of *dimissum* to indicate losses in the text cf. p. 32. The places where notes of this kind are found are:

N. D. iii. 13 (f. 29r): ego autem a te rationes *** Secuntur

So edd. (*rationes requiro B*: A^1 has *recuntur* for *secuntur*). *A* has in the margin *R*, also (erased) ⊢ ∂″.

N. D. iii. 65 (f. 33v): efficiam profecto ut fateare. Sed ***

A has in the margin ⊢ ∂″.

Div. i. 51 (f. 42r): exercitum obsidione liberavit.

In *A liberavit* is added above the line after *obsidione* and *h'* preceded by a rude *m* is added above the line before *obsidione.*

Div. ii. 46 (f. 56^{v}): signum Iovis biennio post quam erat locatum in Capitolio conlocabatur.

A has in the margin ∂^{w} ⊢, with a note of reference to *Capitolio.* There is no lacuna here. Shortly above A^{1} omits:

> unde fulmen venerit, quo concesserit, quid significet autem nulla ratio docet

It seems probable that ∂^{w} ⊢ refers to this omission, and has been put in the wrong place.

Div. ii. 62 (f. 58^{v}): C. Gracchus ad M. Pomponium scripsit duobus anguibus domi conprehensis haruspices a patre convocatos

A mg. has ∂^{w} ⊢, with a reference mark to *convocatos.* Here again there is no lacuna. Shortly before in the passage:

> nihil habendum esse quod fieri posset ostentum

B^{1} and V^{1} omit *ostentum,* for which V^{2} gives *portentum.* I can only conjecture that ∂^{w} ⊢ refers to this omission, and that the note is out of place.

Fat. 46 (f. 75^{v}): ab iis fatum abesse *** Hoc modo hanc causam disceptari oportet.

A mg. has ⊢ ∂^{w}, with a reference mark after *oportet.* Here it is clear that the note has got out of place.

Fat. 48 (f. 77^{r}): omnibus naturaliter ***

Immediately after this comes:

Top. 4: non potui igitur

A mg. has ⊢ ∂^{w} *a te ñ potui.* The reference here is to the lost ending of the *de Fato* and *Top.* 1–3.

Top. 28 (f. 78^{v}): auctoritate edictis magis-

This is followed by § 73 *ergo argumentatio.* *A mg.* has ⊢ ∂^{w}. The reference is to the loss of §§ 28–72.

Leg. iii. 20 (f. 118^{r}): C. vero Gracchi tribunatus iis sicis quas ipse se proiecisse in forum dixit.

So edd.: for *iis sicis A* has *inscitiis.* *A mg.* has *excidiis*[li], with the note ∂^{w}, which here merely indicates a corruption.[1]

[1] This note *dimissum* to mark a corruption may be the source of the variants in *Sex. Rosc.* 11, where Σ gives *omnes hanc quaestionem te praetore manifestis maleficiis cotidiano-*

The fact that in *Div.* ii. 46, 62, *Fat.* 46 these notes are out of place shows that they must have been inherited from a predecessor.

I add a few words concerning the marks for the quaternions in *A* :

Quaternions i–iii are marked simply.

Quaternions iv–vi are marked *R* after the numeral, e.g. iv *R*.

The next quire consists of six folios only.

Quaternion viii is marked simply.

Quaternions ix–xiv have two sets of signatures. On f. 70^{v} there is (1) viiii, and (2) $\tilde{Q}$; on f. 79^{v} (1) x, (2) $\tilde{Q}$. iii; on f. 90^{v} (1) xi, (2) $\tilde{Q}$. iiii; on f. 98^{v} (1) xii, (2) $\tilde{Q}$. v; on f. 106^{v} (1) xiii (erased), (2) $\tilde{Q}$. vi. The next quaternion is not signed (possibly the signature has been erased). It is followed by six folios, without signature.

Chatelain says:

> 'Un premier copiste du nom de *R.* a exécuté les cahiers i–vii; un autre les cahiers viii–xv (qui portent aussi la numérotation i–viii, sauf dans les endroits où la reliure l'a fait disparaître).'

It is obvious that the gatherings were at one time bound up differently. I take *R* to be the common critical sign to indicate doubt (*require*), not the name of the copyist.[1]

I now go on to *B*, in which we have a complicated series of dislocations. In order to explain these clearly, I must practise a certain amount of repetition.

It is clear that *B* is derived from the same archetype as *A*, but after the leaves of the archetype had been greatly disarranged. While *B* agrees with all other MSS. in transposing *N. D.* ii. 16–86 and 86–156, also with *A* in transposing *Tim.* 38–43 and 44–58, and in omitting *Top.* 1–3 and 28–72, it has a large number of fresh dislocations.

We have already seen that the order in *Q* was: *Nat. D.*, *Div.*, *Tim.*, *Fat.*, *Top.*, *Parad.*, *Lucull.*, *Leg.* The evidence of *B* combined with that previously given shows that the *corpus* was broken up into the following sections:

que sanguine dimissui (*al. dimissius*) *sperant futuram.* The Scholiasta Gronovianus here has the strange note:

Dimisso] *Id est prae contempto relicto habitorum* (? = *abiturum*).

These scholia are of uncertain date and seem to be the work of three or four authors. They have been preserved in a Leiden MS., Voss. Q. 138, cent. x.

[1] Plasberg explains *R* as = *recognovi*.

(1) *N. D.* i. 1–64 : cum multae . . . impurus fuisset
(2) i. 64–91 : nonne igitur . . . cognationes
(3) i. 91–ii. 16 : agnoscerem . . . quam deum
(4) ii. 16–86 : etenim si di . . . ferant aliquid
(5) ii. 86–156 : ex sese . . . cum maxima
(6) ii. 156–iii end : largitate fundit . . . esse propensior }
Div. i. 1–ii. 127 : vetus opinio . . . quam derecto }

Since these are given by *B* in the same order, as in *Q*, I treat them as one block.

(7) *Div.* ii. 127–end : deus si quidem . . . surreximus
(8) *Tim.* 1–38 : multa sunt . . . confirmatur
(9) 38–43 : quia de suis . . . aptissimus
(10) 44–48 : sed cum duplex . . . modo illuc
(11) *Tim.* 49–end : sed si in . . . neque dabitur }
Fat. 1–4 : quia pertinet . . . considamus hic }

Here again the order of the archetype is preserved, so the two passages form one block.

(12) *Fat.* 5–41 : quorum in . . . diceremus et cum
(13) *Fat.* 41–48 : eae causae . . . naturaliter }
Top. 4–28 : non potui . . . edictis magis- }

Here again the two passages form one block. Between them intervened the following passage, viz.:

(14) *Top.* 1–3 : maiores . . . suavitate

This, as previously pointed out, was omitted by A^1 and B^1.

(15) *Top.* 28–72 : divisionum . . . possimus hic
(16) *Top.* 72–end : ergo argumentatio . . . debita accedere }
Parad. 1–37 : animadverti . . . dignum Aetionis }

Here again the passages were contiguous in *Q*.

(17) *Parad.* 37–end : tabula te . . . existimandi sunt }
Lucull. 1–2 : magnum ingenium . . . tali ingenio }

This also is one block.

(18) *Lucull.* 2–13 : praeditus Lucullus . . . et P. Scaevo-
(19) *Lucull.* 13–end : -lam aiunt Ti. Graccho . . . descendimus }
Leg. i. 1–21 : lucus quidem . . . condiscipulorum }

Here also is one block.

(20) *Leg.* i. 21–ii. 4 : ne quis exaudiat . . . studiose eorum
(21) ii. 4–13 : etiam sepulcra . . . si latrones
(22) ii. 13–iii. 38 : aliquas concessu . . . video legem
(23) iii. 38–42 : antiquastis sine . . . qui permovet
(24) 42–48 : cum agi nihil . . . religione.

In *B* these sections succeed each other in the following order. I give in brackets the order which they occupied in *Q*.

(1) *N. D.* i. 1–64
(7) *Div.* ii. 127–end
(3) *N. D.* i. 91–ii. 16
(5) ii. 86–156
(4) ii. 16–86
(6) ii. 156–iii end + *Div.* i. 1–ii. 127
(13) *Fat.* 41-end + *Top.* 4–28
(16) *Top.* 72–end + *Parad.* 1–37
(18) *Lucull.* 2–13
(17) *Parad.* 37–end + *Lucull.* 1-2
(19) *Lucull.* 13–end + *Leg.* i. 1–21
(12) *Fat.* 5–41
(21) *Leg.* ii. 4–13
(20) *Leg.* i. 21–ii. 4
(8) *Tim.* i.–38
(10) *Tim.* 44–48
(9) *Tim.* 38–43
(11) *Tim.* 49–end + *Fat.* 1–4
(2) *N. D.* i. 64-91
(22) *Leg.* ii. 13–iii. 38
(24) *Leg.* iii. 42–48
(23) *Leg.* iii. 38–42

The last passage, *Leg.* iii. 38–42, came at the end of *B*. The last page has been torn out and so the passage as given in *B* is not complete. It ends at § 40 *fit ambitione.*

To these are to be added:

(14) *Top.* 1–3: inserted on fly-leaf
(15) *Top.* 28–72: inserted on three additional folios.

B contains a number of notes, some of them tachygraphic, referring to these losses and dislocations. They are interesting as specimens of mediaeval criticism. I take them in the order in which they occur in the MS. Sometimes there are two or three notes on the same passage:

f. 10v, *N. D.* i. 64: tam impurus fuisset + *Div.* ii. 127: deus si quidem

(1) Quod hic sequitur in libro Thimei repperies assignatum
(2) Hic interpositum est de secundo libro divinationis, quod illic in extremitate deest et notatum est asterisco ⁜ quemadmodum et hic qui liber secundus post iii folia terminatur ut in margine scriptum ÷
(3) Recipe hic quod reperies infra folio xxi a fine libri citra ad signum o+o

f. 14ʳ, *Div.* ii. 150: nihil potest + *N. D.* i. 91: agnoscerem non

(1) ·|· ẽẽ iucundius. Quę cũ ẽẽnt dicta surreximus. M. TVL. CICERONIS DE DIVINATIONE LĪB SĒCDS EXPL

(2) iterum incipit de natura deorum

f. 46ʳ, *N. D.* iii. 13: rationes requiro secuntur

So *B*: in the margin is ⊢ ∂ᵛ, as in *A*.

f. 53ʳ, *N. D.* iii. 65: ut fateare sed

Here *hic dimissũ* is written in full, so also *hic pmutatũ ẽ*, with tachygraphical equivalents for both. Here again cf. *A*.

f. 102ʳ, *Div.* ii. 127: quam derecto + *Fat.* 41: eae causae

Quod hic sequitur requiritur in primo libro de natura deorum sub asterisco adnotatum

f. 103ʳ, *Fat.* 48: omnibus naturaliter + *Top.* 4: non potui

(1) ∂ᵛ (= *dimissum*)

(2) Hic deest finis huius libri quem invenies quaternione xxi folio secundo ※

f. 114ʳ, *Parad.* 37

B has: si in amplissima familia natus sit appellandum puto atque ut in magna familia stultorum sunt alii lautiores ut sibi uidentur serui

In the margin is ⊢ ∂ᵛ.

f. 114ᵛ, *Parad.* 37: dignum actionis (*sic*) + *Lucull.* 2: praeditus Lucullus

(1) hic interpositum est, ut videtur, de libro achademico

(2) ordo verus orationis post duo folia repraesentatur

f. 116ᵛ, *Lucull.* 13: et P. Scaevo- + *Parad.* 37: tabula te

(1) quod hic sequitur in libro Luculli redditur suo textui

(2) redditur hic textus superiori orationi

f. 119ʳ, *Lucull.* 2: tali ingenio + *Lucull.* 13: -lam aiunt

Hic intermissum est sed redditur in libro Paradoxae

f. 147ᵛ, *Leg.* i. 21: condiscipulorum + *Fat.* 5: quorum in aliis

(1) hic quod in libro Timei sequitur

(2) falsa est haec notula quoniam quae secuntur ad librum de divinatione pertinent, non ad Timaeum. Quod qui utrumque legerit verum inveniet. TEGANO correxit.

Tegano, however, was wrong, as well as his predecessor.[1]

f. 154ʳ, *Fat.* 41: diceremus ut cum + *Leg.* ii. 4: ut cum

Ab eo loco quo superius de corpore Timei interpositum est usque huc pervenit, quod usque sequitur in fine est libri secundi de divinatione usque quo de topicis incipit loqui

[1] Cf. Pertz, vol. ix, p. 219. Taginus, Abbot of Benedictbeuern, is said to have been made Archbishop of Mainz. Pertz discredits this statement, but thinks that he may have been made Archbishop of Magdeburg in 1004.

f. 155^{v}, *Leg.* ii. 13: quam non latores (*sic*) + *Leg.* i. 21: ne quis exaudiat
 (1) hic usque quod sequitur abhinc xx foliis pertransitis suo loco reddentur
 (2) hic sequitur ordo primi libri de legibus qui in isto libro superius incipit sed pluribus interpositis hic tandem consequentia redditur pertingens usque ad finem libri

f. 163^{v}, *Leg.* ii. 4: studioseque eorum + *Tim.* 1: multa sunt a
 Quod hic sequitur numeratis retro x foliis reppéritur

f. 169^{r}, *Tim.* 38: confirmatur + *Tim.* 44: sed cum duplex
 (1) deẽ
 (2) quod deẽ verso folio invenies ※

f. 169^{v}, *Tim.* 48: modo huc modo illuc + *Tim.* 38: quia de suis
 ⊢∂ᴺ ※

f. 171^{v}, *Fat.* 4: considamus hic + *N. D.* i. 64: nonne igitur tam
 (1) abhinc retroversus xxiii foliis sequitur de eiusdem corpore orationis sed omissis in medio pluribus
 (2) hic interpositum est quod in primo libro de natura deorum dimissum est ubi de secundo libro divinationis est interpositum
 (3) istud est de primo libro de natura deorum in folio x et durat iiii folia usque ad signum σ̄o o

f. 175^{v}, *N. D.* i. 91: cognationes + *Leg.* ii. 13: aliquas concessu
 A superiori exordio interpositioni usque huc de primo libro naturae deorum

f. 182^{v}, *Leg.* iii. 38: video legem + *Leg.* iii. 42: cum agi nihil
 Quod sequi debet verso folio sequenti occurrit

f. 192^{v}, *Leg.* iii. 48: de religione + *Leg.* iii. 38: antiquastis
 Hic redditur quod superius dimissum est.

It will be noticed that *B* has tachygraphic notes on *N. D.* iii. 13 and 65, *Fat.* 48, similar to those found in *A* at the same place. It is very probable that the attempts to correct the dislocations in *B* were made with the assistance of *A*.

I now exhibit the various sections of the *corpus* in order of magnitude. I give the number of lines occupied by the passages in the Teubner text.

(27) *Top.* 1–3
(52) *Tim.* 38–43
(54) *Tim.* 44–48
(65) *Leg.* iii. 38–42
(70) *Leg.* iii. 42–48
(100) *Tim.* 49–*Fat.* 4
(129) *Leg.* ii. 4–13
(198) *Lucull.* 2–13
(205) *Parad.* 27–*Lucull.* 2
(257) *Fat.* 41–*Top.* 28
(305) *Div.* ii. 127–150

(321) *N. D.* i. 64–91
(408) *Tim.* i. 38
(430) *Top.* 28–72
(494) *Fat.* 5–41
(600) *Leg.* i. 21–ii. 4
(604) *N. D.* i. 91–ii. 16
(655) *Top.* 72–*Parad.* 37
(760) *N. D.* 1–64
(864) *N. D.* ii. 16–86
(882) *N. D.* ii. 86–156
(1217) *Leg.* ii. 13–iii. 38
(2379) *Lucull.* 13–*Leg.* i. 21
(4721) *N. D.* ii. 156–*Div.* ii. 127

With the exception of 65, 70, and 129, all of which belong to the *de Legibus*, these figures hang together in a remarkable way. The unit is given by 52–4 and the higher numbers rise by multiples of about 50. Thus 100 + 105 = 205, 305 + 103 = 408, 655 + 105 = 760, 760 + 104 = 864. The relation of 430 to 864 and of 604 to 1217 is very striking. The largest block 4721 is a little more than twice 2379.

I now take the blocks singly as they occurred in *Q*:

(1) *Nat. D.* i. 1–64 = 760
$54 \times 14 = 756$

It would appear that the title did not take up much room.

(2) *N. D.* i. 64–91 = 321
$54 \times 6 = 324$
(3) *N. D.* i. 91–ii. 16 = 604

Here allowance has to be made for the subscription to bk. i and the title to bk. ii. I postpone for a moment the consideration of this figure, merely remarking that $55 \times 11 = 605$, and $50 \times 12 = 600$.

(4) *N. D.* ii. 16–86 = 864
$54 \times 16 = 864$
(5) *N. D.* ii. 86–156 = 882
$55 \times 16 = 880$

It is here obvious that two blocks, each consisting of two quaternions, have changed place. We must, therefore, recognize 55 as a unit. *N. D.* ii. 16–156, therefore, represents four quaternions of *Q*. If so, we should expect blocks 1–3 to coincide with the division by quaternions. Here (1) and (2) = 14 + 6. If we take (3) as 50×12, this gives a total of 32 folios, i. e. four quaternions.

(6) *N. D.* ii. 156–*Div.* ii. 127 = 4721
  54 × 88 = 4752

This large block seems to have formed 11 quaternions in *Q*. It will be remembered that there are lacunae at *N. D.* iii. 13 and 65. These may have been already present in *Q* or so short as not to affect the reckoning.

(7) *Div.* ii. 127–end = 305
  51 × 6 = 306

Here allowance has to be made for the subscription, also for a possible blank space as the end of the work came at, or towards, the end of a folio.

(8) *Timaeus* 1–38 = 408
  51 × 8 = 408

Here also the title must be taken into consideration.

(9) *Timaeus* 38–43 = 52
(10) *Timaeus* 44–48 = 54
(11) *Timaeus* 49–*Fat.* 4 = 100 (*Tim.* 49–end = 46 : *Fat.* 1–4 = 54)

We must make allowance for a possible subscription to the *Timaeus* and the title to the *de Fato*.

(12) *Fat.* 5–41 = 494

This is a little short of the normal equivalent for ten folios.

(13) *Fat.* 41–48 (end) + *Top.* 4–28 = 257
  51 × 5 = 255
(14) *Top.* 1–3 = 27

This must, of course, have come between *Fat.* 48 and *Top.* 4. If 54 = a folio, then 27 must equal a page. The question, therefore, arises how a page came to be omitted by *A* and B^1. It is to be remembered that the end of the *de Fato* is lost. The most probable suggestion is that a dislocated folio contained this on one side and *Top.* 1–3 on the other. The corrector of *B* used this for the fly-sheet containing *Top.* 1–3, but did not make a copy of the other side containing the end of the *de Fato*. It may have had no subscription, in which case he would not be able to identify the work to which it belonged. If so, blocks 13 and 14 would = 255 + 27 + 27 = 309, i. e. six folios.

(15) *Top.* 28–72 = 430
  54 × 8 = 432

This quaternion must have been missing, but was afterwards utilized by B^2 for the three extra leaves inserted in that MS.

(16) *Top.* 72–*Parad.* 27 = 655
54 × 12 = 648
(17) *Parad.* 27–*Lucull.* 2 = 205
51 × 4 = 204

Allowance must be made for the subscription and title.

(18) *Lucull.* 2–13 = 198

This is a little short of the normal content for four folios.

(19) *Lucull.* 13–*Leg.* i. 21 = 2379
(20) *Leg.* i. 21–ii. 4 = 600
(21) *Leg.* ii. 4–13 = 129
(22) *Leg.* ii. 13–iii. 38 = 1217
(23) *Leg.* iii. 38–42 = 65
(24) *Leg.* iii. 42–8 = 70

I take these six blocks together. It is to be noted that 65, 70, and 129 are recalcitrant to the explanation which applies elsewhere. The relation of 129 to 65 suggests that another unit is here at work. Also, 1217 appears to be in relation to 600.

The natural explanation is that towards the end of the MS. the writer contracted his hand, with the result that the unit has risen from 50–4 to 65–70. Such a contraction is very frequent in MSS., e. g. in *V* at the end of the *Philippics* (p. 168). I therefore incline to explain the figures as follows :

65, 70 = 1 f.
129 = 2 ff.
600 = 10 ff.
1217 = 20 ff.

With regard to the large block 2379, it is interesting to notice that it seems to be in relation to the largest block 4721 (2379 × 2 = 4758). It is, therefore, probable that the contraction took place after this point. If so, 54 × 44 = 2376.

I have already pointed out lacunae in the works contained in this *corpus*. The chief gaps are in the *Timaeus* and the *de Fato*. These may be accounted for in two ways, viz. either that the loss is prior to *Q*, or that folios of *Q* itself have perished.

This question can be settled in the case of the *Timaeus* by comparison with the original Greek. The key is given by the two passages which have changed places in *A* and *B*, viz.:

(52) §§ 38–43: quia de suis . . . aptissimum
(54) §§ 44–8 : sed iam duplex . . . modo illuc

The first is a translation of:

40 E–41 E: ὡς οἰκεῖα . . . θεοσεβέστατον

and the second of:

41 E–43 B: διπλῆς δὲ οὔσης . . . καὶ πάντῃ

Cicero's translation is fairly literal, as may be seen from the edition of his version by Plasberg, who prints the Latin rendering interlineally with the Greek above it.

In Stallbaum's text, 40 E–41 E = 46 lines.
41 E–43 B = 49 lines.

We thus find that 52–4 lines of Latin in the Teubner text correspond to 46–9 lines of Greek in Stallbaum's text.

I now take the lacuna in Cicero's version at § 28. Here the words *sed intellegentia continentur* are followed in the MSS. by *ius natura converteret* and a lacuna is marked by editors. Plato's equivalents are 37 C νοῦς ἐπιστήμη τε ἐξ ἀνάγκης ἀποτελεῖται and 38 C θατέρου περίοδος ᾔειν. It follows that *ius* is part of *alterius* (θατέρου).

The passage of Plato for which there is no Latin rendering is 37 C–38 C τούτῳ δὲ ἐν ᾧ . . . περιφορὰς ἃς ᾗ. This in Stallbaum's text = 46 lines. This is exactly the same number of lines as that occupied by 40 E–41 E, which in Cicero's version = 52 lines of Teubner, i.e. one folio of *Q*.

It follows that Cicero's rendering of 37 C–38 C, now lost, which = 46 lines in Stallbaum, should also = 52 lines of Teubner, i.e. one folio of *Q*.

We are now in a position to compare the original with the fragments of the translation.

(1) Cicero begins with a short introduction, §§ 1–2, for which there is no equivalent in Plato. This is followed by a lacuna. His version then begins at § 3, quid est quod.

This is a translation of 27 D ἔστιν οὖν δή. Thus we have no equivalent for 17 A εἷς, δύο, τρεῖς . . . 27 D ἐνδειξαίμην.

This passage occupies 417 lines in Stallbaum. We have already found that 46 lines of Stallbaum correspond to a folio of *Q*. It is therefore interesting to notice that 46 × 9 = 414. It therefore appears that after Cicero's brief introduction, which in *Q* belonged to the previous block, nine folios have been lost.

(2) 27 D–37 C: ἔστιν οὖν δὴ . . . ἐξ ἀνάγκης ἀποτελεῖται = (Cic.) *Tim.* 3–28: quid est quod . . . intellegentia continentur

Here the Greek = 278 lines of Stallbaum. Here the same unit appears (46 × 6 = 276).

The Latin equivalent is 292 lines of Teubner. This is less than might have been anticipated. In view of the figures for the Greek it would appear that six folios of *Q* have been lost. If so, the script must have been a little larger at this point.

(3) 37 C–38 C: τούτῳ δὲ ἐν ᾧ . . . περιφορὰς ἃς ᾗ = 46 lines of Stallbaum.

I have already discussed this passage.

(4) 38 C–40 E: θατέρου περίοδος . . . ἀποδείξεων λέγουσιν, ἀλλ' = (Cic.) *Tim.* 29–38: -ius natura . . . confirmatur.

= 96½ lines of Stallbaum. Here 48 × 2 = 96. For the unit cf. 41 E–43 B (49). The Latin equivalent here is 100 lines of Teubner.

(5) 40 E–41 E: ὡς οἰκεῖα . . . θεοσεβέστατον = (Cic.) *Tim.* 38–43: quia de suis . . . aptissimum = 46 lines, Stallbaum.

(6) 41 E–43 B: διπλῆς δ' οὔσης . . . καὶ πάντῃ = (Cic.) *Tim.* 44–8: sed cum duplex . . . modo illuc = 49 lines, Stallbaum.

I have already discussed these two passages.

(7) 43 B–46 A: κατὰ τοὺς ἕξ . . . ἑνός τε αὖ = 161 lines, Stallbaum.

Here the unit shrinks. If Cicero's version covered four folios of *Q*, as seems likely, he must have expanded somewhat.

(8) 46 A–47 B: περὶ τὴν λειότητα . . . δωρηθὲν ἐκ θεῶν = (Cic.) *Tim.* 49–52: sed si in . . . neque dabitur = 44 lines, Stallbaum.

Cicero's *Timaeus* in its present form ends here. This last portion formed in *Q* one block with *Fat.* 1–4. While *Fat.* 1–4 = 54 lines in Teubner, the normal amount for a folio, *Tim.* 49–52, which must also have formed a folio = 46 lines only. There must have been some irregularity here.

(9) 47 B–92 B (end): λέγω δὴ τοῦτο . . . μονογενὴς ὤν = 1862 lines, Stallbaum.

If we employ the usual unit 46, this corresponds roughly to about 40 folios (46 × 40 = 1840), i. e. 5 quaternions have been lost.

It appears, therefore, that the mutilations in Cicero's *Timaeus* are due to the loss of folios in *Q*. When perfect it seems to have occupied 65 folios, i. e. eight quaternions and one folio, thus distributed. I mark with an asterisk those parts of Cicero's version now extant:

17 A–27 D	correspond to	9	folios	of *Q*
*27 D–37 C	,,	6	,,	,,
37 C–38 C	,,	1	,,	,,
*38 C–40 E	,,	2	,,	,,
*40 E–41 E	,,	1	,,	,,
*41 E–43 B	,,	1	,,	,,
43 B–46 A	,,	4	,,	,,
*46 A–47 B	,,	1	,,	,,
47 B–92 B	,,	40	,,	,,

Out of 65 folios only 11 have survived.

The other work in the *corpus* which has suffered from extensive mutilation is the *de Fato*. This has lost both beginning and end and also has a lacuna at § 4, probably also another at § 45. If we leave out of consideration for the moment these and other lacunae, also *Top.* 1–3, the contents of *Q* seem to have been as follows:

N. D. i. 1–ii. 156	= 32 ff.
N. D. ii. 156–*Div.* ii. 127	= 88
Div. ii. 127–end	= 6
Timaeus	= 65
Fat. 1–4	= 1
5–41	= 10
41–*Top.* 28	= 5
Top. 28–72	= 8
72–*Parad.* 27	= 12
Parad. 27–*Lucull.* 2	= 4
Lucull. 2–13	= 4
13–*Leg.* i. 21	= 44
Leg. i. 21–iii. 48 (end)	= 34
	313

To this must be added one folio for *Top.* 1–3 and the missing end of the *de Fato*; also allowance must be made for the various lacunae. In all probability *Q* contained not less than 40 quaternions (= 320 ff.), very possibly more.

I now proceed to discuss the content of a folio in *Q*.

Here we must go for information to:

Tim. 38–43: quia de suis . . . aptissimum = 52 lines, Teubner
44–8: sed iam duplex . . . modo illuc = 54 " "
Fat. 1–4: quia pertinet . . . considamus hic = 54 " "

The last passage is preceded and followed by a lacuna. It therefore represents a folio of *Q*.

The contents of these three passages in letters are:

Tim. 38–43 = 2189
44–8 = 2362
Fat. 1–4 = 2271

If we take the average for the three passages, the result is 2274. This would give us 1137 for a page and 568 for a column, if it was written in two columns.

I now turn to:

Top. 1–3: maiores nos . . . suavitate = 27 lines, Teubner.

I have previously given my reasons for taking this to represent a page of *Q*. The passage consists of 1149 letters. This is fairly close to 1137.

I have already called attention to:

N. D. i. 1–2: esse debeat . . . sententias = $17\frac{1}{3}$ lines, Teubner.

This passage is omitted by AC^1, but found in *B*. It consists of 558 letters. This again is very near to the average previously arrived at, 568. I am, therefore, inclined to think that AC^1 here omitted a column of *Q*.

It now remains to inquire the length of a line in *Q*. I have already suggested that it was written in columns. The formation of the principal MSS. is as follows. *A* is written in long lines, which frequently consist of some 80 letters. Several leaves, however, of the *de Divinatione*, in which there are long quotations from poetry, are written in two columns, this arrangement being adopted for the intermediate portions of prose, as well as for the quotations. This looks like a survival from a more ancient formation (cf. p. 96). *B* is written throughout in long lines with an average of about 50 letters. *V* and *P* are written in double columns.

I now proceed to consider the internal evidence furnished by the principal MSS.

A has been carefully corrected, as will be seen from the following list of additions made by A^2, where A^1 omits. I have included with them one passage, *Top.* 28, which is not supplied by A^2:

(12) *Tim.* 44: iuste vixerit
(13) *N.D.* i. 120: quam Democrito
(14) *N.D.* i. 72: ex Lycio nihil ne
Leg. i. 35: et beniuolentia
(15) *Div.* ii. 93: hoc modo illo modo
(17) *N.D.* ii. 10: * commemorare possum
Div. ii. 80: deinde inventionem
(18) *Div.* ii. 103: est igitur divinatio
(19) *N.D.* iii. 4: causa quam refellendi
Top. 90: et instituto et natura
Leg. i. 49: quoi referant gratiam
(20) *Div.* i. 123: quaesivisse quid esset
ii. 38: exta esse qualia cuique
(21) *Lucull.* 93: te paucorum neque primum
99: esse alia non probabilia
(22) *N. D.* ii. 72: diligenter retractarent
Fat. 8: tecum quam cum alio Idibus
Lucull. 24: si se ignorabit sapientia
Leg. i. 45: ingenia iuvenum non ita at
(24) *Fat.* 30: medicum sive non adhibueris
(26) *N. D.* ii. 107: revolvens sese conficiensque
Lucull. 12: disserentem et item Antiochum
(29) *Top.* 28: ** -tratuum more aequitate consistat (*om. A*)
Lucull. 67: * haec primum conclusio quam habeat
(30) *Div.* i. 67: * est ut vaticinari furor vera soleat
(31) *N.D.* i. 120: ** -tate rerum tum principia mentis quae
(32) *N.D.* ii. 87: ad usum meliores potuerint esse neque
Div. ii. 55: ** -res causas rerum non quaerere tu vates [1]
Fat. 12: oriente canicula natum esse et Fabium
(33) *N.D.* iii. 5: fundamenta iecisse nostrae civitatis
Div. ii. 38: vestem autem deus potest non inpertire
Lucull. 122: * ut videamus terra penitusne defixa sit
(34) *Fat.* 34: antecedat id ei causa sit sed quod cuique
(35) *Top.* 84: quale quid sit aut simpliciter quaeritur
Tim. 30: tardiusque maiorem celeriusque minorem
Leg. ii. 24: impie commissum est quod expiari poterit
(40) *Lucull.* 62: * assensione omnem et motum animorum et rationem
Leg. iii. 31: eorum libidines nisi illi ipsi qui eas frangere

[1] A^1 has:

magna stultitia ẽ earũ rerũ deos facere effecto boeotios credis thebaide uidisse ex gallorũ gallinaceorũ cantu uictoriam esse thebanorum.

(50) *Lucull.* 106: meminit Sciron Epicuri dogmata. Vera igitur illa sunt omnia
(53) *Tim.* 3: et interit nec umquam esse vere potest. Omne autem quod gignitur
(54) *Div.* i. 60: agrestis immanitas cum sit inmoderato obstupefacta potu atque
(56) *Fat.* 16: medii inter se dividuntur, possum dicere si in sphaera maximi orbes
(59) *Leg.* i. 20: nobis omnis est disputatio explicanda rectissime et quidem ista duce
(65) *Div.* ii. 45: unde fulmen venerit, quo concesserit, quid significet autem nulla ratio docet
(77) *Div.* ii. 48: Praxitelia capita. Illa enim ipsa efficiuntur detractione neque quicquam illud adfertur a
(78) *Lucull.* 99: * quae percipi possint, alia quae percipi non possint. In altero autem alia visa esse probabilia
(83) *Div.* i. 34: persecuntur veteres observatione didicerunt. Carent autem arte ii qui non ratione aut coniectura.

To these must be added the following dittography:

(44) *N. D.* i. 123: dixerit invidiae detestandae gratia dixisse neque *bis scr.*

In this list there are three telescoped passages of 29, 31, 32 letters. The first of these is omitted by B^1 as well as by *A*. It seems clear that 29–32 is the average length of line in a common ancestor. It is to be noticed that omissions of 29 (*Lucull.* 67), 30 (*Div.* i. 67), 33 (*Lucull.* 122) are not due to ὁμ. like most of the other omissions.

I would draw special attention to one of the telescoped passages:

N. D. i. 120: censet imagines divinitate praeditas inesse in universitate rerum, tum principia mentis quae sint in eodem universo deos esse dicit.

For this *A* has:

censet imagines diuinitate praeditas inesse in uniuersi sunt in eodem uniuerso deos esse ịṇ ụṇịụẹṛṣịṭạṭẹ dicit

In the margin is:

tate rerum tū principia mentes quae sunt

There is a reference mark for insertion after *universi*. A previous MS. seems to have had:

inesse in uniuersi
tate rerum tum principia mentis quae (31)
sunt in eodem uniuerso deos esse

Here l. 2 was omitted. I take *in universitate* to be a correction for *in universi*, which made its way into the text. If so, an intermediary MS. may have had:

in uniuersi *mg.* in uniuersitate
sunt in eodem uniuerso deos esse (27)

The variant was received into the text a line further down. Subsequently the missing words were recovered by A^2 from another source.

The following corruptions are interesting:

Div. i. 58: praedictum est fore eos eventus rerum dictum est *A*

This suggests in an ancestor:

prae
dictum est fore eos euentus rerum (28)

N. D. i. 24: quodque in nostro corpore molestum sit, cur hoc idem non habeatur molestum [cur] in deo? *A*.

This indicates:

molestum sit
cur hoc idem non habeatur molestum (29)
in deo

N. D. ii. 123: cum parva squilla quasi societatem coit comparandi cibi; itaque cum pisciculi parvi in concham hiantem innataverunt.

For *pisciculi A* has *pisculi*, and inserts *pisciculi* before *parva squilla*. This indicates:

cum
parua squilla quasi societatem (27)
coit comparandi cibi itaque cum (27)
mg. pisciculi pisculi parui

There are also two longer passages, viz.:

(94) *N. D.* iii. 24: eorumque certis temporibus vel accessus vel recessus sine deo fieri non possunt. Vide, quaeso, si omnis motus omniaque quae certis temporibus ordinem suum conservant.

A^1 repeats *vel accessus* before *ordinem*. This indicates:

eorumque certis temporibus
uel accessus uel recessus sine deo fi (31)
eri non possunt uide quaeso si omnis mo (32)
tus omniaque quae certis temporibus (31)
ordinem suum conseruant

(124) *Div.* ii. 13: divinationem esse earum rerum praedictionem et praesensionem quae essent fortuitae. Primum eodem revolveris. Nam et medici et gubernatoris et imperatoris praesensio est rerum fortuitarum.

A^1 repeats *praedictionem* before *fortuitarum*. This indicates:

rerum
praedictionem et praesensionem quae (32)
essent fortuitae primum eodem reuol (31)
ueris nam et medici et gubernatoris (30)
et imperatoris praesensio est rerum (31)
fortuitarum

Special interest attaches to the telescoped passage *Top.* 28, *-tratuum more aequitate consistat* (29), since it comes between two blocks of text, viz. *Top.* 4–28 and 28–72, and is also omitted by *B*.

With this omission is to be coupled a curious repetition, or anticipation, in ii. 16, where the large dislocation in all MSS. takes place. Here *A* before going on with § 86, *ex sese perfectiores*, inserts from § 156:

largitate fundit, ea ferarumne an hominum causa gignere videtur (54)

There seems to be a relation between these two passages.

B.

Omissions of *B*[1] (except where otherwise noted):

(11) *N. D.* i. 94: verendum est
ii. 64: maximus quia
86: sicut membra
128: ad perpetuam
(14) *N. D.* i. 2: atque moueantur
(15) *N. D.* iii. 64: di discere possim
(16) *N. D.* ii. 142: ** -cos oculos fecit et
(17) *N. D.* iii. 34: innumerabilia sunt
ib.: ut voluptas ut dolor
(18) *N. D.* ii. 64: divum hunc perhibeto
(19) *N. D.* i. 90: si quidem aeterni sunt
ii. 140: sed quasi spectatores
Div. ii. 87: * ergo hoc divinationis
Lucull. 22: ennoeas enim notitias
(20) *Div.* i. 61: * sedata atque restincta
ii. 51: dicam an hominem, si deum
(21) *N. D.* ii. 74: * Ariopagi sic cum dicimus
Div. ii. 90: natura et ad quam quisque
Parad. 30: potes autem esse tu civis
(24) *N. D.* i. 86: an si quod sit id esse mortale
Div. ii. 66: sed ut in cunis fuerit anguis
(25) *N. D.* iii. 32: est et quod est contra naturam
Div. ii. 11: utendum pecunia quem ad modum
Lucull. 99: alia quae percipi non possint

(28) *Parad.* 25: quicquid non oportet scelus esse
Leg. ii. 49: pecuniae capiat aut si maior pars
(29) *Top.* 28: ** -tratuum more aequitate consistat
(31) *N.D.* ii. 50: tum defectibus in initia recurrendo [1]
(33) *Div.* i. 21: atque una fixi ac signati temporis hora
i. 35: aut eandem gentem in fulgoribus errare
(34) *Lucull.* 6: * enitimur gloriam vero non modo non minui
(35) *Fat.* 17: quod non necesse fuerit et quicquid fieri
(37) *N.D.* ii. 61: * inest maior aliqua sic appellatur ut ea ipsa
(38) *Fat.* 36: non possit an eius modi cum quo effici aliquid
(39) *Tim.* 3: quod adfert opinionem sensus rationis expers (*om.* B, not B^1)
(41) *N.D.* iii. 87: * Iovemque optimum et maximum ob eas res appellant
Div. ii. 150: * esse iucundius. Quae cum essent dicta, surreximus
(43) *N.D.* ii. 18: a terra sumpsimus, aliud ab umore, aliud ab igni, aliud
(44) *N.D.* iii. 87: * salvos incolumes opulentos copiosos neque Herculi
(45) *N.D.* ii. 7: * Mopsum, Tiresiam, Amphiaraum, Calchantem, Helenum quos [2]
Div. ii. 19: * locus est divinationi quae a te fortuitarum rerum est
(46) *N.D.* i. 51: nihil enim agit, nullis occupationibus est implicatus
Tim. 23: eadem parte praestantem extremis eademque superatam *bis scr.*[3]
(48) *N.D.* i. 95: immortalisque sit. Quid autem obstat quo minus sit beatus
Div. i. 14: vocibus instat et adsiduas iacit ore querelas cum primum
(49) *N.D.* iii. 80: ** Reguli corpus est praebitum. Cur Africanum domestici pari-
(51) *Leg.* i. 54: bonum esse decreverint, hic nisi quod honestum esset, putarit
(52) *Div.* i. 130: * extiterit pingue et concretum esse caelum ut eius adspiratio
(58) *N.D.* iii. 69: ** esse ratione nec vero scaena solum referta est his sceleribus sed mul- [4]
(61) *Div.* ii. 83: et eius verbum aliquod apte ceciderit ad id quod ages aut cogitabis ea res *bis scr.*
Top. 9: de quo disseritur, tum definitio adhibetur, quae quasi involutam evolvit
(65) *N.D.* iii. 32: ** ullo sensu iucunda accipere non accipere contraria. Si igitur voluptatis sen-
(67) *N.D.* iii. 29: ad accipiendam vim externam et ferundam paratum est. Mortale igitur omne animal
(395) *N.D.* ii. 16: Chrysippus quidem . . . quam deum

[1] These words omitted *loco suo* are inserted immediately afterwards.

[2] This passage, which is omitted *loco suo*, is inserted in § 8 after *paruissent*.

[3] The dittography of this passage is corrupt, so also that in *Div.* ii. 83. Cf. *Top.* 14. Possibly two variants have been combined.

[4] Schwenke reports B as omitting *ratione . . . multo*. According to my collation B^1 wrote *summato* (*om. med.*) for *summa esse . . . multo*. B^2 adds *esse* over the erased letters *-to* (after *summa*).

The following case requires explanation:

Top. 14: si ita Fabiae pecunia legata est a viro, si ei viro mater familias esset, si ea in manum non convenerat

B^1 has: si ita fabiae pecunia ·/ in manum non convenerat

B mg. adds: p. e. cum non iam legata est a uiro si ei uiro mater familias esset, si ea in (*del.*) gr̃

Here *p. e. cum non iam* = *pecuniam*. *A* has *pecunia p̃ ẽ cum non iam*. The dittography therefore was present in the archetype. If so, *B* omits 52 letters. This agreement is a striking example of the close connexion between *A* and *B*.

Here there are several telescoped passages, viz.:

16 (*N. D.* ii. 142)	58 (*N. D.* iii. 69)
29 (*Top.* 28)	65 (*N. D.* iii. 32)
49 (*N. D.* iii. 80)	

The most striking point here is the relation of 58 to 29. This is all the more significant because the words:

-tratuum more aequitate consistat (29)

form a connecting link between two blocks of text, the second of which, *Top.* 28–72, was omitted by *A* and B^1. It would appear that they formed a line in some ancestor.

I cannot attach any importance to 16 (*N. D.* ii. 142) in spite of the fact that $16 \times 3 = 48$, and $16 \times 4 = 64$. There is no trace of so small a unit in the omissions either of *B* or of any other MS. in the case of this *corpus*. I must, therefore, look upon this omission as a *proprius error* due to chance.

There remain the figures 49 and 65, which admit of more than one explanation, which, therefore, I reserve for the moment.

I would call especial attention to:

N. D. ii. 50: neque solum eius species ac forma mutatur tum crescendo tum defectibus in initia recurrendo sed etiam regio, quae tum est aquilenta tum[1] australis. In lunae quoque cursu est et brumae quaedam et solstitii similitudo

B has:

neque solum
eius species ac forma mutatur tum crescendo sed etiam regio quae tum est a
quilenta aut australis in lunae quoque cursu tum defectibus in inicia recurren
est (*in ras. ex* do) et brumae quaedam

The corrector inserts the words *tum . . . recurrendo* (31) in their proper place after *crescendo*.

[1] So editors with *v*, aut *cett.*

Here the intervening passage, *sed etiam regio . . . quoque cursu*, consists of 62 letters. This suggests the following arrangement in a predecessor:

tum crescendo
tum defectibus in initia recurrendo (31)
sed etiam regio quae tum est aquilenta (32)
aut australis in lunae quoque cursu (30)
est et

In connexion with this I would take another passage:

N. D. i. 6: desertaeque disciplinae et iam pridem relictae patrocinium necopinatum a nobis esse susceptum. Nos enim nec subito coepimus philosophari nec mediocrem a primo tempore aetatis in eo studio operam curamque consumpsimus

B has:

desertęque disciplinę c̣ọp̣ịṇạṭụṃ ṃẹḍịọc̣ṛẹṃ ạ
p̣ṛịṃọ ṭẹṃp̣ọṛę ạęṭạṭịṣ et iam pridem relictę patrocinium
necopinatum a nobis esse susceptum. nos autem nec subito cepimus phi
losophari nec mediocrema primo tempore aetatis in eo studio operam
curamque consumpsimus

Here the words *et iam pridem . . . philosophari nec* = 99 letters. It is to be observed that the obelized passage in *B* consists of two parts, viz. (1) *copinatum*, (2) *mediocrem . . . aetatis*. The error is, therefore, complicated. The simplest solution seems to be that the words *mediocrem . . . aetatis* (29) were in the margin of a MS. written thus:

disciplinę
et iam pridem relictę patrocinium ne (31)
copinatum a nobis esse susceptum nos au (33)
tem nec subito cepimus philosophari nec (34) *mg.* mediocrem a primo tempore aetatis

The scribe was puzzled by ὁμ., viz. -*nę*, *ne*, *nec*. He first skipped a line and wrote *copinatum*, then he inserted the marginal addition meant to come after *nec* in l. 4.

The comparison of these figures with those previously obtained by the analysis of *A*, and especially with the repetition of *vel accessus* after an interval of 94 letters in *N. D.* iii. 24, and that of *praedictiones* after an interval of 123 letters in *Div.* ii. 13, suggests that at the back of *A* and *B* there is a MS. with an average of 31 letters to the line.

I now return to the other telescoped passages, viz. 49 (*N. D.* iii.

80) and 65 (*N. D.* iii. 32). Here it is necessary to walk warily, since there are several possibilities. It is possible to look on them as multiples of a smaller unit, e. g. 23–5. When, however, we are dealing with a MS. in long lines like *B*, there is always the possibility that the immediate model was a MS. much like itself. If so, 49 would be a very suitable length for a line in the model, while 65 can be explained as 32 + 33. Thus:

> *Div.* ii. 150 (end): mihi vero, inquit ille, nihil potest esse iucundius. Quae cum essent dicta surreximus.

B^1 after *nihil potest* goes on immediately with the block, *N. D.* i. 91–ii. 16, *agnoscerem non invitus*, &c., which comes here in this MS. B^2 adds in the margin *esse iucundius . . . surreximus* (41).

There is a very interesting passage in *N. D.* ii. 7:

> Quod si ea ficta credimus licentia fabularum, Mopsum, Tiresiam, Amphiaraum, Calchantem, Helenum, quos tamen augures ne ipsae quidem fabulae adscivissent

B^1 omitted *Mopsum . . . quos* (45) *suo loco* and inserted the words subsequently in § 8 after *qui religionibus paruissent.* The intermediate passage, viz. *tamen augures . . . paruissent*, consists of 650 letters. This is the sort of error which may throw light upon the pagination of an ancestor.

It is to be noted that, out of ten omissions of 41–9 letters, six cases, including the telescoped passage (*N. D.* iii. 80), are not due to ὁμ. This is a larger proportion than elsewhere.

On the whole, the evidence inclines me to think that we are here on the track of an immediate ancestor in longer lines.

It is to be observed that the longest omission of *B*, 395, appears to be in relation to the two which precede it, 65 and 67 (66 × 6 = 396). The passage is one which demands special mention, since it is in the troubled zone, ii. 15–16, where the first great dislocation took place.

B^1 reads as follows:

> multo ma
> gis in tantis motionib; tantisq: uicissitudinib; tã multarum rerum at
> que tantarum ordinationibus in quib; nihil umquam inmensa et infi
> nita uetustas mentita sit statuat necesse est ab aliqua mente tantos natu
> rę motus gubernari ex sese perfectiores

Here *ex sese perfectiores* is the beginning of the dislocated block, ii. 86–156. B^1 has omitted (after *gubernari*):

> Chrysippus quidem quamquam est acerrimo ingenio, tamen ea dicit ut ab

ipsa natura didicisse non ut ipse repperisse videatur. Si enim, inquit, est aliquid in rerum natura quod hominis mens quod ratio quod vis quod potestas humana efficere non possit, est certe id quod illud efficit homine melius : atqui res caelestes omnesque eae quarum est ordo sempiternus ab homine confici non possunt: est igitur id a quo illa conficiuntur homine melius. Id autem quid potius dixeris quam deum? (395)

The missing passage, together with:

tam multarum rerum atque tantarum ordinibus in quibus nihil umquam immensa et infinita uetustas mentita sit statuat necesse est ab aliqua mente tantos naturae motus gubernari (149)

occurs later on in *B*, after the end of §§ 86–156, before the next block, ii. 16–86, *etenim si di . . . ferant aliquid*, to which they belong.

In the present passage the words *Chrysippus . . . quam deum* have been added at the foot of the page, but subsequently erased. Also, a corrector has struck out in the text the words *tam multarum . . . gubernari*.

It is to be remembered that the writer of *A* after ii. 16, *dixeris quam deum*, inserts ii. 156:

largitate fundit, ea ferarumne an hominum causa gignere videtur? (54)

and then goes on with §§ 86–156.

I am not clear what conclusion is to be drawn from these errors, but would merely point out that the omission of 395 letters here by *B* may = 12 lines of 33 (= 396).

V.

Whereas in *A* and *B* nearly all omissions have been remedied by the corrector, in *V* a number have not been rectified.

(11) *N. D.* ii. 72: et religioso *om.* V^1
Div. i. 95: et discrimen *om.* *V*
105: aut scientia *om.* *V*
(13) *Parad.* 10: * ii qui hanc rem p. *om.* *V*
(14) *N. D.* ii. 58: vel providentia *om.* V^1
72: ex intellegendo *om.* V^1
(15) *N. D.* iii. 21: quid dicis melius *om.* V^1
(19) *Fat.* 18: id enim fore diceretur *om.* V^1
Lucull. 20: qui doleat et inter eum *om.* V^1
(20) *N. D.* ii. 103: cum sole tum degrediens *om.* V^1
(23) *Lucull.* 67: percipi ab iis quae possint *om.* *V*

(24) *N. D.* ii. 72 : tamquam legendo delegendis *om.* V^1
Div. ii. 129 : * nisi sapientem divinum esse *om.* *V*
Lucull. 9 : quam apud Catulum fuissemus *om.* V^1
(25) *Fat.* 8 : in campo ambulemus tecum quam *om.* *V*
(26) *N. D.* ii. 52 : duodecim signorum orbem annis *om.* V^1
83 : nobiscum videt, nobiscum audit *om.* V^1
Fat. 30 : adversarium sive non habuerit *om.* V^1
Tim. 8 : et me qui disseram hominem esse *om.* *V*
(27) *Lucull.* 19 : aut deducimus multaque facimus *om.* *V*
(28) *Tim.* 38 : ** quamquam nec argumentis nec rati- *om.* *V*
(37) *N. D.* iii. 64 : disputemus dicaliusu ignais immortalibus *om.* V^1
(38) *Div.* ii. 98 : * non in hominibus solum verum in bestiis etiam *om.* V^1
(41) *Fat.* 38 : non falsum esse aut quod falsum non est qui potest *om.* V^1
(44) *Lucull.* 91 : quasi disceptatricem et iudicem. Cuius veri et falsi *om.* V^1
(44) *Div.* i. 125 : praedictum praesensumque ut cum evenerit ita cadat *om.* V^1 (*corr. m.* 1 *in mg.*)
(47) *N. D.* iii. 29 : si omne animal tale est, immortale nullum est. Ergo itidem *om.* V^1
(49) *Fat.* 35 : utinam ne in Pelio nata ulla umquam esset arbor etiam supra *om.* *V*
(52) *N. D.* iii. 36 : nisi ignem probabilius enim videtur tale quiddam esse animum *om.* V^1
(56) *Fat.* 4 : volo. An mihi, inquam, potest quicquam esse molestum quod tibi gratum *om.* *V*
(59) *Fat.* 27 : ne illa quidem eversa vera est haec enuntiatio, cepit Numantiam Scipio *om.* V^1
(64) *Fat.* 33 : quocirca si Stoicis qui omnia fato fieri dicunt consentaneum est huius modi *om.* V^1
(66) *Div.* ii. 103 : hoc quoque est concedendum. At quod omne est, id non cernitur ex alio extrinsecus *om.* *V*

Here the telescoped passage, *Tim.* 38, is of special interest. An ancestor must have had

fidem non habere
quamquam nec argumentis nec rati (28)
onibus certis

V gives *fidem non habere onibus certis* (*med. om.*).

It is to be noticed that there is an omission of 56 letters in *Fat.* 4; also that neither here nor in *Fat.* 4 does V^2 supply the omission.

There is a good deal of evidence for a shorter unit. Thus we have four cases of 26 and three of 24, to which 52, 49, 47 appear to correspond. It is to be noticed that the omission of 45 in *Div.* i. 125 is supplied by the first hand. *V* is written in double columns with an average of 28–30 letters. It is more likely that its model was in some such formation, possibly in somewhat larger letters, than that it was in long lines. If so, the scribe may here have missed two lines of his model.

C.

Omissions of *C*, or *C*[1]:

(12) *N.D.* ii. 58 : prudentia vel *om.* *C*[1]
(13) *N.D.* ii. 142 : * si quid noceret *om.* *C*[1]
(14) *N.D.* iii. 33 : et quod ea sentit *om.* *C*
(15) *N.D.* ii. 146 : et parte tangendi *om.* *C*
(16) *N.D.* i. 96 : * atque ut animi item *om.* *C*
(17) *N.D.* ii. 49 : modici tum recessus *om.* *C*
(18) *Div.* i. 116 : nisi eadem docuisset *om.* *C*
Leg. ii. 52 : -dem caperent quantum *om.* *C*
(19) *Div.* i. 102 : * primus miles fiat bono *om.* *C*
Leg. iii. 9 : auspicia patrum sunto *om.* *C*[1]
(20) *N.D.* i. 43 : nec intellegi quicquam *om.* *C*
98 : nisi in eo qui didicerit *om.* *C*[1]
ii. 103 : cum sole tum degrediens *om.* *C*
(22) *N.D.* ii. 9 : nulla perennia servantur *om.* *C*[1]
118 : flammeae quocirca terrae *om.* *C*
(23) *N.D.* iii. 57 : alvi dentisque evolsionem *om.* *C*
Leg. ii. 8 : ignoremusque vim sermonis *om.* *C*
(24) *N.D.* ii. 37 : contemplandum et imitandum *om.* *C*[1]
121 : alias esse cornibus armatas *om.* *C*[1]
154 : Lacedaemonem Atheniensium *om.* *C*
(25) *N.D.* i. 12 : me non profiteor secutum esse *om.* *C*
(26) *Div.* i. 77 : censeret cum ille quiescendum *om.* *C*
78 : atque in amnes mare influxerit *om.* *C*
(31) 133 : tantum laborare. Quorum igitur causa *om.* *C*
(32) *N.D.* ii. 32 : esse ponit ab hisque principium motus *om.* *C*[1]
iii. 8 : argumentari soleo, perspicuitas enim *om.* *C*
(35) *Div.* i. 103 : mea Tertia, quid tristis es? Mi pater, inquit *om.* *C*
(37) *Div.* i. 76 : * in quo inerant sortes collocavissent simia *om.* *C*
(42) *N.D.* i. 81 : eos opiniones esse de bestiis quibusdam quam apud *om.* *C*
(44) *N.D.* ii. 95 : nubium magnitudinem ventorumque vim cognovissent *om.* *C*
(47) *N.D.* ii. 37 : quodque undique aptum atque perfectum expletumque sit *om.* *C*
(81) *N.D.* iii. 77 : philosophorum disputationem interpretarentur tacere praestaret philosophis quam iis qui se *om.* *C*
(451) *N.D.* iii. 58–9 : tertiae pater Upis . . . natum accepimus *om.* *C*
(558) *N.D.* i. 1–2 : esse debeat . . . dinumerare sententias *om.* *C*[1]

To these should be added a dittography:

(37) *N.D.* iii. 36 : quod si ignis ex sese animal est nulla se alia *bis scr.*

I have hesitated to mark *Leg*. ii. 52 (18) as a telescoped passage. Here the other MSS. give:

eos qui tantumdem caperent quantum omnes heredes

C has *eos qui tantum omnes heredes* (*med. om.*). Here the omission seems due to ὁμ.

The omissions of *C* are not so instructive as those of *A* and *B*. It will be seen that nearly all are due to ὁμ.

There is little trace of the ancestor in 29–32 letters which we have observed in the case of *AB*, though the three omissions of 32 letters may be thus explained.

The interesting point is that *C* seems to have passed through an ancestor written in shorter lines. Thus, in ii. 37 we have an omission of 24 letters in close proximity to one of 47. The intervening words contain 297 letters (24 × 12 = 288). I write out the passage as it appears to have stood in this ancestor:

cui nihil absit	
quodque undique aptum atque	(24)
perfectum expletumque sit	(23)
omnibus suis numeris et parti	(25)
bus scite enim chrysippus ut	(24)
clipei causa inuolucrum uagi	(25)
nam autem gladii sic praeter	(24)
mundum cetera omnia aliorum cau	(27)
sa esse generata ut eas fruges	(25)
atque fructus quos terra gig	(24)
nit animantium causa animan	(24)
tes autem hominum ut equum ue	(24)
hendi causa arandi bouem uenan	(26)
di et custodiendi canem ipse	(24)
autem homo ortus est ad mundum	(25)
contemplandum et imitandum	(24)

C has omitted lines 2–3 and 16, the omission in each case being due to ὁμ.

I would also call attention to an interesting corruption:

N. D. i. 85: sententiis quas appellatis κυρίας δόξας (cyrias doxas *codd.*)

C adds *GR.* (= *Graecum*) before *quas*. This indicates:

sententiis		
quas appellatis cyrias doxas	(25)	*mg.* GR.

This gloss is found in the margin of Harl. 2622, which has

senten
gr̃. ciis quas appellatis cyrias doxas haec ut opinor

In view of this evidence it is interesting to notice that 451 = 81 × 5 + 46. There seems to be a relation between these figures. The largest omission (558) is shared by *A*, and goes back to an earlier stage in the tradition.

P.

There is little to be learnt from *P*, and I only give its omissions for the sake of completeness. None of them have been supplied by a second hand.

(12) *N. D.* iii. 88: ac potestatem
(15) *N. D.* ii. 128: et ad procreandum
(25) *N. D.* iii. 14: quis cornicis cantum notavit
(28) *N. D.* iii. 120: *atque ita se erigunt ut animantes
(32) *N. D.* ii. 122: partim unguium tenacitate arripiunt
(40) *N. D.* iii. 91: portenta enim ab utrisque et prodigia dicuntur
(50) *N. D.* ii. 112: *cuius propter laevum genu Vergilias tenui cum luce videbis
(94) *N. D.* iii. 24: vel accessus vel recessus sine deo fieri non possunt. Vide, quaeso, si omnis motus omniaque quae certis temporibus

The following repetition is recorded:

N. D. iii. 14: dicatis omnia, quod autem semper ex omni aeternitate verum fuerit, id esse fatum [dicatis]

Here *dicatis . . . fatum* = 66.

This corruption, in connexion with ii. 122 (32), may possibly indicate a line of 32–3 letters in an ancestor.

I now proceed to consider the light which these lists throw upon the common archetype. The chief evidence is given by the telescoped passages in *ABV*. I have given reasons for thinking that one of these, *N. D.* iii. 80, where *B* omits 49 letters, may represent a line in the model of *B*. Apart from this, we have the following cases:

(28) *Tim.* 38: **quamquam nec argumentis nec rati- *om. V*
(29) *Top.* 28: **-tratuum more aequitate consistat *om. AB*[1]
(31) *N. D.* i. 120: **-tate rerum, tum principia mentis quae *om. A*[1]
(32) *Div.* ii. 55: **-res causas rerum non quaerere tu vates *om. A*[1]

(59) *N. D.* iii. 69: **esse ratione nec vero scaena solum referta est his sceleribus sed mult- *om.* B^1

(65) *N. D.* iii. 32: **ullo sensu iucunda accipere, non accipere contraria. Si igitur voluptatis sen- *om.* B^1

Next to these the most significant passage is *N. D.* ii. 16, where *A* inserts from § 156.

(54) largitate fundit, ea ferarumne an hominum causa gignere videtur?

The natural interpretation to put on these figures is that *Q* was written in two columns, and had an average of 28–9 lines in one column and 31–2 in another.

In such a MS. there would be abnormally short and long lines. For this reason special interest attaches to a passage preserved by *V* only, viz.:

(24) *Lucull.* 109: si quicquam comprendi[1] posse *om. AB*

I have not mentioned this previously, since it is not supplied by the second hand in either MS.

I mention with more reserve another passage given by V^2 only, viz.:

(34) *Fat.* 41: ne ille quidem esset in nostra potestate *om.* ABV^1

I now call attention to the formation of *V*. It is written in two columns, with 24 lines to the page. In the page reproduced by Chatelain, if we exclude abbreviations, col. 1 has an average of 28 letters and col. 2 of 30 letters to the line. It appears probable that the formation of *Q* was somewhat similar.

Tim. 44–8, which appears to represent a folio of *Q*, contains 2,362 letters. If we suppose that *Q* was written in two columns, this gives an average of 1,181 letters to a page and 590 to a column. If so, a column appears to have contained about 21 lines ($28 \times 21 = 588$).

We have now to consider whether it is possible to push back the inquiry to a further stage, and to investigate the antecedents of *Q*.

Certain corruptions found in all our MSS. must have been already present in the archetype. The most striking case is:

Div. i. 97: quotiens senatus decemviros ad libros ire iussit! quantis in rebus quamque saepe responsis haruspicum paruit!

The words *quotiens . . . iussit* (42) occur here *loco suo* in the MSS.,

[1] So *V*. If *comprehendi* is written, the total is 26.

but the next colon *quantis in . . . paruit* (51) has been inserted by editors from § 98, where the MSS. give:

> Nonne et haruspices ea responderunt quae evenerunt et in Sibyllae libris eaedem repertae praedictiones sunt? Quotiens senatus decemviros ad libros ire iussit! quantis in rebus quamque saepe responsis haruspicum paruit!

It looks as if the whole passage *quotiens . . . paruit* (93) was originally omitted, then inserted in the wrong place, and finally a portion of it *quotiens . . . iussit* reinserted *loco suo*, while the whole remained *loco alieno*.

The intermediate passage, viz. §§ 97–8, *nam et cum . . . praedictiones sunt*, consists of 821 letters.

In connexion with this I would take another curious passage:

Div. i. 70: humani autem animi eam partem quae sensum quae motum quae adpetitum habeat non esse ab actione corporis seiugatam; quae autem pars animi rationis atque intellegentiae sit particeps, eam tum maxime vigere cum plurimum absit a corpore

Here A^1CV after *pars animi* repeat *eam partem quae sensum* (19). *B* inserts the words in § 69, thus:

> et naves subito [eam partemque sensum] perterriti metu conscendistis

where they violently disturb the sense.

The reading of A^1CV seems due to an initial omission of the words *eam partem quae sensum*, which were then inserted after *pars animi*, instead of after *autem animi*. The corruption in *B* is more striking since there is nothing to explain the insertion of the words here. The natural conclusion is that a page or column in an ancestor ended at *subito*, and that the words were inserted here instead of after *pars animi*. If so, the passage §§ 69–70, *perterriti . . . pars animi*, should correspond to some division in a remote ancestor.

As a matter of fact this passage, if we omit the words *eam partem quae sensum*, consists of 411 letters.

We have previously seen that in *Div.* i. 97–8 the intervening passage consists of 821 letters. The relation of 411 to 821 is very striking. I therefore suggest that the number 411 corresponds to the content of a column in a distant ancestor.

In connexion with these dislocations, I mention certain corruptions, also present in *Q*, which seem to indicate a shorter line in a previous MS.:

N. D. i. 2: quo omnes duce natura venimus deos esse dixerunt

B, which is practically our only authority for this passage (*defic. A*), adds *sese* after *omnes.* This looks like a variant for *esse.* If so, an ancestor may have had:

quo omnes
duce natura uenimus deos esse (25) *mg.* sese
dixerunt

ib.: in primis magna dissensio est, eaque nisi diiudicatur

So editors: the MSS. add *quae* after *primis.* This may be a variant for *-que.* This indicates:

in primis
magna dissensio est eaque (22) *mg.* quae
nisi diiudicatur

N. D. i. 89: quem tibi hoc daturum putas? si enim ita esset, quid opus erat te gradatim istuc pervenire? sumpsisses tuo iure. Quid autem est istuc gradatim? nam a beatis ad virtutem, a virtute ad rationem video te venisse gradibus

So editors, after Facciolati. The MSS. place *quid autem est istuc gradatim* (25) before *sumpsisses tuo iure.* The transposition seems required by the sense.

N. D. ii. 111: minorem autem Septentrionem Cepheus passis palmis terga subsequitur. Namque ipse ad tergum Cynosurae vertitur Arcti

So the MSS. For *terga* editors read *a tergo.* I look on *terga* as a variant for *tergum*, which has got into the wrong place. This indicates:

palmis
subsequitur namque ipse ad (23)
mg. terga tergum

N. D. iii. 50: itemque Leonaticum est delubrum Athenis, quod Leocorion nominatur

Leonaticum appears to be a variant for *Leocorion*, which has got into the wrong place. This indicates:

itemque
est delubrum athenis quod (22)
mg. leonaticum leocorion nominatur

N. D. iii. 84: in suo lectulo mortuus in typanidis rogum inlatus est eamque potestatem quam ipse per scelus erat nanctus . . . filio tradidit

So the MSS., except *B*, which has *tyrannidis.* I accept the reading of *B*, and regard *tyrannidis* as a gloss on *potestatem*, which has got into the text in the wrong place. This indicates:

mortuus in
rogum inlatus est eamque (21)
mg. tyrannidis potestatem

Lucull. 126: nec enim divinationem quam probatis ullam esse arbitror fatumque illud quo omnia contineri dicitis contemno

So editors: the MSS. repeat *esse* after *illud*. This suggests:

ullam
esse arbitror fatumque illud (25)
quo omnia

On the strength of these passages, I venture to suggest the following transposition:

N. D. ii. 123: ut in araneolis aliae quasi rete texunt, ut si quid inhaeserit conficiant, aliae autem ex inopinato observant et si quid incidit arripiunt

The words *ex inopinato* seem out of place. They should go with *arripiunt*. It seems likely that they have been inserted in the wrong place after omission. An ancestor may have had:

aliae autem
obseruant et si quid incidit
mg. ex inopinato arripiunt

There are other corruptions which show a multiple of this unit (46–8), viz.:

N. D. ii. 98: speluncarum concavas altitudines, saxorum asperitates, impendentium montium altitudines

So the MSS. Lambinus suggests *latitudines* (after *concavas*).

An ancestor may have had:

concauas
latitudines saxorum asperi (24)
tates impendentium montium (24)
altitudines

N. D. iii. 8: primum illud cur quod perspicuum in istam partem ne egere quidem oratione dixisses quod est perspicuum et inter omnes constaret, de eo ipso tam multa dixeris

So the MSS., except that for *est* (so *A* V^1) *B* V^2 give *esset* and *C* has *et*. Editors omit *perspicuum* after *cur quod* and read *in ista partitione* for *in istam partem*.

It is clear that *perspicuum* has been inserted from the context, the corruption being due to ὁμ. (*quod* . . . *quod*). The variants seem to show that *est* is an accretion. This indicates in an ancestor:

quod
in istam partem ne egere qui (23)
dem oratione dixisses quod (23)
perspicuum

N. D. iii. 24: vide . . . ne tertianas quidem febres et quartanas divinas esse dicendum sit, quarum reversione et motu quid potest esse constantius?

So the MSS.: editors read *quoque* with Lambinus for *quidem*. It seems more likely that *quidem* should come after *quarum*. This indicates:

ne tertianas
febres et quartanas diuinas (24)
esse dicendum sit quarum (21) *mg.* quidem
reuersione

N. D. iii. 45: Quid? Aristaeus, qui olivae dicitur inventor, Apollinis filius, Theseus [qui] Neptuni, reliqui quorum patres di, non erunt in deorum numero?

So the MSS.: *qui* is struck out by editors. This indicates:

aristaeus
qui oliuae dicitur inuentor (24)
apollinis filius theseus (22)
neptuni

The repetition is due to ὁμ.

N. D. iii. 61: aut enim in nobismet insunt ipsis, ut mens, ut spes, ut fides, ut virtus, ut concordia, aut optandae nobis sunt, ut honos, ut salus, ut victoria

Baiter says: '*ut spes* vel delenda vel ante *ut honos* transponenda censuit Walkerus, coll. § 88'. In § 88 we find:

quamvis licet Menti delubra et Virtuti et Fidei consecremus, tamen haec in nobis ipsis sita videmus: Spei, Salutis, Opis, Victoriae facultas a dis expetenda est

The contradiction is obvious. An ancestor seems to have had:

ut mens
ut fides ut uirtus ut concor (23)
dia aut optandae nobis sunt (23)
mg. ut spes ut honos, ut salus

I should like to stop at this point, since I have no wish to multiply ancestors *praeter necessitatem*. As, however, I have noticed traces of a slightly shorter line, I feel bound to point them out. The clearest case is:

N. D. iii. 42: tertius est ex Idaeis Digitis, cui inferias adferunt [cui]

So the MSS.: editors remove *cui*. The word is clearly repeated from the context. This indicates in an ancestor:

digitis
cui inferias adferunt (19)

N. D. iii. 81: duodequadraginta Dionysius tyrannus annos fuit

So the MSS., except that *V* has a transposition mark over *annos*. Editors place the word before *Dionysius*. This indicates:

mg. annos dionysius tyrannus (17)
fuit

N. D. iii. 35: non omnes interpretantur uno modo, quoniam quid diceret [quod] intellegi noluit, omittamus

Editors here insert *qui* before *quoniam*, so V^2, and strike out *quod*, which is in all MSS. It seems probable that *quod* is a variant for the missing *qui*, which has got into the text out of place. This indicates:

uno modo *mg.* quod
quoniam quid diceret (18)
intellegi

I would here point out that in *Div.* i. 70 the words which have been repeated out of place in all MSS., viz. *eam partem quae sensum*, consist of 19 letters.

It is possible that we are here dealing with short lines of the ancestor previously discussed. A passage, however, already mentioned, *N.D.* i. 89, is somewhat significant. Here there is a transposition of *sumpsisses tuo iure* (17) and *quid autem est istuc gradatim?* (25). The most probable explanation seems to be that a line of 17 letters was here omitted and reinserted in a subsequent MS. written in longer lines.

I now mention some corruptions which seem to be connected with this unit:

N. D. iii. 1: quae cum Balbus dixisset, tum adridens Cotta (37)

These words are written twice by $A^1B^1V^1$, viz. at the end of ii, as well as at the beginning of iii. This seems to be a very ancient error, due to the repetition of two lines ($19+18=37$).

N. D. ii. 123: aliae quasi rete texunt ut si quid inhaeserit conficiant, aliae autem [ut] . . . observant

So *ABC*. *ut* is repeated from the context. This indicates:

texunt
ut si quid inhaeserit (18)
conficiant aliae autem (20)

Div. ii. 74: fulmen sinistrum auspicium optimum [quod] habemus ad omnes res praeterquam ad comitia, quod quidem institutum rei publicae causa est

So the MSS.: *quod* is inserted by anticipation from the context. This indicates:

optimum
habemus ad omnes res (17)
praeterquam ad comitia (20)
quod quidem

Tim. 44: cum autem animos corporibus necessitate insevisset cumque ad corpora [necessitate] tum accessio fieret, tum abscessio

So the MSS. The repetition seems due to the arrangement:

corporibus
necessitate inseuis (18)
set cumque ad corpora (18)
tum accessio

I now draw attention to a case where there seems to be a transposition, viz.:

Div. i. 115: similiter Marcius et Publicius vates cecinisse dicuntur, quo de genere Apollinis operta prolata sunt. Credo etiam anhelitus quosdam fuisse terrarum quibus inflatae mentes oracla funderent

Meyer transposes *quo de . . . sunt* (37), placing the words after *credo . . . funderent* (75). The transposition produces an excellent sense. The distant ancestor seems to have had:

crėdo etiam anhelitus (19)
quosdam fuisse terra (18)
rum quibus inflatae men (20)
tes oracla funderent (18)
quo de genere apolli (17)
nis operta prolata sunt (20)

In view of this transposition of 37 and 75 letters, I mention the following corrupt passages:

N. D. i. 77: [omnium] quis tam caecus in contemplandis rebus umquam fuit ut non videret species istas hominum conlatas in deos?

Davis conjectures *omnino* for *omnium*. I look on *omnium* as a variant for *hominum*, which has been inserted in the wrong place. The words *quis tam . . . hominum* consist of 74 letters.

N. D. ii. 132 : multa praetereunda sunt et tamen multa dicuntur. Enumerari autem non possunt fluminum opportunitates, aestus maritimi [multum] accedentes et recedentes

So the MSS. : *multum* seems to be a variant for *multa*. The words *multa dicuntur . . . maritimi* consist of 73 letters.

N. D. ii. 145 : nam et virtutes et vitia cognoscunt, iratum propitium, laetantem dolentem, fortem ignavum, audacem timidumque cognoscunt

Baiter says of *cognoscunt* after *vitia*, 'vel hic vel infra malim abesse'. To me a verb seems desirable here, but the repetition of the same word is odd. It is possible that *cognoscunt* has taken the place of another verb. The words *iratum . . . cognoscunt* consist of 72 letters.

N. D. ii. 146 : nariumque item et gustandi et [parte] tangendi magna iudicia sunt. Ad quos sensus capiendos et perfruendos plures etiam quam vellem artes

So the MSS. : I look on *parte* as a variant for *artes*. The words *tangendi . . . vellem* contain 79 letters.

Fat. 41 : quam ob rem cum dicimus omnia fato fieri causis antecedentibus, non hoc intellegi volumus, causis perfectis et principalibus sed causis adiuvantibus [antecedentibus] et proximis

So the MSS. : *antecedentibus* was struck out by Davis. The word is repeated from the context. The passage *antecedentibus . . . causis* consists of 75 letters.

There is a striking similarity between these passages.

I mention, but do not attempt to classify, two other cases :

N. D. ii. 100 : partim submersarum, partim fluitantium et innantium beluarum, partim ad saxa nativis testis inhaerentium. Ipsum autem mare sic terram appetens litoribus eludit ut una ex duabus naturis conflata videatur

For *saxa nativis* (edd.) the MSS. have various corruptions, viz. *saxa sanati uis A*, *saxas anatiuis B* : *saxa ṣạnatiuis V*. Also for *eludit* some inferior MSS. give *alludit*, which seems right (so Lambinus and Davis). The corruption *sa* seems due to *litoribus* $\overset{a}{e}$*ludit*, i.e. the combination of a variant with a dittography of *-s*. This was subsequently inserted after *saxa*.

N. D. ii. 137: ex intestinis autem [alvo] secretus a reliquo cibo sucus is quo alimur permanat ad iecur per quasdam a medio intestino usque ad portas iecoris—sic enim appellantur—ductas et directas, vias quae pertinent ad iecur eique adhaerent. Atque inde aliae pertinentes sunt, per quas cadit cibus a iecore dilapsus

So the MSS.: editors strike out *alvo*. After *atque inde aliae*, Heindorf inserts *alio*, i.e. *aliae alio pertinentes*. Orelli says 'sane excidit aliquid'. It appears to me that the superfluous *alvo* is a variant for the missing *alio*. In § 136 *alvo* is corrupted to *alio* in *P*.

CHAPTER XI

ASCONIUS AND PSEUDO-ASCONIUS.

THESE works were discovered by Poggio at St. Gallen in 1416. The Sangallensis (Σ) itself is lost, but its readings are known from three copies, made by Poggio, Sozomenus of Pistoia, and Bartolommeo da Montepulciano. These copies are represented by:

P = Matritensis x. 81.

S = Pistoriensis, Forteguerri 37.

M = Laur. liv. 5.

P appears to be written by Poggio himself, but it is not clear whether it is his original transcript or a 'fair copy' made afterwards. *S* was written by Sozomenus at Constance in 1417. *M* is not the original transcript made by Bartolommeo in 1416, but a copy of this written by an ignorant scribe.

There can be no doubt that *S* is the most faithful witness to the readings of Σ. Poggio's aim was to produce an edition which should present the newly-discovered texts in an intelligible form, while Bartolommeo adopted many conjectures made by his more brilliant colleague. Sozomenus was content to play a more humble rôle, and generally reproduced the corruption which he found in Σ.

The latest editor, T. Stangl, speaks severely of Poggio, and looks upon all his efforts with great suspicion. He frequently, but not always, prints in italics words given by *P*, but omitted by *S*, and considers all Poggio's supplements as due to conjecture. I am disposed to think that he goes too far. This may be seen from the following passage:—

238. 17[1]: *εἰρωνεία μετὰ συγχωρήσεως*

For this *P* gives:

hironiã et asynchores eos

The passage is omitted by *S*[2] and *M*. It is wholly inconceivable

[1] The reference is to Stangl's *Ciceronis Orationum Scholiastae* (1912).

[2] Stangl does not here mention the reading of *S*.

that Poggio invented this corrupt passage. How then are we to account for its omission both by *S* and *M*? I can only suppose that Sozomenus and Bartolommeo failed to decipher it, or did not recognize that it formed part of the text. If the latter explanation is adopted, we may conjecture that the words were written in the margin.

I would also draw attention to:

241. 5-7 : sed POSCUNT PROVOCANT intelligendum est, ut sit sensus: provocant se invicem. POSCUNT a pincerna petunt: MAIORIBUS autem POCULIS, ut subaudiatur bibere

Here *SM* omit the words *poscunt a pincerna petunt.* It is very unlikely that Poggio introduced so rare a word as *pincerna* (=butler) in a conjectural supplement.

Also, Sozomenus was not unwilling to emend the text on occasions. Thus:

68. 17 (88. 2): P^1M give *ut repente gladiatores poculo non debitos polliceretur*

Here *S* has the correction *populo* in the text (so P^2).

42. 20 (50. 1): dixerunt a manu Milonis occisum esse Clodium

So *PM* in the scholium: *S* adds *consilio vero maioris alicuius* from the lemma, or from Cicero (*Mil.* 47). The hypothesis of insertion from the context by one writer is here more simple than that of omission by two.

The formation of the Sangallensis can be settled with some degree of accuracy by the help of the lacunae, which in certain places, especially in the commentary of Asconius upon the Corneliana, recur at regular intervals. This subject was investigated by Kiessling and Schöll, who came to the conclusion that Σ had 39-40 lines to a page and 30-40 letters to a line. I made an independent examination of the question, writing out the passages from which most of the evidence is derived, and came to the same conclusion. I found the average content of a line in Σ to be 36 letters.

I will now call attention to a large omission of *S*, viz.:

244. 8-246. 12 : *a Verre L. Magio . . . quia nec superioris

Stangl here says '*duas archetypi paginas om. S*'.

The omitted passage contains 2,892 letters. If we divide this figure by 36, we obtain as result 80 ($80 \times 36 = 2,880$). This gives

40 lines to a page, i.e. *S* has omitted a folio. This is a striking confirmation of the result arrived at by Kiessling and Schöll. We are therefore entitled to conclude that Σ contained 40 lines to a page, with an average of 36 letters to the line.

I now turn to the evidence given by omissions, dittographies, &c., in our MSS.[1] It will be noticed that most of it comes from *S*, also that on several occasions *M* agrees with *S* in an omission.

(23) 238. 17: *hironiam et asynchores eos *om. SM*

(27) 70. 18 (91. 6): cum et imperitos se homines esse *om. S*

(35) 53. 12 (66. 9): et consulatus candidatum se ostendisset *om. S*

235. 6: causit ut diceret Sylla mihi iussit Sylla *om. M*

(37) 215. 6: persolvisse vult enim illum Verris pecunia *om. SM*

34. 11 (36. 20): idque ipse ipsum in superioribus circa quos *bis scr. S* (after an interval of 31 letters)

(47) 45. 7 (53. 21): IIII tribuni aerarii condemnaverunt XIII absolverunt *om. S*

230. 25: et rursum comperendinato iudicio dicit prior defensor *om. S*

(49) 48. 14 (59. 1): in senatu legibus solveretur nisi CC adfuissent neve quis *om. S*

(54) 26. 28 (25. 11): *idem inter primos temporis sui oratores et tragicus poeta bonus *om. S*

(56) 61. 4 (78. 2): qua lege suffragiorum vis potestasque convaluit, alteram Cassiam *om. S*

241. 16: poscunt a pincerna petunt, maioribus autem poculis ut subaudiatur *om. SM*

260. 15: testimonium publicum mandataque acceperant a civitatibus suis s. *bis scr. PM*

(63) 195. 1: *quod hinc pendet suscipitur solum aliquid propter se recipitur ut mihi non *om. S*

(64) 251. 15: ergo simpliciter accipiendum est: vult enim patrem Verris divisorem fuisse *om. S*

(66) 224. 15: *crimina repetundarum et alia pleraque ante acta vita saepe firmantur. Sumitur *om. S*

(67) 26. 8 (24. 9): quave ratione ut hoc loco Cicero hoc verbo ita usus sit, praesertim cum adiecerit *om. S*

228. 31: qui vero contra facit et sit impedimento ceteris astu tegat de hoc intelligitur *om. S*

(70) 16. 8 (9. 1): eius lege censuram quae magistra pudoris et modestiae est sublatam adit. Paulo post. Persequere. *PM*

S^1 here has a curious error, viz. after a capital *P*, the first letter of *Persequere*, Sozomenus wrote *eius lege censuram*. This indicates in Σ:

[1] The references are to Stangl's edition. In the case of Asconius I add in brackets references to my own edition.

eius lege censuram quae magistra pudoris (35)
et modestiae est sublatam adit. Paulo post (35)
Persequere

(83) 231. 26: nomina sua exegisse. Tituli debitorum nomina dicuntur praesertim in his debitis in quibus hominum *bis scr. S*

(108) 19. 17 (14. 22): triumphus mortuus est ante diem triumphi cum cicatrix vulneris eius quod ante plures annos in proelio acceperat rescissa esset *om. S*

(140) 222. 27: *si quis erit qui perpetuam orationem. Vides quia argumentis se usurum non negat iam modo, quamquam perpetuam orationem se neget habiturum in hac oratione quae prima est. *om. M*

(146) 220. 11: flagitabat. Hoc Cicero utitur ad invidiam iudiciorum, infamiam senatu iudicante. Qui Cn. Pompeio invidia tunc Pompeius fuit quod cons. redderet populo tribuniciam potestatem *om. M*

(331) 50. 14–18 (62. 6–12): in hac causa tres sunt quaestiones: prima, cum sit Cornelius reus maiestatis legis Corneliae, utrum certae aliquae res sunt ex lege comprehensae quibus solis reus maiestatis teneatur, quod patronus defendit: an libera eius interpretatione iudicii relicta sit, quod accusator proponit. Secunda est an quod Cornelius fecit ne ca maiestatis teneatur. Tertia, an minuendae maiestatis animum habuerit. *om. P*

Here we have to notice in the first place errors due to the lineation of Σ itself. To this we may attribute the following examples[1]:

(35) 53. 12: *om. S*
235. 6: *om. M*
(37) 215. 6: *om. SM*
34. 11: *bis scr. S*
(66) 224. 15: *om. S*
(67) 26. 8: *om. S*
228. 31: *om. S*
(70) 16. 8: repetition in *S*
(140) 222. 27: *om. M*
(146) 220. 11: *om. S*

I omit for the present some cases which admit of more than one explanation.

What then are we to say of the remaining figures? Are they due to mere chance? It will be observed that there are some singular sequences. Thus we have:

(27) 70. 18: *om. S*
(54) 26. 28: *om. S*
(56) 61. 4: *om. S*
241. 16: *om. SM*
260. 15: *bis scr. PM*

[1] The omissions of 66–7 letters admit of a rival explanation, see *infra*.

(83) 231. 26: *bis scr.* *S* (27 × 3 = 81)
(108) 19. 17: *om.* *S* (27 × 4 = 108)
(327) 50. 14: *om.* *P* (27 × 12 = 324)

Here some light is to be obtained from 260. 15, where we have the following readings:

testimonium publicum mandata que acceperant a civitatibus suis testimonium publicum mandataque acceperant a suis civitatibus scilicet *P*

testimonium publicum madataque acceperant a civitatibus suis testimonium pu. madataque acceperant a civitatibus suis .s. *M*

testimonium publicum mandata que acceperant a civitatibus suis .s. *S*

It is difficult to suppose that Poggio and Bartolommeo both made the same dittography at the same spot. The easier explanation is that the dittography existed in the Sangallensis, being inherited from a previous MS. If so, we may attribute to this ancestor the reading:

testimonium publicum mandata que (29)
acceperant a ciuitatibus suis .s. (27)

The passage was written twice in Σ.

Conversely, in 231. 26, where *S* has a dittography of 83 letters, it appears to preserve a corruption existing in Σ. The previous ancestor seems to have had:

nomina sua exegisse tituli debi (27)
torum nomina dicuntur praesertim (29)
in his debitis in quibus hominum (27)

I now turn to 241. 16. Here we have the following readings:

maioribus autem poculis ut subaudiatur poscunt a pincerna petunt maioribus autem poculis ut subaudiatur *P*
maioribus autem poculis ut subaudiatur *SM* (*med. om.*)

This suggests in a previous MS.:

maiori
bus autem poculis ut subaudiatur (28)
poscunt a pincerna petunt maiori (28)
bus autem poculis ut subaudiatur (28)

The writer omitted two lines (ὁμ.). How then are we to account for the omission of the passage by *SM*, while it is given by *P*? The answer must be that it was in the margin of Σ, and was only noticed or deciphered by Poggio.

I therefore conclude that Σ possessed a number of marginalia, which were omitted by one, or more, of the transcribers. Thus on one occasion (50. 14–18) Poggio himself, who scarcely ever omits anything, left out 327 letters, i.e. 12 lines of this previous ancestor ($27 \times 12 = 324$).

It now remains to ask if any significance is to be attached to the figures which have not yet been considered. Here also there are some curious points to notice. Thus we have two cases where *S* omits 47 letters, and one where *SM* omit 23. There are five omissions of 63–7 letters. I have doubtfully assigned those of 66–7 letters to Σ, since it is easier to suppose that Sozomenus omitted lines of his model. It is, however, possible that they are multiples of 21–2 letters, and represent lines of a more remote ancestor preserved in the marginalia of Σ.

If the results of this analysis are well founded, we should expect to find embedded in the text corruptions due to the lineation of these ancestors. Such evidence is not lacking. I take first the ancestor in lines of 27–8 letters.

(26) 44. 4 (52. 4): unum tum excuti priusquam in senatum intraret priusquam iusserat Σ

Here *priusquam* has been repeated by error. This indicates:

unum tum excuti
priusquam in senatum intraret (26)
iusserat

(27) 24. 7 (21. 6): multam irrogavit quod eius opera sacra multa populi R. deminuta esse diceret Σ

Here *multa* appears to be a variant for *multam*. This indicates:

multam *mg.* multa
irrogauit quod eius opera sacra (27)
P. R. deminuta esse diceret

(27) 226. 11: repetitio verris in qua uidetur insaniae verris causa velle monstrari Σ

Here *uerris* (before *in qua*) appears to be an error for *furoris* (edd.). This points to:

repetitio
furoris in qua uidetur insaniae (27)
uerris causa uelle monstrari

The scribe looked forward to the next line.

(54) 206. 14: ut haec res non solum compendio moram ac brevitatem temporis

tollat sed etiam circa artificium dicendi breuiter etiam in hac parte vim oratoris ostendat Σ

Here Stangl reads *tarditatem* for *brevitatem*, which seems due to the occurrence of *breviter* shortly afterwards. The error points to the following arrangement:

moram ac	
tarditatem temporis tollat sed	(27)
etiam circa artificium dicendi	(27)
breuiter etiam	

(82) 41. 27 (48. 24): de vi accusante Clodio obiecit et ut legimus apud Tironem libertum Ciceronis in libro IIII de vita eius oppressum Clodio L. Caecilium Σ

Here *Clodio* (after *oppressum*) seems to be repeated from *Clodio* (before *obiecit*).

This indicates:

de ui accusante	
clodio obiecit et ut legimus apud	(28)
tironem libertum ciceronis in	(26)
libro IIII de uita eius oppressum	(28)
L. caecilium	

The scribe looked back three lines.

(84) 228. 1: de nominibus Sabinarum plures fecit (*so S*: factae *PM*) quibus precatricibus parentum bellum maritorumque finitum est: ad postremum XXX et V factae Σ

For *fecit* (*factae*) Stangl reads *dictae*, which seems to be the necessary correction. It seems probable that *fecit* is a variant for *factae* (after V), which has got into the wrong place. This points to:

	plures	
	dictae quibus precatricibus pa	(27)
	rentum bellum maritorumque fini	(28)
mg. fecit	tum est ad postremum XXX et V factae	(29)

(85) 41. 11 (48. 3): Flavius sine comite Romam vix perfugit. Haec eadem longo intervallo conversa rursus est in me, nuper quidem, ut scitis, ad Regiam paene confugit (*so S*: confecit *PM*) Σ

Here *S* seems to preserve a corruption from Σ, which points to the following arrangement:

uix per	
fugit haec eadem longo interuallo	(29)
conuersa rursus est in me nuper qui	(29)

dem ut scitis ad regiam paene con (27)
fecit

These three cases of corruption after 82–5 letters should be compared with the dittography of 83 letters in *S* (231. 26).

In view of these corruptions it is probable that the following omissions of Σ represent lines of this ancestor:

(27) 42. 21 (50. 1): consilio vero maioris alicuius *om. PM*
202. 5: etenim fides mea speculatorem r. *Stangl* (*ex Cic.*): *om.* Σ
(28) 229. 13: contra honorem meum nihil posse d. *Stangl* (*ex Cic.*): *om.* Σ

I now turn to the evidence for a shorter line in a previous ancestor:

(19) 44. 12 (52. 16): incidebantur iam domi leges quae nos iam servis nostris addicerent Σ

Here *iam* (after *nos*) is omitted by the MSS. of Cicero. In all probability it is due to repetition. This indicates:

incidebantur
iam domi leges quae nos (19)
seruis nostris

(20) 201. 19: causis eiusmodi soliti

Stangl points out that these words are out of place in Σ.

(21) 238. 17: cum imperio ac securibus. hironiã et asynchores eos. Cum imperio ac securibus *P*

Here *SM* omit *cum imperio . . . eos*. Stangl reads:

mercator signorum. Εἰρωνεία μετὰ συγχωρήσεως. Cum imperio ac securibus

Here *mercator signorum* is supplied from Cicero (*Verr.* i. 60).

The more distant ancestor seems to have had:

mercator signorum
hironiã et asynchores eos (22)
cum imperio ac securibus (21)

l. 3 was inserted by anticipation before l. 2, taking the place of the lemma.

(22) 41. 12 (48. 5): ad Regiam paene confecerit nusquam paene inveni Σ

The repetition of *paene* indicates the arrangement:

ad regiam
paene confecerit nusquam (22)
inueni

The repetition is made easy by ὁμ.

(22) 256. 17 : decuriam modo 'ordinem' ac per hoc ex 'vobis' quia honestiorum decurie per hec ex vobis Σ

The words *per hec* (*hoc*) *ex vobis* are repeated from the context, as Stangl points out. This indicates :

per hoc ex uobis   *mg.* per hec ex uobis
quia honestiorum decurie   (22)

The variant has got into the wrong place. It is to be noticed that *P* has *et* for *ex* in the first place and $\overset{ex}{et}$ in the second. Possibly the variant was *per hec et uobis.*

(38) 228. 9 : alia enim sortitione nunc sedent, illa divinatione constituendi accusatoris alia fuit Σ

Here editors read *alia* for *illa* and omit the word before *fuit.* It looks as if a *duplex lectio* had got into the wrong line. If so, an ancestor may have had :

sedent
mg. alia   illa diuinatione con   (18)
stituendi accusatoris   (20)
fuit

(42) 257. 5 : quae quia magis adiuvant accusationem quam ipsae quae (*so S* : *om.* quae *PM*) sunt principales Σ

Stangl points out that *quae* is repeated from the context. This indicates:

quae quia magis adiuuant   (21)
accusationem quam ipsae   (21)
sunt principales

(43) 27. 16 (26. 11) : ceteras (*so S* : steteras *PM*) eas sibi inimicitias non susceptas sed relictas et cetera Σ

Here *ceteras* appears to be a variant for *cetera*, which has got into the wrong place. Probably the distant ancestor had :

eas sibi inimicitias non   (21)
susceptas sed relictas et   (22)
mg. ceteras   cetera

(43) 238. 20 : habeo istius et patris legitur accepti tabulas. Id est acceptarum pecuniarum. Legitur et habeo et accepti Σ

Here *legitur* after *patris* is an error for *eius* (Cic.). This indicates :

patris
eius accepti tabulas id   (20)

est acceptarum pecuniarum (23)
legitur

The following omission of Σ may represent a line of this more remote ancestor:

(22) 211. 15: aperte palamque dixisset *om. sine lac. PM*: *in lac.* 7 *litt. S*

I have already indicated the possibility that some of the omissions of 63–7 letters in *S* may represent multiples of this lower unit.

I add here for the sake of completeness the other passages which I have noticed where Σ omits passages of Cicero's text:

(31) 198. 1: quod mihi ab amicorum negotiis datur *Lodoicus* (*ex Cic.*): *om.* Σ
(32) 190. 21: scit is qui est in consilio C. Marcellus *Cic.*: *om.* Σ
262. 17: omnia de pecuniis repetundis iudicia *Cic.*: *om.* Σ
(33) 44. 28 (53. 10): fecisse·commemorat ut non modo virtute *Cic.*: *om.* Σ

In the last case there is some uncertainty, since for *se fecisse* Harl. 2682, which so frequently agrees with Asconius, has *suam se fecisse.* It is possible that the text of Asconius may have had *se suam fecisse*, in which case *suam* must be added to the omission.

I have not here included:

14. 13 (6. 7): in vagina reconditum *om. sine lac. S*: *in lac. PM*

since here I would suggest that the letters *i.u.r.* may have dropped out before *circa*, which follows.

Nor, similarly, 16. 29 (10. 2), where Σ gives:

Seplasia he . . . te (Seplasia me hercule, ut dici audiebam *Cic.*)

since there is here some further corruption.

I do not propose to do more than point out the similarity of these omissions of 31–3 letters, and indicate the possibility that they may represent rather longer lines of the more immediate ancestor. I do not like to pass them over in view of the following corruptions found in *S*:

(31) 251. 14: qui putant hironicos pronuntiandum non [putat] vident *S*

This seems to indicate:

qui
mg. putat putant hironicos pronuntiandum non (31)
uident

(32) 211. 14: de eorum compellatione nuda quos negotium [iam] tangeret. Curionem autem patrem dicit. Tam Σ

Stangl says of *iam* 'e v. 15 pro *tam*'.

This suggests:

negotium
tangeret curionem autem patrem dicit (32)
mg. iam tam

I now proceed to discuss an extraordinary series of dislocations found in the pseudo-Asconius. In Asconius proper there is only one, 55. 5–11 (68. 19–69. 7) and 55. 1–4 (69. 8–12).

These dislocations vary in character. Many of them are simple cases of transposition. In others, where the text is considerably disturbed, there are consecutive transpositions. Sometimes blocks of text have changed places in what seems to be a very arbitrary manner. The true order has been restored by editors from Cicero.

There are some curious relations to be observed between the transposed passages. Thus, to take a simple instance, in 195. 14–23 four blocks which have been transposed consist of 62, 63, 66, 189 letters. I have therefore taken the trouble to put together the facts.

I give first a list of the passages in question, placing them in the true order, and adding in brackets their order in Σ, also the number of letters which they contain. In all cases I adopt corruptions found in Σ, as against emendations:

(1)	(*b*)	55. 5–11 (68. 19–69. 7):	quartum . . . populum	(428)
	(*a*)	55. 1–4 (69. 8–13):	tertium . . . adiecta	(214)
(2)	(*a*)	186. 23:	eorum . . . stantem	(54)
	(*f*)	24–5:	in causis . . . fecit	(78)
	(*b*)	26–187. 2:	causis . . . anteponendus	(227)
	(*d*)	187. 3–5:	cum quaestor . . . effectus sit	(177)
	(*c*)	6–8:	Siculis . . . dixit	(175)
	(*e*)	9–17:	veteribus . . . coniuncti	(473)
	(*g*)	18–19:	causam . . . accusationem	(95)
(3)	(*b*)	191. 19–22:	quod in . . . iuris habui	(217)
	(*a*)	22–32:	sestertium . . . protulisset	(620)
	(*d*)	192. 1–2:	accedere . . . advertere	(118)
	(*c*)	3–8:	si tacent . . . sequitur	(323)
	(*f*)	9–10:	te ipsum . . . intellegemus	(79)
	(*e*)	11–30:	et quis . . . vita vis	(1071)
	(*h*)	193. 1–5:	cui metus . . . eiusmodi	(264)
	(*k*)	5–6:	certos . . . perscripsisset	(87)
	(*i*)	7–11:	non enim . . . liquere	(272)
	(*l*)	11–28:	et ideo . . . invenitur	(1098)
	(*g*)	29–194. 13:	a pueris . . . criminum	(850)

(4)	(*c*)	195. 14–17 :	rationem . . . esset	(189)
	(*b*)	18–19 :	ut est . . . dictura	(66)
	(*d*)	20–1 :	deportare . . . locum	(62)
	(*a*)	22–3 :	deinde . . . velit	(63)
(5)	(*c*)	199. 3–6 :	transigere . . . monstretur	(214)
	(*b*)	7–8 :	ipse . . . suum	(95)
	(*a*)	9–10 :	ex illius . . . reddere	(66)
(6)	(*b*)	200. 6–10 :	hunc . . . vocat	(240)
	(*a*)	11–23 :	totum . . . populum	(593)
(7)	(*b*)	201. 7–9 :	de populo . . . dicuntur	(149)
	(*a*)	9–14 :	oblique . . . potestatem	(292)
	(*d*)	15–19 :	ad columnam . . . vocitata est	(280)
	(*c*)	20–2 :	vestri . . . solent	(124)
	(*e*)	19 :	causis eiusmodi soliti	(20)

I here adopt Stangl's suggestion as to the proper place of (*e*).

(8)	(*b*)	202. 26 :	Circes . . . faciebat	(37)
	(*a*)	203. 1 :	redit ad se . . . homines	(44)
(9)	(*b*)	203. 27–8 :	hic est . . . coniurationem	(69)
	(*a*)	204. 1–2 :	accusavit . . . accusatus est	(62)
(10)	(*b*)	207. 18–20 :	invenit . . . reum	(144)
	(*a*)	21–2 :	petit . . . petit	(65)
(11)	(*b*)	211. 5–7 :	ecce . . . Tenedo	(108)
	(*a*)	8–9 :	comitiis . . . comitia	(67)
(12)	(*b*)	212. 1–3 :	his diebus . . . comitiis	(173)
	(*a*)	4–12 :	et M. Metello . . . solet	(505)
(13)	(*b*)	212. 24–9 :	divisores . . . dixisset	(258)
	(*a*)	213. 1–4 :	qui se . . . suscepta	(197)
(14)	(*b*)	213. 17 :	et optima hironia est	(18)
	(*a*)	18–19 :	patris . . . seni s.	(57)
(15)	(*b*)	219. 14–19 :	qui ambo . . . positum est	(349)
	(*a*)	20–1 :	qui C. . . . praetore	(85)
(16)	(*b*)	226. 20 :	non is . . . nocentissimus	(28)
	(*a*)	21 :	non id . . . senatui est	(35)
(17)	(*b*)	230. 19–231. 22 :	adimo . . . dixi	(1941)
	(*a*)	231. 23 :	in hoc . . . scilicet	(45)
(18)	(*b*)	234. 1–4 :	pro quaestore . . . nummos	(182)
	(*a*)	5–8 :	cohorti . . . praetorio	(201)
(19)	(*b*)	238. 17–19 :	cum imperio . . . et privatis	(105)
	(*a*)	20–239. 4 :	habeo . . . potest	(735)

Here (*b*) requires some explanation. In *P cum imperio ac securibus*

(21) occurs twice, viz. before and after *hironiā et asynchores eos* (22). *SM* are defective. After this comes:

Cum imperio ac securibus. Bene, quia licet negotiari equitibus et privatis (62)

(20)	(*b*)	240. 16–17:	videant . . . positum	(73)
	(*a*)	18–20:	homo . . . procreare	(150)
(21)	(*b*)	242. 33:	ad inimicos . . . causarum	(41)
	(*a*)	243. 1–2:	nisi damnato . . . valeret	(119)
(22)	(*b*)	247. 8–20:	tabulas . . . possideret	(614)
	(*e*)	20–3:	more . . . vocabantur	(103)
	(*c*)	23–7:	alii . . . praebiturus	(236)
	(*a*)	27–8:	Terentius . . . tentatum ad-	(41)
	(*d*)	248. 1–20:	appellat . . . iudicii	(949)
	(*f*)	21–2:	bona . . . eorum	(68)
	(*h*)	23–5:	eripis . . . servabatur	(141)
	(*g*)	26–249. 3:	hoc P. R. . . . praetorium	(206)
(23)	(*b*)	250. 18–20:	quam plena . . . orator	(142)
	(*a*)	21:	tr. pl. M. iolaus palicanus	(20)
	(*d*)	22–3:	cuius . . . crudelitatis	(69)
	(*c*)	24:	suo tempore de suppliciis	(22)
	(*f*)	25–7:	is viros . . . crediderat	(157)
	(*e*)	28–30:	dat . . . permanere	(134)
(24)	(*b*)	252. 9–10:	foro . . . dabantur	(57)
	(*a*)	11:	renuntiata . . . nuntiat	(38)
(25)	(*b*)	253. 1–2:	et praedibus . . . dicuntur	(108)
	(*a*)	3:	populo . . . scilicet	(30)
(26)	(*b*)	254. 1–2:	istam . . . diem	(47)
	(*a*)	3–5:	neque . . . possimus	(161)
	(*d*)	6–8:	putabat . . . retuli	(140)
	(*c*)	9–10:	ut uno . . . detrahere	(63)
(27)	(*b*)	260. 4–5:	una . . . iudicum	(63)
	(*a*)	6:	in laudando . . . repetundarum	(45)
(28)	(*b*)	263. 1:	ut praetor . . . composito	(36)
	(*a*)	2–3:	Loctanus . . . laudat	(74)
	(*d*)	4:	iuris . . . virtutem	(54)
	(*c*)	5–6:	L. Octavius . . . improbum	(98)

These figures exhibit some striking correspondences. Thus $1a = 214$ and $1b = 428$ ($214 \times 2 = 428$), $2f = 78$ and $2b = 227$ ($76 \times 3 = 228$), $2d = 177$ and $2c = 175$, $2e = 473$ and $2g = 95$ ($95 \times 5 = 475$). In (3) we may notice that $c = 323$ and $f = 79$ ($80 \times 4 = 320$), so $k = 87$ and $h = 264$ ($87 \times 3 = 261$), so $i = 272$ and $l = 1098$ ($272 \times 4 = 1088$). In (4) we have the unmistakable series 62, 63, 66, 189. Similar features are to be found in other groups. Thus in (19) *b* = 105 and *a* = 735 (105 × 7 = 735); in (22) *f* = 68 and *h* = 141 (70 × 2 = 140), *a*=41 and *g*=206 (41 × 5 = 205), so *e* = 103 and *b*=614 (103 × 6 = 618), so *c* = 236 and *d* = 949 (237 × 4 = 948).

I have not here written out all the passages in full on account of the length of some. I give the following examples in case that any reader desires to check some figures.

(1) (*b*) tertium est de legum abrogationibus quo de genere persaepe S. C. fiunt ut nuper de ipsa lege Calpurnia que derogaretur. Lex haec Calpurnia de ambitu erat, tulerat eam ante biennium C. Calpurnius Piso cos. in qua praeter alias poenas poena pecuniaria erat adiecta (214)

(*a*) quartum quae lex lata esse dicatur, ea non videri populum teneri ut L. Marcio Sex. Iulio cos. de legibus uiuis. Puto uos reminisci has esse leges iuuias quasi illi consulibus M. Iubilius Drusus tr. pl. tulerit qui cum senatus partes tuendas suscepisset et leges pro optimatibus tulisset, postea ea licentia est progressus ut nullum in his morem servaret. Itaque Philippus cos. qui ei inimicus erat obtinuit a senatu ut leges eius omnes uno S. C. tollerentur. Decretum est enim contra auspicia esse latas neque his teneri populum (428)

I here write *cos.* (*bis*), but *consulibus*, so Σ.

(2) (*f*) in causis iudiciisque publicis iam hoc contra Caecilium est qui numquam sui periculum fecit (78)

(*b*) causis iudiciisque publicis. Causae etiam privatae sunt arepetundarum ambitus maiestatis et cetera rei p. causa constituta sunt. Una et id quod facio probavit. Principalis divisio huius causae bipartita est, utrum recte Cicero accuset et utrum Caecilio sit anteponendus (227)

(*c*) Siculis omnibus oslatorie. Cum enim a duobus quaestoribus Sicilia regi soleat, uno Lilybitano, altero Syracusano, ipse vero Lilybitanus quaestor fuerit Sex. Peducaeo praetore, omnibus tamen se placuisse dixit (175)

I write *praetore* with Σ.

(*d*) Cum quaestor. Narrationem in exordio multi admirantur hac reprehensione sed non recte. Est enim argumentalis narratio ad priorem divisionem in qua queritur an recte Cicero ex defensore accusator effectus sit (177)

(*g*) Causam defensionemque. Causae ingerunt quas iusto defensionem e inire defensionem vult esse non accusationem (95)

(*e*) Veteribus patronis multis. Siculi veteres patronos habent in quibus Marcellus a Marcello ortus qui Syracusas victor servavit incolumes: Scipiones quorum auctor P. Scipio Africanus Carthagine excisa Siciliae ornamenta retulit sua quibus quondam a Poenis victoribus spoliata erat, Metellus, quorum familia proxime Siculis patrocinium praebuit, cum fuerit Lepidus in ea provincia praetor, instantibus ad accusandum eum Metellum duobus Celere et Nepote. Populati atque vexati. Populati avaritia, vexati libidine et crudelitate. Cuncti, simul omnes quasi coniuncti (473)

Here also I give *praetor* with Σ.

(4) (*d*) Deportare litteras, portare aliquid ut intereat, deportare ut mutet locum (62)

(*a*) Deinde accusatorem firmum verumque esse offirmum ut possit verum ut velit (63)

(*b*) Ut est hominum genus. Amariora dicturus ad Siculorum personam contula dictura (66)

(*c*) Rationem vitae reposcere. Accusatorem esse, suae reddere defensorem. Nisi a Siculis potuisse cognosci. Quia aut Siculus ipse est aut quia nisi quaestor in Sicilia nihil aliud fuit Caecilius, in quo nosceretur quid hominis esset (189)

It will be seen that in these cases there is a numerical relation between transposed blocks. For fuller information I add a list of all the passages concerned arranged in order of magnitude:

(18)	213. 17
(20)	201. 19
	250. 21
(21)	238. 17 (*cum imperio ac securibus*)
(22)	250. 24
	238. 17 (*hironiā et asynchores eos*)
(28)	226. 20
(30)	253. 3
(35)	226. 21
(36)	263. 1
(37)	202. 26
(38)	252. 11
(41)	242. 33
	247. 27–8
(44)	203. 1
(45)	231. 23
	260. 6
(47)	254. 1–2
(54)	186. 23
	263. 4
(57)	213. 18–19
	252. 9–10
(62)	195. 20–1
	204. 1–2
	238. 19–20
(63)	195. 22–3
	254. 9–10
	260. 4–5
(65)	207. 21–2
(66)	195. 18–19
	199. 9–10
(67)	211. 8–9
(68)	248. 21–2
(69)	203. 27–8
	250. 22–3
(73)	240. 16–17
(74)	263. 2–3
(78)	186. 24–5
(79)	192. 9–10
(85)	219. 20–1
(87)	193. 5–6
(95)	187. 18–19
	199. 7–8
(98)	263. 5–6
(103)	247. 20–3
(108)	211. 5–7

253. 1–2
(118) 192. 1–2
(119) 243. 1–2
(124) 201. 20–2
(134) 250. 28–30
(140) 254. 6–8
(141) 248. 23–5
(142) 250. 18–20
(144) 207. 18–20
(149) 201. 7–9
(150) 240. 18–20
(157) 250. 25–7
(161) 254. 3–5
(173) 212. 1–3
(175) 187. 6–8
(177) 187. 3–5
(182) 234. 1–4
(189) 195. 14–17
(197) 213. 1–4
(201) 234. 5–8
(206) 248. 26–249. 3
(214) 55. 1–4
199. 3–6
(217) 191. 19–22
(227) 186. 26–187. 2
(236) 247. 23–7
(240) 200. 6–10
(258) 212. 24–9
(264) 193. 1–5
(272) 193. 7–11
(280) 201. 15–19
(292) 201. 9–14
(323) 192. 3–8
(349) 219. 14–19
(428) 55. 5–11
(473) 187. 9–17
(505) 212. 4–12
(593) 200. 11–23
(614) 247. 8–20
(620) 191. 23–32
(735) 238. 20–239. 4
(850) 193. 29–194. 13
(949) 248. 1–20
(1071) 192. 11–30
(1098) 193. 11–28
(1941) 230. 19–231. 22

There are some singular correspondences to be observed in these figures. I would call attention to the following sequences :

(28) 226. 20
(54) 186. 23, 263. 4
(57) 213. 18, 252. 9
(108) 211. 5, 253. 1
(214) 55. 1, 199. 3
(428) 55. 5
(850) 193. 29

So also we have:

(118) 192. 1
(119) 243. 1
(236) 247. 23
(240) 200. 6
(473) 187. 9
(949) 248. 1

I now call attention to the omissions and dittographies of *SPM* already considered. I showed that, apart from those cases where one or more of the MSS. omitted lines of Σ, the omissions fall into two classes. For the first of these we had the figures :

27
54
56 (3 exx.)
83
108
327

For the omission of 327 we may compare the dislocation of 323

(192. 3), and for the dittography of 83 the dislocation of 85 (219. 20). In both lists the same unit 27–8 appears.

I also gave examples where corruptions have been embedded in the text at a distance of 26, 27 (two exx.), 54, 82, 84, 85 letters.

All this evidence converges in the same direction, and appears to verify the conjecture that Σ contained marginalia, which represented omitted lines of this ancestor.

The second class of omissions (p. 369) shows the operation of a smaller unit. Thus we have 23, 47 (two exx.), also five cases of 63–7 letters, in the case of which more than one explanation was possible. In connexion with these omissions I mentioned various corruptions embedded in the text at a distance of 19, 20, 21, 22, 38, 42, 43 letters.

The same unit seems to appear in the list of dislocations. Thus we have five cases of 20–3, then there is a break until 28, so we have six cases of 41–7, followed by a break until 54, then thirteen cases of 62–9. The large number of examples between 60–70 suggests that another factor is at work, and in view of the four passages, where Σ omits 31–3 letters of Cicero's text, it appears likely that the immediate ancestor of Σ was a MS. very much like itself.

The conclusion appears to be that these remarkable dislocations were the result of a gradual process in which at least two, and probably three, units appear.

I now proceed to discuss some further evidence which throws light upon the pagination of one of these ancestors.

One of the most disturbed areas is 247. 8–248. 20. This falls into the following blocks :

247. 8-20 :	tabulas . . . possideret	(610)
20-3 :	more . . . vocabantur	(103)
23-7 :	alii . . . praebiturus	(236)
27-8 :	Terentius . . . tentatum ad-	(41)
248. 1-20 :	appellat . . . iudicii	(949)

The order in Σ is :

247. 27–8 :	Terentius . . . tentatum ad-	(41)
8–20 :	tabulas . . . possideret	(610)
23–7 :	alii . . . praebiturus	(236)
248. 1–20 :	appellat . . . iudicii	(949)
247. 20–3 :	more . . . vocabantur	(103)

Here $610+236+103=949$.

This is a very remarkable agreement. It appears that if 247. 8–20, 20–3, 23–7 are put into the right order, they contain exactly the same number of letters as 248. 1–20. The solution seems to be that the passage 247. 20–3 was accidentally omitted and then entered by error at the end of the following page. The transposition of 247. 27–8 *Terentius . . . tentatum ad-* seems due to a separate dislocation.

In order to make the point clear I write out the passage in the correct order:

(610) 247. 8–20: Tabulas cum conficeret. Quomodo ergo dicit Verrem tabulas non habere sed aliquo tempore cepisse non scribere? Haec ergo tempore rationis tabulas confectas habent. His expensum non ferres. Expensum ferre est scribere te pecuniam dedisse. Acceptum cur tu referrent. Accepisse a te se scriberent expensum talis se te ei scribere. Ut ex utroque genere. Summa divisionis et actionis praeturae urbanae et criminum C. Verris in duobus constituta iuri ditione et sartis tectis. Qui auspicato a Chelidone. Aves pascere dicuntur hi euntes magistratus et qui Chelidonis est hirundo urbem frequentat facete urbanam provinciam Chelidonis auspicio meretricis dicit esse susceptam. Neque census esset. Neque centum milia sestertium possideret

(103) 20–3: More veterum censi dicebantur qui centum milia in professione detulissent. Huius modi adeo facultates census vocabantur

(236) 23–7: Alii sic intelligunt. Neque census esset, hoc est neque census eius in quinquennium dives factus quorum annorum spatio instaurari census solet apud censores, quorum administratio per lustrum, hoc est quinquennium tenditur. Tamquam sciret quis vellet quidem se P. R. foret praebiturus

610 + 103 + 236 = 949.

After this comes the dislocated passage:

(41) Terentius, en non dico quasi non noris tentatum ad-

This is followed by:

(949) 248. 1–20: Appellat heredem. Iniuriosum verbum in personam praetoris, appellatio enim est inferioris ad potiorem. Cum intelligam legem Voconiam. Voconius legem tulerat ne quis census, hoc est pecuniosus, heredem relinqueret filium. Hoc ergo caput edicti est legem Voconiam probantis praetoris. Non improbum, non inofficiosum, non inhumanum. Haec enim testamenta non solent valere, nam improbum contra leges inofficiosum contra merita inhumanum contra pietatem. Sua sponte scelerata ac nefaria est. Beneficia sponte et non disputatione iuris consultorum sed naturali interpretatione fugienda sunt ut veneficium parricidium et cetera quae etiam nullo modo prohibente evitanda sunt

Cornelia testamentaria nummaria. Ut Cornelia testamentaria quae de moneta ne quis privatim pecuniam faceret. A certo tempore ut et quod semper reprehensum est tamen a certo tempore in iudicium veniat et a certo tempore plecti posset. Rata esse patietur. Hoc totum εν υποκρινη ut quasi per indignationem dici videatur et interrogative. Cedo mihi leges Atinias Furias Fusias. Istae omnes de iure civili sunt, nihil continent criminum capitalium publicique iudicii.

I write *praetoris* with Σ.

The largest figure in the dislocations is 1,941. If this is divided by 2, the result is 970. This is interesting in view of the evidence just adduced.

Perhaps the most singular corruption found in Σ is:

234. 24: Malleolo occiso. Oratorie pro mortuo occisum dixit.

244. 26–7: Occiso. Suspicioso verbo usus est, nam non institit ut probet a Verre occisum esse, sed ita vult videri, quia Verri mors eius lucro fuit. Alteram tutelae. Filii Malleoli tutor factus est Verres.

The scholia here have changed places in Σ. After *Malleolo occiso* Σ adds *suspicioso . . . Verres*, and after *Occiso* Σ adds *oratorie . . . dixit*. This is most remarkable.

The suspicion arises that *Malleolo occiso* and *Occiso* may have come at the beginning of two quaternions, and that confusion was caused thus. It is worth while to inquire whether there is any relation between 234. 24, 244. 26–7, and the passage 248. 1–20, *appellat . . . iudicii*, which appears to represent a page in an ancestor of Σ.

The best method of comparison is to take the *editio princeps*, in which the text is printed continuously, instead of being broken up into irregular lines, as in a modern edition.

In this 248. 1–20 occupies $16\frac{1}{2}$ lines. The passage 234. 24–244. 26, *Malleolo occiso . . . occiso*, occupies 263 lines. Here $16\frac{1}{2} \times 16 = 264$. No result could be more satisfactory. It appears that if a page in an ancestor of Σ, containing 949 letters, corresponds to $16\frac{1}{2}$ lines of the *editio princeps*, the passages *Malleolo occiso* and *Occiso* would be separated by an interval of 16 pages, i.e. one quaternion, in the same ancestor.

CHAPTER XII

THE MANUSCRIPTS OF PLATO

THE dialogues of Plato were at some ancient date arranged in tetralogies, i.e. collections of four dialogues without reference to their length. The traditional order, which is given by Diogenes Laertius iii. 58–61, is preserved by our MSS. He connects the arrangement with a person called Thrasylus. Recent writers generally attribute the tetralogies to Thrasylus, or Thrasyllus, and identify him with the well-known astrologer at the court of Tiberius. This identification rests on Schol. ad Juv. vii. 576: *Thrasillus multarum artium scientiam professus postremo se dedit Platonicae sectae ac deinde mathesi, in qua praecipue viguit apud Tiberium, cum quo sub honore eiusdem artis familiariter vixit.* It has been questioned by W. Christ, who points out that Varro, *Ling. Lat.* vii. 37, when referring to the *Phaedo*, says *Plato in quarto*, this being the place which it occupies in the first tetralogy.[1] If so, the arrangement goes back to an earlier date.

Our information comes from two sources, viz. Diogenes Laertius and Albinus, Εἰσαγωγή iv, p. 149. Diogenes says: Θρασύλος δέ φησι καὶ κατὰ τὴν τραγικὴν τετραλογίαν ἐκδοῦναι αὐτὸν τοὺς διαλόγους. He then quotes Thrasylus (φησί) as to the number of genuine dialogues and their order (πρώτην μὲν οὖν τετραλογίαν τίθησι). After giving the order he says, καὶ οὗτος μὲν οὕτω διαιρεῖ καί τινες. He then mentions a different order by trilogies, which he attributes to Aristophanes the grammarian.

Albinus says: οἱ μὲν ἀπὸ τῶν Ἐπιστολῶν ἄρχονται, οἱ δ' ἀπὸ τοῦ Θεάγους· εἰσὶ δὲ οἱ κατὰ τετραλογίαν διελόντες αὐτοὺς καὶ τάττουσι πρώτην τετραλογίαν περιέχουσαν τὸν Εὐθύφρονα . . . ταύτης τῆς δόξης εἰσὶ Δερκυλλίδης καὶ Θράσυλλος.

It will be seen that (1) Thrasylus attributes the arrangement to Plato himself; (2) Albinus associates Dercyllides, whom he puts

[1] *Platonische Studien* (1886), p. 3.

first, with Thrasylus, while Diogenes speaks of τινές as holding the same view. It looks, therefore, as if Thrasylus was one of several scholars who advocated an ancient arrangement, attributed to Plato. The identification with the astrologer is probably a guess of the Scholiast.

The MSS. to which the attention of scholars has been chiefly directed are as follows. I adopt the symbols used by Burnet (after Schanz), adding those used by Bekker and others.

A = Paris. 1807, cent. ix.

B = Bodl. Clark. 39, cent. ix (Bekker's 𝔄).

D = Venet. 185, cent. xii (Bekker's Π).

F = Vindob. 55, cent. xiv.

T = Venet. Append. Class. 4. 1, cent. xii (Bekker's 𝔱).

W = Vindob. 54, suppl. phil. Gr. 7, cent. xii (Stallbaum's Vind. 1).

A complete list of MSS. then known, 147 in number, is given by Wohlrab with bibliographical details.[1]

B contains *Tetr.* i–vi and *A* has *Tetr.* viii–ix. Between them, therefore, they contain all the Platonic corpus, except *Tetr.* vii (*Hippias Ma.*, *Hippias Min.*, *Io*, *Menexenus*). At the end of the *Menexenus* *T* and some inferior MSS. have the note, τέλος τοῦ α' βιβλίου. It has been inferred that at one time the corpus was divided into two volumes, consisting of *Tetr.* i–vii and viii–ix. The two last tetralogies include the *Republic* and the *Laws*, and are therefore unusually long.

It is possible that *B* has lost *Tetr.* vii. The first dialogue in *A*, the *Clitopho*, has the number 29. It has been inferred that there was once a previous volume containing 1–28 (*Tetr.* i–vii). This seems quite likely. It has also been suggested that *B* is similarly imperfect, having lost vol. ii.

The tendency at one time was to look on *A* and *B* as the sole sources of information. Cobet says of the other MSS., *vile damnum, si omnes ad unum flammis comburerentur.*[2] He thus states the theory of the 'one best MS.', which was fashionable in the middle of the last century, but is now gravely discredited. Schanz, who

[1] *Jahrb. f. kl. Phil.*, Suppl. xv (1887), pp. 666–726. Immisch adds Paris. Suppl. Grec. 668, cent. xi.

[2] *Mnem.* ix (1860), p. 337.

started by expressing approval of Cobet's position, showed that *T* was independent of *B* in *Tetr.* i–vi, and *D* of *A* in the *Republic.* He met this difficulty, however, by supposing that *T* represented a missing volume of *A*, and *D* a missing volume of *B*.

Of late years the tendency has been to look for MSS. which contain traces of an 'unrevised text' and appear to be independent of *A* and *B*. The chief of these are *F* and *W*.

We have now to consider two sources of evidence which militate against the theory of Cobet. The first is supplied by ancient citations which go back to an earlier period than any of our MSS. The quotations of Stobaeus, Eusebius, and others show that their texts frequently agree with *F*, *W*, and inferior MSS. as against *A* and *B*. Also, they preserve passages omitted by all our MSS., e.g. *Alcib.* i, 115 e, 128 a, 133 c. The second source of evidence is to be found in the papyri. These exhibit an eclectic text and frequently contain marginalia, which reappear in late MSS. Their agreements extend impartially to both families, but they support *W* or *F* quite as frequently as *A* or *B*. Some interesting remarks are made by the editors of the Oxyrhynchus papyri. Thus of Ox. 843 (*Symposium*), cent. ii/iii, we are told: 'The text, as so often with papyri, is of an eclectic character, showing a decided affinity with no single MS. Compared with the three principal witnesses for the *Symposium* it agrees now with *B* against *TW*, now with the two latter as against the former, rarely with *T* against *BW* or with *W* against *BT*.' The editors remark: 'In many cases the papyrus once more proves the antiquity of readings which modern criticism rejects or suspects.'

Other interesting papyri are Ox. 1016 and 1017 (*Phaedrus*). We are told of 1016 that 'as between the two principal MSS., *B* and *T*, the papyrus shows, as usual, little preference, agreeing first with one and then with the other.' In 1017 there are a number of variants given in the margin. The most interesting of these is 240 b ἡδίστοισιν (so *B*), while the text has ἡδίστοις with *T* and Stobaeus. In connexion with this we may mention *Phaedo* 68 b, where the Petrie papyrus supports the reading ἄλλοθι δυνατὸν εἶναι καθαρῶς, which B^1 adds in the margin with the sign γρ. (Cf. p. 399.)

The evidence of the papyri, therefore, utterly routs the theory of Cobet.

The versions of Plato also deserve notice. Mr. F. C. Conybeare discovered and published collations of an Armenian version of the *Laws*, also of some other dialogues.[1] He attributes the translation of the *Laws* to Gregory Magistros, early in cent. xi. It is, therefore, later than some of our MSS., and, as I show later on, there is a remarkable agreement between it and one existing MS. (Ω). Burnet notices that the text of the *Euthyphro*, *Crito*, and *Apology* used by the translator was very like that of *W*. The version of the *Laws* omits freely. Conybeare records a few cases only, saying: 'Of lacunae in the Armenian text, the frequency of which accuses the translator of great want of care, I take no notice, unless some other authority exhibits them, or unless there is antecedent probability in their favour.' A full list would be very interesting and might throw light on the formation of the translator's text, such as is given by *Syr. Sin* in the case of the Gospels.[2]

Immisch considers that the Sicilian translator, Aristippus, cent. xii, also used an eclectic text,[3] but Burnet holds that his MS. resembled *W*.

I now proceed to discuss the various MSS. In the passages which I quote a change of speakers is denoted by a colon, according to the practice of papyri and MSS. For this I allow one letter in the figures which I give. I also use *iota* adscript with the MSS. The papyri vary in this respect.

I take first *A*, although it contains *Tetr.* viii–ix, since the question is less complicated than in the case of *B*, which contains *Tetr.* i–vi. For the characteristics of *A* I refer to a valuable paper of Mr. T. W. Allen in 'A group of ninth-century Greek MSS.'[4] He considers Paris. 1962, Heidelb. Palat. 398, Ven. 246 to be written by the same scribe as *A*,[5] and mentions six other MSS. proceeding from the same scriptorium.

A facsimile of *A*, with a preface by M. Omont, has been published by the authorities of the *Bibliothèque Nationale*. It consists of 43 quaternions, and is written in two columns with 44 lines to the page. I have counted the letters on f. 201^r, with the result: col. i = 1022, col. ii = 980 letters. The average for col. i is slightly

[1] *Am. J. Phil.* xii, xiv, xv, xvi.

[2] *Primitive Text*, pp. 36–41.

[3] *Studien*, p. 34.

[4] *J. Phil.* xxi (1893), pp. 47–54. Cf. *Mélanges Graux*, p. 527.

[5] D. Serruys, *Rev. Phil.* xxxviii. 3. 14, adds Paris. Suppl. Grec. 921.

over 23 letters, and for col. ii slightly over 22. The limits of variation are (18) 1 ex., (19) 1 ex., and (26) 6 exx.

A number of corrections in *A* come from a contemporary διορθωτής. The script resembles closely that of the scribe, and editors are disposed to identify the hands. There are also a number of corrections in a hand ascribed to the twelfth century. The supplements in *Leg.* 745 a–c, 783 b–d, and the numerous additions in the Ὅροι proceed from this writer. On f. 344ᵛ there is a colophon, ὠρθώθη ἡ βίβλος αὕτη ὑπὸ Κωνσταντίνου μητροπολίτου Ἱεραπόλεως τοῦ καὶ ὠνησαμένου, written in a fourteenth-century hand.

For the purposes of this inquiry the corrections of the διορθωτής are of great importance, since they may have been taken from the model. Those which proceed from the twelfth-century hand (A^3) are taken from another source, and may therefore be disregarded; so also corrections of Constantine and other writers of later date.

The subject of telescoped passages in this MS. demands a few words. I take as an example *Leg.* 849 d (f. 241ʳ) τοῖς ξένοις καθ' ὅσον ἂν βούληται καὶ ὁπόταν βούληται. Here A^1 has

ξένοις καθόσον ἂν βούλη
ται

The words καὶ ὁπόταν βούληται are omitted. The twelfth-century corrector (A^3), instead of adding καὶ ὁπόταν βούληται after βούληται, prefers to add -ται καὶ ὁπόταν βούλη- after βούλη. So 920 b (f. 270ᵛ) τοὺς δὲ μὴ τοιούτους ἐπιτηδεύματά τε ἐπιτηδεύοντας. A^1 gives:

δὲ μὴ τοιούτους ἐπιτηδεύ
οντας

A^3, instead of adding ἐπιτηδεύματά τε after τοιούτους, adds -ματά τε ἐπιτηδεύ- after ἐπιτηδεύ. Here it is obvious that we are dealing with a mannerism on the part of A^3, who affected this method of correction. We have no reason to look on the passages as telescoped.

I wish to speak with caution about some of the additions made by the διορθωτής. I take as an example *Tim.* 58 e καὶ διαλύοντος αὐτὸ τὴν ὁμαλότητα ἀποβάλλει, ταύτην δὲ ἀπολέσαν. Here A^1 wrote (f. 130ʳ)

καὶ διαλύον
τος αὐτὸ τὴν ὁμαλότητα ἀ
πολέσαν

Instead of adding ἀποβάλλει ταύτην δὲ after ὁμαλότητα, the διορθωτής adds -ποβάλλει ταύτην δὲ ἀ- in the margin after ἀ.

It is possible that he also preferred this method of correction. In dealing with these passages I have thought it best to mark as telescoped, subject to this reservation, passages corrected by the διορθωτής, but to treat those filled up by A^3 as simple omissions.

I now give a list of omissions, affixing *corr.* to those filled up by the διορθωτής and disregarding additions of A^3. I reserve for separate treatment the omissions of *A* in the Ὅροι, as they present some peculiar features.

(10) *Critias* 116 d : καὶ ἀργύρωι *F*: *om. A*
Epp. 337 b : καὶ ἀγαθούς *om. A*
346 a : ὁ δὲ οὐδέν με *om. A*
350 b : ἤγγελλον τά *om.* A^1 (*corr.*)
(11) *Leg.* 903 d : προσηκούσης *om. A*
907 c : * σφοδρότερον *om. A*
949 e : ἢ πομπεύσεων *om. A*
(12) *Leg.* 812 e : καὶ ἀντίφωνον *om. A*
896 c : καὶ βουλήσεις *om. A*
(13) *Epp.* 322 b : ἀλλ' οἰκουμένας *om. A*
Leg. 732 a : τε καὶ αὑτῶι ἐάν *om.* A^1 (*corr.*)
842 a : τε καὶ οὐκ ὀρθῶς *om. A*
941 a : ἕληι ὡς ἰασίμωι *om. A*
Rep. 381 a : καὶ ἀμφιέσματα *om. A*
400 d : καὶ ἀνάρμοστον *om. A*
Tim. 68 e : καὶ τὸ μὲν θεῖον *om.* A^1 (*corr.*)
(14) *Epp.* 322 e : τούτων προσδεῖν *om. A*
328 b : καὶ ὑπακουστέον *om. A*
Leg. 773 c : καὶ βραδυτέρους *om. A*
920 b : ἐπιτηδεύματά τε *om. A*
c : τὰ δὲ ἀγρονόμους *om. A*
Rep. 328 d : *ὡς παρὰ φίλους τε *om.* A^1 (*corr.*)
366 a : αὖ μέγα δύνανται *om. A*
374 b : ἀλλὰ σκυτοτόμον *D*: *om. AF*
379 a : ἐάντε ἐν μέλεσιν *om. A*
(15) *Epp.* 314 a : καὶ ἀεὶ ἀκουόμενα *om. A*
Leg. 639 c : ** ἢ μετὰ κακῶν ἄρχον- *om.* A^1 (*corr.*)
716 a : καί κεκοσμημένος *om.* A^1 (*corr.*)
847 b : ὁ κτείνας ἐφ' οἷς τε *om. A*
877 e : ἧι κειμένη ἢ καὶ ἐν *om. A*
954 d : * τοῦ λοιποῦ χρόνου *om. A*
Rep. 364 a : τε καὶ δικαιοσύνη *om. A*
373 e : καὶ τὴν ποικιλίαν *om. A*

(16) *Leg.* 626 b : οὔτ' ἐπιτηδευμάτων *om.* A^1 (*corr.*)
778 e : τὰ δὲ ταφρεύσοντας *om.* *A*
925 e : νομοθέτου καὶ ὑπὲρ *om.* *A*
(17) *Leg.* 669 c : καὶ μέλος ἀποδοῦναι *om.* A^1 (*corr.*)
705 b : πολυφόρος τε εἴη καί *om.* A^1 (*corr.*)
829 a : μήθ' ἑαυτοὺς ἀδικεῖν *om.* A^1 (*corr.*)
849 a : ἀγορανόμους τὰ περί[1] *om.* *A*
d : καὶ ὁπόταν βούληται *om.* *A*
937 d : ὁπότερος δ' ἂν κριθῆι *om.* *A*
Min. 314 a : ὅτι αἰσθήσει ταύτηι *om.* A^1 (*corr.*)
Rep. 358 a : ἀδικία δ' ἐπαινεῖται *om.* *A*
360 a : * τῶν παρὰ τὸν βασιλέα *om.* A^1 (*corr.*)
382 e : οὔτε κατὰ φαντασίας *om.* *A*
Tim. 58 e : ** -ποβάλλει ταύτην δὲ ἀ- *om.* A^1 (*corr.*)
(18) *Epp.* 347 c : παρ' αὐτὸν γράμματα τά *om.* *A*
Leg. 668 d : ** τὸ τοιόνδε οἷον τοὺς ἀ- *om.* A^1 (*corr.*)
708 c : τε καὶ νομοθετεῖσθαι *om.* *A*
731 c : ** -τον ἐν οὖν τῶι τιμιωτά- *om.* A^1 (*corr.*)
Rep. 386 c : * ὧι μὴ βίοτος πολὺς εἴη *om.* *A*
400 a : ** -μι ποῖα δὲ ὁποίου βίου *om.* *A*
(19) *Rep.* 373 e : * καὶ ἰδίαι καὶ δημοσίαι *om.* A^1 (*corr.*)
(21) *Leg.* 874 b : ** -τος δὴ νόμος εἷς ἡμῖν ἔστω *om.* *A*
Tim. 47 a : καὶ ἰσημερίαι καὶ τροπαί *F* : *om.* *A Y*
(22) *Leg.* 841 c : γίγνοιτο ἐν πάσαις πόλεσι *om.* *A*
868 e : ἢ ἀδελφὴ ἀδελφὸν ἢ ἀδελφήν *om.* *A*
(25) *Leg.* 902 e : τ' ἐπιμελεῖσθαι καὶ δυνάμενον *om.* *A*
(28) *Leg.* 903 c : μὴν ἕνεκα ὅλου καὶ οὐχ ὅλον μέρους *om.* A^1 (*corr.*)
913 d : ἐὰν δὲ τῆς ἄλλης χώρας ἀγρονόμοις *om.* *A*
(29) *Epp.* 312 a : ἐθέλειν ἑτέρους δὲ μεταπέμψασθαι *om.* *A*
Leg. 861 c : * καὶ τὸ μή : καλῶς ἡμῖν φαίνηι λέγειν *om.* *A*
Min. 313 c : καὶ ἄλλο μὲν ὄψις, ἄλλο δὲ τὰ ὁρώμενα *om.* *A*
(30) *Leg.* 925 e : γαμεῖν ἢ γαμεῖσθαι γίγνηται· τούτων *om.* *A*
Rep. 380 e : καὶ κινεῖται οἷον σῶμα ὑπὸ σιτίων τε *om.* A^1 (*corr.*)
(35) *Leg.* 764 c : παιδείας αὐτῶν ἕνεκα, τοὺς δὲ ἀγωνιστικῆς *om.* *A*
(36) *Leg.* 684 d : τῶν τοιούτων τι πᾶς ἀπαντᾶι λέγων μὴ κινεῖν *om.* A^1 (*corr.*)
(37) *Rep.* 376 d : * ἵνα μὴ ἐῶμεν ἱκανὸν λόγον ἢ συχνὸν διεξίωμεν *om.* A^1 (*corr.*)
379 b : μὴ βλάπτει κακόν τι ποιεῖ : οὐδὲ τοῦτο : ὅ δέ γε *om.* A^1 (*corr.*)
(39) *Rep.* 601 a : * αὐτὸν οὐκ ἐπαΐοντα ἀλλὰ μιμεῖσθαι ὥστε ἐν τοῖς[2] *om.* A^1 (*corr.*)
(40) *Leg.* 822 b : μὲν ὡς βραδύτατον, τὸν δὲ βραδύτατον ὡς τάχιστον *om.* *A*
(41) *Rep.* 504 d : * ἢ γυμναζομένωι ἢ ὃ νῦν δὴ ἐλέγομεν τοῦ μεγίστου τε *om.* *A*
(44) *Rep.* 493 d : εἴτε δὴ ἐν πολιτικῆι ὅτι μὲν γὰρ ἄν τις τούτοις ὁμιλῆι *om.* A^1 (*corr.*)
(46) *Rep.* 443 d : * αὐτὸν αὑτοῦ καὶ κοσμήσαντα καὶ φίλον γενόμενον ἑαυτῶι *om.* *A*

[1] *A* has here been doctored by altering δὴ ἀγοράν to δι' ἀγοράν.
[2] So the corrector : ὥστε ἑτέροις *FD*.

Rep. 609 b: * ψυχῆι ἆρ' οὐκ ἔστιν ὃ ποιεῖ αὐτὴν κακήν: καὶ μάλα ἔφη· ἃ νῦν *om.* A¹ (*corr.*)

(48) *Rep.* 556 e: ἔξωθεν ἐπαγομένων ἢ τῶν ἑτέρων ἐξ ὀλιγαρχουμένης πόλεως *om.* A¹ (*corr.*)

601 a: ἐν μέτρωι καὶ ῥυθμῶι καὶ ἁρμονίαι πάνυ εὖ δοκεῖν λέγεσθαι *om.* A¹ (*corr.*)

(51) *Rep.* 528 c: * οὐκ ἂν πείθοιντο οἱ περὶ ταῦτα ζητητικοὶ μεγαλοφρονούμενοι *om.* A¹ (*corr.*)

(213) *Critias* 111 e–112 a: πρῶτον μὲν τὸ τῆς ἀκροπόλεως εἶχε τότε οὐχ ὡς τὰ νῦν ἔχει· νῦν μὲν γὰρ μία γενομένη νὺξ ὑγρὰ διαφερόντως γῆς αὐτὴν ψιλὴν περιτήξασα πεποίηκε, σεισμῶν ἅμα καὶ πρὸ τῆς ἐπὶ Δευκαλίωνος φθορᾶς τρίτου πρότερον ὕδατος ἐξαισίου γενομένου. τὸ δὲ πρὶν ἐν ἑτέρωι χρόνωι *om.* A

(700) *Leg.* 783 b–d: * παίδων δὲ δὴ γένεσιν μετὰ τοὺς γάμους θῶμεν, καὶ μετὰ γένεσιν τροφὴν καὶ παιδείαν. καὶ τάχ' ἂν οὕτω προϊόντων τῶν λόγων ὅ τε νόμος ἡμῖν ἕκαστος περαίνοιτο εἰς τοὔμπροσθεν ἐπὶ συσσίτια ἡνίκα ἀφικόμεθα—τὰς τοιαύτας κοινωνίας εἴτε ἄρα γυναικῶν εἴτε ἀνδρῶν δεῖ μόνων γίγνεσθαι, προσμίξαντες αὐτοῖς ἐγγύθεν ἴσως μᾶλλον κατοψόμεθα—τά τε ἐπίπροσθεν αὐτῶν, ἔτι νῦν ὄντα ἀνομοθέτητα, τάξαντες αὐτά, ἐπίπροσθεν ποιησόμεθα, καὶ ὅπερ ἐρρήθη νῦν δή, κατοψόμεθά τε αὐτὰ ἀκριβέστερον, μᾶλλόν τε τοὺς προσήκοντας αὐτοῖς καὶ πρέποντας νόμους ἂν θείημεν: ὀρθότατα λέγεις: φυλάξωμεν τοίνυν τῆι μνήμηι τὰ νῦν δὴ λεχθέντα. ἴσως γὰρ χρείαν ποτ' αὐτῶν πάντων ἕξομεν: τὰ ποῖα δὴ διακελεύηι: ἃ τοῖς τρισὶ διωριζόμεθα ῥήμασι. βρῶσιν μὲν ἐλέγομέν που καὶ δεύτερον πόσιν, καὶ ἀφροδισίων δέ τινα διαπτόησιν τρίτον: πάντως, ὦ ξένε, μεμνησόμεθά που ὧν τὰ νῦν διακελεύηι: καλῶς[1] *om.* A

(717) *Leg.* 745 a–c: * θεοῖς ἀπονέμων εὐδόκιμός τε καὶ ἀζήμιος ἂν εἴη· ἐὰν δέ τις ἀπειθῆι τούτωι τῶι νόμωι, φανεῖ μὲν ὁ βουλόμενος ἐπὶ τοῖς ἡμίσεσιν, ὁ δὲ ὀφλὼν ἄλλο τοσοῦτον μέρος ἀποτίσει τῆς αὑτοῦ κτήσεως τὰ δ' ἡμίσεα τῶν θεῶν· ἡ δὲ κτῆσις χωρὶς τοῦ κλήρου πάντων πᾶσα ἐν τῶι φανερῶι γεγράφθω παρὰ φύλαξιν ἄρχουσιν, οἷς ἂν ὁ νόμος προστάξηι, ὅπως ἂν αἱ δίκαι περὶ πάντων, ὅσαι εἰς χρήματα, ῥάιδιαί τε ὦσι καὶ σφόδρα σαφεῖς. τὸ δὴ μετὰ τοῦτο πρῶτον μὲν τὴν πόλιν ἱδρῦσθαι δεῖ τῆς χώρας ὅτι μάλιστα ἐν μέσωι, καὶ τἆλλα ὅσα πρόσφορα πόλει τῶν ὑπαρχόντων ἔχοντα τόπον ἐκλεξάμενον, ἃ νοῆσαί τε καὶ εἰπεῖν οὐδὲν χαλεπόν. μετὰ δὲ ταῦτα μέρη δώδεκα διελέσθαι, θέμενον Ἑστίας πρῶτον καὶ Διὸς καὶ Ἀθηνᾶς ἱερόν, ἀκρόπολιν ὀνομάζοντα, κύκλον περιβάλλοντα, ἀφ' οὗ τὰ δώδεκα μέρη τέμνειν τήν τε πόλιν αὐτὴν καὶ πᾶσαν τὴν χώραν· ἴσα δὲ δεῖ γίγνεσθαι τὰ δώδεκα μέρη τῶι τὰ μὲν ἀγαθῆς γῆς εἶναι σμικρά, τὰ δὲ χείρονος μείζω. κλήρους *om.* A

It will be seen that six passages of 15–21 letters are marked as telescoped. Schanz, who has anticipated the conclusions at which I arrived, draws especial attention to *Leg.* 668 d λέγω δὲ τὸ τοιόνδε, οἷον τοὺς ἀριθμοὺς τοῦ σώματος καὶ ἑκάστων.

[1] I here give Burnet's text. There are some minute differences, and the supplement of A³ seems corrupt in places.

A[1] (f. 171ᵛ) has:

λέγω δὲ
ριθμοὺς τοῦ σώματος καὶ ἑ
κάστων

The diorthotes adds in the margin (after λέγω δὲ):

τὸ τοιόνδε οἷον τοὺς ἀ

This implies in the model:

λέγω δὲ
τὸ τοιόνδε οἷον τοὺς ἀ (18)
ριθμοὺς

Schanz says: '*die Auslassung lässt sich kaum anders als durch Ueberspringen einer Zeile erklären.*'

An equally important passage is *Rep.* 400 a τεθεαμένος ἂν εἴποιμι· ποῖα δὲ ὁποίου βίου μιμήματα, λέγειν οὐκ ἔχω. *A* here gives τεθεαμένος ἂν εἴποι μιμήματα *med. om.* This indicates in the model:

τεθεαμένος ἂν εἴποι
μι ποῖα δὲ ὁποίου βίου (18)
μιμήματα

I have already mentioned (p. 387) that the omissions of *A*[1] in *Leg.* 639 c (15), *Tim.* 58 e (17), *Leg.* 731 c (18), admit of another explanation, but in view of these passages I think it most probable that there also lines have been omitted. The case of *Leg.* 731 c is especially interesting. *A* has in the last line of col. i, f. 195ʳ:

ληθεῖαι γέ ἐστιν πᾶσιν τιμιώτα

Col. ii begins with

τωι τὸ μέγιστον κακὸν οὐ

The diorthotes adds as an extra line at the foot of col. i:

τον ἐν οὖν τῶι τιμιωτά (18)

It seems probable that the writer lost his place when beginning a fresh column and omitted a line of his copy.

The example of 21 in *Leg.* 874 b requires some explanation. *A* has (f. 252ʳ):

ἐκβληθησό
μενον ἄταφον οὗ κυρίως κεί
μενος

A long variant is added at the top of the page by *A*[3] (cent. xii), preceded by the note ἐν ἄλλῳ οὕτως εὗρον, in which the passage is completed by -τος δὴ νόμος εἷς ἡμῖν ἔστω, after οὗ. This indicates:

οὗ
τος δὴ νόμος εἷς ἡμῖν ἔστω (21)
κυρίως κείμενος

The unit here is slightly longer than in the other examples.

Schanz[1] calls attention to the large number of omissions of similar length: '*sind es Weglassungen von* 15, 16, 17, 18, 19 *Buchstaben*'. The favourite number is 17.

The three omissions of 36 letters, all of which are supplied by the διορθωτής, are of special interest. It is also to be noted that he has remedied the omission of 51 (= 17 × 3) and the two cases of 48. The evidence seems to show that the unit varied a good deal, probably in different columns.

Burnet only quotes *F* for the passage of 213 letters omitted by *A* in *Critias* 111 e–112 a. A reference to Bekker's apparatus, however, shows that the omission is peculiar to *A*. We may note that 212 ÷ 4 = 53.

The striking resemblance between the two largest numbers 700, 717 has been noticed by Schanz,[2] who suggests that in each case *A* has omitted a column of the model. If we take the average between them and allow 17 for the average length of line, this would give about 42 lines to the page (17 × 42 = 714). He concludes that the formation of the model resembled that of *A*: '*so hat der Schreiber des Paris. auch in der Höhe sein Exemplar der Vorlage angepasst, denn auch hier bedingt der verschiedene Character der Schrift in Paris. A das kleine Plus.*' This explanation may be right, but in my experience omission of columns is less common than that of folios, and it is possible that folios of a remote ancestor have been lost.

The two passages each occupy 18 lines in Stallbaum's text.[3] The intervening space between them occupies 808 lines, to which must be added something for the title to Bk. vi. We may note that 18 × 45 = 810. There is an interval of 45 columns, or folios, between the omissions.

[1] *Rhein. Mus.* xxxiii (1878), p. 305.

[2] Schanz gives them as 674 and 699. (*Rhein. Mus.* xxxiii, p. 306.)

[3] Ed. Lips. stereotypa.

Before I quit *A*, I must draw attention to an interesting passage, *Tim.* 66 b–c. In *A*, f. 133ʳ, col. 2 ends with:

τὸ δὲ
τούτων αἴτιον τῶν παθημά
των ὀξὺ προσρηθῆναι ξύμ
πασι δὲ τοῖς περὶ ταῦτα

F. 133ᵛ, col. 1 continues:

εἰρημένοις πάθος ἐναντίον
ἀπ' ἐναντίας ἐστὶ προφάσε
ως ὁπόταν ἡ τῶν εἰσιόντων
ξύστασις ἐν ὑγροῖς οἰκεία τῆι
τῆς γλώσσης ἕξει πεφυκυῖ
α λεαίνηι μὲν ἐπαλείφου
σα τὰ τραχυνθέντα τὰ δὲ
παρὰ φύσιν ξυνεστῶτα ἢ κε
χυμένα τὰ μὲν ξυνάγηι τὰ
δὲ χαλᾶι καὶ πᾶν

The διορθωτής adds in the margin, with a reference mark for insertion after χαλᾷ καὶ πᾶν, the words δὲ τούτων τῶν παθημάτων ὀξὺ προσρηθῆναι (34). This is a variant (*om.* αἴτιον) for the words which occur at the beginning of the passage. The variant may have been already out of place in the model or may have been inserted in the wrong place by the διορθωτής. We may notice that the intervening passage ξύμπασι δὲ . . . χαλᾶι καὶ πᾶν consists of 226 letters (17 × 13 = 221). The relation of this to 34 (17 × 2) suggests that the model was preceded by a MS. in similar formation.

Another error which must go back to the model occurs in *Epp.* 311 d–e.

εἰ ἐξείη αὐτοῖς ἐπανορθώσασθαι τὰς αὐτῶν συνουσίας πάνυ ἂν σπουδάσαι ὥστε βελτίω λέγεσθαι περὶ αὐτῶν ἢ νῦν. τοῦτο οὖν ἡμῖν ἔτι, σὺν θεῷ εἰπεῖν, ἔξεστιν, εἴ τι ἄρα μὴ καλῶς πέπρακται κατὰ τὴν ἔμπροσθεν συνουσίαν ἐπανορθώσασθαι καὶ ἔργῳ καὶ λόγῳ· περὶ γὰρ φιλοσοφίαν φημὶ ἐγὼ τὴν ἀληθινὴν δόξαν ἔσεσθαι

A here has a dislocation. The words τὰς αὐτῶν συνουσίας . . . ἐπανορθώσασθαι are placed after καὶ ἔργῳ . . . δόξαν ἔσεσθαι (63). They appear to have been omitted by the model and inserted in the wrong place by *A*. The correct order is given by the twelfth-century corrector (A^3), with some variants, and the note ἐν ἄλλῳ οὕτως εὗρον.

I now turn to the Ὅροι, which exhibit a remarkable series of omissions differing in character from those found elsewhere in *A*. Most of them have been supplied by *A*³ (cent. xii), but these additions are obviously taken from another source.

(11) 414 d: συγκείμενος *om. A*
(13) 414 e: καλὸν τὸ ἀγαθόν *om. A*
(25) 412 c: ὑπομονὴ πόνων ἕνεκα τοῦ καλοῦ *om. A*
415 a: κατὰ διάνοιαν ἀποτελούμενον *om. A*
(30) 415 e: ** -ληξις φόβος ἐπὶ προσδοκίαι κακοῦ κο- *om. A*
(31) 412 e: * χάριτος σχέσις· μνήμη μετ' εὐεργεσίας *om. A*
(37) 416 a: * παίδευσις παιδείας παράδοσις: νομοθετική *om. A*
(45) 412 c: * καταλαβὴ ἑκουσία τοῦ βελτίστου· εὐλάβεια ὀρθοῦ ψόγου *om. A*
(57) 412 d: * ἕξις πρὸς τὸ χρηματίζεσθαι ὡς δεῖ· πρόσθεσις καὶ κτῆσις οὐσίας ὡς χρή *om. A*
(73) 411 d: * διάθεσις καθ' ἣν τὸ ἔχον διακείμενον τελείως σπουδαῖον λέγεται. ἕξις ποιητικὴ εὐνομίας *om. A*
(116) 411 e: * αὐτοπραγία κατὰ φύσιν· εὐταξία ψυχῆς. λογιστικὴ ὁμιλία ψυχῆς περὶ καλῶν καὶ αἰσχρῶν. ἕξις καθ' ἣν ὁ ἔχων αἱρετικός ἐστι καὶ εὐλαβητικὸς ὧν χρή *om. A*
(128) 412 a: * ἠρεμία ψυχῆς περὶ τὰ δεινὰ καὶ θαρσαλέα κατὰ τὸν ὀρθὸν λόγον φαινόμενα. σωτηρία δογμάτων ἀδήλων περὶ τὰ δεινὰ καὶ ἐμπειρία πολέμου. ἕξις ἐμμενητικὴ νόμου *om. A*

The telescoped passage (30) is striking. F. 324ʳ, col. ii, ends:

τά
ξεως ψυχῆς ἀλογίστου ἐκπ [1]

The verso begins with

λακεία· ὁμιλία ἡ πρὸς ἡδο
νήν

The writer of *A* lost his place after turning over the page.

It is to be noticed that none of the larger omissions are to be explained by ὁμ. The hypothesis of accident is out of the question. We are here dealing with deliberate interpolation or deliberate abridgement. Here the numerical test is decisive. If there is no relation between the figures, the probability is in favour of interpolation. If, however, there is a numerical relation between the passages omitted and those retained, it appears more probable that

[1] The method of division is odd, but the π seems to be original. The twelfth-century corrector adds λη in mg., ξις φόβος ἐπὶ προσδοκίαι κακοῦ as an extra line, and κο- before λακεία on the verso.

an abbreviator has been at work, his method being, so far as possible, to cut out lines of his text.

The two longest omissions, 116 and 128, are in close proximity to each other (411 e–412 a). The intermediate words *ἀνδρεία ἕξις . . . πρὸς ἀρετήν* contain 253 letters. Here 128 × 2 = 256. This is somewhat striking. I now exhibit the whole of this troubled zone, 411 d–412 e, marking with an asterisk passages omitted by *A*.

* διάθεσις καθ' ἣν . . . εὐνομίας	(73)
φρόνησις δύναμις . . . ἄρχεσθαι	(514)
* αὐτοπραγία . . . ὧν χρή	(116)
ἀνδρεία ἕξις . . . πρὸς ἀρετήν	(253)
* ἠρεμία ψυχῆς . . . ἐμμενητικὴ νόμου	(128)
ἐγκράτεια . . . λύπης ἕνεκα τοῦ καλοῦ	(311)
* ὑπομονὴ . . . τοῦ καλοῦ	(25)
θάρσος . . . βέλτιστον φανέν	(226)
* καταλαβὴ . . . ὀρθοῦ ψόγου	(45)
ἐλευθερία . . . ἐλευθεριότης	(111)
* ἕξις πρὸς . . . ὡς χρή	(57)
πρᾳότης . . . εὐεργετικὴ ἀνθρώπων	(578)
* χάριτος . . . εὐεργεσίας	(31)

A glance at these figures shows some curious relations. Thus 73 is followed by 514 (73 × 7 = 511), 253 is followed by 128 (128 × 2 = 256), 25 by 226 (25 × 9 = 225), 57 is preceded by 111 and followed by 578. I now place them in order of magnitude:

25, 31, 45, 57, 73, 111, 116, 128, 226, 253, 311, 514, 578.

The following multiples of 25 are illuminating: 25 × 3 = 75, 25 × 5 = 125, 25 × 9 = 225, 25 × 10 = 250, 25 × 23 = 575.

The next number to 25 is 31. In view of the telescoped passage of 30 in 415 e we must allow considerable variety in the unit. If the average is 25, there must have been lower numbers. It is therefore possible that 45 may equal two lines.

The conclusion therefore is that *A* gives a 'shorter text' in the Ὅροι, the result of abridgement, and that it comes from a different source, with longer lines than those found in the model of *A* (average 25, as against average 17).

I now turn to a MS. which has had a somewhat romantic history. Bekker in his Apparatus gives readings from a Vatican MS. no. 796, which he terms Ω. At that time (1811) it was in Paris among other

Italian MSS. brought there by Napoleon. Peipers,[1] using Bekker's collation, was of opinion that a number of MSS. were derived from Ω. Jordan showed that Ω was itself derived from *A*, the proof being that omissions of Ω occupy lines of *A*.[2] The MS. itself, however, could not be found in the Vatican. Schanz says: '*ist in der Vaticana unter dieser Nr. nicht bekannt*'. Burnet, who calls it *O*, and uses it in *Tetr.* ix, calls it cod. Vaticanus 796 (?). He does not refer to Jordan's theory of its derivation from *A*.

In Cavalieri and Lietzmann's *Specimina Codicum Graecorum Vaticanorum*, Plate 9 reproduces a page from this MS., which in the Introduction (p. vii) is called '*Vat. Gr.* I (*olim* 796) saecl. ix/x'. It has, therefore, come to light again.[3] The striking point is that instead of being a comparatively late MS., as Jordan supposed, it turns out to be the oldest known MS. of Plato after *A* and *B*. It has 40 lines to the page.

I now add Jordan's proofs that Ω (*O*) is derived from *A*. I have corrected some of his statements by the help of the facsimile of *A*, and have added some examples which I have myself noticed when looking through Bekker's variants. I have to thank the Rev. H. M. Bannister for verifying the readings of Vat. I in some passages where I was in doubt. The references which I give are to the folios of *A*.

(*a*) Ω omits complete lines of *A*:

(20) *Epp.* 354 c (f. 318ʳ): ἡ τοῖς ἀνθρώποις θεὸς δέ
(22) *Leg.* 902 e (f. 263ᵛ): φασὶν οἱ λιθολόγοι λίθους
(25) *Leg.* 862 e (f. 246ᵛ): τε αὐτοῖς ἔτι ζῆν ἄμεινον τούς

(*b*) Ω passes from one line of *A* to another. I enclose in brackets the passages omitted by Ω:

(19) *Leg.* 922 c (f. 271ᵛ):

ἡ
γώμεθα τελευτᾶν: [πῶς τοῦ
το ὦ ξένε λέγεις] χαλεπόν

924 c (f. 272ʳ):

κατ' ἐνιαυτὸν [τρεῖς καὶ κα
τ' ἐνιαυτὸν] ἄλλον ἕτεροι τρεῖς

[1] *Quaestiones de legibus Platon.*, p. 39.

[2] *Hermes* xii (1877), pp. 161–72.

[3] A note in Ω states that its place in the library was changed by Mai. A description of the MS. is given by Rabe in *Rhein. Mus.* lxiii (1908), pp. 235–8.

(20) *Leg.* 705 e (f. 185ʳ):

νό
μον [ὀρθῶς ὑποτίθεμαι μό
νον]

This is a striking case.

(21) *Leg.* 844 e (f. 239ʳ):

ἐκ τῶν ἑαυτοῦ δρέπῃ [ἐὰν δ' ἐκ
τῶν γειτόνων μνᾶν] ἐὰν δ' ἐξ ἄλ
λης

876 a (f. 262ᵛ):

νομοθετητέον [ποῖα
δὴ νομοθετητέον καὶ] ποῖα

(22) *Laws* 943 b (f. 279ᵛ):

τὰς μὲν [εἰς τοὺς ὁπλίτας ἱπ
πέας δὲ] εἰς τοὺς ἱππέας καί

The following case is interesting (*Leg.* 717 b). *A* has (f. 190ʳ):

ὀρθότα
τα φέροιτ' ἂν πρῶτον μέν

Ω omits φέροιτ' ἂν . . . μέν, but has ὀρθότατα. Probably a line was first omitted and then ὀρθότα was corrected by conjecture.

In one case Ω skips two lines of *A*:

(45) *Demodoc.* 386 a (f. 330ᵛ):

καὶ τοῖς τυχοῦσιν [οἶμαι δεῖν
πιστεύειν εἰ δὲ μὴ πιστεύειν
τοῖς τυχοῦσιν] ἔφη οἴει δεῖν

These instances seem sufficient to prove Jordan's contention. It is probable that an exact collation of Vat. Gr. I would reveal a number of others.

It must now be noticed that Ω is not copied immediately from *A*. This may be shown from the lacunae in the *Laws* (745 a–c, 783 b–d). In both cases *A* is supplemented by the twelfth-century corrector, in 745 a without comment and in 783 b with the note ἔν τισι τῶν ἀντιγράφων φέρεται καὶ ταῦτα. If the dating is right, it did not contain either supplement when Ω was written. Ω^1 agrees with *A* in omitting 783 b–d, the passage being added by Ω^2 with the same note. Ω, however, has 745 a–c in the text. There must, therefore, have been an intermediate MS. between *A* and Ω in which the lacuna in 745 a–c was filled up. I have noticed a large number of such cases. Thus, in the telescoped passage, *Rep.* 400 a, where *A* omits -μι ποῖα δὲ ὁποίου βίου, and the loss is not repaired by any of the correctors, Ω, if we may trust Bekker's collation, is not defective. In some cases corrections in *A* are found in the text of Ω, but frequently there are the same marginalia in both MSS. It is probable that a further study of the relation of Ω to *A* would be remunerative. It may be noticed that Ω contains many references to τοῦ πατριάρχου τὸ βιβλίον,[1] from which it has been inferred that it was written at Constantinople.

I now point out a very curious point of agreement between Ω and the Armenian version, namely that the version like Ω has *Leg.* 745 a–c in the text, but omits 783 b–d with Ω[1] and *A*. It is possible that the version was founded on Ω or a kindred MS.

A facsimile of *B* has been published in the Leiden series with a preface by Mr. T. W. Allen. The MS. was found in the Isle of Patmos by E. D. Clarke in 1801. It has a colophon which states that it was written in A. D. 895 by a scribe named John, for Arethas the deacon of Patras. Arethas, afterwards Archbishop of Caesarea in Cappadocia, collected MSS., several of which still survive. He was accustomed to write scholia in his MSS., also to add colophons. Kougeas, in his recent monograph upon Arethas,[2] gives facsimiles from Paris 451 (Eusebius), Harl. 5694 (Lucian), Dres. Da. 129 (Nicephorus). He says of *B*: τὸ μὲν κείμενον ἔγραψεν ὁ Ἰωάννης, τὸ βιβλιογραφικὸν ὑπόγραμμα μετὰ τῶν κοσμημάτων ὁ Ἀρέθας.

Mr. Allen recognizes three contemporary correctors, whom he terms *A*, *B*, *C*. The first of these is the writer of the scholia and the colophon, i. e. Arethas. The identification was originally made by E. Maas. Mr. Allen had some doubts whether Arethas would undertake in person the labour of writing such extensive scholia, but he tells me that he now agrees. He assigns *B* and *C* to the same period. Other correctors have been at work, one of whom at least belongs to cent. x.

The MS. consists of 53 quaternions and has 34 lines to the page. The contents of three pages which I examined are as follows:

f. 106r (*Theaet.* 192 c–193 c) = 1,697 letters.
f. 169r (*Parmen.* 157 d–158 d) = 1,783 „
f. 169v (*Parmen.* 158 d–159 d) = 1,760 „

[1] Rabe, *l. c.*

[2] S. B. Kougeas, ὁ Καισαρείας Ἀρέθας, Athens, 1913.

The average on f. 106^{r} is 50 letters to the line and on f. 169 about 52. I noticed three exceptionally short lines of 42, 44, 45, and two exceptionally long ones of 58 and 59.

On one occasion, f. 31^{v} (*Phaedo* 68 b), John himself adds in the margin γρ. ἄλλοθι δυνατὸν εἶναι καθαρῶς. This ancient variant clearly existed in the model.

A number of additions have been made by Arethas. It is probable that these were taken from the model. The contemporary correctors *B* and *C* may also have had access to the model. On one occasion, f. 105^{v} (*Theaet.* 192 b), the corrector *B* writes ἐν ἄλλοις καὶ ταῦτα before a supplement, which must come from another source.

In the following list I ascribe the corrections of *A* to Arethas, and unite *B* and *C* under the symbol *corr.* I take no account of the later correctors.

(10) 133 d : ὅτι ἡμέτερα *om. B*
Meno 99 a : τινος ὀρθῶς *F*, *om. B*, *cett.*
Phaedo 90 d : * τοὺς λόγους *om. B*
Polit. 296 e : διοικήσεως *om. B*
(11) *Alcib.* i. 129 b : ὀρθῶς λέγεις *om. B*
Polit. 307 c : βαρύτερα καί *om. B*
310 a : οὔτε ἐννοεῖν *om. B*
310 e : καὶ ἀτιμίαις *om. B*
Soph. 241 d : διαμαχητέον *om. B*
(12) *Alcib.* ii. 141 b : οὐκ ἄν μοι δοκῶ *om. B*
Meno 99 c : ἐνθουσιῶντες *F*, *om. B*, *cett.*
Symp. 175 c : ἁπτόμενός σου *om. B*
(13) *Euthyd.* 281 b : τοῖς ἀνθρώποις *om. B*
Phaedo 42 c : καὶ διακρίσεσι *om. B*
80 e : * αὐτὴ εἰς ἑαυτήν *om..B*
Phaedr. 272 a : τε καὶ ἀκαιρίαν *om. B*
Prot. 330 b : * ἔχει ὦ Σώκρατες *om. B*
(14) *Alcib.* i. 130 c : ἀλλὰ καὶ μετρίως *om. B*
Crat. 387 d : ὀνομάζειν τε καί *om.* B^1 (*corr.*)
388 d : ὁ τὴν τέχνην ἔχων *om.* B^1 (*add. Areth.*)
Euthyd. 291 b : παρέχουσά τε καί *om. B*
Gorg. 492 b : καὶ δικαιοσύνης *F*, *om. B*, *cett.*
Phaedo 80 c : καὶ διαπνεῖσθαι *om. B*
Phaedr. 231 c : ἕτοιμοί εἰσι καί *om. B*
Polit. 291 b : * καὶ γὰρ δὴ καὶ νῦν *om. B*
(15) *Alcib.* i. 130 b : * τίς οὖν ὁ ἄνθρωπος *om. B*
Apol. 37 c : ὦ ἄνδρες Ἀθηναῖοι *om. B*

Gorg. 460 e: καὶ ἀδίκως χρῆται *F*, *om*. *B*, *cett*.
480 d: * μὴ φειδόμενον ἀλλ' *F*, *om*. *B*, *cett*.
Phaedo 100 c: πλὴν αὐτὸ τὸ καλόν *om*. B^1 (*add*. *Areth*.)
(17) *Theaet*. 168 a: αὐτοὺς δὲ μισήσουσι *om*. B^1 (*corr*.)
(18) *Crito*. 52 b: * ὅτι μὴ ἅπαξ εἰς 'Ισθμόν *T*, *Athenaeus*, *om*. *B*, *cett*.
(19) *Phil*. 43 b: ἅπαν δή που τοὐναντίον T^2, *om*. BT^1
(21) *Polit*. 287 e: καὶ ἐμπύροις καὶ ἀπύροις *om*. *B*
(23) *Crat*. 383 b: αὐτῶι γε τούτωι ὄνομα εἶναι [1] *om*. B^1 (*corr*.)
Gorg. 514 b: τὴν τέχνην ἣ οὐκ ἐπιστάμεθα *F*, *om*. B^1 (*corr*.) T^1
(25) *Gorg*. 483 a: αἴσχιον λέγοντος σὺ τὸν νόμον *om*. *BW*
(26) *Crito* 47 a: οὐδὲ πάντων ἀλλὰ τῶν μὲν τῶν δ' οὔ *TW*, *Eusebius*, *om* B^1 (*add*. *Areth*.)
Gorg. 452 e: καὶ ἐν βουλευτηρίωι βουλευτάς *om*. B^1 (*add*. *Areth*.)
Theaet. 160 c: οὔτ' ἄλλου λέγοντος ἀποδεκτέον *om*. B^1 (*corr*.)
(28) *Phaedo* 71 c: ἐγρηγορέναι καὶ ἐκ τοῦ καθεύδειν *om*. *B*
Theaet. 164 b: ἐστιν εἴπερ καὶ τὸ ὁρᾶι ἐπίσταται *om*. B^1 (*corr*.)
192 b: καὶ ὃ μὴ αἰσθάνεται ὧν αἰσθάνεται *om*. B^1 (*corr*.)
(34) *Crat*. 391 a: ἀλλὰ δοκῶ μοι ὧδε ἂν μᾶλλον πεισθήσεσθαι *om*. B^1 (*corr*.)
(36) *Theaet*. 174 c: λοιδορεῖν ἅτ' οὐκ εἰδὼς κακὸν οὐδὲν οὐδενός (*om*. B^1 *corr*.)
(37) *Phil*. 54 c: γίγνεσθαι σύμπασαν δὲ γένεσιν οὐσίας ἕνεκα *om*. *B*
(39) *Meno* 75 d: ἀποκρίνεσθαι· ἔστι δὲ ἴσως τὸ διαλεκτικώτερον *om*. *B*
(41) *Alcib*. i. 120 e: ἔκγονοι, τὸ δ' Ἡρακλέους τε γένος καὶ τὸ 'Αχαιμένους [2] *om*. B^1 (*corr*.)
Apol. 33 b: πώποτε μάθημα μήτε ἐδίδαξα, εἰ δέ τίς φησι παρ' ἐμοῦ [3] *om*. *B*
Parm. 160 d: οὐδὲν ἧττον γιγνώσκεται τί τὸ λεγόμενον μὴ εἶναι *om*. B^1 *at end of line* (*corr*.): *D*
(42) *Euthyd*. 296 b: ἀεὶ δ' ἐπιστάμενος πότερον τὰ μὲν τούτωι ἐπίστασαι *om*. *B*
(44) *Theaet*. 192 c: ὃ μὴ οἶδε καὶ ὃ μὴ οἶδε μηδὲ αἰσθάνεται ὃ μὴ αἰσθάνεται *om*. *B*
(45) *Phil*. 23 c: μᾶλλον [4] δ' εἰ βούλει τριχῆι: καθ' ὅτι φράζοις ἄν: λάβωμεν *om*. B^1 (*corr*.)
(46) *Phaedo* 96 a: βούλομαί γε: ἄκουε τοίνυν ὡς ἐροῦντος. ἐγὼ γὰρ ἔφη ὁ Κέβης *om*. B^1 (*add*. *Areth*.)
(49) *Euthyd*. 303 d: μήτε ἀγαθὸν πρᾶγμα μήτε λευκὸν μηδ' ἄλλο τῶν τοιούτων μηδέν *om*. *B*
(57) *Euthyphro* 8 d: ** -τοῦσιν ὡς οὐ τὸν ἀδικοῦντα δεῖ διδόναι δίκην ἀλλ' ἐκεῖνο ἴσως ἀμφισβη- *om*. B^1 (*add*. *Areth*.)
(60) *Hipparch*. 227 d: εἶναι ὠφελεῖσθαι: τί οὖν δὴ τοῦτο: ὅτι καὶ τόδε αὐτῶι προσωμολογήσαμεν *om*. B^1 (*corr*.)

[1] John wrote ὁ δὲ ὁμολογεῖ τί δέ *med*. *om*. The corrector erased τί δέ, and wrote αὐτῶι . . . εἶναι τί δαί in the margin.

[2] For the method of correction here employed, cf. p. 406.

[3] The passage is added in a tenth-cent. hand.

[4] μᾶλλον is written in a later hand, but probably the corrector rewrote a word which had become illegible.

(61) *Crat.* 389 b: οὔκουν ἐκεῖνο δικαιότατ' ἂν αὐτὸ ὃ ἔστιν κερκὶς καλέσαιμεν: ἔμοιγε δοκεῖ *om. B*

Crito 51 d: καὶ οὐδεὶς ἡμῶν τῶν νόμων ἐμποδών ἐστι οὐδ' ἀπαγορεύει ἐάν τέ τις βούληται *om.* B^1 (*add. Areth.*)

(62) *Theaet.* 192 b: τὸ μνημεῖον ὀρθῶς ὃ οἶδεν οἰηθῆναι ἀδύνατον καὶ ὃ οἶδε καὶ αἰσθάνεται ἔχων *om.* B^1 (*corr.* ἐν ἄλλοις καὶ ταῦτα)

(71) *Theaet.* 192 e: ἔστιν δὲ αἰσθάνεσθαι: ἀληθῆ: οὐκοῦν καὶ ἃ μὴ οἶδε πολλάκις μὲν ἔστι μηδὲ αἰσθάνεσθαι *om. B*

(75) *Alcib.* i. 105 d: ἐνδείξασθαι ὅτι αὐτῆι παντὸς ἄξιος εἶ, ἐνδειξάμενος δὲ οὐδὲν ὅτι οὐ παραυτίκα δυνήσεσθαι *om. B*

(84) *Euthyph.* 12 b: ἐγὼ οὖν τούτωι διαφέρομαι τῶι ποιητῆι. εἴπω σοι ὅπῆι: πάνυ γε: οὐ δοκεῖ μοι εἶναι ἵνα δέος ἔνθα καὶ αἰδὼς *om.* B^1 (*add. Areth.*)

(97) *Protag.* 312 e: περὶ οὗπερ καὶ ἐπιστήμονα περὶ κιθαρίσεως· ἦ γάρ: ναί: εἶεν. ὁ δὲ δὴ σοφιστὴς περὶ τίνος δεινὸν ποιεῖ λέγειν: δῆλον ὅτι *om. B, at the end of a line.*

(98) *Alcib.* i. 134 a: οὐκ ἄρα οἷόν τε ἐὰν μή τις σώφρων καὶ ἀγαθὸς ἦι εὐδαίμονα εἶναι: οὐχ οἷόν τε: οἱ ἄρα κακοὶ τῶν ἀνθρώπων ἄθλιοι: σφόδρα γε *om. B*

(591) *Theaet.* 208 d–209 a: * πάνυ μὲν οὖν: λαβὲ δὴ οὗ χάριν εἴρηται. ἔστι δὲ ὅπερ ἄρτι ἐλέγομεν ὡς ἄρα τὴν διαφορὰν ἑκάστου ἂν λαμβάνηις ἧι τῶν ἄλλων διαφέρει λόγον ὥς φασί τινες λήψηι ἕως δ' ἂν κοινοῦ τινος ἐφάπτηι ἐκείνων πέρι σοι ἔσται ὁ λόγος ὧν ἂν ἡ κοινότης ἦι: μανθάνω καί μοι δοκεῖ καλῶς ἔχειν λόγον τὸ τοιοῦτον καλεῖν: ὅς δ' ἂν μετ' ὀρθῆς δόξης περὶ ὁτουοῦν τῶν ὄντων τὴν διαφορὰν τῶν ἄλλων προσλάβηι αὐτοῦ ἐπιστήμων γεγονὼς ἔσται ὧν πρότερον ἦν δοξαστής: φαμέν γε μὴν οὕτω: νῦν δῆτα, ὦ Θεαίτητε, παντάπασιν ἔγωγε, ἐπειδὴ ἐγγὺς ὥσπερ σκιαγραφήματος γέγονα τοῦ λεγομένου, συνίημι οὐδὲ σμικρόν. ἕως δὲ ἀφειστήκη πόρρωθεν, ἐφαίνετό τί μοι λέγεσθαι: πῶς τί τοῦτο: φράσω ἐὰν οἷός τε γένωμαι. ὀρθὴν ἔγωγε ἔχων δόξαν περὶ σοῦ ἐὰν μὲν προσλάβω τὸν σὸν λόγον *om. B*

I have marked 57 (*Euthyph.* 8 d) as a telescoped passage, but without any conviction. John wrote (f. 4r):

φασιν ἀδικεῖν· ἦ γάρ: ἀληθῆ λέγεις: οὐκ ἄρα ἐκεῖνό γε ἀμφισβη
τοῦσιν τὸ τίς ἐστιν ὁ ἀδικῶν

He here omitted ὡς οὐ τὸν ἀδικοῦντα δεῖ διδόναι δίκην ἀλλ' ἐκεῖνο ἴσως ἀμφισβητοῦσιν. Arethas, instead of inserting ὡς . . . ἀμφισβητοῦσιν after ἀμφισβητοῦσιν, added -τοῦσιν ὡς οὐ . . . ἴσως ἀμφισβη- in the margin. The same method is followed by the correctors *B* and *C* on more than one occasion, e.g. *Theaet.* 160 b (26). Here John wrote (f. 91r):

ρη
τέον αὐτῶι εἴτε γίγνεσθαι αὐτὸ δὲ ἐφ' αὑτοῦ τι ἢ ὂν ἢ γιγνόμενον οὔτ'
αὐτῶι λεκτέον ὡς ὁ λόγος

He here omitted οὔτ' ἄλλου λέγοντος ἀποδεκτέον after λεκτέον. The corrector (*B*), instead of inserting the missing words after λεκτέον, wrote αὐτῶι λεκτέον οὔτ' ἄλλου λέγον- in the right-hand margin and in the next line wrote -τος ἀπο- *in ras.* (over αὐτῶι) and changed λ (in λεκτέον) to δ. There are a number of other passages in which the correctors rewrite the passage instead of making a simple addition.

The most striking point in this list is the agreement of 97 and 98. We may notice that 98 × 6 = 588, which is very near to 591; but in the absence of intermediate figures I would not lay stress on this. The next point which calls for attention is the large number of examples between 40 and 50. It is to be observed that 46 (*Phaedo* 96 a) and 84 (*Euthyph.* 12 b) are both added by Arethas.

In the case of a MS. written in long lines like *B* it is always probable that it was preceded by one or more ancestors written in somewhat similar formation. Since *B* contains an average of 50–52 letters to the line, nothing would be more natural than that the content of a line in the model would vary between 40 and 50.

The omission of 97 letters in *Protag.* 312 e is of special interest since it comes at the end of a line. Here John wrote (f. 337[v]):

δει
νὸν ποιεῖ λέγειν ὥσπερ ὁ κιθαριστὴς δεινὸν δήπου ποιεῖ λέγειν (52)
περὶ οὗπερ καὶ ἐπίσταται : εἰκός γε : τί δή ἐστιν τοῦτο περὶ οὗ (50)
αὐτὸς

Here he has omitted 97 letters after ποιεῖ λέγειν. It is tempting to arrange as lines of the model

περὶ οὗπερ καὶ ἐπιστήμονα περὶ κιθαρίσεως ἢ γάρ : ναί : εἶεν (49)
ὁ δὲ δὴ σοφιστὴς περὶ τίνος δεινὸν ποιεῖ λέγειν : δῆλον ὅτι (48)

It may now be asked if there is any evidence for the formation of more remote ancestors. Here it is necessary to speak with some caution. The three examples of 26 and 28 are interesting, also the sharp break after 28. Also we may notice that two omissions of 26 are remedied by Arethas, a fact which may indicate that they were in the margin of the model and neglected by John. I have noticed the following corruptions in *B* which may be instructive:

Euthyd. 276 b: οἱ ἀμαθεῖς ἄρα μανθάνουσιν, ὦ Κλεινία, ἀλλ' οὐχ οἱ σοφοί.

B has σοφοί after ἄρα as well as *loco suo*. This may indicate in a previous MS.

ἄρα
μανθάνουσιν ὦ κλεινία ἀλλ' οὐχ οἱ (27)
σοφοί

Charm. 172 a: ἀναγκαῖον καλῶς καὶ εὖ πράττειν *TW*, *edd. plerique.*

B has καλῶς πράττειν ἀναγκαῖον καλῶς καὶ εὖ πράττειν. This may indicate in a previous ancestor

ἀναγκαῖον καλῶς καὶ εὖ πράττειν (27) *mg.* καλῶς πράττειν.

Two of the omissions of 28 occur in the *Theaetetus*, both being added by the corrector (*B*), who may have found them as marginalia in the model. It is to be noticed that one of them, 192 b, comes in a part of the *Theaetetus* where we have a long series of omissions due to bewildering repetitions of αἰσθάνεται αἰσθάνεσθαι. One of these 192 b (62) has been remedied by the corrector with the note ἐν ἄλλοις καὶ ταῦτα to which I have previously referred. This was clearly taken from another source, not from the model. It therefore goes back to a previous ancestor.

In a passage so full of repetitions it is not likely that the omissions would represent whole lines, at least as a rule, but rather that the writer would skip from one line to another on account of ὁμ. We should not therefore expect to find exact correspondence.

I now exhibit the whole of this troubled zone, *Theaet.* 192 b–e (ff. 105ᵛ, 106ʳ), marking with asterisks the portions omitted by *B*.

* καὶ ὃ μὴ . . . αἰσθάνεται	(28)
καὶ ἔτι γε . . . αἰσθάνεται ἔχων	(197)
* τὸ μνημεῖον . . . αἰσθάνεται ἔχων	(62)
κατὰ ταῦτα . . . μηδὲ αἰσθάνεται	(91)
* ὃ μὴ οἶδε . . . μὴ αἰσθάνεται	(44)
πάντα ταῦτα . . . μὴ αἰσθάνεσθαι	(657)
* ἔστιν δὲ αἰσθάνεσθαι . . . μηδὲ αἰσθάνεσθαι	(71)

Here $28 \times 7 = 196$. The other figures do not at first look encouraging. If, however, the scribe skipped from line to line, we may find some connexion between the figures, if we add up the blocks.

Here $62 + 91 + 44 = 197$. This is a very surprising result. If we add 657 and 71, the result is 728. This $= 28 \times 26$ exactly.

The whole passage, therefore, $28 + 197 + 197 + 728 = 1150$, i.e. 41 lines of 28 ($= 1148$).

If this analysis is correct, a previous ancestor had in one line

καὶ ὃ μὴ αἰσθάνεται ὧν αἰσθάνεται (28)

This was succeeded by seven lines containing καὶ ἔτι γε . . . αἰσθάνεται ἔχων (197), then seven lines containing τὸ μνημεῖον . . . μὴ αἰσθάνεται (197), then 26 lines containing πάντα ταῦτα . . . μηδὲ αἰσθάνεσθαι (728).

I do not venture to suggest previous ancestors, and would only point out that *F* preserves two passages of 15 letters, omitted by *B cett.*, also one of 14. The additions of Arethas in *Crat.* 388 d (14) and *Phaedo* 100 c (15) may possibly represent marginalia in the model. It is to be noticed that both the additions in *B* come from Arethas.

Before I quit *B* I must make a reference to three passages, all of them belonging to the same dialogue, where Stobaeus and others appear to have had a longer text than that given by our MSS.

(45) *Alcib.* i. 128 a: καὶ ἱμάτια καὶ στρώματα τοῦ ἄλλου σώματος ὁμοίως: ναί *Stobaeus*, *om. codd.*

(66) *Alcib.* i. 115 e: *πάνυ γε: ἐν τοῖς ἀρίστοις ἄρα σὺ ἡγῆι ἀνδρείαν εἶναι κἂν τοῖς κακίστοις θάνατον *Stobaeus*, *om. codd. et Proclus*

(321) *Alcib.* i. 133 c: ἆρ' οὖν ὅθ' ὥσπερ κάτοπτρά ἐστι σαφέστερα τοῦ ἐν τῶι ὀφθαλμῶι ἐνόπτρου καὶ καθαρώτερα καὶ λαμπρότερα, οὕτω καὶ ὁ θεὸς τοῦ ἐν τῆι ἡμετέραι ψυχῆι βελτίστου καθαρώτερόν τε καὶ λαμπρότερον τυγχάνει ὄν: ἔοικέ γε, ὦ Σώκρατες: εἰς τὸν θεὸν ἄρα βλέποντες ἐκείνωι καλλίστωι ἐνόπτρωι χρώιμεθ' ἂν καὶ τῶν ἀνθρωπίνων εἰς τὴν ψυχῆς ἀρετήν, καὶ οὕτως ἂν μάλιστα ὁρῶιμεν καὶ γιγνώσκοιμεν ἡμᾶς αὐτούς: ναί *Eusebius*, *sic fere Stobaeus*, *Theodoretus*, *Iulianus*: *om. codd.*

Here 45 is the average length of a line in the model of *B*. We cannot, however, explain the omission in this way, since it is common to all MSS. The relation of 45 to 66 suggests that the omission goes back to an ancestor with 22 letters to the line. There seems to be a relation between 66 and 321 ($64 \times 5 = 320$).

I conclude with a reference to *B* as a parent. Schanz considers that a number of MSS. are derived from it. In the case of one he proves his case by citing examples of line omissions. The MS. in question, which consists of two parts, viz. Vat. 225 and 226, termed by Bekker Δ and Θ, has played a considerable part in Platonic criticism. Schanz gives the following instances. I add references to the folios of *B*:

(45) *Laches* 198 d: γέγονεν ἄλλη δὲ περὶ γιγνομένων ὅπηι γίγνεται ἄλλη δέ *om.* Θ (f. 305^v)

(47) *Theages* 123 c: **-σθα οὐ μέντοι τό γε ὄνομα ἢ καὶ τὸ ὄνομα: καὶ τὸ ὄνομα ἔγωγε *om.* Θ (f. 278^r)

(50) *Crat.* 404 b: **-μητράν τε καὶ Ἥραν καὶ Ἀπόλλω καὶ Ἀθηνᾶν καὶ Ἥφαιστον καὶ Ἄρη *om.* Δ (f. 67^r)

The question of the relation of *B* to *D* (*Ven.* 185) will be considered subsequently.

D

This MS., Bekker's Π, contains *Tetr.* i–iv and a portion of *Tetr.* viii, viz. *Clitopho* and *Republic* i–x, where it ends at 612 e ἔστι ταῦτα, having lost a few pages at the end. Its tradition for the rest of *Rep.* x is known from Paris. 1810 and other MSS. derived from it before it was mutilated.

In *Tetr.* i–iv it is most closely connected with *B.* Schanz originally thought that it was not derived from *B*, but from a *gemellus*, but afterwards changed his mind. Most recent writers speak of it as an apograph of *B.* In *Tetr.* viii, however, which is not contained by *B*, its tradition is independent of *A* and its value is not disputed. It has been suggested that it is derived from the supposed missing volume of *B.*

D, which is assigned to cent. xii, is said to be carelessly written and, in particular, to contain a number of dittographies. In the *Parmenides* it has recently been collated by Waddell: otherwise we are dependent upon Bekker's collation.

The chief reason for supposing *D* to be derived from *B* in *Tetr.* i–iv is a curious fact noticed by Waddell.. He observed in the *Parmenides* an extraordinary similarity between the lineation of *B* and *D.* 'The first three lines in *D* are identical with those found in *B*, the fourth is longer by η and the fifth by φω, then they diverge, but tend to revert to identity and then again separate.'[1] A striking agreement is that the last three lines on f. 169ʳ and the first three lines on f. 169ᵛ are identical in the two MSS. Waddell with great self-restraint says that 'we have very considerable support for the view that *D* descends from *B.* It is not, however, so strong as in the case of Vat. 225–6 (ΔΘ), and the counter evidence is stronger.'

I would remark in the first place that *D* cannot be a direct copy of *B.* An intermediate MS. is required. This may be seen from certain dislocations in *D*, mentioned by Schanz, though he does not point out their significance.

On f. 30ᵛ after *Phaedo* 68 b ἀλλά τις *D* has in the middle of the page *Crito* 51 a–53 a καὶ σὺ δὲ ἡμᾶς . . . ἀπεδή-. This block of the *Crito* which has got out of place = 87 lines in Stallbaum's text.

[1] *Parm.*, p. lxxxv.

Subsequently there is a dislocated passage of the *Phaedo*, viz. 68 c–69 b φιλοσώματος ὁ αὐτὸς . . . ἀρετῇ καὶ τῷ, which = 43 lines of Stallbaum's text. Also in the *Apology D* originally omitted 35 d–37 e γὰρ ὦ ἄνδρες . . . θεῷ ἀπειθεῖν. This = 84 lines in Stallbaum's text. The relation between 43, 84, 87 shows that folios of an ancestor have been displaced.

The contents of the three pages of *B* which I have already mentioned, viz. ff. 106ʳ, 169ʳ, 169ᵛ, are respectively equal to 48, 43, 45 lines of Stallbaum's text. These figures agree admirably with 43, 84, 87. We should therefore expect to find that on one occasion a folio of *B* has been transposed, on another a page, and on a third a folio has been omitted.

If, however, we look at *B* we find that *Crito* 51 a–53 a comes on f. 24ʳ, l. 23, after -ναι, and ends f. 25ʳ, l. 25 in the middle of a line: *Phaedo* 68 c–69 b begins on f. 32ᵛ, l. 2, towards the end of a line, and ends on 32ᵛ, l. 4, in the middle of a line, while *Apol.* 35 d–37 e begins on f. 17ʳ, l. 33, in the middle of a line, and ends on f. 18ʳ, l. 29, before τοῦ-.

The MS. in question, therefore, though extremely like *B*, was not *B*. If we assume the existence of an intermediate MS., we are left with the singular fact that in the *Parmenides* at any rate we have whole lines exactly the same in *B* and *D*, after passing through an intermediate MS. If so, it is also possible that a further ancestor of *B* and *D* had the same traditional formation, in which case *D* may after all not be derived from *B* itself.

Schanz has already given a number of readings which make it difficult to derive *D* from *B*,[1] and it is probably in consequence of these that Waddell speaks so guardedly. The most striking case which I have myself noticed is:

Alcib. i. 120 e: οἱ μὲν Ἡρακλέους, οἱ δὲ Ἀχαιμένους ἔκγονοι, τὸ δ' Ἡρακλέους τε γένος καὶ τὸ Ἀχαιμένους εἰς Περσέα

Here John wrote (f. 256ʳ)

λακεδαιμο
νίων καὶ περσῶν βασιλεῖς. ἢ οὐκ ἴσμεν ὡς οἱ μὲν ἡρακλέους
οἱ δὲ ἀχαιμένους εἰς περσέα τὸν διὸς ἀναφέρεται καὶ γὰρ τὸ

omitting ἔκγονοι . . . Ἀχαιμένους. The contemporary corrector (*C*),

[1] Platocodex (1877), p. 56.

instead of inserting the missing passage after Ἀχαιμένους, preferred to join it to the margin of the previous line. He therefore wrote *οἱ δὲ Ἀχαιμένους . . . γένος καί* in the right-hand margin, erased *οἱ δέ* at the beginning of the next line, and wrote *τό in ras.*, followed by a small blank space. The addition is made in a bold hand, and could not possibly be overlooked. *D*, however, if Bekker's collation is to be trusted, makes the same omission as John, viz. ἔκγονοι . . . Ἀχαιμένους. He expressly distinguishes it from *B*, to which he assigns οἱ δὲ Ἀχαιμένους . . . γένος καί according to the marginal correction.

Omissions and Dittographies.

I pass over a few omissions of less than 20 letters, also omissions shared by *B*. In *Rep.* x. 612 e–end, I use the symbol *d* for apographs of *D*.

(20) *Rep.* 535 a: καὶ τοὺς ἀνδρειοτάτους *om. D*
(23) *Theaet.* 165 c: καὶ τὸ μὴ ὁρᾶν μὴ ἐπίστασθαι *om. D*
(24) *Rep.* 534 a: μὲν ταῦτα δόξαν συναμφότερα *om. D*
(33) *Rep.* 394 d: ἐγὼ ἴσως δὲ καὶ πλείω ἔτι τούτων· οὐ γὰρ δή *om. D*
(36) *Parm.* 148 d: τὸ ἓν αὐτοῦ καὶ τῶν ἄλλων καὶ τοῦ μὴ ἅπτεσθαι *om. D*[1]
(37) *Rep.* 563 e: ὅθεν τυραννὶς φύεται ὡς ἐμοὶ δοκεῖ: νεανική *om. D*
(39) *Amat.* 138 a: φημί: οὐκοῦν ἧι μὲν κολάζειν ὀρθῶς ἐπιστάμεθα *om. D*
Rep. 400 b: * ἄλλον τροχαῖον ὠνόμαζε μήκη δὲ καὶ βραχύτητας *om. D*
(40) *Parm.* 160 c: ἔστι γάρ: ἔστιν ἄρα καὶ μέγεθός τε καὶ σμικρότης *om. D*
(42) *Parm.* 153 a: οὐκ ἔχω λέγειν: τόδε γε μὴν ἔχεις λέγειν ὅτι τὰ ἄλλα *om. D*
Phaedo 64 e: ὅ γε ὡς ἀληθῶς φιλόσοφος: οὐκοῦν ὅλως δοκεῖ σοι ἔφη *om. D*
(43) *Parm.* 134 d: οὔτ' ἂν ἡ δεσποτεία ἡ ἐκείνων ἡμῶν ποτε ἂν δεσπόσειεν *om. D*[1] *T*
Phaedo 64 e: καθ' ὅσον μὴ πολλὴ ἀνάγκη μετέχειν αὐτῶν: ἀτιμάζειν *om. D*
Phaedr. 274 b: ἱκανῶς ἐχέτω: τί μήν: τὸ δ' εὐπρεπείας δὴ γραφῆς περί *om. D*
(44) *Polit.* 258 b: * δεῖ δὲ ἴσως ἔτι ἧττον τἀμὰ διακωλύειν, ἀλλὰ δὴ μετὰ τόν *om. D*
Rep. 588 c: λέγονται συμπεφυκυῖαι ἰδέαι πολλαὶ εἰς ἓν γενέσθαι *om. D*
Rep. 367 d: * φρονεῖν καὶ ὑγιαίνειν δὴ καὶ ὅσ' ἄλλα ἀγαθὰ γόνιμα τῆι *om. D*
(45) *Rep.* 335 d: πάνυ γε: οὐδὲ δὴ τοῦ ἀγαθοῦ βλάπτειν ἀλλὰ τοῦ ἐναντίου *om. D*
469 a: ** -θρώπων: πεισόμεθα μὲν οὖν: διαπυθόμενοι ἄρα τοῦ θεοῦ *om. D*
479 d: μὴ εἶναι φανήσεται οὔτε φανότερα ὄντος πρὸς τὸ μᾶλλον *om. D*
602 a: πάνυ γε: ὁ δὲ μιμητὴς πότερον ἐκ τοῦ χρῆσθαι ἐπιστήμην *om. D*
607 a: ** -μνους θεοῖς καὶ ἐγκώμια τοῖς ἀγαθοῖς ποιήσεως παραδε- *om. D*
(46) *Rep.* 335 c: ἀμούσους δύνανται ποιεῖν: ἀδύνατον: ἀλλὰ τῆι ἱππικῆι *om. D*
(48) *Parm.* 136 a: μᾶλλον γυμνασθῆναι: πῶς λέγεις φάναι: οἷον ἔφη εἰ βούλει *om. D*

Parm. 147 a: τοῦ ἑνὸς ἄρα μόριά ἐστιν ἢ κἂν οὕτω μετεῖχε τοῦ ἑνὸς τὰ μὴ ἓν *om.* D

Rep. 616 c: ** -ναι γὰρ τοῦτο τὸ φῶς σύνδεσμον τοῦ οὐρανοῦ οἷον τὰ ὑποζώμα- *om.* d

(50) *Phil.* 23 e: ἐσχισμένον καὶ διεσπαρμένον ἰδόντες εἰς ἓν πάλιν ἑκάτερον *om.* D

Rep. 330 a: πάνυ τι ῥαιδίως γῆρας μετὰ πενίας ἐνέγκοι οὔθ' ὁ μὴ ἐπιεικὴς *om.* D

(51) *Rep.* 328 d: ἀλλ' ἡμεῖς ἂν παρά σε ἦιμεν· νῦν δέ σε χρὴ πυκνότερον δεῦρο ἰέναι *om.* D

Parmen. 134 a: οὐ τῆς παρ' ἡμῖν ἂν ἀληθείας εἴη καὶ αὖ ἑκάστη ἡ παρ' ἡμῖν ἐπιστήμη *om.* Dt[1]

(53) *Alcib.* i. 124 e: ναί: ἀλλὰ τὰ ναυτικὰ λέγεις: οὔ: παρὰ τοὺς ναυτικοὺς γὰρ ἂν ἦμεν *om.* D

(55) *Rep.* 462 c: κομιδῆι μὲν οὖν: ἐν ἧιτινι δὴ πόλει πλεῖστοι ἐπὶ τὸ αὐτὸ κατὰ ταὐτά *om.* D

(59) *Rep.* 353 b: ἔστιν: ἆρ' οὖν καὶ ἀρετὴ ὀφθαλμῶν ἐστιν: καὶ ἀρετή: τί δὲ ὤτων ἦν τι ἔργον *om.* D

(61) *Amat.* 137 c: φαίνεταί μοι ἦ δ' ὅς: τί δὲ πότερον ἧπερ βελτίους τε ποιεῖ καὶ κολάζει ὀρθῶς *om.* D

(62) *Clitoph.* 408 e: μηδὲν προνοοῦντας ὁρῶν καθάπερ παῖδας ὡς ἔστι τις γυμναστικὴ καὶ ἰατρικὴ *bis scr.* D

(64) *Crito* 44 d: ὦ Κρίτων οἷοί τε εἶναι οἱ πολλοὶ τὰ μέγιστα κακὰ ἐξεργάζεσθαι ἵνα οἷοί τε ἦσαν *om.* D

(66) *Rep.* 543 d: τὸν ἐκείνηι ὅμοιον καὶ ταῦτα ὡς ἔοικας καλλίω ἔτι ἔχων εἰπεῖν πόλιν τε καὶ ἄνδρα *bis scr.* D

(80) *Rep.* 410 d: ὅσοι ἂν τοὐναντίον διατεθῶσιν: τίνος δὲ ἦ δ' ὃς πέρι λέγεις: ἀγριότητός τε καὶ σκληρότητος καὶ αὖ *om.* D

(87) *Rep.* 554 a: ἐπιθυμίας: καὶ μάλα ἦ δ' ὃς σφόδρα: οὐκ ἄρ' ἂν εἴη ἀστασίαστος ὁ τοιοῦτος ἐν ἑαυτῶι οὐδὲ εἷς ἀλλὰ διπλοῦς τις *om.* D

(89) *Rep.* 335 b: εἰς τὴν τῶν ἵππων: ἆρ' οὖν καὶ κύνες βλαπτόμενοι χείρους γίγνονται εἰς τὴν τῶν κυνῶν ἀλλ' οὐκ εἰς τὴν τῶν ἵππων *om.* D

(91) *Rep.* 583 d: καὶ ἀγαπητὸν γίγνεται ἡσυχία: καὶ ὅταν παύσηται ἄρα εἶπον χαίρων τις ἡ τῆς ἡδονῆς ἡσυχία λυπηρὸν ἔσται: ἴσως *om.* D

(92) *Phil.* 32 a: διάκρισις δέ γ' αὖ καὶ διάλυσις ἡ παρὰ φύσιν τοῦ πνίγους πάθη λύπη. κατὰ φύσιν δ' ἡ πάλιν ἀπόδοσίς τε καὶ ψῦξις ἡδονή *om.* D

(112) *Phaedo* 97 e: τὴν αἰτίαν καὶ τὴν ἀνάγκην λέγοντα τὸ ἄμεινον καὶ ὅτι αὐτὴν ἄμεινον ἦν τοιαύτην εἶναι καὶ εἰ ἐν μέσωι φαίη εἶναι αὐτὴν ἐπεκδιηγήσεσθαι *om.* D

(141) *Polit.* 265 e: πεζονομικὴν διελὼν ἀπόδος ἑκατέρων τῶι μέρει λόγωι χρώμενος. ἂν γὰρ ὀνομάζειν αὐτὰ βουληθῆις ἔσται σοι περιπεπλεγμένον μᾶλλον τοῦ δέοντος: πῶς οὖν χρὴ λέγειν: ὧδε τῆς *om.* D

(155) *Phil.* 62 a: ἑπόμενον τῶι νοεῖν καὶ δὴ καὶ περὶ τῶν ἄλλων ἁπάντων τῶν ὄντων ὡσαύτως διανοούμενος: ἔστω γὰρ οὖν: ἆρ' οὖν οὗτος ἱκανῶς ἐπιστήμης ἕξει κύκλου μὲν καὶ σφαίρας αὐτῆς τῆς θείας τὸν λόγον ἔχων *om.* D

I omit for the moment a longer passage in *Cratyl.* 438 a, since its authenticity is disputed.

In the above list there are two telescoped passages of 45 letters and one of 48. A previous MS. had:

Rep. 469 a: ἀν
θρώπων : πεισόμεθα μὲν οὖν : διαπυθόμενοι ἄρα τοῦ θεοῦ.
πῶς

D has ἂν πῶς *med. om.*

Rep. 607 a: ὕ
μνους θεοῖς καὶ ἐγκώμια τοῖς ἀγαθοῖς ποιήσεως παραδε
κτέον

D has ὑκτέον *med. om.* This error is shared by a number of later MSS., apparently derived from *D*, e.g. ὑκτέον, *Ven. C*, ἑκτέον *Par. DK*, οὐχ ἑκτέον *q*. Others are said to omit ὕμνους . . . παραδεκτέον.[1]

Rep. 616 c: εἶ
ναι γὰρ τοῦτο τὸ φῶς σύνδεσμον τοῦ οὐρανοῦ οἷον τὰ ὑποζώμα
τα

d has εἶτα *med. om.*

There are 18 omissions of 40–8 letters, the bulge being at 43–5. This fact is interesting in view of the problem as to whether *D* is derived from *B*. We have seen that the average length of a line in *B*, if we may judge from the pages which I examined, is 50–2. If *D* is derived from *B* in *Tetr.* i–vi and from a missing volume of *B* in the *Republic*, we should expect to find a striking bulge in the omissions of *D* at 50–2. As a matter of fact there are five omissions of 50–3, but, as Waddell points out (p. 91), an example of a complete line in *B* omitted by *D* has yet to be found.

I would call attention to *Phaedo* 64 e. Here an omission of 42 letters comes immediately after one of 43. Between them comes ἔμοιγε δοκεῖ ἔφη. This indicates

καθ' ὅσον μὴ πολλὴ ἀνάγκη μετέχειν αὐτῶν : ἀτιμάζειν (43)
ἔμοιγε δοκεῖ ἔφη ὅ γε ὡς ἀληθῶς φιλόσοφος : οὐκοῦν ὅ (42)
λως δοκεῖ σοι ἔφη

D omits l. 1 and ὅ γε ὡς . . . ἔφη.

In *Rep.* 335 b–c there are neighbouring omissions of 89 and 46 letters. The intermediate passage consists of 249 letters (= 41·5 × 6).

It appears, therefore, that the MS. which has left most traces on *D* was not *B*, but one in which the lines were slightly shorter. It is

[1] Cf. Schanz in *Hermes* xii (1877), p. 178.

possible that this was an intermediate MS. between *B* and *D*, but it is also possible that it was the model of *B*. It is to be noticed that an omission of 40 letters in *Parm.* 160 c comes at the end of a line in *B*.

There is a curious similarity between the omissions of the two MSS.

In *B* we have eight omissions of 41–9, followed after an interval by 84, 97, 98. In *D* there are 18 omissions of 40–8, followed after an interval by 80, 87, 89, 91, 92. It is possible that a further collation of *D* might throw further light upon this puzzling question.

I now come to *Crat.* 438 a. Here, according to Bekker, a '*m. rec.*' adds in *D* after ἐάσωμεν :

(395) τάδε δὲ ἐπισκεψώμεθα εἰ ἡμῖν καὶ τῇδε ὁμολογεῖς εἴτε καὶ οὔ. φέρε τοὺς τὰ ὀνόματα ἐν ταῖς πόλεσι τιθεμένους ἑκάστοτε ἔν τε ταῖς Ἑλληνικαῖς καὶ βαρβαρικαῖς οὐκ ἀρτίως ὁμολογοῦμεν νομοθέτας εἶναι καὶ τὴν τέχνην τὴν τοῦτο δυναμένην νομοθετικήν : πάνυ γε : λέγε δὴ οἱ πρῶτοι νομοθέται τὰ πρῶτα ὀνόματα πότερον γιγνώσκοντες τὰ πράγματα οἷς ἐτίθεντο ἐτίθεντο ἢ ἀγνοοῦντες : οἶμαι μὲν ἐγώ, ὦ Σώκρατες, γιγνώσκοντες : οὐ γάρ πω, ὦ ἑταῖρε Κρατύλε, ἀγνοοῦντές γε : οὔ μοι δοκεῖ : ἐκ ποίων δέ

The words introduce a fresh point and make a good sense. Former editors adopt the passage except ἐκ ποίων δέ, but Bekker gives a sense by proposing to assign the words to Socrates, explaining ἐκ ποίων δὲ γιγνώσκοντες.

I do not understand Burnet's note 'add. eadem manus ἐκ ποίων δὲ ut significet a 1 ἐπανέλθωμεν . . . a 7 εἰδότα omittenda esse.'

I observe that in the *Parmenides* Bekker ascribes additions to *m. rec.*, which, according to Waddell, are made by the corrector. Burnet, in his Preface to *Clit.*, *Tim.*, *Crit.*, notices that Bekker also sometimes ascribes to *m. rec.* corrections made by the ancient diorthotes in *A*. It would, therefore, be helpful to know more definitely what is meant by *m. rec.* here. As a matter of fact, the passage does not rest on this supplement in *D* alone, but, according to Král, it is also found in *W*,[1] which, like *F*, has a curious knack of preserving passages lost by other MSS., as well as in two dett. The support of *W* is a *fait nouveau* of considerable importance. We must, therefore, take into account the possibility that the passage was omitted by a common parent of *B D*, but has survived in *W*

[1] Immisch, p. 66.

and in the supplement to *D*, from whatever source this was obtained. It is difficult to say why an interpolator should have forged it, and there is no similar case of extensive interpolation in the text of Plato. On the other hand there are long omissions in particular MSS., e.g. *Leg.* 745 a–c, 783 b–d in *A*, *Theaet.* 208 d–209 a in *B*, and, in all our MSS., *Alcib.* I, 133 c. It is easier to omit than to invent.

T

The ancient part of this MS. (cent. xii), ff. 5–212v, contains *Tetr.* i–vii, and part of viii, viz. *Clitopho*, *Rep.* i–iii (ending 389 d ἄρα δεήσει). The remaining folios, 213r–265v are late (cent. xv/xvi) and come from a different source.

In *Tetr.* i–vi *T* represents the *altera familia* as against *B*. The theory that it is derived from a missing volume of *A* has been mentioned. For *Tetr.* vii, which is not in *B* or *A*, it is the chief authority. At the end of *Tetr.* vii it has after the *Menexenus* (f. 197v) the interesting note τέλος τοῦ α′ βιβλίου. In the portion of *Tetr.* viii which it contains it agrees with *A*.

A minute collation of so interesting a MS. is much to be desired. Unfortunately our knowledge is incomplete. Bekker gives it in his list of MSS., but does not use it except for the *Symposium*, where he quotes some trivial variants in the first part of the dialogue. Its merits were pointed out by Schanz, who gives the more important readings for the dialogues edited by him. Burnet has also published selected readings in the *Phaedo*, *Politicus*, and *Philebus*, while Waddell has used it for the *Parmenides*.

T is written in two columns, with 50 lines to the page. If we may judge from a page reproduced by Waddell (p. cxxii), it contains 35–40 letters to a line.

The following omissions are recorded. I pass over some unimportant cases of 10–13 letters.

(14) *Apol.* 33 d: καὶ τιμωρεῖσθαι *om.* *T*
Crat. 385 e: * ἑκάσταις ἐνίοις *om.* *T*
Phaedo 64 b: καὶ οἵου θανάτου *om.* *T*
(15) *Euthyd.* 286 e: οὐδὲ κελεύεις ὅτι *om.* *T*
(19) *Phil.* 43 b: ἅπαν δή που τοὐναντίον *om.* T^1B
Phaedo 77 b: * ἐστὶν πρὸς τὸ ἀπιστεῖν *om.* T^1
(21) *Crat.* 388 d: ὅταν τῶι τρυπάνωι χρῆται *om.* *T*

(22) *Hipp. Min.* 365 e : ὅτι ποιοῦσιν ἢ ἐπίστανται *F*, *om. TW*
(23) *Gorg.* 514 b : τὴν τέχνην ἢ οὐκ ἐπιστάμεθα *om. TB*[1]
Soph. 248 d : ἢ τὸ μὲν πάθημα τὸ δὲ θάτερον *om. T*
(24) *Laches* 179 c : πολέμωι ἠργάσαντο καὶ ὅσα ἐν *om. T*[1]
Phaedr. 247 e : * ἃ λόγος πολὺς ἂν εἴη διελθεῖν *om. T*
(28) *Amat.* 138 d : * περὶ τῶν λεγομένων ἢ πραττομένων *om. T*
(29) *Amat.* 133 e : * ἡγοῦμαι γὰρ ὀρθῶς : ἠρώτησα οὖν ἐγὼ *om. T*
(34) *Gorg.* 467 d : δῆλον ὅτι τὸ ὑγιαίνειν οὗ ἕνεκα πίνουσιν *om. T*[1] ('*add. m.* 1, *ut videtur*' *Schanz*)
(35) *Soph.* 260 c : *ἀναγκαῖον ἀληθῆ πάντ' εἶναι μιγνυμένου δέ *om. T*[1]
(53) *Theaet.* 177 e : λεγέτω τὸ ὄνομα ἀλλὰ τὸ πρᾶγμα τὸ ὀνομαζόμενον θεωρείτω : μὴ γάρ *om. T*
(54) *Crat.* 384 a : * οὐδὲν ἧττον τοῦτ' εἶναι ὀρθὸν τὸ μετατεθὲν τοῦ πρότερον κειμένου *om. T.*
(59) *Theaet.* 190 c : * ἐπὶ τῶν ἐν μέρει ἐπειδὴ τὸ ῥῆμα ἕτερον τῶι ἑτέρωι κατὰ ῥῆμα ταὐτόν ἐστιν *om. T*
(64) *Phaedo* 103 d : πάνυ γε : καὶ τὸ πῦρ γε αὖ προσιόντος τοῦ ψυχροῦ αὐτῶι ἢ ὑπεξιέναι ἢ ἀπολεῖσθαι *om. T*
(87) *Crat.* 433 d : γε : ἀλλὰ τὸ εἶναι τῶν ὀνομάτων τὰ μὲν ἐκ προτέρων συγκείμενα, τὰ δὲ πρῶτα, οὐ καλῶς σοι δοκεῖ λέγεσθαι : ἐμοί *om. T*[1]
(103) *Parmen.* 143 e : τε δύο τὸ δὶς ἓν καὶ τῶι τρία τὸ τρὶς ἕν : ἀνάγκη : δυοῖν. δὲ ὄντοιν καὶ δὶς οὐκ ἀνάγκη δύο δὶς εἶναι καὶ τριῶν καὶ τρὶς οὐκ ἀνάγκη αὖ *om. T*[1]
(119) *Polit.* 275 a : * θεὸν ἀντὶ θνητοῦ ταύτηι μὲν πάμπολυ παρηνέχθημεν· ὅτι δὲ συμπάσης τῆς πόλεως ἄρχοντα αὐτὸν ἀπεφήναμεν ὅντινα δὲ τρόπον οὐ διείπομεν ταύτηι δέ *om. T*[1]

The last case is doubtful, since for τρόπον οὐ διείπομεν T^2 gives τρόπομεν. If this corruption was in the model, the total is 110.

Schanz has already drawn attention to the case of 35, which is not explained by ὁμ. He compares it with the omission of λοιδορεῖν ἅτ' οὐκ εἰδὼς κακὸν οὐδὲν οὐδενός (36) by B^1 (*corr.*) in *Theaet.* 174 c, and suggests that 35–6 represents a line in the archetype of the two families.[1] The statistics which I have given from *B* do not support this view.

On the other hand, as *T* contains 35–40 letters to the line, the omissions of 34 and 35 by T^1 may represent lines of the model, especially if, as Schanz thinks, the addition of 34 is made by the first hand. Also, there appears to be a relation between 34, 35, 64.

The three cases of 53–9, two of which are not explained by ὁμ., are also interesting, and it is to be noticed that three cases of 24–9

[1] p. 101.

are not explained by *ὁμ*. There seems, therefore, to be a second series.

The two largest numbers, 103, 119, may be explained in connexion with either series. The fact that both are repaired by the corrector suggests connexion with 34–5, in which case probably *τρόπομεν* should be credited to the model and the passage reckoned as 110 (35 × 3 = 105).

The important variants which show a cleavage between the different families are *Phil.* 43 b (19), *Hipp. Min.* 365 e (22), *Gorg.* 514 b (23), and it is more probable that here we have indications of the archetype.

The evidence is very unfavourable to the hypothesis that *T* represents a missing volume of *A*. If this were so, we should expect to find a number of omissions of 22–3 letters. As a matter of fact the few which occur seem to belong to an early period in the transmission of the text.

With regard to the recent part of *T*, i. e. after *Rep.* 389 d, Schanz points out two interesting omissions of the fifteenth-century writer (*t*).

Rep. 511 a. The model here had:

> *ἐκεῖ*
> *να ὡς ἐναργέσι δεδοξασμένοις τε καὶ τετιμημένοις μανθάνω*. (49)
> *ἐκεῖ t*, omitting *-να . . . μανθάνω*

394 b: * *καὶ τοῦτο ἔφη μανθάνω ὅτι ἔστιν τὸ περὶ τὰς τραγωιδίας τοιοῦτον* (53) *om. t*

These omissions reveal the lineation of the model.

T appears to have been a prolific parent. One of its descendants is Paris. Coisl. 155, cent. xiv/xv, Bekker's *F*. Schanz produces the following cases in which Coisl. omits lines of *T*:

(33) *Phaedo* 80 b: * *κατὰ ταῦτα ἔχοντι ἑαυτῶι ὁμοιότατον αὖ*
(41) *Cratyl.* 437 b: * *βούλει ἡ ἁμαρτία καὶ ἡ συμφορὰ εἰ κατὰ τὸ ὄνομά τις*
Hipp. Ma. 284 e: *οἱ εἰδότες ἢ οἱ μὴ εἰδότες: οἱ πολλοί: εἰσὶ δ' οὗτοι*
(42) *Alcib.* i. 106 c: * *Ἀθηναίοις ἐντὸς οὐ πολλοῦ χρόνου. εἰ οὖν μέλλοντος*
(44) *Meno* 93 b: * *ἀνθρώπωι οὐδὲ παραληπτὸν ἄλλωι παρ' ἄλλου τοῦτ' ἔστιν*

In *Phil.* 18 c *T* has:

> *ἄφωνα*
> *ἡμῖν τὸ μετὰ τοῦτο διῄρει τά τε ἄφθογγα καὶ ἄφωνα* (41)
> *μέχρι ἑνὸς ἑκάστου*

Coisl. omits *ἡμῖν . . . ἄφωνα* and inserts the words after *ἑκάστου*. This shows that the words were inserted by an intervening MS. in the margin after *ἑκάστου*.

Another MS. which he derives from *T* is Paris. 1808, which omits the following lines of *T*:

(36) *Parmen.* 143 e : * τρία τρὶς εἶναι : πῶς δ' οὔ : τί δαὶ τριῶν ὄντων
(43) *Parmen.* 164 d : * μὴ ὄντος ἄλλα ἐστίν : κομιδῆι μὲν οὖν : οὐκοῦν πολλοί

T also has a grandson in Paris. 1809, which omits the following line of Paris. 1808 :

(61) *Prot.* 322 d : ἧι λόγος ἢ ἄλλης τινὸς δημιουργικῆς ὀλίγοις οἴονται μετεῖναι συμβουλῆς

Also, in two instances, the writer of Paris. 1809 passes from one line of its model to the same place in the next, the omission being due to ὁμ., viz. :

(56) *Lys.* 213 c : πολλάκις δ' ἐχθρὸν εἶναι μὴ ἐχθροῦ ἢ καὶ φίλου ὅταν ἢ μισοῦν τις φιλῆι
(59) *Phil.* 23 e : διάκρισίν τινος δυναμένου : τάχ' ἄν. οὐ μὴν οἶμαί γε ἐν τῶι νῦν, ἂν δέ τι δέηι

F

This MS. contains *Tetr.* vii–viii, together with two dialogues from *Tetr.* vi (Gorgias, Meno) and one from ix (Minos). It consists of 263 ff., and once belonged to F. Barbaro. According to Schneider on *Rep.* 586 b the words

-τελῶς ἔφη ὁ Γλαύκων τὸν τῶν πολλῶν ὦ Σώκρατες χρησμωιδεῖς βίον (52)

form a line.

F was first used by Schneider in his edition of the *Republic* (1830). He does not call particular attention to it in his notes, but in the Index, p. 311, makes the remarkable statement *veterem vulgatam repraesentat et fere cum Stobaeo Eusebio . . . consentit.* Professor Burnet, who did not at first observe the statement in the Index, arrived at the same conclusion from the variants quoted by Schneider. In an important article he pointed out agreements of F with Stobaeus and Eusebius, and also argued from errors which it contains that it was derived from a MS. older than our oldest MSS.[1] Objections have been raised with some reason to the phrase 'ancient vulgate',[2] and perhaps it is better to speak of an 'unrevised text'.[3]

[1] *Cl. R.* xvi (1902), pp. 98–101.
[2] Stuart Jones in *Cl. R.* xvi, pp. 388–91.
[3] Immisch, p. 15.

As *F* is the chief enigma of Platonic criticism, it would be very helpful if we had a facsimile. As it is, we have Schneider's apparatus for the *Republic*, and Král has furnished Burnet with readings in other dialogues. It is probable that the MS. contains much evidence, yet unpublished, which would throw light upon its pedigree. For this purpose minute flaws, such as are not recorded in the Oxford text, are of chief importance. Without further knowledge it is impossible to say whether *F* is substantially independent, or whether it is of vulgar origin, but corrected by means of marginalia derived from an excellent source.

The following omissions and dittographies are recorded:

(10) *Rep.* 407 c: * εἰκός γε ἔφη *om. FD*
(11) *Rep.* 380 d: * φαντάζεσθαι *om. F*
(12) *Hipp. Ma.* 285 e: τοὺς ἄρχοντας *om. F*
Rep. 438 a: λέγειν ὁ ταῦτα *om. F*
459 a: ἐκ τῶν ἀρίστων *om. F*
(13) *Hipp. Ma.* 303 c: δὲ μὴ ἢ ἑκάτερον *om. F*
(14) *Gorg.* 507 c: εἰ δέ ἐστιν ἀληθῆ *om.* F^1
Hipp. Ma. 302 b: καὶ ἃ ἂν ἑκάτερος *om. F*
303 d: ὁμολογοῦμεν γάρ *om. F*
Rep. 374 b: ἀλλὰ σκυτοτόμον *om. FA*
(15) *Rep.* 420 e: μακαρίους ποιεῖν *om.* F^1
(17) *Rep.* 373 e: ὁ πόλεμος ἐργάζεται *om. F*
421 c: ποιεῖν καὶ πειστέον *om.* F^1
558 a: * οὐ κομψὴ ἢ οὔπω εἶδες *om. F*
(19) *Gorg.* 467 c: δῆλον ὅτι τὸ ὑγιαίνειν [1] *om.* F^1
Rep. 463 e: ὅτι τὸ ἐμὸν εὖ πράττει ἢ *om. F*
(20) *Hipp. Ma.* 285 a: ἀλλὰ μὴν ὠφεληθήσονται *om. F*
Tim. 32 a: τότε τὸ μέσον μὲν πρῶτον *om. F*
(23) *Meno* 93 b: ἀρετὴν ἣν αὐτοὶ ἀγαθοὶ ἦσαν *om.* F^1 *in lac.*
(24) *Gorg.* 456 c: τῆι ῥητορικῆι χρῆσθαι ὥσπερ *om.* F^1 *in lac.*
(25) *Rep.* 462 c: τὰ τοιάδε ῥήματα τό τε ἐμὸν καί *bis scr.*
(26) *Rep.* 576 c: * τοῖς δὲ πολλοῖς πολλὰ καὶ δοκεῖ *om. F*
(28) *Rep.* 372 d: τί ἂν αὐτὰς ἄλλο ἢ ταῦτα ἐχόρταζες *om.* F^1
(31) *Rep.* 457 d: οὐκ οἶμαι, ἦν δ' ἐγώ, περί γε τοῦ ὠφελίμου *om. F*
(33) *Rep.* 466 b: μή πηι κατὰ τὸν τῶν σκυτοτόμων φαίνεται *om. F*
(35) *Min.* 317 b: οὔ: οὐδὲ μεταθήσονταί ποτε περὶ τῶν αὐτῶν *om. F*
Rep. 367 b: οὐδὲ τὸ ἄδικον εἶναι ψέγειν ἀλλὰ τὸ δοκεῖν *om.* F^1
505 d: τί δὲ τόδε οὐ φανερόν, ὡς δίκαια μὲν καὶ καλά *om. F*
(36) *Rep.* 438 b: καὶ τὸ ἐσόμενον μεῖζον ἐσομένου ἐλάττονος *om. F*
Clit. 410 d: καὶ τἆλλα πάντα οἷου με νῦν οὕτως εἰρηκέναι *om.* F^1

[1] *T* here has a further omission.

(38) *Rep.* 475 c: * φήσομεν φιλομαθῆ οὐδὲ φιλόσοφον εἶναι ὥσπερ *om. F*
506 a: * ποτὲ ἀγαθά ἐστιν, οὐ πολλοῦ τινος ἄξιον φύλακα *om. F*
532 d: εἶναι ἄλλον δ' αὖ τρόπον χαλεπὰ μὴ ἀποδέχεσθαι *bis scr.*

(40) *Rep.* 495 a: * ὡς ἄρα καὶ αὐτὰ τὰ τῆς φιλοσόφου φύσεως μέρη ὅταν *om. F*

(47) *Rep.* 416 c: ὅτι δεῖ αὐτοὺς τῆς ὀρθῆς τυχεῖν παιδείας ἥτις ποτέ ἐστιν *om. F*[1]

(49) *Rep.* 553 a: * ἣν ὀλιγαρχίαν καλοῦσιν ἐκ τιμημάτων ἔχουσα τοὺς ἄρχοντας *om. F*

(50) *Rep.* 510 e: γράφουσιν καὶ τἆλλα οὕτως αὐτὰ μὲν ταῦτα ἃ πλάττουσίν τε καί *om. F*

(51) *Hipp. Ma.* 303 a: ἐπιγίγνοιτο καὶ ἑκατέρωι καὶ εἴπερ ἑκατέρωι καὶ ἀμφοτέροις *om. F*[1]

(52) *Meno* 75 d: ἀποκρίνεσθαι· ἔστι δὲ ἴσως τὸ διαλεκτικώτερον μὴ μόνον τἀληθῆ *om. F*[1]

(57) *Rep.* 544 c: ἡ Κρητική τε καὶ Λακωνικὴ αὕτη καὶ δευτέρα καὶ δευτέρως ἐπαινουμένη *om. F*

(58) *Rep.* 426 b: ἔφη. τὸ γὰρ τῶι εὖ λέγοντι χαλεπαίνειν οὐκ ἔχει χάριν: οὐκ ἐπαινέτης εἶ *om. F*

(59) *Rep.* 585 b: τί μήν: ἄγνοια δὲ καὶ ἀφροσύνη ἆρ' οὐ κενότης ἐστὶ τῆς περὶ ψυχὴν αὖ ἕξεως *om. F*

(65) *Gorg.* 465 c: ὅτι ὃ κομμωτικὴ πρὸς γυμναστικὴν τοῦτο ὀψοποιικὴ πρὸς ἰατρικήν, μᾶλλον δὲ ὧδε *om. F*, *Aristides* (*cent.* ii *A.D.*)

(85) *Rep.* 350 d: κακίαν τε καὶ ἀμαθίαν, εἶεν, ἦν δ' ἐγώ, τοῦτο μὲν ἡμῖν οὕτω κείσθω, ἔφαμεν δὲ δὴ καὶ ἰσχυρὸν εἶναι τὴν ἀδικίαν *bis scr.*

(96) *Rep.* 354 a: ὁ μὲν δίκαιος ἄρα εὐδαίμων, ὁ δ' ἄδικος ἄθλιος: ἔστω ἔφη: ἀλλὰ μὴν ἄθλιόν γε εἶναι οὐ λυσιτελεῖ, εὐδαίμονα δέ: πῶς γὰρ οὔ *om. F*

(107) *Rep.* 465 d: σωτηρίαν τροφῆι τε καὶ τοῖς ἄλλοις πᾶσιν ὅσων βίος δεῖται αὐτοί τε καὶ παῖδες ἀναδοῦνται καὶ γέρα δέχονται παρὰ τῆς αὐτῶν πόλεως *bis scr.*

(127) *Rep.* 506 d: γὰρ ἡμῖν κἂν ὥσπερ δικαιοσύνης πέρι καὶ σωφροσύνης καὶ τῶν ἄλλων διῆλθες οὕτω καὶ περὶ τοῦ ἀγαθοῦ διέλθηις: καὶ γὰρ ἐμοί, ἦν δ' ἐγώ, ὦ ἑταῖρε, καὶ μάλα ἀρκέσει *bis scr.*

To these may be added:

(183) *Minos* 313 b: ἢ καὶ λόγος σοι δοκεῖ εἶναι τὰ λεγόμενα ἢ ὄψις τὰ ὁρώμενα ἢ ἀκοὴ τὰ ἀκουόμενα; ἢ ἄλλο μὲν λόγος, ἄλλο δὲ τὰ λεγόμενα; καὶ ἄλλο μὲν ὄψις ἄλλο δὲ τὰ ὁρώμενα, καὶ ἄλλο μὲν ἀκοή, ἄλλο δὲ τὰ ἀκουόμενα καὶ ἄλλο δὴ νόμος, ἄλλο δὲ τὰ νομιζόμενα;

The passage is written twice in *F*, but on the second occasion the words ἢ ἄλλο μὲν λόγος . . . ἄλλο δὲ τὰ ἀκουόμενα (89) are omitted. The omission seems accidental and due to ὁμ.

In this list we observe a striking bulge at 33–8 (9 exx.), of which there are three cases of 35. We may also observe that 65 + 31 = 96, and 96 + 31 = 127. It seems probable that we are here on the track of an ancestor.

We have also to notice the six cases of 50–59. In view of the fact that a line of *F* quoted by Schneider (*Rep.* 586 b) contains 52 letters, it is possible that some of these may represent lines in an immediate ancestor.

There is little evidence for any smaller unit. The omissions of 23 and 24 *in lac.* are interesting, but probably due to accident.

It may be convenient to collect here the passages preserved by *F* as against other MSS.

(10) *Meno* 99 a : τινος ὀρθῶς
(12) *Meno* 99 c : ἐνθουσιῶντες
(14) *Gorg.* 492 b : καὶ δικαιοσύνης
(15) *Gorg.* 460 e : καὶ ἀδίκως χρῆται
480 d : * μὴ φειδόμενον ἀλλ'
(21) *Tim.* 47 a : καὶ ἰσημερίαι καὶ τροπαί
(22) *Hip. Min.* 365 e : ὅ τι ποιοῦσιν ἢ ἐπίστανται

W

This MS. contains *Tetr.* i.–vii., with the exception of two dialogues in *Tetr.* iv. (*Alcib.* ii., *Amat.*). There appears to be some doubt as to its date. It was used by Stallbaum, who calls it *Vind.* 1, but his collations were extremely superficial. Thus, he does not mention that it contains *Cratyl.* 438 a τάδε δὲ . . . οὔ μοι δοκεῖ, for which he quotes an inferior MS. (Gud.). Burnet has used some readings communicated to him by Král. Grenfell and Hunt on Oxyrhynchus 843 (*Symposium*) refer to a collation placed at their disposal by Prof. H. Schöne of Bâle, from which they mention an interesting omission in 208 d.

The omissions mentioned by Král and Schöne are:

(27) *Lys.* 209 c : ἐν οἷς δὲ ἄρτι ἐλέγομεν κωλύουσι *om.* W^1
(35) *Meno* 97 c : τότε δ' οὔ : πῶς λέγεις, ὁ ἀεὶ ἔχων ὀρθὴν δόξαν *om.* *W*
(43) *Symp.* 208 d : ἂν ἢ Ἀχιλλέα Πατρόκλωι ἐναποθανεῖν ἢ προαποθανεῖν *om.* *W*
(87) *Meno* 77 c : ἀμφότερα ἔμοιγε δοκεῖ : ἢ γὰρ δοκεῖ τίς σοι, ὦ Μένων, γιγνώσκων τὰ κακὰ ὅτι κακά ἐστιν, ὅμως ἐπιθυμεῖν αὐτῶν *om.* W^1
(88) *Meno* 74 e : σχῆμα εἶναι ἢ τὸ εὐθὺ ἢ οὐχ οὕτω λέγεις : ἔγωγε : ἆρ' οὖν ὅταν οὕτω λέγῃς τότε οὐδὲν μᾶλλον φῄς τὸ στρογγύλον *om.* W^1

The relation between 43, 87, 88 is very striking.

CHAPTER XIII

THE PARIS MANUSCRIPT OF DEMOSTHENES

PARIS. 2934 (*S*), cent. x, is a large MS., consisting of 534 ff., i. e. nearly 67 quaternions. It is written in two columns, with 32 lines to the page. I have counted the letters on the verso of f. 36, and find the contents to be 793 letters in col. i and 768 in col. ii. This gives a total of 1561 in a page, i. e. about 3,122 in a folio. The average content of a line in f. 36ᵛ is nearly 25 letters in col. I and exactly 24 in col. ii. Single lines vary from 20 to 30 letters, the numbers being distributed thus:

(20) 1 ex.	(25) 13 exx.
(21) 5 exx.	(26) 11 exx.
(22) 5 exx.	(27) 2 exx.
(23) 11 exx.	(28) 3 exx.
(24) 11 exx.	(30) 2 exx.

Out of a total of 64 lines, 46 contain 23–6 letters.

S contains a quantity of marginalia written in hands ranging from the twelfth to the fifteenth century. It is to be noticed that on some occasions a late hand adds in the margin or elsewhere a passage already present in the text of *S*. The most striking case is on f. 161ᵛ (xviii. 34–5). Here the words ἀξιῶ δὲ ὑμᾶς . . . ἅπαντ' ἀπώλετο are written a second time at the foot of the page with a reference mark in the margin λείπει ἐκ τοῦ κειμένου, ζήτει κάτω. Dindorf points out that the passage must have been omitted by some MS. with which *S* was collated. In xxi. 69 οὐδ' ἐνεανιεύσατο . . . ὑπέστην οὕτω the annotator, who repeats the passage with some variants, ends with ὑπέστην οὕ-. The presumption here is that in the MS. which he was using a line ended with οὕ-. These marginalia on account of their late date cannot cast any light upon the model of *S*, and as they only confuse the issue I think it best to disregard them. I therefore only employ the formula *om.* S^1 when the omission is repaired by the scribe or by a contemporary hand.

The model of *S* appears to have contained some variants. Thus xviii. 95 for εἰδότας ἡγοῦμαι *S* has εἰδότας εἰδέναι. Here εἰδέναι is a variant for εἰδότας, which has expelled ἡγοῦμαι. So liii. 13 for συνοικίαν *S* has συνθήκην συνοικίαν. Also some marginal notes written by the first hand seem to have been taken over from the model, e. g. f. 134ʳ ὁρικὸν τὸ κεφάλαιον.

Various small omissions are repaired by the scribe, e. g. ff. 103ᵛ πρὸς αὐτὸν οὐ, 128ʳ ὁ δῆμος, 143ᵛ πρὸς τόν, 243ʳ τῆς ἡμέρας, 384ᵛ καθ' ἕκαστον, 402ʳ περιγενέσθαι, Ὀλυμπιόδωρος, 471ᵛ τῆς ἀδελφῆς. The first of these (xxiii. 162) is interesting. *S* has:

γράψας
δὲ ὡς ἀλεξάνδρου πρεσβευ
σαμένου προσεδέξατο τοῖς
λῃσταῖς

The words πρὸς αὐτὸν οὐ are inserted before, instead of after, πρεσβευσαμένου.

There are also some longer passages which suggest that *S* was copied from a model written in similar formation. The most important is on f. 36ᵛ (ix. 17). Here other MSS. give:

εἰ μὴ καὶ τοὺς τὰ μηχανήματα ἐφιστάντας εἰρήνην ἄγειν φήσετε ἕως ἂν αὐτὰ τοῖς τείχεσιν ἤδη προσαγάγωσιν· ἀλλ' οὐ φήσετε.

S has in the text:

εἰ μὴ καὶ τοὺς τὰ μηχανήματα ἐφι (26)
στάντας εἰρήνην ἄγειν φήσετε ἕως (28)

The scribe adds two lines in the margin written thus:

ἂν αὐτὰ τοῖς τείχεσιν ἤδη (21)
προσαγάγωσιν ἀλλ' οὐ φήσετε (23) = 44

The omission is not recorded by Dindorf, probably because the work of the first hand is so manifest. Fuhr says "ἕως . . . φήσετε *om.* S¹, *scriba ipse* ὁ *mutavit in* ἕως *et* ἂν . . . ὁ *add. in mg.*' I am inclined to think that he is right, since there are traces of an erasure under ἕως, and ὁ in the next line may have been added subsequently. If so, the original omission consisted of 47 letters. In any case the suspicion arises that the scribe dropped two lines of his model.

A second case is on f. 501ᵛ (lviii. 62), where the scribe adds in the space between the columns a passage omitted in col. ii, viz. ἀλλὰ τοὺς λέγοντας ἀεὶ γραφόμενοι χρήματα λαμβάνουσιν (47). The supplement here is not arranged in lines, since the space was inadequate for this purpose. It is to be noticed that for *λέγοντας ἀεί* other MSS. (so edd.) give *ἐκεῖθεν*.

Other passages ascribed by Dindorf to *m.* 1 are:

(27) f. 334v (xxxv. 56): ἐψηφισμένοι καὶ περιαιρήσεσθε
f. 412r (xlvii. 32): τετελευτηκότος τοῦ Δημοχάρους
(34) f. 486v (lvii. 10): οὐ πλείους ἢ τριάκοντα· ἐν δὲ τούτοις ἦσαν
(54) f. 388v (xxxi. 14): καὶ δι' ὀρφανίαν ἠδικημένον καὶ προικὸς ἀληθινῆς ἀπεστερημένον

After some hesitation I incline to agree with Dindorf in ascribing the last example to the first hand. I do not feel so positive about the other three cases, but am quite prepared to agree with his verdict.

Dindorf speaks of another addition as entered '*a manu antiquissima, fortasse prima*', viz.:

(22) f. 108r (xxiii. 198) * τῶν τιμῶν ταῖς ὑπερβολαῖς

There can be no doubt that this is written by a second hand, though possibly that of a contemporary corrector.

I now tabulate the evidence given by these ancient additions:

(22) xxiii. 198
(27) xxxv. 56, xlvii. 32
(34) lvii. 10
(47) ix. 17: lviii. 62
(54) xxxi. 14

With the exception of 34, the figures reveal a unit of 22–7 letters.

I now mention three occasions where *S* has an omission *in lacuna*, viz.:

(17) f. 250v (lix. 9): * ὡς Κυρηναῖοι εἴησαν
(29) f. 250r (lix. 8): * τοὺς δικαστὰς δίκαιον ὀργίζεσθαι

Here *S* leaves blank a small space at the end of a line, also a complete line. The probability is that the model had

τοὺς
δικαστὰς δίκαιον ὀργίζεσθαι (25)

(88) f. 389r (liv. 2): * ἃ πέπονθ' ἀκούσητε. δεινῆς γὰρ οὔσης τῆς τότε συμβάσης ὕβρεως οὐκ ἐλάττων ἡ μετὰ ταῦτ' ἀσέλγειά ἐστι τουτουί

The relation of 88 to 22, 47 *bis* suggests that four lines of the model were here omitted.

It is to be noticed that 17 appears to be in relation to the omission of 34 previously mentioned. It is, however, necessary to be cautious, since these omissions *in lacuna* are most easily explained by supposing that a single MS. was damaged in places, and it may have been only a portion of a line which was illegible.

There are a number of passages omitted by *S* which might be here produced as examples of line omission. It will, however, be more convenient to treat these together with the other omissions, some of which may go back to a previous ancestor. I therefore reserve this evidence for the present, and merely give that which is furnished by various corruptions.

The most important passage is Ep. iii. 10:

παρ' ἑτέρων ἔδει δόντας ἐκ τῶν προσιόντων

For προσιόντων *S* has προτέρων σιόντων. This indicates in the model

παρ' ἑ
τέρων ἔδει δόντας ἐκ τῶν προ (23)
σιόντων

The scribe after writing -τέρων . . . προ- began to repeat the line.

The error may be illustrated from Aristotle, *Eth.* iv. 3. 20 ἀξιοῦσιν οὔτε ὀρθῶς μεγαλόψυχοι λέγονται. ἄνευ γὰρ ἀρετῆς. Here an Oxford MS. (Corpus Christi cxii) after ἄνευ γὰρ has ἀρέσιν οὔτε ὀρθῶς μεγαλόψυχοι λέγονται ἄνευ γὰρ ἀρετῆς. The MS. in question is derived from Laur. lxxxi. 11, which has:

ἀξιοῦ
σιν οὔτε ὀρθῶς μεγαλόψυχοι λέγονται ἄνευ γὰρ ἀρε
τῆς

Here the whole line was repeated by the scribe.[1]

I now add other examples. For the sake of brevity I give first the distribution which I attribute to the model, and then add the corruption found in *S*:

xxi. 40: πάντα μᾶλλον ἢ ταῦτα λεκτέον (24)
πᾶν γάρ

πάντα (before γάρ) *S*.

150: οὐδένα οἶμαι τρόπον φέρειν (23)
οὐδέ

οὐδένα (for οὐδέ) *S*.

[1] J. A. Stewart, English MSS. of the *Nicomachean Ethics*, p. 44.

xxvii. 42 : τὰ δύο τάλαντα δημοφῶντι καὶ τάς (24)

καὶ τὰ δύο τάλαντα τάς *S*.

xxviii. 4 : ἡγεμόνα με τῆς συμμορίας καταστήσας (24)

S repeats με after καταστήσας.

xxxv. 3 : μὲν οὖν τοιοῦτοί εἰσιν· ἐγὼ δ' ὦ ἄνδρες (22)

ἐγὼ μὲν δ' *S*.

xxxix. 3 : ἐξαπατηθεὶς ὑπὸ τῆς τουτουὶ μητρὸς ὀμοσάσης (24)

ἐξαπατησάσης for μητρὸς ὀμοσάσης *S*.

xliii. 32 : καὶ ἐκ τοῦ οἴκου οὖσα τοῦ Ἁγνίου ἐπειδάν (26)

S repeats καί before ἐπειδάν.

lviii. 62 : ὑμᾶς οὐδεὶς ὡς ἐπιλείψουσιν οἱ (24)

S has ὑμᾶς before οἱ.

68 : μετασχεῖν τῆς καὶ τοῖς ξένοις δεδομένης. (25)

μετὰ δεδομένης *S*.

lx. 5 : χώραν εἶναι τῶν ἡμετέρων προγόνων (24)

προγόνων εἶ *S*.

The example found in lviii. 62 is of special interest, since in the same section there is a passage of 47 letters added by the first hand. (Cf. p. 419.) The intermediate words between the two passages consist of 234 letters (23 × 10 = 230). We can now arrange the model:

ὑμᾶς οὐδεὶς ὡς ἐπιλείψουσιν (24)
οἱ τοιοῦτοι ῥήτορες οὐδ' ὡς (22)
διὰ τοῦτο χεῖρον ἡ πόλις οἰκή (24)
σεται· τοὐναντίον γάρ ἐστιν (23)
ὡς ἐγὼ τῶν πρεσβυτέρων ἀκούω (24)
τότε γάρ φασιν ἄριστα πρᾶξαι (24)
τὴν πόλιν ὅτε μέτριοι καὶ σώ (23)
φρονες ἄνδρες ἐπολιτεύοντο (24)

πότερον γὰρ συμβούλους εὕροι (25)
τις ἂν τούτους ἀγαθοὺς ἀλλ' (22)
οὐδὲν ἐν τῶι δήμωι λέγουσιν (23)
ἀλλὰ τοὺς λέγοντας ἀεὶ γραφό (24)
μενοι χρήματα λαμβάνουσιν (23)

S[1] repeats ὑμᾶς at the beginning of l. 2 and omits ll. 12–13.

I now take corruptions which exhibit multiples of the unit. (*a*) Two lines:

xviii. 257: ταυ
την ποίαι τινὶ κέχρησαι τύχηι (25)
δι' ἣν παῖς μὲν ὢν μετὰ πολλῆς (23) = 48
ἐνδείας

S has τ̣η̣ν̣ before ἐνδείας (τῆς *L*).

xxvii. 35: δύο τάλαντα
δημοφῶν δ' ἑπτὰ καὶ ὀγδοήκοντα (25)
μνᾶς· τοῦτο δ' ἐστὶ πέντε τάλαντα (26) = 51
καὶ πεντεκαίδεκα μναῖ

S inserts καὶ πεντεκαίδεκα μνᾶς (from l. 4) after τάλαντα in l. 1

xlvii. 27: κλητῆρες
μεμαρτυρήκασιν· ὡς δὲ εἰσή (22)
χθη εἰς τὸ δικαστήριον λαβέ (23) = 45
μοι

S has μοι before μεμαρτυρήκασιν as well as after λαβέ.

xxxi. 3: εὐθὺς ἀδικεῖν βουλόμενος ψευ (25)
δεῖς ἔθηκεν ἐκείνους εἰκὸς καὶ (26) = 51
τούτους

S substitutes τούτους for εὐθύς in l. 1.

lvii. 40: τῶν φρατέρων τῶν συγγενῶν (22)
τῶν τῆς μητρὸς καὶ δημοτῶν (22) = 44
μαρτυρίας

S has μαρτυρίας before τῶν φρατέρων as well as after δημοτῶν.

(*b*) Three lines:

xviii. 56: ἃ μὲν
διώκει τοῦ ψηφίσματος ὦ ἄν (22)
δρες ἀθηναῖοι ταῦτ' ἐστίν. ἐ (22)
γὼ δ' ἀπ' αὐτῶν τούτων πρῶτον (22) = 66
mg. οἴομαι οἶμαι

S has ἃ μεν ο̣ἴ̣ο̣μ̣α̣ι̣ διώκει. This is a clear case of a variant which has got into the text higher up. Cf. Dindorf, p. xiii (*ed. min.*).

(*c*) Four lines:

xv. 9: ἀριοβαρζάνηι
προσγράψαντες τῶι ψηφίσμα (23)
τι μὴ λύοντα τὰς σπονδὰς τὰς (23)
πρὸς τὸν βασιλέα· ἰδὼν δ' ἐκεῖ (23)
νος τὸν μὲν ἀριοβαρζάνην (21) = 90
φανερῶς ἀφεστῶτα βασιλέως

S has φανερῶς . . . βασιλέως after Ἀριοβαρζάνῃ as well as *suo loco*. With this we may probably connect:

xviii. 25: τὴν εἰρήνην ἡ πόλις ἐνταῦθα πά (25)
λιν σκέψασθε τί ἡμῶν ἑκάτερος (25)
προείλετο πράττειν καὶ γὰρ ἐκ (25)
τούτων εἴσεσθε τίς ἦν ὁ φιλίππωι (27) = 102
πάντα

For πάντα *SL*[1] have τε τὴν εἰρήνην. The scribe seems to have looked back to l. 1. The unit here is longer than in xv. 9, but the two examples of 51 (xxvii. 35, xxxi. 3) justify the arrangement.

(*d*) Six lines:

x. 69–70: τῆι μὲν
κατὰ τὴν ἀγορὰν εὐετηρίαι λαμ (25)
προὶ τῆι δ' ὧν προσῆκε παρασκευ (25)
ῆι καταγέλαστοι· οὐ τὸν αὐτὸν (24)
δὲ τρόπον περί τε ὑμῶν καὶ πε (23)
ρὶ αὐτῶν ἐνίους τῶν λεγόντων (24)
ὁρῶ βουλευομένους· ὑμᾶς μὲν (23) = 144
γάρ

S has γὰρ from l. 8 after τῇ μὲν in l. 1 (ὁμ).

(*e*) Eight lines:

lv. 26–7: εἰς τὴν ὁδὸν
ἐξάγειν εἰώθατε ἀλλ' οὐ μὰ (21)
δί' εἴσω τὸ ἐκ τῆς ὁδοῦ δέχε (21)
σθαι τί δεῖ πλείω λέγειν οὐ (22)
δὲ γὰρ ἐκ τούτων ἄδηλον ὅτι (22)
φανερῶς συκοφαντοῦμαι οὔ (22)
τ' ἀδικῶν οὐδὲν οὔτε βεβλαμ (22)
μένων ἅ φασιν· ἵνα δ' εἰδῆτε ὅ (22)
τι καὶ τὸν χλῆδον εἰς τὴν ὅδον (24) = 176
ἐκβεβλήκασιν

S has ἐκβεβλήκασιν after ὁδὸν in l. 1.

xl. 54:

	ὑπὲρ ὧν ἂν λέγηι καὶ μὴ ὑμᾶς	(22)
	φάσκοντα εἰδέναι περὶ ὧν αὐ	(23)
	τὸς οὐδὲν ἕξει εἰπεῖν δίκαι	(23)
	ον ἀποδιδράσκειν τὴν ἀλή	(21)
	θειαν ἐπεὶ καὶ ἐγὼ ὦ ἄνδρες	(22)
	δικασταὶ πάντων ὑμῶν εἰδό	(22)
	των ὃν τρόπον ἀναγκασθεὶς ὁ	(23)
	πατήρ μου ἐποιήσατο τούτους	(24) = 180
	οὐδέν	

S inserts ὑπερων (*sic*) from l. 1 before οὐδέν in l. 9. The relation of 180 to 90 (xv. 9) is to be noticed.

(*f*) Twelve lines:

xlvii. 74–5	ψευδομαρτυριῶν	
	ὥστε ἀπολαβεῖν με τὰ ἐνέχυρα	(24)
	καὶ ἐπειδὴ ἐδεήθην αὐτοῦ ἀνα	(24)
	βαλέσθαι μοι τὴν ὑπερημερίαν	(25)
	ἄσμενος ἤκουσεν ἵνα ὑπερήμε	(24)
	ρος αὐτῶι γενοίμην καὶ ἐκφο	(23)
	ρήσαιτό μου ὡς πλεῖστα καὶ δι	(24)
	ὰ τοῦτο ἀκάκως καὶ ταχύ μοι ὡμο	(25)
	λόγησεν ἵνα πιθανὸς γένηται	(24)
	καὶ μὴ καταφανὴς ἐπιβουλεύ	(23)
	ων ἡγούμενος οὐκ εἶναι αὐτῶι	(24)
	δι' ἄλλου τρόπου τοὺς μάρτυρας	(25)
	ἀφεθῆναι τῶν ψευδομαρτυριῶν	(25) = 290
	ἢ διὰ τοῦ ἐξαπατῆσαι	

S has ἢ διὰ τοῦ ἐξαπατῆσαι after ψευδομαρτυριῶν in l. 1, as well as after the same word in l. 13. The relation of 290 to 144 (x. 69–70) is to be observed.

I add a conspectus of these corruptions:

(22)	xxxv. 3	(51)	xxvii. 35, xxxi. 3
(23)	xxi. 150, Ep. iii. 10	(66)	xviii. 56
(24)	xxi. 40, xxvii. 42, xxviii. 4, xxxix. 3, lviii. 62, lx. 5	(90)	xv. 9
		(102)	xviii. 25
(25)	lviii. 68	(144)	x. 69–70
(26)	xliii. 32	(176)	lv. 26–7
(44)	lvii. 40	(180)	xl. 54
(45)	xlvii. 27	(290)	xlvii. 74–5
(48)	xviii. 257		

I have not included in this list one passage in which a repetition takes place at a greater distance. In *Prooem.* xxxix we have ἐγὼ δὲ οὐδαμῶς μὲν ἂν ἐβουλόμην. In *Prooem.* xl *S* gives βουλεύεσθαι ἐγὼ δὲ οὐδαμῶς. The intermediate passage here consists of 597 letters. This might be connected with 290 in xlvii. 74–5 and explained as 24 lines (290 × 2 = 580). The correspondence, however, is not very close, and it will be seen further on that there is reason for referring this with some other corruptions to a previous stage in the tradition.

I now proceed to discuss a dislocation in *S*, which throws light upon the foliation of an ancestor, viz.:

lix. 83–9: οἱ Ἀρεοπαγῖται . . . ἀκούοντας αὐτῶν
89–107: βελτίους ἔσεσθε . . . ὁμολογουμένως ἀρίστους

These blocks of text are transposed in *S*.[1] They do not coincide with folios in *S*, and therefore represent folios in an ancestor.

The first point to notice is that §§ 83–9 contain two headings, viz. MAPTUPIA and NOMOS MOIXEIAS, while §§ 89–107 contain one, viz. ΨΗΦΙΣΜΑ ΠΕΡΙ ΠΛΑΤΑΙΕΩΝ. In *S* a separate line is given to each heading. In order, therefore, to make the comparison exact, we must allow the average content of a line for each heading. I put this at 24, but any other figure will do equally well.

The second point is that the longest omission of *S*, τὰ δημοτελῆ . . . περὶ τὰ ἱερά (170) occurs in §§ 87–8. This omission may have been made by the writer of *S*, or it may have been already present in the model. The following figures favour the second hypothesis.

§§ 83–9 consist of 1,964 letters. If we add 48 for the two headings the total is 2,012.

§§ 89–107 consist of 7,358 letters, to which must be added 24 for the heading, = 7,382.

This result is not satisfactory. If, however, we subtract 170 from 2,012, the result is 1,842. If we divide 7,382 by 4, the result is 1,845·5, which is exceedingly close. It appears that a folio in a previous MS. got out of place and was inserted after four folios in the same MS.

The next point to notice is that this previous MS. does not appear to have been the model of *S*. All the evidence furnished by omissions of the first hand, lacunas, and corruptions shows that, so

[1] A late hand has corrected the dislocation by adding in the margin μετὰ δύο φύλλα ἔνθα τὸ (.

far as length of line is concerned, the model was much like *S*. We should expect to find that the model more or less resembled *S* in the number of lines to a page. The ancestor, however, which is revealed by this dislocation appears to have contained about 1,845 letters to a folio, while *S* has about 3,122. If written in two columns, it could only contain 20 lines of 23–4 letters, as compared with 32 in *S*. This does not seem probable. It is more likely that the dislocation took place in a previous MS. written in narrower columns. We have seen that the omission of 170 letters (lix. 87–8) was prior to the dislocation. We must, therefore, be prepared to find traces of a previous MS. in narrower columns among the evidence furnished by omissions and corruptions in *S*.

It will be convenient to collect here corruptions in *S* which indicate a previous ancestor, or ancestors. I take first two examples which are somewhat doubtful, since they might be explained as due to short lines in the model.

xxiv. 27: ὅπως ἂν τὰ ἱερὰ θύηται καὶ ἡ διοίκησις

S inserts πως after καί. This clearly indicates:

ὅ
πως ἂν τὰ ἱερὰ θύηται καὶ (20)
ἡ διοίκησις

xviii. 87: ὁ Φίλιππος ἐξηλάθη τοῖς μὲν ὅπλοις ὑφ' ὑμῶν, τῇ δὲ πολιτείᾳ καὶ τοῖς ψηφίσμασι . . . ὑπ' ἐμοῦ

S has ὑφ' ἡμῶν (*sic*) before ἐξηλάθη instead of after ὅπλοις. The words appear to have been inserted in the wrong place after previous omission. This indicates:

φίλιππος
ἐξηλάθη τοῖς μὲν ὅπλοις (20)
mg. ὑφ' ὑμῶν τῆι δὲ πολιτείαι

Apart from these doubtful cases, the evidence indicates a line of 16–18 letters in a previous ancestor. I take first a striking case:

xx. 104: οὐ λέγεις κακῶς τοὺς τετελευτηκότας τῶν εὐεργετῶν

S inserts εὖ after τούς. This indicates:

τοὺς
τετελευτηκότας τῶν (17)
εὐεργετῶν

Other examples are:

iv. 30: ἐν τοῖς ψηφίσμασι καί (18)

S repeats ἐν after καί.

xviii. 305: κατὰ τὰ ἐμὰ ψηφίσματα (18)

These words, which are omitted *suo loco*, before the heading ΑΡΙΘΜΟΣ ΒΟΗΘΕΙΩΝ, are inserted after it in *S*.

xxiii. 160: τὴν πρὸς ὑμᾶς ἔπεμπεν (18)
ἐπιστολήν

S[1] repeated τήν before ἐπιστολήν. It was subsequently erased.

xxxvii. 16: οὐδ'
ἂν εἴ τι γένοιτ' ᾠήθην (18)

S repeats ἄν after ᾠήθην (so *A*).

xlix. 45: καὶ ὡς μὲν ἀληθῆ λέγει (18)
οὐδένα

S repeats καί before οὐδένα.

lii. 4: ἀρχεβιά
δηι καὶ τῶι φρασίαι (16)
προσέταξεν

S adds δῃ after Φρασίᾳ.

lix. 15: ποιεῖν
τι τῶν νομιζομένων (16)
ὑπέρ

S repeats τι before ὑπέρ.

lx. 20: οὔτε καλλίω πρόφασιν (18)
τοῦ τῆς

S has οὔτε for τοῦ.

I would also call attention to:

xxiii. 157: ἐξηλέγχθη τὸ πρᾶγμ'· ἐπ' αὐτοφώρῳ

S inserts φανερῶς, an obvious gloss, before τό. This indicates:

ἐξηλέγχθη
τὸ πρᾶγμ' ἐπ' αὐτοφώρωι (18) *mg.* φανερῶς

In the following cases the writer seems to have looked forward, or backward, two lines:

xxi. 137: τὴν κατ' ἀξίαν τῶν πε (16)
πραγμένων παρὰ τούτων (19) = 35
δίκην

S[1] repeated τήν before δίκην.

lx. 15 : προσιστάμενα γὰρ
πάντα εἰς ἕνα καιρὸν (17)
δύσκριτον καθίστησί (18) = 35
μοι

S has μοι after γάρ as well as *suo loco* (so *FO*).

lxi. 12–13 : σοῦ καταστῆσαι καὶ μὲν (19)
δὴ καὶ τῶν ὁρωμένων (16) = 35
ἐπιφανεστάτου

S has σοιφανεστάτου in l. 3. Here either the writer looked back to σου, or a variant σοι has got out of place and been conflated with ἐπιφανεστάτου.

I do not attempt to pursue the subject further, since it would be difficult to distinguish multiples of this unit and the one previously discussed. I will only make an observation about two passages mentioned above. In xlvii. 74–5 *S* inserts ἢ διὰ τοῦ ἐξαπατῆσαι (17) before 290 letters. It is possible that the words formed a line in a previous ancestor and after omission were inserted after the first ψευδομαρτυριῶν as well as after the second. In lix. 83–9 the omission of 170 letters by *S* has been shown to be prior to the model. It is tempting to suppose that it = 17 × 10.

Two of the corruptions just mentioned, xxxvii. 16 and lx. 15, are shared with *S*, in one case by *A*, and in another by *FO*. It is interesting to find a similar unit in corruptions common to all MSS. I take first a striking example:

xl. 5 : οὐκ ἐγὼ τούτου αἴτιός (18)
εἰμι

The MSS. repeat οὐκ before εἰμί.

With this we may compare:

iii. 7 : τοῦτο πέπρακται νυνί (18)

So edd. *S* has τοῦτο πέπρακται νυνί τοῦτο, and so apparently F^1. Other MSS. give πέπρακται νυνὶ τοῦτο. Here a common ancestor seems to have added τοῦτο from the previous line; a corrector struck out the first τοῦτο instead of the second.

xviii. 112 : εἰς
δὲ τοὺς συκοφάντας (16)
ἄγειν

So *FL*. *S* repeats δέ before ἄγειν, while *A Y* have εἰς τοὺς συκοφάντας δ' ἄγειν.

lx. 4: δικαίως ἄν τις ὑπολάβοι τοὺς μὲν ἐπήλυδας ἐλθόντας εἰς τὰς πόλεις καὶ τούτων πολίτας προσαγορευομένους ὁμοίους εἶναι τοῖς εἰσποιητοῖς τῶν παίδων

The MSS. place εἰς τὰς (τοὺς *S*) before ἐπήλυδας. The words appear to have been inserted in the wrong place after previous omission. This suggests:

τοὺς μὲν
ἐπήλυδας ἐλθόντας (16)
mg. εἰς τὰς πόλεις

I add an interesting transposition:

l. 17: δανεισάμενος ἐγὼ ἀργύριον παρ' Ἀρχεδήμου μὲν τοῦ Ἀναφλυστίου πεντεκαίδεκα μνᾶς ἐπίτοκον, ὀκτακοσίας δὲ δραχμὰς παρὰ Νικίππου τοῦ ναυκλήρου ναυτικὸν ἀνειλόμην, ὃς ἔτυχεν ὢν ἐν Σηστῷ, ἐπόγδοον

So the MSS. The words ὃς ἔτυχεν ὢν ἐν Σηστῶι (18) appear to be out of place. Boeckh says that 'they can only be referred to Nicippus by a very forced translation. Most probably they should come after Ἀναφλυστίου, for, since it might appear strange that the Anaphlystian should be mentioned as being in Sestos, it was natural to add that he was there by accident.'

The following transposition variants are significant:

vi. 13: τοὺς Θηβαίους ἢ ὑμᾶς (17)

ἀξιοῦν is placed after ὑμᾶς by *S*, and before τοὺς by other MSS.

lv. 5: δυσχερὲς πρὸς ἀλλήλους (20)

ἦν is placed before δυσχερὲς by *S*, and after ἀλλήλους by other MSS.

lviii. 49: λαβὲ τὸν νόμον τοῦτον (18)

πάλιν is placed before λαβέ by *S*, and after τοῦτον by other MSS.

In lv. 5 the unit is slightly longer than elsewhere. The same phenomenon has already been noticed in the case of corruptions peculiar to *S*. This fact may throw light upon a curious repetition in i. 19 τί οὖν, ἄν τις εἴποι, σὺ γράφεις ταῦτ' εἶναι στρατιωτικά; μὰ Δί' οὐκ ἔγωγε. ἐγὼ μὲν γὰρ ἡγοῦμαι στρατιώτας δεῖν κατασκευασθῆναι καὶ ταῦτ' εἶναι στρατιωτικὰ καὶ μίαν σύνταξιν εἶναι. Here editors strike out καὶ ταῦτ' εἶναι στρατιωτικά. It is to be noticed that the repeated words, ταῦτ' εἶναι στρατιωτικά consist of 20 letters, while μὰ Δί' οὐκ . . . κατασκευασθῆναι καί consist of 60.

I now recall attention to the list of additions made by the first hand or a contemporary corrector in *S*, viz.: 22, 27 (*bis*), 34, 47 (*bis*), 54. Here 34 is a recalcitrant figure, which has no connexion with the others. In view of the facts now produced it appears probable that 34 = 17 × 2, i.e. two lines of a previous MSS. We may compare the following corruptions:

xxiv. 100: *τὰς πράξεις κατὰ τοὺς ὑπάρχοντας νόμους* (34)

These words are given twice by the MSS. in the same sentence, viz. after *τῶν ἐγγυητῶν* and *suo loco* (after *κατὰ τούτων εἶναι*). The intermediate passage consists of 113 letters (17 × 7 = 119).

lix. 63: *Φράστορα δ' ἐκβαλόντα τε τὴν θυγατέρα τὴν Νεαίρας ταυτησὶ γήμαντα . . . καὶ τὴν προῖκα οὐκ ἀποδόντα*

So edd., the MSS. place *τε* after *γήμαντα*. This suggests:

ἐκβαλόντα *mg. τε*
τὴν θυγατέρα τὴν νεαί (18)
ρας ταυτησὶ γήμαντα (17) = 35

xxi. 100: *τίς οὖν ὑβρίζων πάυσεται . . . εἰ τοῦτον μὲν ὥσπερ δεινὰ πάσχοντα ἐλεήσετε, εἰ δέ τις πένης μηδὲν ἠδικηκώς . . . ὑπὸ τούτου περιπέπτωκε, τούτῳ δ' οὐδὲ συνοργισθήσεσθε;*

Here *μὲν* after *τοῦτον* is supplied by editors. It is to be noticed that *F* has *μέν* for *μηδέν* after *πένης*. This suggests:

τοῦτον
mg. μὲν *ὥσπερ δεινὰ πάσχοντα ἐ* (19)
λεήσετε εἰ δέ τις πένης (19) = 38
μηδέν

I now take a curious passage, xxii. 23. Blass here accepts from the citation of Maximus (*Rhet. Gr.* v. 579) the words *ὕστερον ἐπειδὰν νῦν περὶ ὧν εἴσηκται δῶι λόγον* (39), which are omitted by all the MSS.

I have reserved until the last the most striking passage, viz.:

lix. 5: *ὡς ὦφλε τῶι δημοσίωι ἐκ πέντε καὶ εἴκοσιν ἐτῶν* (38)

The words are placed here (after *μάρτυρας παρασχόμενος*) by edd. In the MSS. they come in § 9 after *αἰτίαν ψευδῆ*, where they destroy the sense. The intermediate passage *καὶ ἔξω . . . αἰτίαν ψευδῆ* consists of 1,190 letters. In view of the distance which intervenes between the correct place and that which they occupy in the MSS., the suspicion arises that after omission they were entered on the wrong folio of a common ancestor.

I have noticed cases of corruptions involving more than two units, but prefer not to carry the inquiry further, since to do so would require more time than I have at my disposal. I would only say that both in *S* and in all the MSS. there are indications of a shorter line in a previous MS. in addition to the line in the model of 23–4 letters attested by the bulk of the corruptions in *S*. It is tempting to suppose that this previous MS. was the archetype. It is, however, possible that there were intervening MSS. written in similar formation.

I now proceed to tabulate the omissions of *S* in the usual way. The first point to notice is the absence of telescoped passages. The only one which I have come across is in *Prooem.* 29:

ἐπειδὰν πράττειν τι δέῃ· εἰ μὲν οὖν ἀποδόντων ὑμῶν.

S here omits εἰ μὲν οὖν ἀποδόν- (14). This instance is deprived of importance by the fact that it comes after the last line of col. 2. The omission seems due to the scribe's having lost his place when turning over a page. Apart from it, I do not find any clear indication of so small a unit. In order, therefore, to lighten the inquiry I begin with omissions of 16 letters. I reserve for the moment all cases which occur in *Phil.* iii.

(16) viii. 7 : καὶ ἀναγκαιότατον *om.* *SL*
17 : διαφθαρήσεται καί *om.* *SL*
xviii. 100 : ἐν οἷς ἐπιστεύθητε *om.* *S*
257 : * μὲν ὄντι φοιτᾶν εἰς *om.* *SL*
xix. 25 : καὶ κατηγοροῦντος *om.* *SL*[1]
xx. 15 : καὶ τῆι βεβαιότητι *om.* *SYOPQ*
xxiii. 152 : καὶ τοῦ ψηφίσματος *om.* *S*
xxv. 28 : εἰς τὸ ἐντὸς τούτων *om.* *S*
xxxv. 36 : * Φασηλίτηι πολίτηι *om.* *S*
xlv. 69 : * ἢ τίνα εὖ πεποίηκας *om.* *S*
l. 22 : καὶ πλοῖα ἑλκόντων *om.* *S*
Prooem. 3 : * εἰ φανερὸν γένοιτο *om.* *S*
(17) xviii. 67 : * ῥαιδίως καὶ ἑτοίμως *om.* *SL*[1]
xix. 280 : καὶ Ἀριστογείτονος *om.* *SL*[1]
xx. 18 : καὶ Ἀριστογείτονος *om.* *SAP*[1]*Q*[1]
xxi. 76 : κατὰ τῶν ἀδικούντων *om.* *SA*
xxxiv. 7 : * τὰ χρήματ' ἐνέθετ' εἰς *om.* *S*
lix. 9 : * ὡς Κυρηναῖοι εἴησαν *om.* *S* (*in lac.*)
lx. 12 : * παρὰ τοῖς προγόνοις *om.* *S*
(18) ii. 21 : τῶν καθ' ἕκαστα σαθρῶν *om.* *S*
iv. 28 : τοῖς στρατευομένοις *om.* *S*
x. 73 : ὑπὸ τῶν προγόνων ἡμῶν *om.* *SA*[1]

xviii. 279 : καὶ πᾶσαν ἔχει κακίαν *om.* *S*

xxiii. 15 : εἴ τι πάθοι Χαρίδημος *om.* *SF*

xlii. 16 : * πρὸς τοὺς στρατηγούς *om.* *S*

xliii. 71 : καὶ παρανενομήκασιν *om.* *S*

xlviii. 56 : ἄλλως τε καὶ τοιαύτηι *om.* *S*

(19) xvii. 3 : * εἴποιτ' ἂν οἶμαι πάντες *om.* SA^1

xix. 320 : * τοῖς ὅπλοις δυνήσεται *om.* *S*

(20) x. 43 : * οἶμαι ἀλλ' οὐδὲ τῶν ἄλλων *om.* *S*

xxv. 82 : * δὴ παμπόνηρος ἄνθρωπος *om.* *S*

xxxiv. 47 : * νῦν τὰ ἐναντία μαρτυρεῖ *om.* *SF*

(21) viii. 76 : * ὅσα ἂν δύνωνται τῆι πόλει *om.* SL^1

xviii. 253 : καὶ τὸν Ἀπόλλω τὸν Πύθιον *om.* $SL^1A^1B^1$

265 : ἐχόρευες, ἐγὼ δ' ἐχορήγουν *om* SL^1, *rhet. duo*

(22) xix. 278 : * εἶναι κελεύει τὴν εἰρήνην *om.* *SA*

xxi. 161 : * κἂν ἄνωθεν ἄρχεσθαι δοκῆι *om.* *SA*

xxiii. 198 : * τῶν τιμῶν ταῖς ὑπερβολαῖς *om.* S^1 (*add. m. antiqua*)

(23) xxv. 14 : * τοῖς ὑμετέροις βουλεύμασι *om.* *S*

xlix. 52 : * τὰ ἐνέχυρα τῶν δανεισμάτων *om.* *S*

xxv. 40 : * οὓς συκοφαντῶν παρέρχεται *om.* *S*

(24) xxxviii. 18 : * τοτὲ δ' ὡς παραδόντος διώκετε *om.* *S*

(25) viii. 75 : * νυνὶ καὶ περὶ ὧν ἂν ὁ δεῖν' εἴπηι *om.* *S*

(26) xviii. 154 : καὶ τῶι κοινῶι τῶν Ἀμφικτυόνων *om.* *SL*

xxxvii. 27 : τὰ ἐμαυτοῦ εἰλόμην κομίσασθαι *om.* *S*

lx. 17 : τί πρακτέον ἐστὶ τῆι δὲ σώζεται *om.* *S*

(27) xxv. 87 : τὸ καθ' αὑτόν. ἴδοιτε δ' ἂν ἐντεῦθεν *om.* *S*

xxxv. 56 : ἐψηφισμένοι καὶ περιαιρήσεσθε *om.* S^1 (*add. m.* 1)

xxxix. 40 : τίς δ' ὧι μήπω παῖδές εἰσι θήσεται *om.* *S*

xlvii. 32 : τετελευτηκότος τοῦ Δημοχάρους *om.* S^1 (*add. m.* 1)

(29) lix. 5 : * τοὺς δικαστὰς δίκαιον ὀργίζεσθαι *om.* *S* (*in lac.*)

(30) xiii. 23 : καὶ λυσιτελοῦντες αὐτοῖς ἐδίδοσαν *om.* *S*

(32) xviii. 129 : ἀλλὰ πάντες ἴσασι ταῦτα, κἂν ἐγὼ μὴ λέγω *om.* SL^1BFQY

(33) xviii. 235 : οὐδ' ὑπὸ τῶν συκοφαντούντων κρινόμενος *om.* *S*

(34) lvii. 10 : οὐ πλείους ἢ τριάκοντα· ἐν δὲ τούτοις ἦσαν *om.* S^1 (*add. m.* 1)

(37) xl. 54 : * ὑπὲρ ὧν ἂν λέγηι καὶ μὴ ὑμᾶς φάσκοντα εἰδέναι *om.* *S*

(38) xxiv. 184 : * ἃς ὅταν σοι δοκῆι πάλιν γράψεις καταχωνεύειν *om.* *S*

(40) xliii. 26 : οὑτοσὶ ὁ παῖς ἀνεψίου παῖς ὢν Ἁγνίαι πρὸς πατρός *om.* *S*

lv. 7 : * εἰ ἠνέγκατε τότε μάρτυρα καὶ ἐπεμαρτύρασθε νῦν *om.* *SA*

(42) x. 16 : καὶ τῶν ἔργων τῶν ἀργυρείων καὶ τοσούτων προσόδων *om.* *S*

xiv. 18 : * δευτέρων ἑκατὸν πέντε καὶ τῶν τρίτων ἑκατὸν πέντε *om.* *S* (*in fine col.*)

xxiv. 86 : * ἐφ' ὧι κατέστησε τοὺς ἐγγυητὰς ἀφεῖσθαι τοῦ δεσμοῦ *om.* *SAYO*

(46) lviii. 46 : εἰ δ' ἐγράψατ' ἄν, πῶς οὐ δεινόν ἐστιν ἑτέρου μὲν γράψαντος *om.* *S*

(47) lviii. 62 : ἀλλὰ τοὺς λέγοντας ἀεὶ γραφόμενοι χρήματα λαμβάνουσιν *om.* S^1 (*add m.* 1)

(49) xxxvi. 11 : καὶ λαβὼν αἵρεσιν Ἀπολλόδωρος αἱρεῖται τὸ ἀσπιδοπηγεῖον *om.* *S*

(51) xlv. 25 : ἐπίσχες· ἐνθυμεῖσθε ὅτι τῶν διαθηκῶν γέγραπται τῶν Πασίωνος *om. S*
(52) xix. 147 : * νῦν δὲ ἡ μὲν πόλις τῶν αὐτῆς ἀφέστηκεν, οὗτος δὲ χρήματα εἴληφεν *A : om. S, plerique.*
xxii. 67 : * μετέχουσιν ὧν ἀδικοῦσιν ὑμᾶς τινες, ἀπὸ δὲ τῶν εἰσπραττομένων *om. SL*[1]*YO*
(53) xiii. 32 : ἃ πρὸς Φλιασίους ὅτε ἐξέπεσον τὸ ἔναγχος βοηθεῖν μὴ ἐπιτρέπειν *om. S*
xxix. 49 : παρ' ὑμῶν ἐλέου τούτοις χρῆται τοῖς λόγοις· πολλὰ μὲν οὖν ἔγωγ' ἔχω *om. S*
(54) xxxi. 14 : καὶ δι' ὀρφανίαν ἠδικημένον καὶ προικὸς ἀληθινῆς ἀπεστερημένον *om. S*[1] (*add. m.* 1)
(59) xiv. 23 : * καθ' ἕκαστον νεώριον ἵνα ὦσι συμμορίαι δύο, τριήρεις τριάκοντα, φυλὴ μία *om. SA*
(63) xlv. 37 : καὶ ὁ ἐπιτροπευθῆναι κατὰ διαθήκας μαρτυρῶν δῆλον ὅτι καθ' ὁποίας ἂν εἰδείη *om. S*
(64) xxi. 101 : * οὐ τοῦτον μόνον ὃν συλλέγουσι καὶ οὗ πληρωταὶ γίγνονταί τινες ἀλλὰ καὶ ἄλλων *om. S, plerique*
(71) xix. 86 : * εἰ τὸν μηδὲ τοὺς θεοὺς καθ' ὃ πάτριον ἦν τιμᾶσθαι ποιήσαντα τοῦτον ἀτιμώρητον ἀφήσετε *om. SLY*[1]
(79) viii. 61 : * ὑπηρετοῦντας ἐκείνῳ ἀλλ' ἀνάγκη τούτοις ὥσπερ προβόλοις προσπταίοντας ὑστερίζειν ἐκείνων *om. SL*
(88) liv. 2 : * ἃ πέπονθ' ἀκούσητε. δεινῆς γὰρ οὔσης τῆς τότε συμβάσης ὕβρεως οὐκ ἐλάττων ἡ μετὰ ταῦτ' ἀσέλγειά ἐστι τουτουί *om. S* (*in lac.*)
(108) lx. 21 : * περὶ ὧν δ' ὁ τῶν ἐναντίων ἡγεμὼν ὑπερῆιρε τοὺς ἐπὶ τούτῳ ταχθέντας, οὐχὶ τοὺς πολλοὺς οὔτ' ἐκείνων οὔθ' ἡμῶν αἰτιάσαιτ' ἄν τις εἰκότως *om. S*
(128) xxxvi. 25 : καὶ ὅσα τις ἀφῆκεν ἢ ἀπήλλαξεν. εἰκότως. εἰ γάρ ἐστι δίκαιον ὧν ἂν ἅπαξ γένηται δίκη μηκέτ' ἐξεῖναι δικάζεσθαι, πολὺ τῶν ἀφεθέντων δικαιότερον μὴ εἶναι δίκας *om. S*
(137) vii. 5 : ἀλλ' εἰ καί τις ἄλλος ἐπιστάμενος παρακρουσθῆναι ἂν ὑμᾶς οἴεται ὑπὸ τῶν ἐνταῦθα διοικήσειν ὡς ἂν αὐτὸς ἐκεῖνος βούληται καὶ πρὶν ὑπεσχημένων καὶ νῦν δὲ πραττόντων *om. SL*[1]
(170) lix. 87–8 : τὰ δημοτελῆ ἐφ' ᾗ ἂν μοιχὸς ἁλῷ· ἐὰν δ' εἰσίῃ νηποινεὶ πασχέτω ὅ τι ἂν πάσχῃ πλὴν θανάτου. βούλομαι τοίνυν ὑμῖν, ὦ ἄνδρες Ἀθηναῖοι, καὶ τοῦ δήμου τοῦ Ἀθηναίων μαρτυρίαν παρασχέσθαι ὡς σπουδάζει περὶ τὰ ἱερά *om. S*

In the absence of telescoped passages special importance attaches to those where the omission is not explained by ὁμ. It is to be noticed that all the omissions of 22–5 letters, eight in number, fell into this class. I have entered lix. 5 as 28, but, as a space for τούς is left in the preceding line, this also is really a case of 24 and may be added to the list. We cannot, however, restrict the unit to this figure in view of xxxv. 56, xlvii. 32, in both of which 27 letters are added by m. 1. We must, therefore, assume a line of 22–7 letters in the model. In the multiples, the addition of the first hand lviii. 62 (47) and xxxi. 14 (54) are of special interest. It is to be remembered that the first hand also adds 47 letters in ix. 17 (*Phil.* iii), a passage not included in this list. The conclusion seems to be that the model varied somewhat in length of line; in all probability one column, as so frequently happens, was narrower than the other. The fact that there are three examples of 42, two of them not explained by ὁμ., deserves notice, and there is a striking bulge at 52–3 (four examples). Among the larger numbers 88, 108, 128 form an interesting sequence.

It has already been shown (p. 426) that the largest omission of *S*, 170 (lix. 87–8), goes back beyond the model, the passage having been already omitted in a MS. smaller than the model, a leaf of which, containing §§ 83–9, was placed after four other leaves, containing §§ 89–107. We must therefore be prepared to find at least another unit present.

I now turn to the smaller figures. Most of these are explained by ὁμ., and the number of cases in which the omission is due to a repetition of καί is to be remarked. The two most noticeable passages are:

xviii. 257: ἐμοὶ μὲν τοίνυν ὑπῆρξεν, Αἰσχίνη, παιδὶ μὲν ὄντι φοιτᾶν εἰς τὰ προσήκοντα διδασκαλεῖα καὶ ἔχειν ὅσα χρὴ . . . . ἐξελθόντι δὲ ἐκ παίδων

xxxiv. 7: οὔτε γὰρ τὴν ὑποθήκην παρέσχετο οὔτε τὰ χρήματ' ἐνέθετ' εἰς τὴν ναῦν, κελευούσης τῆς συγγραφῆς ἐπάναγκες ἐντίθεσθαι

The omission of μὲν ὄντι φοιτᾶν εἰς (16) and τὰ χρήματ' ἐνέθετ' εἰς (17) destroys the sense.

I have already indicated (p. 420) the importance of the addition of 34 letters by m. 1 in lvii. 10, this being the only passage added by m. 1 which does not appear to be a line, or lines, of the model.

I now call attention to the two passages of 52. These may both be explained as 26 × 2, and, if the omission were peculiar to *S*, I should without hesitation accept this solution. It is, however, to be noticed that in both cases the omission is common to a number of MSS. As I have only examined the pedigree of *S*, I speak with some reserve, but it is *prima facie* probable that the omission goes back to an earlier stage (17 × 3 = 51). The second passage, xxii. 67, runs as follows:

τὸ τούτων αἴτιον ἐγὼ ὑμῖν εἴπω; ὅτι τούτων μὲν μετέχει ὧν ἀδικοῦσιν ὑμᾶς τινες, ἀπὸ δὲ τῶν εἰσπραττομένων ὑφαιρεῖται

The omission (without ὁμ.) of μετέχει . . . εἰσπραττομένων produces nonsense.

I now turn to the largest number, 170. In view of what has already been said, it seems extremely likely that this = 17 × 10. It is interesting to notice that the next largest number, 137, is almost exactly a multiple of 17 (17 × 8 = 136).

It will be seen that the evidence furnished by omissions agrees in a remarkable way with that obtained from the corruptions previously considered.

I now take omissions of *S* in *Phil.* iii, beginning as elsewhere at 16 letters:

(16) § 50: καὶ τεταραγμένοις *A*, *om. S cett.*
(17) § 3: καὶ τῶν ἁμαρτημάτων *om. SL*[1]
§ 18: καὶ κατασκευάζοντα *om. SL*[1]
(20) § 14: καὶ κρίνειν βουλομένων *om. SL*[1]
(23) § 44: ἀλλ' εὐαγὲς ᾖι τὸ ἀποκτεῖναι *om. SL*
(24) § 43: καὶ θεωρεῖτε παρ' ὑμῖν αὐτοῖς *om. S*
§ 39: * συγγνώμη τοῖς ἐλεγχομένοις *om. SL*[1]
(26) § 72: καὶ Κλειτόμαχος καὶ Λυκοῦργος *om. SFYO*, *post* βέλτιστος *hab. A*
(28) § 37: * οὐδὲν ποικίλον οὐδὲ σοφὸν ἀλλ' ὅτι *om. SL*[1]*Y*
(29) § 2: οὐκοῦν οὐδ' ὑμᾶς οἴονται δεῖν ἔχειν *om. SL*[1]
(33) § 37: * καὶ παραίτησις οὐδεμί' ἦν οὐδὲ συγγνώμη *om. SL*[1]*Y*
(34) § 26: * καὶ τοῦτ' ἐκ βραχέος λόγου ῥάιδιον δεῖξαι *om. SL*[1]
(35) § 65: * καὶ προέσθαι τῶν ὑπὲρ ὑμῶν λεγόντων τινάς *om. SL*[1]
(47) § 17: ἕως ἂν αὐτὰ τοῖς τείχεσιν ἤδη προσαγάγωσιν· ἀλλ' οὐ φήσετε *om. S*[1] (*add. m.* 1)
(57) § 20: * καὶ τοῖς οὖσιν ἐκεῖ νῦν στρατιώταις πάνθ' ὅσων ἂν δέωνται ἀποστεῖλαι *om. SL*
§ 38: καὶ τοῖς μηδὲν ἐθέλουσι ποιεῖν κατὰ τῶν πάντα ἃ προσήκει πραττόντων *om. SL*[1]
(61) § 58: * τότε μὲν πέμψας τοὺς μετ' Εὐρυλόχου ξένους, πάλιν δὲ τοὺς μετὰ Παρμενίωνος *om. SL*[1]
(71) § 75: * εἰ γὰρ ἦσαν, εὕρηντ' ἂν πάλαι, ἕνεκά γε τοῦ μηδὲν ἡμᾶς αὐτοὺς ποιεῖν ἐθέλειν, ἀλλ' οὐκ εἰσίν *om. SF*

Dobree transposes this passage after ποιήσοντας.

(110) § 65: καὶ τοὺς εἰς τοῦθ' ὑπάγοντας ὑμᾶς ὁρῶν οὐκ ὀρρωδῶ, ἀλλὰ δυσωποῦμαι· ἢ γὰρ ἐξεπίτηδες ἢ δι' ἄγνοιαν εἰς χαλεπὸν πρᾶγμα ὑπάγουσι τὴν πόλιν *om. SLFYO*
(121) § 71: * πανταχοῖ εἰς Πελοπόννησον εἰς Ῥόδον εἰς Χίον ὡς βασιλέα λέγω, οὐδὲ γὰρ τῶν ἐκείνωι συμφερόντων ἀφέστηκε τὸ μὴ τοῦτον ἐᾶσαι πάντα καταστρέψασθαι *om. S*

(160) § 41 : * οὐχ ἵνα αὐτοῖς ᾖι χρήσιμα· καὶ γὰρ ἄνευ τούτων τῶν γραμμάτων τὰ δέοντα ἐφρόνουν, ἀλλ' ἵν' ὑμεῖς ἔχητε ὑπομνήματα καὶ παραδείγματα ὡς ὑπὲρ τῶν τοιούτων σπουδάζειν προσήκει. τί οὖν λέγει τὰ γράμματα; *om.* SL^1

(172) § 46 : * ἴστ' αὐτοί· τί γὰρ δεῖ περὶ πάντων ὑμῶν κατηγορεῖν; παραπλησίως δὲ καὶ οὐδὲν βέλτιον ὑμῶν ἅπαντες οἱ λοιποὶ Ἕλληνες· διόπερ φημὶ ἔγωγε καὶ σπουδῆς πολλῆς καὶ βουλῆς ἀγαθῆς τὰ παρόντα πράγματα προσδεῖσθαι. τίνος *om.* S^1L^1

(204) § 32 : * κύριος δὲ Πυλῶν καὶ τῶν ἐπὶ τοὺς Ἕλληνας παρόδων ἐστὶ καὶ φρουραῖς καὶ ξένοις τοὺς τόπους τούτους κατέχει; ἔχει δὲ καὶ τὴν προμαντείαν τοῦ θεοῦ, παρώσας ἡμᾶς καὶ Θετταλοὺς καὶ Δωριέας καὶ τοὺς ἄλλους Ἀμφικτύονας, ἧς οὐδὲ τοῖς Ἕλλησιν ἅπασι μέτεστι; *om.* SL^1

(596) § 6 : εἰ μὲν οὖν ἅπαντες ὡμολογοῦμεν Φίλιππον τῆι πόλει πολεμεῖν καὶ τὴν εἰρήνην παραβαίνειν, οὐδὲν ἄλλ' ἔδει τὸν παριόντα λέγειν καὶ συμβουλεύειν ἢ ὅπως ἀσφαλέστατα καὶ ῥᾷστ' αὐτὸν ἀμυνούμεθα· ἐπειδὴ δ' οὕτως ἀτόπως ἔνιοι διακεῖνται, ὥστε πόλεις καταλαμβάνοντος ἐκείνου καὶ πολλὰ τῶν ὑμετέρων ἔχοντος καὶ πάντας ἀνθρώπους ἀδικοῦντος ἀνέχεσθαί τινων ἐν ταῖς ἐκκλησίαις λεγόντων πολλάκις ὡς ἡμῶν τινές εἰσιν οἱ ποιοῦντες τὸν πόλεμον, ἀνάγκη φυλάττεσθαι καὶ διορθοῦσθαι περὶ τούτου· ἔστι γὰρ δέος μήποθ' ὡς ἀμυνούμεθα γράψας τις καὶ συμβουλεύσας εἰς τὴν αἰτίαν ἐμπέσηι τοῦ πεποιηκέναι τὸν πόλεμον. ἐγὼ δὴ τοῦτο πρῶτον ἁπάντων λέγω καὶ διορίζομαι· εἰ ἐφ' ἡμῖν ἐστι τὸ βουλεύεσθαι περὶ τοῦ πότερον εἰρήνην ἄγειν ἢ πολεμεῖν δεῖ *om.* SL^1

The evidence of Harpocration *sub voc.* ἄτιμος is quoted in favour of the omission of 23 letters in § 44. The words, however, seem genuine. Blass says 'haec interpolatori tribuere non ausim'. In the same citation he agrees with *S* in a short omission, not included in this list, viz. ἀλλ' οὐ τοῦτο λέγει (15). On the other hand Harpocration quotes twice *sub vocc.* δυσωποῦμαι and ὑπάγουσιν from the important passage in § 65 (110).

The first point to notice in this list is the omission of 47 letters in § 17, remedied by the scribe himself, considered at the beginning of this discussion (p. 419). Here, without doubt, the writer omitted two lines of his model. It seems reasonable to connect with this the omissions of 23–4 letters, possibly others.

Among the shorter omissions we may notice that the three omissions of 33–5 letters are not explained by ὁμ.: also, we have a passage, probably transposed, of 71 letters. In view of previous evidence, it is not unlikely that these are due to a unit of 17–18 letters.

The large figures in this list must be considered in connexion with the evidence already obtained from omissions and corruptions in *S*. It must be remembered that this evidence is a farrago gathered partly from the model, and partly from at least one previous ancestor.

I take first all omissions of more than 100 letters in *S*:

(108) lx. 21	(170) lix. 87–8
(110) *Phil.* iii. 65	(172) *Phil.* iii. 46
(120) *Phil.* iii. 71	(204) *Phil.* iii. 32
(137) vii. 5	(596) *Phil.* iii. 6
(158) *Phil.* iii. 41	

The most striking point here is the resemblance between 170 and 172, which is interesting, since, as has already been shown, the omission of 170 letters in lix. 87–8 goes back to considerable antiquity. We may also notice the similarity of 108 and 110.

I now take the corruptions, viz.:

(102) xviii. 25	(290) xlvii. 74–5
(144) x. 69–70	(597) *Prooem.* xl
(176) lv. 26–7	(1,190) lix. 5
(180) xl. 54	

If we combine these lists, the three largest figures are 596, 597, 1,190. Here 1,190÷2 = 595. This is a very extraordinary result. I now recall attention to 1,190 (p. 431). Here there is an error common to all the MSS., viz. that a passage of 38 letters is placed in § 5 instead of in § 9. The natural explanation is that, after omission, it was placed on the wrong folio of the archetype from which all our MSS. are descended. If so, 1,190 = a folio of this, and 596–7 = a page. When speaking of the corruption peculiar to *S* in *Prooem.* xl (597), I left the question open whether the error was made by the writer of *S*, or whether it went back to a previous MS. (p. 426). In view of these figures, it would appear that the second explanation is correct.

The conclusion, then, is that the longest omission of *S* in *Phil.* iii represents a division, in all probability a page, or column, of the archetype.

It is to be noticed that the words εἰ μὲν οὖν, with which the omitted passage begins, occur also at the beginning of the next sentence. The omission, therefore, is due to ὁμ. This has already been pointed out by Voemel, who says *aberravit oculus scribae a priore* εἰ μὲν οὖν *ad alterum* εἰ μὲν οὖν, but this simple explanation has not found favour with recent editors.

It is to be observed that the four largest omissions before 596 are not assisted by ὁμ. In view of the rarity of long omissions in other speeches of Demosthenes, the hypothesis of deliberate abridgement here seems probable. We have already seen that the favourite method of abbreviators was to strike out lines of their copy. The converging evidence shows that the archetype of Demosthenes contained about 17 letters to the line. The following multiples of 17 are therefore not without interest:

17 × 7 = 119. Cf. 121.
17 × 10 = 170. Cf. 172.
17 × 12 = 204. Cf. 204.
17 × 35 = 595. Cf. 596.

I now call attention to a passage in *Phil.* iii. 73 which I had previously reserved. Here *A vulg.* have φημὶ δεῖν . . . αὐτοὺς δὲ παρασκευάζεσθαι, καὶ πρώτους ἃ χρὴ ποιοῦντας τότε καὶ τοὺς ἄλλους Ἕλληνας συγκαλεῖν. *SFYO* after παρασκευάζεσθαι have τοὺς δ' ἄλλους Ἕλληνας συγκαλεῖν *med. om.* It looks as if the passage had been doctored by the insertion of δέ before ἄλλους after an omission.

I now proceed to discuss a remarkable series of obelizations in the speech against Midias (xxi).

We know from Hermogenes περὶ ἰδεῶν (*Rhet. Gr.* iii. p. 308) that passages in the speeches of Demosthenes were obelized and expelled on the ground of vulgarity (διὰ τὸ ἄγαν εὐτελές). He gives as examples two passages which are not found in existing MSS., viz. κυάμους ἑφθοὺς βοῶσα κατὰ πᾶν τὸ θέρος ἐπλανᾶτο (*De Cor.*) and ἀπὸ τριῶν τρυπημάτων τὴν ἐργασίαν πεποιῆσθαι (*In Neaeram*). He says of the first ὠβέλισάν τινες καὶ ὑπεξείλοντο, ἴσως ὀρθῶς ποιοῦντες.

The subject of obelizations in the MSS. of Demosthenes was first discussed by W. Christ.[1] The MSS. which contain them are *SBF*. There are also references to them in scholia.

Christ says that a long passage in *Phil.* iv. 22–7 οὐκ ἔνεστι . . . λέγειν ἄξιον is obelized in *B*, and quotes a scholium ἀπ' ἐντεῦθεν ἕως τοῦ ἑτέρου ἀστερίσκου τοῦ λόγου τοῦ περὶ τῶν ἐν Χερρονήσῳ ἐπιγραφέντος ἐστίν (i. e. = *Chers.* 48–51). This, however, is only an isolated case. It is in the Midias that the question becomes important. Here

[1] *Die Attikusausgabe des Demosthenes* (1882). For critical signs used in ancient MSS. of Plato cf. Diog. Laert. iii. 39.

a number of passages are obelized, some of which are short, while others are of considerable length. Christ thought that the obels were affixed on subjective grounds by a critic whose abilities he does not rate highly, remarking that 'he was no Aristarchus'. Thus he supposes that §§ 197–9 ὃν γὰρ . . . θεωρήσαιτε were struck out because they are followed in § 199 by τίς γάρ ἐστιν ὅστις and the repetition of γάρ was thought objectionable: so also §§ 217–18 πάντα γὰρ . . . ἡττῆσθαι on account of the following sentence οὐ γὰρ ἐκ πολιτικῆς αἰτίας. He thinks that §§ 205–7 καὶ βοηθοῦσιν . . . ποιήσεις were obelized on account of the numerous asyndeta, and § 218 πότερ' οὖν . . . κοινά because the passage was thought to be obscure. If these were the reasons by which the ancient critic was actuated, we must look on his excisions with grave suspicion.

Christ remarks on one passage § 139 that it may be dispensed with, and suggests that it was obelized on the authority of a good MS. Here he is following the adage *brevior lectio potior*. He has a more suggestive remark on § 99:

ἀλλ' ἴστε δήπου ὅτι τοὺς ἀδίκως τι πάσχοντας, ὃ μὴ δυνήσονται φέρειν, ἐλεεῖν προσήκει, οὐ τοὺς ὧν πεποιήκασι δεινῶν δίκην διδόντας *obel. SBF*

The next sentence begins with καὶ τίς ἂν ταῦτ' ἐλεήσειε δικαίως; Christ says that the critic wished to abridge the text by reading ἀλλὰ τίς ἂν ταῦτ' ἐλεήσειε δικαίως; (*om. med.*). He does not consider the possibility of omission due to ὁμ. in a MS. consulted by the critic. Of this there is a clear case, viz.:

§ 210 μὴ τοίνυν μηδ' οὗτοι τὴν ἄδειαν, ἣν ἡμῖν κοινὴν οὐσίαν οἱ νόμοι παρέχουσι, κωλυόντων κεκτῆσθαι *obel. F*

The previous sentence ends with κεκτῆσθαι, and that before it begins with μὴ τοίνυν. The omission therefore is very simple.

Blass appears to have treated these obelizations more seriously than Christ. In his text they are printed in smaller letters like those passages in *Phil.* iii which are omitted by *S*. This arrangement suggests that the obelized passages are not genuine.

I would here call particular attention to §§ 133–4 καίτοι πότερ' εἰσὶν . . . πάντας ἤλαυνες. The passage is obelized in *S* and Blass prints it in small type. The Scholiast here quotes a variant (ἐξ Ἀργούρας for ἀργυρᾶς), ascribing it to the vulgate (ἡ δημώδης, i.e. ἔκδοσις). On § 147 he refers to ἡ ἀρχαία as giving ἱερά for ἱερὰν ἐσθῆτα. It is clear that in § 133 ἀργυρᾶς was the reading of the ἀρχαία ἔκδοσις, as opposed to the δημώδης. It is, therefore, certain that the section was present in both recensions. Also, a quotation from it by Helladius is preserved by Photius. Its authenticity, therefore, appears to be beyond question.

I now proceed to discuss these obelizations. It will be well first of all to give an example of the way in which these signs are used. I take as an example § 218. Here *S* has:

πό
— τερ' οὖν τούτου γενομένου κρεῖτ
— τον ἦν αὖθις ἢ νυνὶ κολάσαι ἐγὼ
— μὲν οἶμαι νῦν κοινὴ γὰρ ἡ κρίσις
— καὶ τἀδικήματα πάντα ἐφ' οἷς
νῦν κρίνεται κοινά

Editors say that πότερ' οὖν . . . κοινά is obelized, although in *S* no obel is affixed to the last line. Apparently the obelization is meant to include a complete passage.

In most cases the obelization is common to *SBF*. The witnesses, however, do not always agree. In some cases the obelization is more extensive in one MS. than in another. Some passages are obelized in *F* only. These disagreements show that the obels in *B* and *F* cannot have been taken over from *S*, but that all three MSS. derive them from a common source. We have also employment in *B* and *F*, not in *S*, of another sign, the διπλῆ (>—), in combination with the obel. Christ is of opinion that in such cases the passages are regarded as alternatives, that marked by the διπλῆ being retained, while that which is obelized is struck out. It will be seen, therefore, that there are complications in some cases.

In view of previous experience it occurred to me as possible that the author of the obelizations was endeavouring to abridge the text, and went on the method of striking out lines in his copy. I, therefore, thought it worth while to examine the length of some of the shorter passages. I took first:

§ 49: καὶ πολλοὺς ἤδη παραβάντας τὸν νόμον τοῦτον ἐζημιώκασι θανάτωι (54)

The next obelized passage is:

§ 86: τὴν μὲν δίαιταν ἀντιλαχὼν οὐκ ὤμοσεν, ἀλλ' εἴασε καθ' ἑαυτοῦ κυρίαν γενέσθαι, καὶ ἀνώμοτος ἀπηνέχθη· βουλόμενος δὲ τὸ μέλλον λαθεῖν (107)

The relation of 54 to 107 is most striking. Shortly afterwards

I found that two obelized passages, § 92 *εἰ γὰρ . . . φαίνεται*, § 99 *ἀλλ' ἴστε . . . διδόντας*, both contain 110 letters.

I now take the various passages in order, adding a few remarks. Some of them are isolated, while others occur in close proximity to each other. In the latter case evidence is also to be obtained from the intervening blocks of text, since these should exhibit the operation of the same unit. I, therefore, combine them with the obelized passages, which are distinguished from them by an asterisk.

The first passage (§§ 38–41) happens to be uncertain. According to editors *S B F* obelize *ἔτι τοίνυν . . . ἤδη φανερός*. If so, the total number of letters is 1,467. As a matter of fact, however, *S* has:

— *στὶν ἤδη φανερὸς ἀλλὰ μὴν ὁ*
— *πηνίκα καὶ πεποιηκὼς ἃ*
— *κατηγορῶ καὶ ὕβρει πεποι*
— *ηκὼς φαίνεται τοὺς νόμους*

The natural interpretation is that the obelization goes down to *φαίνεται*, after which there is a stop. If so, the total number of letters in the obelized passage is 1,529.

The next passage is:

§ 49 : *καὶ πολλοὺς . . . θανάτωι obel. S* (54)

This passage I have already mentioned.

We now come to three obelized passages which I combine with the intervening blocks of text :

§ 86 : * *τὴν μὲν δίαιταν . . . μέλλον λαθεῖν obel. SBF*	(107)
§§ 86–7 : *φιλάξας τὴν . . . ἔστ' ἀσφαλές*	(448)
§§ 88–92 : * *δεῖ δὴ . . . ἄκυρον ποιεῖ obel. SBF*	(1,374)
§ 92 : *καίτοι εἰ . . . παραβαίνοντος*	(157)
§ 92 : * *εἰ γὰρ . . . θάνατος φαίνεται obel. SF*	(110)

The relation of 107 and 110 to 54 (§ 49) has already been pointed out. We may also notice that 110 × 4 = 440 ; cf. 448.

The next group is found in §§ 97–101, viz.:

§ 97 : * *καὶ μήθ' ἑορτῆς . . . ποιήσετε obel. S* (98)

S here twice has *μήτε* where editors print *μήθ'*, which makes the total, as written in this MS., 100. It is to be noticed that the previous sentence ends with *ἀφήσετε*. The obelization may therefore record an omission due to *ὁμ*.

While the whole passage is obelized in *S*, in *F* διπλαῖ are affixed to the first three lines and obels to the last two. In *B* the whole passage is marked with διπλαῖ. It is, therefore, uncertain what the critical signs mean here.

§§ 98–9 : καὶ τί φήσετε . . . τοῦτο λοιπόν (507)
§ 99 : * ἀλλ' ἴστε . . . δίκην διδόντας *obel. SBF* (110)
ib. : καὶ τίς ἂν . . . τῆς Μειδίου (230)
§§ 100–1 : * τίς οὖν . . . εἶ συλλέξασθαι *obel. SBF* (661)

For 110 cf. § 92. The relation of 110 to 230 and 661 is to be noticed.

There is another group in §§ 133–48, viz. :

§§ 133–4 : * καίτοι πότερ' εἰσίν . . . πάντας ἤλαυνες *obel. S* (438)

B obelizes § 133 only, καίτοι πότερ' εἰσίν . . . ἀπηγγέλλετο (351), while *F* affixes διπλαῖ to the first seven lines and obels to the last seven.

§§ 134–9 : εἰ μὲν γὰρ . . . ἐπινευόντων (1,688)
§ 139 : * οὓς μὰ τοὺς . . . μαρτυρεῖν *obel. SBF* (130)
§§ 140–2 : πάντα δὲ . . . τῇ πολιτείᾳ (812)
§§ 143–8 : * λέγεται τοίνυν . . . ἐνδεικνύμενος *obel. S* (1,711)

In *B* the obelization ends at κόπτειν διαφέρει (§ 147), in which case the total is 1,638, while in *F* another line is obelized after ἐνδεικνύμενος.

The remaining cases are found in §§ 191–218, viz. :

§§ 191–2 : * τάχα τοίνυν . . . τοῦ πράγματος *obel. BF* (568)
§§ 193–7 : οἶμαι τοίνυν . . . τοῦτον τοιοῦτον (1,510)
§§ 197–9 : * ὃν γὰρ οὐχ . . . θεωρήσαιτε *obel. F* (493)
§§ 199–201 : τίς γάρ ἐστιν . . . δεκάκις προσήκει (604)
§ 201 : * οὐδὲ γὰρ . . . διακρούσηται *obel. F* (122)
§§ 202–4 : ἀλλ' ἔγωγε . . . οὐ παύσεσθαι (1,028)
§§ 205–7 : * καὶ βοηθοῦσιν . . . τοῦτο ποιήσεις *obel. SF* (1,235)
§§ 208–10 : πέπυσμαι τοίνυν . . . κωλύει κεκτῆσθαι (890)
§ 210 : * μὴ τοίνυν . . . κωλυόντων κεκτῆσθαι *obel. F* (77)
§§ 211–17 : οὐδὲν δεινὸν . . . ὑμεῖς. μηδαμῶς (1,888)
§§ 217–18 : * πάντα γὰρ . . . τινὸς ἡττῆσθαι *obel. SF* (507)
§ 218 : οὐ γὰρ ἐκ . . . δύνασθαι κρίνεται (133)
ib. : * πότερ' οὖν . . . κρίνεται κοινά *obel. SF* (115)

I now give a conspectus of these figures. In order to be on sure ground, I reserve for the moment those cases in which there is any discrepancy in the MSS. I mark with an asterisk the obelized passages and add in brackets the MSS. in which the obelization occurs.

(54)	* § 49 (*S*)	(507)	§§ 98–9
(77)	* § 210 (*F*)		* §§ 217–18 (*SF*)
(107)	* § 86 (*SBF*)	(568)	* §§ 191–2 (*BF*)
(110)	* § 92 (*SBF*)	(604)	§§ 199–201
	* § 99 (*SBF*)	(661)	* §§ 100–1 (*SBF*)
(115)	* § 218 (*SF*)	(812)	§§ 140–2
(122)	* § 201 (*F*)	(890)	§§ 208–10
(130)	* § 139 (*SBF*)	(1,028)	§§ 202–4
(133)	§ 218	(1,235)	* §§ 205–7 (*SF*)
(157)	§ 92	(1,374)	* §§ 88–92 (*SBF*)
(230)	§ 99	(1,510)	§§ 193–7
(448)	§§ 86–7	(1,688)	§§ 134–9
(493)	* §§ 197–9 (*F*)	(1,888)	§§ 211–17

The striking point in this list is that 507 occurs twice, in one case for an obelized passage and in another for an intervening block. We have also to notice the relation between 507, 1,028, 1,510. Among the lower figures we have the sequence 54, 107, 110 *bis*, 448: also 115 × 2 = 230.

It seems probable that 54 is not a unit, but a multiple (= 27 × 2). If so, 77 represents 26 × 3 (= 78), and 107–10 represent 26 × 4 (= 104). As usual, the unit varies somewhat in the smaller numbers and becomes more constant in the larger. It will be found that multiples of 26 account for a large proportion of the figures. I add the following list:

26 × 5 = 130. Cf. 130, 133.
26 × 6 = 156. Cf. 157.
26 × 9 = 234. Cf. 230.
26 × 17 = 442. Cf. 448.
26 × 19 = 494. Cf. 493.
26 × 23 = 598. Cf. 604.
26 × 31 = 806. Cf. 812.
26 × 34 = 884. Cf. 890.
26 × 53 = 1,378. Cf. 1,374.
26 × 58 = 1,508. Cf. 1,510.
26 × 65 = 1,690. Cf. 1,688.

I here add for the sake of completeness the passages where our authorities differ, following *S* as against *B* and *F*:

(100) § 97 : (μήτε *bis*, as in *S*)	(1,529) §§ 38–41
(438) §§ 133–4	(1,711) §§ 143–8

If we accept the obelization given by *S* in §§ 38–41, the figure 1,529 seems to be connected with the sequence 507, 1,028, 1,510, to which attention has been already drawn. We may notice that 26 × 66 = 1,716.

The natural interpretation to put on these figures is that an ancient critic, who wished to abridge the speech, obelized passages which frequently, though not always, coincided with lines in his text. Curiously enough, his copy appears to have been written in lines which coincided very closely with those actually found in *S*. This fact suggests an objection to the conclusions which I have drawn, viz. that, as *S* itself contains 24–5 letters to the line and the obelized passages consist more or less roughly with lines in *S*, the figures must necessarily exhibit some such multiples as those which I have put together.

This objection would be fatal, if the obelizations were all found in *S*, and in *S* only. As a matter of fact, however, some of them do not occur in *S* at all, while others are common to *B* and *F*, which, presumably, are written in a different formation. There is, therefore, no possible explanation, apart from that of mere chance, except that the obelized passages formed lines in a MS. previous to *SBF*. In all probability the obelizations go back to remote antiquity, probably to a capital MS. written in long lines, not in columns.

If the results of this analysis are sound, these obelizations reveal to us an abridged text in the act of making.

ADDENDA

p. 6. SINCE this work was in print Mr. Percy Simpson has called my attention to two interesting doublets in *Romeo and Juliet*.

In II. ii. 187–III. i. 4 the Second Quarto (1599) gives:

Rom. Would I were sleepe and peace, so sweet to rest!
[The grey eyde morne smiles on the frowning night
Chekring the Easterne Clouds with streaks of light,
And darknesse fleckted like a drunkard reeles
From forth daies pathway, made by Tytan's wheeles.]
Hence will I to my ghostly Frier's close cell,
His help to crave, and my deare hap to tell.
Enter Friar alone, with a basket.
Fri. The grey-eyed morne smiles on the frowning night
Checking the Easterne clowdes with streaks of light:
And fleckeld darknesse like a drunkard reeles,
From forth daies path and Titan's burning wheeles.

Here the bracketed lines have been introduced from the beginning of Act III. The differences between the two versions suggest that an alternative draft was inserted in the margin of the MS. (cf. pp. 167, 177). The error survives in the 1609 Quarto and the First Folio.

In V. iii. 106 sqq. our editions give:

For fear of that I still will stay with thee,
And never from this palace of dim night
Depart again: here, here will I remain
With worms that are thy chambermaids.

Then, after nine lines:

Here 's to my love! O true apothecary!
Thy drugs are quick. Thus with a kiss I die.

The Second Quarto, followed by the First Folio, has:

For feare of that I still will staie with thee,
And never from this Pallace of dym night
Depart again: come lye thou in my armes.
Heer 's to thy health, where ere thou tumblest in.

[O true Appothecarie !
Thy drugs are quicke. Thus with a kisse I die.]
Depart again : here, here will I remain
With wormes that are thy Chambermaids.

The two lines *Here's to . . . I die* occur subsequently in their proper place.

Here the corruption is somewhat complicated. In addition to the doublet we have to notice the intrusion of a variant in l. 3 after *depart again*, while *depart again* is repeated in l. 7.

T. H. Burton, in *Book Hunter*, p. 75, referring to a work called *Men of the Time*, says :

> A few lines dropping out of the life of Robert Owen, the parallelogram Communist, were hustled, as the nearest place of refuge, into the biography of his closest alphabetical neighbour 'Oxford, Bishop of'. The consequence is that the article begins as follows :—
>
> *Oxford*, The Right Rev. Samuel Wilberforce, Bishop of, was born in 1805. A more kind hearted and truly benevolent man does not exist. A sceptic, as regards religious revelation, he is nevertheless an out and out believer in spirit movements.

I owe this reference to Mr. Gordon Duff.

I have observed a curious error in copies (undated) of Valla's tract, *de Donatione Constantini.* This edition is a reprint of a previous edition (undated), which I have used in the Bodleian Library (Bodl. Th. 4° H. 22). The previous edition has at the foot of the page (E i^{v}) :

> moderare imperiũ arbitrantur. Haec tamen omnia eo per
> tinent ut appareat Constantinũ inter tot impedimẽta nun

and at the foot of the next page (E ii^{r}) :

> Gallias. Adiit Hispanias. Adiit Germanos ceterũʒ occidẽ
> tem. Aut si grauabant˜ ambo tantũ obire terraꝝ quibusnam

In the reprint, a copy of which belongs to Queen's College (347 A. 1), the last line on E ii^{r} in the previous edition has been transferred to the place of the last line in E i^{v}.

The reprint therefore has :

> moderare imperiũ arbitrantur. Haec tamen omnia eo per
> tem. Aut si grauabant˜ ambo tantũ obire terraꝝ quibusnam

The next page of the reprint begins with:

tinent ut appareat Constantinũ inter tot impedimẽta nun

and ends with:

Gallias. Adiit Hispanias. Adiit Germanos ceterũq; occidẽ

The missing line:

tem. Aut si grauabant˜ ambo tantũ obire terrarꝫ quibusnam

has been added in thicker type at the top of the next page (E ii[v]), but has not been deleted where it occurs out of place (E i[v]).

A curious dittography in the text of Hesychius may be mentioned here. The MS. has:

φαῖ· δῆμος
φαίακες· ἔθνος
φαίδει· ὄψει
φαίδιμος· ὄνομα κύριον ἢ λαμπρός

Here φαῖ· δῆμος is a corruption of φαίδιμος, which has got into the text.

p. 5. The *Statesman* of August 24, 1917, contained the following transposition:

> The severe winter on the east coast was invalided early this year. He went to reside with his sister in Brighton, and died too much for him, however, and he was there as stated on June 28th from cancer on the liver.

Here line 4 should come after line 1.

p. 22. Corruptions similar to that found in Σ, in *Rosc. Am.* 45, are frequent in MSS. and papyri, e. g.:

Herondas v. 3–4:

ἀλλ' Ἀμφυταίῃ τῇ Μένωνος ἐγκεῖσαι.
ἐγὼ Ἀμφυταίην τὴν λέγεις ὁρώρηκα.

The writer of the papyrus (cent. i/ii A. D.) originally gave μένων for λέγεις.

Theocritus xiii. 29–30:

Ἑλλάσποντον ἵκοντο νότῳ τρίτον ἆμαρ ἀέντι,
εἴσω δ' ὅρμον ἔθεντο Προποντίδος, ἔνθα Κιανῶν

The Oxyrhynchus papyrus, No. 694 (cent. ii A. D.), substitutes ἵκοντο in l. 30 for ἔθεντο.

Sophocles, *Ichneutae* 78-9:

> ἐμοί τ' ἂν εἴη προσφιλὴς φράσας τόδε,
> Φοίβῳ τ' ἄνακτι συντελὴς εὐεργέτης

The papyrus, Ox. 1174 (cent. ii A. D.), has προστελής for συντελής in l. 79.

p. 29. For *et rt* cf. καὶ τὰ ἑξῆς in a MS. (*K*) containing the Axiochus, which belongs to the College of Jesuits at Antwerp. According to Bekker's collation, this symbol is used on four occasions where the text has been abridged.

p. 33. Cf. Cic. *Att.* xiii. 33. 2 Cum Balbo autem puto te aliquid fecisse H. in Capitolio.

Boot thought that *H. in Capitolio* is a corruption for *hinc incipit alia epistula.* Bosius conjectured *hodie in Capitolio.* It is simpler to suppose that *H.* is the omission symbol which has been embedded in the text (cf. p. 108). Probably the words *in Capitolio* are out of place, having been at one time omitted. In the previous sentence Cicero has been speaking of a *professio*, or return of property, which he had to make. He says:

> Neglegentiam miram! semelne putas mihi dixisse Balbum et Faberium professionem relatam? qui etiam eorum iussu miserim qui profiteretur. Ita enim oportere dicebant.

The words *in Capitolio* would give a good sense, if inserted after *profiteretur.* The *tabularium* in which the return was to be entered was close to the Capitol (Shuckburgh). Cicero's informants told him where the return should be made.

The edition of Pliny's *Letters* by Beroaldus (1503) contains an example of an omission note printed in the text. Most MSS. have a lacuna from viii. 8. 3 *etiam navium patiens* to 18. 11 *eodem quo emerat.* Beroaldus prints (f. 136[r]):

> etiam nauium
> patiens hic mutilus Codex. eodem quo emerat in
> struxit

p. 35. The symbol ζη, or ζτ, for ζήτει is found in papyri, e.g. in Ox. 1174, Sophocles, *Ichneutae* (cent. ii A. D.), col. ix, l. 22. In a Tebtunis papyrus, ii. 343 (*Land Survey*), cent. ii, it occurs five times in the text as an abbreviation for ζητητέον. In MSS. it is frequently used to express doubt, e.g. in the *codex Palatinus* of the

Anthology. Preisendanz, in his preface to the Leiden facsimile of this MS., says (p. cxxi) of the corrector *C*, '*ζητήσεως nota ./. vel* ζ^τ *locos permultos instruxit*' (cf. pp. lxi, lxxiv, cxiii). The MS. of Hesychius has the following gloss:

τεῖν: ζητεῖν. ἄλλοι δέ σοι

Here ζητεῖν is a conflation of ζη (ζτ) with τεῖν (= σοι).

I have elsewhere (*Primitive Text*, p. 97) suggested that a confusion of this sign with ζ′ (= ἑπτά) is responsible for the conversion of Sceva's two sons (Acts xix. 16) into seven in *v.* 14, in all MSS. except *D*. M. Havet, in *Rev. Phil.* xxxvii (1913), p. 131, has drawn attention to a large number of passages in which a mysterious *L* occurs in MSS. of Varro, *de Re Rustica*. He considers *L* to be a corruption of *Z*. This sign occurs three times in i. 55. In one of these it comes in the middle of a word, after *bi-* in *bivium*. In another the MSS. give *laudabilior L*, where *laudabilior* is a conjecture for *L*. The doublet *L. laudabiliter* is also found in i. 59. 2. Cf. *Rosc. Am.* 132, where *hoc iudicium* appears to be a corruption of *hd̄*, to mark a lacuna.

p. 48. The signatures in Vat. Reg. 762 have recently been discussed with great minuteness by E. K. Rand and G. Howe in *Memoirs of the American Academy in Rome*, i. (1917), pp. 19–54.

p. 49. For insertion in the wrong place cf. the Hibeh papyrus, No. 26, Ῥητορικὴ πρὸς Ἀλέξανδρον (cent. iii B.C.), 159–63:

τωι πολεμωι τελευτησασι ταφην
δημοσιον χωριον εγ καλωι προ της
πολεως αφωρισθαι καιτοι πασιν αν
των εως ηβησωσι εις τροφην διδοναι

Here εἰς, which has been omitted in l. 159 before ταφήν, has been inserted in l. 163 before τροφήν.

The same papyrus contains an example of 'botching' after the repetition of a word, which deserves mention on account of its early date.

Lines 116–19 are written thus:

ιερων τριττως αναγκαιον λε
γειν η γαρ ερουμεν ως αναγκαιον
τα καθεστωτα διαφυλαττειν

The MSS. have διαφυλακτέον in l. 119, omitting ἀναγκαῖον in l. 118.

This is clearly a superior reading. The writer of the papyrus, after repeating ἀναγκαῖον (l. 116) changed the verbal adjective to the infinitive.

p. 52. An interesting example of a long variant out of place occurs in a papyrus, Ox. 844, containing fragments of Isocrates, *Panegyricus*, cent. ii. In § 74 after παραλελεῖφθαι the MSS. have:

> ὅμως δ' ἐκ τῶν ὑπολοίπων, ἐπειδὴ συμφέρει τοῖς πράγμασιν, οὐκ ὀκνητέον μνησθῆναι περὶ αὐτῶν

In this section the papyrus is deficient, but in § 70, after κατοικισθῆναι, it has an alternative form of the sentence:

> τούτων δὲ οὕτως ἐχόντων οὐκ ὀκνητέον ἐστι περὶ τῶν ὑπολοίπων εἰπεῖν ἃ δὴ συμφέρει τοῖς πράγμασι μνησθῆναι.

For similar cases in Cicero, *Philippics*, cf. pp. 167, 177.

p. 53. An example no less striking than that provided by Harl. 3063 may be found in *Spicilegium Palimpsestorum*, vol. i (*Beuronae* 1913). The upper script in this, which contains homilies, was written about 800 A. D. Apart from an omission of *tum splendescere* (15) on p. 86, I have only noticed two passages where a supplement is added by a second hand. These are:

(62) p. 59: usq: ad finē glorosū uirlit' cōpletas. Ñ enī qui coepert sed qui pseuerauert
(i above glorosū, uirlit', coepert, pseuerauert)

(125) p. 67: cū tantis et p tantis ęterna p̄mia possidebis, si uero, quod absit, supbia iracundia murmurationes vel in oboedientię formā ad imitandū te aliis dederis

Here 62 × 2 = 124.

p. 189. After the example from *Phil.* ix. 4 add:

> xii. 22 ad eum qui mihi fuit propositus exitum.

For *exitum* the MSS. have *exitus* (*corr.* Manutius): while *ns* have *exitum* after *eum*, as well as *exitus* at the end. This indicates in *P*:

ad eum
qui mihi fuit propositus exitus (27) *mg.* exitum

p. 202. Mr. Gordon Duff has pointed out to me a singular case where a marginal note has found its way into the text of an English printed book. In T. Greenhill's Νεκροκηδεία, *or the Art of Embalming*, London, 1705, p. 347, the writer is speaking of a tomb, said to be that of Cicero's daughter, Tullia, in which, when it was opened, a lamp was found still burning. According to the printed text, 'Judaeus Apella thinks it not to have been reduced to ashes by burning, but by the inmission of air or contact with the body'. This must have its origin in a marginal comment *credat Iudaeus Apella.* Still more curiously, the name of *Iudaeus Apella* figures among the list of authorities given at the end of the book.

A marginal note in Poggio's copy of Asconius (*Matrit.* x. 81), apparently written by him, has had a curious history. After reading the arguments of Asconius to show that Cicero did not defend Catiline, as asserted by Fenestella, he wrote in the margin:

> Vincis me. Itaque puto non defendisse sed tantum de defendendo cogitasse, quod per epistulam negari non potest

This note was reproduced in various MSS. derived from Poggio's copy and received into the text by early editors (omitting *vincis me*). It remained there until 1833, when it was struck out by Baiter.

p. 309. Cf. Lucr. vi. 840:

> frigidior porro in puteis aestate fit umor.

Here there is a lacuna between lines 839 and 840. In the *Oblongus frigidior* is preceded by *que*, in the *Quadratus* by *quae*, in the Italian copies by *cur*. These variants appear to be corruptions of $\tilde{Q}$ (= *quaere*), a marginal sign to mark the lacuna (cf. p. 35).

p. 315. According to Baiter in Marc. 25 *A* omits *si tibi soli viveres aut* (20). *H*, however, omits *viveres aut si tibi etiam soli* (25). We should expect to find the same omission in *AH*. It is possible that Baiter has misreported *A*. I have, therefore, not included this passage.

p. 439. I have not referred to the thorny question of stichometry in connexion with *Phil.* iii. According to a note found both in Σ and in *B*, it consisted of 580 στίχοι. This suits the shorter version, given by Σ, better than the longer version, found in *B*. W. Christ, who maintains that the στίχοι refer to the edition of Atticus, allows that the longer text was in existence before the date of this edition. It is noticeable that Dionysius (p. 947 Reiske) lays stress on the length of the speech (ἐν δὲ τῇ μεγίστῃ τῶν κατὰ Φιλίππου δημηγοριῶν).

INDEXES

I. GENERAL INDEX

II. LIST OF MSS.

(A) PAPYRI

(1) GREEK.

Hibeh 26. Ῥητορικὴ πρὸς Ἀλέξανδρον, cent. iii B.C. pp. 11–12.
Oxyrhynch. 16. Thucydides, cent. i A.D. pp. 1, 310.
463. Xenophon, cent. ii/iii A.D. p. 311.
843. Plato, cent. ii/iii A.D. pp. 385, 417.
1016. Plato, cent. ii/iii A.D. pp. 311, 385.

(2) LATIN.

Berol. 13229. Cicero, Planc., cent. v A.D. p. 15.
Oxyrhynch. 1251. Cicero, Cael., cent. v A.D. pp. 266–8, 311.

(B) GREEK MSS.

Florence, Laur. lxxxi. 11. Aristotle, cent. x. p. 421.
Oxford, Bodl., Clark. 39. Plato, cent. ix. pp. 384 sqq.
Coll. Corp. Christi 112. Aristotle, cent. xv. p. 421.
Paris 1807. Plato, cent. ix. pp. 384 sqq.
1808. Plato, cent. xiii. p. 414.
1809. Plato, cent. xv. p. 414.
2934. Demosthenes, cent. x. pp. 418 sqq.
Rome, Vat. 1. Plato, cent. ix/x. p. 396.
225–6. Plato, cent. xv. p. 404.
Venice 185. Plato, cent. xii. pp. 384, 405–11.
App. Class. 4, 1. Plato, cent. xii. pp. 384, 411–14.
Vienna 55. Plato, cent. xiv. pp. 384, 414–17.
Suppl. phil. Gr. 7. Plato, cent. xii. pp. 384, 417.

(C) PALIMPSESTS (LATIN)

Milan E 147 sup. Schol. Bobiensis, cent. v. pp. 46, 156–61.
R 57 sup. Cic. Oratt., cent. v. pp. 13, 153–6, 281–2.
Rome, Vat. 5750. Schol. Bobiensis, cent. v. pp. 46, 156–61.
5751. Cic. Rep., cent. iv. pp. 12, 45, 124–38, 235.
Pal. 24. Cic. Font., cent. iv. p. 281.
Reg. 2077. Cic. Verr., cent. iv. pp. 14, 45–6, 212–26.
Turin, A. ii. 2*. Cic. Oratt., cent. iv. pp. 14, 45, 138–56, 226, 291–4.

(D) LATIN MSS.

III. LIST OF NAMES AND PLACES

IV. LIST OF CHIEF PASSAGES REFERRED TO

www.ingramcontent.com/pod-product-compliance
Lightning Source LLC
Chambersburg PA
CBHW070928100726
47908CB00001B/138

* 9 7 8 1 5 9 7 5 2 5 7 6 3 *